William Wilkie Collins (8 January 1824 – 23 September 1889) was an English novelist, playwright, and short story writer, best known for The Woman in White (1859), No Name (1862), Armadale (1866) and The Moonstone (1868). The last has been called the first modern English detective novel. Born to the family of painter William Collins in London, he grew up in Italy and France, learning French and Italian. He began work as a clerk for a tea merchant. After his first novel, Antonina, appeared in 1850, he met Charles Dickens, who became a close friend and mentor. Some of Collins's works appeared first in Dickens's journals All the Year Round and Household Words and they collaborated on drama and fiction. Collins published his best known works in the 1860s, achieving financial stability and an international following. However, he began suffering from gout. Taking opium for the pain developed into an addiction. In the 1870s and 1880s the quality of his writing declined along with his health. Collins was critical of the institution of marriage: he split his time between Caroline Graves, except for a two-year separation, and his common-law wife Martha Rudd, with whom he had three children. (Source: Wikipedia)

Literary works:
Basil (1852)
Hide and Seek (1854)
The Dead Secret (1856)
The Frozen Deep (1857)
"A House to Let" (1858)
"The Haunted House"
The Woman in White (1860)
No Name (1862)
Armadale (1866)
No Thoroughfare (1867)
The Moonstone (1868)
Man and Wife (1870)
Poor Miss Finch (1872)
The Law and the Lady (1875)
The Fallen Leaves (1879)

Throne Classics

MY LADY'S MONEY,
I SAY NO
&
LITTLE NOVELS
Wilkie Collins

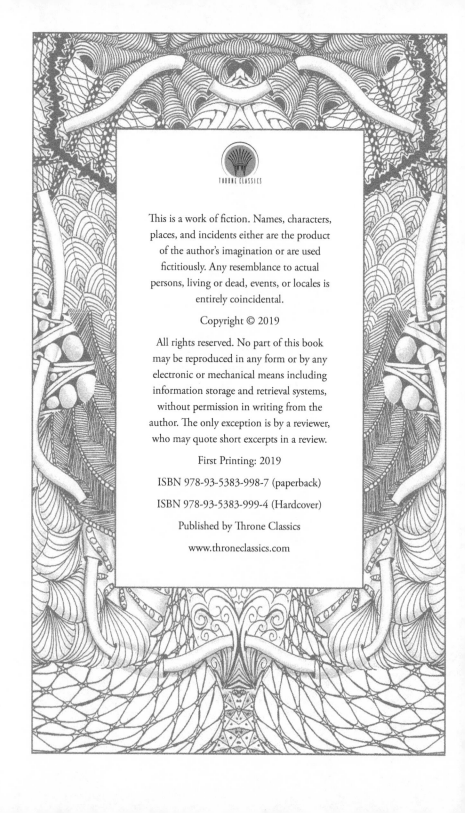

Copyright © 2019

First Printing: 2019

ISBN 978-93-5383-998-7 (paperback)

ISBN 978-93-5383-999-4 (Hardcover)

Published by Throne Classics

www.throneclassics.com

Contents

MY LADY'S MONEY,
I SAY NO
&
LITTLE NOVELS

MY LADY'S MONEY

PERSONS OF THE STORY

Women:

Lady Lydiard (Widow of Lord Lydiard)

Isabel Miller (her Adopted Daughter)

Miss Pink (of South Morden)

The Hon. Mrs. Drumblade (Sister to the Hon. A. Hardyman)

Men

The Hon. Alfred Hardyman (of the Stud Farm)

Mr. Felix Sweetsir (Lady Lydiard's Nephew)

Robert Moody (Lady Lydiard's Steward)

Mr. Troy (Lady Lydiard's Lawyer)

Old Sharon (in the Byways of Legal Bohemia)

Animal

Tommie (Lady Lydiard's Dog)

PART THE FIRST.

THE DISAPPEARANCE.

CHAPTER I.

OLD Lady Lydiard sat meditating by the fireside, with three letters lying open on her lap.

Time had discolored the paper, and had turned the ink to a brownish hue. The letters were all addressed to the same person—"THE RT. HON. LORD LYDIARD"—and were all signed in the same way—"Your affectionate cousin, James Tollmidge." Judged by these specimens of his correspondence, Mr. Tollmidge must have possessed one great merit as a letter-writer—the merit of brevity. He will weary nobody's patience, if he is allowed to have a hearing. Let him, therefore, be permitted, in his own high-flown way, to speak for himself.

First Letter.—"My statement, as your Lordship requests, shall be short and to the point. I was doing very well as a portrait-painter in the country; and I had a wife and children to consider. Under the circumstances, if I had been left to decide for myself, I should certainly have waited until I had saved a little money before I ventured on the serious expense of taking a house and studio at the west end of London. Your Lordship, I positively declare, encouraged me to try the experiment without waiting. And here I am, unknown and unemployed, a helpless artist lost in London—with a sick wife and hungry children, and bankruptcy staring me in the face. On whose shoulders does this dreadful responsibility rest? On your Lordship's!"

Second Letter.—"After a week's delay, you favor me, my Lord, with a curt reply. I can be equally curt on my side. I indignantly deny that I or my wife ever presumed to see your Lordship's name as a means of recommendation to sitters without your permission. Some enemy has slandered us. I claim as my right to know the name of that enemy."

Third (and last) Letter.—"Another week has passed—and not a word of answer has reached me from your Lordship. It matters little. I have employed the interval in making inquiries, and I have at last discovered the hostile influence which has estranged you from me. I have been, it seems, so unfortunate as to offend Lady Lydiard (how, I cannot imagine); and the all-powerful influence of this noble lady is now used against the struggling artist who is united to you by the sacred ties of kindred. Be it so. I can fight my way upwards, my Lord, as other men have done before me. A day may yet come when the throng of carriages waiting at the door of the fashionable portrait-painter will include her Ladyship's vehicle, and bring me the tardy expression of her Ladyship's regret. I refer you, my Lord Lydiard, to that day!"

Having read Mr. Tollmidge's formidable assertions relating to herself for the second time, Lady Lydiard's meditations came to an abrupt end. She rose, took the letters in both hands to tear them up, hesitated, and threw them back in the cabinet drawer in which she had discovered them, among other papers that had not been arranged since Lord Lydiard's death.

"The idiot!" said her Ladyship, thinking of Mr. Tollmidge, "I never even heard of him, in my husband's lifetime; I never even knew that he was really related to Lord Lydiard, till I found his letters. What is to be done next?"

She looked, as she put that question to herself, at an open newspaper thrown on the table, which announced the death of "that accomplished artist Mr. Tollmidge, related, it is said, to the late well-known connoisseur, Lord Lydiard." In the next sentence the writer of the obituary notice deplored the destitute condition of Mrs. Tollmidge and her children, "thrown helpless on the mercy of the world." Lady Lydiard stood by the table with her eyes on those lines, and saw but too plainly the direction in which they pointed—the direction of her check-book.

Turning towards the fireplace, she rang the bell. "I can do nothing in this matter," she thought to herself, "until I know whether the report about Mrs. Tollmidge and her family is to be depended on. Has Moody come back?" she asked, when the servant appeared at the door. "Moody" (otherwise her

Ladyship's steward) had not come back. Lady Lydiard dismissed the subject of the artist's widow from further consideration until the steward returned, and gave her mind to a question of domestic interest which lay nearer to her heart. Her favorite dog had been ailing for some time past, and no report of him had reached her that morning. She opened a door near the fireplace, which led, through a little corridor hung with rare prints, to her own boudoir. "Isabel!" she called out, "how is Tommie?"

A fresh young voice answered from behind the curtain which closed the further end of the corridor, "No better, my Lady."

A low growl followed the fresh young voice, and added (in dog's language), "Much worse, my Lady—much worse!"

Lady Lydiard closed the door again, with a compassionate sigh for Tommie, and walked slowly to and fro in her spacious drawing-room, waiting for the steward's return.

Accurately described, Lord Lydiard's widow was short and fat, and, in the matter of age, perilously near her sixtieth birthday. But it may be said, without paying a compliment, that she looked younger than her age by ten years at least. Her complexion was of that delicate pink tinge which is sometimes seen in old women with well-preserved constitutions. Her eyes (equally well preserved) were of that hard light blue color which wears well, and does not wash out when tried by the test of tears. Add to this her short nose, her plump cheeks that set wrinkles at defiance, her white hair dressed in stiff little curls; and, if a doll could grow old, Lady Lydiard, at sixty, would have been the living image of that doll, taking life easily on its journey downwards to the prettiest of tombs, in a burial-ground where the myrtles and roses grew all the year round.

These being her Ladyship's personal merits, impartial history must acknowledge, on the list of her defects, a total want of tact and taste in her attire. The lapse of time since Lord Lydiard's death had left her at liberty to dress as she pleased. She arrayed her short, clumsy figure in colors that were far too bright for a woman of her age. Her dresses, badly chosen as to their hues, were perhaps not badly made, but were certainly badly worn. Morally, as well as physically, it must be said of Lady Lydiard that her outward side was her worst side. The anomalies of her dress were matched by the anomalies of her character. There were moments when she felt and spoke as became a lady of rank; and there were other moments when she felt and spoke as might have become the cook in the kitchen. Beneath these superficial inconsistencies, the great heart, the essentially true and generous nature of the woman, only waited the sufficient occasion to assert themselves. In the trivial intercourse of society she was open to ridicule on every side of her. But when a serious emergency tried the metal of which she was really made, the people who were loudest in laughing at her stood aghast, and wondered what had become of the familiar companion of their everyday lives.

Her Ladyship's promenade had lasted but a little while, when a man in black clothing presented himself noiselessly at the great door which opened on the staircase. Lady Lydiard signed to him impatiently to enter the room.

"I have been expecting you for some time, Moody," she said. "You look tired. Take a chair."

The man in black bowed respectfully, and took his seat.

CHAPTER II.

ROBERT MOODY was at this time nearly forty years of age. He was a shy, quiet, dark person, with a pale, closely-shaven face, agreeably animated by large black eyes, set deep in their orbits. His mouth was perhaps his best feature; he had firm, well-shaped lips, which softened on rare occasions into a particularly winning smile. The whole look of the man, in spite of his habitual reserve, declared him to be eminently trustworthy. His position in Lady Lydiard's household was in no sense of the menial sort. He acted as her almoner and secretary as well as her steward—distributed her charities, wrote her letters on business, paid her bills, engaged her servants, stocked her wine-cellar, was authorized to borrow books from her library, and was served with his meals in his own room. His parentage gave him claims to these special favors; he was by birth entitled to rank as a gentleman. His father had failed at a time of commercial panic as a country banker, had paid a good dividend, and had died in exile abroad a broken-hearted man. Robert had tried to hold his place in the world, but adverse fortune kept him down. Undeserved disaster followed him from one employment to another, until he abandoned the struggle, bade a last farewell to the pride of other days, and accepted the position considerately and delicately offered to him in Lady Lydiard's house. He had now no near relations living, and he had never made many friends. In the intervals of occupation he led a lonely life in his little room. It was a matter of secret wonder among the women in the servants' hall, considering his personal advantages and the opportunities which must surely have been thrown in his way, that he had never tempted fortune in the character of a married man. Robert Moody entered into no explanations on that subject. In his own sad and quiet way he continued to lead his own sad and quiet life. The women all failing, from the handsome housekeeper downward, to make the smallest impression on him, consoled themselves by prophetic visions of his future relations with the sex, and predicted vindictively that "his time would come."

"Well," said Lady Lydiard, "and what have you done?"

"Your Ladyship seemed to be anxious about the dog," Moody answered, in the low tone which was habitual to him. "I went first to the veterinary surgeon. He had been called away into the country; and—"

Lady Lydiard waved away the conclusion of the sentence with her hand. "Never mind the surgeon. We must find somebody else. Where did you go next?"

"To your Ladyship's lawyer. Mr. Troy wished me to say that he will have the honor of waiting on you—"

"Pass over the lawyer, Moody. I want to know about the painter's widow. Is it true that Mrs. Tollmidge and her family are left in helpless poverty?"

"Not quite true, my Lady. I have seen the clergyman of the parish, who takes an interest in the case—"

Lady Lydiard interrupted her steward for the third time. "Did you mention my name?" she asked sharply.

"Certainly not, my Lady. I followed my instructions, and described you as a benevolent person in search of cases of real distress. It is quite true that Mr. Tollmidge has died, leaving nothing to his family. But the widow has a little income of seventy pounds in her own right."

"Is that enough to live on, Moody?" her Ladyship asked.

"Enough, in this case, for the widow and her daughter," Moody answered. "The difficulty is to pay the few debts left standing, and to start the two sons in life. They are reported to be steady lads; and the family is much respected in the neighborhood. The clergyman proposes to get a few influential names to begin with, and to start a subscription."

"No subscription!" protested Lady Lydiard. "Mr. Tollmidge was Lord Lydiard's cousin; and Mrs. Tollmidge is related to his Lordship by marriage. It would be degrading to my husband's memory to have the begging-box sent round for his relations, no matter how distant they may be. Cousins!" exclaimed her Ladyship, suddenly descending from the lofty ranges of sentiment to the low. "I hate the very name of them! A person who is near

20

enough to me to be my relation and far enough off from me to be my sweetheart, is a double-faced sort of person that I don't like. Let's get back to the widow and her sons. How much do they want?"

"A subscription of five hundred pounds, my Lady, would provide for everything—if it could only be collected."

"It shall be collected, Moody! I will pay the subscription out of my own purse." Having asserted herself in those noble terms, she spoilt the effect of her own outburst of generosity by dropping to the sordid view of the subject in her next sentence. "Five hundred pounds is a good bit of money, though; isn't it, Moody?"

"It is, indeed, my Lady." Rich and generous as he knew his mistress to be, her proposal to pay the whole subscription took the steward by surprise. Lady Lydiard's quick perception instantly detected what was passing in his mind.

"You don't quite understand my position in this matter," she said. "When I read the newspaper notice of Mr. Tollmidge's death, I searched among his Lordship's papers to see if they really were related. I discovered some letters from Mr. Tollmidge, which showed me that he and Lord Lydiard were cousins. One of those letters contains some very painful statements, reflecting most untruly and unjustly on my conduct; lies, in short," her Ladyship burst out, losing her dignity, as usual. "Lies, Moody, for which Mr. Tollmidge deserved to be horsewhipped. I would have done it myself if his Lordship had told me at the time. No matter; it's useless to dwell on the thing now," she continued, ascending again to the forms of expression which became a lady of rank. "This unhappy man has done me a gross injustice; my motives may be seriously misjudged, if I appear personally in communicating with his family. If I relieve them anonymously in their present trouble, I spare them the exposure of a public subscription, and I do what I believe his Lordship would have done himself if he had lived. My desk is on the other table. Bring it here, Moody; and let me return good for evil, while I'm in the humor for it!"

Moody obeyed in silence. Lady Lydiard wrote a check.

"Take that to the banker's, and bring back a five-hundred pound note," she said. "I'll inclose it to the clergyman as coming from 'an unknown friend.' And be quick about it. I am only a fallible mortal, Moody. Don't leave me time enough to take the stingy view of five hundred pounds."

Moody went out with the check. No delay was to be apprehended in obtaining the money; the banking-house was hard by, in St. James's Street. Left alone, Lady Lydiard decided on occupying her mind in the generous direction by composing her anonymous letter to the clergyman. She had just taken a sheet of note-paper from her desk, when a servant appeared at the door announcing a visitor—

"Mr. Felix Sweetsir!"

CHAPTER III.

"MY nephew!" Lady Lydiard exclaimed in a tone which expressed astonishment, but certainly not pleasure as well. "How many years is it since you and I last met?" she asked, in her abruptly straightforward way, as Mr. Felix Sweetsir approached her writing-table.

The visitor was not a person easily discouraged. He took Lady Lydiard's hand, and kissed it with easy grace. A shade of irony was in his manner, agreeably relieved by a playful flash of tenderness.

"Years, my dear aunt?" he said. "Look in your glass and you will see that time has stood still since we met last. How wonderfully well you wear! When shall we celebrate the appearance of your first wrinkle? I am too old; I shall never live to see it."

He took an easychair, uninvited; placed himself close at his aunt's side, and ran his eye over her ill-chosen dress with an air of satirical admiration. "How perfectly successful!" he said, with his well-bred insolence. "What a chaste gayety of color!"

"What do you want?" asked her Ladyship, not in the least softened by the compliment.

"I want to pay my respects to my dear aunt," Felix answered, perfectly impenetrable to his ungracious reception, and perfectly comfortable in a spacious arm-chair.

No pen-and-ink portrait need surely be drawn of Felix Sweetsir—he is too well-known a picture in society. The little lithe man, with his bright, restless eyes, and his long iron-gray hair falling in curls to his shoulders, his airy step and his cordial manner; his uncertain age, his innumerable accomplishments, and his unbounded popularity—is he not familiar everywhere, and welcome everywhere? How gratefully he receives, how prodigally he repays, the cordial appreciation of an admiring world! Every man he knows is "a charming fellow." Every woman he sees is "sweetly pretty." What picnics he gives on the banks of the Thames in the summer season! What a well-earned little income he derives from the whist-table! What an inestimable actor he is at private theatricals of all sorts (weddings included)! Did you never read Sweetsir's novel, dashed off in the intervals of curative perspiration at a German bath? Then you don't know what brilliant fiction really is. He has never written a second work; he does everything, and only does it once. One song—the despair of professional composers. One picture—just to show how easily a gentleman can take up an art and drop it again. A really multiform man, with all the graces and all the accomplishments scintillating perpetually at his fingers' ends. If these poor pages have achieved nothing else, they have done a service to persons not in society by presenting them to Sweetsir. In his gracious company the narrative brightens; and writer and reader (catching reflected brilliancy) understand each other at last, thanks to Sweetsir.

"Well," said Lady Lydiard, "now you are here, what have you got to say for yourself? You have been abroad, of course! Where?"

"Principally at Paris, my dear aunt. The only place that is fit to live in—for this excellent reason, that the French are the only people who know how to make the most of life. One has relations and friends in England and every now and then one returns to London—"

"When one has spent all one's money in Paris," her Ladyship interposed. "That's what you were going to say, isn't it?"

Felix submitted to the interruption with his delightful good-humor.

"What a bright creature you are!" he exclaimed. "What would I not give for your flow of spirits! Yes—one does spend money in Paris, as you say. The clubs, the stock exchange, the race-course: you try your luck here, there, and everywhere; and you lose and win, win and lose—and you haven't a dull day to complain of." He paused, his smile died away, he looked inquiringly at Lady Lydiard. "What a wonderful existence yours must be," he resumed. "The everlasting question with your needy fellow-creatures, 'Where am I to get money?' is a question that has never passed your lips. Enviable woman!" He paused once more—surprised and puzzled this time. "What is the matter, my dear aunt? You seem to be suffering under some uneasiness."

"I am suffering under your conversation," her Ladyship answered sharply. "Money is a sore subject with me just now," she went on, with her eyes on her nephew, watching the effect of what she said. "I have spent five hundred pounds this morning with a scrape of my pen. And, only a week since, I yielded to temptation and made an addition to my picture-gallery." She looked, as she said those words, towards an archway at the further end of the room, closed by curtains of purple velvet. "I really tremble when I think of what that one picture cost me before I could call it mine. A landscape by Hobbema; and the National Gallery bidding against me. Never mind!" she concluded, consoling herself, as usual, with considerations that were beneath her. "Hobbema will sell at my death for a bigger price than I gave for him—that's one comfort!" She looked again at Felix; a smile of mischievous satisfaction began to show itself in her face. "Anything wrong with your watch-chain?" she asked.

Felix, absently playing with his watch-chain, started as if his aunt had suddenly awakened him. While Lady Lydiard had been speaking, his vivacity had subsided little by little, and had left him looking so serious and so old that his most intimate friend would hardly have known him again. Roused by the sudden question that had been put to him, he seemed to be casting about in his mind in search of the first excuse for his silence that might turn up.

"I was wondering," he began, "why I miss something when I look round this beautiful room; something familiar, you know, that I fully expected to find here."

"Tommie?" suggested Lady Lydiard, still watching her nephew as maliciously as ever.

"That's it!" cried Felix, seizing his excuse, and rallying his spirits. "Why don't I hear Tommie snarling behind me; why don't I feel Tommie's teeth in my trousers?"

The smile vanished from Lady Lydiard's face; the tone taken by her nephew in speaking of her dog was disrespectful in the extreme. She showed him plainly that she disapproved of it. Felix went on, nevertheless, impenetrable to reproof of the silent sort. "Dear little Tommie! So delightfully fat; and such an infernal temper! I don't know whether I hate him or love him. Where is he?"

"Ill in bed," answered her ladyship, with a gravity which startled even Felix himself. "I wish to speak to you about Tommie. You know everybody. Do you know of a good dog-doctor? The person I have employed so far doesn't at all satisfy me."

"Professional person?" inquired Felix.

"Yes."

"All humbugs, my dear aunt. The worse the dog gets the bigger the bill grows, don't you see? I have got the man for you—a gentleman. Knows more about horses and dogs than all the veterinary surgeons put together. We met in the boat yesterday crossing the Channel. You know him by name, of course? Lord Rotherfield's youngest son, Alfred Hardyman."

"The owner of the stud farm? The man who has bred the famous racehorses?" cried Lady Lydiard. "My dear Felix, how can I presume to trouble such a great personage about my dog?"

Felix burst into his genial laugh. "Never was modesty more woefully out of place," he rejoined. "Hardyman is dying to be presented to your Ladyship. He has heard, like everybody, of the magnificent decorations of this house, and he is longing to see them. His chambers are close by, in Pall Mall. If he is at home we will have him here in five minutes. Perhaps I had better see the dog first?"

Lady Lydiard shook her head. "Isabel says he had better not be disturbed," she answered. "Isabel understands him better than anybody."

Felix lifted his lively eyebrows with a mixed expression of curiosity and surprise. "Who is Isabel?"

Lady Lydiard was vexed with herself for carelessly mentioning Isabel's name in her nephew's presence. Felix was not the sort of person whom she was desirous of admitting to her confidence in domestic matters. "Isabel is an addition to my household since you were here last," she answered shortly.

"Young and pretty?" inquired Felix. "Ah! you look serious, and you don't answer me. Young and pretty, evidently. Which may I see first, the addition to your household or the addition to your picture-gallery? You look at the picture-gallery—I am answered again." He rose to approach the archway, and stopped at his first step forward. "A sweet girl is a dreadful responsibility, aunt," he resumed, with an ironical assumption of gravity. "Do you know, I shouldn't be surprised if Isabel, in the long run, cost you more than Hobbema. Who is this at the door?"

The person at the door was Robert Moody, returned from the bank. Mr. Felix Sweetsir, being near-sighted, was obliged to fit his eye-glass in position before he could recognize the prime minister of Lady Lydiard's household.

"Ha! our worthy Moody. How well he wears! Not a gray hair on his head—and look at mine! What dye do you use, Moody? If he had my open disposition he would tell. As it is, he looks unutterable things, and holds his tongue. Ah! if I could only have held my tongue—when I was in the diplomatic service, you know—what a position I might have occupied by this time! Don't let me interrupt you, Moody, if you have anything to say to Lady Lydiard."

Having acknowledged Mr. Sweetsir's lively greeting by a formal bow, and a grave look of wonder which respectfully repelled that vivacious gentleman's flow of humor, Moody turned towards his mistress.

"Have you got the bank-note?" asked her Ladyship.

Moody laid the bank-note on the table.

"Am I in the way?" inquired Felix.

"No," said his aunt. "I have a letter to write; it won't occupy me for more than a few minutes. You can stay here, or go and look at the Hobbema, which you please."

Felix made a second sauntering attempt to reach the picture-gallery. Arrived within a few steps of the entrance, he stopped again, attracted by an open cabinet of Italian workmanship, filled with rare old china. Being nothing if not a cultivated amateur, Mr. Sweetsir paused to pay his passing tribute of admiration before the contents of the cabinet. "Charming! charming!" he said to himself, with his head twisted appreciatively a little on one side. Lady Lydiard and Moody left him in undisturbed enjoyment of the china, and went on with the business of the bank-note.

"Ought we to take the number of the note, in case of accident?" asked her Ladyship.

Moody produced a slip of paper from his waistcoat pocket. "I took the number, my Lady, at the bank."

"Very well. You keep it. While I am writing my letter, suppose you direct the envelope. What is the clergyman's name?"

Moody mentioned the name and directed the envelope. Felix, happening to look round at Lady Lydiard and the steward while they were both engaged in writing, returned suddenly to the table as if he had been struck by a new idea.

"Is there a third pen?" he asked. "Why shouldn't I write a line at once to Hardyman, aunt? The sooner you have his opinion about Tommie the better—don't you think so?"

Lady Lydiard pointed to the pen tray, with a smile. To show consideration for her dog was to seize irresistibly on the high-road to her favor. Felix set to work on his letter, in a large scrambling handwriting, with plenty of ink and a noisy pen. "I declare we are like clerks in an office," he remarked, in his cheery way. "All with our noses to the paper, writing as if we lived by it! Here, Moody, let one of the servants take this at once to Mr. Hardyman's."

The messenger was despatched. Robert returned, and waited near his mistress, with the directed envelope in his hand. Felix sauntered back slowly towards the picture-gallery, for the third time. In a moment more Lady Lydiard finished her letter, and folded up the bank-note in it. She had just taken the directed envelope from Moody, and had just placed the letter inside it, when a scream from the inner room, in which Isabel was nursing the sick dog, startled everybody. "My Lady! my Lady!" cried the girl, distractedly,

28

"Tommie is in a fit? Tommie is dying!"

Lady Lydiard dropped the unclosed envelope on the table, and ran—yes, short as she was and fat as she was, ran—into the inner room. The two men, left together, looked at each other.

"Moody," said Felix, in his lazily-cynical way, "do you think if you or I were in a fit that her Ladyship would run? Bah! these are the things that shake one's faith in human nature. I feel infernally seedy. That cursed Channel passage—I tremble in my inmost stomach when I think of it. Get me something, Moody."

"What shall I send you, sir?" Moody asked coldly.

"Some dry curacoa and a biscuit. And let it be brought to me in the picture-gallery. Damn the dog! I'll go and look at Hobbema."

This time he succeeded in reaching the archway, and disappeared behind the curtains of the picture-gallery.

CHAPTER IV.

LEFT alone in the drawing-room, Moody looked at the unfastened envelope on the table.

Considering the value of the inclosure, might he feel justified in wetting the gum and securing the envelope for safety's sake? After thinking it over, Moody decided that he was not justified in meddling with the letter. On reflection, her Ladyship might have changes to make in it or might have a postscript to add to what she had already written. Apart too, from these considerations, was it reasonable to act as if Lady Lydiard's house was a hotel, perpetually open to the intrusion of strangers? Objects worth twice five hundred pounds in the aggregate were scattered about on the tables and in the unlocked cabinets all round him. Moody withdrew, without further hesitation, to order the light restorative prescribed for himself by Mr. Sweetsir.

The footman who took the curacoa into the picture gallery found Felix recumbent on a sofa, admiring the famous Hobbema.

"Don't interrupt me," he said peevishly, catching the servant in the act of staring at him. "Put down the bottle and go!" Forbidden to look at Mr. Sweetsir, the man's eyes as he left the gallery turned wonderingly towards the famous landscape. And what did he see? He saw one towering big cloud in the sky that threatened rain, two withered mahogany-colored trees sorely in want of rain, a muddy road greatly the worse for rain, and a vagabond boy running home who was afraid of the rain. That was the picture, to the footman's eye. He took a gloomy view of the state of Mr. Sweetsir's brains on his return to the servants' hall. "A slate loose, poor devil!" That was the footman's report of the brilliant Felix.

Immediately on the servant's departure, the silence in the picture-gallery was broken by voices penetrating into it from the drawing-room. Felix rose to a sitting position on the sofa. He had recognized the voice of Alfred Hardyman saying, "Don't disturb Lady Lydiard," and the voice of Moody answering, "I will just knock at the door of her Ladyship's room, sir; you will find Mr. Sweetsir in the picture-gallery."

The curtains over the archway parted, and disclosed the figure of a tall man, with a closely cropped head set a little stiffly on his shoulders. The immovable gravity of face and manner which every Englishman seems to acquire who lives constantly in the society of horses, was the gravity which this gentleman displayed as he entered the picture-gallery. He was a finely made, sinewy man, with clearly cut, regular features. If he had not been affected with horses on the brain he would doubtless have been personally popular with the women. As it was, the serene and hippic gloom of the handsome horse-breeder daunted the daughters of Eve, and they failed to make up their minds about the exact value of him, socially considered. Alfred Hardyman was nevertheless a remarkable man in his way. He had been offered the customary alternatives submitted to the younger sons of the nobility—the Church or the diplomatic service—and had refused the one and the other. "I like horses," he said, "and I mean to get my living out of them. Don't talk to me about my position in the world. Talk to my eldest brother, who gets the money and the title." Starting in life with these sensible views, and with a small capital of five thousand pounds, Hardyman took his own place in the sphere that was fitted for him. At the period of this narrative he was already a rich man, and one of the greatest authorities on horse-breeding in England. His prosperity made no change in him. He was always the same grave, quiet, obstinately resolute man—true to the few friends whom he admitted to his intimacy, and sincere to a fault in the expression of his feelings among persons whom he distrusted or disliked. As he entered the picture-gallery and paused for a moment looking at Felix on the sofa, his large, cold, steady gray eyes rested on the little man with an indifference that just verged on contempt. Felix, on the other hand, sprang to his feet with alert politeness and greeted his friend with exuberant cordiality.

"Dear old boy! This is so good of you," he began. "I feel it—I do assure you I feel it!"

"You needn't trouble yourself to feel it," was the quietly-ungracious answer. "Lady Lydiard brings me here. I come to see the house—and the dog."

31

He looked round the gallery in his gravely attentive way. "I don't understand pictures," he remarked resignedly. "I shall go back to the drawing-room."

After a moment's consideration, Felix followed him into the drawing-room, with the air of a man who was determined not to be repelled.

"Well?" asked Hardyman. "What is it?"

"About that matter?" Felix said, inquiringly.

"What matter?"

"Oh, you know. Will next week do?"

"Next week won't do."

Mr. Felix Sweetsir cast one look at his friend. His friend was too intently occupied with the decorations of the drawing-room to notice the look.

"Will to-morrow do?" Felix resumed, after an interval.

"Yes."

"At what time?"

"Between twelve and one in the afternoon."

"Between twelve and one in the afternoon," Felix repeated. He looked again at Hardyman and took his hat. "Make my apologies to my aunt," he said. "You must introduce yourself to her Ladyship. I can't wait here any longer." He walked out of the room, having deliberately returned the contemptuous indifference of Hardyman by a similar indifference on his own side, at parting.

Left by himself, Hardyman took a chair and glanced at the door which led into the boudoir. The steward had knocked at that door, had disappeared through it, and had not appeared again. How much longer was Lady Lydiard's visitor to be left unnoticed in Lady Lydiard's house?

As the question passed through his mind the boudoir door opened. For once in his life, Alfred Hardyman's composure deserted him. He started to his feet, like an ordinary mortal taken completely by surprise.

Instead of Mr. Moody, instead of Lady Lydiard, there appeared in the open doorway a young woman in a state of embarrassment, who actually quickened the beat of Mr. Hardyman's heart the moment he set eyes on her. Was the person who produced this amazing impression at first sight a person of importance? Nothing of the sort. She was only "Isabel" surnamed "Miller." Even her name had nothing in it. Only "Isabel Miller!"

Had she any pretensions to distinction in virtue of her personal appearance?

It is not easy to answer the question. The women (let us put the worst judges first) had long since discovered that she wanted that indispensable elegance of figure which is derived from slimness of waist and length of limb. The men (who were better acquainted with the subject) looked at her figure from their point of view; and, finding it essentially embraceable, asked for nothing more. It might have been her bright complexion or it might have been the bold luster of her eyes (as the women considered it), that dazzled the lords of creation generally, and made them all alike incompetent to discover her faults. Still, she had compensating attractions which no severity of criticism could dispute. Her smile, beginning at her lips, flowed brightly and instantly over her whole face. A delicious atmosphere of health, freshness, and good humor seemed to radiate from her wherever she went and whatever she did. For the rest her brown hair grew low over her broad white forehead, and was topped by a neat little lace cap with ribbons of a violet color. A plain collar and plain cuffs encircled her smooth, round neck, and her plump dimpled hands. Her merino dress, covering but not hiding the charming outline of her bosom, matched the color of the cap-ribbons, and was brightened by a white muslin apron coquettishly trimmed about the pockets, a gift from Lady Lydiard. Blushing and smiling, she let the door fall to behind her, and, shyly approaching the stranger, said to him, in her small, clear voice, "If you please, sir, are you Mr. Hardyman?"

The gravity of the great horse-breeder deserted him at her first question. He smiled as he acknowledged that he was "Mr. Hardyman"—he smiled as he offered her a chair.

"No, thank you, sir," she said, with a quaintly pretty inclination of her head. "I am only sent here to make her Ladyship's apologies. She has put the poor dear dog into a warm bath, and she can't leave him. And Mr. Moody can't come instead of me, because I was too frightened to be of any use, and so he had to hold the dog. That's all. We are very anxious sir, to know if the warm bath is the right thing. Please come into the room and tell us."

She led the way back to the door. Hardyman, naturally enough, was slow to follow her. When a man is fascinated by the charm of youth and beauty, he is in no hurry to transfer his attention to a sick animal in a bath. Hardyman seized on the first excuse that he could devise for keeping Isabel to himself—that is to say, for keeping her in the drawing-room.

"I think I shall be better able to help you," he said, "if you will tell me something about the dog first."

Even his accent in speaking had altered to a certain degree. The quiet, dreary monotone in which he habitually spoke quickened a little under his present excitement. As for Isabel, she was too deeply interested in Tommie's welfare to suspect that she was being made the victim of a stratagem. She left the door and returned to Hardyman with eager eyes. "What can I tell you, sir?" she asked innocently.

Hardyman pressed his advantage without mercy.

"You can tell me what sort of dog he is?"

"Yes, sir."

"How old he is?"

"Yes, sir."

"What his name is?—what his temper is?—what his illness is? what diseases his father and mother had?—what—"

Isabel's head began to turn giddy. "One thing at a time, sir!" she interposed, with a gesture of entreaty. "The dog sleeps on my bed, and I had a bad night with him, he disturbed me so, and I am afraid I am very stupid this morning. His name is Tommie. We are obliged to call him by it, because he won't answer to any other than the name he had when my Lady bought him. But we spell it with an i e at the end, which makes it less vulgar than Tommy with a y. I am very sorry, sir—I forget what else you wanted to know. Please to come in here and my Lady will tell you everything."

She tried to get back to the door of the boudoir. Hardyman, feasting his eyes on the pretty, changeful face that looked up at him with such innocent confidence in his authority, drew her away from the door by the one means at his disposal. He returned to his questions about Tommie.

"Wait a little, please. What sort of dog is he?"

Isabel turned back again from the door. To describe Tommie was a labor of love. "He is the most beautiful dog in the world!" the girl began, with kindling eyes. "He has the most exquisite white curly hair and two light brown patches on his back—and, oh! such lovely dark eyes! They call him a Scotch terrier. When he is well his appetite is truly wonderful—nothing comes amiss to him, sir, from pate de foie gras to potatoes. He has his enemies, poor dear, though you wouldn't think it. People who won't put up with being bitten by him (what shocking tempers one does meet with, to be sure!) call him a mongrel. Isn't it a shame? Please come in and see him, sir; my Lady will be tired of waiting."

Another journey to the door followed those words, checked instantly by a serious objection.

"Stop a minute! You must tell me what his temper is, or I can do nothing for him."

Isabel returned once more, feeling that it was really serious this time. Her gravity was even more charming than her gayety. As she lifted her face to him, with large solemn eyes, expressive of her sense of responsibility, Hardyman would have given every horse in his stables to have had the privilege of taking her in his arms and kissing her.

"Tommie has the temper of an angel with the people he likes," she said.

"When he bites, it generally means that he objects to strangers. He loves my Lady, and he loves Mr. Moody, and he loves me, and—and I think that's all. This way, sir, if you please, I am sure I heard my Lady call."

"No," said Hardyman, in his immovably obstinate way. "Nobody called. About this dog's temper? Doesn't he take to any strangers? What sort of people does he bite in general?"

Isabel's pretty lips began to curl upward at the corners in a quaint smile. Hardyman's last imbecile question had opened her eyes to the true state of the case. Still, Tommie's future was in this strange gentleman's hands; she felt bound to consider that. And, moreover, it was no everyday event, in Isabel's experience, to fascinate a famous personage, who was also a magnificent and perfectly dressed man. She ran the risk of wasting another minute or two, and went on with the memoirs of Tommie.

"I must own, sir," she resumed, "that he behaves a little ungratefully— even to strangers who take an interest in him. When he gets lost in the streets (which is very often), he sits down on the pavement and howls till he collects a pitying crowd round him; and when they try to read his name and address on his collar he snaps at them. The servants generally find him and bring him back; and as soon as he gets home he turns round on the doorstep and snaps at the servants. I think it must be his fun. You should see him sitting up in his chair at dinner-time, waiting to be helped, with his fore paws on the edge of the table, like the hands of a gentleman at a public dinner making a speech. But, oh!" cried Isabel, checking herself, with the tears in her eyes, "how can I talk of him in this way when he is so dreadfully ill! Some of them say it's bronchitis, and some say it's his liver. Only yesterday I took him to the front door to give him a little air, and he stood still on the pavement, quite stupefied. For the first time in his life, he snapped at nobody who went by; and, oh, dear, he hadn't even the heart to smell a lamp-post!"

Isabel had barely stated this last afflicting circumstance when the memoirs of Tommie were suddenly cut short by the voice of Lady Lydiard— really calling this time—from the inner room.

"Isabel! Isabel!" cried her Ladyship, "what are you about?"

Isabel ran to the door of the boudoir and threw it open. "Go in, sir! Pray go in!" she said.

"Without you?" Hardyman asked.

"I will follow you, sir. I have something to do for her Ladyship first."

She still held the door open, and pointed entreatingly to the passage which led to the boudoir "I shall be blamed, sir," she said, "if you don't go in."

This statement of the case left Hardyman no alternative. He presented himself to Lady Lydiard without another moment of delay.

Having closed the drawing-room door on him, Isabel waited a little, absorbed in her own thoughts.

She was now perfectly well aware of the effect which she had produced on Hardyman. Her vanity, it is not to be denied, was flattered by his admiration—he was so grand and so tall, and he had such fine large eyes. The girl looked prettier than ever as she stood with her head down and her color heightened, smiling to herself. A clock on the chimney-piece striking the half-hour roused her. She cast one look at the glass, as she passed it, and went to the table at which Lady Lydiard had been writing.

Methodical Mr. Moody, in submitting to be employed as bath-attendant upon Tommie, had not forgotten the interests of his mistress. He reminded her Ladyship that she had left her letter, with a bank-note inclosed in it, unsealed. Absorbed in the dog, Lady Lydiard answered, "Isabel is doing nothing, let Isabel seal it. Show Mr. Hardyman in here," she continued, turning to Isabel, "and then seal a letter of mine which you will find on the table." "And when you have sealed it," careful Mr. Moody added, "put it back on the table; I will take charge of it when her Ladyship has done with me."

Such were the special instructions which now detained Isabel in the drawing-room. She lighted the taper, and closed and sealed the open envelope, without feeling curiosity enough even to look at the address. Mr. Hardyman was the uppermost subject in her thoughts. Leaving the sealed letter on the table, she returned to the fireplace, and studied her own charming face attentively in the looking-glass. The time passed—and Isabel's reflection was still the subject of Isabel's contemplation. "He must see many beautiful ladies," she thought, veering backward and forward between pride and humility. "I wonder what he sees in Me?"

The clock struck the hour. Almost at the same moment the boudoir-door opened, and Robert Moody, released at last from attendance on Tommie, entered the drawing-room.

CHAPTER V.

"WELL?" asked Isabel eagerly, "what does Mr. Hardyman say? Does he think he can cure Tommie?"

Moody answered a little coldly and stiffly. His dark, deeply-set eyes rested on Isabel with an uneasy look.

"Mr. Hardyman seems to understand animals," he said. "He lifted the dog's eyelid and looked at his eyes, and then he told us the bath was useless."

"Go on!" said Isabel impatiently. "He did something, I suppose, besides telling you that the bath was useless?"

"He took a knife out of his pocket, with a lancet in it."

Isabel clasped her hands with a faint cry of horror. "Oh, Mr. Moody! did he hurt Tommie?"

"Hurt him?" Moody repeated, indignant at the interest which she felt in the animal, and the indifference which she exhibited towards the man (as represented by himself). "Hurt him, indeed! Mr. Hardyman bled the brute—"

"Brute?" Isabel reiterated, with flashing eyes. "I know some people, Mr. Moody, who really deserve to be called by that horrid word. If you can't say 'Tommie,' when you speak of him in my presence, be so good as to say 'the dog.'"

Moody yielded with the worst possible grace. "Oh, very well! Mr. Hardyman bled the dog, and brought him to his senses directly. I am charged to tell you—" He stopped, as if the message which he was instructed to deliver was in the last degree distasteful to him.

"Well, what were you charged to tell me?"

"I was to say that Mr. Hardyman will give you instructions how to treat the dog for the future."

Isabel hastened to the door, eager to receive her instructions. Moody stopped her before she could open it.

"You are in a great hurry to get to Mr. Hardyman," he remarked.

Isabel looked back at him in surprise. "You said just now that Mr. Hardyman was waiting to tell me how to nurse Tommie."

"Let him wait," Moody rejoined sternly. "When I left him, he was sufficiently occupied in expressing his favorable opinion of you to her Ladyship."

The steward's pale face turned paler still as he said those words. With the arrival of Isabel in Lady Lydiard's house "his time had come"—exactly as the women in the servants' hall had predicted. At last the impenetrable man felt the influence of the sex; at last he knew the passion of love misplaced, ill-starred, hopeless love, for a woman who was young enough to be his child. He had already spoken to Isabel more than once in terms which told his secret plainly enough. But the smouldering fire of jealousy in the man, fanned into flame by Hardyman, now showed itself for the first time. His looks, even more than his words, would have warned a woman with any knowledge of the natures of men to be careful how she answered him. Young, giddy, and inexperienced, Isabel followed the flippant impulse of the moment, without a thought of the consequences. "I'm sure it's very kind of Mr. Hardyman to speak favorably of me," she said, with a pert little laugh. "I hope you are not jealous of him, Mr. Moody?"

Moody was in no humor to make allowances for the unbridled gayety of youth and good spirits.

"I hate any man who admires you," he burst out passionately, "let him be who he may!"

Isabel looked at her strange lover with unaffected astonishment. How unlike Mr. Hardyman, who had treated her as a lady from first to last! "What an odd man you are!" she said. "You can't take a joke. I'm sure I didn't mean to offend you."

"You don't offend me—you do worse, you distress me."

Isabel's color began to rise. The merriment died out of her face; she looked at Moody gravely. "I don't like to be accused of distressing people when I don't deserve it," she said. "I had better leave you. Let me by, if you please."

Having committed one error in offending her, Moody committed another in attempting to make his peace with her. Acting under the fear that she would really leave him, he took her roughly by the arm.

"You are always trying to get away from me," he said. "I wish I knew how to make you like me, Isabel."

"I don't allow you to call me Isabel!" she retorted, struggling to free herself from his hold. "Let go of my arm. You hurt me."

Moody dropped her arm with a bitter sigh. "I don't know how to deal with you," he said simply. "Have some pity on me!"

If the steward had known anything of women (at Isabel's age) he would never have appealed to her mercy in those plain terms, and at the unpropitious moment. "Pity you?" she repeated contemptuously. "Is that all you have to say to me after hurting my arm? What a bear you are!" She shrugged her shoulders and put her hands coquettishly into the pockets of her apron. That was how she pitied him! His face turned paler and paler—he writhed under it.

"For God's sake, don't turn everything I say to you into ridicule!" he cried. "You know I love you with all my heart and soul. Again and again I have asked you to be my wife—and you laugh at me as if it was a joke. I haven't deserved to be treated in that cruel way. It maddens me—I can't endure it!"

Isabel looked down on the floor, and followed the lines in the pattern of the carpet with the end of her smart little shoe. She could hardly have been further away from really understanding Moody if he had spoken in Hebrew. She was partly startled, partly puzzled, by the strong emotions which she had unconsciously called into being. "Oh dear me!" she said, "why can't you talk of something else? Why can't we be friends? Excuse me for mentioning it," she went on, looking up at him with a saucy smile, "you are old enough to be my father."

Moody's head sank on his breast. "I own it," he answered humbly. "But there is something to be said for me. Men as old as I am have made good husbands before now. I would devote my whole life to make you happy. There isn't a wish you could form which I wouldn't be proud to obey. You must not reckon me by years. My youth has not been wasted in a profligate life; I can be truer to you and fonder of you than many a younger man. Surely my heart is not quite unworthy of you, when it is all yours. I have lived such a lonely, miserable life—and you might so easily brighten it. You are kind to everybody else, Isabel. Tell me, dear, why are you so hard on me?"

His voice trembled as he appealed to her in those simple words. He had taken the right way at last to produce an impression on her. She really felt for him. All that was true and tender in her nature began to rise in her and take his part. Unhappily, he felt too deeply and too strongly to be patient, and give her time. He completely misinterpreted her silence—completely mistook the motive that made her turn aside for a moment, to gather composure enough to speak to him. "Ah!" he burst out bitterly, turning away on his side, "you have no heart."

She instantly resented those unjust words. At that moment they wounded her to the quick.

"You know best," she said. "I have no doubt you are right. Remember one thing, however, that though I have no heart, I have never encouraged you, Mr. Moody. I have declared over and over again that I could only be your friend. Understand that for the future, if you please. There are plenty of nice women who will be glad to marry you, I have no doubt. You will always have my best wishes for your welfare. Good-morning. Her Ladyship will wonder what has become of me. Be so kind as to let me pass."

Tortured by the passion that consumed him, Moody obstinately kept his place between Isabel and the door. The unworthy suspicion of her, which had been in his mind all through the interview, now forced its way outwards to expression at last.

"No woman ever used a man as you use me without some reason for it," he said. "You have kept your secret wonderfully well—but sooner or later all secrets get found out. I know what is in your mind as well as you know it yourself. You are in love with some other man."

Isabel's face flushed deeply; the defensive pride of her sex was up in arms in an instant. She cast one disdainful look at Moody, without troubling herself to express her contempt in words. "Stand out of my way, sir!"—that was all she said to him.

"You are in love with some other man," he reiterated passionately. "Deny it if you can!"

"Deny it?" she repeated, with flashing eyes. "What right have you to ask the question? Am I not free to do as I please?"

He stood looking at her, meditating his next words with a sudden and sinister change to self-restraint. Suppressed rage was in his rigidly set eyes, suppressed rage was in his trembling hand as he raised it emphatically while he spoke his next words.

"I have one thing more to say," he answered, "and then I have done. If I am not your husband, no other man shall be. Look well to it, Isabel Miller. If there is another man between us, I can tell him this—he shall find it no easy matter to rob me of you!"

She started, and turned pale—but it was only for a moment. The high spirit that was in her rose brightly in her eyes, and faced him without shrinking.

"Threats?" she said, with quiet contempt. "When you make love, Mr. Moody, you take strange ways of doing it. My conscience is easy. You may try to frighten me, but you will not succeed. When you have recovered your temper I will accept your excuses." She paused, and pointed to the table. "There is the letter that you told me to leave for you when I had sealed it," she went on. "I suppose you have her Ladyship's orders. Isn't it time you began to think of obeying them?"

The contemptuous composure of her tone and manner seemed to act on Moody with crushing effect. Without a word of answer, the unfortunate steward took up the letter from the table. Without a word of answer, he walked mechanically to the great door which opened on the staircase—turned on the threshold to look at Isabel—waited a moment, pale and still—and suddenly left the room.

That silent departure, that hopeless submission, impressed Isabel in spite of herself. The sustaining sense of injury and insult sank, as it were, from under her the moment she was alone. He had not been gone a minute before she began to be sorry for him once more. The interview had taught her nothing. She was neither old enough nor experienced enough to understand the overwhelming revolution produced in a man's character when he feels the passion of love for the first time in the maturity of his life. If Moody had stolen a kiss at the first opportunity, she would have resented the liberty he had taken with her; but she would have thoroughly understood him. His terrible earnestness, his overpowering agitation, his abrupt violence—all these evidences of a passion that was a mystery to himself—simply puzzled her. "I'm sure I didn't wish to hurt his feelings" (such was the form that her reflections took, in her present penitent frame of mind); "but why did he provoke me? It is a shame to tell me that I love some other man—when there is no other man. I declare I begin to hate the men, if they are all like Mr. Moody. I wonder whether he will forgive me when he sees me again? I'm sure I'm willing to forget and forgive on my side—especially if he won't insist on my being fond of him because he is fond of me. Oh, dear! I wish he would come back and shake hands. It's enough to try the patience of a saint to be treated in this way. I wish I was ugly! The ugly ones have a quiet time of it—the men let them be. Mr. Moody! Mr. Moody!" She went out to the landing and called to him softly. There was no answer. He was no longer in the house. She stood still for a moment in silent vexation. "I'll go to Tommie!" she decided. "I'm sure he's the more agreeable company of the two. And—oh, good gracious! there's Mr. Hardyman waiting to give me my instructions! How do I look, I wonder?"

She consulted the glass once more—gave one or two corrective touches to her hair and her cap—and hastened into the boudoir.

CHAPTER VI.

FOR a quarter of an hour the drawing-room remained empty. At the end of that time the council in the boudoir broke up. Lady Lydiard led the way back into the drawing-room, followed by Hardyman, Isabel being left to look after the dog. Before the door closed behind him, Hardyman turned round to reiterate his last medical directions—or, in plainer words, to take a last look at Isabel.

"Plenty of water, Miss Isabel, for the dog to lap, and a little bread or biscuit, if he wants something to eat. Nothing more, if you please, till I see him to-morrow."

"Thank you, sir. I will take the greatest care—"

At that point Lady Lydiard cut short the interchange of instructions and civilities. "Shut the door, if you please, Mr. Hardyman. I feel the draught. Many thanks! I am really at a loss to tell you how gratefully I feel your kindness. But for you my poor little dog might be dead by this time."

Hardyman answered, in the quiet melancholy monotone which was habitual with him, "Your Ladyship need feel no further anxiety about the dog. Only be careful not to overfeed him. He will do very well under Miss Isabel's care. By the bye, her family name is Miller—is it not? Is she related to the Warwickshire Millers of Duxborough House?"

Lady Lydiard looked at him with an expression of satirical surprise. "Mr. Hardyman," she said, "this makes the fourth time you have questioned me about Isabel. You seem to take a great interest in my little companion. Don't make any apologies, pray! You pay Isabel a compliment, and, as I am very fond of her, I am naturally gratified when I find her admired. At the same time," she added, with one of her abrupt transitions of language, "I had my eye on you, and I had my eye on her, when you were talking in the next room; and I don't mean to let you make a fool of the girl. She is not in your line of life, and the sooner you know it the better. You make me laugh when you ask if she is related to gentlefolks. She is the orphan daughter of a chemist in the country. Her relations haven't a penny to bless themselves with, except an old aunt, who lives in a village on two or three hundred a year. I heard of the girl by accident. When she lost her father and mother, her aunt offered to take her. Isabel said, 'No, thank you; I will not be a burden on a relation who has only enough for herself. A girl can earn an honest living if she tries; and I mean to try'—that's what she said. I admired her independence," her Ladyship proceeded, ascending again to the higher regions of thought and expression. "My niece's marriage, just at that time, had left me alone in this great house. I proposed to Isabel to come to me as companion and reader for a few weeks, and to decide for herself whether she liked the life or not. We have never been separated since that time. I could hardly be fonder of her if she were my own daughter; and she returns my affection with all her heart. She has excellent qualities—prudent, cheerful, sweet-tempered; with good sense enough to understand what her place is in the world, as distinguished from her place in my regard. I have taken care, for her own sake, never to leave that part of the question in any doubt. It would be cruel kindness to deceive her as to her future position when she marries. I shall take good care that the man who pays his addresses to her is a man in her rank of life. I know but too well, in the case of one of my own relatives, what miseries unequal marriages bring with them. Excuse me for troubling you at this length on domestic matters. I am very fond of Isabel; and a girl's head is so easily turned. Now you know what her position really is, you will also know what limits there must be to the expression of your interest in her. I am sure we understand each other; and I say no more."

Hardyman listened to this long harangue with the immovable gravity which was part of his character—except when Isabel had taken him by surprise. When her Ladyship gave him the opportunity of speaking on his side, he had very little to say, and that little did not suggest that he had greatly profited by what he had heard. His mind had been full of Isabel when Lady Lydiard began, and it remained just as full of her, in just the same way, when Lady Lydiard had done.

"Yes," he remarked quietly, "Miss Isabel is an uncommonly nice girl, as you say. Very pretty, and such frank, unaffected manners. I don't deny that I feel an interest in her. The young ladies one meets in society are not much to my taste. Miss Isabel is my taste."

Lady Lydiard's face assumed a look of blank dismay. "I am afraid I have failed to convey my exact meaning to you," she said.

Hardyman gravely declared that he understood her perfectly. "Perfectly!" he repeated, with his impenetrable obstinacy. "Your Ladyship exactly expresses my opinion of Miss Isabel. Prudent, and cheerful, and sweet-tempered, as you say—all the qualities in a woman that I admire. With good looks, too—of course, with good looks. She will be a perfect treasure (as you remarked just now) to the man who marries her. I may claim to know something about it. I have twice narrowly escaped being married myself; and, though I can't exactly explain it, I'm all the harder to please in consequence. Miss Isabel pleases me. I think I have said that before? Pardon me for saying it again. I'll call again to-morrow morning and look at the dog as early as eleven o'clock, if you will allow me. Later in the day I must be off to France to attend a sale of horses. Glad to have been of any use to your Ladyship, I am sure. Good-morning."

Lady Lydiard let him go, wisely resigning any further attempt to establish an understanding between her visitor and herself.

"He is either a person of very limited intelligence when he is away from his stables," she thought, "or he deliberately declines to take a plain hint when it is given to him. I can't drop his acquaintance, on Tommie's account. The only other alternative is to keep Isabel out of his way. My good little girl shall not drift into a false position while I am living to look after her. When Mr. Hardyman calls to-morrow she shall be out on an errand. When he calls the next time she shall be upstairs with a headache. And if he tries it again she shall be away at my house in the country. If he makes any remarks on her absence—well, he will find that I can be just as dull of understanding as he is when the occasion calls for it."

Having arrived at this satisfactory solution of the difficulty, Lady Lydiard became conscious of an irresistible impulse to summon Isabel to her presence and caress her. In the nature of a warm-hearted woman, this was only the inevitable reaction which followed the subsidence of anxiety about the girl, after her own resolution had set that anxiety at rest. She threw open the door and made one of her sudden appearances at the boudoir. Even in the fervent outpouring of her affection, there was still the inherent abruptness of manner which so strongly marked Lady Lydiard's character in all the relations of life.

"Did I give you a kiss, this morning?" she asked, when Isabel rose to receive her.

"Yes, my Lady," said the girl, with her charming smile.

"Come, then, and give me a kiss in return. Do you love me? Very well, then, treat me like your mother. Never mind 'my lady' this time. Give me a good hug!"

Something in those homely words, or something perhaps in the look that accompanied them, touched sympathies in Isabel which seldom showed themselves on the surface. Her smiling lips trembled, the bright tears rose in her eyes. "You are too good to me," she murmured, with her head on Lady Lydiard's bosom. "How can I ever love you enough in return?"

Lady Lydiard patted the pretty head that rested on her with such filial tenderness. "There! there!" she said, "Go back and play with Tommie, my dear. We may be as fond of each other as we like; but we mustn't cry. God bless you! Go away—go away!"

She turned aside quickly; her own eyes were moistening, and it was part of her character to be reluctant to let Isabel see it. "Why have I made a fool of myself?" she wondered, as she approached the drawing-room door. "It doesn't matter. I am all the better for it. Odd, that Mr. Hardyman should have made me feel fonder of Isabel than ever!"

With those reflections she re-entered the drawing-room—and suddenly checked herself with a start. "Good Heavens!" she exclaimed irritably, "how you frightened me! Why was I not told you were here?"

Having left the drawing-room in a state of solitude, Lady Lydiard on her return found herself suddenly confronted with a gentleman, mysteriously planted on the hearth-rug in her absence. The new visitor may be rightly described as a gray man. He had gray hair, eyebrows, and whiskers; he wore a gray coat, waistcoat, and trousers, and gray gloves. For the rest, his appearance was eminently suggestive of wealth and respectability and, in this case, appearances were really to be trusted. The gray man was no other than Lady Lydiard's legal adviser, Mr. Troy.

"I regret, my Lady, that I should have been so unfortunate as to startle you," he said, with a certain underlying embarrassment in his manner. "I had the honor of sending word by Mr. Moody that I would call at this hour, on some matters of business connected with your Ladyship's house property. I presumed that you expected to find me here, waiting your pleasure—"

Thus far Lady Lydiard had listened to her legal adviser, fixing her eyes on his face in her usually frank, straightforward way. She now stopped him in the middle of a sentence, with a change of expression in her own face which was undisguisedly a change to alarm.

"Don't apologize, Mr. Troy," she said. "I am to blame for forgetting your appointment and for not keeping my nerves under proper control." She paused for a moment and took a seat before she said her next words. "May I ask," she resumed, "if there is something unpleasant in the business that brings you here?"

"Nothing whatever, my Lady; mere formalities, which can wait till to-morrow or next day, if you wish it."

Lady Lydiard's fingers drummed impatiently on the table. "You have known me long enough, Mr. Troy, to know that I cannot endure suspense. You have something unpleasant to tell me."

The lawyer respectfully remonstrated. "Really, Lady Lydiard!—" he began.

"It won't do, Mr. Troy! I know how you look at me on ordinary occasions, and I see how you look at me now. You are a very clever lawyer; but, happily for the interests that I commit to your charge, you are also a thoroughly honest man. After twenty years' experience of you, you can't deceive me. You bring me bad news. Speak at once, sir, and speak plainly."

Mr. Troy yielded—inch by inch, as it were. "I bring news which, I fear, may annoy your Ladyship." He paused, and advanced another inch. "It is news which I only became acquainted with myself on entering this house."

He waited again, and made another advance. "I happened to meet your Ladyship's steward, Mr. Moody, in the hall—"

"Where is he?" Lady Lydiard interposed angrily. "I can make him speak out, and I will. Send him here instantly."

The lawyer made a last effort to hold off the coming disclosure a little longer. "Mr. Moody will be here directly," he said. "Mr. Moody requested me to prepare your Ladyship—"

"Will you ring the bell, Mr. Troy, or must I?"

Moody had evidently been waiting outside while the lawyer spoke for him. He saved Mr. Troy the trouble of ringing the bell by presenting himself in the drawing-room. Lady Lydiard's eyes searched his face as he approached. Her bright complexion faded suddenly. Not a word more passed her lips. She looked, and waited.

In silence on his part, Moody laid an open sheet of paper on the table. The paper quivered in his trembling hand.

Lady Lydiard recovered herself first. "Is that for me?" she asked.

"Yes, my Lady."

She took up the paper without an instant's hesitation. Both the men watched her anxiously as she read it.

The handwriting was strange to her. The words were these:—

"I hereby certify that the bearer of these lines, Robert Moody by name, has presented to me the letter with which he was charged, addressed to myself, with the seal intact. I regret to add that there is, to say the least of it, some mistake. The inclosure referred to by the anonymous writer of the letter, who signs 'a friend in need,' has not reached me. No five-hundred pound bank-note was in the letter when I opened it. My wife was present when I broke the seal, and can certify to this statement if necessary. Not knowing who my charitable correspondent is (Mr. Moody being forbidden to give me any information), I can only take this means of stating the case exactly as it stands, and hold myself at the disposal of the writer of the letter. My private address is at the head of the page.—Samuel Bradstock, Rector, St. Anne's, Deansbury, London."

Lady Lydiard dropped the paper on the table. For the moment, plainly as the Rector's statement was expressed, she appeared to be incapable of understanding it. "What, in God's name, does this mean?" she asked.

The lawyer and the steward looked at each other. Which of the two was entitled to speak first? Lady Lydiard gave them no time to decide. "Moody," she said sternly, "you took charge of the letter—I look to you for an explanation."

Moody's dark eyes flashed. He answered Lady Lydiard without caring to conceal that he resented the tone in which she had spoken to him.

"I undertook to deliver the letter at its address," he said. "I found it, sealed, on the table. Your Ladyship has the clergyman's written testimony that I handed it to him with the seal unbroken. I have done my duty; and I have no explanation to offer."

Before Lady Lydiard could speak again, Mr. Troy discreetly interfered. He saw plainly that his experience was required to lead the investigation in the right direction.

"Pardon me, my Lady," he said, with that happy mixture of the positive and the polite in his manner, of which lawyers alone possess the secret. "There is only one way of arriving at the truth in painful matters of this sort. We must begin at the beginning. May I venture to ask your Ladyship a question?"

Lady Lydiard felt the composing influence of Mr. Troy. "I am at your disposal, sir," she said, quietly.

"Are you absolutely certain that you inclosed the bank-note in the letter?" the lawyer asked.

"I certainly believe I inclosed it," Lady Lydiard answered. "But I was so alarmed at the time by the sudden illness of my dog, that I do not feel justified in speaking positively."

"Was anybody in the room with your Ladyship when you put the inclosure in the letter—as you believe?"

"I was in the room," said Moody. "I can swear that I saw her Ladyship put the bank-note in the letter, and the letter in the envelope."

"And seal the envelope?" asked Mr. Troy.

"No, sir. Her Ladyship was called away into the next room to the dog, before she could seal the envelope."

Mr. Troy addressed himself once more to Lady Lydiard. "Did your Ladyship take the letter into the next room with you?"

"I was too much alarmed to think of it, Mr. Troy. I left it here, on the table."

"With the envelope open?"

"Yes."

"How long were you absent in the other room?"

"Half an hour or more."

"Ha!" said Mr. Troy to himself. "This complicates it a little." He reflected for a while, and then turned again to Moody. "Did any of the servants know of this bank-note being in her Ladyship's possession?"

"Not one of them," Moody answered.

"Do you suspect any of the servants?"

"Certainly not, sir."

"Are there any workmen employed in the house?"

"No, sir."

"Do you know of any persons who had access to the room while Lady Lydiard was absent from it?"

"Two visitors called, sir."

"Who were they?"

"Her Ladyship's nephew, Mr. Felix Sweetsir, and the Honorable Alfred Hardyman."

Mr. Troy shook his head irritably. "I am not speaking of gentlemen of high position and repute," he said. "It's absurd even to mention Mr. Sweetsir and Mr. Hardyman. My question related to strangers who might have obtained access to the drawing-room—people calling, with her Ladyship's sanction, for subscriptions, for instance; or people calling with articles of dress or ornament to be submitted to her Ladyship's inspection."

"No such persons came to the house with my knowledge," Moody answered.

Mr. Troy suspended the investigation, and took a turn thoughtfully in the room. The theory on which his inquiries had proceeded thus far had failed to produce any results. His experience warned him to waste no more time on it, and to return to the starting-point of the investigation—in other words, to the letter. Shifting his point of view, he turned again to Lady Lydiard, and tried his questions in a new direction.

"Mr. Moody mentioned just now," he said, "that your Ladyship was called into the next room before you could seal your letter. On your return to this room, did you seal the letter?"

"I was busy with the dog," Lady Lydiard answered. "Isabel Miller was of no use in the boudoir, and I told her to seal it for me."

Mr. Troy started. The new direction in which he was pushing his inquiries began to look like the right direction already. "Miss Isabel Miller," he proceeded, "has been a resident under your Ladyship's roof for some little time, I believe?"

"For nearly two years, Mr. Troy."

"As your Ladyship's companion and reader?"

"As my adopted daughter," her Ladyship answered, with marked emphasis.

Wise Mr. Troy rightly interpreted the emphasis as a warning to him to suspend the examination of her Ladyship, and to address to Mr. Moody the far more serious questions which were now to come.

"Did anyone give you the letter before you left the house with it?" he said to the steward. "Or did you take it yourself?"

"I took it myself, from the table here."

"Was it sealed?"

"Yes."

"Was anybody present when you took the letter from the table?"

"Miss Isabel was present."

"Did you find her alone in the room?"

"Yes, sir."

Lady Lydiard opened her lips to speak, and checked herself. Mr. Troy, having cleared the ground before him, put the fatal question.

"Mr. Moody," he said, "when Miss Isabel was instructed to seal the letter, did she know that a bank-note was inclosed in it?"

Instead of replying, Robert drew back from the lawyer with a look of horror. Lady Lydiard started to her feet—and checked herself again, on the point of speaking.

"Answer him, Moody," she said, putting a strong constraint on herself.

Robert answered very unwillingly. "I took the liberty of reminding her ladyship that she had left her letter unsealed," he said. "And I mentioned as my excuse for speaking,"—he stopped, and corrected himself—"I believe I mentioned that a valuable inclosure was in the letter."

"You believe?" Mr. Troy repeated. "Can't you speak more positively than that?"

"I can speak positively," said Lady Lydiard, with her eyes on the lawyer. "Moody did mention the inclosure in the letter—in Isabel Miller's hearing as well as in mine." She paused, steadily controlling herself. "And what of that, Mr. Troy?" she added, very quietly and firmly.

Mr. Troy answered quietly and firmly, on his side. "I am surprised that your Ladyship should ask the question," he said.

"I persist in repeating the question," Lady Lydiard rejoined. "I say that Isabel Miller knew of the inclosure in my letter—and I ask, What of that?"

"And I answer," retorted the impenetrable lawyer, "that the suspicion of theft rests on your Ladyship's adopted daughter, and on nobody else."

"It's false!" cried Robert, with a burst of honest indignation. "I wish to God I had never said a word to you about the loss of the bank-note! Oh, my Lady! my Lady! don't let him distress you! What does he know about it?"

"Hush!" said Lady Lydiard. "Control yourself, and hear what he has to say." She rested her hand on Moody's shoulder, partly to encourage him, partly to support herself; and, fixing her eyes again on Mr. Troy, repeated his last words, "'Suspicion rests on my adopted daughter, and on nobody else.' Why on nobody else?"

"Is your Ladyship prepared to suspect the Rector of St. Anne's of embezzlement, or your own relatives and equals of theft?" Mr. Troy asked. "Does a shadow of doubt rest on the servants? Not if Mr. Moody's evidence is to be believed. Who, to our own certain knowledge, had access to the letter while it was unsealed? Who was alone in the room with it? And who knew of the inclosure in it? I leave the answer to your Ladyship."

"Isabel Miller is as incapable of an act of theft as I am. There is my answer, Mr. Troy."

The lawyer bowed resignedly, and advanced to the door.

"Am I to take your Ladyship's generous assertion as finally disposing of the question of the lost bank-note?" he inquired.

Lady Lydiard met the challenge without shrinking from it.

"No!" she said. "The loss of the bank-note is known out of my house. Other persons may suspect this innocent girl as you suspect her. It is due to Isabel's reputation—her unstained reputation, Mr. Troy!—that she should know what has happened, and should have an opportunity of defending herself. She is in the next room, Moody. Bring her here."

Robert's courage failed him: he trembled at the bare idea of exposing Isabel to the terrible ordeal that awaited her. "Oh, my Lady!" he pleaded, "think again before you tell the poor girl that she is suspected of theft. Keep it a secret from her—the shame of it will break her heart!"

"Keep it a secret," said Lady Lydiard, "when the Rector and the Rector's wife both know of it! Do you think they will let the matter rest where it is, even if I could consent to hush it up? I must write to them; and I can't write anonymously after what has happened. Put yourself in Isabel's place, and tell me if you would thank the person who knew you to be innocently exposed to a disgraceful suspicion, and who concealed it from you? Go, Moody! The longer you delay, the harder it will be."

With his head sunk on his breast, with anguish written in every line of his face, Moody obeyed. Passing slowly down the short passage which connected the two rooms, and still shrinking from the duty that had been imposed on him, he paused, looking through the curtains which hung over the entrance to the boudoir.

CHAPTER VII.

THE sight that met Moody's view wrung him to the heart.

Isabel and the dog were at play together. Among the varied accomplishments possessed by Tommie, the capacity to take his part at a game of hide-and-seek was one. His playfellow for the time being put a shawl or a handkerchief over his head, so as to prevent him from seeing, and then hid among the furniture a pocketbook, or a cigar-case, or a purse, or anything else that happened to be at hand, leaving the dog to find it, with his keen sense of smell to guide him. Doubly relieved by the fit and the bleeding, Tommie's spirits had revived; and he and Isabel had just begun their game when Moody looked into the room, charged with his terrible errand. "You're burning, Tommie, you're burning!" cried the girl, laughing and clapping her hands. The next moment she happened to look round and saw Moody through the parted curtains. His face warned her instantly that something serious had happened. She advanced a few steps, her eyes resting on him in silent alarm. He was himself too painfully agitated to speak. Not a word was exchanged between Lady Lydiard and Mr. Troy in the next room. In the complete stillness that prevailed, the dog was heard sniffing and fidgeting about the furniture. Robert took Isabel by the hand and led her into the drawing-room. "For God's sake, spare her, my Lady!" he whispered. The lawyer heard him. "No," said Mr. Troy. "Be merciful, and tell her the truth!"

He spoke to a woman who stood in no need of his advice. The inherent nobility in Lady Lydiard's nature was aroused: her great heart offered itself patiently to any sorrow, to any sacrifice.

Putting her arm round Isabel—half caressing her, half supporting her—Lady Lydiard accepted the whole responsibility and told the whole truth.

Reeling under the first shock, the poor girl recovered herself with admirable courage. She raised her head, and eyed the lawyer without uttering a word. In its artless consciousness of innocence the look was nothing less than sublime. Addressing herself to Mr. Troy, Lady Lydiard pointed to Isabel. "Do you see guilt there?" she asked.

Mr. Troy made no answer. In the melancholy experience of humanity to which his profession condemned him, he had seen conscious guilt assume the face of innocence, and helpless innocence admit the disguise of guilt: the keenest observation, in either case, failing completely to detect the truth. Lady Lydiard misinterpreted his silence as expressing the sullen self-assertion of a heartless man. She turned from him, in contempt, and held out her hand to Isabel.

"Mr. Troy is not satisfied yet," she said bitterly. "My love, take my hand, and look me in the face as your equal; I know no difference of rank at such a time as this. Before God, who hears you, are you innocent of the theft of the bank-note?"

"Before God, who hears me," Isabel answered, "I am innocent."

Lady Lydiard looked once more at the lawyer, and waited to hear if he believed that.

Mr. Troy took refuge in dumb diplomacy—he made a low bow. It might have meant that he believed Isabel, or it might have meant that he modestly withdrew his own opinion into the background. Lady Lydiard did not condescend to inquire what it meant.

"The sooner we bring this painful scene to an end the better," she said. "I shall be glad to avail myself of your professional assistance, Mr. Troy, within certain limits. Outside of my house, I beg that you will spare no trouble in tracing the lost money to the person who has really stolen it. Inside of my house, I must positively request that the disappearance of the note may never be alluded to, in any way whatever, until your inquiries have been successful in discovering the thief. In the meanwhile, Mrs. Tollmidge and her family must not be sufferers by my loss: I shall pay the money again." She paused, and pressed Isabel's hand with affectionate fervor. "My child," she said, "one last word to you, and I have done. You remain here, with my trust in you, and my love for you, absolutely unshaken. When you think of what has been said here to-day, never forget that."

Isabel bent her head, and kissed the kind hand that still held hers. The high spirit that was in her, inspired by Lady Lydiard's example, rose equal to the dreadful situation in which she was placed.

"No, my Lady," she said calmly and sadly; "it cannot be. What this gentleman has said of me is not to be denied—the appearances are against me. The letter was open, and I was alone in the room with it, and Mr. Moody told me that a valuable inclosure was inside it. Dear and kind mistress! I am not fit to be a member of your household, I am not worthy to live with the honest people who serve you, while my innocence is in doubt. It is enough for me now that you don't doubt it. I can wait patiently, after that, for the day that gives me back my good name. Oh, my Lady, don't cry about it! Pray, pray don't cry!"

Lady Lydiard's self-control failed her for the first time. Isabel's courage had made Isabel dearer to her than ever. She sank into a chair, and covered her face with her handkerchief. Mr. Troy turned aside abruptly, and examined a Japanese vase, without any idea in his mind of what he was looking at. Lady Lydiard had gravely misjudged him in believing him to be a heartless man.

Isabel followed the lawyer, and touched him gently on the arm to rouse his attention.

"I have one relation living, sir—an aunt—who will receive me if I go to her," she said simply. "Is there any harm in my going? Lady Lydiard will give you the address when you want me. Spare her Ladyship, sir, all the pain and trouble that you can."

At last the heart that was in Mr. Troy asserted itself. "You are a fine creature!" he said, with a burst of enthusiasm. "I agree with Lady Lydiard—I believe you are innocent, too; and I will leave no effort untried to find the proof of it." He turned aside again, and had another look at the Japanese vase.

As the lawyer withdrew himself from observation, Moody approached Isabel.

Thus far he had stood apart, watching her and listening to her in silence.

59

Not a look that had crossed her face, not a word that had fallen from her, had escaped him. Unconsciously on her side, unconsciously on his side, she now wrought on his nature with a purifying and ennobling influence which animated it with a new life. All that had been selfish and violent in his passion for her left him to return no more. The immeasurable devotion which he laid at her feet, in the days that were yet to come—the unyielding courage which cheerfully accepted the sacrifice of himself when events demanded it at a later period of his life—struck root in him now. Without attempting to conceal the tears that were falling fast over his cheeks—striving vainly to express those new thoughts in him that were beyond the reach of words—he stood before her the truest friend and servant that ever woman had.

"Oh, my dear! my heart is heavy for you. Take me to serve you and help you. Her Ladyship's kindness will permit it, I am sure."

He could say no more. In those simple words the cry of his heart reached her. "Forgive me, Robert," she answered, gratefully, "if I said anything to pain you when we spoke together a little while since. I didn't mean it." She gave him her hand, and looked timidly over her shoulder at Lady Lydiard. "Let me go!" she said, in low, broken tones, "Let me go!"

Mr. Troy heard her, and stepped forward to interfere before Lady Lydiard could speak. The man had recovered his self-control; the lawyer took his place again on the scene.

"You must not leave us, my dear," he said to Isabel, "until I have put a question to Mr. Moody in which you are interested. Do you happen to have the number of the lost bank-note?" he asked, turning to the steward.

Moody produced his slip of paper with the number on it. Mr. Troy made two copies of it before he returned the paper. One copy he put in his pocket, the other he handed to Isabel.

"Keep it carefully," he said. "Neither you nor I know how soon it may be of use to you."

Receiving the copy from him, she felt mechanically in her apron for her pocketbook. She had used it, in playing with the dog, as an object to hide from him; but she had suffered, and was still suffering, too keenly to be capable of the effort of remembrance. Moody, eager to help her even in the most trifling thing, guessed what had happened. "You were playing with Tommie," he said; "is it in the next room?"

The dog heard his name pronounced through the open door. The next moment he trotted into the drawing-room with Isabel's pocketbook in his mouth. He was a strong, well-grown Scotch terrier of the largest size, with bright, intelligent eyes, and a coat of thick curling white hair, diversified by two light brown patches on his back. As he reached the middle of the room, and looked from one to another of the persons present, the fine sympathy of his race told him that there was trouble among his human friends. His tail dropped; he whined softly as he approached Isabel, and laid her pocketbook at her feet.

She knelt as she picked up the pocketbook, and raised her playfellow of happier days to take her leave of him. As the dog put his paws on her shoulders, returning her caress, her first tears fell. "Foolish of me," she said, faintly, "to cry over a dog. I can't help it. Good-by, Tommie!"

Putting him away from her gently, she walked towards the door. The dog instantly followed. She put him away from her, for the second time, and left him. He was not to be denied; he followed her again, and took the skirt of her dress in his teeth, as if to hold her back. Robert forced the dog, growling and resisting with all his might, to let go of the dress. "Don't be rough with him," said Isabel. "Put him on her ladyship's lap; he will be quieter there." Robert obeyed. He whispered to Lady Lydiard as she received the dog; she seemed to be still incapable of speaking—she bowed her head in silent assent. Robert hurried back to Isabel before she had passed the door. "Not alone!" he said entreatingly. "Her Ladyship permits it, Isabel. Let me see you safe to your aunt's house."

Isabel looked at him, felt for him, and yielded.

"Yes," she answered softly; "to make amends for what I said to you when I was thoughtless and happy!" She waited a little to compose herself before she spoke her farewell words to Lady Lydiard. "Good-by, my Lady. Your kindness has not been thrown away on an ungrateful girl. I love you, and thank you, with all my heart."

Lady Lydiard rose, placing the dog on the chair as she left it. She seemed to have grown older by years, instead of by minutes, in the short interval that had passed since she had hidden her face from view. "I can't bear it!" she cried, in husky, broken tones. "Isabel! Isabel! I forbid you to leave me!"

But one person could venture to resist her. That person was Mr. Troy—and Mr. Troy knew it.

"Control yourself," he said to her in a whisper. "The girl is doing what is best and most becoming in her position—and is doing it with a patience and courage wonderful to see. She places herself under the protection of her nearest relative, until her character is vindicated and her position in your house is once more beyond a doubt. Is this a time to throw obstacles in her way? Be worthy of yourself, Lady Lydiard and think of the day when she will return to you without the breath of a suspicion to rest on her!"

There was no disputing with him—he was too plainly in the right. Lady Lydiard submitted; she concealed the torture that her own resolution inflicted on her with an endurance which was, indeed, worthy of herself. Taking Isabel in her arms she kissed her in a passion of sorrow and love. "My poor dear! My own sweet girl! don't suppose that this is a parting kiss! I shall see you again—often and often I shall see you again at your aunt's!" At a sign from Mr. Troy, Robert took Isabel's arm in his and led her away. Tommie, watching her from his chair, lifted his little white muzzle as his playfellow looked back on passing the doorway. The long, melancholy, farewell howl of the dog was the last sound Isabel Miller heard as she left the house.

PART THE SECOND.

THE DISCOVERY.

CHAPTER VIII.

ON the day after Isabel's departure, diligent Mr. Troy set forth for the Head Office in Whitehall to consult the police on the question of the missing money. He had previously sent information of the robbery to the Bank of England, and had also advertised the loss in the daily newspapers.

The air was so pleasant, and the sun was so bright, that he determined on proceeding to his destination on foot. He was hardly out of sight of his own offices when he was overtaken by a friend, who was also walking in the direction of Whitehall. This gentleman was a person of considerable worldly wisdom and experience; he had been officially associated with cases of striking and notorious crime, in which Government had lent its assistance to discover and punish the criminals. The opinion of a person in this position might be of the greatest value to Mr. Troy, whose practice as a solicitor had thus far never brought him into collision with thieves and mysteries. He accordingly decided, in Isabel's interests, on confiding to his friend the nature of his errand to the police. Concealing the name, but concealing nothing else, he described what had happened on the previous day at Lady Lydiard's house, and then put the question plainly to his companion.

"What would you do in my place?"

"In your place," his friend answered quietly, "I should not waste time and money in consulting the police."

"Not consult the police!" exclaimed Mr. Troy in amazement. "Surely, I have not made myself understood? I am going to the Head Office; and I have got a letter of introduction to the chief inspector in the detective department. I am afraid I omitted to mention that?"

"It doesn't make any difference," proceeded the other, as coolly as ever. "You have asked for my advice, and I give you my advice. Tear up your letter of introduction, and don't stir a step further in the direction of Whitehall."

Mr. Troy began to understand. "You don't believe in the detective police?" he said.

"Who can believe in them, who reads his newspaper and remembers what he reads?" his friend rejoined. "Fortunately for the detective department, the public in general forgets what it reads. Go to your club, and look at the criminal history of our own time, recorded in the newspapers. Every crime is more or less a mystery. You will see that the mysteries which the police discover are, almost without exception, mysteries made penetrable by the commonest capacity, through the extraordinary stupidity exhibited in the means taken to hide the crime. On the other hand, let the guilty man or woman be a resolute and intelligent person, capable of setting his (or her) wits fairly against the wits of the police—in other words, let the mystery really be a mystery—and cite me a case if you can (a really difficult and perplexing case) in which the criminal has not escaped. Mind! I don't charge the police with neglecting their work. No doubt they do their best, and take the greatest pains in following the routine to which they have been trained. It is their misfortune, not their fault, that there is no man of superior intelligence among them—I mean no man who is capable, in great emergencies, of placing himself above conventional methods, and following a new way of his own. There have been such men in the police—men naturally endowed with that faculty of mental analysis which can decompose a mystery, resolve it into its component parts, and find the clue at the bottom, no matter how remote from ordinary observation it may be. But those men have died, or have retired. One of them would have been invaluable to you in the case you have just mentioned to me. As things are, unless you are wrong in believing in the young lady's innocence, the person who has stolen that bank-note will be no easy person to find. In my opinion, there is only one man now in London who is likely to be of the slightest assistance to you—and he is not in the police."

"Who is he?" asked Mr. Troy.

"An old rogue, who was once in your branch of the legal profession," the friend answered. "You may, perhaps, remember the name: they call him 'Old Sharon.'"

"What! The scoundrel who was struck off the Roll of Attorneys, years since? Is he still alive?"

"Alive and prospering. He lives in a court or lane running out of Long Acre, and he offers advice to persons interested in recovering missing objects of any sort. Whether you have lost your wife, or lost your cigar-case, Old Sharon is equally useful to you. He has an inbred capacity for reading the riddle the right way in cases of mystery, great or small. In short, he possesses exactly that analytical faculty to which I alluded just now. I have his address at my office, if you think it worth while to try him."

"Who can trust such a man?" Mr. Troy objected. "He would be sure to deceive me."

"You are entirely mistaken. Since he was struck off the Rolls Old Sharon has discovered that the straight way is, on the whole, the best way, even in a man's own interests. His consultation fee is a guinea; and he gives a signed estimate beforehand for any supplementary expenses that may follow. I can tell you (this is, of course, strictly between ourselves) that the authorities at my office took his advice in a Government case that puzzled the police. We approached him, of course, through persons who were to be trusted to represent us, without betraying the source from which their instructions were derived; and we found the old rascal's advice well worth paying for. It is quite likely that he may not succeed so well in your case. Try the police, by all means; and, if they fail, why, there is Sharon as a last resort."

This arrangement commended itself to Mr. Troy's professional caution. He went on to Whitehall, and he tried the detective police.

They at once adopted the obvious conclusion to persons of ordinary capacity—the conclusion that Isabel was the thief.

Acting on this conviction, the authorities sent an experienced woman from the office to Lady Lydiard's house, to examine the poor girl's clothes and ornaments before they were packed up and sent after her to her aunt's.

The search led to nothing. The only objects of any value that were discovered had been presents from Lady Lydiard. No jewelers' or milliners' bills were among the papers found in her desk. Not a sign of secret extravagance in dress was to be seen anywhere. Defeated so far, the police proposed next to have Isabel privately watched. There might be a prodigal lover somewhere in the background, with ruin staring him in the face unless he could raise five hundred pounds. Lady Lydiard (who had only consented to the search under stress of persuasive argument from Mr. Troy) resented this ingenious idea as an insult. She declared that if Isabel was watched the girl should know of it instantly from her own lips. The police listened with perfect resignation and decorum, and politely shifted their ground. A certain suspicion (they remarked) always rested in cases of this sort on the servants. Would her Ladyship object to private inquiries into the characters and proceedings of the servants? Her Ladyship instantly objected, in the most positive terms. Thereupon the "Inspector" asked for a minute's private conversation with Mr. Troy. "The thief is certainly a member of Lady Lydiard's household," this functionary remarked, in his politely-positive way. "If her Ladyship persists in refusing to let us make the necessary inquiries, our hands are tied, and the case comes to an end through no fault of ours. If her Ladyship changes her mind, perhaps you will drop me a line, sir, to that effect. Good-morning."

So the experiment of consulting the police came to an untimely end. The one result obtained was the expression of purblind opinion by the authorities of the detective department which pointed to Isabel, or to one of the servants, as the undiscovered thief. Thinking the matter over in the retirement of his own office—and not forgetting his promise to Isabel to leave no means untried of establishing her innocence—Mr. Troy could see but one alternative left to him. He took up his pen, and wrote to his friend at the Government office. There was nothing for it now but to run the risk, and try Old Sharon.

CHAPTER IX.

THE next day, Mr. Troy (taking Robert Moody with him as a valuable witness) rang the bell at the mean and dirty lodging-house in which Old Sharon received the clients who stood in need of his advice.

They were led up stairs to a back room on the second floor of the house. Entering the room, they discovered through a thick cloud of tobacco smoke, a small, fat, bald-headed, dirty, old man, in an arm-chair, robed in a tattered flannel dressing-gown, with a short pipe in his mouth, a pug-dog on his lap, and a French novel in his hands.

"Is it business?" asked Old Sharon, speaking in a hoarse, asthmatical voice, and fixing a pair of bright, shameless, black eyes attentively on the two visitors.

"It is business," Mr. Troy answered, looking at the old rogue who had disgraced an honorable profession, as he might have looked at a reptile which had just risen rampant at his feet. "What is your fee for a consultation?"

"You give me a guinea, and I'll give you half an hour." With this reply Old Sharon held out his unwashed hand across the rickety ink-splashed table at which he was sitting.

Mr. Troy would not have touched him with the tips of his own fingers for a thousand pounds. He laid the guinea on the table.

Old Sharon burst into a fierce laugh—a laugh strangely accompanied by a frowning contraction of his eyebrows, and a frightful exhibition of the whole inside of his mouth. "I'm not clean enough for you—eh?" he said, with an appearance of being very much amused. "There's a dirty old man described in this book that is a little like me." He held up his French novel. "Have you read it? A capital story—well put together. Ah, you haven't read it? You have got a pleasure to come. I say, do you mind tobacco-smoke? I think faster while I smoke—that's all."

Mr. Troy's respectable hand waved a silent permission to smoke, given under dignified protest.

"All right," said Old Sharon. "Now, get on."

He laid himself back in his chair, and puffed out his smoke, with eyes lazily half closed, like the eyes of the pug-dog on his lap. At that moment, indeed there was a curious resemblance between the two. They both seemed to be preparing themselves, in the same idle way, for the same comfortable nap.

Mr. Troy stated the circumstances under which the five hundred pound note had disappeared, in clear and consecutive narrative. When he had done, Old Sharon suddenly opened his eyes. The pug-dog suddenly opened his eyes. Old Sharon looked hard at Mr. Troy. The pug looked hard at Mr. Troy. Old Sharon spoke. The pug growled.

"I know who you are—you're a lawyer. Don't be alarmed! I never saw you before; and I don't know your name. What I do know is a lawyer's statement of facts when I hear it. Who's this?" Old Sharon looked inquisitively at Moody as he put the question.

Mr. Troy introduced Moody as a competent witness, thoroughly acquainted with the circumstances, and ready and willing to answer any questions relating to them. Old Sharon waited a little, smoking hard and thinking hard. "Now, then!" he burst out in his fiercely sudden way. "I'm going to get to the root of the matter."

He leaned forward with his elbows on the table, and began his examination of Moody. Heartily as Mr. Troy despised and disliked the old rogue, he listened with astonishment and admiration—literally extorted from him by the marvelous ability with which the questions were adapted to the end in view. In a quarter of an hour Old Sharon had extracted from the witness everything, literally everything down to the smallest detail, that Moody could tell him. Having now, in his own phrase, "got to the root of the matter," he relighted his pipe with a grunt of satisfaction, and laid himself back in his old armchair.

"Well?" said Mr. Troy. "Have you formed your opinion?"

"Yes; I've formed my opinion."

"What is it?"

Instead of replying, Old Sharon winked confidentially at Mr. Troy, and put a question on his side.

"I say! is a ten-pound note much of an object to you?"

"It depends on what the money is wanted for," answered Mr. Troy.

"Look here," said Old Sharon; "I give you an opinion for your guinea; but, mind this, it's an opinion founded on hearsay—and you know as a lawyer what that is worth. Venture your ten pounds—in plain English, pay me for my time and trouble in a baffling and difficult case—and I'll give you an opinion founded on my own experience."

"Explain yourself a little more clearly," said Mr. Troy. "What do you guarantee to tell us if we venture the ten pounds?"

"I guarantee to name the person, or the persons, on whom the suspicion really rests. And if you employ me after that, I guarantee (before you pay me a halfpenny more) to prove that I am right by laying my hand on the thief."

"Let us have the guinea opinion first," said Mr. Troy.

Old Sharon made another frightful exhibition of the whole inside of his mouth; his laugh was louder and fiercer than ever. "I like you!" he said to Mr. Troy, "you are so devilish fond of your money. Lord! how rich you must be! Now listen. Here's the guinea opinion: Suspect, in this case, the very last person on whom suspicion could possibly fall."

Moody, listening attentively, started, and changed color at those last words. Mr. Troy looked thoroughly disappointed and made no attempt to conceal it.

"Is that all?" he asked.

"All?" retorted the cynical vagabond. "You're a pretty lawyer! What more can I say, when I don't know for certain whether the witness who has given me my information has misled me or not? Have I spoken to the girl and formed my own opinion? No! Have I been introduced among the servants (as errand-boy, or to clean the boots and shoes, or what not), and have I formed my own judgement of them? No! I take your opinions for granted, and I tell you how I should set to work myself if they were my opinions too—and that's a guinea's-worth, a devilish good guinea's-worth to a rich man like you!"

Old Sharon's logic produced a certain effect on Mr. Troy, in spite of himself. It was smartly put from his point of view—there was no denying that.

"Even if I consented to your proposal," he said, "I should object to your annoying the young lady with impertinent questions, or to your being introduced as a spy into a respectable house."

Old Sharon doubled his dirty fists and drummed with them on the rickety table in a comical frenzy of impatience while Mr. Troy was speaking.

"What the devil do you know about my way of doing my business?" he burst out when the lawyer had done. "One of us two is talking like a born idiot—and (mind this) it isn't me. Look here! Your young lady goes out for a walk, and she meets with a dirty, shabby old beggar—I look like a shabby old beggar already, don't I? Very good. This dirty old wretch whines and whimpers and tells a long story, and gets sixpence out of the girl—and knows her by that time, inside and out, as well as if he had made her—and, mark! hasn't asked her a single question, and, instead of annoying her, has made her happy in the performance of a charitable action. Stop a bit! I haven't done with you yet. Who blacks your boots and shoes? Look here!" He pushed his pug-dog off his lap, dived under the table, appeared again with an old boot and a bottle of blackening, and set to work with tigerish activity. "I'm going out for a walk, you know, and I may as well make myself smart." With that announcement, he began to sing over his work—a song of sentiment, popular in England in the early part of the present century—"She's all my fancy painted her; she's lovely, she's divine; but her heart it is another's; and it never can be mine! Too-ral-loo-ral-loo'. I like a love-song. Brush away!

brush away! till I see my own pretty face in the blacking. Hey! Here's a nice, harmless, jolly old man! sings and jokes over his work, and makes the kitchen quite cheerful. What's that you say? He's a stranger, and don't talk to him too freely. You ought to be ashamed of yourself to speak in that way of a poor old fellow with one foot in the grave. Mrs. Cook will give him a nice bit of dinner in the scullery; and John Footman will look out an old coat for him. And when he's heard everything he wants to hear, and doesn't come back again the next day to his work—what do they think of it in the servants' hall? Do they say, 'We've had a spy among us!' Yah! you know better than that, by this time. The cheerful old man has been run over in the street, or is down with the fever, or has turned up his toes in the parish dead-house—that's what they say in the servants' hall. Try me in your own kitchen, and see if your servants take me for a spy. Come, come, Mr. Lawyer! out with your ten pounds, and don't waste any more precious time about it!"

"I will consider and let you know," said Mr. Troy.

Old Sharon laughed more ferociously than ever, and hobbled round the table in a great hurry to the place at which Moody was sitting. He laid one hand on the steward's shoulder, and pointed derisively with the other to Mr. Troy.

"I say, Mr. Silent-man! Bet you five pounds I never hear of that lawyer again!"

Silently attentive all through the interview (except when he was answering questions), Moody only replied in the fewest words. "I don't bet," was all he said. He showed no resentment at Sharon's familiarity, and he appeared to find no amusement in Sharon's extraordinary talk. The old vagabond seemed actually to produce a serious impression on him! When Mr. Troy set the example of rising to go, he still kept his seat, and looked at the lawyer as if he regretted leaving the atmosphere of tobacco smoke reeking in the dirty room.

"Have you anything to say before we go?" Mr. Troy asked.

Moody rose slowly and looked at Old Sharon. "Not just now, sir," he replied, looking away again, after a moment's reflection.

Old Sharon interpreted Moody's look and Moody's reply from his own peculiar point of view. He suddenly drew the steward away into a corner of the room.

"I say!" he began, in a whisper. "Upon your solemn word of honor, you know—are you as rich as the lawyer there?"

"Certainly not."

"Look here! It's half price to a poor man. If you feel like coming back, on your own account—five pounds will do from you. There! there! Think of it!—think of it!"

"Now, then!" said Mr. Troy, waiting for his companion, with the door open in his hand. He looked back at Sharon when Moody joined him. The old vagabond was settled again in his armchair, with his dog in his lap, his pipe in his mouth, and his French novel in his hand; exhibiting exactly the picture of frowzy comfort which he had presented when his visitors first entered the room.

"Good-day," said Mr. Troy, with haughty condescension.

"Don't interrupt me!" rejoined Old Sharon, absorbed in his novel. "You've had your guinea's worth. Lord! what a lovely book this is! Don't interrupt me!"

"Impudent scoundrel!" said Mr. Troy, when he and Moody were in the street again. "What could my friend mean by recommending him? Fancy his expecting me to trust him with ten pounds! I consider even the guinea completely thrown away."

"Begging your pardon, sir," said Moody, "I don't quite agree with you there."

"What! you don't mean to tell me you understand that oracular sentence of his—'Suspect the very last person on whom suspicion could possibly fall.' Rubbish!"

"I don't say I understand it, sir. I only say it has set me thinking."

"Thinking of what? Do your suspicions point to the thief?"

"If you will please to excuse me, Mr. Troy, I should like to wait a while before I answer that."

Mr. Troy suddenly stood still, and eyed his companion a little distrustfully.

"Are you going to turn detective-policeman on your own account?" he asked.

"There's nothing I won't turn to, and try, to help Miss Isabel in this matter," Moody answered, firmly. "I have saved a few hundred pounds in Lady Lydiard's service, and I am ready to spend every farthing of it, if I can only discover the thief."

Mr. Troy walked on again. "Miss Isabel seems to have a good friend in you," he said. He was (perhaps unconsciously) a little offended by the independent tone in which the steward spoke, after he had himself engaged to take the vindication of the girl's innocence into his own hands.

"Miss Isabel has a devoted servant and slave in me!" Moody answered, with passionate enthusiasm.

"Very creditable; I haven't a word to say against it," Mr. Troy rejoined. "But don't forget that the young lady has other devoted friends besides you. I am her devoted friend, for instance—I have promised to serve her, and I mean to keep my word. You will excuse me for adding that my experience and discretion are quite as likely to be useful to her as your enthusiasm. I know the world well enough to be careful in trusting strangers. It will do you no harm, Mr. Moody, to follow my example."

Moody accepted his reproof with becoming patience and resignation. "If you have anything to propose, sir, that will be of service to Miss Isabel," he said, "I shall be happy if I can assist you in the humblest capacity."

"And if not?" Mr. Troy inquired, conscious of having nothing to propose as he asked the question.

"In that case, sir, I must take my own course, and blame nobody but myself if it leads me astray."

Mr. Troy said no more: he parted from Moody at the next turning.

Pursuing the subject privately in his own mind, he decided on taking the earliest opportunity of visiting Isabel at her aunt's house, and on warning her, in her future intercourse with Moody, not to trust too much to the steward's discretion. "I haven't a doubt," thought the lawyer, "of what he means to do next. The infatuated fool is going back to Old Sharon!"

CHAPTER X.

RETURNING to his office, Mr. Troy discovered, among the correspondence that was waiting for him, a letter from the very person whose welfare was still the uppermost subject in his mind. Isabel Miller wrote in these terms:

"Dear Sir—My aunt, Miss Pink, is very desirous of consulting you professionally at the earliest opportunity. Although South Morden is within little more than half an hour's railway ride from London, Miss Pink does not presume to ask you to visit her, being well aware of the value of your time. Will you, therefore, be so kind as to let me know when it will be convenient to you to receive my aunt at your office in London? Believe me, dear sir, respectfully yours, ISABEL MILLER. P.S.—I am further instructed to say that the regrettable event at Lady Lydiard's house is the proposed subject of the consultation. The Lawn, South Morden. Thursday."

Mr. Troy smiled as he read the letter. "Too formal for a young girl!" he said to himself. "Every word of it has been dictated by Miss Pink." He was not long in deciding what course he should take. There was a pressing necessity for cautioning Isabel, and here was his opportunity. He sent for his head clerk, and looked at his list of engagements for the day. There was nothing set down in the book which the clerk was not quite as well able to do as the master. Mr. Troy consulted his railway-guide, ordered his cab, and caught the next train to South Morden.

South Morden was then (and remains to this day) one of those primitive agricultural villages, passed over by the march of modern progress, which are still to be found in the near neighborhood of London. Only the slow trains stopped at the station and there was so little to do that the station-master and his porter grew flowers on the embankment, and trained creepers over the waiting-room window. Turning your back on the railway, and walking along the one street of South Morden, you found yourself in the old England of two centuries since. Gabled cottages, with fast-closed windows; pigs and poultry in quiet possession of the road; the venerable church surrounded by its shady burial-ground; the grocer's shop which sold everything, and the butcher's shop which sold nothing; the scarce inhabitants who liked a good look at a stranger, and the unwashed children who were pictures of dirty health; the clash of the iron-chained bucket in the public well, and the thump of the falling nine-pins in the skittle-ground behind the public-house; the horse-pond on the one bit of open ground, and the old elm-tree with the wooden seat round it on the other—these were some of the objects that you saw, and some of the noises that you heard in South Morden, as you passed from one end of the village to the other.

About half a mile beyond the last of the old cottages, modern England met you again under the form of a row of little villas, set up by an adventurous London builder who had bought the land a bargain. Each villa stood in its own little garden, and looked across a stony road at the meadow lands and softly-rising wooded hills beyond. Each villa faced you in the sunshine with the horrid glare of new red brick, and forced its nonsensical name on your attention, traced in bright paint on the posts of its entrance gate. Consulting the posts as he advanced, Mr. Troy arrived in due course of time at the villa called The Lawn, which derived its name apparently from a circular patch of grass in front of the house. The gate resisting his efforts to open it, he rang the bell.

Admitted by a trim, clean, shy little maid-servant, Mr. Troy looked about him in amazement. Turn which way he might, he found himself silently confronted by posted and painted instructions to visitors, which forbade him to do this, and commanded him to do that, at every step of his progress from the gate to the house. On the side of the lawn a label informed him that he was not to walk on the grass. On the other side a painted hand pointed along a boundary-wall to an inscription which warned him to go that way if he had business in the kitchen. On the gravel walk at the foot of the housesteps words, neatly traced in little white shells, reminded him not to "forget the scraper". On the doorstep he was informed, in letters of lead, that he was "Welcome!" On the mat in the passage bristly black words burst on his attention, commanding him to "wipe his shoes." Even the hat-stand in the hall was not allowed to speak for itself; it had "Hats and Cloaks" inscribed on it, and it issued its directions imperatively in the matter of your wet umbrella—"Put it here!"

Giving the trim little servant his card, Mr. Troy was introduced to a reception-room on the lower floor. Before he had time to look round him the door was opened again from without, and Isabel stole into the room on tiptoe. She looked worn and anxious. When she shook hands with the old lawyer the charming smile that he remembered so well was gone.

"Don't say you have seen me," she whispered. "I am not to come into the room till my aunt sends for me. Tell me two things before I run away again. How is Lady Lydiard? And have you discovered the thief?"

"Lady Lydiard was well when I last saw her; and we have not yet succeeded in discovering the thief." Having answered the questions in those terms, Mr. Troy decided on cautioning Isabel on the subject of the steward while he had the chance. "One question on my side," he said, holding her back from the door by the arm. "Do you expect Moody to visit you here?"

"I am sure he will visit me," Isabel answered warmly. "He has promised to come here at my request. I never knew what a kind heart Robert Moody had till this misfortune fell on me. My aunt, who is not easily taken with strangers, respects and admires him. I can't tell you how good he was to me on the journey here—and how kindly, how nobly, he spoke to me when we parted." She paused, and turned her head away. The tears were rising in her eyes. "In my situation," she said faintly, "kindness is very keenly felt. Don't notice me, Mr. Troy."

The lawyer waited a moment to let her recover herself.

"I agree entirely, my dear, in your opinion of Moody," he said. "At the same time, I think it right to warn you that his zeal in your service may possibly outrun his discretion. He may feel too confidently about penetrating the mystery of the missing money; and, unless you are on your guard, he may raise false hopes in you when you next see him. Listen to any advice that he may give you, by all means. But, before you decide on being guided by his opinion, consult my older experience, and hear what I have to say on the subject. Don't suppose that I am attempting to make you distrust this good friend," he added, noticing the look of uneasy surprise which Isabel fixed on him. "No such idea is in my mind. I only warn you that Moody's eagerness to be of service to you may mislead him. You understand me."

"Yes, sir," replied Isabel coldly; "I understand you. Please let me go now. My aunt will be down directly; and she must not find me here." She curtseyed with distant respect, and left the room.

"So much for trying to put two ideas together into a girl's mind!" thought Mr. Troy, when he was alone again. "The little fool evidently thinks I am jealous of Moody's place in her estimation. Well! I have done my duty—and I can do no more."

He looked round the room. Not a chair was out of its place, not a speck of dust was to be seen. The brightly-perfect polish of the table made your eyes ache; the ornaments on it looked as if they had never been touched by mortal hand; the piano was an object for distant admiration, not an instrument to be played on; the carpet made Mr. Troy look nervously at the soles of his shoes; and the sofa (protected by layers of white crochet-work) said as plainly as if in words, "Sit on me if you dare!" Mr. Troy retreated to a bookcase at the further end of the room. The books fitted the shelves to such absolute perfection that he had some difficulty in taking one of them out. When he had succeeded, he found himself in possession of a volume of the History of England. On the fly-leaf he encountered another written warning:—"This book belongs to Miss Pink's Academy for Young Ladies, and is not to be removed from the library." The date, which was added, referred to a period of ten years since. Miss Pink now stood revealed as a retired schoolmistress, and Mr. Troy began to understand some of the characteristic peculiarities of that lady's establishment which had puzzled him up to the present time.

He had just succeeded in putting the book back again when the door opened once more, and Isabel's aunt entered the room.

If Miss Pink could, by any possible conjuncture of circumstances, have disappeared mysteriously from her house and her friends, the police would have found the greatest difficulty in composing the necessary description of the missing lady. The acutest observer could have discovered nothing that was noticeable or characteristic in her personal appearance. The pen of the present writer portrays her in despair by a series of negatives. She was not young, she was not old; she was neither tall nor short, nor stout nor thin; nobody could call her features attractive, and nobody could call them ugly; there was nothing in her voice, her expression, her manner, or her dress that differed in any appreciable degree from the voice, expression, manner, and dress of five hundred thousand other single ladies of her age and position in the world. If you had asked her to describe herself, she would have answered, "I am a gentlewoman"; and if you had further inquired which of her numerous accomplishments took highest rank in her own esteem, she would have replied, "My powers of conversation." For the rest, she was Miss Pink, of South Morden; and, when that has been said, all has been said.

"Pray be seated, sir. We have had a beautiful day, after the long-continued wet weather. I am told that the season is very unfavorable for wall-fruit. May I offer you some refreshment after your journey?" In these terms and in the smoothest of voices, Miss Pink opened the interview.

Mr. Troy made a polite reply, and added a few strictly conventional remarks on the beauty of the neighborhood. Not even a lawyer could sit in Miss Pink's presence, and hear Miss Pink's conversation, without feeling himself called upon (in the nursery phrase) to "be on his best behavior".

"It is extremely kind of you, Mr. Troy, to favor me with this visit," Miss Pink resumed. "I am well aware that the time of professional gentlemen is of especial value to them; and I will therefore ask you to excuse me if I proceed abruptly to the subject on which I desire to consult your experience."

Here the lady modestly smoothed out her dress over her knees, and the lawyer made a bow. Miss Pink's highly-trained conversation had perhaps one fault—it was not, strictly speaking, conversation at all. In its effect on her hearers it rather resembled the contents of a fluently conventional letter, read aloud.

"The circumstances under which my niece Isabel has left Lady Lydiard's house," Miss Pink proceeded, "are so indescribably painful—I will go further, I will say so deeply humiliating—that I have forbidden her to refer to them again in my presence, or to mention them in the future to any living creature besides myself. You are acquainted with those circumstances, Mr. Troy; and you will understand my indignation when I first learnt that my sister's child had been suspected of theft. I have not the honor of being acquainted with Lady Lydiard. She is not a Countess, I believe? Just so! Her husband was only a Baron. I am not acquainted with Lady Lydiard; and I will not trust myself to say what I think of her conduct to my niece."

"Pardon me, madam," Mr. Troy interposed. "Before you say any more about Lady Lydiard, I really must beg leave to observe—"

"Pardon me," Miss Pink rejoined. "I never form a hasty judgment. Lady Lydiard's conduct is beyond the reach of any defense, no matter how ingenious it may be. You may not be aware, sir, that in receiving my niece under her roof her Ladyship was receiving a gentlewoman by birth as well as by education. My late lamented sister was the daughter of a clergyman of the Church of England. I need hardly remind you that, as such, she was a born lady. Under favoring circumstances, Isabel's maternal grandfather might have been Archbishop of Canterbury, and have taken precedence of the whole House of Peers, the Princes of the blood Royal alone excepted. I am not prepared to say that my niece is equally well connected on her father's side. My sister surprised—I will not add shocked—us when she married a chemist. At the same time, a chemist is not a tradesman. He is a gentleman at one end of the profession of Medicine, and a titled physician is a gentleman at the other end. That is all. In inviting Isabel to reside with her, Lady Lydiard, I repeat, was bound to remember that she was associating herself with a young gentlewoman. She has not remembered this, which is one insult; and she has suspected my niece of theft, which is another."

Miss Pink paused to take breath. Mr. Troy made a second attempt to get a hearing.

"Will you kindly permit me, madam, to say a few words?"

"No!" said Miss Pink, asserting the most immovable obstinacy under the blandest politeness of manner. "Your time, Mr. Troy, is really too valuable! Not even your trained intellect can excuse conduct which is manifestly inexcusable on the face of it. Now you know my opinion of Lady Lydiard, you will not be surprised to hear that I decline to trust her Ladyship. She may, or she may not, cause the necessary inquiries to be made for the vindication of my niece's character. In a matter so serious as this—I may say, in a duty which I owe to the memories of my sister and my parents—I will not leave the responsibility to Lady Lydiard. I will take it on myself. Let me add that I am able to pay the necessary expenses. The earlier years of my life, Mr. Troy, have been passed in the tuition of young ladies. I have been happy in meriting the confidence of parents; and I have been strict in observing the golden rules of economy. On my retirement, I have been able to invest a modest, a very modest, little fortune in the Funds. A portion of it is at the service of my niece for the recovery of her good name; and I desire to place the necessary investigation confidentially in your hands. You are acquainted with the case, and the case naturally goes to you. I could not prevail on myself—I really could not prevail on myself—to mention it to a stranger. That is the business on which I wished to consult you. Please say nothing more about Lady Lydiard—the subject is inexpressibly disagreeable to me. I will only trespass on your kindness to tell me if I have succeeded in making myself understood."

Miss Pink leaned back in her chair, at the exact angle permitted by the laws of propriety; rested her left elbow on the palm of her right hand, and lightly supported her cheek with her forefinger and thumb. In this position she waited Mr. Troy's answer—the living picture of human obstinacy in its most respectable form.

If Mr. Troy had not been a lawyer—in other words, if he had not been professionally capable of persisting in his own course, in the face of every conceivable difficulty and discouragement—Miss Pink might have remained in undisturbed possession of her own opinions. As it was, Mr. Troy had got his hearing at last; and no matter how obstinately she might close her eyes to it, Miss Pink was now destined to have the other side of the case presented to her view.

"I am sincerely obliged to you, madam, for the expression of your confidence in me," Mr. Troy began; "at the same time, I must beg you to excuse me if I decline to accept your proposal."

Miss Pink had not expected to receive such an answer as this. The lawyer's brief refusal surprised and annoyed her.

"Why do you decline to assist me?" she asked.

"Because," answered Mr. Troy, "my services are already engaged, in Miss Isabel's interest, by a client whom I have served for more than twenty years. My client is—"

Miss Pink anticipated the coming disclosure. "You need not trouble yourself, sir, to mention your client's name," she said.

"My client," persisted Mr. Troy, "loves Miss Isabel dearly."

"That is a matter of opinion," Miss Pink interposed.

"And believes in Miss Isabel's innocence," proceeded the irrepressible lawyer, "as firmly as you believe in it yourself."

Miss Pink (being human) had a temper; and Mr. Troy had found his way to it.

"If Lady Lydiard believes in my niece's innocence," said Miss Pink, suddenly sitting bolt upright in her chair, "why has my niece been compelled, in justice to herself, to leave Lady Lydiard's house?"

"You will admit, madam," Mr. Troy answered cautiously, "that we are all of us liable, in this wicked world, to be the victims of appearances. Your niece is a victim—an innocent victim. She wisely withdraws from Lady Lydiard's house until appearances are proved to be false and her position is cleared up."

Miss Pink had her reply ready. "That is simply acknowledging, in other words, that my niece is suspected. I am only a woman, Mr. Troy—but it is not quite so easy to mislead me as you seem to suppose."

Mr. Troy's temper was admirably trained. But it began to acknowledge that Miss Pink's powers of irritation could sting to some purpose.

"No intention of misleading you, madam, has ever crossed my mind," he rejoined warmly. "As for your niece, I can tell you this. In all my experience of Lady Lydiard, I never saw her so distressed as she was when Miss Isabel left the house!"

"Indeed!" said Miss Pink, with an incredulous smile. "In my rank of life, when we feel distressed about a person, we do our best to comfort that person by a kind letter or an early visit. But then I am not a lady of title."

"Lady Lydiard engaged herself to call on Miss Isabel in my hearing," said Mr. Troy. "Lady Lydiard is the most generous woman living!"

"Lady Lydiard is here!" cried a joyful voice on the other side of the door.

At the same moment, Isabel burst into the room in a state of excitement which actually ignored the formidable presence of Miss Pink. "I beg your pardon, aunt! I was upstairs at the window, and I saw the carriage stop at the gate. And Tommie has come, too! The darling saw me at the window!" cried the poor girl, her eyes sparkling with delight as a perfect explosion of barking made itself heard over the tramp of horses' feet and the crash of carriage wheels outside.

Miss Pink rose slowly, with a dignity that looked capable of adequately receiving—not one noble lady only, but the whole peerage of England.

"Control yourself, dear Isabel," she said. "No well-bred young lady permits herself to become unduly excited. Stand by my side—a little behind me."

Isabel obeyed. Mr. Troy kept his place, and privately enjoyed his triumph over Miss Pink. If Lady Lydiard had been actually in league with him, she could not have chosen a more opportune time for her visit. A momentary interval passed. The carriage drew up at the door; the horses trampled on the gravel; the bell rung madly; the uproar of Tommie, released from the carriage and clamoring to be let in, redoubled its fury. Never before had such an unruly burst of noises invaded the tranquility of Miss Pink's villa!

CHAPTER XI.

THE trim little maid-servant ran upstairs from her modest little kitchen, trembling at the terrible prospect of having to open the door. Miss Pink, deafened by the barking, had just time to say, "What a very ill-behaved dog!" when a sound of small objects overthrown in the hall, and a scurrying of furious claws across the oil-cloth, announced that Tommie had invaded the house. As the servant appeared, introducing Lady Lydiard, the dog ran in. He made one frantic leap at Isabel, which would certainly have knocked her down but for the chair that happened to be standing behind her. Received on her lap, the faithful creature half smothered her with his caresses. He barked, he shrieked, in his joy at seeing her again. He jumped off her lap and tore round and round the room at the top of his speed; and every time he passed Miss Pink he showed the whole range of his teeth and snarled ferociously at her ankles. Having at last exhausted his superfluous energy, he leaped back again on Isabel's lap, with his tongue quivering in his open mouth—his tail wagging softly, and his eye on Miss Pink, inquiring how she liked a dog in her drawing-room!

"I hope my dog has not disturbed you, ma'am?" said Lady Lydiard, advancing from the mat at the doorway, on which she had patiently waited until the raptures of Tommie subsided into repose.

Miss Pink, trembling between terror and indignation, acknowledged Lady Lydiard's polite inquiry by a ceremonious bow, and an answer which administered by implication a dignified reproof. "Your Ladyship's dog does not appear to be a very well-trained animal," the ex-schoolmistress remarked.

"Well trained?" Lady Lydiard repeated, as if the expression was perfectly unintelligible to her. "I don't think you have had much experience of dogs, ma'am." She turned to Isabel, and embraced her tenderly. "Give me a kiss, my dear—you don't know how wretched I have been since you left me." She looked back again at Miss Pink. "You are not, perhaps, aware, ma'am, that my dog is devotedly attached to your niece. A dog's love has been considered by many great men (whose names at the moment escape me) as the most touching and disinterested of all earthly affections." She looked the other way, and discovered the lawyer. "How do you do, Mr. Troy? It's a pleasant surprise to find you here The house was so dull without Isabel that I really couldn't put off seeing her any longer. When you are more used to Tommie, Miss Pink, you will understand and admire him. You understand and admire him, Isabel—don't you? My child! you are not looking well. I shall take you back with me, when the horses have had their rest. We shall never be happy away from each other."

Having expressed her sentiments, distributed her greetings, and defended her dog—all, as it were, in one breath—Lady Lydiard sat down by Isabel's side, and opened a large green fan that hung at her girdle. "You have no idea, Miss Pink, how fat people suffer in hot weather," said the old lady, using her fan vigorously.

Miss Pink's eyes dropped modestly to the ground—"fat" was such a coarse word to use, if a lady must speak of her own superfluous flesh! "May I offer some refreshment?" Miss Pink asked, mincingly. "A cup of tea?"

Lady Lydiard shook her head.

"A glass of water?"

Lady Lydiard declined this last hospitable proposal with an exclamation of disgust. "Have you got any beer?" she inquired.

"I beg your Ladyship's pardon," said Miss Pink, doubting the evidence of her own ears. "Did you say—beer?"

Lady Lydiard gesticulated vehemently with her fan. "Yes, to be sure! Beer! beer!"

Miss Pink rose, with a countenance expressive of genteel disgust, and rang the bell. "I think you have beer downstairs, Susan?" she said, when the maid appeared at the door.

"Yes, miss."

"A glass of beer for Lady Lydiard," said Miss Pink—under protest.

"Bring it in a jug," shouted her Ladyship, as the maid left the room. "I like to froth it up for myself," she continued, addressing Miss Pink. "Isabel sometimes does it for me, when she is at home—don't you, my dear?"

Miss Pink had been waiting her opportunity to assert her own claim to the possession of her own niece, from the time when Lady Lydiard had coolly declared her intention of taking Isabel back with her. The opportunity now presented itself.

"Your Ladyship will pardon me," she said, "if I remark that my niece's home is under my humble roof. I am properly sensible, I hope, of your kindness to Isabel, but while she remains the object of a disgraceful suspicion she remains with me."

Lady Lydiard closed her fan with an angry snap.

"You are completely mistaken, Miss Pink. You may not mean it—but you speak most unjustly if you say that your niece is an object of suspicion to me, or to anybody in my house."

Mr. Troy, quietly listening up to this point now interposed to stop the discussion before it could degenerate into a personal quarrel. His keen observation, aided by his accurate knowledge of his client's character, had plainly revealed to him what was passing in Lady Lydiard's mind. She had entered the house, feeling (perhaps unconsciously) a jealousy of Miss Pink, as her predecessor in Isabel's affections, and as the natural protectress of the girl under existing circumstances. Miss Pink's reception of her dog had additionally irritated the old lady. She had taken a malicious pleasure in shocking the schoolmistress's sense of propriety—and she was now only too ready to proceed to further extremities on the delicate question of Isabel's justification for leaving her house. For Isabel's own sake, therefore—to say nothing of other reasons—it was urgently desirable to keep the peace between the two ladies. With this excellent object in view, Mr. Troy seized his opportunity of striking into the conversation for the first time.

"Pardon me, Lady Lydiard," he said, "you are speaking of a subject which has been already sufficiently discussed between Miss Pink and myself. I think we shall do better not to dwell uselessly on past events, but to direct our attention to the future. We are all equally satisfied of the complete rectitude of Miss Isabel's conduct, and we are all equally interested in the vindication of her good name."

Whether these temperate words would of themselves have exercised the pacifying influence at which Mr. Troy aimed may be doubtful. But, as he ceased speaking, a powerful auxiliary appeared in the shape of the beer. Lady Lydiard seized on the jug, and filled the tumbler for herself with an unsteady hand. Miss Pink, trembling for the integrity of her carpet, and scandalized at seeing a peeress drinking beer like a washer-woman, forgot the sharp answer that was just rising to her lips when the lawyer interfered. "Small!" said Lady Lydiard, setting down the empty tumbler, and referring to the quality of the beer. "But very pleasant and refreshing. What's the servant's name? Susan? Well, Susan, I was dying of thirst and you have saved my life. You can leave the jug—I dare say I shall empty it before I go."

Mr. Troy, watching Miss Pink's face, saw that it was time to change the subject again.

"Did you notice the old village, Lady Lydiard, on your way here?" he asked. "The artists consider it one of the most picturesque places in England."

"I noticed that it was a very dirty village," Lady Lydiard answered, still bent on making herself disagreeable to Miss Pink. "The artists may say what they please; I see nothing to admire in rotten cottages, and bad drainage, and ignorant people. I suppose the neighborhood has its advantages. It looks dull enough, to my mind."

Isabel had hitherto modestly restricted her exertions to keeping Tommie quiet on her lap. Like Mr. Troy, she occasionally looked at her aunt—and she now made a timid attempt to defend the neighborhood as a duty that she owed to Miss Pink.

"Oh, my Lady! don't say it's a dull neighborhood," she pleaded. "There are such pretty walks all round us. And, when you get to the hills, the view is beautiful."

Lady Lydiard's answer to this was a little masterpiece of good-humored contempt. She patted Isabel's cheek, and said, "Pooh! Pooh!"

"Your Ladyship does not admire the beauties of Nature," Miss Pink remarked, with a compassionate smile. "As we get older, no doubt our sight begins to fail—"

"And we leave off canting about the beauties of Nature," added Lady Lydiard. "I hate the country. Give me London, and the pleasures of society."

"Come! come! Do the country justice, Lady Lydiard!" put in peacemaking Mr. Troy. "There is plenty of society to be found out of London—as good society as the world can show."

"The sort of society," added Miss Pink, "which is to be found, for example, in this neighborhood. Her Ladyship is evidently not aware that persons of distinction surround us, whichever way we turn. I may instance among others, the Honorable Mr. Hardyman—"

Lady Lydiard, in the act of pouring out a second glassful of beer, suddenly set down the jug.

"Who is that you're talking of, Miss Pink?"

"I am talking of our neighbor, Lady Lydiard—the Honorable Mr. Hardyman."

"Do you mean Alfred Hardyman—the man who breeds the horses?"

"The distinguished gentleman who owns the famous stud-farm," said Miss Pink, correcting the bluntly-direct form in which Lady Lydiard had put her question.

"Is he in the habit of visiting here?" the old lady inquired, with a sudden appearance of anxiety. "Do you know him?"

"I had the honor of being introduced to Mr. Hardyman at our last flower show," Miss Pink replied. "He has not yet favored me with a visit."

Lady Lydiard's anxiety appeared to be to some extent relieved.

"I knew that Hardyman's farm was in this county," she said; "but I had no notion that it was in the neighborhood of South Morden. How far away is he—ten or a dozen miles, eh?"

"Not more than three miles," answered Miss Pink. "We consider him quite a near neighbor of ours."

Renewed anxiety showed itself in Lady Lydiard. She looked round sharply at Isabel. The girl's head was bent so low over the rough head of the dog that her face was almost entirely concealed from view. So far as appearances went, she seemed to be entirely absorbed in fondling Tommie. Lady Lydiard roused her with a tap of the green fan.

"Take Tommie out, Isabel, for a run in the garden," she said. "He won't sit still much longer—and he may annoy Miss Pink. Mr. Troy, will you kindly help Isabel to keep my ill-trained dog in order?"

Mr. Troy got on his feet, and, not very willingly, followed Isabel out of the room. "They will quarrel now, to a dead certainty!" he thought to himself, as he closed the door. "Have you any idea of what this means?" he said to his companion, as he joined her in the hall. "What has Mr. Hardyman done to excite all this interest in him?"

Isabel's guilty color rose. She knew perfectly well that Hardyman's unconcealed admiration of her was the guiding motive of Lady Lydiard's inquiries. If she had told the truth, Mr. Troy would have unquestionably returned to the drawing-room, with or without an acceptable excuse for intruding himself. But Isabel was a woman; and her answer, it is needless to say, was "I don't know, I'm sure."

In the mean time, the interview between the two ladies began in a manner which would have astonished Mr. Troy—they were both silent. For once in her life Lady Lydiard was considering what she should say, before she said it. Miss Pink, on her side, naturally waited to hear what object her Ladyship had in view—waited, until her small reserve of patience gave way. Urged by irresistible curiosity, she spoke first.

"Have you anything to say to me in private?" she asked.

Lady Lydiard had not got to the end of her reflections. She said "Yes!"— and she said no more.

"Is it anything relating to my niece?" persisted Miss Pink.

Still immersed in her reflections, Lady Lydiard suddenly rose to the surface, and spoke her mind, as usual.

"About your niece, ma'am. The other day Mr. Hardyman called at my house, and saw Isabel."

"Yes," said Miss Pink, politely attentive, but not in the least interested, so far.

"That's not all ma'am. Mr. Hardyman admires Isabel; he owned it to me himself in so many words."

Miss Pink listened, with a courteous inclination of her head. She looked mildly gratified, nothing more. Lady Lydiard proceeded:

"You and I think differently on many matters," she said. "But we are both agreed, I am sure, in feeling the sincerest interest in Isabel's welfare. I beg to suggest to you, Miss Pink, that Mr. Hardyman, as a near neighbor of yours, is a very undesirable neighbor while Isabel remains in your house."

Saying those words, under a strong conviction of the serious importance of the subject, Lady Lydiard insensibly recovered the manner and resumed the language which befitted a lady of her rank. Miss Pink, noticing the change, set it down to an expression of pride on the part of her visitor which, in referring to Isabel, assailed indirectly the social position of Isabel's aunt.

"I fail entirely to understand what your Ladyship means," she said coldly.

Lady Lydiard, on her side, looked in undisguised amazement at Miss Pink.

"Haven't I told you already that Mr. Hardyman admires your niece?" she asked.

"Naturally," said Miss Pink. "Isabel inherits her lamented mother's personal advantages. If Mr. Hardyman admires her, Mr. Hardyman shows his good taste."

Lady Lydiard's eyes opened wider and wider in wonder. "My good lady!" she exclaimed, "is it possible you don't know that when a man admires a women he doesn't stop there? He falls in love with her (as the saying is) next."

"So I have heard," said Miss Pink.

"So you have heard?" repeated Lady Lydiard. "If Mr. Hardyman finds his way to Isabel I can tell you what you will see. Catch the two together, ma'am—and you will see Mr. Hardyman making love to your niece."

"Under due restrictions, Lady Lydiard, and with my permission first obtained, of course, I see no objection to Mr. Hardyman paying his addresses to Isabel."

"The woman is mad!" cried Lady Lydiard. "Do you actually suppose, Miss Pink, that Alfred Hardyman could, by any earthly possibility, marry your niece!"

Not even Miss Pink's politeness could submit to such a question as this. She rose indignantly from her chair. "As you aware, Lady Lydiard, that the doubt you have just expressed is an insult to my niece, and a insult to Me?"

"Are you aware of who Mr. Hardyman really is?" retorted her Ladyship. "Or do you judge of his position by the vocation in life which he has perversely chosen to adopt? I can tell you, if you do, that Alfred Hardyman is the younger son of one of the oldest barons in the English Peerage, and that his mother is related by marriage to the Royal family of Wurtemberg."

Miss Pink received the full shock of this information without receding from her position by a hair-breadth.

"An English gentlewoman offers a fit alliance to any man living who seeks her hand in marriage," said Miss Pink. "Isabel's mother (you may not be aware of it) was the daughter of an English clergyman—"

"And Isabel's father was a chemist in a country town," added Lady

Lydiard.

"Isabel's father," rejoined Miss Pink, "was attached in a most responsible capacity to the useful and honorable profession of Medicine. Isabel is, in the strictest sense of the word, a young gentlewoman. If you contradict that for a single instant, Lady Lydiard, you will oblige me to leave the room."

Those last words produced a result which Miss Pink had not anticipated—they roused Lady Lydiard to assert herself. As usual in such cases, she rose superior to her own eccentricity. Confronting Miss Pink, she now spoke and looked with the gracious courtesy and the unpresuming self-confidence of the order to which she belonged.

"For Isabel's own sake, and for the quieting of my conscience," she answered, "I will say one word more, Miss Pink, before I relieve you of my presence. Considering my age and my opportunities, I may claim to know quite as much as you do of the laws and customs which regulate society in our time. Without contesting your niece's social position—and without the slightest intention of insulting you—I repeat that the rank which Mr. Hardyman inherits makes it simply impossible for him even to think of marrying Isabel. You will do well not to give him any opportunities of meeting with her alone. And you will do better still (seeing that he is so near a neighbor of yours) if you permit Isabel to return to my protection, for a time at least. I will wait to hear from you when you have thought the matter over at your leisure. In the mean time, if I have inadvertently offended you, I ask your pardon—and I wish you good-evening."

She bowed, and walked to the door. Miss Pink, as resolute as ever in maintaining her pretensions, made an effort to match the great lady on her own ground.

"Before you go, Lady Lydiard, I beg to apologize if I have spoken too warmly on my side," she said. "Permit me to send for your carriage."

"Thank you, Miss Pink. My carriage is only at the village inn. I shall enjoy a little walk in the cool evening air. Mr. Troy, I have no doubt, will give me his arm." She bowed once more, and quietly left the room.

Reaching the little back garden of the villa, through an open door at the further end of the hall, Lady Lydiard found Tommie rolling luxuriously on Miss Pink's flower-beds, and Isabel and Mr. Troy in close consultation on the gravel walk.

She spoke to the lawyer first.

"They are baiting the horses at the inn," she said. "I want your arm, Mr. Troy, as far as the village—and, in return, I will take you back to London with me. I have to ask your advice about one or two little matters, and this is a good opportunity."

"With the greatest pleasure, Lady Lydiard. I suppose I must say good-by to Miss Pink?"

"A word of advice to you, Mr. Troy. Take care how you ruffle Miss Pink's sense of her own importance. Another word for your private ear. Miss Pink is a fool."

On the lawyer's withdrawal, Lady Lydiard put her arm fondly round Isabel's waist. "What were you and Mr. Troy so busy in talking about?" she asked.

"We were talking, my Lady, about tracing the person who stole the money," Isabel answered, rather sadly. "It seems a far more difficult matter than I supposed it to be. I try not to lose patience and hope—but it is a little hard to feel that appearances are against me, and to wait day after day in vain for the discovery that is to set me right."

"You are a dear good child," said Lady Lydiard; "and you are more precious to me than ever. Don't despair, Isabel. With Mr. Troy's means of inquiring, and with my means of paying, the discovery of the thief cannot be much longer delayed. If you don't return to me soon, I shall come back and see you again. Your aunt hates the sight of me—but I don't care two straws for that," remarked Lady Lydiard, showing the undignified side of her character once more. "Listen to me, Isabel! I have no wish to lower your aunt in your estimation, but I feel far more confidence in your good sense than in hers. Mr. Hardyman's business has taken him to France for the present. It is at least possible that you may meet with him on his return. If you do, keep him at a distance, my dear—politely, of course. There! there! you needn't turn red; I am not blaming you; I am only giving you a little good advice. In your position you cannot possibly be too careful. Here is Mr. Troy! You must come to the gate with us, Isabel, or we shall never get Tommie away from you; I am only his second favorite; you have the first place in his affections. God bless and prosper you, my child!—I wish to heaven you were going back to London with me! Well, Mr. Troy, how have you done with Miss Pink? Have you offended that terrible 'gentlewoman' (hateful word!); or has it been all the other way, and has she given you a kiss at parting?"

Mr. Troy smiled mysteriously, and changed the subject. His brief parting interview with the lady of the house was not of a nature to be rashly related. Miss Pink had not only positively assured him that her visitor was the most ill-bred woman she had ever met with, but had further accused Lady Lydiard of shaking her confidence in the aristocracy of her native country. "For the first time in my life," said Miss Pink, "I feel that something is to be said for the Republican point of view; and I am not indisposed to admit that the constitution of the United States has its advantages!"

CHAPTER XII.

THE conference between Lady Lydiard and Mr. Troy, on the way back to London, led to some practical results.

Hearing from her legal adviser that the inquiry after the missing money was for a moment at a standstill, Lady Lydiard made one of those bold suggestions with which she was accustomed to startle her friends in cases of emergency. She had heard favorable reports of the extraordinary ingenuity of the French police; and she now proposed sending to Paris for assistance, after first consulting her nephew, Mr. Felix Sweetsir. "Felix knows Paris as well as he knows London," she remarked. "He is an idle man, and it is quite likely that he will relieve us of all trouble by taking the matter into his own hands. In any case, he is sure to know who are the right people to address in our present necessity. What do you say?"

Mr. Troy, in reply, expressed his doubts as to the wisdom of employing foreigners in a delicate investigation which required an accurate knowledge of English customs and English character. Waiving this objection, he approved of the idea of consulting her Ladyship's nephew. "Mr. Sweetsir is a man of the world," he said. "In putting the case before him, we are sure to have it presented to us from a new point of view." Acting on this favorable expression of opinion, Lady Lydiard wrote to her nephew. On the day after the visit to Miss Pink, the proposed council of three was held at Lady Lydiard's house.

Felix, never punctual at keeping an appointment, was even later than usual on this occasion. He made his apologies with his hand pressed upon his forehead, and his voice expressive of the languor and discouragement of a suffering man.

"The beastly English climate is telling on my nerves," said Mr. Sweetsir—"the horrid weight of the atmosphere, after the exhilarating air of Paris; the intolerable dirt and dullness of London, you know. I was in bed, my dear aunt, when I received your letter. You may imagine the completely demoralised state I was in, when I tell you of the effect which the news of the robbery produced on me. I fell back on my pillow, as if I had been shot. Your Ladyship should really be a little more careful in communicating these disagreeable surprises to a sensitively-organised man. Never mind—my valet is a perfect treasure; he brought me some drops of ether on a lump of sugar. I said, 'Alfred' (his name is Alfred), 'put me into my clothes!' Alfred put me in. I assure you it reminded me of my young days, when I was put into my first pair of trousers. Has Alfred forgotten anything? Have I got my braces on? Have I come out in my shirt-sleeves? Well, dear aunt;—well, Mr. Troy!—what can I say? What can I do?"

Lady Lydiard, entirely without sympathy for nervous suffering, nodded to the lawyer. "You tell him," she said.

"I believe I speak for her Ladyship," Mr. Troy began, "when I say that we should like to hear, in the first place, how the whole case strikes you, Mr. Sweetsir?"

"Tell it me all over again," said Felix.

Patient Mr. Troy told it all over again—and waited for the result.

"Well?" said Felix.

"Well?" said Mr. Troy. "Where does the suspicion of robbery rest in your opinion? You look at the theft of the bank-note with a fresh eye."

"You mentioned a clergyman just now," said Felix. "The man, you know, to whom the money was sent. What was his name?"

"The Reverend Samuel Bradstock."

"You want me to name the person whom I suspect?"

"Yes, if you please," said Mr. Troy.

"I suspect the Reverend Samuel Bradstock," said Felix.

"If you have come here to make stupid jokes," interposed Lady Lydiard, "you had better go back to your bed again. We want a serious opinion."

"You have a serious opinion," Felix coolly rejoined. "I never was more in earnest in my life. Your Ladyship is not aware of the first principle to be adopted in cases of suspicion. One proceeds on what I will call the exhaustive system of reasoning. Thus: Does suspicion point to the honest servants downstairs? No. To your Ladyship's adopted daughter? Appearances are against the poor girl; but you know her better than to trust to appearances. Are you suspicious of Moody? No. Of Hardyman—who was in the house at the time? Ridiculous! But I was in the house at the time, too. Do you suspect Me? Just so! That idea is ridiculous, too. Now let us sum up. Servants, adopted daughter, Moody, Hardyman, Sweetsir—all beyond suspicion. Who is left? The Reverend Samuel Bradstock."

This ingenious exposition of "the exhaustive system of reasoning," failed to produce any effect on Lady Lydiard. "You are wasting our time," she said sharply. "You know as well as I do that you are talking nonsense."

"I don't," said Felix. "Taking the gentlemanly professions all round, I know of no men who are so eager to get money, and who have so few scruples about how they get it, as the parsons. Where is there a man in any other profession who perpetually worries you for money?—who holds the bag under your nose for money?—who sends his clerk round from door to door to beg a few shillings of you, and calls it an 'Easter offering'? The parson does all this. Bradstock is a parson. I put it logically. Bowl me over, if you can."

Mr. Troy attempted to "bowl him over," nevertheless. Lady Lydiard wisely interposed.

"When a man persists in talking nonsense," she said, "silence is the best answer; anything else only encourages him." She turned to Felix. "I have a question to ask you," she went on. "You will either give me a serious reply, or wish me good-morning." With this brief preface, she made her inquiry as to the wisdom and possibility of engaging the services of the French police.

Felix took exactly the view of the matter which had been already expressed by Mr. Troy. "Superior in intelligence," he said, "but not superior in courage, to the English police. Capable of performing wonders on their own ground and among their own people. But, my dear aunt, the two most dissimilar nations on the face of the earth are the English and the French. The French police may speak our language—but they are incapable of understanding our national character and our national manners. Set them to work on a private inquiry in the city of Pekin—and they would get on in time with the Chinese people. Set them to work in the city of London—and the English people would remain, from first to last, the same impenetrable mystery to them. In my belief the London Sunday would be enough of itself to drive them back to Paris in despair. No balls, no concerts, no theaters, not even a museum or a picture-gallery open; every shop shut up but the gin-shop; and nothing moving but the church bells and the men who sell the penny ices. Hundreds of Frenchmen come to see me on their first arrival in England. Every man of them rushes back to Paris on the second Saturday of his visit, rather than confront the horrors of a second Sunday in London! However, you can try it if you like. Send me a written abstract of the case, and I will forward it to one of the official people in the Rue Jerusalem, who will do anything he can to oblige me. Of course," said Felix, turning to Mr. Troy, "some of you have got the number of the lost bank-note? If the thief has tried to pass it in Paris, my man may be of some use to you."

"Three of us have got the number of the note," answered Mr. Troy; "Miss Isabel Miller, Mr. Moody, and myself."

"Very good," said Felix. "Send me the number, with the abstract of the case. Is there anything else I can do towards recovering the money?" he asked, turning to his aunt. "There is one lucky circumstance in connection with this loss—isn't there? It has fallen on a person who is rich enough to take it easy. Good heavens! suppose it had been my loss!"

"It has fallen doubly on me," said Lady Lydiard; "and I am certainly not rich enough to take it that easy. The money was destined to a charitable purpose; and I have felt it my duty to pay it again."

Felix rose and approached his aunt's chair with faltering steps, as became a suffering man. He took Lady Lydiard's hand and kissed it with enthusiastic admiration.

"You excellent creature!" he said. "You may not think it, but you reconcile me to human nature. How generous! how noble! I think I'll go to bed again, Mr. Troy, if you really don't want any more of me. My head feels giddy and my legs tremble under me. It doesn't matter; I shall feel easier when Alfred has taken me out of my clothes again. God bless you, my dear aunt! I never felt so proud of being related to you as I do to-day. Good-morning Mr. Troy! Don't forget the abstract of the case; and don't trouble yourself to see me to the door. I dare say I shan't tumble downstairs; and, if I do, there's the porter in the hall to pick me up again. Enviable porter! as fat as butter and as idle as a pig! Au revoir! au revoir!" He kissed his hand, and drifted feebly out of the room. Sweetsir one might say, in a state of eclipse; but still the serviceable Sweetsir, who was never consulted in vain by the fortunate people privileged to call him friend!

"Is he really ill, do you think?" Mr. Troy asked.

"My nephew has turned fifty," Lady Lydiard answered, "and he persists in living as if he was a young man. Every now and then Nature says to him, 'Felix, you are old!' And Felix goes to bed, and says it's his nerves."

"I suppose he is to be trusted to keep his word about writing to Paris?" pursued the lawyer.

"Oh, yes! He may delay doing it but he will do it. In spite of his lackadaisical manner, he has moments of energy that would surprise you. Talking of surprises, I have something to tell you about Moody. Within the last day or two there has been a marked change in him—a change for the worse."

"You astonish me, Lady Lydiard! In what way has Moody deteriorated?"

"You shall hear. Yesterday was Friday. You took him out with you, on business, early in the morning."

Mr. Troy bowed, and said nothing. He had not thought it desirable to mention the interview at which Old Sharon had cheated him of his guinea.

"In the course of the afternoon," pursued Lady Lydiard, "I happened to want him, and I was informed that Moody had gone out again. Where had he gone? Nobody knew. Had he left word when he would be back? He had left no message of any sort. Of course, he is not in the position of an ordinary servant. I don't expect him to ask permission to go out. But I do expect him to leave word downstairs of the time at which he is likely to return. When he did come back, after an absence of some hours, I naturally asked for an explanation. Would you believe it? he simply informed me that he had been away on business of his own; expressed no regret, and offered no explanation—in short, spoke as if he was an independent gentleman. You may not think it, but I kept my temper. I merely remarked that I hoped it would not happen again. He made me a bow, and he said, 'My business is not completed yet, my Lady. I cannot guarantee that it may not call me away again at a moment's notice.' What do you think of that? Nine people out of ten would have given him warning to leave their service. I begin to think I am a wonderful woman—I only pointed to the door. One does hear sometimes of men's brains softening in the most unexpected manner. I have my suspicions of Moody's brains, I can tell you."

Mr. Troy's suspicions took a different direction: they pointed along the line of streets which led to Old Sharon's lodgings. Discreetly silent as to the turn which his thoughts had taken, he merely expressed himself as feeling too much surprised to offer any opinion at all.

"Wait a little," said Lady Lydiard, "I haven't done surprising you yet. You have seen a boy here in a page's livery, I think? Well, he is a good boy; and he has gone home for a week's holiday with his friends. The proper person to supply his place with the boots and shoes and other small employments, is of course the youngest footman, a lad only a few years older than himself. What do you think Moody does? Engages a stranger, with the house full of idle men-servants already, to fill the page's place. At intervals this morning I heard them wonderfully merry in the servants hall—so merry that the noise and laughter found its way upstairs to the breakfast-room. I like my servants to be in good spirits; but it certainly did strike me that they were getting beyond reasonable limits. I questioned my maid, and was informed that the noise was all due to the jokes of the strangest old man that ever was seen. In other words, to the person whom my steward had taken it on himself to engage in the page's absence. I spoke to Moody on the subject. He answered in an odd, confused way, that he had exercised his discretion to the best of his judgment and that (if I wished it), he would tell the old man to keep his good spirits under better control. I asked him how he came to hear of the man. He only answered, 'By accident, my Lady'—and not one more word could I get out of him, good or bad. Moody engages the servants, as you know; but on every other occasion he has invariably consulted me before an engagement was settled. I really don't feel at all sure about this person who has been so strangely introduced into the house—he may be a drunkard or a thief. I wish you would speak to Moody yourself, Mr. Troy. Do you mind ringing the bell?"

Mr. Troy rose, as a matter of course, and rang the bell.

He was by this time, it is needless to say, convinced that Moody had not only gone back to consult Old Sharon on his own responsibility, but worse still, had taken the unwarrantable liberty of introducing him, as a spy, into the house. To communicate this explanation to Lady Lydiard would, in her present humor, be simply to produce the dismissal of the steward from her service. The only other alternative was to ask leave to interrogate Moody privately, and, after duly reproving him, to insist on the departure of Old Sharon as the one condition on which Mr. Troy would consent to keep Lady Lydiard in ignorance of the truth.

"I think I shall manage better with Moody, if your Ladyship will permit me to see him in private," the lawyer said. "Shall I go downstairs and speak with him in his own room?"

"Why should you trouble yourself to do that?" said her Ladyship. "See him here; and I will go into the boudoir."

As she made that reply, the footman appeared at the drawing-room door.

"Send Moody here," said Lady Lydiard.

The footman's answer, delivered at that moment, assumed an importance which was not expressed in the footman's words. "My Lady," he said, "Mr. Moody has gone out."

CHAPTER XIII.

WHILE the strange proceedings of the steward were the subject of conversation between Lady Lydiard and Mr. Troy, Moody was alone in his room, occupied in writing to Isabel. Being unwilling that any eyes but his own should see the address, he had himself posted his letter; the time that he had chosen for leaving the house proving, unfortunately, to be also the time proposed by her Ladyship for his interview with the lawyer. In ten minutes after the footman had reported his absence, Moody returned. It was then too late to present himself in the drawing-room. In the interval, Mr. Troy had taken his leave, and Moody's position had dropped a degree lower in Lady Lydiard's estimation.

Isabel received her letter by the next morning's post. If any justification of Mr. Troy's suspicions had been needed, the terms in which Moody wrote would have amply supplied it.

"DEAR ISABEL (I hope I may call you 'Isabel' without offending you, in your present trouble?)—I have a proposal to make, which, whether you accept it or not, I beg you will keep a secret from every living creature but ourselves. You will understand my request, when I add that these lines relate to the matter of tracing the stolen bank-note.

"I have been privately in communication with a person in London, who is, as I believe, the one person competent to help us in gaining our end. He has already made many inquiries in private. With some of them I am acquainted; the rest he has thus far kept to himself. The person to whom I allude, particularly wishes to have half an hour's conversation with you in my presence. I am bound to warn you that he is a very strange and very ugly old man; and I can only hope that you will look over his personal appearance in consideration of what he is likely to do for your future advantage.

"Can you conveniently meet us, at the further end of the row of villas in which your aunt lives, the day after to-morrow, at four o'clock? Let me have a line to say if you will keep the appointment, and if the hour named will suit you. And believe me your devoted friend and servant,

"ROBERT MOODY."

The lawyer's warning to her to be careful how she yielded too readily to any proposal of Moody's recurred to Isabel's mind while she read those lines. Being pledged to secrecy, she could not consult Mr. Troy—she was left to decide for herself.

No obstacle stood in the way of her free choice of alternatives. After their early dinner at three o'clock, Miss Pink habitually retired to her own room "to meditate," as she expressed it. Her "meditations" inevitably ended in a sound sleep of some hours; and during that interval Isabel was at liberty to do as she pleased. After considerable hesitation, her implicit belief in Moody's truth and devotion, assisted by a strong feeling of curiosity to see the companion with whom the steward had associated himself, decided Isabel on consenting to keep the appointment.

Taking up her position beyond the houses, on the day and at the hour mentioned by Moody, she believed herself to be fully prepared for the most unfavorable impression which the most disagreeable of all possible strangers could produce.

But the first appearance of Old Sharon—as dirty as ever, clothed in a long, frowzy, gray overcoat, with his pug-dog at his heels, and his smoke-blackened pipe in his mouth, with a tan white hat on his head, which looked as if it had been picked up in a gutter, a hideous leer in his eyes, and a jaunty trip in his walk—took her so completely by surprise that she could only return Moody's friendly greeting by silently pressing his hand. As for Moody's companion, to look at him for a second time was more than she had resolution to do. She kept her eyes fixed on the pug-dog, and with good reason; as far as appearances went, he was indisputably the nobler animal of the two.

Under the circumstances, the interview threatened to begin in a very embarrassing manner. Moody, disheartened by Isabel's silence, made no attempt to set the conversation going; he looked as if he meditated a hasty retreat to the railway station which he had just left. Fortunately, he had at his side the right man (for once) in the right place. Old Sharon's effrontery was equal to any emergency.

"I am not a nice-looking old man, my dear, am I?" he said, leering at Isabel with cunning, half-closed eyes. "Bless your heart! you'll soon get used to me! You see, I am the sort of color, as they say at the linen-drapers, that doesn't wash well. It's all through love; upon my life it is! Early in the present century I had my young affections blighted; and I've neglected myself ever since. Disappointment takes different forms, miss, in different men. I don't think I have had heart enough to brush my hair for the last fifty years. She was a magnificent woman, Mr. Moody, and she dropped me like a hot potato. Dreadful! dreadful! Let us pursue this painful subject no further. Ha! here's a pretty country! Here's a nice blue sky! I admire the country, miss; I see so little of it, you know. Have you any objection to walk along into the fields? The fields, my dear, bring out all the poetry of my nature. Where's the dog? Here, Puggy! Puggy! hunt about, my man, and find some dog-grass. Does his inside good, you know, after a meat diet in London. Lord! how I feel my spirits rising in this fine air! Does my complexion look any brighter, miss? Will you run a race with me, Mr. Moody, or will you oblige me with a back at leap-frog? I'm not mad, my dear young lady; I'm only merry. I live, you see, in the London stink; and the smell of the hedges and the wild flowers is too much for me at first. It gets into my head, it does. I'm drunk! As I live by bread, I'm drunk on fresh air! Oh! what a jolly day! Oh! how young and innocent I do feel!" Here his innocence got the better of him, and he began to sing, "I wish I were a little fly, in my love's bosom for to lie!" "Hullo! here we are on the nice soft grass! and, oh, my gracious! there's a bank running down into a hollow! I can't stand that, you know. Mr. Moody, hold my hat, and take the greatest care of it. Here goes for a roll down the bank!"

He handed his horrible hat to the astonished Moody, laid himself flat on the top of the bank, and deliberately rolled down it, exactly as he might have done when he was a boy. The tails of his long gray coat flew madly in the wind: the dog pursued him, jumping over him, and barking with delight; he shouted and screamed in answer to the dog as he rolled over and over faster and faster; and, when he got up, on the level ground, and called out cheerfully to his companions standing above him, "I say, you two, I feel twenty years younger already!"—human gravity could hold out no longer. The sad and silent Moody smiled, and Isabel burst into fits of laughter.

"There," he said "didn't I tell you-you would get used to me, Miss? There's a deal of life left in the old man yet—isn't there? Shy me down my hat, Mr. Moody. And now we'll get to business!" He turned round to the dog still barking at his heels. "Business, Puggy!" he called out sharply, and Puggy instantly shut up his mouth, and said no more.

"Well, now," Old Sharon resumed when he had joined his friends and had got his breath again, "let's have a little talk about yourself, miss. Has Mr. Moody told you who I am, and what I want with you? Very good. May I offer you my arm? No! You like to be independent, don't you? All right—I don't object. I am an amiable old man, I am. About this Lady Lydiard, now? Suppose you tell me how you first got acquainted with her?"

In some surprise at this question, Isabel told her little story. Observing Sharon's face while she was speaking, Moody saw that he was not paying the smallest attention to the narrative. His sharp, shameless black eyes watched the girl's face absently; his gross lips curled upwards in a sardonic and self-satisfied smile. He was evidently setting a trap for her of some kind. Without a word of warning—while Isabel was in the middle of a sentence—the trap opened, with the opening of Old Sharon's lips.

"I say," he burst out. "How came you to seal her Ladyship's letter—eh?"

The question bore no sort of relation, direct or indirect, to what Isabel happened to be saying at the moment. In the sudden surprise of hearing it, she started and fixed her eyes in astonishment on Sharon's face. The old vagabond chuckled to himself. "Did you see that?" he whispered to Moody. "I beg your pardon, miss," he went on; "I won't interrupt you again. Lord! how interesting it is!—ain't it, Mr. Moody? Please to go on, miss."

But Isabel, though she spoke with perfect sweetness and temper, declined to go on. "I had better tell you, sir, how I came to seal her Ladyship's letter," she said. "If I may venture on giving my opinion, that part of my story seems to be the only part of it which relates to your business with me to-day."

Without further preface she described the circumstances which had led to her assuming the perilous responsibility of sealing the letter. Old Sharon's wandering attention began to wander again: he was evidently occupied in setting another trap. For the second time he interrupted Isabel in the middle of a sentence. Suddenly stopping short, he pointed to some sheep, at the further end of the field through which they happened to be passing at the moment.

"There's a pretty sight," he said. "There are the innocent sheep a-feeding—all following each other as usual. And there's the sly dog waiting behind the gate till the sheep wants his services. Reminds me of Old Sharon and the public!" He chuckled over the discovery of the remarkable similarity between the sheep-dog and himself, and the sheep and the public—and then burst upon Isabel with a second question. "I say! didn't you look at the letter before you sealed it?"

"Certainly not!" Isabel answered.

"Not even at the address?"

"No!"

"Thinking of something else—eh?"

"Very likely," said Isabel.

"Was it your new bonnet, my dear?"

Isabel laughed. "Women are not always thinking of their new bonnets," she answered.

Old Sharon, to all appearance, dropped the subject there. He lifted his lean brown forefinger and pointed again—this time to a house at a short distance from them. "That's a farmhouse, surely?" he said. "I'm thirsty after my roll down the hill. Do you think, Miss, they would give me a drink of milk?"

106

"I am sure they would," said Isabel. "I know the people. Shall I go and ask them?"

"Thank you, my dear. One word more before you go. About the sealing of that letter? What could you have been thinking of while you were doing it?" He looked hard at her, and took her suddenly by the arm. "Was it your sweetheart?" he asked, in a whisper.

The question instantly reminded Isabel that she had been thinking of Hardyman while she sealed the letter. She blushed as the remembrance crossed her mind. Robert, noticing the embarrassment, spoke sharply to Old Sharon. "You have no right to put such a question to a young lady," he said. "Be a little more careful for the future."

"There! there! don't be hard on me," pleaded the old rogue. "An ugly old man like me may make his innocent little joke—eh, miss? I'm sure you're too sweet-tempered to be angry when I meant no offense.. Show me that you bear no malice. Go, like a forgiving young angel, and ask for the milk."

Nobody appealed to Isabel's sweetness of temper in vain. "I will do it with pleasure," she said—and hastened away to the farmhouse.

CHAPTER XIV.

THE instant Isabel was out of hearing, Old Sharon slapped Moody on the shoulder to rouse his attention. "I've got her out of the way," he said, "now listen to me. My business with the young angel is done—I may go back to London."

Moody looked at him with astonishment.

"Lord! how little you know of thieves!" exclaimed Old Sharon. "Why, man alive, I have tried her with two plain tests! If you wanted a proof of her innocence, there it was, as plain as the nose in your face. Did you hear me ask her how she came to seal the letter—just when her mind was running on something else?"

"I heard you," said Moody.

"Did you see how she started and stared at me?"

"I did."

"Well, I can tell you this—if she had stolen the money she would neither have started nor stared. She would have had her answer ready beforehand in her own mind, in case of accidents. There's only one thing in my experience that you can never do with a thief, when a thief happens to be a woman— you can never take her by surprise. Put that remark by in your mind; one day you may find a use for remembering it. Did you see her blush, and look quite hurt in her feelings, pretty dear, when I asked about her sweetheart? Do you think a thief, in her place, would have shown such a face as that? Not she! The thief would have been relieved. The thief would have said to herself, 'All right! the more the old fool talks about sweethearts the further he is from tracing the robbery to Me!' Yes! yes! the ground's cleared now, Master Moody. I've reckoned up the servants; I've questioned Miss Isabel; I've made my inquiries in all the other quarters that may be useful to us—and what's the result? The advice I gave, when you and the lawyer first came to me—I hate that fellow!—remains as sound and good advice as ever. I have got the thief in my mind," said Old Sharon, closing his cunning eyes and then opening them again, "as plain as I've got you in my eye at this minute. No more of that now," he went on, looking round sharply at the path that led to the farmhouse. "I've something particular to say to you—and there's barely time to say it before that nice girl comes back. Look here! Do you happen to be acquainted with Mr.-Honorable-Hardyman's valet?"

Moody's eyes rested on Old Sharon with a searching and doubtful look.

"Mr. Hardyman's valet?" he repeated. "I wasn't prepared to hear Mr. Hardyman's name."

Old Sharon looked at Moody, in his turn, with a flash of sardonic triumph.

"Oho!" he said. "Has my good boy learned his lesson? Do you see the thief through my spectacles, already?"

"I began to see him," Moody answered, "when you gave us the guinea opinion at your lodgings."

"Will you whisper his name?" asked Old Sharon.

"Not yet. I distrust my own judgment. I wait till time proves that you are right."

Old Sharon knitted his shaggy brows and shook his head. "If you had only a little more dash and go in you," he said, "you would be a clever fellow. As it is—!" He finished the sentence by snapping his fingers with a grin of contempt. "Let's get to business. Are you going back by the next train along with me? or are you going to stop with the young lady?"

"I will follow you by a later train," Moody answered.

"Then I must give you my instructions at once," Sharon continued. "You get better acquainted with Hardyman's valet. Lend him money if he wants it—stick at nothing to make a bosom friend of him. I can't do that part of it; my appearance would be against me. You are the man—you are respectable from the top of your hat to the tips of your boots; nobody would suspect You. Don't make objections! Can you fix the valet? Or can't you?"

"I can try," said Moody. "And what then?"

Old Sharon put his gross lips disagreeably close to Moody's ear.

"Your friend the valet can tell you who his master's bankers are," he said; "and he can supply you with a specimen of his master's handwriting."

Moody drew back, as suddenly as if his vagabond companion had put a knife to his throat. "You old villain!" he said. "Are you tempting me to forgery?"

"You infernal fool!" retorted Old Sharon. "Will you hold that long tongue of yours, and hear what I have to say. You go to Hardyman's bankers, with a note in Hardyman's handwriting (exactly imitated by me) to this effect:—'Mr. H. presents his compliments to Messrs. So-and-So, and is not quite certain whether a payment of five hundred pounds has been made within the last week to his account. He will be much obliged if Messrs. So-and-So will inform him by a line in reply, whether there is such an entry to his credit in their books, and by whom the payment has been made.' You wait for the bankers' answer, and bring it to me. It's just possible that the name you're afraid to whisper may appear in the letter. If it does, we've caught our man. Is that forgery, Mr. Muddlehead Moody? I'll tell you what—if I had lived to be your age, and knew no more of the world than you do, I'd go and hang myself. Steady! here's our charming friend with the milk. Remember your instructions, and don't lose heart if my notion of the payment to the bankers comes to nothing. I know what to do next, in that case—and, what's more, I'll take all the risk and trouble on my own shoulders. Oh, Lord! I'm afraid I shall be obliged to drink the milk, now it's come!"

With this apprehension in his mind, he advanced to relieve Isabel of the jug that she carried.

"Here's a treat!" he burst out, with an affectation of joy, which was completely belied by the expression of his dirty face. "Here's a kind and dear young lady, to help an old man to a drink with her own pretty hands." He paused, and looked at the milk very much as he might have looked at a dose of physic. "Will anyone take a drink first?" he asked, offering the jug piteously to Isabel and Moody. "You see, I'm not wed to genuine milk; I'm used to chalk and water. I don't know what effect the unadulterated cow might have on my poor old inside." He tasted the milk with the greatest caution. "Upon my soul, this is too rich for me! The unadulterated cow is a deal too strong to be drunk alone. If you'll allow me I'll qualify it with a drop of gin. Here, Puggy, Puggy!" He set the milk down before the dog; and, taking a flask out of his pocket, emptied it at a draught. "That's something like!" he said, smacking his lips with an air of infinite relief. "So sorry, Miss, to have given you all your trouble for nothing; it's my ignorance that's to blame, not me. I couldn't know I was unworthy of genuine milk till I tried—could I? And do you know," he proceeded, with his eyes directed slyly on the way back to the station, "I begin to think I'm not worthy of the fresh air, either. A kind of longing seems to come over me for the London stink. I'm home-sick already for the soot of my happy childhood and my own dear native mud. The air here is too thin for me, and the sky's too clean; and—oh, Lord!—when you're wed to the roar of the traffic—the 'busses and the cabs and what not—the silence in these parts is downright awful. I'll wish you good evening, miss; and get back to London."

Isabel turned to Moody with disappointment plainly expressed in her face and manner.

"Is that all he has to say?" she asked. "You told me he could help us. You led me to suppose he could find the guilty person."

Sharon heard her. "I could name the guilty person," he answered, "as easily, miss, as I could name you."

"Why don't you do it then?" Isabel inquired, not very patiently

"Because the time's not ripe for it yet, miss—that's one reason. Because, if I mentioned the thief's name, as things are now, you, Miss Isabel, would think me mad; and you would tell Mr. Moody I had cheated him out of his money—that's another reason. The matter's in train, if you will only wait a little longer."

"So you say," Isabel rejoined. "If you really could name the thief, I believe you would do it now."

She turned away with a frown on her pretty face. Old Sharon followed her. Even his coarse sensibilities appeared to feel the irresistible ascendancy of beauty and youth.

"I say!" he began, "we must part friends, you know—or I shall break my heart over it. They have got milk at the farmhouse. Do you think they have got pen, ink, and paper too?"

Isabel answered, without turning to look at him, "Of course they have!"

"And a bit of sealing-wax?"

"I daresay!"

Old Sharon laid his dirty claws on her shoulder and forced her to face him as the best means of shaking them off.

"Come along!" he said. "I am going to pacify you with some information in writing."

"Why should you write it?" Isabel asked suspiciously.

"Because I mean to make my own conditions, my dear, before I let you into the secret."

In ten minutes more they were all three in the farmhouse parlor. Nobody but the farmer's wife was at home. The good woman trembled from head to foot at the sight of Old Sharon. In all her harmless life she had never yet seen humanity under the aspect in which it was now presented to her. "Mercy preserve us, Miss!" she whispered to Isabel, "how come you to be in such company as that?" Instructed by Isabel, she produced the necessary materials for writing and sealing—and, that done, she shrank away to the door. "Please to excuse me, miss," she said with a last horrified look at her venerable visitor; "I really can't stand the sight of such a blot of dirt as that in my nice clean parlor." With those words she disappeared, and was seen no more.

Perfectly indifferent to his reception, Old Sharon wrote, inclosed what he had written in an envelope; and sealed it (in the absence of anything better fitted for his purpose) with the mouthpiece of his pipe.

"Now, miss," he said, "you give me your word of honor,"—he stopped and looked round at Moody with a grin—"and you give me yours, that you won't either of you break the seal on this envelope till the expiration of one week from the present day. There are the conditions, Miss Isabel, on which I'll give you your information. If you stop to dispute with me, the candle's alight, and I'll burn it!"

It was useless to contend with him. Isabel and Moody gave him the promise that he required. He handed the sealed envelope to Isabel with a low bow. "When the week's out," he said, "you will own I'm a cleverer fellow than you think me now. Wish you good evening, Miss. Come along, Puggy! Farewell to the horrid clean country, and back again to the nice London stink!"

He nodded to Moody—he leered at Isabel—he chuckled to himself—he left the farmhouse.

CHAPTER XV.

ISABEL looked down at the letter in her hand—considered it in silence—and turned to Moody. "I feel tempted to open it already," she said.

"After giving your promise?" Moody gently remonstrated.

Isabel met that objection with a woman's logic.

"Does a promise matter?" she asked, "when one gives it to a dirty, disreputable, presuming old wretch like Mr. Sharon? It's a wonder to me that you trust such a creature. I wouldn't!"

"I doubted him just as you do," Moody answered, "when I first saw him in company with Mr. Troy. But there was something in the advice he gave us at that first consultation which altered my opinion of him for the better. I dislike his appearance and his manners as much as you do—I may even say I felt ashamed of bringing such a person to see you. And yet I can't think that I have acted unwisely in employing Mr. Sharon."

Isabel listened absently. She had something more to say, and she was considering how she should say it. "May I ask you a bold question?" she began.

"Any question you like."

"Have you—" she hesitated and looked embarrassed. "Have you paid Mr. Sharon much money?" she resumed, suddenly rallying her courage. Instead of answering, Moody suggested that it was time to think of returning to Miss Pink's villa. "Your aunt may be getting anxious about you," he said.

Isabel led the way out of the farmhouse in silence. She reverted to Mr. Sharon and the money, however, as they returned by the path across the fields.

"I am sure you will not be offended with me," she said gently, "if I own that I am uneasy about the expense. I am allowing you to use your purse as if it was mine—and I have hardly any savings of my own."

Moody entreated her not to speak of it. "How can I put my money to a better use than in serving your interests?" he asked. "My one object in life is to relieve you of your present anxieties. I shall be the happiest man living if you only owe a moment's happiness to my exertions!"

Isabel took his hand, and looked at him with grateful tears in her eyes.

"How good you are to me, Mr. Moody!" she said. "I wish I could tell you how deeply I feel your kindness."

"You can do it easily," he answered, with a smile. "Call me 'Robert'— don't call me 'Mr. Moody.'"

She took his arm with a sudden familiarity that charmed him. "If you had been my brother I should have called you 'Robert,'" she said; "and no brother could have been more devoted to me than you are."

He looked eagerly at her bright face turned up to his. "May I never hope to be something nearer and dearer to you than a brother?" he asked timidly.

She hung her head and said nothing. Moody's memory recalled Sharon's coarse reference to her "sweetheart." She had blushed when he put the question? What had she done when Moody put his question? Her face answered for her—she had turned pale; she was looking more serious than usual. Ignorant as he was of the ways of women, his instinct told him that this was a bad sign. Surely her rising color would have confessed it, if time and gratitude together were teaching her to love him? He sighed as the inevitable conclusion forced itself on his mind.

"I hope I have not offended you?" he said sadly.

"Oh, no."

"I wish I had not spoken. Pray don't think that I am serving you with any selfish motive."

"I don't think that, Robert. I never could think it of you."

He was not quite satisfied yet. "Even if you were to marry some other man," he went on earnestly, "it would make no difference in what I am trying

115

to do for you. No matter what I might suffer, I should still go on—for your sake."

"Why do you talk so?" she burst out passionately. "No other man has such a claim as you to my gratitude and regard. How can you let such thoughts come to you? I have done nothing in secret. I have no friends who are not known to you. Be satisfied with that, Robert—and let us drop the subject."

"Never to take it up again?" he asked, with the infatuated pertinacity of a man clinging to his last hope.

At other times and under other circumstances, Isabel might have answered him sharply. She spoke with perfect gentleness now.

"Not for the present," she said. "I don't know my own heart. Give me time."

His gratitude caught at those words, as the drowning man is said to catch at the proverbial straw. He lifted her hand, and suddenly and fondly pressed his lips on it. She showed no confusion. Was she sorry for him, poor wretch!—and was that all?

They walked on, arm-in-arm, in silence.

Crossing the last field, they entered again on the high road leading to the row of villas in which Miss Pink lived. The minds of both were preoccupied. Neither of them noticed a gentleman approaching on horseback, followed by a mounted groom. He was advancing slowly, at the walking-pace of his horse, and he only observed the two foot-passengers when he was close to them.

"Miss Isabel!"

She started, looked up, and discovered—Alfred Hardyman.

He was dressed in a perfectly-made travelling suit of light brown, with a peaked felt hat of a darker shade of the same color, which, in a picturesque sense, greatly improved his personal appearance. His pleasure at discovering Isabel gave the animation to his features which they wanted on ordinary occasions. He sat his horse, a superb hunter, easily and gracefully. His light

116

amber-colored gloves fitted him perfectly. His obedient servant, on another magnificent horse, waited behind him. He looked the impersonation of rank and breeding—of wealth and prosperity. What a contrast, in a woman's eyes, to the shy, pale, melancholy man, in the ill-fitting black clothes, with the wandering, uneasy glances, who stood beneath him, and felt, and showed that he felt, his inferior position keenly! In spite of herself, the treacherous blush flew over Isabel's face, in Moody's presence, and with Moody's eyes distrustfully watching her.

"This is a piece of good fortune that I hardly hoped for," said Hardyman, his cool, quiet, dreary way of speaking quickened as usual, in Isabel's presence. "I only got back from France this morning, and I called on Lady Lydiard in the hope of seeing you. She was not at home—and you were in the country—and the servants didn't know the address. I could get nothing out of them, except that you were on a visit to a relation." He looked at Moody while he was speaking. "Haven't I seen you before?" he said, carelessly. "Yes; at Lady Lydiard's. You're her steward, are you not? How d'ye do?" Moody, with his eyes on the ground, answered silently by a bow. Hardyman, perfectly indifferent whether Lady Lydiard's steward spoke or not, turned on his saddle and looked admiringly at Isabel. "I begin to think I am a lucky man at last," he went on with a smile. "I was jogging along to my farm, and despairing of ever seeing Miss Isabel again—and Miss Isabel herself meets me at the roadside! I wonder whether you are as glad to see me as I am to see you? You won't tell me—eh? May I ask you something else? Are you staying in our neighborhood?"

There was no alternative before Isabel but to answer this last question. Hardyman had met her out walking, and had no doubt drawn the inevitable inference—although he was too polite to say so in plain words.

"Yes, sir," she answered, shyly, "I am staying in this neighborhood."

"And who is your relation?" Hardyman proceeded, in his easy, matter-of-course way. "Lady Lydiard told me, when I had the pleasure of meeting you at her house, that you had an aunt living in the country. I have a good memory, Miss Isabel, for anything that I hear about You! It's your aunt, isn't it? Yes? I know everybody about hew. What is your aunt's name?"

Isabel, still resting her hand on Robert's arm, felt it tremble a little as Hardyman made this last inquiry. If she had been speaking to one of her equals she would have known how to dispose of the question without directly answering it. But what could she say to the magnificent gentleman on the stately horse? He had only to send his servant into the village to ask who the young lady from London was staying with, and the answer, in a dozen mouths at least, would direct him to her aunt. She cast one appealing look at Moody and pronounced the distinguished name of Miss Pink.

"Miss Pink?" Hardyman repeated. "Surely I know Miss Pink?" (He had not the faintest remembrances of her.) "Where did I meet her last?" (He ran over in his memory the different local festivals at which strangers had been introduced to him.) "Was it at the archery meeting? or at the grammar-school when the prizes were given? No? It must have been at the flower show, then, surely?"

It had been at the flower show. Isabel had heard it from Miss Pink fifty times at least, and was obliged to admit it now.

"I am quite ashamed of never having called," Hardyman proceeded. "The fact is, I have so much to do. I am a bad one at paying visits. Are you on your way home? Let me follow you and make my apologies personally to Miss Pink."

Moody looked at Isabel. It was only a momentary glance, but she perfectly understood it.

"I am afraid, sir, my aunt cannot have the honor of seeing you to-day," she said.

Hardyman was all compliance. He smiled and patted his horse's neck. "To-morrow, then," he said. "My compliments, and I will call in the afternoon. Let me see: Miss Pink lives at—?" He waited, as if he expected Isabel to assist his treacherous memory once more. She hesitated again. Hardyman looked round at his groom. The groom could find out the address, even if he did not happen to know it already. Besides, there was the little row of houses visible at the further end of the road. Isabel pointed to the villas, as a necessary concession to good manners, before the groom could anticipate her. "My aunt lives there, sir; at the house called The Lawn."

"Ah! to be sure!" said Hardyman. "I oughtn't to have wanted reminding; but I have so many things to think of at the farm. And I am afraid I must be getting old—my memory isn't as good as it was. I am so glad to have seen you, Miss Isabel. You and your aunt must come and look at my horses. Do you like horses? Are you fond of riding? I have a quiet roan mare that is used to carrying ladies; she would be just the thing for you. Did I beg you to give my best compliments to your aunt? Yes? How well you are looking! our air here agrees with you. I hope I haven't kept you standing too long? I didn't think of it in the pleasure of meeting you. Good-by, Miss Isabel; good-by, till to-morrow!"

He took off his hat to Isabel, nodded to Moody, and pursued his way to the farm.

Isabel looked at her companion. His eyes were still on the ground. Pale, silent, motionless, he waited by her like a dog, until she gave the signal of walking on again towards the house.

"You are not angry with me for speaking to Mr. Hardyman?" she asked, anxiously.

He lifted his head it the sound of her voice. "Angry with you, my dear! why should I be angry?"

"You seem so changed, Robert, since we met Mr. Hardyman. I couldn't help speaking to him—could I?"

"Certainly not."

They moved on towards the villa. Isabel was still uneasy. There was something in Moody's silent submission to all that she said and all that she did which pained and humiliated her. "You're not jealous?" she said, smiling timidly.

He tried to speak lightly on his side. "I have no time to be jealous while I have your affairs to look after," he answered.

She pressed his arm tenderly. "Never fear, Robert, that new friends will make me forget the best and dearest friend who is now at my side." She paused, and looked up at him with a compassionate fondness that was very pretty to see. "I can keep out of the way to-morrow, when Mr. Hardyman calls," she said. "It is my aunt he is coming to see—not me."

It was generously meant. But while her mind was only occupied with the present time, Moody's mind was looking into the future. He was learning the hard lesson of self-sacrifice already. "Do what you think is right," he said quietly; "don't think of me."

They reached the gate of the villa. He held out his hand to say good-by.

"Won't you come in?" she asked. "Do come in!"

"Not now, my dear. I must get back to London as soon as I can. There is some more work to be done for you, and the sooner I do it the better."

She heard his excuse without heeding it.

"You are not like yourself, Robert," she said. "Why is it? What are you thinking of?"

He was thinking of the bright blush that overspread her face when Hardyman first spoke to her; he was thinking of the invitation to her to see the stud-farm, and to ride the roan mare; he was thinking of the utterly powerless position in which he stood towards Isabel and towards the highly-born gentleman who admired her. But he kept his doubts and fears to himself. "The train won't wait for me," he said, and held out his hand once more.

She was not only perplexed; she was really distressed. "Don't take leave of me in that cold way!" she pleaded. Her eyes dropped before his, and her lips trembled a little. "Give me a kiss, Robert, at parting." She said those bold words softly and sadly, out of the depth of her pity for him. He started; his face brightened suddenly; his sinking hope rose again. In another moment the change came; in another moment he understood her. As he touched her cheek with his lips, he turned pale again. "Don't quite forget me," he said, in low, faltering tones—and left her.

Miss Pink met Isabel in the hall. Refreshed by unbroken repose, the ex-schoolmistress was in the happiest frame of mind for the reception of her niece's news.

Informed that Moody had travelled to South Morden to personally report the progress of the inquiries, Miss Pink highly approved of him as a substitute for Mr. Troy. "Mr. Moody, as a banker's son, is a gentleman by birth," she remarked; "he has condescended, in becoming Lady Lydiard's steward. What I saw of him, when he came here with you, prepossessed me in his favor. He has my confidence, Isabel, as well as yours—he is in every respect a superior person to Mr. Troy. Did you meet any friends, my dear, when you were out walking?"

The answer to this question produced a species of transformation in Miss Pink. The rapturous rank-worship of her nation feasted, so to speak, on Hardyman's message. She looked taller and younger than usual—she was all smiles and sweetness. "At last, Isabel, you have seen birth and breeding under their right aspect," she said. "In the society of Lady Lydiard, you cannot possibly have formed correct ideas of the English aristocracy. Observe Mr. Hardyman when he does me the honor to call to-morrow—and you will see the difference."

"Mr. Hardyman is your visitor, aunt—not mine. I was going to ask you to let me remain upstairs in my room."

Miss Pink was unaffectedly shocked. "This is what you learn at Lady Lydiard's!" she observed. "No, Isabel, your absence would be a breach of good manners—I cannot possibly permit it. You will be present to receive our distinguished friend with me. And mind this!" added Miss Pink, in her most impressive manner, "If Mr. Hardyman should by any chance ask why you have left Lady Lydiard, not one word about those disgraceful circumstances which connect you with the loss of the banknote! I should sink into the earth if the smallest hint of what has really happened should reach Mr. Hardyman's ears. My child, I stand towards you in the place of your lamented mother; I have the right to command your silence on this horrible subject, and I do imperatively command it."

In these words foolish Miss Pink sowed the seed for the harvest of trouble that was soon to come.

CHAPTER XVI.

PAYING his court to the ex-schoolmistress on the next day, Hardyman made such excellent use of his opportunities that the visit to the stud-farm took place on the day after. His own carriage was placed at the disposal of Isabel and her aunt; and his own sister was present to confer special distinction on the reception of Miss Pink.

In a country like England, which annually suspends the sitting of its Legislature in honor of a horse-race, it is only natural and proper that the comfort of the horses should be the first object of consideration at a stud-farm. Nine-tenths of the land at Hardyman's farm was devoted, in one way or another, to the noble quadruped with the low forehead and the long nose. Poor humanity was satisfied with second-rate and third-rate accommodation. The ornamental grounds, very poorly laid out, were also very limited in extent—and, as for the dwelling-house, it was literally a cottage. A parlor and a kitchen, a smoking-room, a bed-room, and a spare chamber for a friend, all scantily furnished, sufficed for the modest wants of the owner of the property. If you wished to feast your eyes on luxury you went to the stables.

The stud-farm being described, the introduction to Hardyman's sister follows in due course.

The Honorable Lavinia Hardyman was, as all persons in society know, married rather late in life to General Drumblade. It is saying a great deal, but it is not saying too much, to describe Mrs. Drumblade as the most mischievous woman of her age in all England. Scandal was the breath of her life; to place people in false positions, to divulge secrets and destroy characters, to undermine friendships, and aggravate enmities—these were the sources of enjoyment from which this dangerous woman drew the inexhaustible fund of good spirits that made her a brilliant light in the social sphere. She was one of the privileged sinners of modern society. The worst mischief that she could work was ascribed to her "exuberant vitality." She had that ready familiarity of manner which is (in her class) so rarely discovered to be insolence in disguise.

Her power of easy self-assertion found people ready to accept her on her own terms wherever she went. She was one of those big, overpowering women, with blunt manners, voluble tongues, and goggle eyes, who carry everything before them. The highest society modestly considered itself in danger of being dull in the absence of Mrs. Drumblade. Even Hardyman himself—who saw as little of her as possible, whose frankly straightforward nature recoiled by instinct from contact with his sister—could think of no fitter person to make Miss Pink's reception agreeable to her, while he was devoting his own attentions to her niece. Mrs. Drumblade accepted the position thus offered with the most amiable readiness. In her own private mind she placed an interpretation on her brother's motives which did him the grossest injustice. She believed that Hardyman's designs on Isabel contemplated the most profligate result. To assist this purpose, while the girl's nearest relative was supposed to be taking care of her, was Mrs. Drumblade's idea of "fun." Her worst enemies admitted that the honorable Lavinia had redeeming qualities, and owned that a keen sense of humor was one of her merits.

Was Miss Pink a likely person to resist the fascinations of Mrs. Drumblade? Alas, for the ex-schoolmistress! before she had been five minutes at the farm, Hardyman's sister had fished for her, caught her, landed her. Poor Miss Pink!

Mrs. Drumblade could assume a grave dignity of manner when the occasion called for it. She was grave, she was dignified, when Hardyman performed the ceremonies of introduction. She would not say she was charmed to meet Miss Pink—the ordinary slang of society was not for Miss Pink's ears—she would say she felt this introduction as a privilege. It was so seldom one met with persons of trained intellect in society. Mrs. Drumblade was already informed of Miss Pink's earlier triumphs in the instruction of youth. Mrs. Drumblade had not been blessed with children herself; but she had nephews and nieces, and she was anxious about their education, especially the nieces. What a sweet, modest girl Miss Isabel was! The fondest wish she could form for her nieces would be that they should resemble Miss Isabel when they grew up. The question was, as to the best method of education. She would own that she had selfish motives in becoming acquainted with

Miss Pink. They were at the farm, no doubt, to see Alfred's horses. Mrs. Drumblade did not understand horses; her interest was in the question of education. She might even confess that she had accepted Alfred's invitation in the hope of hearing Miss Pink's views. There would be opportunities, she trusted, for a little instructive conversation on that subject. It was, perhaps, ridiculous to talk, at her age, of feeling as if she was Miss Pink's pupil; and yet it exactly expressed the nature of the aspiration which was then in her mind.

In these terms, feeling her way with the utmost nicety, Mrs. Drumblade wound the net of flattery round and round Miss Pink until her hold on that innocent lady was, in every sense of the word, secure. Before half the horses had been passed under review, Hardyman and Isabel were out of sight, and Mrs. Drumblade and Miss Pink were lost in the intricacies of the stables. "Excessively stupid of me! We had better go back, and establish ourselves comfortably in the parlor. When my brother misses us, he and your charming niece will return to look for us in the cottage." Under cover of this arrangement the separation became complete. Miss Pink held forth on education to Mrs. Drumblade in the parlor; while Hardyman and Isabel were on their way to a paddock at the farthest limits of the property.

"I am afraid you are getting a little tired," said Hardyman. "Won't you take my arm?"

Isabel was on her guard: she had not forgotten what Lady Lydiard had said to her. "No, thank you, Mr. Hardyman; I am a better walker than you think."

Hardyman continued the conversation in his blunt, resolute way. "I wonder whether you will believe me," he asked, "if I tell you that this is one of the happiest days of my life."

"I should think you were always happy," Isabel cautiously replied, "having such a pretty place to live in as this."

Hardyman met that answer with one of his quietly-positive denials. "A man is never happy by himself," he said. "He is happy with a companion. For instance, I am happy with you."

Isabel stopped and looked back. Hardyman's language was becoming a little too explicit. "Surely we have lost Mrs. Drumblade and my aunt," she said. "I don't see them anywhere."

"You will see them directly; they are only a long way behind." With this assurance, he returned, in his own obstinate way, to his one object in view. "Miss Isabel, I want to ask you a question. I'm not a ladies' man. I speak my mind plainly to everybody—women included. Do you like being here to-day?"

Isabel's gravity was not proof against this very downright question. "I should be hard to please," she said laughing, "if I didn't enjoy my visit to the farm."

Hardyman pushed steadily forward through the obstacle of the farm to the question of the farm's master. "You like being here," he repeated. "Do you like Me?"

This was serious. Isabel drew back a little, and looked at him. He waited with the most impenetrable gravity for her reply.

"I think you can hardly expect me to answer that question," she said

"Why not?"

"Our acquaintance has been a very short one, Mr. Hardyman. And, if you are so good as to forget the difference between us, I think I ought to remember it."

"What difference?"

"The difference in rank."

Hardyman suddenly stood still, and emphasized his next words by digging his stick into the grass.

"If anything I have said has vexed you," he began, "tell me so plainly, Miss Isabel, and I'll ask your pardon. But don't throw my rank in my face. I cut adrift from all that nonsense when I took this farm and got my living out of the horses. What has a man's rank to do with a man's feelings?" he went on, with another emphatic dig of his stick. "I am quite serious in asking if you like me—for this good reason, that I like you. Yes, I do. You remember that day when I bled the old lady's dog—well, I have found out since then that there's a sort of incompleteness in my life which I never suspected before. It's you who have put that idea into my head. You didn't mean it, I dare say, but you have done it all the same. I sat alone here yesterday evening smoking my pipe—and I didn't enjoy it. I breakfasted alone this morning—and I didn't enjoy that. I said to myself, She's coming to lunch, that's one comfort—I shall enjoy lunch. That's what I feel, roughly described. I don't suppose I've been five minutes together without thinking of you, now in one way and now in another, since the day when I first saw you. When a man comes to my time of life, and has had any experience, he knows what that means. It means, in plain English, that his heart is set on a woman. You're the woman."

Isabel had thus far made several attempts to interrupt him, without success. But, when Hardyman's confession attained its culminating point, she insisted on being heard.

"If you will excuse me, sir," she interposed gravely, "I think I had better go back to the cottage. My aunt is a stranger here, and she doesn't know where to look for us."

"We don't want your aunt," Hardyman remarked, in his most positive manner.

"We do want her," Isabel rejoined. "I won't venture to say it's wrong in you, Mr. Hardyman, to talk to me as you have just done, but I am quite sure it's very wrong of me to listen."

He looked at her with such unaffected surprise and distress that she stopped, on the point of leaving him, and tried to make herself better understood.

"I had no intention of offending you, sir," she said, a little confusedly. "I only wanted to remind you that there are some things which a gentleman in your position—" She stopped, tried to finish the sentence, failed, and began another. "If I had been a young lady in your own rank of life," she went on,

"I might have thanked you for paying me a compliment, and have given you a serious answer. As it is, I am afraid that I must say that you have surprised and disappointed me. I can claim very little for myself, I know. But I did imagine—so long as there was nothing unbecoming in my conduct—that I had some right to your respect."

Listening more and more impatiently, Hardyman took her by the hand, and burst out with another of his abrupt questions.

"What can you possibly be thinking of?" he asked.

She gave him no answer; she only looked at him reproachfully, and tried to release herself.

Hardyman held her hand faster than ever.

"I believe you think me an infernal scoundrel!" he said. "I can stand a good deal, Miss Isabel, but I can't stand that. How have I failed in respect toward you, if you please? I have told you-you're the woman my heart is set on. Well? Isn't it plain what I want of you, when I say that? Isabel Miller, I want you to be my wife!"

Isabel's only reply to this extraordinary proposal of marriage was a faint cry of astonishment, followed by a sudden trembling that shook her from head to foot.

Hardyman put his arm round her with a gentleness which his oldest friend would have been surprised to see in him.

"Take your time to think of it," he said, dropping back again into his usual quiet tone. "If you had known me a little better you wouldn't have mistaken me, and you wouldn't be looking at me now as if you were afraid to believe your own ears. What is there so very wonderful in my wanting to marry you? I don't set up for being a saint. When I was a younger man I was no better (and no worse) than other young men. I'm getting on now to middle life. I don't want romances and adventures—I want an easy existence with a nice lovable woman who will make me a good wife. You're the woman, I tell you again. I know it by what I've seen of you myself, and by what I have heard of you from Lady Lydiard. She said you were prudent, and sweet-tempered, and affectionate; to which I wish to add that you have just the face and figure that I like, and the modest manners and the blessed absence of all slang in your talk, which I don't find in the young women I meet with in the present day. That's my view of it: I think for myself. What does it matter to me whether you're the daughter of a Duke or the daughter of a Dairyman? It isn't your father I want to marry—it's you. Listen to reason, there's a dear! We have only one question to settle before we go back to your aunt. You wouldn't answer me when I asked it a little while since. Will you answer now? Do you like me?"

Isabel looked up at him timidly.

"In my position, sir," she asked, "have I any right to like you? What would your relations and friends think, if I said Yes?"

Hardyman gave her waist a little admonitory squeeze with his arm

"What? You're at it again? A nice way to answer a man, to call him 'Sir,' and to get behind his rank as if it was a place of refuge from him! I hate talking of myself, but you force me to it. Here is my position in the world—I have got an elder brother; he is married, and he has a son to succeed him, in the title and the property. You understand, so far? Very well! Years ago I shifted my share of the rank (whatever it may be) on to my brother's shoulders. He is a thorough good fellow, and he has carried my dignity for me, without once dropping it, ever since. As for what people may say, they have said it already, from my father and mother downward, in the time when I took to the horses and the farm. If they're the wise people I take them for, they won't be at the trouble of saying it all over again. No, no. Twist it how you may, Miss Isabel, whether I'm single or whether I'm married, I'm plain Alfred Hardyman; and everybody who knows me knows that I go on my way, and please myself. If you don't like me, it will be the bitterest disappointment I ever had in my life; but say so honestly, all the same."

Where is the woman in Isabel's place whose capacity for resistance would not have yielded a little to such an appeal as this?

"I should be an insensible wretch," she replied warmly, "if I didn't feel the honor you have done me, and feel it gratefully."

"Does that mean you will have me for a husband?" asked downright Hardyman.

She was fairly driven into a corner; but (being a woman) she tried to slip through his fingers at the last moment.

"Will you forgive me," she said, "if I ask you for a little more time? I am so bewildered, I hardly know what to say or do for the best. You see, Mr. Hardyman, it would be a dreadful thing for me to be the cause of giving offense to your family. I am obliged to think of that. It would be so distressing for you (I will say nothing of myself) if your friends closed their doors on me. They might say I was a designing girl, who had taken advantage of your good opinion to raise herself in the world. Lady Lydiard warned me long since not to be ambitious about myself and not to forget my station in life, because she treated me like her adopted daughter. Indeed—indeed, I can't tell you how I feel your goodness, and the compliment—the very great compliment, you pay me! My heart is free, and if I followed my own inclinations—" She checked herself, conscious that she was on the brink of saying too much. "Will you give me a few days," she pleaded, "to try if I can think composedly of all this? I am only a girl, and I feel quite dazzled by the prospect that you set before me."

Hardyman seized on those words as offering all the encouragement that he desired to his suit.

"Have your own way in this thing and in everything!" he said, with an unaccustomed fervor of language and manner. "I am so glad to hear that your heart is open to me, and that all your inclinations take my part."

Isabel instantly protested against this misrepresentation of what she had really said, "Oh, Mr. Hardyman, you quite mistake me!"

He answered her very much as he had answered Lady Lydiard, when she had tried to make him understand his proper relations towards Isabel.

"No, no; I don't mistake you. I agree to every word you say. How can

I expect you to marry me, as you very properly remark, unless I give you a day or two to make up your mind? It's quite enough for me that you like the prospect. If Lady Lydiard treated you as her daughter, why shouldn't you be my wife? It stands to reason that you're quite right to marry a man who can raise you in the world. I like you to be ambitious—though Heaven knows it isn't much I can do for you, except to love you with all my heart. Still, it's a great encouragement to hear that her Ladyship's views agree with mine—"

"They don't agree, Mr. Hardyman!" protested poor Isabel. "You are entirely misrepresenting—"

Hardyman cordially concurred in this view of the matter. "Yes! yes! I can't pretend to represent her Ladyship's language, or yours either; I am obliged to take my words as they come to me. Don't disturb yourself: it's all right—I understand. You have made me the happiest man living. I shall ride over to-morrow to your aunt's house, and hear what you have to say to me. Mind you're at home! Not a day must pass now without my seeing you. I do love you, Isabel—I do, indeed!" He stooped, and kissed her heartily. "Only to reward me," he explained, "for giving you time to think."

She drew herself away from him—resolutely, not angrily. Before she could make a third attempt to place the subject in its right light before him, the luncheon bell rang at the cottage—and a servant appeared evidently sent to look for them.

"Don't forget to-morrow," Hardyman whispered confidentially. "I'll call early—and then go to London, and get the ring."

CHAPTER XVII.

EVENTS succeeded each other rapidly, after the memorable day to Isabel of the luncheon at the farm.

On the next day (the ninth of the month) Lady Lydiard sent for her steward, and requested him to explain his conduct in repeatedly leaving the house without assigning any reason for his absence. She did not dispute his claims to a freedom of action which would not be permitted to an ordinary servant. Her objection to his present course of proceeding related entirely to the mystery in which it was involved, and to the uncertainty in which the household was left as to the hour of his return. On those grounds, she thought herself entitled to an explanation. Moody's habitual reserve—strengthened, on this occasion, by his dread of ridicule, if his efforts to serve Isabel ended in failure—disinclined him to take Lady Lydiard into his confidence, while his inquiries were still beset with obstacles and doubts. He respectfully entreated her Ladyship to grant him a delay of a few weeks before he entered on his explanation. Lady Lydiard's quick temper resented his request. She told Moody plainly that he was guilty of an act of presumption in making his own conditions with his employer. He received the reproof with exemplary resignation; but he held to his conditions nevertheless. From that moment the result of the interview was no longer in doubt. Moody was directed to send in his accounts. The accounts having been examined, and found to be scrupulously correct, he declined accepting the balance of salary that was offered to him. The next day he left Lady Lydiard's service.

On the tenth of the month her Ladyship received a letter from her nephew.

The health of Felix had not improved. He had made up his mind to go abroad again towards the end of the month. In the meantime, he had written to his friend in Paris, and he had the pleasure of forwarding an answer. The letter inclosed announced that the lost five-hundred-pound note had been made the subject of careful inquiry in Paris. It had not been traced. The French police offered to send to London one of their best men, well acquainted with the English language, if Lady Lydiard was desirous of employing him. He would be perfectly willing to act with an English officer in conducting the investigation, should it be thought necessary. Mr. Troy being consulted as to the expediency of accepting this proposal, objected to the pecuniary terms demanded as being extravagantly high. He suggested waiting a little before any reply was sent to Paris; and he engaged meanwhile to consult a London solicitor who had great experience in cases of theft, and whose advice might enable them to dispense entirely with the services of the French police.

Being now a free man again, Moody was able to follow his own inclinations in regard to the instructions which he had received from Old Sharon.

The course that had been recommended to him was repellent to the self-respect and the sense of delicacy which were among the inbred virtues of Moody's character. He shrank from forcing himself as a friend on Hardyman's valet: he recoiled from the idea of tempting the man to steal a specimen of his master's handwriting. After some consideration, he decided on applying to the agent who collected the rents at Hardyman's London chambers. Being an old acquaintance of Moody's, this person would certainly not hesitate to communicate the address of Hardyman's bankers, if he knew it. The experiment, tried under these favoring circumstances, proved perfectly successful. Moody proceeded to Sharon's lodgings the same day, with the address of the bankers in his pocketbook. The old vagabond, greatly amused by Moody's scruples, saw plainly enough that, so long as he wrote the supposed letter from Hardyman in the third person, it mattered little what handwriting was employed, seeing that no signature would be necessary. The letter was at once composed, on the model which Sharon had already suggested to Moody, and a respectable messenger (so far as outward appearances went) was employed to take it to the bank. In half an hour the answer came back. It added one more to the difficulties which beset the inquiry after the lost money. No such sum as five hundred pounds had been paid, within the dates mentioned, to the credit of Hardyman's account.

Old Sharon was not in the least discomposed by this fresh check. "Give my love to the dear young lady," he said with his customary impudence; "and tell her we are one degree nearer to finding the thief."

Moody looked at him, doubting whether he was in jest or in earnest.

"Must I squeeze a little more information into that thick head of yours?" asked Sharon. With this question he produced a weekly newspaper, and pointed to a paragraph which reported, among the items of sporting news, Hardyman's recent visit to a sale of horses at a town in the north of France. "We know he didn't pay the bank-note in to his account," Sharon remarked. "What else did he do with it? Took it to pay for the horses that he bought in France! Do you see your way a little plainer now? Very good. Let's try next if your money holds out. Somebody must cross the Channel in search of the note. Which of us two is to sit in the steam-boat with a white basin on his lap? Old Sharon, of course!" He stopped to count the money still left, out of the sum deposited by Moody to defray the cost of the inquiry. "All right!" he went on. "I've got enough to pay my expenses there and back. Don't stir out of London till you hear from me. I can't tell how soon I may not want you. If there's any difficulty in tracing the note, your hand will have to go into your pocket again. Can't you get the lawyer to join you? Lord! how I should enjoy squandering his money! It's a downright disgrace to me to have only got one guinea out of him. I could tear my flesh off my bones when I think of it."

The same night Old Sharon started for France, by way of Dover and Calais.

Two days elapsed, and brought no news from Moody's agent. On the third day, he received some information relating to Sharon—not from the man himself, but in a letter from Isabel Miller.

"For once, dear Robert," she wrote, "my judgment has turned out to be sounder than yours. That hateful old man has confirmed my worst opinion of him. Pray have him punished. Take him before a magistrate and charge him with cheating you out of your money. I inclose the sealed letter which he gave me at the farmhouse. The week's time before I was to open it expired yesterday. Was there ever anything so impudent and so inhuman? I am too vexed and angry about the money you have wasted on this old wretch to write more. Yours, gratefully and affectionately, Isabel."

The letter in which Old Sharon had undertaken (by way of pacifying Isabel) to write the name of the thief, contained these lines:

"You are a charming girl, my dear; but you still want one thing to make you perfect—and that is a lesson in patience. I am proud and happy to teach you. The name of the thief remains, for the present, Mr. —— (Blank)."

From Moody's point of view, there was but one thing to be said of this: it was just like Old Sharon! Isabel's letter was of infinitely greater interest to him. He feasted his eyes on the words above the signature: she signed herself, "Yours gratefully and affectionately." Did the last words mean that she was really beginning to be fond of him? After kissing the word, he wrote a comforting letter to her, in which he pledged himself to keep a watchful eye on Sharon, and to trust him with no more money until he had honestly earned it first.

A week passed. Moody (longing to see Isabel) still waited in vain for news from France. He had just decided to delay his visit to South Morden no longer, when the errand-boy employed by Sharon brought him this message: "The old 'un's at home, and waitin' to see yer."

CHAPTER XVIII.

SHARON'S news was not of an encouraging character. He had met with serious difficulties, and had spent the last farthing of Moody's money in attempting to overcome them.

One discovery of importance he had certainly made. A horse withdrawn from the sale was the only horse that had met with Hardyman's approval. He had secured the animal at the high reserved price of twelve thousand francs—being four hundred and eighty pounds in English money; and he had paid with an English bank-note. The seller (a French horse-dealer resident in Brussels) had returned to Belgium immediately on completing the negotiations. Sharon had ascertained his address, and had written to him at Brussels, inclosing the number of the lost banknote. In two days he had received an answer, informing him that the horse-dealer had been called to England by the illness of a relative, and that he had hitherto failed to send any address to which his letters could be forwarded. Hearing this, and having exhausted his funds, Sharon had returned to London. It now rested with Moody to decide whether the course of the inquiry should follow the horse-dealer next. Here was the cash account, showing how the money had been spent. And there was Sharon, with his pipe in his mouth and his dog on his lap, waiting for orders.

Moody wisely took time to consider before he committed himself to a decision. In the meanwhile, he ventured to recommend a new course of proceeding which Sharon's report had suggested to his mind.

"It seems to me," he said, "that we have taken the roundabout way of getting to our end in view, when the straight road lay before us. If Mr. Hardyman has passed the stolen note, you know, as well as I do, that he has passed it innocently. Instead of wasting time and money in trying to trace a stranger, why not tell Mr. Hardyman what has happened, and ask him to give us the number of the note? You can't think of everything, I know; but it does seem strange that this idea didn't occur to you before you went to France."

"Mr. Moody," said Old Sharon, "I shall have to cut your acquaintance. You are a man without faith; I don't like you. As if I hadn't thought of Hardyman weeks since!" he exclaimed contemptuously. "Are you really soft enough to suppose that a gentleman in his position would talk about his money affairs to me? You know mighty little of him if you do. A fortnight since I sent one of my men (most respectably dressed) to hang about his farm, and see what information he could pick up. My man became painfully acquainted with the toe of a boot. It was thick, sir; and it was Hardyman's."

"I will run the risk of the boot," Moody replied, in his quiet way.

"And put the question to Hardyman?"

"Yes."

"Very good," said Sharon. "If you get your answer from his tongue, instead of his boot, the case is cleared up—unless I have made a complete mess of it. Look here, Moody! If you want to do me a good turn, tell the lawyer that the guinea-opinion was the right one. Let him know that he was the fool, not you, when he buttoned up his pockets and refused to trust me. And, I say," pursued Old Sharon, relapsing into his customary impudence, "you're in love, you know, with that nice girl. I like her myself. When you marry her invite me to the wedding. I'll make a sacrifice; I'll brush my hair and wash my face in honor of the occasion."

Returning to his lodgings, Moody found two letters waiting on the table. One of them bore the South Morden postmark. He opened that letter first.

It was written by Miss Pink. The first lines contained an urgent entreaty to keep the circumstances connected with the loss of the five hundred pounds the strictest secret from everyone in general, and from Hardyman in particular. The reasons assigned for making the strange request were next expressed in these terms: "My niece Isabel is, I am happy to inform you, engaged to be married to Mr. Hardyman. If the slightest hint reached him of her having been associated, no matter how cruelly and unjustly, with a suspicion of theft, the marriage would be broken off, and the result to herself and to everybody connected with her, would be disgrace for the rest of our lives."

On the blank space at the foot of the page a few words were added in Isabel's writing: "Whatever changes there may be in my life, your place in my heart is one that no other person can fill: it is the place of my dearest friend. Pray write and tell me that you are not distressed and not angry. My one anxiety is that you should remember what I have always told you about the state of my own feelings. My one wish is that you will still let me love you and value you, as I might have loved and valued a brother."

The letter dropped from Moody's hand. Not a word—not even a sigh—passed his lips. In tearless silence he submitted to the pang that wrung him. In tearless silence he contemplated the wreck of his life.

CHAPTER XIX.

THE narrative returns to South Morden, and follows the events which attended Isabel's marriage engagement.

To say that Miss Pink, inflated by the triumph, rose, morally speaking, from the earth and floated among the clouds, is to indicate faintly the effect produced on the ex-schoolmistress when her niece first informed her of what had happened at the farm. Attacked on one side by her aunt, and on the other by Hardyman, and feebly defended, at the best, by her own doubts and misgivings, Isabel ended by surrendering at discretion. Like thousands of other women in a similar position, she was in the last degree uncertain as to the state of her own heart. To what extent she was insensibly influenced by Hardyman's commanding position in believing herself to be sincerely attached to him, it was beyond her power of self-examination to discover. He doubly dazzled her by his birth and by his celebrity. Not in England only, but throughout Europe, he was a recognized authority on his own subject. How could she—how could any woman—resist the influence of his steady mind, his firmness of purpose, his manly resolution to owe everything to himself and nothing to his rank, set off as these attractive qualities were by the outward and personal advantages which exercise an ascendancy of their own? Isabel was fascinated, and yet Isabel was not at ease. In her lonely moments she was troubled by regretful thoughts of Moody, which perplexed and irritated her. She had always behaved honestly to him; she had never encouraged him to hope that his love for her had the faintest prospect of being returned. Yet, knowing, as she did, that her conduct was blameless so far, there were nevertheless perverse sympathies in her which took his part. In the wakeful hours of the night there were whispering voices in her which said: "Think of Moody!" Had there been a growing kindness towards this good friend in her heart, of which she herself was not aware? She tried to detect it—to weigh it for what it was really worth. But it lay too deep to be discovered and estimated, if it did really exist—if it had any sounder origin than her own morbid fancy. In the broad light of day, in the little bustling duties of life, she forgot it again. She could think of what she ought to wear on the wedding day; she could even try privately how her new signature, "Isabel Hardyman," would look when she had the right to use it. On the whole, it may be said that the time passed smoothly—with some occasional checks and drawbacks, which were the more easily endured seeing that they took their rise in Isabel's own conduct. Compliant as she was in general, there were two instances, among others, in which her resolution to take her own way was not to be overcome. She refused to write either to Moody or to Lady Lydiard informing them of her engagement; and she steadily disapproved of Miss Pink's policy of concealment, in the matter of the robbery at Lady Lydiard's house. Her aunt could only secure her as a passive accomplice by stating family considerations in the strongest possible terms. "If the disgrace was confined to you, my dear, I might leave you to decide. But I am involved in it, as your nearest relative; and, what is more, even the sacred memories of your father and mother might feel the slur cast on them." This exaggerated language—like all exaggerated language, a mischievous weapon in the arsenal of weakness and prejudice— had its effect on Isabel. Reluctantly and sadly, she consented to be silent.

Miss Pink wrote word of the engagement to Moody first; reserving to a later day the superior pleasure of informing Lady Lydiard of the very event which that audacious woman had declared to be impossible. To her aunt's surprise, just as she was about to close the envelope Isabel stepped forward, and inconsistently requested leave to add a postscript to the very letter which she had refused to write! Miss Pink was not even permitted to see the postscript. Isabel secured the envelope the moment she laid down her pen, and retired to her room with a headache (which was heartache in disguise) for the rest of the day.

While the question of marriage was still in debate, an event occurred which exercised a serious influence on Hardyman's future plans.

He received a letter from the Continent which claimed his immediate attention. One of the sovereigns of Europe had decided on making some radical changes in the mounting and equipment of a cavalry regiment; and he required the assistance of Hardyman in that important part of the contemplated reform which was connected with the choice and purchase of horses. Setting his own interests out of the question, Hardyman owed obligations to the kindness of his illustrious correspondent which made it impossible for him to send an excuse. In a fortnight's time, at the latest, it would be necessary for him to leave England; and a month or more might elapse before it would be possible for him to return.

Under these circumstances, he proposed, in his own precipitate way, to hasten the date of the marriage. The necessary legal delay would permit the ceremony to be performed on that day fortnight. Isabel might then accompany him on his journey, and spend a brilliant honeymoon at the foreign Court. She at once refused, not only to accept his proposal, but even to take it into consideration. While Miss Pink dwelt eloquently on the shortness of the notice, Miss Pink's niece based her resolution on far more important grounds. Hardyman had not yet announced the contemplated marriage to his parents and friends; and Isabel was determined not to become his wife until she could be first assured of a courteous and tolerant reception by the family—if she could hope for no warmer welcome at their hands.

Hardyman was not a man who yielded easily, even in trifles. In the present case, his dearest interests were concerned in inducing Isabel to reconsider her decision. He was still vainly trying to shake her resolution, when the afternoon post brought a letter for Miss Pink which introduced a new element of disturbance into the discussion. The letter was nothing less than Lady Lydiard's reply to the written announcement of Isabel's engagement, despatched on the previous day by Miss Pink.

Her Ladyship's answer was a surprisingly short one. It only contained these lines:

"Lady Lydiard begs to acknowledge the receipt of Miss Pink's letter requesting that she will say nothing to Mr. Hardyman of the loss of a bank-note in her house, and, assigning as a reason that Miss Isabel Miller is engaged to be married to Mr. Hardyman, and might be prejudiced in his estimation if the facts were made known. Miss Pink may make her mind easy. Lady Lydiard had not the slightest intention of taking Mr. Hardyman into her confidence on the subject of her domestic affairs. With regard to the proposed marriage, Lady Lydiard casts no doubt on Miss Pink's perfect sincerity and good faith; but, at the same time, she positively declines to believe that Mr. Hardyman means to make Miss Isabel Miller his wife. Lady L. will yield to the evidence of a properly-attested certificate—and to nothing else."

A folded piece of paper, directed to Isabel, dropped out of this characteristic letter as Miss Pink turned from the first page to the second. Lady Lydiard addressed her adopted daughter in these words:

"I was on the point of leaving home to visit you again, when I received your aunt's letter. My poor deluded child, no words can tell how distressed I am about you. You are already sacrificed to the folly of the most foolish woman living. For God's sake, take care you do not fall a victim next to the designs of a profligate man. Come to me instantly, Isabel, and I promise to take care of you."

Fortified by these letters, and aided by Miss Pink's indignation, Hardyman pressed his proposal on Isabel with renewed resolution. She made no attempt to combat his arguments—she only held firmly to her decision. Without some encouragement from Hardyman's father and mother she still steadily refused to become his wife. Irritated already by Lady Lydiard's letters, he lost the self-command which so eminently distinguished him in the ordinary affairs of life, and showed the domineering and despotic temper which was an inbred part of his disposition. Isabel's high spirit at once resented the harsh terms in which he spoke to her. In the plainest words, she released him from his engagement, and, without waiting for his excuses, quitted the room.

Left together, Hardyman and Miss Pink devised an arrangement which paid due respect to Isabel's scruples, and at the same time met Lady Lydiard's insulting assertion of disbelief in Hardyman's honor, by a formal and public announcement of the marriage.

It was proposed to give a garden party at the farm in a week's time for the express purpose of introducing Isabel to Hardyman's family and friends in the character of his betrothed wife. If his father and mother accepted the invitation, Isabel's only objection to hastening the union would fall to the ground. Hardyman might, in that case, plead with his Imperial correspondent for a delay in his departure of a few days more; and the marriage might still take place before he left England. Isabel, at Miss Pink's intercession, was induced to accept her lover's excuses, and, in the event of her favorable reception by Hardyman's parents at the farm, to give her consent (not very willingly even yet) to hastening the ceremony which was to make her Hardyman's wife.

On the next morning the whole of the invitations were sent out, excepting the invitation to Hardyman's father and mother. Without mentioning it to Isabel, Hardyman decided on personally appealing to his mother before he ventured on taking the head of the family into his confidence.

The result of the interview was partially successful—and no more. Lord Rotherfield declined to see his youngest son; and he had engagements which would, under any circumstances, prevent his being present at the garden party. But at the express request of Lady Rotherfield, he was willing to make certain concessions.

"I have always regarded Alfred as a barely sane person," said his Lordship, "since he turned his back on his prospects to become a horse dealer. If we decline altogether to sanction this new act—I won't say, of insanity, I will say, of absurdity—on his part, it is impossible to predict to what discreditable extremities he may not proceed. We must temporise with Alfred. In the meantime I shall endeavor to obtain some information respecting this young person—named Miller, I think you said, and now resident at South Morden. If I am satisfied that she is a woman of reputable character, possessing an average education and presentable manners, we may as well let Alfred take his own way. He is out of the pale of Society, as it is; and Miss Miller has no father and mother to complicate matters, which is distinctly a merit on her part and, in short, if the marriage is not absolutely disgraceful, the wisest way (as we have no power to prevent it) will be to submit. You will say nothing to Alfred about what I propose to do. I tell you plainly I don't trust him. You will simply inform him from me that I want time to consider, and that, unless he hears to the contrary in the interval, he may expect to have the sanction of your presence at his breakfast, or luncheon, or whatever it is. I must go to town in a day or two, and I shall ascertain what Alfred's friends know about this last of his many follies, if I meet any of them at the club."

Returning to South Morden in no serene frame of mind, Hardyman found Isabel in a state of depression which perplexed and alarmed him.

The news that his mother might be expected to be present at the garden party failed entirely to raise her spirits. The only explanation she gave of the change in her was, that the dull heavy weather of the last few days made her feel a little languid and nervous. Naturally dissatisfied with this reply to his inquiries, Hardyman asked for Miss Pink. He was informed that Miss Pink could not see him. She was constitutionally subject to asthma, and, having warnings of the return of the malady, she was (by the doctor's advice) keeping her room. Hardyman returned to the farm in a temper which was felt by everybody in his employment, from the trainer to the stable-boys.

While the apology made for Miss Pink stated no more than the plain truth, it must be confessed that Hardyman was right in declining to be satisfied with Isabel's excuse for the melancholy that oppressed her. She had that morning received Moody's answer to the lines which she had addressed to him at the end of her aunt's letter; and she had not yet recovered from the effect which it had produced on her spirits.

"It is impossible for me to say honestly that I am not distressed (Moody wrote) by the news of your marriage engagement. The blow has fallen very heavily on me. When I look at the future now, I see only a dreary blank. This is not your fault—you are in no way to blame. I remember the time when I should have been too angry to own this—when I might have said or done things which I should have bitterly repented afterwards. That time is past. My temper has been softened, since I have befriended you in your troubles. That good at least has come out of my foolish hopes, and perhaps out of the true sympathy which I have felt for you. I can honestly ask you to accept my heart's dearest wishes for your happiness—and I can keep the rest to myself.

"Let me say a word now relating to the efforts that I have made to help you, since that sad day when you left Lady Lydiard's house.

"I had hoped (for reasons which it is needless to mention here) to interest Mr. Hardyman himself in aiding our inquiry. But your aunt's wishes, as expressed in her letter to me, close my lips. I will only beg you, at some convenient time, to let me mention the last discoveries that we have made; leaving it to your discretion, when Mr. Hardyman has become your husband, to ask him the questions which, under other circumstances, I should have put to him myself.

"It is, of course, possible that the view I take of Mr. Hardyman's capacity to help us may be a mistaken one. In this case, if you still wish the investigation to be privately carried on, I entreat you to let me continue to direct it, as the greatest favor you can confer on your devoted old friend.

"You need be under no apprehension about the expense to which you are likely to put me. I have unexpectedly inherited what is to me a handsome fortune.

"The same post which brought your aunt's letter brought a line from a lawyer asking me to see him on the subject of my late father's affairs. I waited a day or two before I could summon heart enough to see him, or to see anybody; and then I went to his office. You have heard that my father's bank stopped payment, at a time of commercial panic. His failure was mainly attributable to the treachery of a friend to whom he had lent a large sum of money, and who paid him the yearly interest, without acknowledging that every farthing of it had been lost in unsuccessful speculations. The son of this man has prospered in business, and he has honorably devoted a part of his wealth to the payment of his father's creditors. Half the sum due to my father has thus passed into my hands as his next of kin; and the other half is to follow in course of time. If my hopes had been fulfilled, how gladly I should have shared my prosperity with you! As it is, I have far more than enough for my wants as a lonely man, and plenty left to spend in your service.

"God bless and prosper you, my dear. I shall ask you to accept a little present from me, among the other offerings that are made to you before the wedding day.—R.M."

The studiously considerate and delicate tone in which these lines were written had an effect on Isabel which was exactly the opposite of the effect intended by the writer. She burst into a passionate fit of tears; and in the safe solitude of her own room, the despairing words escaped her, "I wish I had died before I met with Alfred Hardyman!"

As the days wore on, disappointments and difficulties seemed by a kind of fatality to beset the contemplated announcement of the marriage.

Miss Pink's asthma, developed by the unfavorable weather, set the doctor's art at defiance, and threatened to keep that unfortunate lady a prisoner in her room on the day of the party. Hardyman's invitations were in some cases refused; and in others accepted by husbands with excuses for the absence of their wives. His elder brother made an apology for himself as well as for his wife. Felix Sweetsir wrote, "With pleasure, dear Alfred, if my health permits me to leave the house." Lady Lydiard, invited at Miss Pink's special request, sent no reply. The one encouraging circumstance was the silence of Lady Rotherfield. So long as her son received no intimation to the contrary, it was a sign that Lord Rotherfield permitted his wife to sanction the marriage by her presence.

Hardyman wrote to his Imperial correspondent, engaging to leave England on the earliest possible day, and asking to be pardoned if he failed to express himself more definitely, in consideration of domestic affairs, which it was necessary to settle before he started for the Continent. If there should not be time enough to write again, he promised to send a telegraphic announcement of his departure. Long afterwards, Hardyman remembered the misgivings that had troubled him when he wrote that letter. In the rough draught of it, he had mentioned, as his excuse for not being yet certain of his own movements, that he expected to be immediately married. In the fair copy, the vague foreboding of some accident to come was so painfully present to his mind, that he struck out the words which referred to his marriage, and substituted the designedly indefinite phrase, "domestic affairs."

CHAPTER XX.

THE day of the garden party arrived. There was no rain; but the air was heavy, and the sky was overcast by lowering clouds.

Some hours before the guests were expected, Isabel arrived alone at the farm, bearing the apologies of unfortunate Miss Pink, still kept a prisoner in her bed-chamber by the asthma. In the confusion produced at the cottage by the preparations for entertaining the company, the one room in which Hardyman could receive Isabel with the certainty of not being interrupted was the smoking-room. To this haven of refuge he led her—still reserved and silent, still not restored to her customary spirits. "If any visitors come before the time," Hardyman said to his servant, "tell them I am engaged at the stables. I must have an hour's quiet talk with you," he continued, turning to Isabel, "or I shall be in too bad a temper to receive my guests with common politeness. The worry of giving this party is not to be told in words. I almost wish I had been content with presenting you to my mother, and had let the rest of my acquaintances go to the devil."

A quiet half hour passed; and the first visitor, a stranger to the servants, appeared at the cottage-gate. He was a middle-aged man, and he had no wish to disturb Mr. Hardyman. "I will wait in the grounds," he said, "and trouble nobody." The middle-aged man, who expressed himself in these modest terms, was Robert Moody.

Five minutes later, a carriage drove up to the gate. An elderly lady got out of it, followed by a fat white Scotch terrier, who growled at every stranger within his reach. It is needless to introduce Lady Lydiard and Tommie.

Informed that Mr. Hardyman was at the stables, Lady Lydiard gave the servant her card. "Take that to your master, and say I won't detain him five minutes." With these words, her Ladyship sauntered into the grounds. She looked about her with observant eyes; not only noticing the tent which had been set up on the grass to accommodate the expected guests, but entering it, and looking at the waiters who were engaged in placing the luncheon on the table. Returning to the outer world, she next remarked that Mr. Hardyman's lawn was in very bad order. Barren sun-dried patches, and little holes and crevices opened here and there by the action of the summer heat, announced that the lawn, like everything else at the farm, had been neglected, in the exclusive attention paid to the claims of the horses. Reaching a shrubbery which bounded one side of the grounds next, her Ladyship became aware of a man slowly approaching her, to all appearance absorbed in thought. The man drew a little nearer. She lifted her glasses to her eyes and recognized—Moody.

No embarrassment was produced on either side by this unexpected meeting. Lady Lydiard had, not long since, sent to ask her former steward to visit her; regretting, in her warm-hearted way, the terms on which they had separated, and wishing to atone for the harsh language that had escaped her at their parting interview. In the friendly talk which followed the reconciliation, Lady Lydiard not only heard the news of Moody's pecuniary inheritance— but, noticing the change in his appearance for the worse, contrived to extract from him the confession of his ill-starred passion for Isabel. To discover him now, after all that he had acknowledged, walking about the grounds at Hardyman's farm, took her Ladyship completely by surprise. "Good Heavens!" she exclaimed, in her loudest tones, "what are you doing here?"

"You mentioned Mr. Hardyman's garden party, my Lady, when I had the honor of waiting on you," Moody answered. "Thinking over it afterward, it seemed the fittest occasion I could find for making a little wedding present to Miss Isabel. Is there any harm in my asking Mr. Hardyman to let me put the present on her plate, so that she may see it when she sits down to luncheon? If your Ladyship thinks so, I will go away directly, and send the gift by post."

Lady Lydiard looked at him attentively. "You don't despise the girl," she asked, "for selling herself for rank and money? I do—I can tell you!"

Moody's worn white face flushed a little. "No, my Lady," he answered, "I can't hear you say that! Isabel would not have engaged herself to Mr. Hardyman unless she had been fond of him—as fond, I dare say, as I once hoped she might be of me. It's a hard thing to confess that; but I do confess it, in justice to her—God bless her!"

The generosity that spoke in those simple words touched the finest sympathies in Lady Lydiard's nature. "Give me your hand," she said, with her own generous spirit kindling in her eyes. "You have a great heart, Moody. Isabel Miller is a fool for not marrying you—and one day she will know it!"

Before a word more could pass between them, Hardyman's voice was audible on the other side of the shrubbery, calling irritably to his servant to find Lady Lydiard.

Moody retired to the further end of the walk, while Lady Lydiard advanced in the opposite direction, so as to meet Hardyman at the entrance to the shrubbery. He bowed stiffly, and begged to know why her Ladyship had honored him with a visit.

Lady Lydiard replied without noticing the coldness of her reception.

"I have not been very well, Mr. Hardyman, or you would have seen me before this. My only object in presenting myself here is to make my excuses personally for having written of you in terms which expressed a doubt of your honor. I have done you an injustice, and I beg you to forgive me."

Hardyman acknowledged this frank apology as unreservedly as it had been offered to him. "Say no more, Lady Lydiard. And let me hope, now you are here, that you will honor my little party with your presence."

Lady Lydiard gravely stated her reasons for not accepting the invitation.

"I disapprove so strongly of unequal marriages," she said, walking on slowly towards the cottage, "that I cannot, in common consistency, become one of your guests. I shall always feel interested in Isabel Miller's welfare; and I can honestly say I shall be glad if your married life proves that my old-fashioned prejudices are without justification in your case. Accept my thanks for your invitation; and let me hope that my plain speaking has not offended you."

She bowed, and looked about her for Tommie before she advanced to the carriage waiting for her at the gate. In the surprise of seeing Moody she had forgotten to look back for the dog when she entered the shrubbery. She now called to him, and blew the whistle at her watch-chain. Not a sign of Tommie was to be seen. Hardyman instantly directed the servants to search in the cottage and out of the cottage for the dog. The order was obeyed with all needful activity and intelligence, and entirely without success. For the time being at any rate, Tommie was lost.

Hardyman promised to have the dog looked for in every part of the farm, and to send him back in the care of one of his own men. With these polite assurances Lady Lydiard was obliged to be satisfied. She drove away in a very despondent frame of mind. "First Isabel, and now Tommie," thought her Ladyship. "I am losing the only companions who made life tolerable to me."

Returning from the garden gate, after taking leave of his visitor, Hardyman received from his servant a handful of letters which had just arrived for him. Walking slowly over the lawn as he opened them, he found nothing but excuses for the absence of guests who had already accepted their invitations. He had just thrust the letters into his pocket, when he heard footsteps behind him, and, looking round, found himself confronted by Moody.

"Hullo! have you come to lunch?" Hardyman asked, roughly.

"I have come here, sir, with a little gift for Miss Isabel, in honor of her marriage," Moody answered quietly, "and I ask your permission to put it on the table, so that she may see it when your guests sit down to luncheon."

He opened a jeweler's case as he spoke, containing a plain gold bracelet with an inscription engraved on the inner side: "To Miss Isabel Miller, with the sincere good wishes of Robert Moody."

Plain as it was, the design of the bracelet was unusually beautiful. Hardyman had noticed Moody's agitation on the day when he had met Isabel near her aunt's house, and had drawn his own conclusions from it. His face darkened with a momentary jealousy as he looked at the bracelet. "All right, old fellow!" he said, with contemptuous familiarity. "Don't be modest. Wait and give it to her with your own hand."

"No, sir," said Moody "I would rather leave it, if you please, to speak for itself."

Hardyman understood the delicacy of feeling which dictated those words, and, without well knowing why, resented it. He was on the point of speaking, under the influence of this unworthy motive, when Isabel's voice reached his ears, calling to him from the cottage.

Moody's face contracted with a sudden expression of pain as he, too, recognized the voice. "Don't let me detain you, sir," he said, sadly. "Good-morning!"

Hardyman left him without ceremony. Moody, slowly following, entered the tent. All the preparations for the luncheon had been completed; nobody was there. The places to be occupied by the guests were indicated by cards bearing their names. Moody found Isabel's card, and put his bracelet inside the folded napkin on her plate. For a while he stood with his hand on the table, thinking. The temptation to communicate once more with Isabel before he lost her forever, was fast getting the better of his powers of resistance.

"If I could persuade her to write a word to say she liked her bracelet," he thought, "it would be a comfort when I go back to my solitary life." He tore a leaf out of his pocket book and wrote on it, "One line to say you accept my gift and my good wishes. Put it under the cushion of your chair, and I shall find it when the company have left the tent." He slipped the paper into the case which held the bracelet, and instead of leaving the farm as he had intended, turned back to the shelter of the shrubbery.

150

CHAPTER XXI.

HARDYMAN went on to the cottage. He found Isabel in some agitation. And there, by her side, with his tail wagging slowly, and his eye on Hardyman in expectation of a possible kick—there was the lost Tommie!

"Has Lady Lydiard gone?" Isabel asked eagerly.

"Yes," said Hardyman. "Where did you find the dog?"

As events had ordered it, the dog had found Isabel, under these circumstances.

The appearance of Lady Lydiard's card in the smoking-room had been an alarming event for Lady Lydiard's adopted daughter. She was guiltily conscious of not having answered her Ladyship's note, inclosed in Miss Pink's letter, and of not having taken her Ladyship's advice in regulating her conduct towards Hardyman. As he rose to leave the room and receive his visitor in the grounds, Isabel begged him to say nothing of her presence at the farm, unless Lady Lydiard exhibited a forgiving turn of mind by asking to see her. Left by herself in the smoking-room, she suddenly heard a bark in the passage which had a familiar sound in her ears. She opened the door—and in rushed Tommie, with one of his shrieks of delight! Curiosity had taken him into the house. He had heard the voices in the smoking-room; had recognized Isabel's voice; and had waited, with his customary cunning and his customary distrust of strangers, until Hardyman was out of the way. Isabel kissed and caressed him, and then drove him out again to the lawn, fearing that Lady Lydiard might return to look for him. Going back to the smoking-room, she stood at the window watching for Hardyman's return. When the servants came to look for the dog, she could only tell them that she had last seen him in the grounds, not far from the cottage. The useless search being abandoned, and the carriage having left the gate, who should crawl out from the back of a cupboard in which some empty hampers were placed but Tommie himself! How he had contrived to get back to the smoking-room (unless she had omitted to completely close the door on her return) it was impossible to say. But there he was, determined this time to stay with Isabel, and keeping in his hiding place until he heard the movement of the carriage-wheels, which informed him that his lawful mistress had left the cottage! Isabel had at once called Hardyman, on the chance that the carriage might yet be stopped. It was already out of sight, and nobody knew which of two roads it had taken, both leading to London. In this emergency, Isabel could only look at Hardyman and ask what was to be done.

"I can't spare a servant till after the party," he answered. "The dog must be tied up in the stables."

Isabel shook her head. Tommie was not accustomed to be tied up. He would make a disturbance, and he would be beaten by the grooms. "I will take care of him," she said. "He won't leave me."

"There's something else to think of besides the dog," Hardyman rejoined irritably. "Look at these letters!" He pulled them out of his pocket as he spoke. "Here are no less than seven men, all calling themselves my friends, who accepted my invitation, and who write to excuse themselves on the very day of the party. Do you know why? They're all afraid of my father—I forgot to tell you he's a Cabinet Minister as well as a Lord. Cowards and cads. They have heard he isn't coming and they think to curry favor with the great man by stopping away. Come along, Isabel! Let's take their names off the luncheon table. Not a man of them shall ever darken my doors again!"

"I am to blame for what has happened," Isabel answered sadly. "I am estranging you from your friends. There is still time, Alfred, to alter your mind and let me go."

He put his arm round her with rough fondness. "I would sacrifice every friend I have in the world rather than lose you. Come along!"

They left the cottage. At the entrance to the tent, Hardyman noticed the dog at Isabel's heels, and vented his ill-temper, as usual with male humanity, on the nearest unoffending creature that he could find. "Be off, you mongrel brute!" he shouted. The tail of Tommie relaxed from its customary tight curve over the small of his back; and the legs of Tommie (with his tail between them) took him at full gallop to the friendly shelter of the cupboard in the smoking-room. It was one of those trifling circumstances which women notice seriously. Isabel said nothing; she only thought to herself, "I wish he had shown his temper when I first knew him!"

They entered the tent.

"I'll read the names," said Hardyman, "and you find the cards and tear them up. Stop! I'll keep the cards. You're just the sort of woman my father likes. He'll be reconciled to me when he sees you, after we are married. If one of those men ever asks him for a place, I'll take care, if it's years hence, to put an obstacle in his way! Here; take my pencil, and make a mark on the cards to remind me; the same mark I set against a horse in my book when I don't like him—a cross, inclosed in a circle." He produced his pocketbook. His hands trembled with anger as he gave the pencil to Isabel and laid the book on the table. He had just read the name of the first false friend, and Isabel had just found the card, when a servant appeared with a message. "Mrs. Drumblade has arrived, sir, and wishes to see you on a matter of the greatest importance."

Hardyman left the tent, not very willingly. "Wait here," he said to Isabel; "I'll be back directly."

She was standing near her own place at the table. Moody had left one end of the jeweler's case visible above the napkin, to attract her attention. In a minute more the bracelet and note were in her hands. She dropped on her chair, overwhelmed by the conflicting emotions that rose in her at the sight of the bracelet, at the reading of the note. Her head drooped, and the tears filled her eyes. "Are all women as blind as I have been to what is good and noble in the men who love them?" she wondered, sadly. "Better as it is," she thought, with a bitter sigh; "I am not worthy of him."

As she took up the pencil to write her answer to Moody on the back of her dinner-card, the servant appeared again at the door of the tent.

"My master wants you at the cottage, miss, immediately."

Isabel rose, putting the bracelet and the note in the silver-mounted leather pocket (a present from Hardyman) which hung at her belt. In the hurry of passing round the table to get out, she never noticed that her dress touched Hardyman's pocketbook, placed close to the edge, and threw it down on the grass below. The book fell into one of the heat cracks which Lady Lydiard had noticed as evidence of the neglected condition of the cottage lawn.

"You ought to hear the pleasant news my sister has just brought me," said Hardyman, when Isabel joined him in the parlor. "Mrs. Drumblade has been told, on the best authority, that my mother is not coming to the party."

"There must be some reason, of course, dear Isabel," added Mrs. Drumblade. "Have you any idea of what it can be? I haven't seen my mother myself; and all my inquiries have failed to find it out."

She looked searchingly at Isabel as she spoke. The mask of sympathy on her face was admirably worn. Nobody who possessed only a superficial acquaintance with Mrs. Drumblade's character would have suspected how thoroughly she was enjoying in secret the position of embarrassment in which her news had placed her brother. Instinctively doubting whether Mrs. Drumblade's friendly behavior was quite as sincere as it appeared to be, Isabel answered that she was a stranger to Lady Rotherfield, and was therefore quite at a loss to explain the cause of her ladyship's absence. As she spoke, the guests began to arrive in quick succession, and the subject was dropped as a matter of course.

It was not a merry party. Hardyman's approaching marriage had been made the topic of much malicious gossip, and Isabel's character had, as usual in such cases, become the object of all the false reports that scandal could invent. Lady Rotherfield's absence confirmed the general conviction that Hardyman was disgracing himself. The men were all more or less uneasy. The women resented the discovery that Isabel was—personally speaking, at least—beyond the reach of hostile criticism. Her beauty was viewed as a downright offense; her refined and modest manners were set down as perfect acting; "really disgusting, my dear, in so young a girl." General Drumblade, a large and mouldy veteran, in a state of chronic astonishment (after his own matrimonial experience) at Hardyman's folly in marrying at all, diffused a wide circle of gloom, wherever he went and whatever he did. His accomplished wife, forcing her high spirits on everybody's attention with a sort of kittenish playfulness, intensified the depressing effect of the general dullness by all the force of the strongest contrast. After waiting half an hour for his mother, and waiting in vain, Hardyman led the way to the tent in despair. "The sooner I fill their stomachs and get rid of them," he thought savagely, "the better I shall be pleased!"

The luncheon was attacked by the company with a certain silent ferocity, which the waiters noticed as remarkable, even in their large experience. The men drank deeply, but with wonderfully little effect in raising their spirits; the women, with the exception of amiable Mrs. Drumblade, kept Isabel deliberately out of the conversation that went on among them. General Drumblade, sitting next to her in one of the places of honor, discoursed to Isabel privately on "my brother-in-law Hardyman's infernal temper." A young marquis, on her other side—a mere lad, chosen to make the necessary speech in acknowledgment of his superior rank—rose, in a state of nervous trepidation, to propose Isabel's health as the chosen bride of their host. Pale and trembling, conscious of having forgotten the words which he had learnt beforehand, this unhappy young nobleman began: "Ladies and gentlemen, I haven't an idea—" He stopped, put his hand to his head, stared wildly, and sat down again; having contrived to state his own case with masterly brevity and perfect truth, in a speech of seven words.

While the dismay, in some cases, and the amusement in others, was still at its height, Hardyman's valet made his appearance, and, approaching his master, said in a whisper, "Could I speak to you, sit, for a moment outside?"

"What the devil do you want?" Hardyman asked irritably. "Is that a letter in your hand? Give it to me."

The valet was a Frenchman. In other words, he had a sense of what was due to himself. His master had forgotten this. He gave up the letter with a certain dignity of manner, and left the tent. Hardyman opened the letter. He turned pale as he read it; crumpled it in his hand, and threw it down on the table. "By G—d! it's a lie!" he exclaimed furiously.

The guests rose in confusion. Mrs. Drumblade, finding the letter within her reach, coolly possessed herself of it; recognized her mother's handwriting; and read these lines:

"I have only now succeeded in persuading your father to let me write to you. For God's sake, break off your marriage at any sacrifice. Your father has heard, on unanswerable authority, that Miss Isabel Miller left her situation in Lady Lydiard's house on suspicion of theft."

While his sister was reading this letter, Hardyman had made his way to Isabel's chair. "I must speak to you, directly," he whispered. "Come away with me!" He turned, as he took her arm, and looked at the table. "Where is my letter?" he asked. Mrs. Drumblade handed it to him, dexterously crumpled up again as she had found it. "No bad news, dear Alfred, I hope?" she said, in her most affectionate manner. Hardyman snatched the letter from her, without answering, and led Isabel out of the tent.

"Read that!" he said, when they were alone. "And tell me at once whether it's true or false."

Isabel read the letter. For a moment the shock of the discovery held her speechless. She recovered herself, and returned the letter.

"It is true," she answered.

Hardyman staggered back as if she had shot him.

"True that you are guilty?" he asked.

"No; I am innocent. Everybody who knows me believes in my innocence. It is true the appearances were against me. They are against me still." Having said this, she waited, quietly and firmly, for his next words.

He passed his hand over his forehead with a sigh of relief. "It's bad enough as it is," he said, speaking quietly on his side. "But the remedy for it is plain enough. Come back to the tent."

She never moved. "Why?" she asked.

"Do you suppose I don't believe in your innocence too?" he answered. "The one way of setting you right with the world now is for me to make you my wife, in spite of the appearances that point to you. I'm too fond of you, Isabel, to give you up. Come back with me, and I will announce our marriage to my friends."

She took his hand, and kissed it. "It is generous and good of you," she said; "but it must not be."

He took a step nearer to her. "What do you mean?" he asked.

"It was against my will," she pursued, "that my aunt concealed the truth from you. I did wrong to consent to it, I will do wrong no more. Your mother is right, Alfred. After what has happened, I am not fit to be your wife until my innocence is proved. It is not proved yet."

The angry color began to rise in his face once more. "Take care," he said; "I am not in a humor to be trifled with."

"I am not trifling with you," she answered, in low, sad tones.

"You really mean what you say?"

"I mean it."

"Don't be obstinate, Isabel. Take time to consider."

"You are very kind, Alfred. My duty is plain to me. I will marry you—if you still wish it—when my good name is restored to me. Not before."

He laid one hand on her arm, and pointed with the other to the guests in the distance, all leaving the tent on the way to their carriages.

"Your good name will be restored to you," he said, "on the day when I make you my wife. The worst enemy you have cannot associate my name with a suspicion of theft. Remember that and think a little before you decide. You see those people there. If you don't change your mind by the time they have got to the cottage, it's good-by between us, and good-by forever. I refuse to wait for you; I refuse to accept a conditional engagement. Wait, and think. They're walking slowly; you have got some minutes more."

He still held her arm, watching the guests as they gradually receded from view. It was not until they had all collected in a group outside the cottage door that he spoke himself, or that he permitted Isabel to speak again.

"Now," he said, "you have had your time to get cool. Will you take my arm, and join those people with me? or will you say good-by forever?"

"Forgive me, Alfred!" she began, gently. "I cannot consent, in justice to you, to shelter myself behind your name. It is the name of your family; and they have a right to expect that you will not degrade it—"

"I want a plain answer," he interposed sternly. "Which is it? Yes, or No?"

She looked at him with sad compassionate eyes. Her voice was firm as she answered him in one word as he had desired. The word was—

"No."

Without speaking to her, without even looking at her, he turned and walked back to the cottage.

Making his way silently through the group of visitors—every one of whom had been informed of what had happened by his sister—with his head down and his lips fast closed, he entered the parlor and rang the bell which communicated with his foreman's rooms at the stables.

"You know that I am going abroad on business?" he said, when the man appeared.

"Yes, sir."

"I am going to-day—going by the night train to Dover. Order the horse to be put to instantly in the dogcart. Is there anything wanted before I am off?"

The inexorable necessities of business asserted their claims through the obedient medium of the foreman. Chafing at the delay, Hardyman was obliged to sit at his desk, signing checks and passing accounts, with the dogcart waiting in the stable yard.

A knock at the door startled him in the middle of his work. "Come in," he called out sharply.

He looked up, expecting to see one of the guests or one of the servants. It was Moody who entered the room. Hardyman laid down his pen, and fixed his eyes sternly on the man who had dared to interrupt him.

"What the devil do you want?" he asked.

"I have seen Miss Isabel, and spoken with her," Moody replied. "Mr. Hardyman, I believe it is in your power to set this matter right. For the young lady's sake, sir, you must not leave England without doing it."

Hardyman turned to his foreman. "Is this fellow mad or drunk?" he asked.

Moody proceeded as calmly and as resolutely as if those words had not been spoken. "I apologize for my intrusion, sir. I will trouble you with no explanations. I will only ask one question. Have you a memorandum of the number of that five-hundred pound note you paid away in France?"

Hardyman lost all control over himself.

"You scoundrel!" he cried, "have you been prying into my private affairs? Is it your business to know what I did in France?"

"Is it your vengeance on a woman to refuse to tell her the number of a bank-note?" Moody rejoined, firmly.

That answer forced its way, through Hardyman's anger, to Hardyman's sense of honor. He rose and advanced to Moody. For a moment the two men faced each other in silence. "You're a bold fellow," said Hardyman, with a sudden change from anger to irony. "I'll do the lady justice. I'll look at my pocketbook."

He put his hand into the breast-pocket of his coat; he searched his other pockets; he turned over the objects on his writing-table. The book was gone.

Moody watched him with a feeling of despair. "Oh! Mr. Hardyman, don't say you have lost your pocketbook!"

He sat down again at his desk, with sullen submission to the new disaster. "All I can say is you're at liberty to look for it," he replied. "I must have dropped it somewhere." He turned impatiently to the foreman, "Now then! What is the next check wanted? I shall go mad if I wait in this damned place much longer!"

Moody left him, and found his way to the servants' offices. "Mr. Hardyman has lost his pocketbook," he said. "Look for it, indoors and out—on the lawn, and in the tent. Ten pounds reward for the man who finds it!"

Servants and waiters instantly dispersed, eager for the promised reward. The men who pursued the search outside the cottage divided their forces. Some of them examined the lawn and the flower-beds. Others went straight to the empty tent. These last were too completely absorbed in pursuing the object in view to notice that they disturbed a dog, eating a stolen lunch of his own from the morsels left on the plates. The dog slunk away under the canvas when the men came in, waited in hiding until they had gone, then returned to the tent, and went on with his luncheon.

Moody hastened back to the part of the grounds (close to the shrubbery) in which Isabel was waiting his return.

She looked at him, while he was telling her of his interview with Hardyman, with an expression in her eyes which he had never seen in them before—an expression which set his heart beating wildly, and made him break off in his narrative before he had reached the end.

"I understand," she said quietly, as he stopped in confusion. "You have made one more sacrifice to my welfare. Robert! I believe you are the noblest man that ever breathed the breath of life!"

His eyes sank before hers; he blushed like a boy. "I have done nothing for you yet," he said. "Don't despair of the future, if the pocketbook should not be found. I know who the man is who received the bank note; and I have only to find him to decide the question whether it is the stolen note or not."

She smiled sadly as his enthusiasm. "Are you going back to Mr. Sharon to help you?" she asked. "That trick he played me has destroyed my belief in him. He no more knows than I do who the thief really is."

"You are mistaken, Isabel. He knows—and I know." He stopped there, and made a sign to her to be silent. One of the servants was approaching them.

"Is the pocketbook found?" Moody asked.

"No, sir."

"Has Mr. Hardyman left the cottage?"

"He has just gone, sir. Have you any further instructions to give us?"

"No. There is my address in London, if the pocketbook should be found."

The man took the card that was handed to him and retired. Moody offered his arm to Isabel. "I am at your service," he said, "when you wish to return to your aunt."

They had advanced nearly as far as the tent, on their way out of the grounds, when they were met by a gentleman walking towards them from the cottage. He was a stranger to Isabel. Moody immediately recognized him as Mr. Felix Sweetsir.

"Ha! our good Moody!" cried Felix. "Enviable man! you look younger than ever." He took off his hat to Isabel; his bright restless eyes suddenly became quiet as they rested on her. "Have I the honor of addressing the future Mrs. Hardyman? May I offer my best congratulations? What has become of our friend Alfred?"

Moody answered for Isabel. "If you will make inquiries at the cottage, sir," he said, "you will find that you are mistaken, to say the least of it, in addressing your questions to this young lady."

Felix took off his hat again—with the most becoming appearance of surprise and distress.

"Something wrong, I fear?" he said, addressing Isabel. "I am, indeed, ashamed if I have ignorantly given you a moment's pain. Pray accept my most sincere apologies. I have only this instant arrived; my health would not allow me to be present at the luncheon. Permit me to express the earnest hope that matters may be set right to the satisfaction of all parties. Good-afternoon!"

He bowed with elaborate courtesy, and turned back to the cottage.

"Who is that?" Isabel asked.

"Lady Lydiard's nephew, Mr. Felix Sweetsir," Moody answered, with a sudden sternness of tone, and a sudden coldness of manner, which surprised Isabel.

"You don't like him?" she said.

As she spoke, Felix stopped to give audience to one of the grooms, who had apparently been sent with a message to him. He turned so that his face was once more visible to Isabel. Moody pressed her hand significantly as it rested on his arm.

"Look well at that man," he whispered. "It's time to warn you. Mr. Felix Sweetsir is the worst enemy you have!"

Isabel heard him in speechless astonishment. He went on in tones that trembled with suppressed emotion.

"You doubt if Sharon knows the thief. You doubt if I know the thief. Isabel! as certainly as the heaven is above us, there stands the wretch who stole the bank-note!"

She drew her hand out of his arm with a cry of terror. She looked at him as if she doubted whether he was in his right mind.

He took her hand, and waited a moment trying to compose himself.

"Listen to me," he said. "At the first consultation I had with Sharon he gave this advice to Mr. Troy and to me. He said, 'Suspect the very last person on whom suspicion could possibly fall.' Those words, taken with the questions he had asked before he pronounced his opinion, struck through me as if he had struck me with a knife. I instantly suspected Lady Lydiard's nephew. Wait! From that time to this I have said nothing of my suspicion to any living soul. I knew in my own heart that it took its rise in the inveterate

162

dislike that I have always felt for Mr. Sweetsir, and I distrusted it accordingly. But I went back to Sharon, for all that, and put the case into his hands. His investigations informed me that Mr. Sweetsir owed 'debts of honor' (as gentlemen call them), incurred through lost bets, to a large number of persons, and among them a bet of five hundred pounds lost to Mr. Hardyman. Further inquiries showed that Mr. Hardyman had taken the lead in declaring that he would post Mr. Sweetsir as a defaulter, and have him turned out of his clubs, and turned out of the betting-ring. Ruin stared him in the face if he failed to pay his debt to Mr. Hardyman on the last day left to him—the day after the note was lost. On that very morning, Lady Lydiard, speaking to me of her nephew's visit to her, said, 'If I had given him an opportunity of speaking, Felix would have borrowed money of me; I saw it in his face.' One moment more, Isabel. I am not only certain that Mr. Sweetsir took the five-hundred pound note out of the open letter, I am firmly persuaded that he is the man who told Lord Rotherfield of the circumstances under which you left Lady Lydiard's house. Your marriage to Mr. Hardyman might have put you in a position to detect the theft. You, not I, might, in that case, have discovered from your husband that the stolen note was the note with which Mr. Sweetsir paid his debt. He came here, you may depend on it, to make sure that he had succeeded in destroying your prospects. A more depraved villain at heart than that man never swung from a gallows!"

He checked himself at those words. The shock of the disclosure, the passion and vehemence with which he spoke, overwhelmed Isabel. She trembled like a frightened child.

While he was still trying to soothe and reassure her, a low whining made itself heard at her feet. They looked down, and saw Tommie. Finding himself noticed at last, he expressed his sense of relief by a bark. Something dropped out of his mouth. As Moody stooped to pick it up, the dog ran to Isabel and pushed his head against her feet, as his way was when he expected to have the handkerchief thrown over him, preparatory to one of those games at hide-and-seek which have been already mentioned. Isabel put out her hand to caress him, when she was stopped by a cry from Moody. It was his turn to tremble now. His voice faltered as he said the words, "The dog has found the pocketbook!"

He opened the book with shaking hands. A betting-book was bound up in it, with the customary calendar. He turned to the date of the day after the robbery.

There was the entry: "Felix Sweetsir. Paid 500 pounds. Note numbered, N 8, 70564; dated 15th May, 1875."

Moody took from his waistcoat pocket his own memorandum of the number of the lost bank-note. "Read it Isabel," he said. "I won't trust my memory."

She read it. The number and date of the note entered in the pocketbook exactly corresponded with the number and date of the note that Lady Lydiard had placed in her letter.

Moody handed the pocketbook to Isabel. "There is the proof of your innocence," he said, "thanks to the dog! Will you write and tell Mr. Hardyman what has happened?" he asked, with his head down and his eyes on the ground.

She answered him, with the bright color suddenly flowing over her face.

"You shall write to him," she said, "when the time comes."

"What time?" he asked.

She threw her arms round his neck, and hid her face on his bosom.

"The time," she whispered, "when I am your wife."

A low growl from Tommie reminded them that he too had some claim to be noticed.

Isabel dropped on her knees, and saluted her old playfellow with the heartiest kisses she had ever given him since the day when their acquaintance began. "You darling!" she said, as she put him down again, "what can I do to reward you?"

Tommie rolled over on his back—more slowly than usual, in consequence of his luncheon in the tent. He elevated his four paws in the air and looked lazily at Isabel out of his bright brown eyes. If ever a dog's look spoke yet, Tommie's look said, "I have eaten too much; rub my stomach."

POSTSCRIPT.

Persons of a speculative turn of mind are informed that the following document is for sale, and are requested to mention what sum they will give for it.

"IOU, Lady Lydiard, five hundred pounds (L500), Felix Sweetsir."

Her Ladyship became possessed of this pecuniary remittance under circumstances which surround it with a halo of romantic interest. It was the last communication she was destined to receive from her accomplished nephew. There was a Note attached to it, which cannot fail to enhance its value in the estimation of all right-minded persons who assist the circulation of paper money.

The lines that follow are strictly confidential:

"Note.—Our excellent Moody informs me, my dear aunt, that you have decided (against his advice) on 'refusing to prosecute.' I have not the slightest idea of what he means; but I am very much obliged to him, nevertheless, for reminding me of a circumstance which is of some interest to yourself personally.

"I am on the point of retiring to the Continent in search of health. One generally forgets something important when one starts on a journey. Before Moody called, I had entirely forgotten to mention that I had the pleasure of borrowing five hundred pounds of you some little time since.

"On the occasion to which I refer, your language and manner suggested that you would not lend me the money if I asked for it. Obviously, the only course left was to take it without asking. I took it while Moody was gone to get some curacoa; and I returned to the picture-gallery in time to receive that delicious liqueur from the footman's hands.

"You will naturally ask why I found it necessary to supply myself (if I may borrow an expression from the language of State finance) with this 'forced loan.' I was actuated by motives which I think do me honor. My position at the time was critical in the extreme. My credit with the money-lenders was at an end; my friends had all turned their backs on me. I must either take the money or disgrace my family. If there is a man living who is sincerely attached to his family, I am that man. I took the money.

"Conceive your position as my aunt (I say nothing of myself), if I had adopted the other alternative. Turned out of the Jockey Club, turned out of Tattersalls', turned out of the betting-ring; in short, posted publicly as a defaulter before the noblest institution in England, the Turf—and all for want of five hundred pounds to stop the mouth of the greatest brute I know of, Alfred Hardyman! Let me not harrow your feelings (and mine) by dwelling on it. Dear and admirable woman! To you belongs the honor of saving the credit of the family; I can claim nothing but the inferior merit of having offered you the opportunity.

"My IOU, it is needless to say, accompanies these lines. Can I do anything for you abroad?—F. S."

To this it is only necessary to add (first) that Moody was perfectly right in believing F. S. to be the person who informed Hardyman's father of Isabel's position when she left Lady Lydiard's house; and (secondly) that Felix did really forward Mr. Troy's narrative of the theft to the French police, altering nothing in it but the number of the lost bank-note.

What is there left to write about? Nothing is left—but to say good-by (very sorrowfully on the writer's part) to the Persons of the Story.

Good-by to Miss Pink—who will regret to her dying day that Isabel's answer to Hardyman was No.

Good-by to Lady Lydiard—who differs with Miss Pink, and would have regretted it, to her dying day, if the answer had been Yes.

Good-by to Moody and Isabel—whose history has closed with the closing of the clergyman's book on their wedding-day.

Good-by to Hardyman—who has sold his farm and his horses, and has begun a new life among the famous fast trotters of America.

Good-by to Old Sharon—who, a martyr to his promise, brushed his hair and washed his face in honor of Moody's marriage; and catching a severe cold as the necessary consequence, declared, in the intervals of sneezing, that he would "never do it again."

And last, not least, good-by to Tommie? No. The writer gave Tommie his dinner not half an hour since, and is too fond of him to say good-by.

I SAY NO

BOOK THE FIRST—AT SCHOOL.

CHAPTER I. THE SMUGGLED SUPPER.

Outside the bedroom the night was black and still. The small rain fell too softly to be heard in the garden; not a leaf stirred in the airless calm; the watch-dog was asleep, the cats were indoors; far or near, under the murky heaven, not a sound was stirring.

Inside the bedroom the night was black and still.

Miss Ladd knew her business as a schoolmistress too well to allow night-lights; and Miss Ladd's young ladies were supposed to be fast asleep, in accordance with the rules of the house. Only at intervals the silence was faintly disturbed, when the restless turning of one of the girls in her bed betrayed itself by a gentle rustling between the sheets. In the long intervals of stillness, not even the softly audible breathing of young creatures asleep was to be heard.

The first sound that told of life and movement revealed the mechanical movement of the clock. Speaking from the lower regions, the tongue of Father Time told the hour before midnight.

A soft voice rose wearily near the door of the room. It counted the strokes of the clock—and reminded one of the girls of the lapse of time.

"Emily! eleven o'clock."

There was no reply. After an interval the weary voice tried again, in louder tones:

"Emily!"

A girl, whose bed was at the inner end of the room, sighed under the heavy heat of the night—and said, in peremptory tones, "Is that Cecilia?"

"Yes."

"What do you want?"

"I'm getting hungry, Emily. Is the new girl asleep?"

The new girl answered promptly and spitefully, "No, she isn't."

Having a private object of their own in view, the five wise virgins of Miss Ladd's first class had waited an hour, in wakeful anticipation of the falling asleep of the stranger—and it had ended in this way! A ripple of laughter ran round the room. The new girl, mortified and offended, entered her protest in plain words.

"You are treating me shamefully! You all distrust me, because I am a stranger."

"Say we don't understand you," Emily answered, speaking for her schoolfellows; "and you will be nearer the truth."

"Who expected you to understand me, when I only came here to-day? I have told you already my name is Francine de Sor. If want to know more, I'm nineteen years old, and I come from the West Indies."

Emily still took the lead. "Why do you come here?" she asked. "Who ever heard of a girl joining a new school just before the holidays? You are nineteen years old, are you? I'm a year younger than you—and I have finished my education. The next big girl in the room is a year younger than me—and she has finished her education. What can you possibly have left to learn at your age?"

"Everything!" cried the stranger from the West Indies, with an outburst of tears. "I'm a poor ignorant creature. Your education ought to have taught you to pity me instead of making fun of me. I hate you all. For shame, for shame!"

Some of the girls laughed. One of them—the hungry girl who had counted the strokes of the clock—took Francine's part.

"Never mind their laughing, Miss de Sor. You are quite right, you have good reason to complain of us."

Miss de Sor dried her eyes. "Thank you—whoever you are," she answered briskly.

"My name is Cecilia Wyvil," the other proceeded. "It was not, perhaps, quite nice of you to say you hated us all. At the same time we have forgotten our good breeding—and the least we can do is to beg your pardon."

This expression of generous sentiment appeared to have an irritating effect on the peremptory young person who took the lead in the room. Perhaps she disapproved of free trade in generous sentiment.

"I can tell you one thing, Cecilia," she said; "you shan't beat ME in generosity. Strike a light, one of you, and lay the blame on me if Miss Ladd finds us out. I mean to shake hands with the new girl—and how can I do it in the dark? Miss de Sor, my name's Brown, and I'm queen of the bedroom. I—not Cecilia—offer our apologies if we have offended you. Cecilia is my dearest friend, but I don't allow her to take the lead in the room. Oh, what a lovely nightgown!"

The sudden flow of candle-light had revealed Francine, sitting up in her bed, and displaying such treasures of real lace over her bosom that the queen lost all sense of royal dignity in irrepressible admiration. "Seven and sixpence," Emily remarked, looking at her own night-gown and despising it. One after another, the girls yielded to the attraction of the wonderful lace. Slim and plump, fair and dark, they circled round the new pupil in their flowing white robes, and arrived by common consent at one and the same conclusion: "How rich her father must be!"

Favored by fortune in the matter of money, was this enviable person possessed of beauty as well?

In the disposition of the beds, Miss de Sor was placed between Cecilia on the right hand, and Emily on the left. If, by some fantastic turn of events, a man—say in the interests of propriety, a married doctor, with Miss Ladd to look after him—had been permitted to enter the room, and had been asked what he thought of the girls when he came out, he would not even have mentioned Francine. Blind to the beauties of the expensive night-gown, he would have noticed her long upper lip, her obstinate chin, her sallow complexion, her eyes placed too close together—and would have turned his attention to her nearest neighbors. On one side his languid interest would have been instantly roused by Cecilia's glowing auburn hair, her exquisitely pure skin, and her tender blue eyes. On the other, he would have discovered a bright little creature, who would have fascinated and perplexed him at one and the same time. If he had been questioned about her by a stranger, he would have been at a loss to say positively whether she was dark or light: he would have remembered how her eyes had held him, but he would not have known of what color they were. And yet, she would have remained a vivid picture in his memory when other impressions, derived at the same time, had vanished. "There was one little witch among them, who was worth all the rest put together; and I can't tell you why. They called her Emily. If I wasn't a married man—" There he would have thought of his wife, and would have sighed and said no more.

While the girls were still admiring Francine, the clock struck the half-hour past eleven.

Cecilia stole on tiptoe to the door—looked out, and listened—closed the door again—and addressed the meeting with the irresistible charm of her sweet voice and her persuasive smile.

"Are none of you hungry yet?" she inquired. "The teachers are safe in their rooms; we have set ourselves right with Francine. Why keep the supper waiting under Emily's bed?"

Such reasoning as this, with such personal attractions to recommend it, admitted of but one reply. The queen waved her hand graciously, and said, "Pull it out."

Is a lovely girl—whose face possesses the crowning charm of expression, whose slightest movement reveals the supple symmetry of her figure—less lovely because she is blessed with a good appetite, and is not ashamed to acknowledge it? With a grace all her own, Cecilia dived under the bed, and produced a basket of jam tarts, a basket of fruit and sweetmeats, a basket of sparkling lemonade, and a superb cake—all paid for by general subscriptions, and smuggled into the room by kind connivance of the servants. On this occasion, the feast was especially plentiful and expensive, in commemoration not only of the arrival of the Midsummer holidays, but of the coming freedom of Miss Ladd's two leading young ladies. With widely different destinies before them, Emily and Cecilia had completed their school life, and were now to go out into the world.

The contrast in the characters of the two girls showed itself, even in such a trifle as the preparations for supper.

Gentle Cecilia, sitting on the floor surrounded by good things, left it to the ingenuity of others to decide whether the baskets should be all emptied at once, or handed round from bed to bed, one at a time. In the meanwhile, her lovely blue eyes rested tenderly on the tarts.

Emily's commanding spirit seized on the reins of government, and employed each of her schoolfellows in the occupation which she was fittest to undertake. "Miss de Sor, let me look at your hand. Ah! I thought so. You have got the thickest wrist among us; you shall draw the corks. If you let the lemonade pop, not a drop of it goes down your throat. Effie, Annis, Priscilla, you are three notoriously lazy girls; it's doing you a true kindness to set you to work. Effie, clear the toilet-table for supper; away with the combs, the brushes, and the looking-glass. Annis, tear the leaves out of your book of exercises, and set them out for plates. No! I'll unpack; nobody touches the baskets but me. Priscilla, you have the prettiest ears in the room. You shall act as sentinel, my dear, and listen at the door. Cecilia, when you have done devouring those tarts with your eyes, take that pair of scissors (Miss de Sor, allow me to apologize for the mean manner in which this school is carried on; the knives and forks are counted and locked up every night)—I say take that pair of scissors, Cecilia, and carve the cake, and don't keep the largest bit for yourself. Are we all ready? Very well. Now take example by me. Talk as much as you like, so long as you don't talk too loud. There is one other thing before we begin. The men always propose toasts on these occasions; let's be like the men. Can any of you make a speech? Ah, it falls on me as usual. I propose the first toast. Down with all schools and teachers—especially the new teacher, who came this half year. Oh, mercy, how it stings!" The fixed gas in the lemonade took the orator, at that moment, by the throat, and effectually checked the flow of her eloquence. It made no difference to the girls. Excepting the ease of feeble stomachs, who cares for eloquence in the presence of a supper-table? There were no feeble stomachs in that bedroom. With what inexhaustible energy Miss Ladd's young ladies ate and drank! How merrily they enjoyed the delightful privilege of talking nonsense! And— alas! alas!—how vainly they tried, in after life, to renew the once unalloyed enjoyment of tarts and lemonade!

In the unintelligible scheme of creation, there appears to be no human happiness—not even the happiness of schoolgirls—which is ever complete. Just as it was drawing to a close, the enjoyment of the feast was interrupted by an alarm from the sentinel at the door.

"Put out the candle!" Priscilla whispered "Somebody on the stairs."

CHAPTER II. BIOGRAPHY IN THE BEDROOM.

The candle was instantly extinguished. In discreet silence the girls stole back to their beds, and listened.

As an aid to the vigilance of the sentinel, the door had been left ajar. Through the narrow opening, a creaking of the broad wooden stairs of the old house became audible. In another moment there was silence. An interval passed, and the creaking was heard again. This time, the sound was distant and diminishing. On a sudden it stopped. The midnight silence was disturbed no more.

What did this mean?

Had one among the many persons in authority under Miss Ladd's roof heard the girls talking, and ascended the stairs to surprise them in the act of violating one of the rules of the house? So far, such a proceeding was by no means uncommon. But was it within the limits of probability that a teacher should alter her opinion of her own duty half-way up the stairs, and deliberately go back to her own room again? The bare idea of such a thing was absurd on the face of it. What more rational explanation could ingenuity

176

discover on the spur of the moment?

Francine was the first to offer a suggestion. She shook and shivered in her bed, and said, "For heaven's sake, light the candle again! It's a Ghost."

"Clear away the supper, you fools, before the ghost can report us to Miss Ladd."

With this excellent advice Emily checked the rising panic. The door was closed, the candle was lit; all traces of the supper disappeared. For five minutes more they listened again. No sound came from the stairs; no teacher, or ghost of a teacher, appeared at the door.

Having eaten her supper, Cecilia's immediate anxieties were at an end; she was at leisure to exert her intelligence for the benefit of her schoolfellows. In her gentle ingratiating way, she offered a composing suggestion. "When we heard the creaking, I don't believe there was anybody on the stairs. In these old houses there are always strange noises at night—and they say the stairs here were made more than two hundred years since."

The girls looked at each other with a sense of relief—but they waited to hear the opinion of the queen. Emily, as usual, justified the confidence placed in her. She discovered an ingenious method of putting Cecilia's suggestion to the test.

"Let's go on talking," she said. "If Cecilia is right, the teachers are all asleep, and we have nothing to fear from them. If she's wrong, we shall sooner or later see one of them at the door. Don't be alarmed, Miss de Sor. Catching us talking at night, in this school, only means a reprimand. Catching us with a light, ends in punishment. Blow out the candle."

Francine's belief in the ghost was too sincerely superstitious to be shaken: she started up in bed. "Oh, don't leave me in the dark! I'll take the punishment, if we are found out."

"On your sacred word of honor?" Emily stipulated.

"Yes—yes."

The queen's sense of humor was tickled.

"There's something funny," she remarked, addressing her subjects, "in a big girl like this coming to a new school and beginning with a punishment. May I ask if you are a foreigner, Miss de Sor?"

"My papa is a Spanish gentleman," Francine answered, with dignity.

"And your mamma?"

"My mamma is English."

"And you have always lived in the West Indies?"

"I have always lived in the Island of St. Domingo."

Emily checked off on her fingers the different points thus far discovered in the character of Mr. de Sor's daughter. "She's ignorant, and superstitious, and foreign, and rich. My dear (forgive the familiarity), you are an interesting girl—and we must really know more of you. Entertain the bedroom. What have you been about all your life? And what in the name of wonder, brings you here? Before you begin I insist on one condition, in the name of all the young ladies in the room. No useful information about the West Indies!"

Francine disappointed her audience.

She was ready enough to make herself an object of interest to her companions; but she was not possessed of the capacity to arrange events in their proper order, necessary to the recital of the simplest narrative. Emily was obliged to help her, by means of questions. In one respect, the result justified the trouble taken to obtain it. A sufficient reason was discovered for the extraordinary appearance of a new pupil, on the day before the school closed for the holidays.

Mr. de Sor's elder brother had left him an estate in St. Domingo, and a fortune in money as well; on the one easy condition that he continued to reside in the island. The question of expense being now beneath the notice of the family, Francine had been sent to England, especially recommended to Miss Ladd as a young lady with grand prospects, sorely in need of a fashionable education. The voyage had been so timed, by the advice of the schoolmistress, as to make the holidays a means of obtaining this object privately. Francine

178

was to be taken to Brighton, where excellent masters could be obtained to assist Miss Ladd. With six weeks before her, she might in some degree make up for lost time; and, when the school opened again, she would avoid the mortification of being put down in the lowest class, along with the children.

The examination of Miss de Sor having produced these results was pursued no further. Her character now appeared in a new, and not very attractive, light. She audaciously took to herself the whole credit of telling her story:

"I think it's my turn now," she said, "to be interested and amused. May I ask you to begin, Miss Emily? All I know of you at present is, that your family name is Brown."

Emily held up her hand for silence.

Was the mysterious creaking on the stairs making itself heard once more? No. The sound that had caught Emily's quick ear came from the beds, on the opposite side of the room, occupied by the three lazy girls. With no new alarm to disturb them, Effie, Annis, and Priscilla had yielded to the composing influences of a good supper and a warm night. They were fast asleep—and the stoutest of the three (softly, as became a young lady) was snoring!

The unblemished reputation of the bedroom was dear to Emily, in her capacity of queen. She felt herself humiliated in the presence of the new pupil.

"If that fat girl ever gets a lover," she said indignantly, "I shall consider it my duty to warn the poor man before he marries her. Her ridiculous name is Euphemia. I have christened her (far more appropriately) Boiled Veal. No color in her hair, no color in her eyes, no color in her complexion. In short, no flavor in Euphemia. You naturally object to snoring. Pardon me if I turn my back on you—I am going to throw my slipper at her."

The soft voice of Cecilia—suspiciously drowsy in tone—interposed in the interests of mercy.

"She can't help it, poor thing; and she really isn't loud enough to disturb us."

"She won't disturb you, at any rate! Rouse yourself, Cecilia. We are wide awake on this side of the room—and Francine says it's our turn to amuse her."

A low murmur, dying away gently in a sigh, was the only answer. Sweet Cecilia had yielded to the somnolent influences of the supper and the night. The soft infection of repose seemed to be in some danger of communicating itself to Francine. Her large mouth opened luxuriously in a long-continued yawn.

"Good-night!" said Emily.

Miss de Sor became wide awake in an instant.

"No," she said positively; "you are quite mistaken if you think I am going to sleep. Please exert yourself, Miss Emily—I am waiting to be interested."

Emily appeared to be unwilling to exert herself. She preferred talking of the weather.

"Isn't the wind rising?" she said.

There could be no doubt of it. The leaves in the garden were beginning to rustle, and the pattering of the rain sounded on the windows.

Francine (as her straight chin proclaimed to all students of physiognomy) was an obstinate girl. Determined to carry her point she tried Emily's own system on Emily herself—she put questions.

"Have you been long at this school?"

"More than three years."

"Have you got any brothers and sisters?"

"I am the only child."

"Are your father and mother alive?"

Emily suddenly raised herself in bed.

"Wait a minute," she said; "I think I hear it again."

"The creaking on the stairs?"

"Yes."

Either she was mistaken, or the change for the worse in the weather made it not easy to hear slight noises in the house. The wind was still rising. The passage of it through the great trees in the garden began to sound like the fall of waves on a distant beach. It drove the rain—a heavy downpour by this time—rattling against the windows.

"Almost a storm, isn't it?" Emily said

Francine's last question had not been answered yet. She took the earliest opportunity of repeating it:

"Never mind the weather," she said. "Tell me about your father and mother. Are they both alive?"

Emily's reply only related to one of her parents.

"My mother died before I was old enough to feel my loss."

"And your father?"

Emily referred to another relative—her father's sister. "Since I have grown up," she proceeded, "my good aunt has been a second mother to me. My story is, in one respect, the reverse of yours. You are unexpectedly rich; and I am unexpectedly poor. My aunt's fortune was to have been my fortune, if I outlived her. She has been ruined by the failure of a bank. In her old age, she must live on an income of two hundred a year—and I must get my own living when I leave school."

"Surely your father can help you?" Francine persisted.

"His property is landed property." Her voice faltered, as she referred to him, even in that indirect manner. "It is entailed; his nearest male relative inherits it."

The delicacy which is easily discouraged was not one of the weaknesses in the nature of Francine.

181

"Do I understand that your father is dead?" she asked.

Our thick-skinned fellow-creatures have the rest of us at their mercy: only give them time, and they carry their point in the end. In sad subdued tones—telling of deeply-rooted reserves of feeling, seldom revealed to strangers—Emily yielded at last.

"Yes," she said, "my father is dead."

"Long ago?"

"Some people might think it long ago. I was very fond of my father. It's nearly four years since he died, and my heart still aches when I think of him. I'm not easily depressed by troubles, Miss de Sor. But his death was sudden— he was in his grave when I first heard of it—and—Oh, he was so good to me; he was so good to me!"

The gay high-spirited little creature who took the lead among them all—who was the life and soul of the school—hid her face in her hands, and burst out crying.

Startled and—to do her justice—ashamed, Francine attempted to make excuses. Emily's generous nature passed over the cruel persistency that had tortured her. "No no; I have nothing to forgive. It isn't your fault. Other girls have not mothers and brothers and sisters—and get reconciled to such a loss as mine. Don't make excuses."

"Yes, but I want you to know that I feel for you," Francine insisted, without the slightest approach to sympathy in face, voice, or manner. "When my uncle died, and left us all the money, papa was much shocked. He trusted to time to help him."

"Time has been long about it with me, Francine. I am afraid there is something perverse in my nature; the hope of meeting again in a better world seems so faint and so far away. No more of it now! Let us talk of that good creature who is asleep on the other side of you. Did I tell you that I must earn my own bread when I leave school? Well, Cecilia has written home and found an employment for me. Not a situation as governess—something quite out of the common way. You shall hear all about it."

In the brief interval that had passed, the weather had begun to change again. The wind was as high as ever; but to judge by the lessening patter on the windows the rain was passing away.

Emily began.

She was too grateful to her friend and school-fellow, and too deeply interested in her story, to notice the air of indifference with which Francine settled herself on her pillow to hear the praises of Cecilia. The most beautiful girl in the school was not an object of interest to a young lady with an obstinate chin and unfortunately-placed eyes. Pouring warm from the speaker's heart the story ran smoothly on, to the monotonous accompaniment of the moaning wind. By fine degrees Francine's eyes closed, opened and closed again. Toward the latter part of the narrative Emily's memory became, for the moment only, confused between two events. She stopped to consider—noticed Francine's silence, in an interval when she might have said a word of encouragement—and looked closer at her. Miss de Sor was asleep.

"She might have told me she was tired," Emily said to herself quietly. "Well! the best thing I can do is to put out the light and follow her example."

As she took up the extinguisher, the bedroom door was suddenly opened from the outer side. A tall woman, robed in a black dressing-gown, stood on the threshold, looking at Emily.

CHAPTER III. THE LATE MR. BROWN.

The woman's lean, long-fingered hand pointed to the candle.

"Don't put it out." Saying those words, she looked round the room, and satisfied herself that the other girls were asleep.

Emily laid down the extinguisher. "You mean to report us, of course," she said. "I am the only one awake, Miss Jethro; lay the blame on me."

"I have no intention of reporting you. But I have something to say."

She paused, and pushed her thick black hair (already streaked with gray) back from her temples. Her eyes, large and dark and dim, rested on Emily with a sorrowful interest. "When your young friends wake to-morrow morning," she went on, "you can tell them that the new teacher, whom nobody likes, has left the school."

For once, even quick-witted Emily was bewildered. "Going away," she said, "when you have only been here since Easter!"

Miss Jethro advanced, not noticing Emily's expression of surprise. "I am not very strong at the best of times," she continued, "may I sit down on your bed?" Remarkable on other occasions for her cold composure, her voice trembled as she made that request—a strange request surely, when there were chairs at her disposal.

Emily made room for her with the dazed look of a girl in a dream. "I beg your pardon, Miss Jethro, one of the things I can't endure is being puzzled. If you don't mean to report us, why did you come in and catch me with the light?"

Miss Jethro's explanation was far from relieving the perplexity which her conduct had caused.

"I have been mean enough," she answered, "to listen at the door, and I heard you talking of your father. I want to hear more about him. That is why I came in."

"You knew my father!" Emily exclaimed.

"I believe I knew him. But his name is so common—there are so many thousands of 'James Browns' in England—that I am in fear of making a mistake. I heard you say that he died nearly four years since. Can you mention any particulars which might help to enlighten me? If you think I am taking a liberty—"

Emily stopped her. "I would help you if I could," she said. "But I was in poor health at the time; and I was staying with friends far away in Scotland, to try change of air. The news of my father's death brought on a relapse. Weeks passed before I was strong enough to travel—weeks and weeks before

I saw his grave! I can only tell you what I know from my aunt. He died of heart-complaint."

Miss Jethro started.

Emily looked at her for the first time, with eyes that betrayed a feeling of distrust. "What have I said to startle you?" she asked.

"Nothing! I am nervous in stormy weather—don't notice me." She went on abruptly with her inquiries. "Will you tell me the date of your father's death?"

"The date was the thirtieth of September, nearly four years since."

She waited, after that reply.

Miss Jethro was silent.

"And this," Emily continued, "is the thirtieth of June, eighteen hundred and eighty-one. You can now judge for yourself. Did you know my father?"

Miss Jethro answered mechanically, using the same words.

"I did know your father."

Emily's feeling of distrust was not set at rest. "I never heard him speak of you," she said.

In her younger days the teacher must have been a handsome woman. Her grandly-formed features still suggested the idea of imperial beauty—perhaps Jewish in its origin. When Emily said, "I never heard him speak of you," the color flew into her pallid cheeks: her dim eyes became alive again with a momentary light. She left her seat on the bed, and, turning away, mastered the emotion that shook her.

"How hot the night is!" she said: and sighed, and resumed the subject with a steady countenance. "I am not surprised that your father never mentioned me—to you." She spoke quietly, but her face was paler than ever. She sat down again on the bed. "Is there anything I can do for you," she asked, "before I go away? Oh, I only mean some trifling service that would lay you under no obligation, and would not oblige you to keep up your acquaintance with me."

Her eyes—the dim black eyes that must once have been irresistibly beautiful—looked at Emily so sadly that the generous girl reproached herself for having doubted her father's friend. "Are you thinking of him," she said gently, "when you ask if you can be of service to me?"

Miss Jethro made no direct reply. "You were fond of your father?" she added, in a whisper. "You told your schoolfellow that your heart still aches when you speak of him."

"I only told her the truth," Emily answered simply.

Miss Jethro shuddered—on that hot night!—shuddered as if a chill had struck her.

Emily held out her hand; the kind feeling that had been roused in her glittered prettily in her eyes. "I am afraid I have not done you justice," she said. "Will you forgive me and shake hands?"

Miss Jethro rose, and drew back. "Look at the light!" she exclaimed.

The candle was all burned out. Emily still offered her hand—and still Miss Jethro refused to see it.

"There is just light enough left," she said, "to show me my way to the door. Good-night—and good-by."

Emily caught at her dress, and stopped her. "Why won't you shake hands with me?" she asked.

The wick of the candle fell over in the socket, and left them in the dark. Emily resolutely held the teacher's dress. With or without light, she was still bent on making Miss Jethro explain herself.

They had throughout spoken in guarded tones, fearing to disturb the sleeping girls. The sudden darkness had its inevitable effect. Their voices sank to whispers now. "My father's friend," Emily pleaded, "is surely my friend?"

"Drop the subject."

"Why?"

"You can never be my friend."

"Why not?"

"Let me go!"

Emily's sense of self-respect forbade her to persist any longer. "I beg your pardon for having kept you here against your will," she said—and dropped her hold on the dress.

Miss Jethro instantly yielded on her side. "I am sorry to have been obstinate," she answered. "If you do despise me, it is after all no more than I have deserved." Her hot breath beat on Emily's face: the unhappy woman must have bent over the bed as she made her confession. "I am not a fit person for you to associate with."

"I don't believe it!"

Miss Jethro sighed bitterly. "Young and warm hearted—I was once like you!" She controlled that outburst of despair. Her next words were spoken in steadier tones. "You will have it—you shall have it!" she said. "Some one (in this house or out of it; I don't know which) has betrayed me to the mistress of the school. A wretch in my situation suspects everybody, and worse still, does it without reason or excuse. I heard you girls talking when you ought to have been asleep. You all dislike me. How did I know it mightn't be one of you? Absurd, to a person with a well-balanced mind! I went halfway up the stairs, and felt ashamed of myself, and went back to my room. If I could only have got some rest! Ah, well, it was not to be done. My own vile suspicions kept me awake; I left my bed again. You know what I heard on the other side of that door, and why I was interested in hearing it. Your father never told me he had a daughter. 'Miss Brown,' at this school, was any 'Miss Brown,' to me. I had no idea of who you really were until to-night. I'm wandering. What does all this matter to you? Miss Ladd has been merciful; she lets me go without exposing me. You can guess what has happened. No? Not even yet? Is it innocence or kindness that makes you so slow to understand? My dear, I have obtained admission to this respectable house by means of false references, and I have been discovered. Now you know why you must not be the friend of such a woman as I am! Once more, good-night—and good-by."

Emily shrank from that miserable farewell.

"Bid me good-night," she said, "but don't bid me good-by. Let me see you again."

"Never!"

The sound of the softly-closed door was just audible in the darkness. She had spoken—she had gone—never to be seen by Emily again.

Miserable, interesting, unfathomable creature—the problem that night of Emily's waking thoughts: the phantom of her dreams. "Bad? or good?" she asked herself. "False; for she listened at the door. True; for she told me the tale of her own disgrace. A friend of my father; and she never knew that he had a daughter. Refined, accomplished, lady-like; and she stoops to use a false reference. Who is to reconcile such contradictions as these?"

Dawn looked in at the window—dawn of the memorable day which was, for Emily, the beginning of a new life. The years were before her; and the years in their course reveal baffling mysteries of life and death.

CHAPTER IV. MISS LADD'S DRAWING-MASTER.

Francine was awakened the next morning by one of the housemaids, bringing up her breakfast on a tray. Astonished at this concession to laziness, in an institution devoted to the practice of all virtues, she looked round. The bedroom was deserted.

"The other young ladies are as busy as bees, miss," the housemaid explained. "They were up and dressed two hours ago: and the breakfast has been cleared away long since. It's Miss Emily's fault. She wouldn't allow them to wake you; she said you could be of no possible use downstairs, and you had better be treated like a visitor. Miss Cecilia was so distressed at your missing your breakfast that she spoke to the housekeeper, and I was sent up to you. Please to excuse it if the tea's cold. This is Grand Day, and we are all topsy-turvy in consequence."

Inquiring what "Grand Day" meant, and why it produced this extraordinary result in a ladies' school, Francine discovered that the first day of the vacation was devoted to the distribution of prizes, in the presence of parents, guardians and friends. An Entertainment was added, comprising those merciless tests of human endurance called Recitations; light refreshments and musical performances being distributed at intervals, to encourage the exhausted audience. The local newspaper sent a reporter to describe the proceedings, and some of Miss Ladd's young ladies enjoyed the intoxicating luxury of seeing their names in print.

"It begins at three o'clock," the housemaid went on, "and, what with practicing and rehearsing, and ornamenting the schoolroom, there's a hubbub fit to make a person's head spin. Besides which," said the girl, lowering her voice, and approaching a little nearer to Francine, "we have all been taken by surprise. The first thing in the morning Miss Jethro left us, without saying good-by to anybody."

"Who is Miss Jethro?"

"The new teacher, miss. We none of us liked her, and we all suspect there's something wrong. Miss Ladd and the clergyman had a long talk together yesterday (in private, you know), and they sent for Miss Jethro—which looks bad, doesn't it? Is there anything more I can do for you, miss? It's a beautiful day after the rain. If I was you, I should go and enjoy myself in the garden."

Having finished her breakfast, Francine decided on profiting by this sensible suggestion.

The servant who showed her the way to the garden was not favorably impressed by the new pupil: Francine's temper asserted itself a little too plainly in her face. To a girl possessing a high opinion of her own importance it was not very agreeable to feel herself excluded, as an illiterate stranger, from the one absorbing interest of her schoolfellows. "Will the time ever come," she wondered bitterly, "when I shall win a prize, and sing and play before all the company? How I should enjoy making the girls envy me!"

A broad lawn, overshadowed at one end by fine old trees—flower beds and shrubberies, and winding paths prettily and invitingly laid out—made the garden a welcome refuge on that fine summer morning. The novelty of the scene, after her experience in the West Indies, the delicious breezes cooled by the rain of the night, exerted their cheering influence even on the sullen disposition of Francine. She smiled, in spite of herself, as she followed the pleasant paths, and heard the birds singing their summer songs over her head.

Wandering among the trees, which occupied a considerable extent of ground, she passed into an open space beyond, and discovered an old fish-pond, overgrown by aquatic plants. Driblets of water trickled from a dilapidated fountain in the middle. On the further side of the pond the ground sloped downward toward the south, and revealed, over a low paling, a pretty view of a village and its church, backed by fir woods mounting the heathy sides of a range of hills beyond. A fanciful little wooden building, imitating the form of a Swiss cottage, was placed so as to command the prospect. Near it, in the shadow of the building, stood a rustic chair and table—with a color-box on one, and a portfolio on the other. Fluttering over the grass, at the mercy of the capricious breeze, was a neglected sheet of drawing-paper. Francine ran round the pond, and picked up the paper just as it was on the point of being tilted into the water. It contained a sketch in water colors of the village and the woods, and Francine had looked at the view itself with indifference—the picture of the view interested her. Ordinary visitors to Galleries of Art, which admit students, show the same strange perversity. The work of the copyist commands their whole attention; they take no interest in the original picture.

Looking up from the sketch, Francine was startled. She discovered a man, at the window of the Swiss summer-house, watching her.

"When you have done with that drawing," he said quietly, "please let me have it back again."

He was tall and thin and dark. His finely-shaped intelligent face—hidden, as to the lower part of it, by a curly black beard—would have been absolutely handsome, even in the eyes of a schoolgirl, but for the deep furrows that marked it prematurely between the eyebrows, and at the sides of the mouth. In the same way, an underlying mockery impaired the attraction

190

of his otherwise refined and gentle manner. Among his fellow-creatures, children and dogs were the only critics who appreciated his merits without discovering the defects which lessened the favorable appreciation of him by men and women. He dressed neatly, but his morning coat was badly made, and his picturesque felt hat was too old. In short, there seemed to be no good quality about him which was not perversely associated with a drawback of some kind. He was one of those harmless and luckless men, possessed of excellent qualities, who fail nevertheless to achieve popularity in their social sphere.

Francine handed his sketch to him, through the window; doubtful whether the words that he had addressed to her were spoken in jest or in earnest.

"I only presumed to touch your drawing," she said, "because it was in danger."

"What danger?" he inquired.

Francine pointed to the pond. "If I had not been in time to pick it up, it would have been blown into the water."

"Do you think it was worth picking up?"

Putting that question, he looked first at the sketch—then at the view which it represented—then back again at the sketch. The corners of his mouth turned upward with a humorous expression of scorn. "Madam Nature," he said, "I beg your pardon." With those words, he composedly tore his work of art into small pieces, and scattered them out of the window.

"What a pity!" said Francine.

He joined her on the ground outside the cottage. "Why is it a pity?" he asked.

"Such a nice drawing."

"It isn't a nice drawing."

"You're not very polite, sir."

191

He looked at her—and sighed as if he pitied so young a woman for having a temper so ready to take offense. In his flattest contradictions he always preserved the character of a politely-positive man.

"Put it in plain words, miss," he replied. "I have offended the predominant sense in your nature—your sense of self-esteem. You don't like to be told, even indirectly, that you know nothing of Art. In these days, everybody knows everything—and thinks nothing worth knowing after all. But beware how you presume on an appearance of indifference, which is nothing but conceit in disguise. The ruling passion of civilized humanity is, Conceit. You may try the regard of your dearest friend in any other way, and be forgiven. Ruffle the smooth surface of your friend's self-esteem—and there will be an acknowledged coolness between you which will last for life. Excuse me for giving you the benefit of my trumpery experience. This sort of smart talk is my form of conceit. Can I be of use to you in some better way? Are you looking for one of our young ladies?"

Francine began to feel a certain reluctant interest in him when he spoke of "our young ladies." She asked if he belonged to the school.

The corners of his mouth turned up again. "I'm one of the masters," he said. "Are you going to belong to the school, too?"

Francine bent her head, with a gravity and condescension intended to keep him at his proper distance. Far from being discouraged, he permitted his curiosity to take additional liberties. "Are you to have the misfortune of being one of my pupils?" he asked.

"I don't know who you are."

"You won't be much wiser when you do know. My name is Alban Morris."

Francine corrected herself. "I mean, I don't know what you teach."

Alban Morris pointed to the fragments of his sketch from Nature. "I am a bad artist," he said. "Some bad artists become Royal Academicians. Some take to drink. Some get a pension. And some—I am one of them—

find refuge in schools. Drawing is an 'Extra' at this school. Will you take my advice? Spare your good father's pocket; say you don't want to learn to draw."

He was so gravely in earnest that Francine burst out laughing. "You are a strange man," she said.

"Wrong again, miss. I am only an unhappy man."

The furrows in his face deepened, the latent humor died out of his eyes. He turned to the summer-house window, and took up a pipe and tobacco pouch, left on the ledge.

"I lost my only friend last year," he said. "Since the death of my dog, my pipe is the one companion I have left. Naturally I am not allowed to enjoy the honest fellow's society in the presence of ladies. They have their own taste in perfumes. Their clothes and their letters reek with the foetid secretion of the musk deer. The clean vegetable smell of tobacco is unendurable to them. Allow me to retire—and let me thank you for the trouble you took to save my drawing."

The tone of indifference in which he expressed his gratitude piqued Francine. She resented it by drawing her own conclusion from what he had said of the ladies and the musk deer. "I was wrong in admiring your drawing," she remarked; "and wrong again in thinking you a strange man. Am I wrong, for the third time, in believing that you dislike women?"

"I am sorry to say you are right," Alban Morris answered gravely.

"Is there not even one exception?"

The instant the words passed her lips, she saw that there was some secretly sensitive feeling in him which she had hurt. His black brows gathered into a frown, his piercing eyes looked at her with angry surprise. It was over in a moment. He raised his shabby hat, and made her a bow.

"There is a sore place still left in me," he said; "and you have innocently hit it. Good-morning."

Before she could speak again, he had turned the corner of the summer-house, and was lost to view in a shrubbery on the westward side of the grounds.

CHAPTER V. DISCOVERIES IN THE GARDEN.

Left by herself, Miss de Sor turned back again by way of the trees.

So far, her interview with the drawing-master had helped to pass the time. Some girls might have found it no easy task to arrive at a true view of the character of Alban Morris. Francine's essentially superficial observation set him down as "a little mad," and left him there, judged and dismissed to her own entire satisfaction.

Arriving at the lawn, she discovered Emily pacing backward and forward, with her head down and her hands behind her, deep in thought. Francine's high opinion of herself would have carried her past any of the other girls, unless they had made special advances to her. She stopped and looked at Emily.

It is the sad fate of little women in general to grow too fat and to be born with short legs. Emily's slim finely-strung figure spoke for itself as to the first of these misfortunes, and asserted its happy freedom from the second, if she only walked across a room. Nature had built her, from head to foot, on a skeleton-scaffolding in perfect proportion. Tall or short matters little to the result, in women who possess the first and foremost advantage of beginning well in their bones. When they live to old age, they often astonish thoughtless men, who walk behind them in the street. "I give you my honor, she was as easy and upright as a young girl; and when you got in front of her and looked—white hair, and seventy years of age."

Francine approached Emily, moved by a rare impulse in her nature—the impulse to be sociable. "You look out of spirits," she began. "Surely you don't regret leaving school?"

In her present mood, Emily took the opportunity (in the popular phrase) of snubbing Francine. "You have guessed wrong; I do regret," she answered. "I have found in Cecilia my dearest friend at school. And school brought with it the change in my life which has helped me to bear the loss of my father. If you must know what I was thinking of just now, I was thinking of my aunt. She has not answered my last letter—and I'm beginning to be afraid she is ill."

194

"I'm very sorry," said Francine.

"Why? You don't know my aunt; and you have only known me since yesterday afternoon. Why are you sorry?"

Francine remained silent. Without realizing it, she was beginning to feel the dominant influence that Emily exercised over the weaker natures that came in contact with her. To find herself irresistibly attracted by a stranger at a new school—an unfortunate little creature, whose destiny was to earn her own living—filled the narrow mind of Miss de Sor with perplexity. Having waited in vain for a reply, Emily turned away, and resumed the train of thought which her schoolfellow had interrupted.

By an association of ideas, of which she was not herself aware, she now passed from thinking of her aunt to thinking of Miss Jethro. The interview of the previous night had dwelt on her mind at intervals, in the hours of the new day.

Acting on instinct rather than on reason, she had kept that remarkable incident in her school life a secret from every one. No discoveries had been made by other persons. In speaking to her staff of teachers, Miss Ladd had alluded to the affair in the most cautious terms. "Circumstances of a private nature have obliged the lady to retire from my school. When we meet after the holidays, another teacher will be in her place." There, Miss Ladd's explanation had begun and ended. Inquiries addressed to the servants had led to no result. Miss Jethro's luggage was to be forwarded to the London terminus of the railway—and Miss Jethro herself had baffled investigation by leaving the school on foot. Emily's interest in the lost teacher was not the transitory interest of curiosity; her father's mysterious friend was a person whom she honestly desired to see again. Perplexed by the difficulty of finding a means of tracing Miss Jethro, she reached the shady limit of the trees, and turned to walk back again. Approaching the place at which she and Francine had met, an idea occurred to her. It was just possible that Miss Jethro might not be unknown to her aunt.

Still meditating on the cold reception that she had encountered, and still feeling the influence which mastered her in spite of herself, Francine interpreted Emily's return as an implied expression of regret. She advanced with a constrained smile, and spoke first.

"How are the young ladies getting on in the schoolroom?" she asked, by way of renewing the conversation.

Emily's face assumed a look of surprise which said plainly, Can't you take a hint and leave me to myself?

Francine was constitutionally impenetrable to reproof of this sort; her thick skin was not even tickled. "Why are you not helping them," she went on; "you who have the clearest head among us and take the lead in everything?"

It may be a humiliating confession to make, yet it is surely true that we are all accessible to flattery. Different tastes appreciate different methods of burning incense—but the perfume is more or less agreeable to all varieties of noses. Francine's method had its tranquilizing effect on Emily. She answered indulgently, "Miss de Sor, I have nothing to do with it."

"Nothing to do with it? No prizes to win before you leave school?"

"I won all the prizes years ago."

"But there are recitations. Surely you recite?"

Harmless words in themselves, pursuing the same smooth course of flattery as before—but with what a different result! Emily's face reddened with anger the moment they were spoken. Having already irritated Alban Morris, unlucky Francine, by a second mischievous interposition of accident, had succeeded in making Emily smart next. "Who has told you," she burst out; "I insist on knowing!"

"Nobody has told me anything!" Francine declared piteously.

"Nobody has told you how I have been insulted?"

"No, indeed! Oh, Miss Brown, who could insult you?"

In a man, the sense of injury does sometimes submit to the discipline of silence. In a woman—never. Suddenly reminded of her past wrongs (by

196

the pardonable error of a polite schoolfellow), Emily committed the startling inconsistency of appealing to the sympathies of Francine!

"Would you believe it? I have been forbidden to recite—I, the head girl of the school. Oh, not to-day! It happened a month ago—when we were all in consultation, making our arrangements. Miss Ladd asked me if I had decided on a piece to recite. I said, 'I have not only decided, I have learned the piece.' 'And what may it be?' 'The dagger-scene in Macbeth.' There was a howl—I can call it by no other name—a howl of indignation. A man's soliloquy, and, worse still, a murdering man's soliloquy, recited by one of Miss Ladd's young ladies, before an audience of parents and guardians! That was the tone they took with me. I was as firm as a rock. The dagger-scene or nothing. The result is—nothing! An insult to Shakespeare, and an insult to Me. I felt it—I feel it still. I was prepared for any sacrifice in the cause of the drama. If Miss Ladd had met me in a proper spirit, do you know what I would have done? I would have played Macbeth in costume. Just hear me, and judge for yourself. I begin with a dreadful vacancy in my eyes, and a hollow moaning in my voice: 'Is this a dagger that I see before me—?'"

Reciting with her face toward the trees, Emily started, dropped the character of Macbeth, and instantly became herself again: herself, with a rising color and an angry brightening of the eyes. "Excuse me, I can't trust my memory: I must get the play." With that abrupt apology, she walked away rapidly in the direction of the house.

In some surprise, Francine turned, and looked at the trees. She discovered—in full retreat, on his side—the eccentric drawing-master, Alban Morris.

Did he, too, admire the dagger-scene? And was he modestly desirous of hearing it recited, without showing himself? In that case, why should Emily (whose besetting weakness was certainly not want of confidence in her own resources) leave the garden the moment she caught sight of him? Francine consulted her instincts. She had just arrived at a conclusion which expressed itself outwardly by a malicious smile, when gentle Cecilia appeared on the lawn—a lovable object in a broad straw hat and a white dress, with a nosegay in her bosom—smiling, and fanning herself.

"It's so hot in the schoolroom," she said, "and some of the girls, poor things, are so ill-tempered at rehearsal—I have made my escape. I hope you got your breakfast, Miss de Sor. What have you been doing here, all by yourself?"

"I have been making an interesting discovery," Francine replied.

"An interesting discovery in our garden? What can it be?"

"The drawing-master, my dear, is in love with Emily. Perhaps she doesn't care about him. Or, perhaps, I have been an innocent obstacle in the way of an appointment between them."

Cecilia had breakfasted to her heart's content on her favorite dish—buttered eggs. She was in such good spirits that she was inclined to be coquettish, even when there was no man present to fascinate. "We are not allowed to talk about love in this school," she said—and hid her face behind her fan. "Besides, if it came to Miss Ladd's ears, poor Mr. Morris might lose his situation."

"But isn't it true?" asked Francine.

"It may be true, my dear; but nobody knows. Emily hasn't breathed a word about it to any of us. And Mr. Morris keeps his own secret. Now and then we catch him looking at her—and we draw our own conclusions."

"Did you meet Emily on your way here?"

"Yes, and she passed without speaking to me."

"Thinking perhaps of Mr. Morris."

Cecilia shook her head. "Thinking, Francine, of the new life before her—and regretting, I am afraid, that she ever confided her hopes and wishes to me. Did she tell you last night what her prospects are when she leaves school?"

"She told me you had been very kind in helping her. I daresay I should have heard more, if I had not fallen asleep. What is she going to do?"

"To live in a dull house, far away in the north," Cecilia answered; "with only old people in it. She will have to write and translate for a great scholar, who is studying mysterious inscriptions—hieroglyphics, I think they are called—found among the ruins of Central America. It's really no laughing matter, Francine! Emily made a joke of it, too. 'I'll take anything but a situation as a governess,' she said; 'the children who have Me to teach them would be to be pitied indeed!' She begged and prayed me to help her to get an honest living. What could I do? I could only write home to papa. He is a member of Parliament: and everybody who wants a place seems to think he is bound to find it for them. As it happened, he had heard from an old friend of his (a certain Sir Jervis Redwood), who was in search of a secretary. Being in favor of letting the women compete for employment with the men, Sir Jervis was willing to try, what he calls, 'a female.' Isn't that a horrid way of speaking of us? and Miss Ladd says it's ungrammatical, besides. Papa had written back to say he knew of no lady whom he could recommend. When he got my letter speaking of Emily, he kindly wrote again. In the interval, Sir Jervis had received two applications for the vacant place. They were both from old ladies—and he declined to employ them."

"Because they were old," Francine suggested maliciously.

"You shall hear him give his own reasons, my dear. Papa sent me an extract from his letter. It made me rather angry; and (perhaps for that reason) I think I can repeat it word for word:—'We are four old people in this house, and we don't want a fifth. Let us have a young one to cheer us. If your daughter's friend likes the terms, and is not encumbered with a sweetheart, I will send for her when the school breaks up at midsummer.' Coarse and selfish—isn't it? However, Emily didn't agree with me, when I showed her the extract. She accepted the place, very much to her aunt's surprise and regret, when that excellent person heard of it. Now that the time has come (though Emily won't acknowledge it), I believe she secretly shrinks, poor dear, from the prospect."

"Very likely," Francine agreed—without even a pretense of sympathy.

"But tell me, who are the four old people?"

"First, Sir Jervis himself—seventy, last birthday. Next, his unmarried sister—nearly eighty. Next, his man-servant, Mr. Rook—well past sixty. And last, his man-servant's wife, who considers herself young, being only a little over forty. That is the household. Mrs. Rook is coming to-day to attend Emily on the journey to the North; and I am not at all sure that Emily will like her."

"A disagreeable woman, I suppose?"

"No—not exactly that. Rather odd and flighty. The fact is, Mrs. Rook has had her troubles; and perhaps they have a little unsettled her. She and her husband used to keep the village inn, close to our park: we know all about them at home. I am sure I pity these poor people. What are you looking at, Francine?"

Feeling no sort of interest in Mr. and Mrs. Rook, Francine was studying her schoolfellow's lovely face in search of defects. She had already discovered that Cecilia's eyes were placed too widely apart, and that her chin wanted size and character.

"I was admiring your complexion, dear," she answered coolly. "Well, and why do you pity the Rooks?"

Simple Cecilia smiled, and went on with her story.

"They are obliged to go out to service in their old age, through a misfortune for which they are in no way to blame. Their customers deserted the inn, and Mr. Rook became bankrupt. The inn got what they call a bad name—in a very dreadful way. There was a murder committed in the house."

"A murder?" cried Francine. "Oh, this is exciting! You provoking girl, why didn't you tell me about it before?"

"I didn't think of it," said Cecilia placidly.

"Do go on! Were you at home when it happened?"

"I was here, at school."

"You saw the newspapers, I suppose?"

"Miss Ladd doesn't allow us to read newspapers. I did hear of it, however, in letters from home. Not that there was much in the letters. They said it was too horrible to be described. The poor murdered gentleman—"

Francine was unaffectedly shocked. "A gentleman!" she exclaimed. "How dreadful!"

"The poor man was a stranger in our part of the country," Cecilia resumed; "and the police were puzzled about the motive for a murder. His pocketbook was missing; but his watch and his rings were found on the body. I remember the initials on his linen because they were the same as my mother's initial before she was married—'J. B.' Really, Francine, that's all I know about it."

"Surely you know whether the murderer was discovered?"

"Oh, yes—of course I know that! The government offered a reward; and clever people were sent from London to help the county police. Nothing came of it. The murderer has never been discovered, from that time to this."

"When did it happen?"

"It happened in the autumn."

"The autumn of last year?"

"No! no! Nearly four years since."

CHAPTER VI. ON THE WAY TO THE VILLAGE.

Alban Morris—discovered by Emily in concealment among the trees— was not content with retiring to another part of the grounds. He pursued his retreat, careless in what direction it might take him, to a footpath across the fields, which led to the highroad and the railway station.

Miss Ladd's drawing-master was in that state of nervous irritability which seeks relief in rapidity of motion. Public opinion in the neighborhood (especially public opinion among the women) had long since decided that his manners were offensive, and his temper incurably bad. The men who happened to pass him on the footpath said "Good-morning" grudgingly.

The women took no notice of him—with one exception. She was young and saucy, and seeing him walking at the top of his speed on the way to the railway station, she called after him, "Don't be in a hurry, sir! You're in plenty of time for the London train."

To her astonishment he suddenly stopped. His reputation for rudeness was so well established that she moved away to a safe distance, before she ventured to look at him again. He took no notice of her—he seemed to be considering with himself. The frolicsome young woman had done him a service: she had suggested an idea.

"Suppose I go to London?" he thought. "Why not?—the school is breaking up for the holidays—and she is going away like the rest of them." He looked round in the direction of the schoolhouse. "If I go back to wish her good-by, she will keep out of my way, and part with me at the last moment like a stranger. After my experience of women, to be in love again—in love with a girl who is young enough to be my daughter—what a fool, what a driveling, degraded fool I must be!"

Hot tears rose in his eyes. He dashed them away savagely, and went on again faster than ever—resolved to pack up at once at his lodgings in the village, and to take his departure by the next train.

At the point where the footpath led into the road, he came to a standstill for the second time.

The cause was once more a person of the sex associated in his mind with a bitter sense of injury. On this occasion the person was only a miserable little child, crying over the fragments of a broken jug.

Alban Morris looked at her with his grimly humorous smile. "So you've broken a jug?" he remarked.

"And spilt father's beer," the child answered. Her frail little body shook with terror. "Mother'll beat me when I go home," she said.

"What does mother do when you bring the jug back safe and sound?" Alban asked.

"Gives me bren-butter."

"Very well. Now listen to me. Mother shall give you bread and butter again this time."

The child stared at him with the tears suspended in her eyes. He went on talking to her as seriously as ever.

"You understand what I have just said to you?"

"Yes, sir."

"Have you got a pocket-handkerchief?"

"No, sir."

"Then dry your eyes with mine."

He tossed his handkerchief to her with one hand, and picked up a fragment of the broken jug with the other. "This will do for a pattern," he said to himself. The child stared at the handkerchief—stared at Alban—took courage—and rubbed vigorously at her eyes. The instinct, which is worth all the reason that ever pretended to enlighten mankind—the instinct that never deceives—told this little ignorant creature that she had found a friend. She returned the handkerchief in grave silence. Alban took her up in his arms.

"Your eyes are dry, and your face is fit to be seen," he said. "Will you give me a kiss?" The child gave him a resolute kiss, with a smack in it. "Now come and get another jug," he said, as he put her down. Her red round eyes opened wide in alarm. "Have you got money enough?" she asked. Alban slapped his pocket. "Yes, I have," he answered. "That's a good thing," said the child; "come along."

They went together hand in hand to the village, and bought the new jug, and had it filled at the beer-shop. The thirsty father was at the upper end of the fields, where they were making a drain. Alban carried the jug until they were within sight of the laborer. "You haven't far to go," he said. "Mind you don't drop it again—What's the matter now?"

"I'm frightened."

"Why?"

"Oh, give me the jug."

She almost snatched it out of his hand. If she let the precious minutes slip away, there might be another beating in store for her at the drain: her father was not of an indulgent disposition when his children were late in bringing his beer. On the point of hurrying away, without a word of farewell, she remembered the laws of politeness as taught at the infant school—and dropped her little curtsey—and said, "Thank you, sir." That bitter sense of injury was still in Alban's mind as he looked after her. "What a pity she should grow up to be a woman!" he said to himself.

The adventure of the broken jug had delayed his return to his lodgings by more than half an hour. When he reached the road once more, the cheap up-train from the North had stopped at the station. He heard the ringing of the bell as it resumed the journey to London.

One of the passengers (judging by the handbag that she carried) had not stopped at the village.

As she advanced toward him along the road, he remarked that she was a small wiry active woman—dressed in bright colors, combined with a deplorable want of taste. Her aquiline nose seemed to be her most striking feature as she came nearer. It might have been fairly proportioned to the rest of her face, in her younger days, before her cheeks had lost flesh and roundness. Being probably near-sighted, she kept her eyes half-closed; there were cunning little wrinkles at the corners of them. In spite of appearances, she was unwilling to present any outward acknowledgment of the march of time. Her hair was palpably dyed—her hat was jauntily set on her head, and ornamented with a gay feather. She walked with a light tripping step, swinging her bag, and holding her head up smartly. Her manner, like her dress, said as plainly as words could speak, "No matter how long I may have lived, I mean to be young and charming to the end of my days." To Alban's surprise she stopped and addressed him.

"Oh, I beg your pardon. Could you tell me if I am in the right road to

Miss Ladd's school?"

She spoke with nervous rapidity of articulation, and with a singularly unpleasant smile. It parted her thin lips just widely enough to show her suspiciously beautiful teeth; and it opened her keen gray eyes in the strangest manner. The higher lid rose so as to disclose, for a moment, the upper part of the eyeball, and to give her the appearance—not of a woman bent on making herself agreeable, but of a woman staring in a panic of terror. Careless to conceal the unfavorable impression that she had produced on him, Alban answered roughly, "Straight on," and tried to pass her.

She stopped him with a peremptory gesture. "I have treated you politely," she said, "and how do you treat me in return? Well! I am not surprised. Men are all brutes by nature—and you are a man. 'Straight on'?" she repeated contemptuously; "I should like to know how far that helps a person in a strange place. Perhaps you know no more where Miss Ladd's school is than I do? or, perhaps, you don't care to take the trouble of addressing me? Just what I should have expected from a person of your sex! Good-morning."

Alban felt the reproof; she had appealed to his most readily-impressible sense—his sense of humor. He rather enjoyed seeing his own prejudice against women grotesquely reflected in this flighty stranger's prejudice against men. As the best excuse for himself that he could make, he gave her all the information that she could possibly want—then tried again to pass on—and again in vain. He had recovered his place in her estimation: she had not done with him yet.

"You know all about the way there," she said "I wonder whether you know anything about the school?"

No change in her voice, no change in her manner, betrayed any special motive for putting this question. Alban was on the point of suggesting that she should go on to the school, and make her inquiries there—when he happened to notice her eyes. She had hitherto looked him straight in the face. She now looked down on the road. It was a trifling change; in all probability it meant nothing—and yet, merely because it was a change, it roused his curiosity. "I ought to know something about the school," he answered. "I am one of the masters."

"Then you're just the man I want. May I ask your name?"

"Alban Morris."

"Thank you. I am Mrs. Rook. I presume you have heard of Sir Jervis Redwood?"

"No."

"Bless my soul! You are a scholar, of course—and you have never heard of one of your own trade. Very extraordinary. You see, I am Sir Jervis's housekeeper; and I am sent here to take one of your young ladies back with me to our place. Don't interrupt me! Don't be a brute again! Sir Jervis is not of a communicative disposition. At least, not to me. A man—that explains it—a man! He is always poring over his books and writings; and Miss Redwood, at her great age, is in bed half the day. Not a thing do I know about this new inmate of ours, except that I am to take her back with me. You would feel some curiosity yourself in my place, wouldn't you? Now do tell me. What sort of girl is Miss Emily Brown?"

The name that he was perpetually thinking of—on this woman's lips! Alban looked at her.

"Well," said Mrs. Rook, "am I to have no answer? Ah, you want leading. So like a man again! Is she pretty?"

Still examining the housekeeper with mingled feelings of interest and distrust, Alban answered ungraciously:

"Yes."

"Good-tempered?"

Alban again said "Yes."

"So much about herself," Mrs. Rook remarked. "About her family now?" She shifted her bag restlessly from one hand to another. "Perhaps you can tell me if Miss Emily's father—" she suddenly corrected herself—"if Miss Emily's parents are living?"

"I don't know."

"You mean you won't tell me."

"I mean exactly what I have said."

"Oh, it doesn't matter," Mrs. Rook rejoined; "I shall find out at the school. The first turning to the left, I think you said—across the fields?"

He was too deeply interested in Emily to let the housekeeper go without putting a question on his side:

"Is Sir Jervis Redwood one of Miss Emily's old friends?" he asked.

"He? What put that into your head? He has never even seen Miss Emily. She's going to our house—ah, the women are getting the upper hand now, and serve the men right, I say!—she's going to our house to be Sir Jervis's secretary. You would like to have the place yourself, wouldn't you? You would like to keep a poor girl from getting her own living? Oh, you may look as fierce as you please—the time's gone by when a man could frighten me. I like her Christian name. I call Emily a nice name enough. But 'Brown'! Good-morning, Mr. Morris; you and I are not cursed with such a contemptibly common name as that! 'Brown'? Oh, Lord!"

She tossed her head scornfully, and walked away, humming a tune.

Alban stood rooted to the spot. The effort of his later life had been to conceal the hopeless passion which had mastered him in spite of himself. Knowing nothing from Emily—who at once pitied and avoided him—of her family circumstances or of her future plans, he had shrunk from making inquiries of others, in the fear that they, too, might find out his secret, and that their contempt might be added to the contempt which he felt for himself. In this position, and with these obstacles in his way, the announcement of Emily's proposed journey—under the care of a stranger, to fill an employment in the house of a stranger—not only took him by surprise, but inspired him with a strong feeling of distrust. He looked after Sir Jervis Redwood's flighty housekeeper, completely forgetting the purpose which had brought him thus far on the way to his lodgings. Before Mrs. Rook was out of sight, Alban Morris was following her back to the school.

CHAPTER VII. "COMING EVENTS CAST THEIR SHADOWS BEFORE."

Miss De Sor and Miss Wyvil were still sitting together under the trees, talking of the murder at the inn.

"And is that really all you can tell me?" said Francine.

"That is all," Cecilia answered.

"Is there no love in it?"

"None that I know of."

"It's the most uninteresting murder that ever was committed. What shall we do with ourselves? I'm tired of being here in the garden. When do the performances in the schoolroom begin?"

"Not for two hours yet."

Francine yawned. "And what part do you take in it?" she asked.

"No part, my dear. I tried once—only to sing a simple little song. When I found myself standing before all the company and saw rows of ladies and gentlemen waiting for me to begin, I was so frightened that Miss Ladd had to make an apology for me. I didn't get over it for the rest of the day. For the first time in my life, I had no appetite for my dinner. Horrible!" said Cecilia, shuddering over the remembrance of it. "I do assure you, I thought I was going to die."

Perfectly unimpressed by this harrowing narrative, Francine turned her head lazily toward the house. The door was thrown open at the same moment. A lithe little person rapidly descended the steps that led to the lawn.

"It's Emily come back again," said Francine.

"And she seems to be rather in a hurry," Cecilia remarked.

Francine's satirical smile showed itself for a moment. Did this appearance of hurry in Emily's movements denote impatience to resume the recital of "the dagger-scene"? She had no book in her hand; she never even looked toward Francine. Sorrow became plainly visible in her face as she approached the two girls.

Cecilia rose in alarm. She had been the first person to whom Emily had confided her domestic anxieties. "Bad news from your aunt?" she asked.

"No, my dear; no news at all." Emily put her arms tenderly round her friend's neck. "The time has come, Cecilia," she said. "We must wish each other good-by."

"Is Mrs. Rook here already?"

"It's you, dear, who are going," Emily answered sadly. "They have sent the governess to fetch you. Miss Ladd is too busy in the schoolroom to see her—and she has told me all about it. Don't be alarmed. There is no bad news from home. Your plans are altered; that's all."

"Altered?" Cecilia repeated. "In what way?"

"In a very agreeable way—you are going to travel. Your father wishes you to be in London, in time for the evening mail to France."

Cecilia guessed what had happened. "My sister is not getting well," she said, "and the doctors are sending her to the Continent."

"To the baths at St. Moritz," Emily added. "There is only one difficulty in the way; and you can remove it. Your sister has the good old governess to take care of her, and the courier to relieve her of all trouble on the journey. They were to have started yesterday. You know how fond Julia is of you. At the last moment, she won't hear of going away, unless you go too. The rooms are waiting at St. Moritz; and your father is annoyed (the governess says) by the delay that has taken place already."

She paused. Cecilia was silent. "Surely you don't hesitate?" Emily said.

"I am too happy to go wherever Julia goes," Cecilia answered warmly; "I was thinking of you, dear." Her tender nature, shrinking from the hard necessities of life, shrank from the cruelly-close prospect of parting. "I thought we were to have had some hours together yet," she said. "Why are we hurried in this way? There is no second train to London, from our station, till late in the afternoon."

"There is the express," Emily reminded her; "and there is time to catch it, if you drive at once to the town." She took Cecilia's hand and pressed it to her bosom. "Thank you again and again, dear, for all you have done for me. Whether we meet again or not, as long as I live I shall love you. Don't cry!" She made a faint attempt to resume her customary gayety, for Cecilia's sake. "Try to be as hard-hearted as I am. Think of your sister—don't think of me. Only kiss me."

Cecilia's tears fell fast. "Oh, my love, I am so anxious about you! I am so afraid that you will not be happy with that selfish old man—in that dreary house. Give it up, Emily! I have got plenty of money for both of us; come abroad with me. Why not? You always got on well with Julia, when you came to see us in the holidays. Oh, my darling! my darling! What shall I do without you?"

All that longed for love in Emily's nature had clung round her school-friend since her father's death. Turning deadly pale under the struggle to control herself, she made the effort—and bore the pain of it without letting a cry or a tear escape her. "Our ways in life lie far apart," she said gently. "There is the hope of meeting again, dear—if there is nothing more."

The clasp of Cecilia's arm tightened round her. She tried to release herself; but her resolution had reached its limits. Her hands dropped, trembling. She could still try to speak cheerfully, and that was all.

"There is not the least reason, Cecilia, to be anxious about my prospects. I mean to be Sir Jervis Redwood's favorite before I have been a week in his service."

She stopped, and pointed to the house. The governess was approaching them. "One more kiss, darling. We shall not forget the happy hours we have spent together; we shall constantly write to each other." She broke down at last. "Oh, Cecilia! Cecilia! leave me for God's sake—I can't bear it any longer!"

210

The governess parted them. Emily dropped into the chair that her friend had left. Even her hopeful nature sank under the burden of life at that moment.

A hard voice, speaking close at her side, startled her.

"Would you rather be Me," the voice asked, "without a creature to care for you?"

Emily raised her head. Francine, the unnoticed witness of the parting interview, was standing by her, idly picking the leaves from a rose which had dropped out of Cecilia's nosegay.

Had she felt her own isolated position? She had felt it resentfully.

Emily looked at her, with a heart softened by sorrow. There was no answering kindness in the eyes of Miss de Sor—there was only a dogged endurance, sad to see in a creature so young.

"You and Cecilia are going to write to each other," she said. "I suppose there is some comfort in that. When I left the island they were glad to get rid of me. They said, 'Telegraph when you are safe at Miss Ladd's school.' You see, we are so rich, the expense of telegraphing to the West Indies is nothing to us. Besides, a telegram has an advantage over a letter—it doesn't take long to read. I daresay I shall write home. But they are in no hurry; and I am in no hurry. The school's breaking up; you are going your way, and I am going mine—and who cares what becomes of me? Only an ugly old schoolmistress, who is paid for caring. I wonder why I am saying all this? Because I like you? I don't know that I like you any better than you like me. When I wanted to be friends with you, you treated me coolly; I don't want to force myself on you. I don't particularly care about you. May I write to you from Brighton?"

Under all this bitterness—the first exhibition of Francine's temper, at its worst, which had taken place since she joined the school—Emily saw, or thought she saw, distress that was too proud, or too shy, to show itself. "How can you ask the question?" she answered cordially.

Francine was incapable of meeting the sympathy offered to her, even half way. "Never mind how," she said. "Yes or no is all I want from you."

"Oh, Francine! Francine! what are you made of! Flesh and blood? or stone and iron? Write to me of course—and I will write back again."

"Thank you. Are you going to stay here under the trees?"

"Yes."

"All by yourself?"

"All by myself."

"With nothing to do?"

"I can think of Cecilia."

Francine eyed her with steady attention for a moment.

"Didn't you tell me last night that you were very poor?" she asked.

"I did."

"So poor that you are obliged to earn your own living?"

"Yes."

Francine looked at her again.

"I daresay you won't believe me," she said. "I wish I was you."

She turned away irritably, and walked back to the house.

Were there really longings for kindness and love under the surface of this girl's perverse nature? Or was there nothing to be hoped from a better knowledge of her?—In place of tender remembrances of Cecilia, these were the perplexing and unwelcome thoughts which the more potent personality of Francine forced upon Emily's mind.

She rose impatiently, and looked at her watch. When would it be her turn to leave the school, and begin the new life?

Still undecided what to do next, her interest was excited by the appearance of one of the servants on the lawn. The woman approached her, and presented a visiting-card; bearing on it the name of Sir Jervis Redwood. Beneath the name, there was a line written in pencil: "Mrs. Rook, to wait on Miss Emily Brown." The way to the new life was open before her at last!

Looking again at the commonplace announcement contained in the line of writing, she was not quite satisfied. Was it claiming a deference toward herself, to which she was not entitled, to expect a letter either from Sir Jervis, or from Miss Redwood; giving her some information as to the journey which she was about to undertake, and expressing with some little politeness the wish to make her comfortable in her future home? At any rate, her employer had done her one service: he had reminded her that her station in life was not what it had been in the days when her father was living, and when her aunt was in affluent circumstances.

She looked up from the card. The servant had gone. Alban Morris was waiting at a little distance—waiting silently until she noticed him.

CHAPTER VIII. MASTER AND PUPIL.

Emily's impulse was to avoid the drawing-master for the second time. The moment afterward, a kinder feeling prevailed. The farewell interview with Cecilia had left influences which pleaded for Alban Morris. It was the day of parting good wishes and general separations: he had only perhaps come to say good-by. She advanced to offer her hand, when he stopped her by pointing to Sir Jervis Redwood's card.

"May I say a word, Miss Emily, about that woman?" he asked

"Do you mean Mrs. Rook?"

"Yes. You know, of course, why she comes here?"

"She comes here by appointment, to take me to Sir Jervis Redwood's house. Are you acquainted with her?"

"She is a perfect stranger to me. I met her by accident on her way here. If Mrs. Rook had been content with asking me to direct her to the school, I should not be troubling you at this moment. But she forced her conversation on me. And she said something which I think you ought to know. Have you heard of Sir Jervis Redwood's housekeeper before to-day?"

"I have only heard what my friend—Miss Cecilia Wyvil—has told me."

"Did Miss Cecilia tell you that Mrs. Rook was acquainted with your father or with any members of your family?"

"Certainly not!"

Alban reflected. "It was natural enough," he resumed, "that Mrs. Rook should feel some curiosity about You. What reason had she for putting a question to me about your father—and putting it in a very strange manner?"

Emily's interest was instantly excited. She led the way back to the seats in the shade. "Tell me, Mr. Morris, exactly what the woman said." As she spoke, she signed to him to be seated.

Alban observed the natural grace of her action when she set him the example of taking a chair, and the little heightening of her color caused by anxiety to hear what he had still to tell her. Forgetting the restraint that he had hitherto imposed on himself, he enjoyed the luxury of silently admiring her. Her manner betrayed none of the conscious confusion which would have shown itself, if her heart had been secretly inclined toward him. She saw the man looking at her. In simple perplexity she looked at the man.

"Are you hesitating on my account?" she asked. "Did Mrs. Rook say something of my father which I mustn't hear?"

"No, no! nothing of the sort!"

"You seem to be confused."

Her innocent indifference tried his patience sorely. His memory went back to the past time—recalled the ill-placed passion of his youth, and the cruel injury inflicted on him—his pride was roused. Was he making himself ridiculous? The vehement throbbing of his heart almost suffocated him. And there she sat, wondering at his odd behavior. "Even this girl is as cold-blooded as the rest of her sex!" That angry thought gave him back his self-control. He made his excuses with the easy politeness of a man of the world.

"I beg your pardon, Miss Emily; I was considering how to put what I have to say in the fewest and plainest words. Let me try if I can do it. If Mrs. Rook had merely asked me whether your father and mother were living, I should have attributed the question to the commonplace curiosity of a gossiping woman, and have thought no more of it. What she actually did say was this: 'Perhaps you can tell me if Miss Emily's father——' There she checked herself, and suddenly altered the question in this way: 'If Miss Emily's parents are living?' I may be making mountains out of molehills; but I thought at the time (and think still) that she had some special interest in inquiring after your father, and, not wishing me to notice it for reasons of her own, changed the form of the question so as to include your mother. Does this strike you as a far-fetched conclusion?"

"Whatever it may be," Emily said, "it is my conclusion, too. How did you answer her?"

"Quite easily. I could give her no information—and I said so."

"Let me offer you the information, Mr. Morris, before we say anything more. I have lost both my parents."

Alban's momentary outbreak of irritability was at an end. He was earnest and yet gentle, again; he forgave her for not understanding how dear and how delightful to him she was. "Will it distress you," he said, "if I ask how long it is since your father died?"

"Nearly four years," she replied. "He was the most generous of men; Mrs. Rook's interest in him may surely have been a grateful interest. He may have been kind to her in past years—and she may remember him thankfully. Don't you think so?"

Alban was unable to agree with her. "If Mrs. Rook's interest in your father was the harmless interest that you have suggested," he said, "why should she have checked herself in that unaccountable manner, when she first asked me if he was living? The more I think of it now, the less sure I feel that she knows anything at all of your family history. It may help me to decide, if you will tell me at what time the death of your mother took place."

"So long ago," Emily replied, "that I can't even remember her death. I was an infant at the time."

"And yet Mrs. Rook asked me if your 'parents' were living! One of two things," Alban concluded. "Either there is some mystery in this matter, which we cannot hope to penetrate at present—or Mrs. Rook may have been speaking at random; on the chance of discovering whether you are related to some 'Mr. Brown' whom she once knew."

"Besides," Emily added, "it's only fair to remember what a common family name mine is, and how easily people may make mistakes. I should like to know if my dear lost father was really in her mind when she spoke to you. Do you think I could find it out?"

"If Mrs. Rook has any reasons for concealment, I believe you would have no chance of finding it out—unless, indeed, you could take her by surprise."

"In what way, Mr. Morris?"

"Only one way occurs to me just now," he said. "Do you happen to have a miniature or a photograph of your father?"

Emily held out a handsome locket, with a monogram in diamonds, attached to her watch chain. "I have his photograph here," she rejoined; "given to me by my dear old aunt, in the days of her prosperity. Shall I show it to Mrs. Rook?"

"Yes—if she happens, by good luck, to offer you an opportunity."

Impatient to try the experiment, Emily rose as he spoke. "I mustn't keep Mrs. Rook waiting," she said.

Alban stopped her, on the point of leaving him. The confusion and hesitation which she had already noticed began to show themselves in his manner once more.

"Miss Emily, may I ask you a favor before you go? I am only one of the masters employed in the school; but I don't think—let me say, I hope I am

216

not guilty of presumption—if I offer to be of some small service to one of my pupils—"

There his embarrassment mastered him. He despised himself not only for yielding to his own weakness, but for faltering like a fool in the expression of a simple request. The next words died away on his lips.

This time, Emily understood him.

The subtle penetration which had long since led her to the discovery of his secret—overpowered, thus far, by the absorbing interest of the moment—now recovered its activity. In an instant, she remembered that Alban's motive for cautioning her, in her coming intercourse with Mrs. Rook, was not the merely friendly motive which might have actuated him, in the case of one of the other girls. At the same time, her quickness of apprehension warned her not to risk encouraging this persistent lover, by betraying any embarrassment on her side. He was evidently anxious to be present (in her interests) at the interview with Mrs. Rook. Why not? Could he reproach her with raising false hope, if she accepted his services, under circumstances of doubt and difficulty which he had himself been the first to point out? He could do nothing of the sort. Without waiting until he had recovered himself, she answered him (to all appearances) as composedly as if he had spoken to her in the plainest terms.

"After all that you have told me," she said, "I shall indeed feel obliged if you will be present when I see Mrs. Rook."

The eager brightening of his eyes, the flush of happiness that made him look young on a sudden, were signs not to be mistaken. The sooner they were in the presence of a third person (Emily privately concluded) the better it might be for both of them. She led the way rapidly to the house.

CHAPTER IX. MRS. ROOK AND THE LOCKET.

As mistress of a prosperous school, bearing a widely-extended reputation, Miss Ladd prided herself on the liberality of her household arrangements. At breakfast and dinner, not only the solid comforts but the elegant luxuries of the table, were set before the young ladies "Other schools may, and no doubt do, offer to pupils the affectionate care to which they have been accustomed under the parents' roof," Miss Ladd used to say. "At my school, that care extends to their meals, and provides them with a cuisine which, I flatter myself, equals the most successful efforts of the cooks at home." Fathers, mothers, and friends, when they paid visits to this excellent lady, brought away with them the most gratifying recollections of her hospitality. The men, in particular, seldom failed to recognize in their hostess the rarest virtue that a single lady can possess—the virtue of putting wine on the table which may be gratefully remembered by her guests the next morning.

An agreeable surprise awaited Mrs. Rook when she entered the house of bountiful Miss Ladd.

Luncheon was ready for Sir Jervis Redwood's confidential emissary in the waiting-room. Detained at the final rehearsals of music and recitation, Miss Ladd was worthily represented by cold chicken and ham, a fruit tart, and a pint decanter of generous sherry. "Your mistress is a perfect lady!" Mrs. Rook said to the servant, with a burst of enthusiasm. "I can carve for myself, thank you; and I don't care how long Miss Emily keeps me waiting."

As they ascended the steps leading into the house, Alban asked Emily if he might look again at her locket.

"Shall I open it for you?" she suggested.

"No: I only want to look at the outside of it."

He examined the side on which the monogram appeared, inlaid with diamonds. An inscription was engraved beneath.

"May I read it?" he said.

"Certainly!"

The inscription ran thus: "In loving memory of my father. Died 30th September, 1877."

"Can you arrange the locket," Alban asked, "so that the side on which the diamonds appear hangs outward?"

She understood him. The diamonds might attract Mrs. Rook's notice; and in that case, she might ask to see the locket of her own accord. "You are beginning to be of use to me, already," Emily said, as they turned into the corridor which led to the waiting-room.

They found Sir Jervis's housekeeper luxuriously recumbent in the easiest chair in the room.

Of the eatable part of the lunch some relics were yet left. In the pint decanter of sherry, not a drop remained. The genial influence of the wine (hastened by the hot weather) was visible in Mrs. Rook's flushed face, and in a special development of her ugly smile. Her widening lips stretched to new lengths; and the white upper line of her eyeballs were more freely and horribly visible than ever.

"And this is the dear young lady?" she said, lifting her hands in over-acted admiration. At the first greetings, Alban perceived that the impression produced was, in Emily's case as in his case, instantly unfavorable.

The servant came in to clear the table. Emily stepped aside for a minute to give some directions about her luggage. In that interval Mrs. Rook's cunning little eyes turned on Alban with an expression of malicious scrutiny.

"You were walking the other way," she whispered, "when I met you." She stopped, and glanced over her shoulder at Emily. "I see what attraction has brought you back to the school. Steal your way into that poor little fool's heart; and then make her miserable for the rest of her life!—No need, miss, to hurry," she said, shifting the polite side of her toward Emily, who returned at the moment. "The visits of the trains to your station here are like the visits of the angels described by the poet, 'few and far between.' Please excuse the quotation. You wouldn't think it to look at me—I'm a great reader."

"Is it a long journey to Sir Jervis Redwood's house?" Emily asked, at a loss what else to say to a woman who was already becoming unendurable to her.

Mrs. Rook looked at the journey from an oppressively cheerful point of view.

"Oh, Miss Emily, you shan't feel the time hang heavy in my company. I can converse on a variety of topics, and if there is one thing more than another that I like, it's amusing a pretty young lady. You think me a strange creature, don't you? It's only my high spirits. Nothing strange about me—unless it's my queer Christian name. You look a little dull, my dear. Shall I begin amusing you before we are on the railway? Shall I tell you how I came by my queer name?"

Thus far, Alban had controlled himself. This last specimen of the housekeeper's audacious familiarity reached the limits of his endurance.

"We don't care to know how you came by your name," he said.

"Rude," Mrs. Rook remarked, composedly. "But nothing surprises me, coming from a man."

She turned to Emily. "My father and mother were a wicked married couple," she continued, "before I was born. They 'got religion,' as the saying is, at a Methodist meeting in a field. When I came into the world—I don't know how you feel, miss; I protest against being brought into the world without asking my leave first—my mother was determined to dedicate me to piety, before I was out of my long clothes. What name do you suppose she had me christened by? She chose it, or made it, herself—the name of 'Righteous'! Righteous Rook! Was there ever a poor baby degraded by such a ridiculous name before? It's needless to say, when I write letters, I sign R. Rook—and leave people to think it's Rosamond, or Rosabelle, or something sweetly pretty of that kind. You should have seen my husband's face when he first heard that his sweetheart's name was 'Righteous'! He was on the point of kissing me, and he stopped. I daresay he felt sick. Perfectly natural under the circumstances."

Alban tried to stop her again. "What time does the train go?" he asked.

Emily entreated him to restrain himself, by a look. Mrs. Rook was still too inveterately amiable to take offense. She opened her traveling-bag briskly, and placed a railway guide in Alban's hands.

"I've heard that the women do the men's work in foreign parts," she said.

"But this is England; and I am an Englishwoman. Find out when the train goes, my dear sir, for yourself."

Alban at once consulted the guide. If there proved to be no immediate need of starting for the station, he was determined that Emily should not be condemned to pass the interval in the housekeeper's company. In the meantime, Mrs. Rook was as eager as ever to show her dear young lady what an amusing companion she could be.

"Talking of husbands," she resumed, "don't make the mistake, my dear, that I committed. Beware of letting anybody persuade you to marry an old man. Mr. Rook is old enough to be my father. I bear with him. Of course, I bear with him. At the same time, I have not (as the poet says) 'passed through the ordeal unscathed.' My spirit—I have long since ceased to believe in anything of the sort: I only use the word for want of a better—my spirit, I say, has become embittered. I was once a pious young woman; I do assure you I was nearly as good as my name. Don't let me shock you; I have lost faith and hope; I have become—what's the last new name for a free-thinker? Oh, I keep up with the times, thanks to old Miss Redwood! She takes in the newspapers, and makes me read them to her. What is the new name? Something ending in ic. Bombastic? No, Agnostic?—that's it! I have become an Agnostic. The inevitable result of marrying an old man; if there's any blame it rests on my husband."

"There's more than an hour yet before the train starts," Alban interposed. "I am sure, Miss Emily, you would find it pleasanter to wait in the garden."

"Not at all a bad notion," Mrs. Rook declared. "Here's a man who can make himself useful, for once. Let's go into the garden."

She rose, and led the way to the door. Alban seized the opportunity of whispering to Emily.

"Did you notice the empty decanter, when we first came in? That horrid woman is drunk."

Emily pointed significantly to the locket. "Don't let her go. The garden will distract her attention: keep her near me here."

Mrs. Rook gayly opened the door. "Take me to the flower-beds," she said. "I believe in nothing—but I adore flowers."

Mrs. Rook waited at the door, with her eye on Emily. "What do you say, miss?"

"I think we shall be more comfortable if we stay where we are."

"Whatever pleases you, my dear, pleases me." With this reply, the compliant housekeeper—as amiable as ever on the surface—returned to her chair.

Would she notice the locket as she sat down? Emily turned toward the window, so as to let the light fall on the diamonds.

No: Mrs. Rook was absorbed, at the moment, in her own reflections. Miss Emily, having prevented her from seeing the garden, she was maliciously bent on disappointing Miss Emily in return. Sir Jervis's secretary (being young) took a hopeful view no doubt of her future prospects. Mrs. Rook decided on darkening that view in a mischievously-suggestive manner, peculiar to herself.

"You will naturally feel some curiosity about your new home," she began, "and I haven't said a word about it yet. How very thoughtless of me! Inside and out, dear Miss Emily, our house is just a little dull. I say our house, and why not—when the management of it is all thrown on me. We are built of stone; and we are much too long, and are not half high enough. Our situation is on the coldest side of the county, away in the west. We are close to the Cheviot hills; and if you fancy there is anything to see when you look out of window, except sheep, you will find yourself woefully mistaken. As for walks, if you go out on one side of the house you may, or may not, be gored by cattle. On the other side, if the darkness overtakes you, you may, or may not, tumble down a deserted lead mine. But the company, inside the house, makes amends for it all," Mrs. Rook proceeded, enjoying the expression of dismay which was beginning to show itself on Emily's face. "Plenty of excitement for you, my dear, in our small family. Sir Jervis will introduce you to plaster casts of hideous Indian idols; he will keep you writing for him, without mercy, from morning to night; and when he does let you go, old Miss Redwood will find she can't sleep, and will send for the pretty young lady-secretary to read to her. My husband I am sure you will like. He is a respectable man, and bears the highest character. Next to the idols, he's the most hideous object in the house. If you are good enough to encourage him, I don't say that he won't amuse you; he will tell you, for instance, he never in his life hated any human being as he hates his wife. By the way, I must not forget—in the interests of truth, you know—to mention one drawback that does exist in our domestic circle. One of these days we shall have our brains blown out or our throats cut. Sir Jervis's mother left him ten thousand pounds' worth of precious stones all contained in a little cabinet with drawers. He won't let the banker take care of his jewels; he won't sell them; he won't even wear one of the rings on his finger, or one of the pins at his breast. He keeps his cabinet on his dressing-room table; and he says, 'I like to gloat over my jewels, every night, before I go to bed.' Ten thousand pounds' worth of diamonds, rubies, emeralds, sapphires, and what not—at the mercy of the first robber who happens to hear of them. Oh, my dear, he would have no choice, I do assure you, but to use his pistols. We shouldn't quietly submit to be robbed. Sir Jervis inherits the spirit of his ancestors. My husband has the temper of a game cock. I myself, in defense of the property of my employers, am capable of becoming a perfect fiend. And we none of us understand the use of firearms!"

While she was in full enjoyment of this last aggravation of the horrors of the prospect, Emily tried another change of position—and, this time, with success. Greedy admiration suddenly opened Mrs. Rook's little eyes to their utmost width. "My heart alive, miss, what do I see at your watch-chain? How they sparkle! Might I ask for a closer view?"

Emily's fingers trembled; but she succeeded in detaching the locket from the chain. Alban handed it to Mrs. Rook.

She began by admiring the diamonds—with a certain reserve. "Nothing like so large as Sir Jervis's diamonds; but choice specimens no doubt. Might I ask what the value—?"

She stopped. The inscription had attracted her notice: she began to read it aloud: "In loving memory of my father. Died—"

Her face instantly became rigid. The next words were suspended on her lips.

Alban seized the chance of making her betray herself—under pretense of helping her. "Perhaps you find the figures not easy to read," he said. "The date is 'thirtieth September, eighteen hundred and seventy-seven'—nearly four years since."

Not a word, not a movement, escaped Mrs. Rook. She held the locket before her as she had held it from the first. Alban looked at Emily. Her eyes were riveted on the housekeeper: she was barely capable of preserving the appearance of composure. Seeing the necessity of acting for her, he at once said the words which she was unable to say for herself.

"Perhaps, Mrs. Rook, you would like to look at the portrait?" he suggested. "Shall I open the locket for you?"

Without speaking, without looking up, she handed the locket to Alban.

He opened it, and offered it to her. She neither accepted nor refused it: her hands remained hanging over the arms of the chair. He put the locket on her lap.

The portrait produced no marked effect on Mrs. Rook. Had the date prepared her to see it? She sat looking at it—still without moving: still without saying a word. Alban had no mercy on her. "That is the portrait of Miss Emily's father," he said. "Does it represent the same Mr. Brown whom you had in your mind when you asked me if Miss Emily's father was still living?"

That question roused her. She looked up, on the instant; she answered loudly and insolently: "No!"

"And yet," Alban persisted, "you broke down in reading the inscription: and considering what talkative woman you are, the portrait has had a strange effect on you—to say the least of it."

She eyed him steadily while he was speaking—and turned to Emily when he had done. "You mentioned the heat just now, miss. The heat has overcome me; I shall soon get right again."

224

The insolent futility of that excuse irritated Emily into answering her. "You will get right again perhaps all the sooner," she said, "if we trouble you with no more questions, and leave you to recover by yourself."

The first change of expression which relaxed the iron tensity of the housekeeper's face showed itself when she heard that reply. At last there was a feeling in Mrs. Rook which openly declared itself—a feeling of impatience to see Alban and Emily leave the room.

They left her, without a word more.

CHAPTER X. GUESSES AT THE TRUTH.

"What are we to do next? Oh, Mr. Morris, you must have seen all sorts of people in your time—you know human nature, and I don't. Help me with a word of advice!"

Emily forgot that he was in love with her—forgot everything, but the effect produced by the locket on Mrs. Rook, and the vaguely alarming conclusion to which it pointed. In the fervor of her anxiety she took Alban's arm as familiarly as if he had been her brother. He was gentle, he was considerate; he tried earnestly to compose her. "We can do nothing to any good purpose," he said, "unless we begin by thinking quietly. Pardon me for saying so—you are needlessly exciting yourself."

There was a reason for her excitement, of which he was necessarily ignorant. Her memory of the night interview with Miss Jethro had inevitably intensified the suspicion inspired by the conduct of Mrs. Rook. In less than twenty-four hours, Emily had seen two women shrinking from secret remembrances of her father—which might well be guilty remembrances— innocently excited by herself! How had they injured him? Of what infamy, on their parts, did his beloved and stainless memory remind them? Who could fathom the mystery of it? "What does it mean?" she cried, looking wildly in Alban's compassionate face. "You must have formed some idea of your own. What does it mean?"

"Come, and sit down, Miss Emily. We will try if we can find out what it means, together."

They returned to the shady solitude under the trees. Away, in front of the house, the distant grating of carriage wheels told of the arrival of Miss Ladd's guests, and of the speedy beginning of the ceremonies of the day.

"We must help each other," Alban resumed.

"When we first spoke of Mrs. Rook, you mentioned Miss Cecilia Wyvil as a person who knew something about her. Have you any objection to tell me what you may have heard in that way?"

In complying with his request Emily necessarily repeated what Cecilia had told Francine, when the two girls had met that morning in the garden.

Alban now knew how Emily had obtained employment as Sir Jervis's secretary; how Mr. and Mrs. Rook had been previously known to Cecilia's father as respectable people keeping an inn in his own neighborhood; and, finally, how they had been obliged to begin life again in domestic service, because the terrible event of a murder had given the inn a bad name, and had driven away the customers on whose encouragement their business depended.

Listening in silence, Alban remained silent when Emily's narrative had come to an end.

"Have you nothing to say to me?" she asked.

"I am thinking over what I have just heard," he answered.

Emily noticed a certain formality in his tone and manner, which disagreeably surprised her. He seemed to have made his reply as a mere concession to politeness, while he was thinking of something else which really interested him.

"Have I disappointed you in any way?" she asked.

"On the contrary, you have interested me. I want to be quite sure that I remember exactly what you have said. You mentioned, I think, that your friendship with Miss Cecilia Wyvil began here, at the school?"

"Yes."

"And in speaking of the murder at the village inn, you told me that the crime was committed—I have forgotten how long ago?"

His manner still suggested that he was idly talking about what she had told him, while some more important subject for reflection was in possession of his mind.

"I don't know that I said anything about the time that had passed since the crime was committed," she answered, sharply. "What does the murder matter to us? I think Cecilia told me it happened about four years since. Excuse me for noticing it, Mr. Morris—you seem to have some interests of your own to occupy your attention. Why couldn't you say so plainly when we came out here? I should not have asked you to help me, in that case. Since my poor father's death, I have been used to fight through my troubles by myself."

She rose, and looked at him proudly. The next moment her eyes filled with tears.

In spite of her resistance, Alban took her hand. "Dear Miss Emily," he said, "you distress me: you have not done me justice. Your interests only are in my mind."

Answering her in those terms, he had not spoken as frankly as usual. He had only told her a part of the truth.

Hearing that the woman whom they had just left had been landlady of an inn, and that a murder had been committed under her roof, he was led to ask himself if any explanation might be found, in these circumstances, of the otherwise incomprehensible effect produced on Mrs. Rook by the inscription on the locket.

In the pursuit of this inquiry there had arisen in his mind a monstrous suspicion, which pointed to Mrs. Rook. It impelled him to ascertain the date at which the murder had been committed, and (if the discovery encouraged further investigation) to find out next the manner in which Mr. Brown had died.

Thus far, what progress had he made? He had discovered that the date of Mr. Brown's death, inscribed on the locket, and the date of the crime committed at the inn, approached each other nearly enough to justify further investigation.

In the meantime, had he succeeded in keeping his object concealed from Emily? He had perfectly succeeded. Hearing him declare that her interests only had occupied his mind, the poor girl innocently entreated him to forgive her little outbreak of temper. "If you have any more questions to ask me, Mr. Morris, pray go on. I promise never to think unjustly of you again."

He went on with an uneasy conscience—for it seemed cruel to deceive her, even in the interests of truth—but still he went on.

"Suppose we assume that this woman had injured your father in some way," he said. "Am I right in believing that it was in his character to forgive injuries?"

"Entirely right."

"In that case, his death may have left Mrs. Rook in a position to be called to account, by those who owe a duty to his memory—I mean the surviving members of his family."

"There are but two of us, Mr. Morris. My aunt and myself."

"There are his executors."

"My aunt is his only executor."

"Your father's sister—I presume?"

"Yes."

"He may have left instructions with her, which might be of the greatest use to us."

"I will write to-day, and find out," Emily replied. "I had already planned to consult my aunt," she added, thinking again of Miss Jethro.

"If your aunt has not received any positive instructions," Alban continued, "she may remember some allusion to Mrs. Rook, on your father's part, at the time of his last illness—"

228

Emily stopped him. "You don't know how my dear father died," she said. "He was struck down—apparently in perfect health—by disease of the heart."

"Struck down in his own house?"

"Yes—in his own house."

Those words closed Alban's lips. The investigation so carefully and so delicately conducted had failed to serve any useful purpose. He had now ascertained the manner of Mr. Brown's death and the place of Mr. Brown's death—and he was as far from confirming his suspicions of Mrs. Rook as ever.

CHAPTER XI. THE DRAWING-MASTER'S CONFESSION.

"Is there nothing else you can suggest?" Emily asked.

"Nothing—at present."

"If my aunt fails us, have we no other hope?"

"I have hope in Mrs. Rook," Alban answered. "I see I surprise you; but I really mean what I say. Sir Jervis's housekeeper is an excitable woman, and she is fond of wine. There is always a weak side in the character of such a person as that. If we wait for our chance, and turn it to the right use when it comes, we may yet succeed in making her betray herself."

Emily listened to him in bewilderment.

"You talk as if I was sure of your help in the future," she said. "Have you forgotten that I leave school to-day, never to return? In half an hour more, I shall be condemned to a long journey in the company of that horrible creature—with a life to look forward to, in the same house with her, among strangers! A miserable prospect, and a hard trial of a girl's courage—is it not, Mr. Morris?"

"You will at least have one person, Miss Emily, who will try with all his heart and soul to encourage you."

"What do you mean?"

"I mean," said Alban, quietly, "that the Midsummer vacation begins to-day; and that the drawing-master is going to spend his holidays in the North."

Emily jumped up from her chair. "You!" she exclaimed. "You are going to Northumberland? With me?"

"Why not?" Alban asked. "The railway is open to all travelers alike, if they have money enough to buy a ticket."

"Mr. Morris! what can you be thinking of? Indeed, indeed, I am not ungrateful. I know you mean kindly—you are a good, generous man. But do remember how completely a girl, in my position, is at the mercy of appearances. You, traveling in the same carriage with me! and that woman putting her own vile interpretation on it, and degrading me in Sir Jervis Redwood's estimation, on the day when I enter his house! Oh, it's worse than thoughtless—it's madness, downright madness."

"You are quite right," Alban gravely agreed, "it is madness. I lost whatever little reason I once possessed, Miss Emily, on the day when I first met you out walking with the young ladies of the school."

Emily turned away in significant silence. Alban followed her.

"You promised just now," he said, "never to think unjustly of me again. I respect and admire you far too sincerely to take a base advantage of this occasion—the only occasion on which I have been permitted to speak with you alone. Wait a little before you condemn a man whom you don't understand. I will say nothing to annoy you—I only ask leave to explain myself. Will you take your chair again?"

She returned unwillingly to her seat. "It can only end," she thought, sadly, "in my disappointing him!"

"I have had the worst possible opinion of women for years past," Alban resumed; "and the only reason I can give for it condemns me out of my own mouth. I have been infamously treated by one woman; and my wounded self-esteem has meanly revenged itself by reviling the whole sex. Wait a little, Miss Emily. My fault has received its fit punishment. I have been thoroughly humiliated—and you have done it."

"Mr. Morris!"

"Take no offense, pray, where no offense is meant. Some few years since it was the great misfortune of my life to meet with a Jilt. You know what I mean?"

"Yes."

"She was my equal by birth (I am a younger son of a country squire), and my superior in rank. I can honestly tell you that I was fool enough to love her with all my heart and soul. She never allowed me to doubt—I may say this without conceit, remembering the miserable end of it—that my feeling for her was returned. Her father and mother (excellent people) approved of the contemplated marriage. She accepted my presents; she allowed all the customary preparations for a wedding to proceed to completion; she had not even mercy enough, or shame enough, to prevent me from publicly degrading myself by waiting for her at the altar, in the presence of a large congregation. The minutes passed—and no bride appeared. The clergyman, waiting like me, was requested to return to the vestry. I was invited to follow him. You foresee the end of the story, of course? She had run away with another man. But can you guess who the man was? Her groom!"

Emily's face reddened with indignation. "She suffered for it? Oh, Mr. Morris, surely she suffered for it?"

"Not at all. She had money enough to reward the groom for marrying her; and she let herself down easily to her husband's level. It was a suitable marriage in every respect. When I last heard of them, they were regularly in the habit of getting drunk together. I am afraid I have disgusted you? We will drop the subject, and resume my precious autobiography at a later date. One showery day in the autumn of last year, you young ladies went out with Miss Ladd for a walk. When you were all trotting back again, under your umbrellas, did you (in particular) notice an ill-tempered fellow standing in the road, and getting a good look at you, on the high footpath above him?"

Emily smiled, in spite of herself. "I don't remember it," she said.

"You wore a brown jacket which fitted you as if you had been born in it—and you had the smartest little straw hat I ever saw on a woman's head. It was the first time I ever noticed such things. I think I could paint a portrait of the boots you wore (mud included), from memory alone. That was the impression you produced on me. After believing, honestly believing, that love was one of the lost illusions of my life—after feeling, honestly feeling, that I would as soon look at the devil as look at a woman—there was the state of mind to which retribution had reduced me; using for his instrument Miss Emily Brown. Oh, don't be afraid of what I may say next! In your presence, and out of your presence, I am man enough to be ashamed of my own folly. I am resisting your influence over me at this moment, with the strongest of all resolutions—the resolution of despair. Let's look at the humorous side of the story again. What do you think I did when the regiment of young ladies had passed by me?"

Emily declined to guess.

"I followed you back to the school; and, on pretense of having a daughter to educate, I got one of Miss Ladd's prospectuses from the porter at the lodge gate. I was in your neighborhood, you must know, on a sketching tour. I went back to my inn, and seriously considered what had happened to me. The result of my cogitations was that I went abroad. Only for a change—not at all because I was trying to weaken the impression you had produced on me! After a while I returned to England. Only because I was tired of traveling— not at all because your influence drew me back! Another interval passed; and luck turned my way, for a wonder. The drawing-master's place became vacant here. Miss Ladd advertised; I produced my testimonials; and took the situation. Only because the salary was a welcome certainty to a poor man— not at all because the new position brought me into personal association with Miss Emily Brown! Do you begin to see why I have troubled you with all this talk about myself? Apply the contemptible system of self-delusion which my confession has revealed, to that holiday arrangement for a tour in the north which has astonished and annoyed you. I am going to travel this afternoon by your train. Only because I feel an intelligent longing to see the northernmost county of England—not at all because I won't let you trust yourself alone with

Mrs. Rook! Not at all because I won't leave you to enter Sir Jervis Redwood's service without a friend within reach in case you want him! Mad? Oh, yes—perfectly mad. But, tell me this: What do all sensible people do when they find themselves in the company of a lunatic? They humor him. Let me take your ticket and see your luggage labeled: I only ask leave to be your traveling servant. If you are proud—I shall like you all the better, if you are—pay me wages, and keep me in my proper place in that way."

Some girls, addressed with this reckless intermingling of jest and earnest, would have felt confused, and some would have felt flattered. With a good-tempered resolution, which never passed the limits of modesty and refinement, Emily met Alban Morris on his own ground.

"You have said you respect me," she began; "I am going to prove that I believe you. The least I can do is not to misinterpret you, on my side. Am I to understand, Mr. Morris—you won't think the worse of me, I hope, if I speak plainly—am I to understand that you are in love with me?"

"Yes, Miss Emily—if you please."

He had answered with the quaint gravity which was peculiar to him; but he was already conscious of a sense of discouragement. Her composure was a bad sign—from his point of view.

"My time will come, I daresay," she proceeded. "At present I know nothing of love, by experience; I only know what some of my schoolfellows talk about in secret. Judging by what they tell me, a girl blushes when her lover pleads with her to favor his addresses. Am I blushing?"

"Must I speak plainly, too?" Alban asked.

"If you have no objection," she answered, as composedly as if she had been addressing her grandfather.

"Then, Miss Emily, I must say—you are not blushing."

She went on. "Another token of love—as I am informed—is to tremble. Am I trembling?"

"No."

"Am I too confused to look at you?"

"No."

"Do I walk away with dignity—and then stop, and steal a timid glance at my lover, over my shoulder?"

"I wish you did!"

"A plain answer, Mr. Morris! Yes or No."

"No—of course."

"In one last word, do I give you any sort of encouragement to try again?"

"In one last word, I have made a fool of myself—and you have taken the kindest possible way of telling me so."

This time, she made no attempt to reply in his own tone. The good-humored gayety of her manner disappeared. She was in earnest—truly, sadly in earnest—when she said her next words.

"Is it not best, in your own interests, that we should bid each other good-by?" she asked. "In the time to come—when you only remember how kind you once were to me—we may look forward to meeting again. After all that you have suffered, so bitterly and so undeservedly, don't, pray don't, make me feel that another woman has behaved cruelly to you, and that I—so grieved to distress you—am that heartless creature!"

Never in her life had she been so irresistibly charming as she was at that moment. Her sweet nature showed all its innocent pity for him in her face.

He saw it—he felt it—he was not unworthy of it. In silence, he lifted her hand to his lips. He turned pale as he kissed it.

"Say that you agree with me?" she pleaded.

"I obey you."

As he answered, he pointed to the lawn at their feet. "Look," he said, "at that dead leaf which the air is wafting over the grass. Is it possible that such sympathy as you feel for Me, such love as I feel for You, can waste, wither, and fall to the ground like that leaf? I leave you, Emily—with the firm conviction that there is a time of fulfillment to come in our two lives. Happen what may in the interval—I trust the future."

The words had barely passed his lips when the voice of one of the servants reached them from the house. "Miss Emily, are you in the garden?"

Emily stepped out into the sunshine. The servant hurried to meet her, and placed a telegram in her hand. She looked at it with a sudden misgiving. In her small experience, a telegram was associated with the communication of bad news. She conquered her hesitation—opened it—read it. The color left her face: she shuddered. The telegram dropped on the grass.

"Read it," she said, faintly, as Alban picked it up.

He read these words: "Come to London directly. Miss Letitia is dangerously ill."

"Your aunt?" he asked.

"Yes—my aunt."

BOOK THE SECOND—IN LONDON.

CHAPTER XII. MRS. ELLMOTHER.

The metropolis of Great Britain is, in certain respects, like no other metropolis on the face of the earth. In the population that throngs the streets, the extremes of Wealth and the extremes of Poverty meet, as they meet nowhere else. In the streets themselves, the glory and the shame of architecture—the mansion and the hovel—are neighbors in situation, as they are neighbors nowhere else. London, in its social aspect, is the city of contrasts.

Toward the close of evening Emily left the railway terminus for the place of residence in which loss of fortune had compelled her aunt to take refuge. As she approached her destination, the cab passed—by merely crossing a road—from a spacious and beautiful Park, with its surrounding houses topped by statues and cupolas, to a row of cottages, hard by a stinking ditch miscalled a canal. The city of contrasts: north and south, east and west, the city of social contrasts.

Emily stopped the cab before the garden gate of a cottage, at the further end of the row. The bell was answered by the one servant now in her aunt's employ—Miss Letitia's maid.

Personally, this good creature was one of the ill-fated women whose appearance suggests that Nature intended to make men of them and altered her mind at the last moment. Miss Letitia's maid was tall and gaunt and awkward. The first impression produced by her face was an impression of bones. They rose high on her forehead; they projected on her cheeks; and they reached their boldest development in her jaws. In the cavernous eyes of this unfortunate person rigid obstinacy and rigid goodness looked out together, with equal severity, on all her fellow-creatures alike. Her mistress (whom she had served for a quarter of a century and more) called her "Bony." She accepted this cruelly appropriate nick-name as a mark of affectionate familiarity which honored a servant. No other person was allowed to take liberties with her: to every one but her mistress she was known as Mrs. Ellmother.

"How is my aunt?" Emily asked.

"Bad."

"Why have I not heard of her illness before?"

"Because she's too fond of you to let you be distressed about her. 'Don't tell Emily'; those were her orders, as long as she kept her senses."

"Kept her senses? Good heavens! what do you mean?"

"Fever—that's what I mean."

"I must see her directly; I am not afraid of infection."

"There's no infection to be afraid of. But you mustn't see her, for all that."

"I insist on seeing her."

"Miss Emily, I am disappointing you for your own good. Don't you know me well enough to trust me by this time?"

"I do trust you."

"Then leave my mistress to me—and go and make yourself comfortable in your own room."

Emily's answer was a positive refusal. Mrs. Ellmother, driven to her last resources, raised a new obstacle.

"It's not to be done, I tell you! How can you see Miss Letitia when she can't bear the light in her room? Do you know what color her eyes are? Red, poor soul—red as a boiled lobster."

With every word the woman uttered, Emily's perplexity and distress increased.

"You told me my aunt's illness was fever," she said—"and now you speak of some complaint in her eyes. Stand out of the way, if you please, and let me go to her."

Mrs. Ellmother, still keeping her place, looked through the open door.

"Here's the doctor," she announced. "It seems I can't satisfy you; ask him what's the matter. Come in, doctor." She threw open the door of the parlor, and introduced Emily. "This is the mistress's niece, sir. Please try if you can keep her quiet. I can't." She placed chairs with the hospitable politeness of the old school—and returned to her post at Miss Letitia's bedside.

Doctor Allday was an elderly man, with a cool manner and a ruddy complexion—thoroughly acclimatized to the atmosphere of pain and grief in which it was his destiny to live. He spoke to Emily (without any undue familiarity) as if he had been accustomed to see her for the greater part of her life.

"That's a curious woman," he said, when Mrs. Ellmother closed the door; "the most headstrong person, I think, I ever met with. But devoted to her mistress, and, making allowance for her awkwardness, not a bad nurse. I am afraid I can't give you an encouraging report of your aunt. The rheumatic fever (aggravated by the situation of this house—built on clay, you know, and close to stagnant water) has been latterly complicated by delirium."

"Is that a bad sign, sir?"

"The worst possible sign; it shows that the disease has affected the heart. Yes: she is suffering from inflammation of the eyes, but that is an unimportant symptom. We can keep the pain under by means of cooling lotions and a dark room. I've often heard her speak of you—especially since the illness assumed a serious character. What did you say? Will she know you, when you go into her room? This is about the time when the delirium usually sets in. I'll see if there's a quiet interval."

He opened the door—and came back again.

"By the way," he resumed, "I ought perhaps to explain how it was that I took the liberty of sending you that telegram. Mrs. Ellmother refused to inform you of her mistress's serious illness. That circumstance, according to my view of it, laid the responsibility on the doctor's shoulders. The form taken by your aunt's delirium—I mean the apparent tendency of the words that escape her in that state—seems to excite some incomprehensible feeling in the mind of her crabbed servant. She wouldn't even let me go into the bedroom, if she could possibly help it. Did Mrs. Ellmother give you a warm welcome when you came here?"

"Far from it. My arrival seemed to annoy her."

"Ah—just what I expected. These faithful old servants always end by presuming on their fidelity. Did you ever hear what a witty poet—I forget his name: he lived to be ninety—said of the man who had been his valet for more than half a century? 'For thirty years he was the best of servants; and for thirty years he has been the hardest of masters.' Quite true—I might say the same of my housekeeper. Rather a good story, isn't it?"

The story was completely thrown away on Emily; but one subject interested her now. "My poor aunt has always been fond of me," she said. "Perhaps she might know me, when she recognizes nobody else."

"Not very likely," the doctor answered. "But there's no laying down any rule in cases of this kind. I have sometimes observed that circumstances which have produced a strong impression on patients, when they are in a state of health, give a certain direction to the wandering of their minds, when they are in a state of fever. You will say, 'I am not a circumstance; I don't see how this encourages me to hope'—and you will be quite right. Instead of talking of my medical experience, I shall do better to look at Miss Letitia, and let you know the result. You have got other relations, I suppose? No? Very distressing—very distressing."

Who has not suffered as Emily suffered, when she was left alone? Are there not moments—if we dare to confess the truth—when poor humanity loses its hold on the consolations of religion and the hope of immortality, and feels the cruelty of creation that bids us live, on the condition that we die, and leads the first warm beginnings of love, with merciless certainty, to the cold conclusion of the grave?

"She's quiet, for the time being," Dr. Allday announced, on his return. "Remember, please, that she can't see you in the inflamed state of her eyes, and don't disturb the bed-curtains. The sooner you go to her the better, perhaps—if you have anything to say which depends on her recognizing your voice. I'll call to-morrow morning. Very distressing," he repeated, taking his hat and making his bow—"Very distressing."

Emily crossed the narrow little passage which separated the two rooms, and opened the bed-chamber door. Mrs. Ellmother met her on the threshold. "No," said the obstinate old servant, "you can't come in."

The faint voice of Miss Letitia made itself heard, calling Mrs. Ellmother by her familiar nick-name.

"Bony, who is it?"

"Never mind."

"Who is it?"

"Miss Emily, if you must know."

"Oh! poor dear, why does she come here? Who told her I was ill?"

"The doctor told her."

"Don't come in, Emily. It will only distress you—and it will do me no good. God bless you, my love. Don't come in."

"There!" said Mrs. Ellmother. "Do you hear that? Go back to the sitting-room."

Thus far, the hard necessity of controlling herself had kept Emily silent. She was now able to speak without tears. "Remember the old times, aunt," she pleaded, gently. "Don't keep me out of your room, when I have come here to nurse you!"

"I'm her nurse. Go back to the sitting-room," Mrs. Ellmother repeated.

True love lasts while life lasts. The dying woman relented.

"Bony! Bony! I can't be unkind to Emily. Let her in."

240

Mrs. Ellmother still insisted on having her way.

"You're contradicting your own orders," she said to her mistress. "You don't know how soon you may begin wandering in your mind again. Think, Miss Letitia—think."

This remonstrance was received in silence. Mrs. Ellmother's great gaunt figure still blocked up the doorway.

"If you force me to it," Emily said, quietly, "I must go to the doctor, and ask him to interfere."

"Do you mean that?" Mrs. Ellmother said, quietly, on her side.

"I do mean it," was the answer.

The old servant suddenly submitted—with a look which took Emily by surprise. She had expected to see anger; the face that now confronted her was a face subdued by sorrow and fear.

"I wash my hands of it," Mrs. Ellmother said. "Go in—and take the consequences."

CHAPTER XIII. MISS LETITIA.

Emily entered the room. The door was immediately closed on her from the outer side. Mrs. Ellmother's heavy steps were heard retreating along the passage. Then the banging of the door that led into the kitchen shook the flimsily-built cottage. Then, there was silence.

The dim light of a lamp hidden away in a corner and screened by a dingy green shade, just revealed the closely-curtained bed, and the table near it bearing medicine-bottles and glasses. The only objects on the chimney-piece were a clock that had been stopped in mercy to the sufferer's irritable nerves, and an open case containing a machine for pouring drops into the eyes. The smell of fumigating pastilles hung heavily on the air. To Emily's excited imagination, the silence was like the silence of death. She approached the bed trembling. "Won't you speak to me, aunt?"

"Is that you, Emily? Who let you come in?"

"You said I might come in, dear. Are you thirsty? I see some lemonade on the table. Shall I give it to you?"

"No! If you open the bed-curtains, you let in the light. My poor eyes! Why are you here, my dear? Why are you not at the school?"

"It's holiday-time, aunt. Besides, I have left school for good."

"Left school?" Miss Letitia's memory made an effort, as she repeated those words. "You were going somewhere when you left school," she said, "and Cecilia Wyvil had something to do with it. Oh, my love, how cruel of you to go away to a stranger, when you might live here with me!" She paused—her sense of what she had herself just said began to grow confused. "What stranger?" she asked abruptly. "Was it a man? What name? Oh, my mind! Has death got hold of my mind before my body?"

"Hush! hush! I'll tell you the name. Sir Jervis Redwood."

"I don't know him. I don't want to know him. Do you think he means to send for you. Perhaps he has sent for you. I won't allow it! You shan't go!"

"Don't excite yourself, dear! I have refused to go; I mean to stay here with you."

The fevered brain held to its last idea. "Has he sent for you?" she said again, louder than before.

Emily replied once more, in terms carefully chosen with the one purpose of pacifying her. The attempt proved to be useless, and worse—it seemed to make her suspicious. "I won't be deceived!" she said; "I mean to know all about it. He did send for you. Whom did he send?"

"His housekeeper."

"What name?" The tone in which she put the question told of excitement that was rising to its climax. "Don't you know that I'm curious about names?" she burst out. "Why do you provoke me? Who is it?"

"Nobody you know, or need care about, dear aunt. Mrs. Rook."

Instantly on the utterance of that name, there followed an unexpected result. Silence ensued.

Emily waited—hesitated—advanced, to part the curtains, and look in at her aunt. She was stopped by a dreadful sound of laughter—the cheerless laughter that is heard among the mad. It suddenly ended in a dreary sigh.

Afraid to look in, she spoke, hardly knowing what she said. "Is there anything you wish for? Shall I call—?"

Miss Letitia's voice interrupted her. Dull, low, rapidly muttering, it was unlike, shockingly unlike, the familiar voice of her aunt. It said strange words.

"Mrs. Rook? What does Mrs. Rook matter? Or her husband either? Bony, Bony, you're frightened about nothing. Where's the danger of those two people turning up? Do you know how many miles away the village is? Oh, you fool—a hundred miles and more. Never mind the coroner, the coroner must keep in his own district—and the jury too. A risky deception? I call it a pious fraud. And I have a tender conscience, and a cultivated mind. The newspaper? How is our newspaper to find its way to her, I should like to know? You poor old Bony! Upon my word you do me good—you make me laugh."

The cheerless laughter broke out again—and died away again drearily in a sigh.

Accustomed to decide rapidly in the ordinary emergencies of her life, Emily felt herself painfully embarrassed by the position in which she was now placed.

After what she had already heard, could she reconcile it to her sense of duty to her aunt to remain any longer in the room?

In the hopeless self-betrayal of delirium, Miss Letitia had revealed some act of concealment, committed in her past life, and confided to her faithful old servant. Under these circumstances, had Emily made any discoveries which convicted her of taking a base advantage of her position at the bedside? Most assuredly not! The nature of the act of concealment; the causes that had led to it; the person (or persons) affected by it—these were mysteries which left her entirely in the dark. She had found out that her aunt was acquainted with Mrs. Rook, and that was literally all she knew.

Blameless, so far, in the line of conduct that she had pursued, might she still remain in the bed-chamber—on this distinct understanding with herself: that she would instantly return to the sitting-room if she heard anything which could suggest a doubt of Miss Letitia's claim to her affection and respect? After some hesitation, she decided on leaving it to her conscience to answer that question. Does conscience ever say, No—when inclination says, Yes? Emily's conscience sided with her reluctance to leave her aunt.

Throughout the time occupied by these reflections, the silence had remained unbroken. Emily began to feel uneasy. She timidly put her hand through the curtains, and took Miss Letitia's hand. The contact with the burning skin startled her. She turned away to the door, to call the servant— when the sound of her aunt's voice hurried her back to the bed.

"Are you there, Bony?" the voice asked.

Was her mind getting clear again? Emily tried the experiment of making a plain reply. "Your niece is with you," she said. "Shall I call the servant?"

Miss Letitia's mind was still far away from Emily, and from the present time.

"The servant?" she repeated. "All the servants but you, Bony, have been sent away. London's the place for us. No gossiping servants and no curious neighbors in London. Bury the horrid truth in London. Ah, you may well say I look anxious and wretched. I hate deception—and yet, it must be done. Why do you waste time in talking? Why don't you find out where the vile woman lives? Only let me get at her—and I'll make Sara ashamed of herself."

Emily's heart beat fast when she heard the woman's name. "Sara" (as she and her school-fellows knew) was the baptismal name of Miss Jethro. Had her aunt alluded to the disgraced teacher, or to some other woman?

She waited eagerly to hear more. There was nothing to be heard. At this most interesting moment, the silence remained undisturbed.

In the fervor of her anxiety to set her doubts at rest, Emily's faith in her own good resolutions began to waver. The temptation to say something which might set her aunt talking again was too strong to be resisted—if she remained at the bedside. Despairing of herself she rose and turned to the door. In the moment that passed while she crossed the room the very words occurred to her that would suit her purpose. Her cheeks were hot with shame—she hesitated—she looked back at the bed—the words passed her lips.

"Sara is only one of the woman's names," she said. "Do you like her other name?"

The rapidly-muttering tones broke out again instantly—but not in answer to Emily. The sound of a voice had encouraged Miss Letitia to pursue her own confused train of thought, and had stimulated the fast-failing capacity of speech to exert itself once more.

"No! no! He's too cunning for you, and too cunning for me. He doesn't leave letters about; he destroys them all. Did I say he was too cunning for us? It's false. We are too cunning for him. Who found the morsels of his letter in the basket? Who stuck them together? Ah, we know! Don't read it, Bony. 'Dear Miss Jethro'—don't read it again. 'Miss Jethro' in his letter; and 'Sara,' when he talks to himself in the garden. Oh, who would have believed it of him, if we hadn't seen and heard it ourselves!"

There was no more doubt now.

But who was the man, so bitterly and so regretfully alluded to?

No: this time Emily held firmly by the resolution which bound her to respect the helpless position of her aunt. The speediest way of summoning Mrs. Ellmother would be to ring the bell. As she touched the handle a faint cry of suffering from the bed called her back.

"Oh, so thirsty!" murmured the failing voice—"so thirsty!"

She parted the curtains. The shrouded lamplight just showed her the green shade over Miss Letitia's eyes—the hollow cheeks below it—the arms laid helplessly on the bed-clothes. "Oh, aunt, don't you know my voice? Don't you know Emily? Let me kiss you, dear!" Useless to plead with her; useless to kiss her; she only reiterated the words, "So thirsty! so thirsty!" Emily raised the poor tortured body with a patient caution which spared it pain, and put the glass to her aunt's lips. She drank the lemonade to the last drop. Refreshed for the moment, she spoke again—spoke to the visionary servant of her delirious fancy, while she rested in Emily's arms.

"For God's sake, take care how you answer if she questions you. If she knew what we know! Are men ever ashamed? Ha! the vile woman! the vile woman!"

Her voice, sinking gradually, dropped to a whisper. The next few words that escaped her were muttered inarticulately. Little by little, the false energy of fever was wearing itself out. She lay silent and still. To look at her now was to look at the image of death. Once more, Emily kissed her—closed the curtains—and rang the bell. Mrs. Ellmother failed to appear. Emily left the room to call her.

Arrived at the top of the kitchen stairs, she noted a slight change. The door below, which she had heard banged on first entering her aunt's room, now stood open. She called to Mrs. Ellmother. A strange voice answered her. Its accent was soft and courteous; presenting the strongest imaginable contrast to the harsh tones of Miss Letitia's crabbed old maid.

"Is there anything I can do for you, miss?"

The person making this polite inquiry appeared at the foot of the stairs—a plump and comely woman of middle age. She looked up at the young lady with a pleasant smile.

"I beg your pardon," Emily said; "I had no intention of disturbing you. I called to Mrs. Ellmother."

The stranger advanced a little way up the stairs, and answered, "Mrs. Ellmother is not here."

"Do you expect her back soon?"

"Excuse me, miss—I don't expect her back at all."

"Do you mean to say that she has left the house?"

"Yes, miss. She has left the house."

CHAPTER XIV. MRS. MOSEY.

Emily's first act—after the discovery of Mrs. Ellmother's incomprehensible disappearance—was to invite the new servant to follow her into the sitting-room.

"Can you explain this?" she began.

"No, miss."

"May I ask if you have come here by Mrs. Ellmother's invitation?"

"By Mrs. Ellmother's request, miss."

"Can you tell me how she came to make the request?"

"With pleasure, miss. Perhaps—as you find me here, a stranger to yourself, in place of the customary servant—I ought to begin by giving you a reference."

"And, perhaps (if you will be so kind), by mentioning your name," Emily added.

"Thank you for reminding me, miss. My name is Elizabeth Mosey. I am well known to the gentleman who attends Miss Letitia. Dr. Allday will speak to my character and also to my experience as a nurse. If it would be in any way satisfactory to give you a second reference—"

"Quite needless, Mrs. Mosey."

"Permit me to thank you again, miss. I was at home this evening, when Mrs. Ellmother called at my lodgings. Says she, 'I have come here, Elizabeth, to ask a favor of you for old friendship's sake.' Says I, 'My dear, pray command me, whatever it may be.' If this seems rather a hasty answer to make, before I knew what the favor was, might I ask you to bear in mind that Mrs. Ellmother put it to me 'for old friendship's sake'—alluding to my late husband, and to the business which we carried on at that time? Through no fault of ours, we got into difficulties. Persons whom we had trusted proved unworthy. Not to trouble you further, I may say at once, we should have been ruined, if our old friend Mrs. Ellmother had not come forward, and trusted us with the savings of her lifetime. The money was all paid back again, before my husband's death. But I don't consider—and, I think you won't consider—that the obligation was paid back too. Prudent or not prudent, there is nothing Mrs. Ellmother can ask of me that I am not willing to do. If I have put myself in an awkward situation (and I don't deny that it looks so) this is the only excuse, miss, that I can make for my conduct."

Mrs. Mosey was too fluent, and too fond of hearing the sound of her own eminently persuasive voice. Making allowance for these little drawbacks, the impression that she produced was decidedly favorable; and, however rashly she might have acted, her motive was beyond reproach. Having said some kind words to this effect, Emily led her back to the main interest of her narrative.

"Did Mrs. Ellmother give no reason for leaving my aunt, at such a time as this?" she asked.

"The very words I said to her, miss."

"And what did she say, by way of reply?"

"She burst out crying—a thing I have never known her to do before, in an experience of twenty years."

"And she really asked you to take her place here, at a moment's notice?"

"That was just what she did," Mrs. Mosey answered. "I had no need to tell her I was astonished; my lips spoke for me, no doubt. She's a hard woman in speech and manner, I admit. But there's more feeling in her than you would suppose. 'If you are the good friend I take you for,' she says, 'don't ask me for reasons; I am doing what is forced on me, and doing it with a heavy heart.' In my place, miss, would you have insisted on her explaining herself, after that? The one thing I naturally wanted to know was, if I could speak to some lady, in the position of mistress here, before I ventured to intrude. Mrs.

Ellmother understood that it was her duty to help me in this particular. Your poor aunt being out of the question she mentioned you."

"How did she speak of me? In an angry way?"

"No, indeed—quite the contrary. She says, 'You will find Miss Emily at the cottage. She is Miss Letitia's niece. Everybody likes her—and everybody is right.'"

"She really said that?"

"Those were her words. And, what is more, she gave me a message for you at parting. 'If Miss Emily is surprised' (that was how she put it) 'give her my duty and good wishes; and tell her to remember what I said, when she took my place at her aunt's bedside.' I don't presume to inquire what this means," said Mrs. Mosey respectfully, ready to hear what it meant, if Emily would only be so good as to tell her. "I deliver the message, miss, as it was delivered to me. After which, Mrs. Ellmother went her way, and I went mine."

"Do you know where she went?"

"No, miss."

"Have you nothing more to tell me?"

"Nothing more; except that she gave me my directions, of course, about the nursing. I took them down in writing—and you will find them in their proper place, with the prescriptions and the medicines."

Acting at once on this hint, Emily led the way to her aunt's room.

Miss Letitia was silent, when the new nurse softly parted the curtains—looked in—and drew them together again. Consulting her watch, Mrs. Mosey compared her written directions with the medicine-bottles on the table, and set one apart to be used at the appointed time. "Nothing, so far, to alarm us," she whispered. "You look sadly pale and tired, miss. Might I advise you to rest a little?"

"If there is any change, Mrs. Mosey—either for the better or the worse—

of course you will let me know?"

"Certainly, miss."

Emily returned to the sitting-room: not to rest (after all that she had heard), but to think.

Amid much that was unintelligible, certain plain conclusions presented themselves to her mind.

After what the doctor had already said to Emily, on the subject of delirium generally, Mrs. Ellmother's proceedings became intelligible: they proved that she knew by experience the perilous course taken by her mistress's wandering thoughts, when they expressed themselves in words. This explained the concealment of Miss Letitia's illness from her niece, as well as the reiterated efforts of the old servant to prevent Emily from entering the bedroom.

But the event which had just happened—that is to say, Mrs. Ellmother's sudden departure from the cottage—was not only of serious importance in itself, but pointed to a startling conclusion.

The faithful maid had left the mistress, whom she had loved and served, sinking under a fatal illness—and had put another woman in her place, careless of what that woman might discover by listening at the bedside— rather than confront Emily after she had been within hearing of her aunt while the brain of the suffering woman was deranged by fever. There was the state of the case, in plain words.

In what frame of mind had Mrs. Ellmother adopted this desperate course of action?

To use her own expression, she had deserted Miss Letitia "with a heavy heart." To judge by her own language addressed to Mrs. Mosey, she had left Emily to the mercy of a stranger—animated, nevertheless, by sincere feelings of attachment and respect. That her fears had taken for granted suspicion which Emily had not felt, and discoveries which Emily had (as yet) not made, in no way modified the serious nature of the inference which her conduct justified. The disclosure which this woman dreaded—who could doubt it now?—directly threatened Emily's peace of mind. There was no disguising it: the innocent niece was associated with an act of deception, which had been, until that day, the undetected secret of the aunt and the aunt's maid.

In this conclusion, and in this only, was to be found the rational explanation of Mrs. Ellmother's choice—placed between the alternatives of submitting to discovery by Emily, or of leaving the house.

Poor Miss Letitia's writing-table stood near the window of the sitting-room. Shrinking from the further pursuit of thoughts which might end in disposing her mind to distrust of her dying aunt, Emily looked round in search of some employment sufficiently interesting to absorb her attention. The writing-table reminded her that she owed a letter to Cecilia. That helpful friend had surely the first claim to know why she had failed to keep her engagement with Sir Jervis Redwood.

After mentioning the telegram which had followed Mrs. Rook's arrival at the school, Emily's letter proceeded in these terms:

"As soon as I had in some degree recovered myself, I informed Mrs. Rook of my aunt's serious illness.

"Although she carefully confined herself to commonplace expressions of sympathy, I could see that it was equally a relief to both of us to feel that we were prevented from being traveling companions. Don't suppose that I have taken a capricious dislike to Mrs. Rook—or that you are in any way to blame for the unfavorable impression which she has produced on me. I will make this plain when we meet. In the meanwhile, I need only tell you that I gave her a letter of explanation to present to Sir Jervis Redwood. I also informed him of my address in London: adding a request that he would forward your letter, in case you have written to me before you receive these lines.

"Kind Mr. Alban Morris accompanied me to the railway-station, and arranged with the guard to take special care of me on the journey to London. We used to think him rather a heartless man. We were quite wrong. I don't know what his plans are for spending the summer holidays. Go where he may, I remember his kindness; my best wishes go with him.

"My dear, I must not sadden your enjoyment of your pleasant visit to the Engadine, by writing at any length of the sorrow that I am suffering. You know how I love my aunt, and how gratefully I have always felt her motherly goodness to me. The doctor does not conceal the truth. At her age, there is no hope: my father's last-left relation, my one dearest friend, is dying.

"No! I must not forget that I have another friend—I must find some comfort in thinking of you.

"I do so long in my solitude for a letter from my dear Cecilia. Nobody comes to see me, when I most want sympathy; I am a stranger in this vast city. The members of my mother's family are settled in Australia: they have not even written to me, in all the long years that have passed since her death. You remember how cheerfully I used to look forward to my new life, on leaving school? Good-by, my darling. While I can see your sweet face, in my thoughts, I don't despair—dark as it looks now—of the future that is before me."

Emily had closed and addressed her letter, and was just rising from her chair, when she heard the voice of the new nurse at the door.

CHAPTER XV. EMILY.

"May I say a word?" Mrs. Mosey inquired. She entered the room—pale and trembling. Seeing that ominous change, Emily dropped back into her chair.

"Dead?" she said faintly.

Mrs. Mosey looked at her in vacant surprise.

"I wish to say, miss, that your aunt has frightened me."

Even that vague allusion was enough for Emily.

"You need say no more," she replied. "I know but too well how my aunt's mind is affected by the fever."

Confused and frightened as she was, Mrs. Mosey still found relief in her customary flow of words.

"Many and many a person have I nursed in fever," she announced. "Many and many a person have I heard say strange things. Never yet, miss, in all my experience—!"

"Don't tell me of it!" Emily interposed.

"Oh, but I must tell you! In your own interests, Miss Emily—in your own interests. I won't be inhuman enough to leave you alone in the house to-night; but if this delirium goes on, I must ask you to get another nurse. Shocking suspicions are lying in wait for me in that bedroom, as it were. I can't resist them as I ought, if I go back again, and hear your aunt saying what she has been saying for the last half hour and more. Mrs. Ellmother has expected impossibilities of me; and Mrs. Ellmother must take the consequences. I don't say she didn't warn me—speaking, you will please to understand, in the strictest confidence. 'Elizabeth,' she says, 'you know how wildly people talk in Miss Letitia's present condition. Pay no heed to it,' she says. 'Let it go in at one ear and out at the other,' she says. 'If Miss Emily asks questions—you know nothing about it. If she's frightened—you know nothing about it. If she bursts into fits of crying that are dreadful to see, pity her, poor thing, but take no notice.' All very well, and sounds like speaking out, doesn't it? Nothing of the sort! Mrs. Ellmother warns me to expect this, that, and the other. But there is one horrid thing (which I heard, mind, over and over again at your aunt's bedside) that she does not prepare me for; and that horrid thing is—Murder!"

At that last word, Mrs. Mosey dropped her voice to a whisper—and waited to see what effect she had produced.

Sorely tried already by the cruel perplexities of her position, Emily's courage failed to resist the first sensation of horror, aroused in her by the climax of the nurse's hysterical narrative. Encouraged by her silence, Mrs. Mosey went on. She lifted one hand with theatrical solemnity—and luxuriously terrified herself with her own horrors.

"An inn, Miss Emily; a lonely inn, somewhere in the country; and a comfortless room at the inn, with a makeshift bed at one end of it, and a makeshift bed at the other—I give you my word of honor, that was how your aunt put it. She spoke of two men next; two men asleep (you understand) in the two beds. I think she called them 'gentlemen'; but I can't be sure, and I wouldn't deceive you—you know I wouldn't deceive you, for the world. Miss Letitia muttered and mumbled, poor soul. I own I was getting tired of listening—when she burst out plain again, in that one horrid word—Oh, miss, don't be impatient! don't interrupt me!"

Emily did interrupt, nevertheless. In some degree at least she had recovered herself. "No more of it!" she said—"I won't hear a word more."

But Mrs. Mosey was too resolutely bent on asserting her own importance, by making the most of the alarm that she had suffered, to be repressed by any ordinary method of remonstrance. Without paying the slightest attention to what Emily had said, she went on again more loudly and more excitably than ever.

"Listen, miss—listen! The dreadful part of it is to come; you haven't heard about the two gentlemen yet. One of them was murdered—what do you think of that!—and the other (I heard your aunt say it, in so many words) committed the crime. Did Miss Letitia fancy she was addressing a lot of people when you were nursing her? She called out, like a person making public proclamation, when I was in her room. 'Whoever you are, good people' (she says), 'a hundred pounds reward, if you find the runaway murderer. Search everywhere for a poor weak womanish creature, with rings on his little white hands. There's nothing about him like a man, except his voice—a fine round voice. You'll know him, my friends—the wretch, the monster—you'll know him by his voice.' That was how she put it; I tell you again, that was how she put it. Did you hear her scream? Ah, my dear young lady, so much the better for you! 'O the horrid murder' (she says)—'hush it up!' I'll take my Bible oath before the magistrate," cried Mrs. Mosey, starting out of her chair, "your aunt said, 'Hush it up!'"

Emily crossed the room. The energy of her character was roused at last. She seized the foolish woman by the shoulders, forced her back in the chair, and looked her straight in the face without uttering a word.

For the moment, Mrs. Mosey was petrified. She had fully expected—

having reached the end of her terrible story—to find Emily at her feet, entreating her not to carry out her intention of leaving the cottage the next morning; and she had determined, after her sense of her own importance had been sufficiently flattered, to grant the prayer of the helpless young lady. Those were her anticipations—and how had they been fulfilled? She had been treated like a mad woman in a state of revolt!

"How dare you assault me?" she asked piteously. "You ought to be ashamed of yourself. God knows I meant well."

"You are not the first person," Emily answered, quietly releasing her, "who has done wrong with the best intentions."

"I did my duty, miss, when I told you what your aunt said."

"You forgot your duty when you listened to what my aunt said."

"Allow me to explain myself."

"No: not a word more on that subject shall pass between us. Remain here, if you please; I have something to suggest in your own interests. Wait, and compose yourself."

The purpose which had taken a foremost place in Emily's mind rested on the firm foundation of her love and pity for her aunt.

Now that she had regained the power to think, she felt a hateful doubt pressed on her by Mrs. Mosey's disclosures. Having taken for granted that there was a foundation in truth for what she herself had heard in her aunt's room, could she reasonably resist the conclusion that there must be a foundation in truth for what Mrs. Mosey had heard, under similar circumstances?

There was but one way of escaping from this dilemma—and Emily deliberately took it. She turned her back on her own convictions; and persuaded herself that she had been in the wrong, when she had attached importance to anything that her aunt had said, under the influence of delirium. Having adopted this conclusion, she resolved to face the prospect of a night's solitude by the death-bed—rather than permit Mrs. Mosey to have a second opportunity of drawing her own inferences from what she might hear in Miss Letitia's room.

"Do you mean to keep me waiting much longer, miss?"

"Not a moment longer, now you are composed again," Emily answered. "I have been thinking of what has happened; and I fail to see any necessity for putting off your departure until the doctor comes to-morrow morning. There is really no objection to your leaving me to-night."

"I beg your pardon, miss; there is an objection. I have already told you I can't reconcile it to my conscience to leave you here by yourself. I am not an inhuman woman," said Mrs. Mosey, putting her handkerchief to her eyes—smitten with pity for herself.

Emily tried the effect of a conciliatory reply. "I am grateful for your kindness in offering to stay with me," she said.

"Very good of you, I'm sure," Mrs. Mosey answered ironically. "But for all that, you persist in sending me away."

"I persist in thinking that there is no necessity for my keeping you here until to-morrow."

"Oh, have it your own way! I am not reduced to forcing my company on anybody."

Mrs. Mosey put her handkerchief in her pocket, and asserted her dignity. With head erect and slowly-marching steps she walked out of the room. Emily was left in the cottage, alone with her dying aunt.

CHAPTER XVI. MISS JETHRO.

A fortnight after the disappearance of Mrs. Ellmother, and the dismissal of Mrs. Mosey, Doctor Allday entered his consulting-room, punctual to the hour at which he was accustomed to receive patients.

An occasional wrinkling of his eyebrows, accompanied by an intermittent restlessness in his movements, appeared to indicate some disturbance of this worthy man's professional composure. His mind was indeed not at ease. Even the inexcitable old doctor had felt the attraction which had already conquered three such dissimilar people as Alban Morris, Cecilia Wyvil, and Francine de Sor. He was thinking of Emily.

A ring at the door-bell announced the arrival of the first patient.

The servant introduced a tall lady, dressed simply and elegantly in dark apparel. Noticeable features, of a Jewish cast—worn and haggard, but still preserving their grandeur of form—were visible through her veil. She moved with grace and dignity; and she stated her object in consulting Doctor Allday with the ease of a well-bred woman.

"I come to ask your opinion, sir, on the state of my heart," she said; "and I am recommended by a patient, who has consulted you with advantage to herself." She placed a card on the doctor's writing-desk, and added: "I have become acquainted with the lady, by being one of the lodgers in her house."

The doctor recognized the name—and the usual proceedings ensued. After careful examination, he arrived at a favorable conclusion. "I may tell you at once," he said—"there is no reason to be alarmed about the state of your heart."

"I have never felt any alarm about myself," she answered quietly. "A sudden death is an easy death. If one's affairs are settled, it seems, on that account, to be the death to prefer. My object was to settle my affairs—such as they are—if you had considered my life to be in danger. Is there nothing the matter with me?"

"I don't say that," the doctor replied. "The action of your heart is very feeble. Take the medicine that I shall prescribe; pay a little more attention to eating and drinking than ladies usually do; don't run upstairs, and don't fatigue yourself by violent exercise—and I see no reason why you shouldn't live to be an old woman."

"God forbid!" the lady said to herself. She turned away, and looked out of the window with a bitter smile.

Doctor Allday wrote his prescription. "Are you likely to make a long stay in London?" he asked.

"I am here for a little while only. Do you wish to see me again?"

"I should like to see you once more, before you go away—if you can make it convenient. What name shall I put on the prescription?"

"Miss Jethro."

"A remarkable name," the doctor said, in his matter-of-fact way.

Miss Jethro's bitter smile showed itself again.

Without otherwise noticing what Doctor Allday had said, she laid the consultation fee on the table. At the same moment, the footman appeared with a letter. "From Miss Emily Brown," he said. "No answer required."

He held the door open as he delivered the message, seeing that Miss Jethro was about to leave the room. She dismissed him by a gesture; and, returning to the table, pointed to the letter.

"Was your correspondent lately a pupil at Miss Ladd's school?" she inquired.

"My correspondent has just left Miss Ladd," the doctor answered. "Are you a friend of hers?"

"I am acquainted with her."

"You would be doing the poor child a kindness, if you would go and see her. She has no friends in London."

"Pardon me—she has an aunt."

"Her aunt died a week since."

"Are there no other relations?"

"None. A melancholy state of things, isn't it? She would have been absolutely alone in the house, if I had not sent one of my women servants to stay with her for the present. Did you know her father?"

Miss Jethro passed over the question, as if she had not heard it. "Has the young lady dismissed her aunt's servants?" she asked.

258

"Her aunt kept but one servant, ma'am. The woman has spared Miss Emily the trouble of dismissing her." He briefly alluded to Mrs. Ellmother's desertion of her mistress. "I can't explain it," he said when he had done. "Can you?"

"What makes you think, sir, that I can help you? I have never even heard of the servant—and the mistress was a stranger to me."

At Doctor Allday's age a man is not easily discouraged by reproof, even when it is administered by a handsome woman. "I thought you might have known Miss Emily's father," he persisted.

Miss Jethro rose, and wished him good-morning. "I must not occupy any more of your valuable time," she said.

"Suppose you wait a minute?" the doctor suggested.

Impenetrable as ever, he rang the bell. "Any patients in the waiting-room?" he inquired. "You see I have time to spare," he resumed, when the man had replied in the negative. "I take an interest in this poor girl; and I thought—"

"If you think that I take an interest in her, too," Miss Jethro interposed, "you are perfectly right—I knew her father," she added abruptly; the allusion to Emily having apparently reminded her of the question which she had hitherto declined to notice.

"In that case," Doctor Allday proceeded, "I want a word of advice. Won't you sit down?"

She took a chair in silence. An irregular movement in the lower part of her veil seemed to indicate that she was breathing with difficulty. The doctor observed her with close attention. "Let me see my prescription again," he said. Having added an ingredient, he handed it back with a word of explanation. "Your nerves are more out of order than I supposed. The hardest disease to cure that I know of is—worry."

The hint could hardly have been plainer; but it was lost on Miss Jethro. Whatever her troubles might be, her medical adviser was not made acquainted with them. Quietly folding up the prescription, she reminded him that he had proposed to ask her advice.

"In what way can I be of service to you?" she inquired.

"I am afraid I must try your patience," the doctor acknowledged, "if I am to answer that question plainly."

With these prefatory words, he described the events that had followed Mrs. Mosey's appearance at the cottage. "I am only doing justice to this foolish woman," he continued, "when I tell you that she came here, after she had left Miss Emily, and did her best to set matters right. I went to the poor girl directly—and I felt it my duty, after looking at her aunt, not to leave her alone for that night. When I got home the next morning, whom do you think I found waiting for me? Mrs. Ellmother!"

He stopped—in the expectation that Miss Jethro would express some surprise. Not a word passed her lips.

"Mrs. Ellmother's object was to ask how her mistress was going on," the doctor proceeded. "Every day while Miss Letitia still lived, she came here to make the same inquiry—without a word of explanation. On the day of the funeral, there she was at the church, dressed in deep mourning; and, as I can personally testify, crying bitterly. When the ceremony was over—can you believe it?—she slipped away before Miss Emily or I could speak to her. We have seen nothing more of her, and heard nothing more, from that time to this."

He stopped again, the silent lady still listening without making any remark.

"Have you no opinion to express?" the doctor asked bluntly.

"I am waiting," Miss Jethro answered.

"Waiting—for what?"

"I haven't heard yet, why you want my advice."

Doctor Allday's observation of humanity had hitherto reckoned want of caution among the deficient moral qualities in the natures of women. He set down Miss Jethro as a remarkable exception to a general rule.

"I want you to advise me as to the right course to take with Miss Emily," he said. "She has assured me she attaches no serious importance to her aunt's wanderings, when the poor old lady's fever was at its worst. I don't doubt that she speaks the truth—but I have my own reasons for being afraid that she is deceiving herself. Will you bear this in mind?"

"Yes—if it's necessary."

"In plain words, Miss Jethro, you think I am still wandering from the point. I have got to the point. Yesterday, Miss Emily told me that she hoped to be soon composed enough to examine the papers left by her aunt."

Miss Jethro suddenly turned in her chair, and looked at Doctor Allday.

"Are you beginning to feel interested?" the doctor asked mischievously.

She neither acknowledged nor denied it. "Go on"—was all she said.

"I don't know how you feel," he proceeded; "I am afraid of the discoveries which she may make; and I am strongly tempted to advise her to leave the proposed examination to her aunt's lawyer. Is there anything in your knowledge of Miss Emily's late father, which tells you that I am right?"

"Before I reply," said Miss Jethro, "it may not be amiss to let the young lady speak for herself."

"How is she to do that?" the doctor asked.

Miss Jethro pointed to the writing table. "Look there," she said. "You have not yet opened Miss Emily's letter."

CHAPTER XVII. DOCTOR ALLDAY.

Absorbed in the effort to overcome his patient's reserve, the doctor had forgotten Emily's letter. He opened it immediately.

After reading the first sentence, he looked up with an expression of annoyance. "She has begun the examination of the papers already," he said.

"Then I can be of no further use to you," Miss Jethro rejoined. She made a second attempt to leave the room.

Doctor Allday turned to the next page of the letter. "Stop!" he cried. "She has found something—and here it is."

He held up a small printed Handbill, which had been placed between the first and second pages. "Suppose you look at it?" he said.

"Whether I am interested in it or not?" Miss Jethro asked.

"You may be interested in what Miss Emily says about it in her letter."

"Do you propose to show me her letter?"

"I propose to read it to you."

Miss Jethro took the Handbill without further objection. It was expressed in these words:

"MURDER. 100 POUNDS REWARD.—Whereas a murder was committed on the thirtieth September, 1877, at the Hand-in-Hand Inn, in the village of Zeeland, Hampshire, the above reward will be paid to any person or persons whose exertions shall lead to the arrest and conviction of the suspected murderer. Name not known. Supposed age, between twenty and thirty years. A well-made man, of small stature. Fair complexion, delicate features, clear blue eyes. Hair light, and cut rather short. Clean shaven, with the exception of narrow half-whiskers. Small, white, well-shaped hands. Wore valuable rings on the two last fingers of the left hand. Dressed neatly in a dark-gray tourist-suit. Carried a knapsack, as if on a pedestrian excursion. Remarkably good voice, smooth, full, and persuasive. Ingratiating manners. Apply to the Chief Inspector, Metropolitan Police Office, London."

Miss Jethro laid aside the Handbill without any visible appearance of agitation. The doctor took up Emily's letter, and read as follows:

"You will be as much relieved as I was, my kind friend, when you look at the paper inclosed. I found it loose in a blank book, with cuttings from newspapers, and odd announcements of lost property and other curious things (all huddled together between the leaves), which my aunt no doubt intended to set in order and fix in their proper places. She must have been thinking of her book, poor soul, in her last illness. Here is the origin of those 'terrible words' which frightened stupid Mrs. Mosey! Is it not encouraging to have discovered such a confirmation of my opinion as this? I feel a new interest in looking over the papers that still remain to be examined—"

Before he could get to the end of the sentence Miss Jethro's agitation broke through her reserve.

"Do what you proposed to do!" she burst out vehemently. "Stop her at once from carrying her examination any further! If she hesitates, insist on it!"

At last Doctor Allday had triumphed! "It has been a long time coming," he remarked, in his cool way; "and it's all the more welcome on that account. You dread the discoveries she may make, Miss Jethro, as I do. And you know what those discoveries may be."

"What I do know, or don't know, is of no importance," she answered sharply.

"Excuse me, it is of very serious importance. I have no authority over this poor girl—I am not even an old friend. You tell me to insist. Help me to declare honestly that I know of circumstances which justify me; and I may insist to some purpose."

Miss Jethro lifted her veil for the first time, and eyed him searchingly.

"I believe I can trust you," she said. "Now listen! The one consideration on which I consent to open my lips, is consideration for Miss Emily's tranquillity. Promise me absolute secrecy, on your word of honor."

He gave the promise.

"I want to know one thing, first," Miss Jethro proceeded. "Did she tell you—as she once told me—that her father had died of heart-complaint?"

"Yes."

"Did you put any questions to her?"

"I asked how long ago it was."

"And she told you?"

"She told me."

"You wish to know, Doctor Allday, what discoveries Miss Emily may yet make, among her aunt's papers. Judge for yourself, when I tell you that she has been deceived about her father's death."

"Do you mean that he is still living?"

"I mean that she has been deceived—purposely deceived—about the manner of his death."

"Who was the wretch who did it?"

"You are wronging the dead, sir! The truth can only have been concealed out of the purest motives of love and pity. I don't desire to disguise the conclusion at which I have arrived after what I have heard from yourself. The person responsible must be Miss Emily's aunt—and the old servant must have been in her confidence. Remember! You are bound in honor not to repeat to any living creature what I have just said."

The doctor followed Miss Jethro to the door. "You have not yet told me," he said, "how her father died."

"I have no more to tell you."

With those words she left him.

He rang for his servant. To wait until the hour at which he was accustomed to go out, might be to leave Emily's peace of mind at the mercy of an accident. "I am going to the cottage," he said. "If anybody wants me, I shall be back in a quarter of an hour."

On the point of leaving the house, he remembered that Emily would probably expect him to return the Handbill. As he took it up, the first lines caught his eye: he read the date at which the murder had been committed, for the second time. On a sudden the ruddy color left his face.

"Good God!" he cried, "her father was murdered—and that woman was concerned in it."

Following the impulse that urged him, he secured the Handbill in his pocketbook—snatched up the card which his patient had presented as her introduction—and instantly left the house. He called the first cab that passed him, and drove to Miss Jethro's lodgings.

"Gone"—was the servant's answer when he inquired for her. He insisted on speaking to the landlady. "Hardly ten minutes have passed," he said, "since she left my house."

"Hardly ten minutes have passed," the landlady replied, "since that message was brought here by a boy."

The message had been evidently written in great haste: "I am unexpectedly obliged to leave London. A bank note is inclosed in payment of my debt to you. I will send for my luggage."

The doctor withdrew.

"Unexpectedly obliged to leave London," he repeated, as he got into the cab again. "Her flight condemns her: not a doubt of it now. As fast as you can!" he shouted to the man; directing him to drive to Emily's cottage.

CHAPTER XVIII. MISS LADD.

Arriving at the cottage, Doctor Allday discovered a gentleman, who was just closing the garden gate behind him.

"Has Miss Emily had a visitor?" he inquired, when the servant admitted him.

"The gentleman left a letter for Miss Emily, sir."

"Did he ask to see her?"

"He asked after Miss Letitia's health. When he heard that she was dead, he seemed to be startled, and went away immediately."

"Did he give his name?"

"No, sir."

The doctor found Emily absorbed over her letter. His anxiety to forestall any possible discovery of the deception which had concealed the terrible story of her father's death, kept Doctor Allday's vigilance on the watch. He doubted the gentleman who had abstained from giving his name; he even distrusted the other unknown person who had written to Emily.

She looked up. Her face relieved him of his misgivings, before she could speak.

"At last, I have heard from my dearest friend," she said. "You remember what I told you about Cecilia? Here is a letter—a long delightful letter—from the Engadine, left at the door by some gentleman unknown. I was questioning the servant when you rang the bell."

"You may question me, if you prefer it. I arrived just as the gentleman was shutting your garden gate."

"Oh, tell me! what was he like?"

"Tall, and thin, and dark. Wore a vile republican-looking felt hat. Had nasty ill-tempered wrinkles between his eyebrows. The sort of man I distrust by instinct."

"Why?"

"Because he doesn't shave."

"Do you mean that he wore a beard?"

"Yes; a curly black beard."

Emily clasped her hands in amazement. "Can it be Alban Morris?" she exclaimed.

The doctor looked at her with a sardonic smile; he thought it likely that he had discovered her sweetheart.

"Who is Mr. Alban Morris?" he asked.

"The drawing-master at Miss Ladd's school."

Doctor Allday dropped the subject: masters at ladies' schools were not persons who interested him. He returned to the purpose which had brought him to the cottage—and produced the Handbill that had been sent to him in Emily's letter.

"I suppose you want to have it back again?" he said.

She took it from him, and looked at it with interest.

"Isn't it strange," she suggested, "that the murderer should have escaped, with such a careful description of him as this circulated all over England?"

She read the description to the doctor.

"'Name not known. Supposed age, between twenty-five and thirty years. A well-made man, of small stature. Fair complexion, delicate features, clear blue eyes. Hair light, and cut rather short. Clean shaven, with the exception of narrow half-whiskers. Small, white, well-shaped hands. Wore valuable rings on the two last fingers of the left hand. Dressed neatly—'"

"That part of the description is useless," the doctor remarked; "he would change his clothes."

"But could he change his voice?" Emily objected. "Listen to this: 'Remarkably good voice, smooth, full, and persuasive.' And here again! 'Ingratiating manners.' Perhaps you will say he could put on an appearance of rudeness?"

"I will say this, my dear. He would be able to disguise himself so effectually that ninety-nine people out of a hundred would fail to identify him, either by his voice or his manner."

"How?"

"Look back at the description: 'Hair cut rather short, clean shaven, with the exception of narrow half-whiskers.' The wretch was safe from pursuit; he had ample time at his disposal—don't you see how he could completely alter the appearance of his head and face? No more, my dear, of this disagreeable subject! Let us get to something interesting. Have you found anything else among your aunt's papers?"

"I have met with a great disappointment," Emily replied. "Did I tell you how I discovered the Handbill?"

"No."

"I found it, with the scrap-book and the newspaper cuttings, under a collection of empty boxes and bottles, in a drawer of the washhand-stand. And I naturally expected to make far more interesting discoveries in this room. My search was over in five minutes. Nothing in the cabinet there, in the corner, but a few books and some china. Nothing in the writing-desk, on that side-table, but a packet of note-paper and some sealing-wax. Nothing here, in the drawers, but tradesmen's receipts, materials for knitting, and old photographs. She must have destroyed all her papers, poor dear, before her last illness; and the Handbill and the other things can only have escaped, because they were left in a place which she never thought of examining. Isn't it provoking?"

With a mind inexpressibly relieved, good Doctor Allday asked permission to return to his patients: leaving Emily to devote herself to her friend's letter.

On his way out, he noticed that the door of the bed-chamber on the opposite side of the passage stood open. Since Miss Letitia's death the room had not been used. Well within view stood the washhand-stand to which Emily had alluded. The doctor advanced to the house door—reflected—hesitated—and looked toward the empty room.

It had struck him that there might be a second drawer which Emily had overlooked. Would he be justified in setting this doubt at rest? If he passed over ordinary scruples it would not be without excuse. Miss Letitia had spoken to him of her affairs, and had asked him to act (in Emily's interest) as co-executor with her lawyer. The rapid progress of the illness had made it impossible for her to execute the necessary codicil. But the doctor had been morally (if not legally) taken into her confidence—and, for that reason, he decided that he had a right in this serious matter to satisfy his own mind.

A glance was enough to show him that no second drawer had been overlooked.

There was no other discovery to detain the doctor. The wardrobe only contained the poor old lady's clothes; the one cupboard was open and empty. On the point of leaving the room, he went back to the washhand-stand. While he had the opportunity, it might not be amiss to make sure that Emily had thoroughly examined those old boxes and bottles, which she had alluded to with some little contempt.

The drawer was of considerable length. When he tried to pull it completely out from the grooves in which it ran, it resisted him. In his present frame of mind, this was a suspicious circumstance in itself. He cleared away the litter so as to make room for the introduction of his hand and arm into the drawer. In another moment his fingers touched a piece of paper, jammed between the inner end of the drawer and the bottom of the flat surface of the washhand-stand. With a little care, he succeeded in extricating the paper. Only pausing to satisfy himself that there was nothing else to be found, and to close the drawer after replacing its contents, he left the cottage.

The cab was waiting for him. On the drive back to his own house, he opened the crumpled paper. It proved to be a letter addressed to Miss Letitia; and it was signed by no less a person than Emily's schoolmistress. Looking back from the end to the beginning, Doctor Allday discovered, in the first sentence, the name of—Miss Jethro.

But for the interview of that morning with his patient he might have doubted the propriety of making himself further acquainted with the letter. As things were, he read it without hesitation.

"DEAR MADAM—I cannot but regard it as providential circumstance that your niece, in writing to you from my house, should have mentioned, among other events of her school life, the arrival of my new teacher, Miss Jethro.

"To say that I was surprised is to express very inadequately what I felt when I read your letter, informing me confidentially that I had employed a woman who was unworthy to associate with the young persons placed under my care. It is impossible for me to suppose that a lady in your position, and possessed of your high principles, would make such a serious accusation as this, without unanswerable reasons for doing so. At the same time I cannot, consistently with my duty as a Christian, suffer my opinion of Miss Jethro to be in any way modified, until proofs are laid before me which it is impossible to dispute.

"Placing the same confidence in your discretion, which you have placed in mine, I now inclose the references and testimonials which Miss Jethro submitted to me, when she presented herself to fill the vacant situation in my school.

"I earnestly request you to lose no time in instituting the confidential inquiries which you have volunteered to make. Whatever the result may be, pray return to me the inclosures which I have trusted to your care, and believe me, dear madam, in much suspense and anxiety, sincerely yours,

"AMELIA LADD."

It is needless to describe, at any length, the impression which these lines produced on the doctor.

If he had heard what Emily had heard at the time of her aunt's last illness, he would have called to mind Miss Letitia's betrayal of her interest in some man unknown, whom she believed to have been beguiled by Miss Jethro— and he would have perceived that the vindictive hatred, thus produced, must have inspired the letter of denunciation which the schoolmistress had acknowledged. He would also have inferred that Miss Letitia's inquiries had proved her accusation to be well founded—if he had known of the new teacher's sudden dismissal from the school. As things were, he was merely confirmed in his bad opinion of Miss Jethro; and he was induced, on reflection, to keep his discovery to himself.

"If poor Miss Emily saw the old lady exhibited in the character of an informer," he thought, "what a blow would be struck at her innocent respect for the memory of her aunt!"

CHAPTER XIX. SIR JERVIS REDWOOD.

In the meantime, Emily, left by herself, had her own correspondence to occupy her attention. Besides the letter from Cecilia (directed to the care of Sir Jervis Redwood), she had received some lines addressed to her by Sir Jervis himself. The two inclosures had been secured in a sealed envelope, directed to the cottage.

If Alban Morris had been indeed the person trusted as messenger by Sir Jervis, the conclusion that followed filled Emily with overpowering emotions of curiosity and surprise.

Having no longer the motive of serving and protecting her, Alban must, nevertheless, have taken the journey to Northumberland. He must have gained Sir Jervis Redwood's favor and confidence—and he might even have been a guest at the baronet's country seat—when Cecilia's letter arrived. What did it mean?

Emily looked back at her experience of her last day at school, and recalled her consultation with Alban on the subject of Mrs. Rook. Was he still bent on clearing up his suspicions of Sir Jervis's housekeeper? And, with that end in view, had he followed the woman, on her return to her master's place of abode?

Suddenly, almost irritably, Emily snatched up Sir Jervis's letter. Before the doctor had come in, she had glanced at it, and had thrown it aside in her impatience to read what Cecilia had written. In her present altered frame of mind, she was inclined to think that Sir Jervis might be the more interesting correspondent of the two.

On returning to his letter, she was disappointed at the outset.

In the first place, his handwriting was so abominably bad that she was obliged to guess at his meaning. In the second place, he never hinted at the circumstances under which Cecilia's letter had been confided to the gentleman who had left it at her door.

She would once more have treated the baronet's communication with

271

contempt—but for the discovery that it contained an offer of employment in London, addressed to herself.

Sir Jervis had necessarily been obliged to engage another secretary in Emily's absence. But he was still in want of a person to serve his literary interests in London. He had reason to believe that discoveries made by modern travelers in Central America had been reported from time to time by the English press; and he wished copies to be taken of any notices of this sort which might be found, on referring to the files of newspapers kept in the reading-room of the British Museum. If Emily considered herself capable of contributing in this way to the completeness of his great work on "the ruined cities," she had only to apply to his bookseller in London, who would pay her the customary remuneration and give her every assistance of which she might stand in need. The bookseller's name and address followed (with nothing legible but the two words "Bond Street"), and there was an end of Sir Jervis's proposal.

Emily laid it aside, deferring her answer until she had read Cecilia's letter.

CHAPTER XX. THE REVEREND MILES MIRABEL.

"I am making a little excursion from the Engadine, my dearest of all dear friends. Two charming fellow-travelers take care of me; and we may perhaps get as far as the Lake of Como.

"My sister (already much improved in health) remains at St. Moritz with the old governess. The moment I know what exact course we are going to take, I shall write to Julia to forward any letters which arrive in my absence. My life, in this earthly paradise, will be only complete when I hear from my darling Emily.

"In the meantime, we are staying for the night at some interesting place, the name of which I have unaccountably forgotten; and here I am in my room, writing to you at last—dying to know if Sir Jervis has yet thrown himself at your feet, and offered to make you Lady Redwood with magnificent settlements.

"But you are waiting to hear who my new friends are. My dear, one of them is, next to yourself, the most delightful creature in existence. Society knows her as Lady Janeaway. I love her already, by her Christian name; she is my friend Doris. And she reciprocates my sentiments.

"You will now understand that union of sympathies made us acquainted with each other.

"If there is anything in me to be proud of, I think it must be my admirable appetite. And, if I have a passion, the name of it is Pastry. Here again, Lady Doris reciprocates my sentiments. We sit next to each other at the table d'hote.

"Good heavens, I have forgotten her husband! They have been married rather more than a month. Did I tell you that she is just two years older than I am?

"I declare I am forgetting him again! He is Lord Janeaway. Such a quiet modest man, and so easily amused. He carries with him everywhere a dirty little tin case, with air holes in the cover. He goes softly poking about among bushes and brambles, and under rocks, and behind old wooden houses. When he has caught some hideous insect that makes one shudder, he blushes with pleasure, and looks at his wife and me, and says, with the prettiest lisp: 'This is what I call enjoying the day.' To see the manner in which he obeys Her is, between ourselves, to feel proud of being a woman.

"Where was I? Oh, at the table d'hote.

"Never, Emily—I say it with a solemn sense of the claims of truth—never have I eaten such an infamous, abominable, maddeningly bad dinner, as the dinner they gave us on our first day at the hotel. I ask you if I am not patient; I appeal to your own recollection of occasions when I have exhibited extraordinary self-control. My dear, I held out until they brought the pastry round. I took one bite, and committed the most shocking offense against good manners at table that you can imagine. My handkerchief, my poor innocent handkerchief, received the horrid—please suppose the rest. My hair stands on end, when I think of it. Our neighbors at the table saw me. The coarse men laughed. The sweet young bride, sincerely feeling for me, said,

'Will you allow me to shake hands? I did exactly what you have done the day before yesterday.' Such was the beginning of my friendship with Lady Doris Janeaway.

"We are two resolute women—I mean that she is resolute, and that I follow her—and we have asserted our right of dining to our own satisfaction, by means of an interview with the chief cook.

"This interesting person is an ex-Zouave in the French army. Instead of making excuses, he confessed that the barbarous tastes of the English and American visitors had so discouraged him, that he had lost all pride and pleasure in the exercise of his art. As an example of what he meant, he mentioned his experience of two young Englishmen who could speak no foreign language. The waiters reported that they objected to their breakfasts, and especially to the eggs. Thereupon (to translate the Frenchman's own way of putting it) he exhausted himself in exquisite preparations of eggs. Eggs a la tripe, au gratin, a l'Aurore, a la Dauphine, a la Poulette, a la Tartare, a la Venitienne, a la Bordelaise, and so on, and so on. Still the two young gentlemen were not satisfied. The ex-Zouave, infuriated; wounded in his honor, disgraced as a professor, insisted on an explanation. What, in heaven's name, did they want for breakfast? They wanted boiled eggs; and a fish which they called a Bloaterre. It was impossible, he said, to express his contempt for the English idea of a breakfast, in the presence of ladies. You know how a cat expresses herself in the presence of a dog—and you will understand the allusion. Oh, Emily, what dinners we have had, in our own room, since we spoke to that noble cook!

"Have I any more news to send you? Are you interested, my dear, in eloquent young clergymen?

"On our first appearance at the public table we noticed a remarkable air of depression among the ladies. Had some adventurous gentleman tried to climb a mountain, and failed? Had disastrous political news arrived from England; a defeat of the Conservatives, for instance? Had a revolution in the fashions broken out in Paris, and had all our best dresses become of no earthly value to us? I applied for information to the only lady present who shone on the company with a cheerful face—my friend Doris, of course. "'What day was yesterday?' she asked.

"'Sunday,' I answered.

"'Of all melancholy Sundays,' she continued, the most melancholy in the calendar. Mr. Miles Mirabel preached his farewell sermon, in our temporary chapel upstairs.'

"'And you have not recovered it yet?'

"'We are all heart-broken, Miss Wyvil.'

"This naturally interested me. I asked what sort of sermons Mr. Mirabel preached. Lady Janeaway said: 'Come up to our room after dinner. The subject is too distressing to be discussed in public.'

"She began by making me personally acquainted with the reverend gentleman—that is to say, she showed me the photographic portraits of him. They were two in number. One only presented his face. The other exhibited him at full length, adorned in his surplice. Every lady in the congregation had received the two photographs as a farewell present. 'My portraits,' Lady Doris remarked, 'are the only complete specimens. The others have been irretrievably ruined by tears.'

"You will now expect a personal description of this fascinating man. What the photographs failed to tell me, my friend was so kind as to complete from the resources of her own experience. Here is the result presented to the best of my ability.

"He is young—not yet thirty years of age. His complexion is fair; his features are delicate, his eyes are clear blue. He has pretty hands, and rings prettier still. And such a voice, and such manners! You will say there are plenty of pet parsons who answer to this description. Wait a little—I have kept his chief distinction till the last. His beautiful light hair flows in profusion over his shoulders; and his glossy beard waves, at apostolic length, down to the lower buttons of his waistcoat.

"What do you think of the Reverend Miles Mirabel now?

"The life and adventures of our charming young clergyman, bear eloquent testimony to the saintly patience of his disposition, under trials which would have overwhelmed an ordinary man. (Lady Doris, please notice, quotes in this place the language of his admirers; and I report Lady Doris.)

"He has been clerk in a lawyer's office—unjustly dismissed. He has given readings from Shakespeare—infamously neglected. He has been secretary to a promenade concert company—deceived by a penniless manager. He has been employed in negotiations for making foreign railways—repudiated by an unprincipled Government. He has been translator to a publishing house—declared incapable by envious newspapers and reviews. He has taken refuge in dramatic criticism—dismissed by a corrupt editor. Through all these means of purification for the priestly career, he passed at last into the one sphere that was worthy of him: he entered the Church, under the protection of influential friends. Oh, happy change! From that moment his labors have been blessed. Twice already he has been presented with silver tea-pots filled with sovereigns. Go where he may, precious sympathies environ him; and domestic affection places his knife and fork at innumerable family tables. After a continental career, which will leave undying recollections, he is now recalled to England—at the suggestion of a person of distinction in the Church, who prefers a mild climate. It will now be his valued privilege to represent an absent rector in a country living; remote from cities, secluded in pastoral solitude, among simple breeders of sheep. May the shepherd prove worthy of the flock!

"Here again, my dear, I must give the merit where the merit is due. This memoir of Mr. Mirabel is not of my writing. It formed part of his farewell sermon, preserved in the memory of Lady Doris—and it shows (once more in the language of his admirers) that the truest humility may be found in the character of the most gifted man.

"Let me only add, that you will have opportunities of seeing and hearing this popular preacher, when circumstances permit him to address congregations in the large towns. I am at the end of my news; and I begin to feel—after this long, long letter—that it is time to go to bed. Need I say that I have often spoken of you to Doris, and that she entreats you to be her friend as well as mine, when we meet again in England?

"Good-by, darling, for the present. With fondest love,

"Your CECILIA."

"P.S.—I have formed a new habit. In case of feeling hungry in the night, I keep a box of chocolate under the pillow. You have no idea what a comfort it is. If I ever meet with the man who fulfills my ideal, I shall make it a condition of the marriage settlement, that I am to have chocolate under the pillow."

CHAPTER XXI. POLLY AND SALLY.

Without a care to trouble her; abroad or at home, finding inexhaustible varieties of amusement; seeing new places, making new acquaintances—what a disheartening contrast did Cecilia's happy life present to the life of her friend! Who, in Emily's position, could have read that joyously-written letter from Switzerland, and not have lost heart and faith, for the moment at least, as the inevitable result?

A buoyant temperament is of all moral qualities the most precious, in this respect; it is the one force in us—when virtuous resolution proves insufficient—which resists by instinct the stealthy approaches of despair. "I shall only cry," Emily thought, "if I stay at home; better go out."

Observant persons, accustomed to frequent the London parks, can hardly have failed to notice the number of solitary strangers sadly endeavoring to vary their lives by taking a walk. They linger about the flower-beds; they sit for hours on the benches; they look with patient curiosity at other people who have companions; they notice ladies on horseback and children at play, with submissive interest; some of the men find company in a pipe, without appearing to enjoy it; some of the women find a substitute for dinner, in little dry biscuits wrapped in crumpled scraps of paper; they are not sociable; they are hardly ever seen to make acquaintance with each other; perhaps they are shame-faced, or proud, or sullen; perhaps they despair of others, being accustomed to despair of themselves; perhaps they have their reasons for never venturing to encounter curiosity, or their vices which dread detection, or their virtues which suffer hardship with the resignation that is sufficient for itself. The one thing certain is, that these unfortunate people resist discovery. We know that they are strangers in London—and we know no more.

And Emily was one of them.

Among the other forlorn wanderers in the Parks, there appeared latterly a trim little figure in black (with the face protected from notice behind a crape veil), which was beginning to be familiar, day after day, to nursemaids and children, and to rouse curiosity among harmless solitaries meditating on benches, and idle vagabonds strolling over the grass. The woman-servant, whom the considerate doctor had provided, was the one person in Emily's absence left to take care of the house. There was no other creature who could be a companion to the friendless girl. Mrs. Ellmother had never shown herself again since the funeral. Mrs. Mosey could not forget that she had been (no matter how politely) requested to withdraw. To whom could Emily say, "Let us go out for a walk?" She had communicated the news of her aunt's death to Miss Ladd, at Brighton; and had heard from Francine. The worthy schoolmistress had written to her with the truest kindness. "Choose your own time, my poor child, and come and stay with me at Brighton; the sooner the better." Emily shrank—not from accepting the invitation—but from encountering Francine. The hard West Indian heiress looked harder than ever with a pen in her hand. Her letter announced that she was "getting on wretchedly with her studies (which she hated); she found the masters appointed to instruct her ugly and disagreeable (and loathed the sight of them); she had taken a dislike to Miss Ladd (and time only confirmed that unfavorable impression); Brighton was always the same; the sea was always the same; the drives were always the same. Francine felt a presentiment that she should do something desperate, unless Emily joined her, and made Brighton endurable behind the horrid schoolmistress's back." Solitude in London was a privilege and a pleasure, viewed as the alternative to such companionship as this.

Emily wrote gratefully to Miss Ladd, and asked to be excused.

Other days had passed drearily since that time; but the one day that had brought with it Cecilia's letter set past happiness and present sorrow together so vividly and so cruelly that Emily's courage sank. She had forced back the tears, in her lonely home; she had gone out to seek consolation and encouragement under the sunny sky—to find comfort for her sore heart in the radiant summer beauty of flowers and grass, in the sweet breathing of the air, in the happy heavenward soaring of the birds. No! Mother Nature is stepmother to the sick at heart. Soon, too soon, she could hardly see where she went. Again and again she resolutely cleared her eyes, under the shelter of her veil, when passing strangers noticed her; and again and again the tears found their way back. Oh, if the girls at the school were to see her now—the girls who used to say in their moments of sadness, "Let us go to Emily and be cheered"—would they know her again? She sat down to rest and recover herself on the nearest bench. It was unoccupied. No passing footsteps were audible on the remote path to which she had strayed. Solitude at home! Solitude in the Park! Where was Cecilia at that moment? In Italy, among the lakes and mountains, happy in the company of her light-hearted friend.

The lonely interval passed, and persons came near. Two sisters, girls like herself, stopped to rest on the bench.

They were full of their own interests; they hardly looked at the stranger in mourning garments. The younger sister was to be married, and the elder was to be bridesmaid. They talked of their dresses and their presents; they compared the dashing bridegroom of one with the timid lover of the other; they laughed over their own small sallies of wit, over their joyous dreams of the future, over their opinions of the guests invited to the wedding. Too joyfully restless to remain inactive any longer, they jumped up again from the seat. One of them said, "Polly, I'm too happy!" and danced as she walked away. The other cried, "Sally, for shame!" and laughed, as if she had hit on the most irresistible joke that ever was made.

Emily rose and went home.

By some mysterious influence which she was unable to trace, the boisterous merriment of the two girls had roused in her a sense of revolt against the life that she was leading. Change, speedy change, to some occupation that would force her to exert herself, presented the one promise of brighter days that she could see. To feel this was to be inevitably reminded of Sir Jervis Redwood. Here was a man, who had never seen her, transformed by the incomprehensible operation of Chance into the friend of whom she stood in need—the friend who pointed the way to a new world of action, the busy world of readers in the library of the Museum.

Early in the new week, Emily had accepted Sir Jervis's proposal, and had so interested the bookseller to whom she had been directed to apply, that he took it on himself to modify the arbitrary instructions of his employer.

"The old gentleman has no mercy on himself, and no mercy on others," he explained, "where his literary labors are concerned. You must spare yourself, Miss Emily. It is not only absurd, it's cruel, to expect you to ransack old newspapers for discoveries in Yucatan, from the time when Stephens published his 'Travels in Central America'—nearly forty years since! Begin with back numbers published within a few years—say five years from the present date—and let us see what your search over that interval will bring forth."

Accepting this friendly advice, Emily began with the newspaper-volume dating from New Year's Day, 1876.

The first hour of her search strengthened the sincere sense of gratitude with which she remembered the bookseller's kindness. To keep her attention steadily fixed on the one subject that interested her employer, and to resist the temptation to read those miscellaneous items of news which especially interest women, put her patience and resolution to a merciless test. Happily for herself, her neighbors on either side were no idlers. To see them so absorbed over their work that they never once looked at her, after the first moment when she took her place between them, was to find exactly the example of which she stood most in need. As the hours wore on, she pursued her weary way, down one column and up another, resigned at least (if not quite reconciled yet) to her task. Her labors ended, for the day, with such encouragement as she might derive from the conviction of having, thus far, honestly pursued a useless search.

News was waiting for her when she reached home, which raised her sinking spirits.

On leaving the cottage that morning she had given certain instructions, relating to the modest stranger who had taken charge of her correspondence—in case of his paying a second visit, during her absence at the Museum. The first words spoken by the servant, on opening the door, informed her that the unknown gentleman had called again. This time he had boldly left his card. There was the welcome name that she had expected to see—Alban Morris.

CHAPTER XXII. ALBAN MORRIS.

Having looked at the card, Emily put her first question to the servant.

"Did you tell Mr. Morris what your orders were?" she asked.

"Yes, miss; I said I was to have shown him in, if you had been at home. Perhaps I did wrong; I told him what you told me when you went out this morning—I said you had gone to read at the Museum."

"What makes you think you did wrong?"

"Well, miss, he didn't say anything, but he looked upset."

"Do you mean that he looked angry?"

The servant shook her head. "Not exactly angry—puzzled and put out."

"Did he leave any message?"

"He said he would call later, if you would be so good as to receive him."

In half an hour more, Alban and Emily were together again. The light fell full on her face as she rose to receive him.

"Oh, how you have suffered!"

The words escaped him before he could restrain himself. He looked at her with the tender sympathy, so precious to women, which she had not seen in the face of any human creature since the loss of her aunt. Even the good doctor's efforts to console her had been efforts of professional routine—the inevitable result of his life-long familiarity with sorrow and death. While Alban's eyes rested on her, Emily felt her tears rising. In the fear that he might misinterpret her reception of him, she made an effort to speak with some appearance of composure.

"I lead a lonely life," she said; "and I can well understand that my face shows it. You are one of my very few friends, Mr. Morris"—the tears rose again; it discouraged her to see him standing irresolute, with his hat in his hand, fearful of intruding on her. "Indeed, indeed, you are welcome," she said, very earnestly.

In those sad days her heart was easily touched. She gave him her hand for the second time. He held it gently for a moment. Every day since they had parted she had been in his thoughts; she had become dearer to him than ever. He was too deeply affected to trust himself to answer. That silence pleaded for him as nothing had pleaded for him yet. In her secret self she remembered with wonder how she had received his confession in the school garden. It was a little hard on him, surely, to have forbidden him even to hope.

Conscious of her own weakness—even while giving way to it—she felt the necessity of turning his attention from herself. In some confusion, she pointed to a chair at her side, and spoke of his first visit, when he had left her letters at the door. Having confided to him all that she had discovered, and all that she had guessed, on that occasion, it was by an easy transition that she alluded next to the motive for his journey to the North.

"I thought it might be suspicion of Mrs. Rook," she said. "Was I mistaken?"

"No; you were right."

"They were serious suspicions, I suppose?"

"Certainly! I should not otherwise have devoted my holiday-time to clearing them up."

"May I know what they were?"

"I am sorry to disappoint you," he began.

"But you would rather not answer my question," she interposed.

"I would rather hear you tell me if you have made any other guess."

"One more, Mr. Morris. I guessed that you had become acquainted with Sir Jervis Redwood."

"For the second time, Miss Emily, you have arrived at a sound conclusion. My one hope of finding opportunities for observing Sir Jervis's housekeeper depended on my chance of gaining admission to Sir Jervis's house."

"How did you succeed? Perhaps you provided yourself with a letter of introduction?"

"I knew nobody who could introduce me," Alban replied. "As the event proved, a letter would have been needless. Sir Jervis introduced himself— and, more wonderful still, he invited me to his house at our first interview."

"Sir Jervis introduced himself?" Emily repeated, in amazement. "From Cecilia's description of him, I should have thought he was the last person in the world to do that!"

Alban smiled. "And you would like to know how it happened?" he suggested.

"The very favor I was going to ask of you," she replied.

Instead of at once complying with her wishes, he paused—hesitated— and made a strange request. "Will you forgive my rudeness, if I ask leave to walk up and down the room while I talk? I am a restless man. Walking up and down helps me to express myself freely."

Her face brightened for the first time. "How like You that is!" she exclaimed.

Alban looked at her with surprise and delight. She had betrayed an interest in studying his character, which he appreciated at its full value. "I should never have dared to hope," he said, "that you knew me so well already."

"You are forgetting your story," she reminded him.

He moved to the opposite side of the room, where there were fewer impediments in the shape of furniture. With his head down, and his hands crossed behind him, he paced to and fro. Habit made him express himself in his usual quaint way—but he became embarrassed as he went on. Was he disturbed by his recollections? or by the fear of taking Emily into his confidence too freely?

"Different people have different ways of telling a story," he said. "Mine is the methodical way—I begin at the beginning. We will start, if you please, in the railway—we will proceed in a one-horse chaise—and we will stop at a village, situated in a hole. It was the nearest place to Sir Jervis's house, and it was therefore my destination. I picked out the biggest of the cottages—I mean the huts—and asked the woman at the door if she had a bed to let. She evidently thought me either mad or drunk. I wasted no time in persuasion; the right person to plead my cause was asleep in her arms. I began by admiring the baby; and I ended by taking the baby's portrait. From that moment I became a member of the family—the member who had his own way. Besides the room occupied by the husband and wife, there was a sort of kennel in which the husband's brother slept. He was dismissed (with five shillings of mine to comfort him) to find shelter somewhere else; and I was promoted to the vacant place. It is my misfortune to be tall. When I went to bed, I slept with my head on the pillow, and my feet out of the window. Very cool and pleasant in summer weather. The next morning, I set my trap for Sir Jervis."

"Your trap?" Emily repeated, wondering what he meant.

"I went out to sketch from Nature," Alban continued. "Can anybody (with or without a title, I don't care), living in a lonely country house, see a stranger hard at work with a color-box and brushes, and not stop to look at what he is doing? Three days passed, and nothing happened. I was quite patient; the grand open country all round me offered lessons of inestimable value in what we call aerial perspective. On the fourth day, I was absorbed over the hardest of all hard tasks in landscape art, studying the clouds straight from Nature. The magnificent moorland silence was suddenly profaned by a man's voice, speaking (or rather croaking) behind me. 'The worst curse of human life,' the voice said, 'is the detestable necessity of taking exercise. I hate losing my time; I hate fine scenery; I hate fresh air; I hate a pony. Go on, you brute!' Being too deeply engaged with the clouds to look round, I had supposed this pretty speech to be addressed to some second person. Nothing of the sort; the croaking voice had a habit of speaking to itself. In a minute more, there came within my range of view a solitary old man, mounted on a rough pony."

"Was it Sir Jervis?"

Alban hesitated.

"It looked more like the popular notion of the devil," he said.

"Oh, Mr. Morris!"

"I give you my first impression, Miss Emily, for what it is worth. He had his high-peaked hat in his hand, to keep his head cool. His wiry iron-gray hair looked like hair standing on end; his bushy eyebrows curled upward toward his narrow temples; his horrid old globular eyes stared with a wicked brightness; his pointed beard hid his chin; he was covered from his throat to his ankles in a loose black garment, something between a coat and a cloak; and, to complete him, he had a club foot. I don't doubt that Sir Jervis Redwood is the earthly alias which he finds convenient—but I stick to that first impression which appeared to surprise you. 'Ha! an artist; you seem to be the sort of man I want!' In those terms he introduced himself. Observe, if you please, that my trap caught him the moment he came my way. Who wouldn't be an artist?"

"Did he take a liking to you?" Emily inquired.

"Not he! I don't believe he ever took a liking to anybody in his life."

"Then how did you get your invitation to his house?"

"That's the amusing part of it, Miss Emily. Give me a little breathing time, and you shall hear."

CHAPTER XXIII. MISS REDWOOD.

"I got invited to Sir Jervis's house," Alban resumed, "by treating the old savage as unceremoniously as he had treated me. 'That's an idle trade of yours,' he said, looking at my sketch. 'Other ignorant people have made the same remark,' I answered. He rode away, as if he was not used to be spoken to in that manner, and then thought better of it, and came back. 'Do you understand wood engraving?' he asked. 'Yes.' 'And etching?' 'I have practiced etching myself.' 'Are you a Royal Academician?' 'I'm a drawing-master at a ladies' school.' 'Whose school?' 'Miss Ladd's.' 'Damn it, you know the girl who ought to have been my secretary.' I am not quite sure whether you will take it as a compliment—Sir Jervis appeared to view you in the light of a reference to my respectability. At any rate, he went on with his questions. 'How long do you stop in these parts?' 'I haven't made up my mind.' 'Look here; I want to consult you—are you listening?' 'No; I'm sketching.' He burst into a horrid scream. I asked if he felt himself taken ill. 'Ill?' he said—'I'm laughing.' It was a diabolical laugh, in one syllable—not 'ha! ha! ha!' only 'ha!'—and it made him look wonderfully like that eminent person, whom I persist in thinking he resembles. 'You're an impudent dog,' he said; 'where are you living?' He was so delighted when he heard of my uncomfortable position in the kennel-bedroom, that he offered his hospitality on the spot. 'I can't go to you in such a pigstye as that,' he said; 'you must come to me. What's your name?' 'Alban Morris; what's yours?' 'Jervis Redwood. Pack up your traps when you've done your job, and come and try my kennel. There it is, in a corner of your drawing, and devilish like, too.' I packed up my traps, and I tried his kennel. And now you have had enough of Sir Jervis Redwood."

"Not half enough!" Emily answered. "Your story leaves off just at the interesting moment. I want you to take me to Sir Jervis's house."

"And I want you, Miss Emily, to take me to the British Museum. Don't let me startle you! When I called here earlier in the day, I was told that you had gone to the reading-room. Is your reading a secret?"

His manner, when he made that reply, suggested to Emily that there was some foregone conclusion in his mind, which he was putting to the test. She answered without alluding to the impression which he had produced on her.

"My reading is no secret. I am only consulting old newspapers."

He repeated the last words to himself. "Old newspapers?" he said—as if he was not quite sure of having rightly understood her.

She tried to help him by a more definite reply.

"I am looking through old newspapers," she resumed, "beginning with the year eighteen hundred and seventy-six."

"And going back from that time," he asked eagerly; "to earlier dates still?"

"No—just the contrary—advancing from 'seventy-six' to the present time."

He suddenly turned pale—and tried to hide his face from her by looking out of the window. For a moment, his agitation deprived him of his presence of mind. In that moment, she saw that she had alarmed him.

"What have I said to frighten you?" she asked.

He tried to assume a tone of commonplace gallantry. "There are limits even to your power over me," he replied. "Whatever else you may do, you can never frighten me. Are you searching those old newspapers with any particular object in view?"

"Yes."

"May I know what it is?"

"May I know why I frightened you?"

He began to walk up and down the room again—then checked himself abruptly, and appealed to her mercy.

"Don't be hard on me," he pleaded. "I am so fond of you—oh, forgive me! I only mean that it distresses me to have any concealments from you. If I could open my whole heart at this moment, I should be a happier man."

She understood him and believed him. "My curiosity shall never embarrass you again," she answered warmly. "I won't even remember that I wanted to hear how you got on in Sir Jervis's house."

His gratitude seized the opportunity of taking her harmlessly into his confidence. "As Sir Jervis's guest," he said, "my experience is at your service. Only tell me how I can interest you."

She replied, with some hesitation, "I should like to know what happened when you first saw Mrs. Rook." To her surprise and relief, he at once complied with her wishes.

"We met," he said, "on the evening when I first entered the house. Sir Jervis took me into the dining-room—and there sat Miss Redwood, with a large black cat on her lap. Older than her brother, taller than her brother, leaner than her brother—with strange stony eyes, and a skin like parchment—she looked (if I may speak in contradictions) like a living corpse. I was presented, and the corpse revived. The last lingering relics of former good breeding showed themselves faintly in her brow and in her smile. You will hear more of Miss Redwood presently. In the meanwhile, Sir Jervis made me reward his hospitality by professional advice. He wished me to decide whether the artists whom he had employed to illustrate his wonderful book had cheated him by overcharges and bad work—and Mrs. Rook was sent to fetch the engravings from his study upstairs. You remember her petrified appearance, when she first read the inscription on your locket? The same result followed when she found herself face to face with me. I saluted her civilly—she was deaf and blind to my politeness. Her master snatched the illustrations out of her hand, and told her to leave the room. She stood stockstill, staring helplessly. Sir Jervis looked round at his sister; and I followed his example. Miss Redwood was observing the housekeeper too attentively to notice anything else; her brother was obliged to speak to her. 'Try Rook with the bell,' he said. Miss Redwood took a fine old bronze hand-bell from the table at her side, and rang it. At the shrill silvery sound of the bell, Mrs. Rook put her hand to her head as if the ringing had hurt her—turned instantly, and left us. 'Nobody can manage Rook but my sister,' Sir Jervis explained; 'Rook is crazy.' Miss Redwood differed with him. 'No!' she said. Only one word, but there were volumes of contradiction in it. Sir Jervis looked at me slyly; meaning, perhaps, that he thought his sister crazy too. The dinner was brought in at the same moment, and my attention was diverted to Mrs. Rook's husband."

"What was he like?" Emily asked.

"I really can't tell you; he was one of those essentially commonplace persons, whom one never looks at a second time. His dress was shabby, his head was bald, and his hands shook when he waited on us at table—and that is all I remember. Sir Jervis and I feasted on salt fish, mutton, and beer. Miss Redwood had cold broth, with a wine-glass full of rum poured into it by Mr. Rook. 'She's got no stomach,' her brother informed me; 'hot things come up again ten minutes after they have gone down her throat; she lives on that beastly mixture, and calls it broth-grog!' Miss Redwood sipped her elixir of life, and occasionally looked at me with an appearance of interest which I was at a loss to understand. Dinner being over, she rang her antique bell. The shabby old man-servant answered her call. 'Where's your wife?' she inquired. 'Ill, miss.' She took Mr. Rook's arm to go out, and stopped as she passed me. 'Come to my room, if you please, sir, to-morrow at two o'clock,' she said. Sir Jervis explained again: 'She's all to pieces in the morning' (he invariably called his sister 'She'); 'and gets patched up toward the middle of the day. Death has forgotten her, that's about the truth of it.' He lighted his pipe and pondered over the hieroglyphics found among the ruined cities of Yucatan; I lighted my pipe, and read the only book I could find in the dining-room—a dreadful record of shipwrecks and disasters at sea. When the room was full of tobacco-smoke we fell asleep in our chairs—and when we awoke again we got up and went to bed. There is the true story of my first evening at Redwood Hall."

Emily begged him to go on. "You have interested me in Miss Redwood," she said. "You kept your appointment, of course?"

"I kept my appointment in no very pleasant humor. Encouraged by my favorable report of the illustrations which he had submitted to my judgment, Sir Jervis proposed to make me useful to him in a new capacity. 'You have nothing particular to do,' he said, 'suppose you clean my pictures?' I gave him one of my black looks, and made no other reply. My interview with his sister tried my powers of self-command in another way. Miss Redwood declared her purpose in sending for me the moment I entered the room. Without any preliminary remarks—speaking slowly and emphatically, in a wonderfully strong voice for a woman of her age—she said, 'I have a favor to ask of you, sir. I want you to tell me what Mrs. Rook has done.' I was so staggered that I stared at her like a fool. She went on: 'I suspected Mrs. Rook, sir, of having guilty remembrances on her conscience before she had been a week in our service.' Can you imagine my astonishment when I heard that Miss Redwood's view of Mrs. Rook was my view? Finding that I still said nothing, the old lady entered into details: 'We arranged, sir,' (she persisted in calling me 'sir,' with the formal politeness of the old school)—'we arranged, sir, that Mrs. Rook and her husband should occupy the bedroom next to mine, so that I might have her near me in case of my being taken ill in the night. She looked at the door between the two rooms—suspicious! She asked if there was any objection to her changing to another room—suspicious! suspicious! Pray take a seat, sir, and tell me which Mrs. Rook is guilty of—theft or murder?'"

"What a dreadful old woman!" Emily exclaimed. "How did you answer her?"

"I told her, with perfect truth, that I knew nothing of Mrs. Rook's secrets. Miss Redwood's humor took a satirical turn. 'Allow me to ask, sir, whether your eyes were shut, when our housekeeper found herself unexpectedly in your presence?' I referred the old lady to her brother's opinion. 'Sir Jervis believes Mrs. Rook to be crazy,' I reminded her. 'Do you refuse to trust me, sir?' 'I have no information to give you, madam.' She waved her skinny old hand in the direction of the door. I made my bow, and retired. She called me back. 'Old women used to be prophets, sir, in the bygone time,' she said. 'I will venture on a prediction. You will be the means of depriving us of the services of Mr. and Mrs. Rook. If you will be so good as to stay here a day or two longer you will hear that those two people have given us notice to quit. It will be her doing, mind—he is a mere cypher. I wish you good-morning.' Will you believe me, when I tell you that the prophecy was fulfilled?"

"Do you mean that they actually left the house?"

"They would certainly have left the house," Alban answered, "if Sir Jervis had not insisted on receiving the customary month's warning. He asserted his resolution by locking up the old husband in the pantry. His sister's suspicions never entered his head; the housekeeper's conduct (he said) simply proved that she was, what he had always considered her to be, crazy. 'A capital servant, in spite of that drawback,' he remarked; 'and you will see, I shall bring her to her senses.' The impression produced on me was naturally of a very different kind. While I was still uncertain how to entrap Mrs. Rook into confirming my suspicions, she herself had saved me the trouble. She had placed her own guilty interpretation on my appearance in the house—I had driven her away!"

Emily remained true to her resolution not to let her curiosity embarrass Alban again. But the unexpressed question was in her thoughts—"Of what guilt does he suspect Mrs. Rook? And, when he first felt his suspicions, was my father in his mind?"

Alban proceeded.

"I had only to consider next, whether I could hope to make any further discoveries, if I continued to be Sir Jervis's guest. The object of my journey had been gained; and I had no desire to be employed as picture-cleaner. Miss Redwood assisted me in arriving at a decision. I was sent for to speak to her again. The success of her prophecy had raised her spirits. She asked, with ironical humility, if I proposed to honor them by still remaining their guest, after the disturbance that I had provoked. I answered that I proposed to leave by the first train the next morning. 'Will it be convenient for you to travel to some place at a good distance from this part of the world?' she asked. I had my own reasons for going to London, and said so. 'Will you mention that to my brother this evening, just before we sit down to dinner?' she continued. 'And will you tell him plainly that you have no intention of returning to the North? I shall make use of Mrs. Rook's arm, as usual, to help me downstairs—and I will take care that she hears what you say. Without venturing on another prophecy, I will only hint to you that I have my own idea of what will happen; and I should like you to see for yourself, sir, whether my anticipations are realized.' Need I tell you that this strange old woman proved to be right once more? Mr. Rook was released; Mrs. Rook made humble apologies, and laid the whole blame on her husband's temper: and Sir Jervis bade me remark that his method had succeeded in bringing the housekeeper to her senses. Such were the results produced by the announcement of my departure for London—purposely made in Mrs. Rook's hearing. Do you agree with me, that my journey to Northumberland has not been taken in vain?"

Once more, Emily felt the necessity of controlling herself.

291

Alban had said that he had "reasons of his own for going to London." Could she venture to ask him what those reasons were? She could only persist in restraining her curiosity, and conclude that he would have mentioned his motive, if it had been (as she had at one time supposed) connected with herself. It was a wise decision. No earthly consideration would have induced Alban to answer her, if she had put the question to him.

All doubt of the correctness of his own first impression was now at an end; he was convinced that Mrs. Rook had been an accomplice in the crime committed, in 1877, at the village inn. His object in traveling to London was to consult the newspaper narrative of the murder. He, too, had been one of the readers at the Museum—had examined the back numbers of the newspaper—and had arrived at the conclusion that Emily's father had been the victim of the crime. Unless he found means to prevent it, her course of reading would take her from the year 1876 to the year 1877, and under that date, she would see the fatal report, heading the top of a column, and printed in conspicuous type.

In the meanwhile Emily had broken the silence, before it could lead to embarrassing results, by asking if Alban had seen Mrs. Rook again, on the morning when he left Sir Jervis's house.

"There was nothing to be gained by seeing her," Alban replied. "Now that she and her husband had decided to remain at Redwood Hall, I knew where to find her in case of necessity. As it happened I saw nobody, on the morning of my departure, but Sir Jervis himself. He still held to his idea of having his pictures cleaned for nothing. 'If you can't do it yourself,' he said, 'couldn't you teach my secretary?' He described the lady whom he had engaged in your place as a 'nasty middle-aged woman with a perpetual cold in her head.' At the same time (he remarked) he was a friend to the women, 'because he got them cheap.' I declined to teach the unfortunate secretary the art of picture-cleaning. Finding me determined, Sir Jervis was quite ready to say good-by. But he made use of me to the last. He employed me as postman and saved a stamp. The letter addressed to you arrived at breakfast-time. Sir Jervis said, 'You are going to London; suppose you take it with you?'"

"Did he tell you that there was a letter of his own inclosed in the envelope?"

"No. When he gave me the envelope it was already sealed."

Emily at once handed to him Sir Jervis's letter. "That will tell you who employs me at the Museum, and what my work is," she said.

He looked through the letter, and at once offered—eagerly offered—to help her.

"I have been a student in the reading-room at intervals, for years past," he said. "Let me assist you, and I shall have something to do in my holiday time." He was so anxious to be of use that he interrupted her before she could thank him. "Let us take alternate years," he suggested. "Did you not tell me you were searching the newspapers published in eighteen hundred and seventy-six?"

"Yes."

"Very well. I will take the next year. You will take the year after. And so on."

"You are very kind," she answered—"but I should like to propose an improvement on your plan."

"What improvement?" he asked, rather sharply.

"If you will leave the five years, from 'seventy-six to 'eighty-one, entirely to me," she resumed, "and take the next five years, reckoning backward from 'seventy-six, you will help me to better purpose. Sir Jervis expects me to look for reports of Central American Explorations, through the newspapers of the last forty years; and I have taken the liberty of limiting the heavy task imposed on me. When I report my progress to my employer, I should like to say that I have got through ten years of the examination, instead of five. Do you see any objection to the arrangement I propose?"

He proved to be obstinate—incomprehensibly obstinate.

"Let us try my plan to begin with," he insisted. "While you are looking through 'seventy-six, let me be at work on 'seventy-seven. If you still prefer your own arrangement, after that, I will follow your suggestion with pleasure. Is it agreed?"

Her acute perception—enlightened by his tone as wall as by his words—detected something under the surface already.

"It isn't agreed until I understand you a little better," she quietly replied. "I fancy you have some object of your own in view."

She spoke with her usual directness of look and manner. He was evidently disconcerted. "What makes you think so?" he asked.

"My own experience of myself makes me think so," she answered. "If I had some object to gain, I should persist in carrying it out—like you."

"Does that mean, Miss Emily, that you refuse to give way?"

"No, Mr. Morris. I have made myself disagreeable, but I know when to stop. I trust you—and submit."

If he had been less deeply interested in the accomplishment of his merciful design, he might have viewed Emily's sudden submission with some distrust. As it was, his eagerness to prevent her from discovering the narrative of the murder hurried him into an act of indiscretion. He made an excuse to leave her immediately, in the fear that she might change her mind.

"I have inexcusably prolonged my visit," he said. "If I presume on your kindness in this way, how can I hope that you will receive me again? We meet to-morrow in the reading-room."

He hastened away, as if he was afraid to let her say a word in reply.

Emily reflected.

"Is there something he doesn't want me to see, in the news of the year 'seventy-seven?" The one explanation which suggested itself to her mind assumed that form of expression—and the one method of satisfying her curiosity that seemed likely to succeed, was to search the volume which Alban had reserved for his own reading.

For two days they pursued their task together, seated at opposite desks.

On the third day Emily was absent.

Was she ill?

She was at the library in the City, consulting the file of The Times for the year 1877.

CHAPTER XXIV. MR. ROOK.

Emily's first day in the City library proved to be a day wasted.

She began reading the back numbers of the newspaper at haphazard, without any definite idea of what she was looking for. Conscious of the error into which her own impatience had led her, she was at a loss how to retrace the false step that she had taken. But two alternatives presented themselves: either to abandon the hope of making any discovery—or to attempt to penetrate Alban 's motives by means of pure guesswork, pursued in the dark.

How was the problem to be solved? This serious question troubled her all through the evening, and kept her awake when she went to bed. In despair of her capacity to remove the obstacle that stood in her way, she decided on resuming her regular work at the Museum—turned her pillow to get at the cool side of it—and made up her mind to go asleep.

In the case of the wiser animals, the Person submits to Sleep. It is only the superior human being who tries the hopeless experiment of making Sleep submit to the Person. Wakeful on the warm side of the pillow, Emily remained wakeful on the cool side—thinking again and again of the interview with Alban which had ended so strangely.

Little by little, her mind passed the limits which had restrained it thus far. Alban's conduct in keeping his secret, in the matter of the newspapers, now began to associate itself with Alban's conduct in keeping that other secret, which concealed from her his suspicions of Mrs. Rook.

She started up in bed as the next possibility occurred to her.

In speaking of the disaster which had compelled Mr. and Mrs. Rook to close the inn, Cecilia had alluded to an inquest held on the body of the murdered man. Had the inquest been mentioned in the newspapers, at the time? And had Alban seen something in the report, which concerned Mrs. Rook?

Led by the new light that had fallen on her, Emily returned to the library the next morning with a definite idea of what she had to look for. Incapable of giving exact dates, Cecilia had informed her that the crime was committed "in the autumn." The month to choose, in beginning her examination, was therefore the month of August.

No discovery rewarded her. She tried September, next—with the same unsatisfactory results. On Monday the first of October she met with some encouragement at last. At the top of a column appeared a telegraphic summary of all that was then known of the crime. In the number for the Wednesday following, she found a full report of the proceedings at the inquest.

Passing over the preliminary remarks, Emily read the evidence with the closest attention.

—————————

The jury having viewed the body, and having visited an outhouse in which the murder had been committed, the first witness called was Mr. Benjamin Rook, landlord of the Hand-in-Hand inn.

On the evening of Sunday, September 30th, 1877, two gentlemen presented themselves at Mr. Rook's house, under circumstances which especially excited his attention.

The youngest of the two was short, and of fair complexion. He carried a knapsack, like a gentleman on a pedestrian excursion; his manners were pleasant; and he was decidedly good-looking. His companion, older, taller, and darker—and a finer man altogether—leaned on his arm and seemed to be exhausted. In every respect they were singularly unlike each other. The younger stranger (excepting little half-whiskers) was clean shaved. The elder wore his whole beard. Not knowing their names, the landlord distinguished them, at the coroner's suggestion, as the fair gentleman, and the dark gentleman.

It was raining when the two arrived at the inn. There were signs in the heavens of a stormy night.

On accosting the landlord, the fair gentleman volunteered the following statement:

Approaching the village, he had been startled by seeing the dark gentleman (a total stranger to him) stretched prostrate on the grass at the roadside—so far as he could judge, in a swoon. Having a flask with brandy in it, he revived the fainting man, and led him to the inn.

This statement was confirmed by a laborer, who was on his way to the village at the time.

The dark gentleman endeavored to explain what had happened to him. He had, as he supposed, allowed too long a time to pass (after an early breakfast that morning), without taking food: he could only attribute the fainting fit to that cause. He was not liable to fainting fits. What purpose (if any) had brought him into the neighborhood of Zeeland, he did not state. He had no intention of remaining at the inn, except for refreshment; and he asked for a carriage to take him to the railway station.

The fair gentleman, seeing the signs of bad weather, desired to remain in Mr. Rook's house for the night, and proposed to resume his walking tour the next day.

Excepting the case of supper, which could be easily provided, the landlord had no choice but to disappoint both his guests. In his small way of business, none of his customers wanted to hire a carriage—even if he could have afforded to keep one. As for beds, the few rooms which the inn contained were all engaged; including even the room occupied by himself and his wife. An exhibition of agricultural implements had been opened in the neighborhood, only two days since; and a public competition between rival machines was to be decided on the coming Monday. Not only was the Hand-in-Hand inn crowded, but even the accommodation offered by the nearest town had proved barely sufficient to meet the public demand.

The gentlemen looked at each other and agreed that there was no help for it but to hurry the supper, and walk to the railway station—a distance of between five and six miles—in time to catch the last train.

While the meal was being prepared, the rain held off for a while. The dark man asked his way to the post-office and went out by himself.

He came back in about ten minutes, and sat down afterward to supper with his companion. Neither the landlord, nor any other person in the public room, noticed any change in him on his return. He was a grave, quiet sort of person, and (unlike the other one) not much of a talker.

As the darkness came on, the rain fell again heavily; and the heavens were black.

A flash of lightning startled the gentlemen when they went to the window to look out: the thunderstorm began. It was simply impossible that two strangers to the neighborhood could find their way to the station, through storm and darkness, in time to catch the train. With or without bedrooms, they must remain at the inn for the night. Having already given up their own room to their lodgers, the landlord and landlady had no other place to sleep in than the kitchen. Next to the kitchen, and communicating with it by a door, was an outhouse; used, partly as a scullery, partly as a lumber-room. There was an old truckle-bed among the lumber, on which one of the gentlemen might rest. A mattress on the floor could be provided for the other. After adding a table and a basin, for the purposes of the toilet, the accommodation which Mr. Rook was able to offer came to an end.

The travelers agreed to occupy this makeshift bed-chamber.

The thunderstorm passed away; but the rain continued to fall heavily. Soon after eleven the guests at the inn retired for the night. There was some little discussion between the two travelers, as to which of them should take possession of the truckle-bed. It was put an end to by the fair gentleman, in his own pleasant way. He proposed to "toss up for it"—and he lost. The dark gentleman went to bed first; the fair gentleman followed, after waiting a while. Mr. Rook took his knapsack into the outhouse; and arranged on the table his appliances for the toilet—contained in a leather roll, and including a razor—ready for use in the morning.

Having previously barred the second door of the outhouse, which led into the yard, Mr. Rook fastened the other door, the lock and bolts of which were on the side of the kitchen. He then secured the house door, and the shutters over the lower windows. Returning to the kitchen, he noticed that the time was ten minutes short of midnight. Soon afterward, he and his wife went to bed.

Nothing happened to disturb Mr. and Mrs. Rook during the night.

At a quarter to seven the next morning, he got up; his wife being still asleep. He had been instructed to wake the gentlemen early; and he knocked at their door. Receiving no answer, after repeatedly knocking, he opened the door and stepped into the outhouse.

At this point in his evidence, the witness's recollections appeared to overpower him. "Give me a moment, gentlemen," he said to the jury. "I have had a dreadful fright; and I don't believe I shall get over it for the rest of my life."

The coroner helped him by a question: "What did you see when you opened the door?"

Mr. Rook answered: "I saw the dark man stretched out on his bed—dead, with a frightful wound in his throat. I saw an open razor, stained with smears of blood, at his side."

"Did you notice the door, leading into the yard?"

"It was wide open, sir. When I was able to look round me, the other traveler—I mean the man with the fair complexion, who carried the knapsack—was nowhere to be seen."

"What did you do, after making these discoveries?"

"I closed the yard door. Then I locked the other door, and put the key in my pocket. After that I roused the servant, and sent him to the constable—who lived near to us—while I ran for the doctor, whose house was at the other end of our village. The doctor sent his groom, on horseback, to the police-office in the town. When I returned to the inn, the constable was there—and he and the police took the matter into their own hands."

"You have nothing more to tell us?"

"Nothing more."

CHAPTER XXV. "J. B."

Mr. Rook having completed his evidence, the police authorities were the next witnesses examined.

They had not found the slightest trace of any attempt to break into the house in the night. The murdered man's gold watch and chain were discovered under his pillow. On examining his clothes the money was found in his purse, and the gold studs and sleeve buttons were left in his shirt. But his pocketbook (seen by witnesses who had not yet been examined) was missing. The search for visiting cards and letters had proved to be fruitless. Only the initials, "J. B.," were marked on his linen. He had brought no luggage with him to the inn. Nothing could be found which led to the discovery of his name or of the purpose which had taken him into that part of the country.

The police examined the outhouse next, in search of circumstantial evidence against the missing man.

He must have carried away his knapsack, when he took to flight, but he had been (probably) in too great a hurry to look for his razor—or perhaps too terrified to touch it, if it had attracted his notice. The leather roll, and the other articles used for his toilet, had been taken away. Mr. Rook identified the blood-stained razor. He had noticed overnight the name of the Belgian city, "Liege," engraved on it.

The yard was the next place inspected. Foot-steps were found on the muddy earth up to the wall. But the road on the other side had been recently mended with stones, and the trace of the fugitive was lost. Casts had been taken of the footsteps; and no other means of discovery had been left untried. The authorities in London had also been communicated with by telegraph.

The doctor being called, described a personal peculiarity, which he had noticed at the post-mortem examination, and which might lead to the identification of the murdered man.

As to the cause of death, the witness said it could be stated in two words. The internal jugular vein had been cut through, with such violence, judging by the appearances, that the wound could not have been inflicted, in the act of suicide, by the hand of the deceased person. No other injuries, and no sign of disease, was found on the body. The one cause of death had been Hemorrhage; and the one peculiarity which called for notice had been discovered in the mouth. Two of the front teeth, in the upper jaw, were false. They had been so admirably made to resemble the natural teeth on either side of them, in form and color, that the witness had only hit on the discovery by accidentally touching the inner side of the gum with one of his fingers.

The landlady was examined, when the doctor had retired. Mrs. Rook was able, in answering questions put to her, to give important information, in reference to the missing pocketbook.

Before retiring to rest, the two gentlemen had paid the bill—intending to leave the inn the first thing in the morning. The traveler with the knapsack paid his share in money. The other unfortunate gentleman looked into his purse, and found only a shilling and a sixpence in it. He asked Mrs. Rook if she could change a bank-note. She told him it could be done, provided the note was for no considerable sum of money. Upon that he opened his pocketbook (which the witness described minutely) and turned out the contents on the table. After searching among many Bank of England notes, some in one pocket of the book and some in another, he found a note of the value of five pounds. He thereupon settled his bill, and received the change from Mrs. Rook—her husband being in another part of the room, attending to the guests. She noticed a letter in an envelope, and a few cards which looked (to her judgment) like visiting cards, among the bank-notes which he had turned out on the table. When she returned to him with the change, he had just put them back, and was closing the pocketbook. She saw him place it in one of the breast pockets of his coat.

The fellow-traveler who had accompanied him to the inn was present all the time, sitting on the opposite side of the table. He made a remark when he saw the notes produced. He said, "Put all that money back—don't tempt a poor man like me!" It was said laughing, as if by way of a joke.

Mrs. Rook had observed nothing more that night; had slept as soundly as usual; and had been awakened when her husband knocked at the outhouse door, according to instructions received from the gentlemen, overnight.

Three of the guests in the public room corroborated Mrs. Rook's evidence. They were respectable persons, well and widely known in that part of Hampshire. Besides these, there were two strangers staying in the house. They referred the coroner to their employers—eminent manufacturers at Sheffield and Wolverhampton—whose testimony spoke for itself.

The last witness called was a grocer in the village, who kept the post-office.

On the evening of the 30th, a dark gentleman, wearing his beard, knocked at the door, and asked for a letter addressed to "J. B., Post-office, Zeeland." The letter had arrived by that morning's post; but, being Sunday evening, the grocer requested that application might be made for it the next morning. The stranger said the letter contained news, which it was of importance to him to receive without delay. Upon this, the grocer made an exception to customary rules and gave him the letter. He read it by the light of the lamp in the passage. It must have been short, for the reading was done in a moment. He seemed to think over it for a while; and then he turned round to go out. There was nothing to notice in his look or in his manner. The witness offered a remark on the weather; and the gentleman said, "Yes, it looks like a bad night"—and so went away.

The postmaster's evidence was of importance in one respect: it suggested the motive which had brought the deceased to Zeeland. The letter addressed to "J. B." was, in all probability, the letter seen by Mrs. Rook among the contents of the pocketbook, spread out on the table.

The inquiry being, so far, at an end, the inquest was adjourned—on the chance of obtaining additional evidence, when the reported proceedings were read by the public.

....

Consulting a later number of the newspaper Emily discovered that the deceased person had been identified by a witness from London.

Henry Forth, gentleman's valet, being examined, made the following statement:

He had read the medical evidence contained in the report of the inquest; and, believing that he could identify the deceased, had been sent by his present master to assist the object of the inquiry. Ten days since, being then out of place, he had answered an advertisement. The next day, he was instructed to call at Tracey's Hotel, London, at six o'clock in the evening, and to ask for Mr. James Brown. Arriving at the hotel he saw the gentleman for a few minutes only. Mr. Brown had a friend with him. After glancing over the valet's references, he said, "I haven't time enough to speak to you this evening. Call here to-morrow morning at nine o'clock." The gentleman who was present laughed, and said, "You won't be up!" Mr. Brown answered, "That won't matter; the man can come to my bedroom, and let me see how he understands his duties, on trial." At nine the next morning, Mr. Brown was reported to be still in bed; and the witness was informed of the number of the room. He knocked at the door. A drowsy voice inside said something, which he interpreted as meaning "Come in." He went in. The toilet-table was on his left hand, and the bed (with the lower curtain drawn) was on his right. He saw on the table a tumbler with a little water in it, and with two false teeth in the water. Mr. Brown started up in bed—looked at him furiously—abused him for daring to enter the room—and shouted to him to "get out." The witness, not accustomed to be treated in that way, felt naturally indignant, and at once withdrew—but not before he had plainly seen the vacant place which the false teeth had been made to fill. Perhaps Mr. Brown had forgotten that he had left his teeth on the table. Or perhaps he (the valet) had misunderstood what had been said to him when he knocked at the door. Either way, it seemed to be plain enough that the gentleman resented the discovery of his false teeth by a stranger.

Having concluded his statement the witness proceeded to identify the

303

remains of the deceased.

He at once recognized the gentleman named James Brown, whom he had twice seen—once in the evening, and again the next morning—at Tracey's Hotel. In answer to further inquiries, he declared that he knew nothing of the family, or of the place of residence, of the deceased. He complained to the proprietor of the hotel of the rude treatment that he had received, and asked if Mr. Tracey knew anything of Mr. James Brown. Mr. Tracey knew nothing of him. On consulting the hotel book it was found that he had given notice to leave, that afternoon.

Before returning to London, the witness produced references which gave him an excellent character. He also left the address of the master who had engaged him three days since.

The last precaution adopted was to have the face of the corpse photographed, before the coffin was closed. On the same day the jury agreed on their verdict: "Willful murder against some person unknown."

....

Two days later, Emily found a last allusion to the crime—extracted from the columns of the South Hampshire Gazette.

A relative of the deceased, seeing the report of the adjourned inquest, had appeared (accompanied by a medical gentleman); had seen the photograph; and had declared the identification by Henry Forth to be correct.

Among other particulars, now communicated for the first time, it was stated that the late Mr. James Brown had been unreasonably sensitive on the subject of his false teeth, and that the one member of his family who knew of his wearing them was the relative who now claimed his remains.

The claim having been established to the satisfaction of the authorities, the corpse was removed by railroad the same day. No further light had been thrown on the murder. The Handbill offering the reward, and describing the suspected man, had failed to prove of any assistance to the investigations of the police.

From that date, no further notice of the crime committed at the Hand-in-Hand inn appeared in the public journals.

....

Emily closed the volume which she had been consulting, and thankfully acknowledged the services of the librarian.

The new reader had excited this gentleman's interest. Noticing how carefully she examined the numbers of the old newspaper, he looked at her, from time to time, wondering whether it was good news or bad of which she was in search. She read steadily and continuously; but she never rewarded his curiosity by any outward sign of the impression that had been produced on her. When she left the room there was nothing to remark in her manner; she looked quietly thoughtful—and that was all.

The librarian smiled—amused by his own folly. Because a stranger's appearance had attracted him, he had taken it for granted that circumstances of romantic interest must be connected with her visit to the library. Far from misleading him, as he supposed, his fancy might have been employed to better purpose, if it had taken a higher flight still—and had associated Emily with the fateful gloom of tragedy, in place of the brighter interest of romance.

There, among the ordinary readers of the day, was a dutiful and affectionate daughter following the dreadful story of the death of her father by murder, and believing it to be the story of a stranger—because she loved and trusted the person whose short-sighted mercy had deceived her. That very discovery, the dread of which had shaken the good doctor's firm nerves, had forced Alban to exclude from his confidence the woman whom he loved, and had driven the faithful old servant from the bedside of her dying mistress—that very discovery Emily had now made, with a face which never changed color, and a heart which beat at ease. Was the deception that had won this cruel victory over truth destined still to triumph in the days which were to come? Yes—if the life of earth is a foretaste of the life of hell. No—if a lie is a lie, be the merciful motive for the falsehood what it may. No—if all deceit contains in it the seed of retribution, to be ripened inexorably in the lapse of time.

CHAPTER XXVI. MOTHER EVE.

The servant received Emily, on her return from the library, with a sly smile. "Here he is again, miss, waiting to see you."

She opened the parlor door, and revealed Alban Morris, as restless as ever, walking up and down the room.

"When I missed you at the Museum, I was afraid you might be ill," he said. "Ought I to have gone away, when my anxiety was relieved? Shall I go away now?"

"You must take a chair, Mr. Morris, and hear what I have to say for myself. When you left me after your last visit, I suppose I felt the force of example. At any rate I, like you, had my suspicions. I have been trying to confirm them—and I have failed."

He paused, with the chair in his hand. "Suspicions of Me?" he asked.

"Certainly! Can you guess how I have been employed for the last two days? No—not even your ingenuity can do that. I have been hard at work, in another reading-room, consulting the same back numbers of the same newspaper, which you have been examining at the British Museum. There is my confession—and now we will have some tea."

She moved to the fireplace, to ring the bell, and failed to see the effect produced on Alban by those lightly-uttered words. The common phrase is the only phrase that can describe it. He was thunderstruck.

"Yes," she resumed, "I have read the report of the inquest. If I know nothing else, I know that the murder at Zeeland can't be the discovery which you are bent on keeping from me. Don't be alarmed for the preservation of your secret! I am too much discouraged to try again."

The servant interrupted them by answering the bell; Alban once more escaped detection. Emily gave her orders with an approach to the old gayety of her school days. "Tea, as soon as possible—and let us have the new cake. Are you too much of a man, Mr. Morris, to like cake?"

In this state of agitation, he was unreasonably irritated by that playful question. "There is one thing I like better than cake," he said; "and that one thing is a plain explanation."

His tone puzzled her. "Have I said anything to offend you?" she asked. "Surely you can make allowance for a girl's curiosity? Oh, you shall have your explanation—and, what is more, you shall have it without reserve!"

She was as good as her word. What she had thought, and what she had planned, when he left her after his last visit, was frankly and fully told. "If you wonder how I discovered the library," she went on, "I must refer you to my aunt's lawyer. He lives in the City—and I wrote to him to help me. I don't consider that my time has been wasted. Mr. Morris, we owe an apology to Mrs. Rook."

Alban's astonishment, when he heard this, forced its way to expression in words. "What can you possibly mean?" he asked.

The tea was brought in before Emily could reply. She filled the cups, and sighed as she looked at the cake. "If Cecilia was here, how she would enjoy it!" With that complimentary tribute to her friend, she handed a slice to Alban. He never even noticed it.

"We have both of us behaved most unkindly to Mrs. Rook," she resumed. "I can excuse your not seeing it; for I should not have seen it either, but for the newspaper. While I was reading, I had an opportunity of thinking over what we said and did, when the poor woman's behavior so needlessly offended us. I was too excited to think, at the time—and, besides, I had been upset, only the night before, by what Miss Jethro said to me."

Alban started. "What has Miss Jethro to do with it?" he asked.

"Nothing at all," Emily answered. "She spoke to me of her own private affairs. A long story—and you wouldn't be interested in it. Let me finish what I had to say. Mrs. Rook was naturally reminded of the murder, when she heard that my name was Brown; and she must certainly have been struck—as I was—by the coincidence of my father's death taking place at the same time when his unfortunate namesake was killed. Doesn't this sufficiently account for her agitation when she looked at the locket? We first took her by

307

surprise: and then we suspected her of Heaven knows what, because the poor creature didn't happen to have her wits about her, and to remember at the right moment what a very common name 'James Brown' is. Don't you see it as I do?"

"I see that you have arrived at a remarkable change of opinion, since we spoke of the subject in the garden at school."

"In my place, you would have changed your opinion too. I shall write to Mrs. Rook by tomorrow's post."

Alban heard her with dismay. "Pray be guided by my advice!" he said earnestly. "Pray don't write that letter!"

"Why not?"

It was too late to recall the words which he had rashly allowed to escape him. How could he reply?

To own that he had not only read what Emily had read, but had carefully copied the whole narrative and considered it at his leisure, appeared to be simply impossible after what he had now heard. Her peace of mind depended absolutely on his discretion. In this serious emergency, silence was a mercy, and silence was a lie. If he remained silent, might the mercy be trusted to atone for the lie? He was too fond of Emily to decide that question fairly, on its own merits. In other words, he shrank from the terrible responsibility of telling her the truth.

"Isn't the imprudence of writing to such a person as Mrs. Rook plain enough to speak for itself?" he suggested cautiously.

"Not to me."

She made that reply rather obstinately. Alban seemed (in her view) to be trying to prevent her from atoning for an act of injustice. Besides, he despised her cake. "I want to know why you object," she said; taking back the neglected slice, and eating it herself.

"I object," Alban answered, "because Mrs. Rook is a coarse presuming woman. She may pervert your letter to some use of her own, which you may have reason to regret."

"Is that all?"

"Isn't it enough?"

"It may be enough for you. When I have done a person an injury, and wish to make an apology, I don't think it necessary to inquire whether the person's manners happen to be vulgar or not."

Alban's patience was still equal to any demands that she could make on it. "I can only offer you advice which is honestly intended for your own good," he gently replied.

"You would have more influence over me, Mr. Morris, if you were a little readier to take me into your confidence. I daresay I am wrong—but I don't like following advice which is given to me in the dark."

It was impossible to offend him. "Very naturally," he said; "I don't blame you."

Her color deepened, and her voice rose. Alban's patient adherence to his own view—so courteously and considerately urged—was beginning to try her temper. "In plain words," she rejoined, "I am to believe that you can't be mistaken in your judgment of another person."

There was a ring at the door of the cottage while she was speaking. But she was too warmly interested in confuting Alban to notice it.

He was quite willing to be confuted. Even when she lost her temper, she was still interesting to him. "I don't expect you to think me infallible," he said. "Perhaps you will remember that I have had some experience. I am unfortunately older than you are."

"Oh if wisdom comes with age," she smartly reminded him, "your friend Miss Redwood is old enough to be your mother—and she suspected Mrs. Rook of murder, because the poor woman looked at a door, and disliked being in the next room to a fidgety old maid."

Alban's manner changed: he shrank from that chance allusion to doubts and fears which he dare not acknowledge. "Let us talk of something else," he said.

She looked at him with a saucy smile. "Have I driven you into a corner at last? And is that your way of getting out of it?"

Even his endurance failed. "Are you trying to provoke me?" he asked. "Are you no better than other women? I wouldn't have believed it of you, Emily."

"Emily?" She repeated the name in a tone of surprise, which reminded him that he had addressed her with familiarity at a most inappropriate time—the time when they were on the point of a quarrel. He felt the implied reproach too keenly to be able to answer her with composure.

"I think of Emily—I love Emily—my one hope is that Emily may love me. Oh, my dear, is there no excuse if I forget to call you 'Miss' when you distress me?"

All that was tender and true in her nature secretly took his part. She would have followed that better impulse, if he had only been calm enough to understand her momentary silence, and to give her time. But the temper of a gentle and generous man, once roused, is slow to subside. Alban abruptly left his chair. "I had better go!" he said.

"As you please," she answered. "Whether you go, Mr. Morris, or whether you stay, I shall write to Mrs. Rook."

The ring at the bell was followed by the appearance of a visitor. Doctor Allday opened the door, just in time to hear Emily's last words. Her vehemence seemed to amuse him.

"Who is Mrs. Rook?" he asked.

"A most respectable person," Emily answered indignantly; "housekeeper to Sir Jervis Redwood. You needn't sneer at her, Doctor Allday! She has not always been in service—she was landlady of the inn at Zeeland."

The doctor, about to put his hat on a chair, paused. The inn at Zeeland

310

reminded him of the Handbill, and of the visit of Miss Jethro.

"Why are you so hot over it?" he inquired

"Because I detest prejudice!" With this assertion of liberal feeling she pointed to Alban, standing quietly apart at the further end of the room. "There is the most prejudiced man living—he hates Mrs. Rook. Would you like to be introduced to him? You're a philosopher; you may do him some good. Doctor Allday—Mr. Alban Morris."

The doctor recognized the man, with the felt hat and the objectionable beard, whose personal appearance had not impressed him favorably.

Although they may hesitate to acknowledge it, there are respectable Englishmen still left, who regard a felt hat and a beard as symbols of republican disaffection to the altar and the throne. Doctor Allday's manner might have expressed this curious form of patriotic feeling, but for the associations which Emily had revived. In his present frame of mind, he was outwardly courteous, because he was inwardly suspicious. Mrs. Rook had been described to him as formerly landlady of the inn at Zeeland. Were there reasons for Mr. Morris's hostile feeling toward this woman which might be referable to the crime committed in her house that might threaten Emily's tranquillity if they were made known? It would not be amiss to see a little more of Mr. Morris, on the first convenient occasion.

"I am glad to make your acquaintance, sir."

"You are very kind, Doctor Allday."

The exchange of polite conventionalities having been accomplished, Alban approached Emily to take his leave, with mingled feelings of regret and anxiety—regret for having allowed himself to speak harshly; anxiety to part with her in kindness.

"Will you forgive me for differing from you?" It was all he could venture to say, in the presence of a stranger.

"Oh, yes!" she said quietly.

"Will you think again, before you decide?"

"Certainly, Mr. Morris. But it won't alter my opinion, if I do."

The doctor, hearing what passed between them, frowned. On what subject had they been differing? And what opinion did Emily decline to alter?

Alban gave it up. He took her hand gently. "Shall I see you at the Museum, to-morrow?" he asked.

She was politely indifferent to the last. "Yes—unless something happens to keep me at home."

The doctor's eyebrows still expressed disapproval. For what object was the meeting proposed? And why at a museum?

"Good-afternoon, Doctor Allday."

"Good-afternoon, sir."

For a moment after Alban's departure, the doctor stood irresolute. Arriving suddenly at a decision, he snatched up his hat, and turned to Emily in a hurry.

"I bring you news, my dear, which will surprise you. Who do you think has just left my house? Mrs. Ellmother! Don't interrupt me. She has made up her mind to go out to service again. Tired of leading an idle life—that's her own account of it—and asks me to act as her reference."

"Did you consent?"

"Consent! If I act as her reference, I shall be asked how she came to leave her last place. A nice dilemma! Either I must own that she deserted her mistress on her deathbed—or tell a lie. When I put it to her in that way, she walked out of the house in dead silence. If she applies to you next, receive her as I did—or decline to see her, which would be better still."

"Why am I to decline to see her?"

"In consequence of her behavior to your aunt, to be sure! No: I have said all I wanted to say—and I have no time to spare for answering idle questions. Good-by."

Socially-speaking, doctors try the patience of their nearest and dearest friends, in this respect—they are almost always in a hurry. Doctor Allday's precipitate departure did not tend to soothe Emily's irritated nerves. She began to find excuses for Mrs. Ellmother in a spirit of pure contradiction. The old servant's behavior might admit of justification: a friendly welcome might persuade her to explain herself. "If she applies to me," Emily determined, "I shall certainly receive her."

Having arrived at this resolution, her mind reverted to Alban.

Some of the sharp things she had said to him, subjected to after-reflection in solitude, failed to justify themselves. Her better sense began to reproach her. She tried to silence that unwelcome monitor by laying the blame on Alban. Why had he been so patient and so good? What harm was there in his calling her "Emily"? If he had told her to call him by his Christian name, she might have done it. How noble he looked, when he got up to go away; he was actually handsome! Women may say what they please and write what they please: their natural instinct is to find their master in a man—especially when they like him. Sinking lower and lower in her own estimation, Emily tried to turn the current of her thoughts in another direction. She took up a book—opened it, looked into it, threw it across the room.

If Alban had returned at that moment, resolved on a reconciliation—if he had said, "My dear, I want to see you like yourself again; will you give me a kiss, and make it up"—would he have left her crying, when he went away? She was crying now.

CHAPTER XXVII. MENTOR AND TELEMACHUS.

If Emily's eyes could have followed Alban as her thoughts were following him, she would have seen him stop before he reached the end of the road in which the cottage stood. His heart was full of tenderness and sorrow: the longing to return to her was more than he could resist. It would be easy to wait, within view of the gate, until the doctor's visit came to an end. He had just decided to go back and keep watch—when he heard rapid footsteps approaching. There (devil take him!) was the doctor himself.

"I have something to say to you, Mr. Morris. Which way are you walking?"

"Any way," Alban answered—not very graciously.

"Then let us take the turning that leads to my house. It's not customary for strangers, especially when they happen to be Englishmen, to place confidence in each other. Let me set the example of violating that rule. I want to speak to you about Miss Emily. May I take your arm? Thank you. At my age, girls in general—unless they are my patients—are not objects of interest to me. But that girl at the cottage—I daresay I am in my dotage—I tell you, sir, she has bewitched me! Upon my soul, I could hardly be more anxious about her, if I was her father. And, mind, I am not an affectionate man by nature. Are you anxious about her too?"

"Yes."

"In what way?"

"In what way are you anxious, Doctor Allday?"

The doctor smiled grimly.

"You don't trust me? Well, I have promised to set the example. Keep your mask on, sir—mine is off, come what may of it. But, observe: if you repeat what I am going to say—"

Alban would hear no more. "Whatever you may say, Doctor Allday, is trusted to my honor. If you doubt my honor, be so good as to let go my arm—I am not walking your way."

The doctor's hand tightened its grasp. "That little flourish of temper, my dear sir, is all I want to set me at my ease. I feel I have got hold of the right man. Now answer me this. Have you ever heard of a person named Miss Jethro?"

Alban suddenly came to a standstill.

"All right!" said the doctor. "I couldn't have wished for a more satisfactory reply."

"Wait a minute," Alban interposed. "I know Miss Jethro as a teacher at

314

Miss Ladd's school, who left her situation suddenly—and I know no more."

The doctor's peculiar smile made its appearance again.

"Speaking in the vulgar tone," he said, "you seem to be in a hurry to wash your hands of Miss Jethro."

"I have no reason to feel any interest in her," Alban replied.

"Don't be too sure of that, my friend. I have something to tell you which may alter your opinion. That ex-teacher at the school, sir, knows how the late Mr. Brown met his death, and how his daughter has been deceived about it."

Alban listened with surprise—and with some little doubt, which he thought it wise not to acknowledge.

"The report of the inquest alludes to a 'relative' who claimed the body," he said. "Was that 'relative' the person who deceived Miss Emily? And was the person her aunt?"

"I must leave you to take your own view," Doctor Allday replied. "A promise binds me not to repeat the information that I have received. Setting that aside, we have the same object in view—and we must take care not to get in each other's way. Here is my house. Let us go in, and make a clean breast of it on both sides."

Established in the safe seclusion of his study, the doctor set the example of confession in these plain terms:

"We only differ in opinion on one point," he said. "We both think it likely (from our experience of the women) that the suspected murderer had an accomplice. I say the guilty person is Miss Jethro. You say—Mrs. Rook."

"When you have read my copy of the report," Alban answered, "I think you will arrive at my conclusion. Mrs. Rook might have entered the outhouse in which the two men slept, at any time during the night, while her husband was asleep. The jury believed her when she declared that she never woke till the morning. I don't."

"I am open to conviction, Mr. Morris. Now about the future. Do you

315

mean to go on with your inquiries?"

"Even if I had no other motive than mere curiosity," Alban answered, "I think I should go on. But I have a more urgent purpose in view. All that I have done thus far, has been done in Emily's interests. My object, from the first, has been to preserve her from any association—in the past or in the future—with the woman whom I believe to have been concerned in her father's death. As I have already told you, she is innocently doing all she can, poor thing, to put obstacles in my way."

"Yes, yes," said the doctor; "she means to write to Mrs. Rook—and you have nearly quarreled about it. Trust me to take that matter in hand. I don't regard it as serious. But I am mortally afraid of what you are doing in Emily's interests. I wish you would give it up."

"Why?"

"Because I see a danger. I don't deny that Emily is as innocent of suspicion as ever. But the chances, next time, may be against us. How do you know to what lengths your curiosity may lead you? Or on what shocking discoveries you may not blunder with the best intentions? Some unforeseen accident may open her eyes to the truth, before you can prevent it. I seem to surprise you?"

"You do, indeed, surprise me."

"In the old story, my dear sir, Mentor sometimes surprised Telemachus. I am Mentor—without being, I hope, quite so long-winded as that respectable philosopher. Let me put it in two words. Emily's happiness is precious to you. Take care you are not made the means of wrecking it! Will you consent to a sacrifice, for her sake?"

"I will do anything for her sake."

"Will you give up your inquiries?"

"From this moment I have done with them!"

"Mr. Morris, you are the best friend she has."

316

"The next best friend to you, doctor."

In that fond persuasion they now parted—too eagerly devoted to Emily to look at the prospect before them in its least hopeful aspect. Both clever men, neither one nor the other asked himself if any human resistance has ever yet obstructed the progress of truth—when truth has once begun to force its way to the light.

For the second time Alban stopped, on his way home. The longing to be reconciled with Emily was not to be resisted. He returned to the cottage, only to find disappointment waiting for him. The servant reported that her young mistress had gone to bed with a bad headache.

Alban waited a day, in the hope that Emily might write to him. No letter arrived. He repeated his visit the next morning. Fortune was still against him. On this occasion, Emily was engaged.

"Engaged with a visitor?" he asked.

"Yes, sir. A young lady named Miss de Sor."

Where had he heard that name before? He remembered immediately that he had heard it at the school. Miss de Sor was the unattractive new pupil, whom the girls called Francine. Alban looked at the parlor window as he left the cottage. It was of serious importance that he should set himself right with Emily. "And mere gossip," he thought contemptuously, "stands in my way!"

If he had been less absorbed in his own interests, he might have remembered that mere gossip is not always to be despised. It has worked fatal mischief in its time.

CHAPTER XXVIII. FRANCINE.

"You're surprised to see me, of course?" Saluting Emily in those terms, Francine looked round the parlor with an air of satirical curiosity. "Dear me, what a little place to live in!"

"What brings you to London?" Emily inquired.

"You ought to know, my dear, without asking. Why did I try to make friends with you at school? And why have I been trying ever since? Because I hate you—I mean because I can't resist you—no! I mean because I hate myself for liking you. Oh, never mind my reasons. I insisted on going to London with Miss Ladd—when that horrid woman announced that she had an appointment with her lawyer. I said, 'I want to see Emily.' 'Emily doesn't like you.' 'I don't care whether she likes me or not; I want to see her.' That's the way we snap at each other, and that's how I always carry my point. Here I am, till my duenna finishes her business and fetches me. What a prospect for You! Have you got any cold meat in the house? I'm not a glutton, like Cecilia—but I'm afraid I shall want some lunch."

"Don't talk in that way, Francine!"

"Do you mean to say you're glad to see me?"

"If you were only a little less hard and bitter, I should always be glad to see you."

"You darling! (excuse my impetuosity). What are you looking at? My new dress? Do you envy me?"

"No; I admire the color—that's all."

Francine rose, and shook out her dress, and showed it from every point of view. "See how it's made: Paris, of course! Money, my dear; money will do anything—except making one learn one's lessons."

"Are you not getting on any better, Francine?"

"Worse, my sweet friend—worse. One of the masters, I am happy to say, has flatly refused to teach me any longer. 'Pupils without brains I am accustomed to,' he said in his broken English; 'but a pupil with no heart is beyond my endurance.' Ha! ha! the mouldy old refugee has an eye for character, though. No heart—there I am, described in two words."

"And proud of it," Emily remarked.

"Yes—proud of it. Stop! let me do myself justice. You consider tears a sign that one has some heart, don't you? I was very near crying last Sunday.

318

A popular preacher did it; no less a person that Mr. Mirabel—you look as if you had heard of him."

"I have heard of him from Cecilia."

"Is she at Brighton? Then there's one fool more in a fashionable watering place. Oh, she's in Switzerland, is she? I don't care where she is; I only care about Mr. Mirabel. We all heard he was at Brighton for his health, and was going to preach. Didn't we cram the church! As to describing him, I give it up. He is the only little man I ever admired—hair as long as mine, and the sort of beard you see in pictures. I wish I had his fair complexion and his white hands. We were all in love with him—or with his voice, which was it?—when he began to read the commandments. I wish I could imitate him when he came to the fifth commandment. He began in his deepest bass voice: 'Honor thy father—' He stopped and looked up to heaven as if he saw the rest of it there. He went on with a tremendous emphasis on the next word. 'And thy mother,' he said (as if that was quite a different thing) in a tearful, fluty, quivering voice which was a compliment to mothers in itself. We all felt it, mothers or not. But the great sensation was when he got into the pulpit. The manner in which he dropped on his knees, and hid his face in his hands, and showed his beautiful rings was, as a young lady said behind me, simply seraphic. We understood his celebrity, from that moment—I wonder whether I can remember the sermon."

"You needn't attempt it on my account," Emily said.

"My dear, don't be obstinate. Wait till you hear him."

"I am quite content to wait."

"Ah, you're just in the right state of mind to be converted; you're in a fair way to become one of his greatest admirers. They say he is so agreeable in private life; I am dying to know him.—Do I hear a ring at the bell? Is somebody else coming to see you?"

The servant brought in a card and a message.

"The person will call again, miss."

Emily looked at the name written on the card.

"Mrs. Ellmother!" she exclaimed.

"What an extraordinary name!" cried Francine. "Who is she?"

"My aunt's old servant."

"Does she want a situation?"

Emily looked at some lines of writing at the back of the card. Doctor Allday had rightly foreseen events. Rejected by the doctor, Mrs. Ellmother had no alternative but to ask Emily to help her.

"If she is out of place," Francine went on, "she may be just the sort of person I am looking for."

"You?" Emily asked, in astonishment.

Francine refused to explain until she got an answer to her question. "Tell me first," she said, "is Mrs. Ellmother engaged?"

"No; she wants an engagement, and she asks me to be her reference."

"Is she sober, honest, middle-aged, clean, steady, good-tempered, industrious?" Francine rattled on. "Has she all the virtues, and none of the vices? Is she not too good-looking, and has she no male followers? In one terrible word—will she satisfy Miss Ladd?"

"What has Miss Ladd to do with it?"

"How stupid you are, Emily! Do put the woman's card down on the table, and listen to me. Haven't I told you that one of my masters has declined to have anything more to do with me? Doesn't that help you to understand how I get on with the rest of them? I am no longer Miss Ladd's pupil, my dear. Thanks to my laziness and my temper, I am to be raised to the dignity of 'a parlor boarder.' In other words, I am to be a young lady who patronizes the school; with a room of my own, and a servant of my own. All provided for by a private arrangement between my father and Miss Ladd, before I left the West Indies. My mother was at the bottom of it, I have not the least doubt.

You don't appear to understand me."

"I don't, indeed!"

Francine considered a little. "Perhaps they were fond of you at home," she suggested.

"Say they loved me, Francine—and I loved them."

"Ah, my position is just the reverse of yours. Now they have got rid of me, they don't want me back again at home. I know as well what my mother said to my father, as if I had heard her. 'Francine will never get on at school, at her age. Try her, by all means; but make some other arrangement with Miss Ladd in case of a failure—or she will be returned on our hands like a bad shilling.' There is my mother, my anxious, affectionate mother, hit off to a T."

"She is your mother, Francine; don't forget that."

"Oh, no; I won't forget it. My cat is my kitten's mother—there! there! I won't shock your sensibilities. Let us get back to matter of fact. When I begin my new life, Miss Ladd makes one condition. My maid is to be a model of discretion—an elderly woman, not a skittish young person who will only encourage me. I must submit to the elderly woman, or I shall be sent back to the West Indies after all. How long did Mrs. Ellmother live with your aunt?"

"Twenty-five years, and more.'

"Good heavens, it's a lifetime! Why isn't this amazing creature living with you, now your aunt is dead? Did you send her away?"

"Certainly not."

"Then why did she go?"

"I don't know."

"Do you mean that she went away without a word of explanation?"

"Yes; that is exactly what I mean."

"When did she go? As soon as your aunt was dead?"

"That doesn't matter, Francine."

"In plain English, you won't tell me? I am all on fire with curiosity—and that's how you put me out! My dear, if you have the slightest regard for me, let us have the woman in here when she comes back for her answer. Somebody must satisfy me. I mean to make Mrs. Ellmother explain herself."

"I don't think you will succeed, Francine."

"Wait a little, and you will see. By-the-by, it is understood that my new position at the school gives me the privilege of accepting invitations. Do you know any nice people to whom you can introduce me?"

"I am the last person in the world who has a chance of helping you," Emily answered. "Excepting good Doctor Allday—" On the point of adding the name of Alban Morris, she checked herself without knowing why, and substituted the name of her school-friend. "And not forgetting Cecilia," she resumed, "I know nobody."

"Cecilia's a fool," Francine remarked gravely; "but now I think of it, she may be worth cultivating. Her father is a member of Parliament—and didn't I hear that he has a fine place in the country? You see, Emily, I may expect to be married (with my money), if I can only get into good society. (Don't suppose I am dependent on my father; my marriage portion is provided for in my uncle's will.) Cecilia may really be of some use to me. Why shouldn't I make a friend of her, and get introduced to her father—in the autumn, you know, when the house is full of company? Have you any idea when she is coming back?"

"No."

"Do you think of writing to her?"

"Of course!"

"Give her my kind love; and say I hope she enjoys Switzerland."

"Francine, you are positively shameless! After calling my dearest friend a fool and a glutton, you send her your love for your own selfish ends; and you

322

expect me to help you in deceiving her! I won't do it."

"Keep your temper, my child. We are all selfish, you little goose. The only difference is—some of us own it, and some of us don't. I shall find my own way to Cecilia's good graces quite easily: the way is through her mouth. You mentioned a certain Doctor Allday. Does he give parties? And do the right sort of men go to them? Hush! I think I hear the bell again. Go to the door, and see who it is."

Emily waited, without taking any notice of this suggestion. The servant announced that "the person had called again, to know if there was any answer."

"Show her in here," Emily said.

The servant withdrew, and came back again.

"The person doesn't wish to intrude, miss; it will be quite sufficient if you will send a message by me."

Emily crossed the room to the door.

"Come in, Mrs. Ellmother," she said. "You have been too long away already. Pray come in."

CHAPTER XXIX. "BONY."

Mrs. Ellmother reluctantly entered the room.

Since Emily had seen her last, her personal appearance doubly justified the nickname by which her late mistress had distinguished her. The old servant was worn and wasted; her gown hung loose on her angular body; the big bones of her face stood out, more prominently than ever. She took Emily's offered hand doubtingly. "I hope I see you well, miss," she said—with hardly a vestige left of her former firmness of voice and manner.

"I am afraid you have been suffering from illness," Emily answered gently.

"It's the life I'm leading that wears me down; I want work and change."

Making that reply, she looked round, and discovered Francine observing her with undisguised curiosity. "You have got company with you," she said to Emily. "I had better go away, and come back another time."

Francine stopped her before she could open the door. "You mustn't go away; I wish to speak to you."

"About what, miss?"

The eyes of the two women met—one, near the end of her life, concealing under a rugged surface a nature sensitively affectionate and incorruptibly true: the other, young in years, without the virtues of youth, hard in manner and hard at heart. In silence on either side, they stood face to face; strangers brought together by the force of circumstances, working inexorably toward their hidden end.

Emily introduced Mrs. Ellmother to Francine. "It may be worth your while," she hinted, "to hear what this young lady has to say."

Mrs. Ellmother listened, with little appearance of interest in anything that a stranger might have to say: her eyes rested on the card which contained her written request to Emily. Francine, watching her closely, understood what was passing in her mind. It might be worth while to conciliate the old woman by a little act of attention. Turning to Emily, Francine pointed to the card lying on the table. "You have not attended yet to Mr. Ellmother's request," she said.

Emily at once assured Mrs. Ellmother that the request was granted. "But is it wise," she asked, "to go out to service again, at your age?"

"I have been used to service all my life, Miss Emily—that's one reason. And service may help me to get rid of my own thoughts—that's another. If you can find me a situation somewhere, you will be doing me a good turn."

"Is it useless to suggest that you might come back, and live with me?" Emily ventured to say.

Mrs. Ellmother's head sank on her breast. "Thank you kindly, miss; it is useless."

"Why is it useless?" Francine asked.

Mrs. Ellmother was silent.

"Miss de Sor is speaking to you," Emily reminded her.

"Am I to answer Miss de Sor?"

Attentively observing what passed, and placing her own construction on looks and tones, it suddenly struck Francine that Emily herself might be in Mrs. Ellmother's confidence, and that she might have reasons of her own for assuming ignorance when awkward questions were asked. For the moment at least, Francine decided on keeping her suspicions to herself.

"I may perhaps offer you the employment you want," she said to Mrs. Ellmother. "I am staying at Brighton, for the present, with the lady who was Miss Emily's schoolmistress, and I am in need of a maid. Would you be willing to consider it, if I proposed to engage you?"

"Yes, miss."

"In that case, you can hardly object to the customary inquiry. Why did you leave your last place?"

Mrs. Ellmother appealed to Emily. "Did you tell this young lady how long I remained in my last place?"

Melancholy remembrances had been revived in Emily by the turn which the talk had now taken. Francine's cat-like patience, stealthily feeling its way to its end, jarred on her nerves. "Yes," she said; "in justice to you, I have mentioned your long term of service."

Mrs. Ellmother addressed Francine. "You know, miss, that I served my late mistress for over twenty-five years. Will you please remember that—and let it be a reason for not asking me why I left my place."

Francine smiled compassionately. "My good creature, you have mentioned the very reason why I should ask. You live five-and-twenty years with your mistress—and then suddenly leave her—and you expect me to pass over this extraordinary proceeding without inquiry. Take a little time to think."

"I want no time to think. What I had in my mind, when I left Miss Letitia, is something which I refuse to explain, miss, to you, or to anybody."

She recovered some of her old firmness, when she made that reply. Francine saw the necessity of yielding—for the time at least, Emily remained silent, oppressed by remembrance of the doubts and fears which had darkened the last miserable days of her aunt's illness. She began already to regret having made Francine and Mrs. Ellmother known to each other.

"I won't dwell on what appears to be a painful subject," Francine graciously resumed. "I meant no offense. You are not angry, I hope?"

"Sorry, miss. I might have been angry, at one time. That time is over."

It was said sadly and resignedly: Emily heard the answer. Her heart ached as she looked at the old servant, and thought of the contrast between past and present. With what a hearty welcome this broken woman had been used to receive her in the bygone holiday-time! Her eyes moistened. She felt the merciless persistency of Francine, as if it had been an insult offered to herself. "Give it up!" she said sharply.

"Leave me, my dear, to manage my own business," Francine replied. "About your qualifications?" she continued, turning coolly to Mrs. Ellmother. "Can you dress hair?"

"Yes."

"I ought to tell you," Francine insisted, "that I am very particular about my hair."

"My mistress was very particular about her hair," Mrs. Ellmother answered.

"Are you a good needlewoman?"

"As good as ever I was—with the help of my spectacles."

Francine turned to Emily. "See how well we get on together. We are beginning to understand each other already. I am an odd creature, Mrs. Ellmother. Sometimes, I take sudden likings to persons—I have taken a liking to you. Do you begin to think a little better of me than you did? I hope you will produce the right impression on Miss Ladd; you shall have every assistance that I can give. I will beg Miss Ladd, as a favor to me, not to ask you that one forbidden question."

Poor Mrs. Ellmother, puzzled by the sudden appearance of Francine in the character of an eccentric young lady, the creature of genial impulse, thought it right to express her gratitude for the promised interference in her favor. "That's kind of you, miss," she said.

"No, no, only just. I ought to tell you there's one thing Miss Ladd is strict about—sweethearts. Are you quite sure," Francine inquired jocosely, "that you can answer for yourself, in that particular?"

This effort of humor produced its intended effect. Mrs. Ellmother, thrown off her guard, actually smiled. "Lord, miss, what will you say next!"

"My good soul, I will say something next that is more to the purpose. If Miss Ladd asks me why you have so unaccountably refused to be a servant again in this house, I shall take care to say that it is certainly not out of dislike to Miss Emily."

"You need say nothing of the sort," Emily quietly remarked.

"And still less," Francine proceeded, without noticing the interruption—"still less through any disagreeable remembrances of Miss Emily's aunt."

Mrs. Ellmother saw the trap that had been set for her. "It won't do, miss," she said.

"What won't do?"

"Trying to pump me."

Francine burst out laughing. Emily noticed an artificial ring in her gayety which suggested that she was exasperated, rather than amused, by the repulse which had baffled her curiosity once more.

Mrs. Ellmother reminded the merry young lady that the proposed arrangement between them had not been concluded yet. "Am I to understand, miss, that you will keep a place open for me in your service?"

"You are to understand," Francine replied sharply, "that I must have Miss Ladd's approval before I can engage you. Suppose you come to Brighton? I will pay your fare, of course."

"Never mind my fare, miss. Will you give up pumping?"

"Make your mind easy. It's quite useless to attempt pumping you. When will you come?"

Mrs. Ellmother pleaded for a little delay. "I'm altering my gowns," she said. "I get thinner and thinner—don't I, Miss Emily? My work won't be done before Thursday."

"Let us say Friday, then," Francine proposed.

"Friday!" Mrs. Ellmother exclaimed. "You forget that Friday is an unlucky day."

"I forgot that, certainly! How can you be so absurdly superstitious."

"You may call it what you like, miss. I have good reason to think as I do. I was married on a Friday—and a bitter bad marriage it turned out to be. Superstitious, indeed! You don't know what my experience has been. My only sister was one of a party of thirteen at dinner; and she died within the year. If we are to get on together nicely, I'll take that journey on Saturday, if you please."

"Anything to satisfy you," Francine agreed; "there is the address. Come in the middle of the day, and we will give you your dinner. No fear of our being thirteen in number. What will you do, if you have the misfortune to spill the salt?"

"Take a pinch between my finger and thumb, and throw it over my left shoulder," Mrs. Ellmother answered gravely. "Good-day, miss."

"Good-day."

Emily followed the departing visitor out to the hall. She had seen and heard enough to decide her on trying to break off the proposed negotiation—with the one kind purpose of protecting Mrs. Ellmother against the pitiless curiosity of Francine.

"Do you think you and that young lady are likely to get on well together?" she asked.

"I have told you already, Miss Emily, I want to get away from my own home and my own thoughts; I don't care where I go, so long as I do that." Having answered in those words, Mrs. Ellmother opened the door, and waited a while, thinking. "I wonder whether the dead know what is going on in the world they have left?" she said, looking at Emily. "If they do, there's one among them knows my thoughts, and feels for me. Good-by, miss—and don't think worse of me than I deserve."

Emily went back to the parlor. The only resource left was to plead with Francine for mercy to Mrs. Ellmother.

"Do you really mean to give it up?" she asked.

"To give up—what? 'Pumping,' as that obstinate old creature calls it?"

Emily persisted. "Don't worry the poor old soul! However strangely she may have left my aunt and me her motives are kind and good—I am sure of that. Will you let her keep her harmless little secret?"

"Oh, of course!"

"I don't believe you, Francine!"

"Don't you? I am like Cecilia—I am getting hungry. Shall we have some lunch?"

"You hard-hearted creature!"

"Does that mean—no luncheon until I have owned the truth? Suppose you own the truth? I won't tell Mrs. Ellmother that you have betrayed her."

"For the last time, Francine—I know no more of it than you do. If you persist in taking your own view, you as good as tell me I lie; and you will

329

oblige me to leave the room."

Even Francine's obstinacy was compelled to give way, so far as appearances went. Still possessed by the delusion that Emily was deceiving her, she was now animated by a stronger motive than mere curiosity. Her sense of her own importance imperatively urged her to prove that she was not a person who could be deceived with impunity.

"I beg your pardon," she said with humility. "But I must positively have it out with Mrs. Ellmother. She has been more than a match for me—my turn next. I mean to get the better of her; and I shall succeed."

"I have already told you, Francine—you will fail."

"My dear, I am a dunce, and I don't deny it. But let me tell you one thing. I haven't lived all my life in the West Indies, among black servants, without learning something."

"What do you mean?"

"More, my clever friend, than you are likely to guess. In the meantime, don't forget the duties of hospitality. Ring the bell for luncheon."

CHAPTER XXX. LADY DORIS.

The arrival of Miss Ladd, some time before she had been expected, interrupted the two girls at a critical moment. She had hurried over her business in London, eager to pass the rest of the day with her favorite pupil. Emily's affectionate welcome was, in some degree at least, inspired by a sensation of relief. To feel herself in the embrace of the warm-hearted schoolmistress was like finding a refuge from Francine.

When the hour of departure arrived, Miss Ladd invited Emily to Brighton for the second time. "On the last occasion, my dear, you wrote me an excuse; I won't be treated in that way again. If you can't return with us now, come to-morrow." She added in a whisper, "Otherwise, I shall think you include me in your dislike of Francine."

There was no resisting this. It was arranged that Emily should go to Brighton on the next day.

330

Left by herself, her thoughts might have reverted to Mrs. Ellmother's doubtful prospects, and to Francine's strange allusion to her life in the West Indies, but for the arrival of two letters by the afternoon post. The handwriting on one of them was unknown to her. She opened that one first. It was an answer to the letter of apology which she had persisted in writing to Mrs. Rook. Happily for herself, Alban's influence had not been without its effect, after his departure. She had written kindly—but she had written briefly at the same time.

Mrs. Rook's reply presented a nicely compounded mixture of gratitude and grief. The gratitude was addressed to Emily as a matter of course. The grief related to her "excellent master." Sir Jervis's strength had suddenly failed. His medical attendant, being summoned, had expressed no surprise. "My patient is over seventy years of age," the doctor remarked. "He will sit up late at night, writing his book; and he refuses to take exercise, till headache and giddiness force him to try the fresh air. As the necessary result, he has broken down at last. It may end in paralysis, or it may end in death." Reporting this expression of medical opinion, Mrs. Rook's letter glided imperceptibly from respectful sympathy to modest regard for her own interests in the future. It might be the sad fate of her husband and herself to be thrown on the world again. If necessity brought them to London, would "kind Miss Emily grant her the honor of an interview, and favor a poor unlucky woman with a word of advice?"

"She may pervert your letter to some use of her own, which you may have reason to regret." Did Emily remember Alban's warning words? No: she accepted Mrs. Rook's reply as a gratifying tribute to the justice of her own opinions.

Having proposed to write to Alban, feeling penitently that she had been in the wrong, she was now readier than ever to send him a letter, feeling compassionately that she had been in the right. Besides, it was due to the faithful friend, who was still working for her in the reading room, that he should be informed of Sir Jervis's illness. Whether the old man lived or whether he died, his literary labors were fatally interrupted in either case; and one of the consequences would be the termination of her employment at the Museum. Although the second of the two letters which she had received was addressed to her in Cecilia's handwriting, Emily waited to read it until she had first written to Alban. "He will come to-morrow," she thought; "and we shall both make apologies. I shall regret that I was angry with him and he will regret that he was mistaken in his judgment of Mrs. Rook. We shall be as good friends again as ever."

In this happy frame of mind she opened Cecilia's letter. It was full of good news from first to last.

The invalid sister had made such rapid progress toward recovery that the travelers had arranged to set forth on their journey back to England in a fortnight. "My one regret," Cecilia added, "is the parting with Lady Doris. She and her husband are going to Genoa, where they will embark in Lord Janeaway's yacht for a cruise in the Mediterranean. When we have said that miserable word good-by—oh, Emily, what a hurry I shall be in to get back to you! Those allusions to your lonely life are so dreadful, my dear, that I have destroyed your letter; it is enough to break one's heart only to look at it. When once I get to London, there shall be no more solitude for my poor afflicted friend. Papa will be free from his parliamentary duties in August—and he has promised to have the house full of delightful people to meet you. Who do you think will be one of our guests? He is illustrious; he is fascinating; he deserves a line all to himself, thus:

"The Reverend Miles Mirabel!

"Lady Doris has discovered that the country parsonage, in which this brilliant clergyman submits to exile, is only twelve miles away from our house. She has written to Mr. Mirabel to introduce me, and to mention the date of my return. We will have some fun with the popular preacher—we will both fall in love with him together.

"Is there anybody to whom you would like me to send an invitation? Shall we have Mr. Alban Morris? Now I know how kindly he took care of you at the railway station, your good opinion of him is my opinion. Your letter also mentions a doctor. Is he nice? and do you think he will let me eat pastry, if we have him too? I am so overflowing with hospitality (all for your sake) that I am ready to invite anybody, and everybody, to cheer you and make you happy. Would you like to meet Miss Ladd and the whole school?

"As to our amusements, make your mind easy.

"I have come to a distinct understanding with Papa that we are to have dances every evening—except when we try a little concert as a change. Private theatricals are to follow, when we want another change after the dancing and the music. No early rising; no fixed hour for breakfast; everything that is most exquisitely delicious at dinner—and, to crown all, your room next to mine, for delightful midnight gossipings, when we ought to be in bed. What do you say, darling, to the programme?

"A last piece of news—and I have done.

"I have actually had a proposal of marriage, from a young gentleman who sits opposite me at the table d'hote! When I tell you that he has white eyelashes, and red hands, and such enormous front teeth that he can't shut his mouth, you will not need to be told that I refused him. This vindictive person has abused me ever since, in the most shameful manner. I heard him last night, under my window, trying to set one of his friends against me. 'Keep clear of her, my dear fellow; she's the most heartless creature living.' The friend took my part; he said, 'I don't agree with you; the young lady is a person of great sensibility.' 'Nonsense!' says my amiable lover; 'she eats too much—her sensibility is all stomach.' There's a wretch for you. What a shameful advantage to take of sitting opposite to me at dinner! Good-by, my love, till we meet soon, and are as happy together as the day is long."

Emily kissed the signature. At that moment of all others, Cecilia was such a refreshing contrast to Francine!

Before putting the letter away, she looked again at that part of it which mentioned Lady Doris's introduction of Cecilia to Mr. Mirabel. "I don't feel the slightest interest in Mr. Mirabel," she thought, smiling as the idea occurred to her; "and I need never have known him, but for Lady Doris—who is a perfect stranger to me."

She had just placed the letter in her desk, when a visitor was announced.

Doctor Allday presented himself (in a hurry as usual).

"Another patient waiting?" Emily asked mischievously. "No time to spare, again?"

"Not a moment," the old gentleman answered. "Have you heard from Mrs. Ellmother?"

"Yes."

"You don't mean to say you have answered her?"

"I have done better than that, doctor—I have seen her this morning."

"And consented to be her reference, of course?"

"How well you know me!"

Doctor Allday was a philosopher: he kept his temper. "Just what I might have expected," he said. "Eve and the apple! Only forbid a woman to do anything, and she does it directly—because you have forbidden her. I'll try the other way with you now, Miss Emily. There was something else that I meant to have forbidden."

"What was it?"

"May I make a special request?"

"Certainly."

"Oh, my dear, write to Mrs. Rook! I beg and entreat of you, write to Mrs. Rook!"

Emily's playful manner suddenly disappeared.

Ignoring the doctor's little outbreak of humor, she waited in grave surprise, until it was his pleasure to explain himself.

Doctor Allday, on his side, ignored the ominous change in Emily; he went on as pleasantly as ever. "Mr. Morris and I have had a long talk about you, my dear. Mr. Morris is a capital fellow; I recommend him as a sweetheart. I also back him in the matter of Mrs. Rook.—What's the matter now? You're as red as a rose. Temper again, eh?"

"Hatred of meanness!" Emily answered indignantly. "I despise a man who plots, behind my back, to get another man to help him. Oh, how I have been mistaken in Alban Morris!"

"Oh, how little you know of the best friend you have!" cried the doctor, imitating her. "Girls are all alike; the only man they can understand, is the man who flatters them. Will you oblige me by writing to Mrs. Rook?"

Emily made an attempt to match the doctor, with his own weapons. "Your little joke comes too late," she said satirically. "There is Mrs. Rook's answer. Read it, and—" she checked herself, even in her anger she was incapable of speaking ungenerously to the old man who had so warmly befriended her. "I won't say to you," she resumed, "what I might have said to another person."

"Shall I say it for you?" asked the incorrigible doctor. "'Read it, and be ashamed of yourself'—That was what you had in your mind, isn't it? Anything to please you, my dear." He put on his spectacles, read the letter, and handed it back to Emily with an impenetrable countenance. "What do you think of my new spectacles?" he asked, as he took the glasses off his nose. "In the experience of thirty years, I have had three grateful patients." He put the spectacles back in the case. "This comes from the third. Very gratifying—very gratifying."

Emily's sense of humor was not the uppermost sense in her at that moment. She pointed with a peremptory forefinger to Mrs. Rook's letter. "Have you nothing to say about this?"

The doctor had so little to say about it that he was able to express himself in one word:

"Humbug!"

He took his hat—nodded kindly to Emily—and hurried away to feverish pulses waiting to be felt, and to furred tongues that were ashamed to show themselves.

CHAPTER XXXI. MOIRA.

When Alban presented himself the next morning, the hours of the night had exercised their tranquilizing influence over Emily. She remembered sorrowfully how Doctor Allday had disturbed her belief in the man who loved her; no feeling of irritation remained. Alban noticed that her manner was unusually subdued; she received him with her customary grace, but not with her customary smile.

"Are you not well?" he asked.

"I am a little out of spirits," she replied. "A disappointment—that is all."

He waited a moment, apparently in the expectation that she might tell him what the disappointment was. She remained silent, and she looked away from him. Was he in any way answerable for the depression of spirits to which she alluded? The doubt occurred to him—but he said nothing.

"I suppose you have received my letter?" she resumed.

"I have come here to thank you for your letter."

"It was my duty to tell you of Sir Jervis's illness; I deserve no thanks."

"You have written to me so kindly," Alban reminded her; "you have referred to our difference of opinion, the last time I was here, so gently and so forgivingly—"

"If I had written a little later," she interposed, "the tone of my letter might have been less agreeable to you. I happened to send it to the post, before I received a visit from a friend of yours—a friend who had something to say to me after consulting with you."

"Do you mean Doctor Allday?"

"Yes."

"What did he say?"

"What you wished him to say. He did his best; he was as obstinate and unfeeling as you could possibly wish him to be; but he was too late. I have written to Mrs. Rook, and I have received a reply." She spoke sadly, not angrily—and pointed to the letter lying on her desk.

Alban understood: he looked at her in despair. "Is that wretched woman doomed to set us at variance every time we meet!" he exclaimed.

Emily silently held out the letter.

He refused to take it. "The wrong you have done me is not to be set right in that way," he said. "You believe the doctor's visit was arranged between us. I never knew that he intended to call on you; I had no interest in sending him here—and I must not interfere again between you and Mrs. Rook."

"I don't understand you."

"You will understand me when I tell you how my conversation with Doctor Allday ended. I have done with interference; I have done with advice. Whatever my doubts may be, all further effort on my part to justify them—all further inquiries, no matter in what direction—are at an end: I made the sacrifice, for your sake. No! I must repeat what you said to me just now; I deserve no thanks. What I have done, has been done in deference to Doctor Allday—against my own convictions; in spite of my own fears. Ridiculous convictions! ridiculous fears! Men with morbid minds are their own tormentors. It doesn't matter how I suffer, so long as you are at ease. I shall never thwart you or vex you again. Have you a better opinion of me now?"

She made the best of all answers—she gave him her hand.

"May I kiss it?" he asked, as timidly as if he had been a boy addressing his first sweetheart.

She was half inclined to laugh, and half inclined to cry. "Yes, if you like," she said softly.

"Will you let me come and see you again?"

"Gladly—when I return to London."

"You are going away?"

"I am going to Brighton this afternoon, to stay with Miss Ladd."

It was hard to lose her, on the happy day when they understood each other at last. An expression of disappointment passed over his face. He rose, and walked restlessly to the window. "Miss Ladd?" he repeated, turning to Emily as if an idea had struck him. "Did I hear, at the school, that Miss de Sor was to spend the holidays under the care of Miss Ladd?"

"Yes."

"The same young lady," he went on, "who paid you a visit yesterday morning?"

"The same."

That haunting distrust of the future, which he had first betrayed and then affected to ridicule, exercised its depressing influence over his better sense. He was unreasonable enough to feel doubtful of Francine, simply because she was a stranger.

"Miss de Sor is a new friend of yours," he said. "Do you like her?"

It was not an easy question to answer—without entering into particulars which Emily's delicacy of feeling warned her to avoid. "I must know a little more of Miss de Sor," she said, "before I can decide."

Alban's misgivings were naturally encouraged by this evasive reply. He began to regret having left the cottage, on the previous day, when he had heard that Emily was engaged. He might have sent in his card, and might have been admitted. It was an opportunity lost of observing Francine. On the morning of her first day at school, when they had accidentally met at the summer house, she had left a disagreeable impression on his mind. Ought he to allow his opinion to be influenced by this circumstance? or ought he to follow Emily's prudent example, and suspend judgment until he knew a little more of Francine?

"Is any day fixed for your return to London?" he asked.

"Not yet," she said; "I hardly know how long my visit will be."

338

"In little more than a fortnight," he continued, "I shall return to my classes—they will be dreary classes, without you. Miss de Sor goes back to the school with Miss Ladd, I suppose?"

Emily was at a loss to account for the depression in his looks and tones, while he was making these unimportant inquiries. She tried to rouse him by speaking lightly in reply.

"Miss de Sor returns in quite a new character; she is to be a guest instead of a pupil. Do you wish to be better acquainted with her?"

"Yes," he said gravely, "now I know that she is a friend of yours." He returned to his place near her. "A pleasant visit makes the days pass quickly," he resumed. "You may remain at Brighton longer than you anticipate; and we may not meet again for some time to come. If anything happens—"

"Do you mean anything serious?" she asked.

"No, no! I only mean—if I can be of any service. In that case, will you write to me?"

"You know I will!"

She looked at him anxiously. He had completely failed to hide from her the uneasy state of his mind: a man less capable of concealment of feeling never lived. "You are anxious, and out of spirits," she said gently. "Is it my fault?"

"Your fault? oh, don't think that! I have my dull days and my bright days—and just now my barometer is down at dull." His voice faltered, in spite of his efforts to control it; he gave up the struggle, and took his hat to go. "Do you remember, Emily, what I once said to you in the garden at the school? I still believe there is a time of fulfillment to come in our lives." He suddenly checked himself, as if there had been something more in his mind to which he hesitated to give expression—and held out his hand to bid her good-by.

"My memory of what you said in the garden is better than yours," she reminded him. "You said 'Happen what may in the interval, I trust the future.' Do you feel the same trust still?"

He sighed—drew her to him gently—and kissed her on the forehead. Was that his own reply? She was not calm enough to ask him the question: it remained in her thoughts for some time after he had gone.

....

On the same day Emily was at Brighton.

Francine happened to be alone in the drawing-room. Her first proceeding, when Emily was shown in, was to stop the servant.

"Have you taken my letter to the post?"

"Yes, miss."

"It doesn't matter." She dismissed the servant by a gesture, and burst into such effusive hospitality that she actually insisted on kissing Emily. "Do you know what I have been doing?" she said. "I have been writing to Cecilia—directing to the care of her father, at the House of Commons. I stupidly forgot that you would be able to give me the right address in Switzerland. You don't object, I hope, to my making myself agreeable to our dear, beautiful, greedy girl? It is of such importance to me to surround myself with influential friends—and, of course, I have given her your love. Don't look disgusted! Come, and see your room.—Oh, never mind Miss Ladd. You will see her when she wakes. Ill? Is that sort of old woman ever ill? She's only taking her nap after bathing. Bathing in the sea, at her age! How she must frighten the fishes!"

Having seen her own bed-chamber, Emily was next introduced to the room occupied by Francine.

One object that she noticed in it caused her some little surprise—not unmingled with disgust. She discovered on the toilet-table a coarsely caricatured portrait of Mrs. Ellmother. It was a sketch in pencil—wretchedly drawn; but spitefully successful as a likeness. "I didn't know you were an artist," Emily remarked, with an ironical emphasis on the last word. Francine laughed scornfully—crumpled the drawing up in her hand—and threw it into the waste-paper basket.

"You satirical creature!" she burst out gayly. "If you had lived a dull life at St. Domingo, you would have taken to spoiling paper too. I might really have turned out an artist, if I had been clever and industrious like you. As it was, I learned a little drawing—and got tired of it. I tried modeling in wax—and got tired of it. Who do you think was my teacher? One of our slaves."

"A slave!" Emily exclaimed.

"Yes—a mulatto, if you wish me to be particular; the daughter of an English father and a negro mother. In her young time (at least she said so herself) she was quite a beauty, in her particular style. Her master's favorite; he educated her himself. Besides drawing and painting, and modeling in wax, she could sing and play—all the accomplishments thrown away on a slave! When her owner died, my uncle bought her at the sale of the property."

A word of natural compassion escaped Emily—to Francine's surprise.

"Oh, my dear, you needn't pity her! Sappho (that was her name) fetched a high price, even when she was no longer young. She came to us, by inheritance, with the estates and the rest of it; and took a fancy to me, when she found out I didn't get on well with my father and mother. 'I owe it to my father and mother,' she used to say, 'that I am a slave. When I see affectionate daughters, it wrings my heart.' Sappho was a strange compound. A woman with a white side to her character, and a black side. For weeks together, she would be a civilized being. Then she used to relapse, and become as complete a negress as her mother. At the risk of her life she stole away, on those occasions, into the interior of the island, and looked on, in hiding, at the horrid witchcrafts and idolatries of the blacks; they would have murdered a half-blood, prying into their ceremonies, if they had discovered her. I followed her once, so far as I dared. The frightful yellings and drummings in the darkness of the forests frightened me. The blacks suspected her, and it came to my ears. I gave her the warning that saved her life (I don't know what I should have done without Sappho to amuse me!); and, from that time, I do believe the curious creature loved me. You see I can speak generously even of a slave!"

"I wonder you didn't bring her with you to England," Emily said.

"In the first place," Francine answered, "she was my father's property, not mine. In the second place, she's dead. Poisoned, as the other half-bloods supposed, by some enemy among the blacks. She said herself, she was under a spell!"

"What did she mean?"

Francine was not interested enough in the subject to explain. "Stupid superstition, my dear. The negro side of Sappho was uppermost when she was dying—there is the explanation. Be off with you! I hear the old woman on the stairs. Meet her before she can come in here. My bedroom is my only refuge from Miss Ladd."

On the morning of the last day in the week, Emily had a little talk in private with her old schoolmistress. Miss Ladd listened to what she had to say of Mrs. Ellmother, and did her best to relieve Emily's anxieties. "I think you are mistaken, my child, in supposing that Francine is in earnest. It is her great fault that she is hardly ever in earnest. You can trust to my discretion; leave the rest to your aunt's old servant and to me."

Mrs. Ellmother arrived, punctual to the appointed time. She was shown into Miss Ladd's own room. Francine—ostentatiously resolved to take no personal part in the affair—went for a walk. Emily waited to hear the result.

After a long interval, Miss Ladd returned to the drawing-room, and announced that she had sanctioned the engagement of Mrs. Ellmother.

"I have considered your wishes, in this respect," she said. "It is arranged that a week's notice, on either side, shall end the term of service, after the first month. I cannot feel justified in doing more than that. Mrs. Ellmother is such a respectable woman; she is so well known to you, and she was so long in your aunt's service, that I am bound to consider the importance of securing a person who is exactly fitted to attend on such a girl as Francine. In one word, I can trust Mrs. Ellmother."

"When does she enter on her service?" Emily inquired.

"On the day after we return to the school," Miss Ladd replied. "You will be glad to see her, I am sure. I will send her here."

"One word more before you go," Emily said.

"Did you ask her why she left my aunt?"

"My dear child, a woman who has been five-and-twenty years in one place is entitled to keep her own secrets. I understand that she had her reasons, and that she doesn't think it necessary to mention them to anybody. Never trust people by halves—especially when they are people like Mrs. Ellmother."

It was too late now to raise any objections. Emily felt relieved, rather than disappointed, on discovering that Mrs. Ellmother was in a hurry to get back to London by the next train. She had found an opportunity of letting her lodgings; and she was eager to conclude the bargain. "You see I couldn't say Yes," she explained, "till I knew whether I was to get this new place or not—and the person wants to go in tonight."

Emily stopped her at the door. "Promise to write and tell me how you get on with Miss de Sor."

"You say that, miss, as if you didn't feel hopeful about me."

"I say it, because I feel interested about you. Promise to write."

Mrs. Ellmother promised, and hastened away. Emily looked after her from the window, as long as she was in view. "I wish I could feel sure of Francine!" she said to herself.

"In what way?" asked the hard voice of Francine, speaking at the door.

It was not in Emily's nature to shrink from a plain reply. She completed her half-formed thought without a moment's hesitation.

"I wish I could feel sure," she answered, "that you will be kind to Mrs. Ellmother."

"Are you afraid I shall make her life one scene of torment?" Francine inquired. "How can I answer for myself? I can't look into the future."

"For once in your life, can you be in earnest?" Emily said.

"For once in your life, can you take a joke?" Francine replied.

Emily said no more. She privately resolved to shorten her visit to Brighton.

BOOK THE THIRD—NETHERWOODS.

CHAPTER XXXII. IN THE GRAY ROOM.

The house inhabited by Miss Ladd and her pupils had been built, in the early part of the present century, by a wealthy merchant—proud of his money, and eager to distinguish himself as the owner of the largest country seat in the neighborhood.

After his death, Miss Ladd had taken Netherwoods (as the place was called), finding her own house insufficient for the accommodation of the increasing number of her pupils. A lease was granted to her on moderate terms. Netherwoods failed to attract persons of distinction in search of a country residence. The grounds were beautiful; but no landed property—not even a park—was attached to the house. Excepting the few acres on which the building stood, the surrounding land belonged to a retired naval officer of old family, who resented the attempt of a merchant of low birth to assume the position of a gentleman. No matter what proposals might be made to the admiral, he refused them all. The privilege of shooting was not one of the attractions offered to tenants; the country presented no facilities for hunting; and the only stream in the neighborhood was not preserved. In consequence of these drawbacks, the merchant's representatives had to choose between a proposal to use Netherwoods as a lunatic asylum, or to accept as tenant the respectable mistress of a fashionable and prosperous school. They decided in favor of Miss Ladd.

The contemplated change in Francine's position was accomplished, in that vast house, without inconvenience. There were rooms unoccupied, even when the limit assigned to the number of pupils had been reached. On the re-opening of the school, Francine was offered her choice between two rooms on one of the upper stories, and two rooms on the ground floor. She chose these last.

344

Her sitting-room and bedroom, situated at the back of the house, communicated with each other. The sitting-room, ornamented with a pretty paper of delicate gray, and furnished with curtains of the same color, had been accordingly named, "The Gray Room." It had a French window, which opened on the terrace overlooking the garden and the grounds. Some fine old engravings from the grand landscapes of Claude (part of a collection of prints possessed by Miss Ladd's father) hung on the walls. The carpet was in harmony with the curtains; and the furniture was of light-colored wood, which helped the general effect of subdued brightness that made the charm of the room. "If you are not happy here," Miss Ladd said, "I despair of you." And Francine answered, "Yes, it's very pretty, but I wish it was not so small."

On the twelfth of August the regular routine of the school was resumed. Alban Morris found two strangers in his class, to fill the vacancies left by Emily and Cecilia. Mrs. Ellmother was duly established in her new place. She produced an unfavorable impression in the servants' hall—not (as the handsome chief housemaid explained) because she was ugly and old, but because she was "a person who didn't talk." The prejudice against habitual silence, among the lower order of the people, is almost as inveterate as the prejudice against red hair.

In the evening, on that first day of renewed studies—while the girls were in the grounds, after tea—Francine had at last completed the arrangement of her rooms, and had dismissed Mrs. Ellmother (kept hard at work since the morning) to take a little rest. Standing alone at her window, the West Indian heiress wondered what she had better do next. She glanced at the girls on the lawn, and decided that they were unworthy of serious notice, on the part of a person so specially favored as herself. She turned sidewise, and looked along the length of the terrace. At the far end a tall man was slowly pacing to and fro, with his head down and his hands in his pockets. Francine recognized the rude drawing-master, who had torn up his view of the village, after she had saved it from being blown into the pond.

She stepped out on the terrace, and called to him. He stopped, and looked up.

"Do you want me?" he called back.

"Of course I do!"

She advanced a little to meet him, and offered encouragement under the form of a hard smile. Although his manners might be unpleasant, he had claims on the indulgence of a young lady, who was at a loss how to employ her idle time. In the first place, he was a man. In the second place, he was not as old as the music-master, or as ugly as the dancing-master. In the third place, he was an admirer of Emily; and the opportunity of trying to shake his allegiance by means of a flirtation, in Emily's absence, was too good an opportunity to be lost.

"Do you remember how rude you were to me, on the day when you were sketching in the summer-house?" Francine asked with snappish playfulness. "I expect you to make yourself agreeable this time—I am going to pay you a compliment."

He waited, with exasperating composure, to hear what the proposed compliment might be. The furrow between his eyebrows looked deeper than ever. There were signs of secret trouble in that dark face, so grimly and so resolutely composed. The school, without Emily, presented the severest trial of endurance that he had encountered, since the day when he had been deserted and disgraced by his affianced wife.

"You are an artist," Francine proceeded, "and therefore a person of taste. I want to have your opinion of my sitting-room. Criticism is invited; pray come in."

He seemed to be unwilling to accept the invitation—then altered his mind, and followed Francine. She had visited Emily; she was perhaps in a fair way to become Emily's friend. He remembered that he had already lost an opportunity of studying her character, and—if he saw the necessity—of warning Emily not to encourage the advances of Miss de Sor.

"Very pretty," he remarked, looking round the room—without appearing to care for anything in it, except the prints.

Francine was bent on fascinating him. She raised her eyebrows and lifted her hands, in playful remonstrance. "Do remember it's my room," she said, "and take some little interest in it, for my sake!"

"What do you want me to say?" he asked.

"Come and sit down by me." She made room for him on the sofa. Her one favorite aspiration—the longing to excite envy in others—expressed itself in her next words. "Say something pretty," she answered; "say you would like to have such a room as this."

"I should like to have your prints," he remarked. "Will that do?"

"It wouldn't do—from anybody else. Ah, Mr. Morris, I know why you are not as nice as you might be! You are not happy. The school has lost its one attraction, in losing our dear Emily. You feel it—I know you feel it." She assisted this expression of sympathy to produce the right effect by a sigh. "What would I not give to inspire such devotion as yours! I don't envy Emily; I only wish—" She paused in confusion, and opened her fan. "Isn't it pretty?" she said, with an ostentatious appearance of changing the subject. Alban behaved like a monster; he began to talk of the weather.

"I think this is the hottest day we have had," he said; "no wonder you want your fan. Netherwoods is an airless place at this season of the year."

She controlled her temper. "I do indeed feel the heat," she admitted, with a resignation which gently reproved him; "it is so heavy and oppressive here after Brighton. Perhaps my sad life, far away from home and friends, makes me sensitive to trifles. Do you think so, Mr. Morris?"

The merciless man said he thought it was the situation of the house.

"Miss Ladd took the place in the spring," he continued; "and only discovered the one objection to it some months afterward. We are in the highest part of the valley here—but, you see, it's a valley surrounded by hills; and on three sides the hills are near us. All very well in winter; but in summer I have heard of girls in this school so out of health in the relaxing atmosphere that they have been sent home again."

Francine suddenly showed an interest in what he was saying. If he had cared to observe her closely, he might have noticed it.

"Do you mean that the girls were really ill?" she asked.

"No. They slept badly—lost appetite—started at trifling noises. In short, their nerves were out of order."

"Did they get well again at home, in another air?"

"Not a doubt of it," he answered, beginning to get weary of the subject. "May I look at your books?"

Francine's interest in the influence of different atmospheres on health was not exhausted yet. "Do you know where the girls lived when they were at home?" she inquired.

"I know where one of them lived. She was the best pupil I ever had—and I remember she lived in Yorkshire." He was so weary of the idle curiosity—as it appeared to him—which persisted in asking trifling questions, that he left his seat, and crossed the room. "May I look at your books?" he repeated.

"Oh, yes!"

The conversation was suspended for a while. The lady thought, "I should like to box his ears!" The gentleman thought, "She's only an inquisitive fool after all!" His examination of her books confirmed him in the delusion that there was really nothing in Francine's character which rendered it necessary to caution Emily against the advances of her new friend. Turning away from the book-case, he made the first excuse that occurred to him for putting an end to the interview.

"I must beg you to let me return to my duties, Miss de Sor. I have to correct the young ladies' drawings, before they begin again to-morrow."

Francine's wounded vanity made a last expiring attempt to steal the heart of Emily's lover.

"You remind me that I have a favor to ask," she said. "I don't attend the other classes—but I should so like to join your class! May I?" She looked up at him with a languishing appearance of entreaty which sorely tried Alban's capacity to keep his face in serious order. He acknowledged the compliment paid to him in studiously commonplace terms, and got a little nearer to the open window. Francine's obstinacy was not conquered yet.

"My education has been sadly neglected," she continued; "but I have had some little instruction in drawing. You will not find me so ignorant as some of the other girls." She waited a little, anticipating a few complimentary words. Alban waited also—in silence. "I shall look forward with pleasure to my lessons under such an artist as yourself," she went on, and waited again, and was disappointed again. "Perhaps," she resumed, "I may become your favorite pupil—Who knows?"

"Who indeed!"

It was not much to say, when he spoke at last—but it was enough to encourage Francine. She called him "dear Mr. Morris"; she pleaded for permission to take her first lesson immediately; she clasped her hands— "Please say Yes!"

"I can't say Yes, till you have complied with the rules."

"Are they your rules?"

Her eyes expressed the readiest submission—in that case. He entirely failed to see it: he said they were Miss Ladd's rules—and wished her good-evening.

She watched him, walking away down the terrace. How was he paid? Did he receive a yearly salary, or did he get a little extra money for each new pupil who took drawing lessons? In this last case, Francine saw her opportunity of being even with him "You brute! Catch me attending your class!"

CHAPTER XXXIII. RECOLLECTIONS OF ST. DOMINGO.

The night was oppressively hot. Finding it impossible to sleep, Francine lay quietly in her bed, thinking. The subject of her reflections was a person who occupied the humble position of her new servant.

Mrs. Ellmother looked wretchedly ill. Mrs. Ellmother had told Emily that her object, in returning to domestic service, was to try if change would relieve her from the oppression of her own thoughts. Mrs. Ellmother believed in vulgar superstitions which declared Friday to be an unlucky day; and which recommended throwing a pinch over your left shoulder, if you happened to spill the salt.

In themselves, these were trifling recollections. But they assumed a certain importance, derived from the associations which they called forth.

They reminded Francine, by some mental process which she was at a loss to trace, of Sappho the slave, and of her life at St. Domingo.

She struck a light, and unlocked her writing desk. From one of the drawers she took out an old household account-book.

The first page contained some entries, relating to domestic expenses, in her own handwriting. They recalled one of her efforts to occupy her idle time, by relieving her mother of the cares of housekeeping. For a day or two, she had persevered—and then she had ceased to feel any interest in her new employment. The remainder of the book was completely filled up, in a beautifully clear handwriting, beginning on the second page. A title had been found for the manuscript by Francine. She had written at the top of the page: Sappho's Nonsense.

After reading the first few sentences she rapidly turned over the leaves, and stopped at a blank space near the end of the book. Here again she had added a title. This time it implied a compliment to the writer: the page was headed: Sappho's Sense.

She read this latter part of the manuscript with the closest attention.

"I entreat my kind and dear young mistress not to suppose that I believe in witchcraft—after such an education as I have received. When I wrote down, at your biding, all that I had told you by word of mouth, I cannot imagine what delusion possessed me. You say I have a negro side to my character, which I inherit from my mother. Did you mean this, dear mistress, as a joke? I am almost afraid it is sometimes not far off from the truth.

"Let me be careful, however, to avoid leading you into a mistake. It is really true that the man-slave I spoke of did pine and die, after the spell had been cast on him by my witch-mother's image of wax. But I ought also to have told you that circumstances favored the working of the spell: the fatal end was not brought about by supernatural means.

"The poor wretch was not in good health at the time; and our owner had occasion to employ him in the valley of the island far inland. I have been told, and can well believe, that the climate there is different from the climate on the coast—in which the unfortunate slave had been accustomed to live. The overseer wouldn't believe him when he said the valley air would be his death—and the negroes, who might otherwise have helped him, all avoided a man whom they knew to be under a spell.

"This, you see, accounts for what might appear incredible to civilized persons. If you will do me a favor, you will burn this little book, as soon as you have read what I have written here. If my request is not granted, I can only implore you to let no eyes but your own see these pages. My life might be in danger if the blacks knew what I have now told you, in the interests of truth."

Francine closed the book, and locked it up again in her desk. "Now I know," she said to herself, "what reminded me of St. Domingo."

When Francine rang her bell the next morning, so long a time elapsed without producing an answer that she began to think of sending one of the house-servants to make inquiries. Before she could decide, Mrs. Ellmother presented herself, and offered her apologies.

"It's the first time I have overslept myself, miss, since I was a girl. Please to excuse me, it shan't happen again."

"Do you find that the air here makes you drowsy?" Francine asked.

Mrs. Ellmother shook her head. "I didn't get to sleep," she said, "till morning, and so I was too heavy to be up in time. But air has got nothing to do with it. Gentlefolks may have their whims and fancies. All air is the same to people like me."

"You enjoy good health, Mrs. Ellmother?"

351

"Why not, miss? I have never had a doctor."

"Oh! That's your opinion of doctors, is it?"

"I won't have anything to do with them—if that's what you mean by my opinion," Mrs. Ellmother answered doggedly. "How will you have your hair done?"

"The same as yesterday. Have you seen anything of Miss Emily? She went back to London the day after you left us."

"I haven't been in London. I'm thankful to say my lodgings are let to a good tenant."

"Then where have you lived, while you were waiting to come here?"

"I had only one place to go to, miss; I went to the village where I was born. A friend found a corner for me. Ah, dear heart, it's a pleasant place, there!"

"A place like this?"

"Lord help you! As little like this as chalk is to cheese. A fine big moor, miss, in Cumberland, without a tree in sight—look where you may. Something like a wind, I can tell you, when it takes to blowing there."

"Have you never been in this part of the country?"

"Not I! When I left the North, my new mistress took me to Canada. Talk about air! If there was anything in it, the people in that air ought to live to be a hundred. I liked Canada."

"And who was your next mistress?"

Thus far, Mrs. Ellmother had been ready enough to talk. Had she failed to hear what Francine had just said to her? or had she some reason for feeling reluctant to answer? In any case, a spirit of taciturnity took sudden possession of her—she was silent.

Francine (as usual) persisted. "Was your next place in service with Miss Emily's aunt?"

"Yes."

"Did the old lady always live in London?"

"No."

"What part of the country did she live in?"

"Kent."

"Among the hop gardens?"

"No."

"In what other part, then?"

"Isle of Thanet."

"Near the sea coast?"

"Yes."

Even Francine could insist no longer: Mrs. Ellmother's reserve had beaten her—for that day at least. "Go into the hall," she said, "and see if there are any letters for me in the rack."

There was a letter bearing the Swiss postmark. Simple Cecilia was flattered and delighted by the charming manner in which Francine had written to her. She looked forward with impatience to the time when their present acquaintance might ripen into friendship. Would "Dear Miss de Sor" waive all ceremony, and consent to be a guest (later in the autumn) at her father's house? Circumstances connected with her sister's health would delay their return to England for a little while. By the end of the month she hoped to be at home again, and to hear if Francine was disengaged. Her address, in England, was Monksmoor Park, Hants.

Having read the letter, Francine drew a moral from it: "There is great use in a fool, when one knows how to manage her."

Having little appetite for her breakfast, she tried the experiment of a walk on the terrace. Alban Morris was right; the air at Netherwoods, in the summer time, was relaxing. The morning mist still hung over the lowest part of the valley, between the village and the hills beyond. A little exercise produced a feeling of fatigue. Francine returned to her room, and trifled with her tea and toast.

Her next proceeding was to open her writing-desk, and look into the old account-book once more. While it lay open on her lap, she recalled what had passed that morning, between Mrs. Ellmother and herself.

The old woman had been born and bred in the North, on an open moor. She had been removed to the keen air of Canada when she left her birthplace. She had been in service after that, on the breezy eastward coast of Kent. Would the change to the climate of Netherwoods produce any effect on Mrs. Ellmother? At her age, and with her seasoned constitution, would she feel it as those school-girls had felt it—especially that one among them, who lived in the bracing air of the North, the air of Yorkshire?

Weary of solitary thinking on one subject, Francine returned to the terrace with a vague idea of finding something to amuse her—that is to say, something she could turn into ridicule—if she joined the girls.

The next morning, Mrs. Ellmother answered her mistress's bell without delay. "You have slept better, this time?" Francine said.

"No, miss. When I did get to sleep I was troubled by dreams. Another bad night—and no mistake!"

"I suspect your mind is not quite at ease," Francine suggested.

"Why do you suspect that, if you please?"

"You talked, when I met you at Miss Emily's, of wanting to get away from your own thoughts. Has the change to this place helped you?"

"It hasn't helped me as I expected. Some people's thoughts stick fast."

"Remorseful thoughts?" Francine inquired.

Mrs. Ellmother held up her forefinger, and shook it with a gesture of reproof. "I thought we agreed, miss, that there was to be no pumping."

354

The business of the toilet proceeded in silence.

A week passed. During an interval in the labors of the school, Miss Ladd knocked at the door of Francine's room.

"I want to speak to you, my dear, about Mrs. Ellmother. Have you noticed that she doesn't seem to be in good health?"

"She looks rather pale, Miss Ladd."

"It's more serious than that, Francine. The servants tell me that she has hardly any appetite. She herself acknowledges that she sleeps badly. I noticed her yesterday evening in the garden, under the schoolroom window. One of the girls dropped a dictionary. She started at that slight noise, as if it terrified her. Her nerves are seriously out of order. Can you prevail upon her to see the doctor?"

Francine hesitated—and made an excuse. "I think she would be much more likely, Miss Ladd, to listen to you. Do you mind speaking to her?"

"Certainly not!"

Mrs. Ellmother was immediately sent for. "What is your pleasure, miss?" she said to Francine.

Miss Ladd interposed. "It is I who wish to speak to you, Mrs. Ellmother. For some days past, I have been sorry to see you looking ill."

"I never was ill in my life, ma'am."

Miss Ladd gently persisted. "I hear that you have lost your appetite."

"I never was a great eater, ma'am."

It was evidently useless to risk any further allusion to Mrs. Ellmother's symptoms. Miss Ladd tried another method of persuasion. "I daresay I may be mistaken," she said; "but I do really feel anxious about you. To set my mind at rest, will you see the doctor?"

"The doctor! Do you think I'm going to begin taking physic, at my time of life? Lord, ma'am! you amuse me—you do indeed!" She burst into a sudden fit of laughter; the hysterical laughter which is on the verge of tears. With a desperate effort, she controlled herself. "Please, don't make a fool of me again," she said—and left the room.

"What do you think now?" Miss Ladd asked.

Francine appeared to be still on her guard.

"I don't know what to think," she said evasively.

Miss Ladd looked at her in silent surprise, and withdrew.

Left by herself, Francine sat with her elbows on the table and her face in her hands, absorbed in thought. After a long interval, she opened her desk—and hesitated. She took a sheet of note-paper—and paused, as if still in doubt. She snatched up her pen, with a sudden recovery of resolution—and addressed these lines to the wife of her father's agent in London:

"When I was placed under your care, on the night of my arrival from the West Indies, you kindly said I might ask you for any little service which might be within your power. I shall be greatly obliged if you can obtain for me, and send to this place, a supply of artists' modeling wax—sufficient for the production of a small image."

CHAPTER XXXIV. IN THE DARK.

A week later, Alban Morris happened to be in Miss Ladd's study, with a report to make on the subject of his drawing-class. Mrs. Ellmother interrupted them for a moment. She entered the room to return a book which Francine had borrowed that morning.

"Has Miss de Sor done with it already?" Miss Ladd asked.

"She won't read it, ma'am. She says the leaves smell of tobacco-smoke."

Miss Ladd turned to Alban, and shook her head with an air of good-humored reproof. "I know who has been reading that book last!" she said.

Alban pleaded guilty, by a look. He was the only master in the school who smoked. As Mrs. Ellmother passed him, on her way out, he noticed the signs of suffering in her wasted face.

"That woman is surely in a bad state of health," he said. "Has she seen the doctor?"

"She flatly refuses to consult the doctor," Miss Ladd replied. "If she was a stranger, I should meet the difficulty by telling Miss de Sor (whose servant she is) that Mrs. Ellmother must be sent home. But I cannot act in that peremptory manner toward a person in whom Emily is interested."

From that moment Mrs. Ellmother became a person in whom Alban was interested. Later in the day, he met her in one of the lower corridors of the house, and spoke to her. "I am afraid the air of this place doesn't agree with you," he said.

Mrs. Ellmother's irritable objection to being told (even indirectly) that she looked ill, expressed itself roughly in reply. "I daresay you mean well, sir—but I don't see how it matters to you whether the place agrees with me or not."

"Wait a minute," Alban answered good-humoredly. "I am not quite a stranger to you."

"How do you make that out, if you please?"

"I know a young lady who has a sincere regard for you."

"You don't mean Miss Emily?"

"Yes, I do. I respect and admire Miss Emily; and I have tried, in my poor way, to be of some little service to her."

Mrs. Ellmother's haggard face instantly softened. "Please to forgive me, sir, for forgetting my manners," she said simply. "I have had my health since the day I was born—and I don't like to be told, in my old age, that a new place doesn't agree with me."

Alban accepted this apology in a manner which at once won the heart of the North-countrywoman. He shook hands with her. "You're one of the right sort," she said; "there are not many of them in this house."

Was she alluding to Francine? Alban tried to make the discovery. Polite

357

circumlocution would be evidently thrown away on Mrs. Ellmother. "Is your new mistress one of the right sort?" he asked bluntly.

The old servant's answer was expressed by a frowning look, followed by a plain question.

"Do you say that, sir, because you like my new mistress?"

"No."

"Please to shake hands again!" She said it—took his hand with a sudden grip that spoke for itself—and walked away.

Here was an exhibition of character which Alban was just the man to appreciate. "If I had been an old woman," he thought in his dryly humorous way, "I believe I should have been like Mrs. Ellmother. We might have talked of Emily, if she had not left me in such a hurry. When shall I see her again?"

He was destined to see her again, that night—under circumstances which he remembered to the end of his life.

The rules of Netherwoods, in summer time, recalled the young ladies from their evening's recreation in the grounds at nine o'clock. After that hour, Alban was free to smoke his pipe, and to linger among trees and flower-beds before he returned to his hot little rooms in the village. As a relief to the drudgery of teaching the young ladies, he had been using his pencil, when the day's lessons were over, for his own amusement. It was past ten o'clock before he lighted his pipe, and began walking slowly to and fro on the path which led to the summer-house, at the southern limit of the grounds.

In the perfect stillness of the night, the clock of the village church was distinctly audible, striking the hours and the quarters. The moon had not risen; but the mysterious glimmer of starlight trembled on the large open space between the trees and the house.

Alban paused, admiring with an artist's eye the effect of light, so faintly and delicately beautiful, on the broad expanse of the lawn. "Does the man live who could paint that?" he asked himself. His memory recalled the works of the greatest of all landscape painters—the English artists of fifty years since. While recollections of many a noble picture were still passing through his mind, he was startled by the sudden appearance of a bareheaded woman on the terrace steps.

She hurried down to the lawn, staggering as she ran—stopped, and looked back at the house—hastened onward toward the trees—stopped again, looking backward and forward, uncertain which way to turn next— and then advanced once more. He could now hear her heavily gasping for breath. As she came nearer, the starlight showed a panic-stricken face—the face of Mrs. Ellmother.

Alban ran to meet her. She dropped on the grass before he could cross the short distance which separated them. As he raised her in his arms she looked at him wildly, and murmured and muttered in the vain attempt to speak. "Look at me again," he said. "Don't you remember the man who had some talk with you to-day?" She still stared at him vacantly: he tried again. "Don't you remember Miss Emily's friend?"

As the name passed his lips, her mind in some degree recovered its balance. "Yes," she said; "Emily's friend; I'm glad I have met with Emily's friend." She caught at Alban's arm—starting as if her own words had alarmed her. "What am I talking about? Did I say 'Emily'? A servant ought to say 'Miss Emily.' My head swims. Am I going mad?"

Alban led her to one of the garden chairs. "You're only a little frightened," he said. "Rest, and compose yourself."

She looked over her shoulder toward the house. "Not here! I've run away from a she-devil; I want to be out of sight. Further away, Mister—I don't know your name. Tell me your name; I won't trust you, unless you tell me your name!"

"Hush! hush! Call me Alban."

"I never heard of such a name; I won't trust you."

"You won't trust your friend, and Emily's friend? You don't mean that, I'm sure. Call me by my other name—call me 'Morris.'"

"Morris?" she repeated. "Ah, I've heard of people called 'Morris.' Look back! Your eyes are young—do you see her on the terrace?"

"There isn't a living soul to be seen anywhere."

With one hand he raised her as he spoke—and with the other he took up the chair. In a minute more, they were out of sight of the house. He seated her so that she could rest her head against the trunk of a tree.

"What a good fellow!" the poor old creature said, admiring him; "he knows how my head pains me. Don't stand up! You're a tall man. She might see you."

"She can see nothing. Look at the trees behind us. Even the starlight doesn't get through them."

Mrs. Ellmother was not satisfied yet. "You take it coolly," she said. "Do you know who saw us together in the passage to-day? You good Morris, she saw us—she did. Wretch! Cruel, cunning, shameless wretch."

In the shadows that were round them, Alban could just see that she was shaking her clinched fists in the air. He made another attempt to control her. "Don't excite yourself! If she comes into the garden, she might hear you."

The appeal to her fears had its effect.

"That's true," she said, in lowered tones. A sudden distrust of him seized her the next moment. "Who told me I was excited?" she burst out. "It's you who are excited. Deny it if you dare; I begin to suspect you, Mr. Morris; I don't like your conduct. What has become of your pipe? I saw you put your pipe in your coat pocket. You did it when you set me down among the trees where she could see me! You are in league with her—she is coming to meet you here—you know she does not like tobacco-smoke. Are you two going to put me in the madhouse?"

She started to her feet. It occurred to Alban that the speediest way of pacifying her might be by means of the pipe. Mere words would exercise no persuasive influence over that bewildered mind. Instant action, of some kind, would be far more likely to have the right effect. He put his pipe and his

360

tobacco pouch into her hands, and so mastered her attention before he spoke.

"Do you know how to fill a man's pipe for him?" he asked.

"Haven't I filled my husband's pipe hundreds of times?" she answered sharply.

"Very well. Now do it for me."

She took her chair again instantly, and filled the pipe. He lighted it, and seated himself on the grass, quietly smoking. "Do you think I'm in league with her now?" he asked, purposely adopting the rough tone of a man in her own rank of life.

She answered him as she might have answered her husband, in the days of her unhappy marriage.

"Oh, don't gird at me, there's a good man! If I've been off my head for a minute or two, please not to notice me. It's cool and quiet here," the poor woman said gratefully. "Bless God for the darkness; there's something comforting in the darkness—along with a good man like you. Give me a word of advice. You are my friend in need. What am I to do? I daren't go back to the house!"

She was quiet enough now, to suggest the hope that she might be able to give Alban some information "Were you with Miss de Sor," he asked, "before you came out here? What did she do to frighten you?"

There was no answer; Mrs. Ellmother had abruptly risen once more. "Hush!" she whispered. "Don't I hear somebody near us?"

Alban at once went back, along the winding path which they had followed. No creature was visible in the gardens or on the terrace. On returning, he found it impossible to use his eyes to any good purpose in the obscurity among the trees. He waited a while, listening intently. No sound was audible: there was not even air enough to stir the leaves.

As he returned to the place that he had left, the silence was broken by the chimes of the distant church clock, striking the three-quarters past ten.

Even that familiar sound jarred on Mrs. Ellmother's shattered nerves. In her state of mind and body, she was evidently at the mercy of any false alarm which might be raised by her own fears. Relieved of the feeling of distrust which had thus far troubled him, Alban sat down by her again—opened his match-box to relight his pipe—and changed his mind. Mrs. Ellmother had unconsciously warned him to be cautious.

For the first time, he thought it likely that the heat in the house might induce some of the inmates to try the cooler atmosphere in the grounds. If this happened, and if he continued to smoke, curiosity might tempt them to follow the scent of tobacco hanging on the stagnant air.

"Is there nobody near us?" Mrs. Ellmother asked. "Are you sure?"

"Quite sure. Now tell me, did you really mean it, when you said just now that you wanted my advice?"

"Need you ask that, sir? Who else have I got to help me?"

"I am ready and willing to help you—but I can't do it unless I know first what has passed between you and Miss de Sor. Will you trust me?"

"I will!"

"May I depend on you?"

"Try me!"

CHAPTER XXXV. THE TREACHERY OF THE PIPE.

Alban took Mrs. Ellmother at her word. "I am going to venture on a guess," he said. "You have been with Miss de Sor to-night."

"Quite true, Mr. Morris."

"I am going to guess again. Did Miss de Sor ask you to stay with her, when you went into her room?"

"That's it! She rang for me, to see how I was getting on with my needlework—and she was what I call hearty, for the first time since I have been in her service. I didn't think badly of her when she first talked of engaging me; and I've had reason to repent of my opinion ever since. Oh, she showed the cloven foot to-night! 'Sit down,' she says; 'I've nothing to read, and I hate work; let's have a little chat.' She's got a glib tongue of her own. All I could do was to say a word now and then to keep her going. She talked and talked till it was time to light the lamp. She was particular in telling me to put the shade over it. We were half in the dark, and half in the light. She trapped me (Lord knows how!) into talking about foreign parts; I mean the place she lived in before they sent her to England. Have you heard that she comes from the West Indies?"

"Yes; I have heard that. Go on."

"Wait a bit, sir. There's something, by your leave, that I want to know. Do you believe in Witchcraft?"

"I know nothing about it. Did Miss de Sor put that question to you?"

"She did."

"And how did you answer?"

"Neither in one way nor the other. I'm in two minds about that matter of Witchcraft. When I was a girl, there was an old woman in our village, who was a sort of show. People came to see her from all the country round— gentlefolks among them. It was her great age that made her famous. More than a hundred years old, sir! One of our neighbors didn't believe in her age, and she heard of it. She cast a spell on his flock. I tell you, she sent a plague on his sheep, the plague of the Bots. The whole flock died; I remember it well. Some said the sheep would have had the Bots anyhow. Some said it was the spell. Which of them was right? How am I to settle it?"

"Did you mention this to Miss de Sor?"

"I was obliged to mention it. Didn't I tell you, just now, that I can't make up my mind about Witchcraft? 'You don't seem to know whether you believe or disbelieve,' she says. It made me look like a fool. I told her I had my reasons, and then I was obliged to give them."

"And what did she do then?"

"She said, 'I've got a better story of Witchcraft than yours.' And she opened a little book, with a lot of writing in it, and began to read. Her story made my flesh creep. It turns me cold, sir, when I think of it now."

He heard her moaning and shuddering. Strongly as his interest was excited, there was a compassionate reluctance in him to ask her to go on. His merciful scruples proved to be needless. The fascination of beauty it is possible to resist. The fascination of horror fastens its fearful hold on us, struggle against it as we may. Mrs. Ellmother repeated what she had heard, in spite of herself.

"It happened in the West Indies," she said; "and the writing of a woman slave was the writing in the little book. The slave wrote about her mother. Her mother was a black—a Witch in her own country. There was a forest in her own country. The devil taught her Witchcraft in the forest. The serpents and the wild beasts were afraid to touch her. She lived without eating. She was sold for a slave, and sent to the island—an island in the West Indies. An old man lived there; the wickedest man of them all. He filled the black Witch with devilish knowledge. She learned to make the image of wax. The image of wax casts spells. You put pins in the image of wax. At every pin you put, the person under the spell gets nearer and nearer to death. There was a poor black in the island. He offended the Witch. She made his image in wax; she cast spells on him. He couldn't sleep; he couldn't eat; he was such a coward that common noises frightened him. Like Me! Oh, God, like me!"

"Wait a little," Alban interposed. "You are exciting yourself again—wait."

"You're wrong, sir! You think it ended when she finished her story, and shut up her book; there's worse to come than anything you've heard yet. I don't know what I did to offend her. She looked at me and spoke to me, as if I was the dirt under her feet. 'If you're too stupid to understand what I have been reading,' she says, 'get up and go to the glass. Look at yourself, and remember what happened to the slave who was under the spell. You're getting paler and paler, and thinner and thinner; you're pining away just as he did. Shall I tell you why?' She snatched off the shade from the lamp, and put

364

her hand under the table, and brought out an image of wax. My image! She pointed to three pins in it. 'One,' she says, 'for no sleep. One for no appetite. One for broken nerves.' I asked her what I had done to make such a bitter enemy of her. She says, 'Remember what I asked of you when we talked of your being my servant. Choose which you will do? Die by inches' (I swear she said it as I hope to be saved); 'die by inches, or tell me—'"

There—in the full frenzy of the agitation that possessed her—there, Mrs. Ellmother suddenly stopped.

Alban's first impression was that she might have fainted. He looked closer, and could just see her shadowy figure still seated in the chair. He asked if she was ill. No.

"Then why don't you go on?"

"I have done," she answered.

"Do you think you can put me off," he rejoined sternly, "with such an excuse as that? What did Miss de Sor ask you to tell her? You promised to trust me. Be as good as your word."

In the days of her health and strength, she would have set him at defiance. All she could do now was to appeal to his mercy.

"Make some allowance for me," she said. "I have been terribly upset. What has become of my courage? What has broken me down in this way? Spare me, sir."

He refused to listen. "This vile attempt to practice on your fears may be repeated," he reminded her. "More cruel advantage may be taken of the nervous derangement from which you are suffering in the climate of this place. You little know me, if you think I will allow that to go on."

She made a last effort to plead with him. "Oh sir, is this behaving like the good kind man I thought you were? You say you are Miss Emily's friend? Don't press me—for Miss Emily's sake!"

"Emily!" Alban exclaimed. "Is she concerned in this?"

There was a change to tenderness in his voice, which persuaded Mrs. Ellmother that she had found her way to the weak side of him. Her one effort now was to strengthen the impression which she believed herself to have produced. "Miss Emily is concerned in it," she confessed.

"In what way?"

"Never mind in what way."

"But I do mind."

"I tell you, sir, Miss Emily must never know it to her dying day!"

The first suspicion of the truth crossed Alban's mind.

"I understand you at last," he said. "What Miss Emily must never know—is what Miss de Sor wanted you to tell her. Oh, it's useless to contradict me! Her motive in trying to frighten you is as plain to me now as if she had confessed it. Are you sure you didn't betray yourself, when she showed the image of wax?"

"I should have died first!" The reply had hardly escaped her before she regretted it. "What makes you want to be so sure about it?" she said. "It looks as if you knew—"

"I do know."

"What!"

The kindest thing that he could do now was to speak out. "Your secret is no secret to me," he said.

Rage and fear shook her together. For the moment she was like the Mrs. Ellmother of former days. "You lie!" she cried.

"I speak the truth."

"I won't believe you! I daren't believe you!"

"Listen to me. In Emily's interests, listen to me. I have read of the murder at Zeeland—"

366

"That's nothing! The man was a namesake of her father."

"The man was her father himself. Keep your seat! There is nothing to be alarmed about. I know that Emily is ignorant of the horrid death that her father died. I know that you and your late mistress have kept the discovery from her to this day. I know the love and pity which plead your excuse for deceiving her, and the circumstances that favored the deception. My good creature, Emily's peace of mind is as sacred to me as it is to you! I love her as I love my own life—and better. Are you calmer, now?"

He heard her crying: it was the best relief that could come to her. After waiting a while to let the tears have their way, he helped her to rise. There was no more to be said now. The one thing to do was to take her back to the house.

"I can give you a word of advice," he said, "before we part for the night. You must leave Miss de Sor's service at once. Your health will be a sufficient excuse. Give her warning immediately."

Mrs. Ellmother hung back, when he offered her his arm. The bare prospect of seeing Francine again was revolting to her. On Alban's assurance that the notice to leave could be given in writing, she made no further resistance. The village clock struck eleven as they ascended the terrace steps.

A minute later, another person left the grounds by the path which led to the house. Alban's precaution had been taken too late. The smell of tobacco-smoke had guided Francine, when she was at a loss which way to turn next in search of Mrs. Ellmother. For the last quarter of an hour she had been listening, hidden among the trees.

CHAPTER XXXVI. CHANGE OF AIR.

The inmates of Netherwoods rose early, and went to bed early. When Alban and Mrs. Ellmother arrived at the back door of the house, they found it locked.

The only light visible, along the whole length of the building, glimmered through the Venetian blind of the window-entrance to Francine's sitting-room. Alban proposed to get admission to the house by that way. In her horror of again encountering Francine, Mrs. Ellmother positively refused to follow him when he turned away from the door. "They can't be all asleep yet," she said—and rang the bell.

One person was still out of bed—and that person was the mistress of the house. They recognized her voice in the customary question: "Who's there?" The door having been opened, good Miss Ladd looked backward and forward between Alban and Mrs. Ellmother, with the bewildered air of a lady who doubted the evidence of her own eyes. The next moment, her sense of humor overpowered her. She burst out laughing.

"Close the door, Mr. Morris," she said, "and be so good as to tell me what this means. Have you been giving a lesson in drawing by starlight?"

Mrs. Ellmother moved, so that the light of the lamp in Miss Ladd's hand fell on her face. "I am faint and giddy," she said; "let me go to my bed."

Miss Ladd instantly followed her. "Pray forgive me! I didn't see you were ill, when I spoke," she gently explained. "What can I do for you?"

"Thank you kindly, ma'am. I want nothing but peace and quiet. I wish you good-night."

Alban followed Miss Ladd to her study, on the front side of the house. He had just mentioned the circumstances under which he and Mrs. Ellmother had met, when they were interrupted by a tap at the door. Francine had got back to her room unperceived, by way of the French window. She now presented herself, with an elaborate apology, and with the nearest approach to a penitent expression of which her face was capable.

"I am ashamed, Miss Ladd, to intrude on you at this time of night. My only excuse is, that I am anxious about Mrs. Ellmother. I heard you just now in the hall. If she is really ill, I am the unfortunate cause of it."

"In what way, Miss de Sor?"

"I am sorry to say I frightened her—while we were talking in my room— quite unintentionally. She rushed to the door and ran out. I supposed she had gone to her bedroom; I had no idea she was in the grounds."

In this false statement there was mingled a grain of truth. It was true that Francine believed Mrs. Ellmother to have taken refuge in her room—for she had examined the room. Finding it empty, and failing to discover the fugitive in other parts of the house, she had become alarmed, and had tried the grounds next—with the formidable result which has been already related. Concealing this circumstance, she had lied in such a skillfully artless manner that Alban (having no suspicion of what had really happened to sharpen his wits) was as completely deceived as Miss Ladd. Proceeding to further explanation—and remembering that she was in Alban's presence—Francine was careful to keep herself within the strict limit of truth. Confessing that she had frightened her servant by a description of sorcery, as it was practiced among the slaves on her father's estate, she only lied again, in declaring that Mrs. Ellmother had supposed she was in earnest, when she was guilty of no more serious offense than playing a practical joke.

In this case, Alban was necessarily in a position to detect the falsehood. But it was so evidently in Francine's interests to present her conduct in the most favorable light, that the discovery failed to excite his suspicion. He waited in silence, while Miss Ladd administered a severe reproof. Francine having left the room, as penitently as she had entered it (with her handkerchief over her tearless eyes), he was at liberty, with certain reserves, to return to what had passed between Mrs. Ellmother and himself.

"The fright which the poor old woman has suffered," he said, "has led to one good result. I have found her ready at last to acknowledge that she is ill, and inclined to believe that the change to Netherwoods has had something to do with it. I have advised her to take the course which you suggested, by leaving this house. Is it possible to dispense with the usual delay, when she gives notice to leave Miss de Sor's service?"

"She need feel no anxiety, poor soul, on that account," Miss Ladd replied. "In any case, I had arranged that a week's notice on either side should be enough. As it is, I will speak to Francine myself. The least she can do, to express her regret, is to place no difficulties in Mrs. Ellmother's way."

The next day was Sunday.

Miss Ladd broke through her rule of attending to secular affairs on week days only; and, after consulting with Mrs. Ellmother, arranged with Francine that her servant should be at liberty to leave Netherwoods (health permitting) on the next day. But one difficulty remained. Mrs. Ellmother was in no condition to take the long journey to her birthplace in Cumberland; and her own lodgings in London had been let.

Under these circumstances, what was the best arrangement that could be made for her? Miss Ladd wisely and kindly wrote to Emily on the subject, and asked for a speedy reply.

Later in the day, Alban was sent for to see Mrs. Ellmother. He found her anxiously waiting to hear what had passed, on the previous night, between Miss Ladd and himself. "Were you careful, sir, to say nothing about Miss Emily?"

"I was especially careful; I never alluded to her in any way."

"Has Miss de Sor spoken to you?"

"I have not given her the opportunity."

"She's an obstinate one—she might try."

"If she does, she shall hear my opinion of her in plain words." The talk between them turned next on Alban's discovery of the secret, of which Mrs. Ellmother had believed herself to be the sole depositary since Miss Letitia's death. Without alarming her by any needless allusion to Doctor Allday or to Miss Jethro, he answered her inquiries (so far as he was himself concerned) without reserve. Her curiosity once satisfied, she showed no disposition to pursue the topic. She pointed to Miss Ladd's cat, fast asleep by the side of an empty saucer.

"Is it a sin, Mr. Morris, to wish I was Tom? He doesn't trouble himself about his life that is past or his life that is to come. If I could only empty my saucer and go to sleep, I shouldn't be thinking of the number of people in this world, like myself, who would be better out of it than in it. Miss Ladd has got me my liberty tomorrow; and I don't even know where to go, when I leave this place."

"Suppose you follow Tom's example?" Alban suggested. "Enjoy to-day (in that comfortable chair) and let to-morrow take care of itself."

To-morrow arrived, and justified Alban's system of philosophy. Emily answered Miss Ladd's letter, to excellent purpose, by telegraph.

"I leave London to-day with Cecilia" (the message announced) "for Monksmoor Park, Hants. Will Mrs. Ellmother take care of the cottage in my absence? I shall be away for a month, at least. All is prepared for her if she consents."

Mrs. Ellmother gladly accepted this proposal. In the interval of Emily's absence, she could easily arrange to return to her own lodgings. With words of sincere gratitude she took leave of Miss Ladd; but no persuasion would induce her to say good-by to Francine. "Do me one more kindness, ma'am; don't tell Miss de Sor when I go away." Ignorant of the provocation which had produced this unforgiving temper of mind, Miss Ladd gently remonstrated. "Miss de Sor received my reproof in a penitent spirit; she expresses sincere sorrow for having thoughtlessly frightened you. Both yesterday and to-day she has made kind inquiries after your health. Come! come! don't bear malice—wish her good-by." Mrs. Ellmother's answer was characteristic. "I'll say good-by by telegraph, when I get to London."

Her last words were addressed to Alban. "If you can find a way of doing it, sir, keep those two apart."

"Do you mean Emily and Miss de Sor?

"Yes."

"What are you afraid of?"

"I don't know."

"Is that quite reasonable, Mrs. Ellmother?"

"I daresay not. I only know that I am afraid."

The pony chaise took her away. Alban's class was not yet ready for him.

He waited on the terrace.

Innocent alike of all knowledge of the serious reason for fear which did really exist, Mrs. Ellmother and Alban felt, nevertheless, the same vague distrust of an intimacy between the two girls. Idle, vain, malicious, false—to know that Francine's character presented these faults, without any discoverable merits to set against them, was surely enough to justify a gloomy view of the prospect, if she succeeded in winning the position of Emily's friend. Alban reasoned it out logically in this way—without satisfying himself, and without accounting for the remembrance that haunted him of Mrs. Ellmother's farewell look. "A commonplace man would say we are both in a morbid state of mind," he thought; "and sometimes commonplace men turn out to be right."

He was too deeply preoccupied to notice that he had advanced perilously near Francine's window. She suddenly stepped out of her room, and spoke to him.

"Do you happen to know, Mr. Morris, why Mrs. Ellmother has gone away without bidding me good-by?"

"She was probably afraid, Miss de Sor, that you might make her the victim of another joke."

Francine eyed him steadily. "Have you any particular reason for speaking to me in that way?"

"I am not aware that I have answered you rudely—if that is what you mean."

"That is not what I mean. You seem to have taken a dislike to me. I should be glad to know why."

"I dislike cruelty—and you have behaved cruelly to Mrs. Ellmother."

"Meaning to be cruel?" Francine inquired.

"You know as well as I do, Miss de Sor, that I can't answer that question."

Francine looked at him again "Am I to understand that we are enemies?"

372

she asked.

"You are to understand," he replied, "that a person whom Miss Ladd employs to help her in teaching, cannot always presume to express his sentiments in speaking to the young ladies."

"If that means anything, Mr. Morris, it means that we are enemies."

"It means, Miss de Sor, that I am the drawing-master at this school, and that I am called to my class."

Francine returned to her room, relieved of the only doubt that had troubled her. Plainly no suspicion that she had overheard what passed between Mrs. Ellmother and himself existed in Alban's mind. As to the use to be made of her discovery, she felt no difficulty in deciding to wait, and be guided by events. Her curiosity and her self-esteem had been alike gratified—she had got the better of Mrs. Ellmother at last, and with that triumph she was content. While Emily remained her friend, it would be an act of useless cruelty to disclose the terrible truth. There had certainly been a coolness between them at Brighton. But Francine—still influenced by the magnetic attraction which drew her to Emily—did not conceal from herself that she had offered the provocation, and had been therefore the person to blame. "I can set all that right," she thought, "when we meet at Monksmoor Park." She opened her desk and wrote the shortest and sweetest of letters to Cecilia. "I am entirely at the disposal of my charming friend, on any convenient day— may I add, my dear, the sooner the better?"

CHAPTER XXXVII. "THE LADY WANTS YOU, SIR."

The pupils of the drawing-class put away their pencils and color-boxes in high good humor: the teacher's vigilant eye for faults had failed him for the first time in their experience. Not one of them had been reproved; they had chattered and giggled and drawn caricatures on the margin of the paper, as freely as if the master had left the room. Alban's wandering attention was indeed beyond the reach of control. His interview with Francine had doubled his sense of responsibility toward Emily—while he was further than ever from seeing how he could interfere, to any useful purpose, in his present position, and with his reasons for writing under reserve.

One of the servants addressed him as he was leaving the schoolroom. The landlady's boy was waiting in the hall, with a message from his lodgings.

"Now then! what is it?" he asked, irritably.

"The lady wants you, sir." With this mysterious answer, the boy presented a visiting card. The name inscribed on it was—"Miss Jethro."

She had arrived by the train, and she was then waiting at Alban's lodgings. "Say I will be with her directly." Having given the message, he stood for a while, with his hat in his hand—literally lost in astonishment. It was simply impossible to guess at Miss Jethro's object: and yet, with the usual perversity of human nature, he was still wondering what she could possibly want with him, up to the final moment when he opened the door of his sitting-room.

She rose and bowed with the same grace of movement, and the same well-bred composure of manner, which Doctor Allday had noticed when she entered his consulting-room. Her dark melancholy eyes rested on Alban with a look of gentle interest. A faint flush of color animated for a moment the faded beauty of her face—passed away again—and left it paler than before.

"I cannot conceal from myself," she began, "that I am intruding on you under embarrassing circumstances."

"May I ask, Miss Jethro, to what circumstances you allude?"

"You forget, Mr. Morris, that I left Miss Ladd's school, in a manner which justified doubt of me in the minds of strangers."

"Speaking as one of those strangers," Alban replied, "I cannot feel that I had any right to form an opinion, on a matter which only concerned Miss Ladd and yourself."

Miss Jethro bowed gravely. "You encourage me to hope," she said. "I think you will place a favorable construction on my visit when I mention my motive. I ask you to receive me, in the interests of Miss Emily Brown."

Stating her purpose in calling on him in those plain terms, she added to the amazement which Alban already felt, by handing to him—as if she was presenting an introduction—a letter marked, "Private," addressed to her by Doctor Allday.

"I may tell you," she premised, "that I had no idea of troubling you, until Doctor Allday suggested it. I wrote to him in the first instance; and there is his reply. Pray read it."

The letter was dated, "Penzance"; and the doctor wrote, as he spoke, without ceremony.

"MADAM—Your letter has been forwarded to me. I am spending my autumn holiday in the far West of Cornwall. However, if I had been at home, it would have made no difference. I should have begged leave to decline holding any further conversation with you, on the subject of Miss Emily Brown, for the following reasons:

"In the first place, though I cannot doubt your sincere interest in the young lady's welfare, I don't like your mysterious way of showing it. In the second place, when I called at your address in London, after you had left my house, I found that you had taken to flight. I place my own interpretation on this circumstance; but as it is not founded on any knowledge of facts, I merely allude to it, and say no more."

Arrived at that point, Alban offered to return the letter. "Do you really mean me to go on reading it?" he asked.

"Yes," she said quietly.

Alban returned to the letter.

"In the third place, I have good reason to believe that you entered Miss Ladd's school as a teacher, under false pretenses. After that discovery, I tell you plainly I hesitate to attach credit to any statement that you may wish to make. At the same time, I must not permit my prejudices (as you will probably call them) to stand in the way of Miss Emily's interests—supposing them to be really depending on any interference of yours. Miss Ladd's drawing-master, Mr. Alban Morris, is even more devoted to Miss Emily's service than I am. Whatever you might have said to me, you can say to him—with this possible advantage, that he may believe you."

There the letter ended. Alban handed it back in silence.

Miss Jethro pointed to the words, "Mr. Alban Morris is even more devoted to Miss Emily's service than I am."

"Is that true?" she asked.

"Quite true."

"I don't complain, Mr. Morris, of the hard things said of me in that letter; you are at liberty to suppose, if you like, that I deserve them. Attribute it to pride, or attribute it to reluctance to make needless demands on your time—I shall not attempt to defend myself. I leave you to decide whether the woman who has shown you that letter—having something important to say to you—is a person who is mean enough to say it under false pretenses."

"Tell me what I can do for you, Miss Jethro: and be assured, beforehand, that I don't doubt your sincerity."

"My purpose in coming here," she answered, "is to induce you to use your influence over Miss Emily Brown—"

"With what object?" Alban asked, interrupting her.

"My object is her own good. Some years since, I happened to become acquainted with a person who has attained some celebrity as a preacher. You have perhaps heard of Mr. Miles Mirabel?"

"I have heard of him."

"I have been in correspondence with him," Miss Jethro proceeded. "He tells me he has been introduced to a young lady, who was formerly one of Miss Ladd's pupils, and who is the daughter of Mr. Wyvil, of Monksmoor Park. He has called on Mr. Wyvil; and he has since received an invitation to stay at Mr. Wyvil's house. The day fixed for the visit is Monday, the fifth of next month."

Alban listened—at a loss to know what interest he was supposed to have in being made acquainted with Mr. Mirabel's engagements. Miss Jethro's next words enlightened him.

"You are perhaps aware," she resumed, "that Miss Emily Brown is Miss Wyvil's intimate friend. She will be one of the guests at Monksmoor Park. If there are any obstacles which you can place in her way—if there is any influence which you can exert, without exciting suspicion of your motive— prevent her, I entreat you, from accepting Miss Wyvil's invitation, until Mr. Mirabel's visit has come to an end."

"Is there anything against Mr. Mirabel?" he asked.

"I say nothing against him."

"Is Miss Emily acquainted with him?"

"No."

"Is he a person with whom it would be disagreeable to her to associate?"

"Quite the contrary."

"And yet you expect me to prevent them from meeting! Be reasonable, Miss Jethro."

"I can only be in earnest, Mr. Morris—more truly, more deeply in earnest than you can suppose. I declare to you that I am speaking in Miss Emily's interests. Do you still refuse to exert yourself for her sake?"

"I am spared the pain of refusal," Alban answered. "The time for interference has gone by. She is, at this moment, on her way to Monksmoor Park."

Miss Jethro attempted to rise—and dropped back into her chair. "Water!" she said faintly. After drinking from the glass to the last drop, she began to revive. Her little traveling-bag was on the floor at her side. She took out a railway guide, and tried to consult it. Her fingers trembled incessantly; she was unable to find the page to which she wished to refer. "Help me," she said, "I must leave this place—by the first train that passes."

"To see Emily?" Alban asked.

"Quite useless! You have said it yourself—the time for interference has gone by. Look at the guide."

"What place shall I look for?"

"Look for Vale Regis."

Alban found the place. The train was due in ten minutes. "Surely you are not fit to travel so soon?" he suggested.

"Fit or not, I must see Mr. Mirabel—I must make the effort to keep them apart by appealing to him."

"With any hope of success?"

"With no hope—and with no interest in the man himself. Still I must try."

"Out of anxiety for Emily's welfare?"

"Out of anxiety for more than that."

"For what?"

"If you can't guess, I daren't tell you."

That strange reply startled Alban. Before he could ask what it meant, Miss Jethro had left him.

In the emergencies of life, a person readier of resource than Alban Morris it would not have been easy to discover. The extraordinary interview that had now come to an end had found its limits. Bewildered and helpless, he stood at the window of his room, and asked himself (as if he had been the weakest man living), "What shall I do?"

BOOK THE FOURTH—THE COUNTRY HOUSE.

CHAPTER XXXVIII. DANCING.

The windows of the long drawing-room at Monksmoor are all thrown open to the conservatory. Distant masses of plants and flowers, mingled in ever-varying forms of beauty, are touched by the melancholy luster of the rising moon. Nearer to the house, the restful shadows are disturbed at intervals, where streams of light fall over them aslant from the lamps in the room. The fountain is playing. In rivalry with its lighter music, the nightingales are singing their song of ecstasy. Sometimes, the laughter of girls is heard—and, sometimes, the melody of a waltz. The younger guests at Monksmoor are dancing.

Emily and Cecilia are dressed alike in white, with flowers in their hair. Francine rivals them by means of a gorgeous contrast of color, and declares that she is rich with the bright emphasis of diamonds and the soft persuasion of pearls.

Miss Plym (from the rectory) is fat and fair and prosperous: she overflows with good spirits; she has a waist which defies tight-lacing, and she dances joyously on large flat feet. Miss Darnaway (officer's daughter with small means) is the exact opposite of Miss Plym. She is thin and tall and faded—poor soul. Destiny has made it her hard lot in life to fill the place of head-nursemaid at home. In her pensive moments, she thinks of the little brothers and sisters, whose patient servant she is, and wonders who comforts them in their tumbles and tells them stories at bedtime, while she is holiday-making at the pleasant country house.

Tender-hearted Cecilia, remembering how few pleasures this young friend has, and knowing how well she dances, never allows her to be without a partner. There are three invaluable young gentlemen present, who are excellent dancers. Members of different families, they are nevertheless fearfully and wonderfully like each other. They present the same rosy complexions and straw-colored mustachios, the same plump cheeks, vacant eyes and low forehead; and they utter, with the same stolid gravity, the same imbecile small talk. On sofas facing each other sit the two remaining guests, who have not joined the elders at the card-table in another room. They are both men. One of them is drowsy and middle-aged—happy in the possession of large landed property: happier still in a capacity for drinking Mr. Wyvil's famous port-wine without gouty results.

The other gentleman—ah, who is the other? He is the confidential adviser and bosom friend of every young lady in the house. Is it necessary to name the Reverend Miles Mirabel?

There he sits enthroned, with room for a fair admirer on either side of him—the clerical sultan of a platonic harem. His persuasive ministry is felt as well as heard: he has an innocent habit of fondling young persons. One of his arms is even long enough to embrace the circumference of Miss Plym—while the other clasps the rigid silken waist of Francine. "I do it everywhere else," he says innocently, "why not here?" Why not indeed—with that delicate complexion and those beautiful blue eyes; with the glorious golden hair that rests on his shoulders, and the glossy beard that flows over his breast? Familiarities, forbidden to mere men, become privileges and condescensions when an angel enters society—and more especially when that angel has enough of mortality in him to be amusing. Mr. Mirabel, on his social side, is an irresistible companion. He is cheerfulness itself; he takes a favorable view of everything; his sweet temper never differs with anybody. "In my humble way," he confesses, "I like to make the world about me brighter." Laughter (harmlessly produced, observe!) is the element in which he lives and breathes. Miss Darnaway's serious face puts him out; he has laid a bet with Emily—not in money, not even in gloves, only in flowers—that he will make Miss Darnaway laugh; and he has won the wager. Emily's flowers are in his button-hole, peeping through the curly interstices of his beard. "Must you leave me?" he asks tenderly, when there is a dancing man at liberty, and it is Francine's turn to claim him. She leaves her seat not very willingly. For a while, the place is vacant; Miss Plym seizes the opportunity of consulting the ladies' bosom friend.

"Dear Mr. Mirabel, do tell me what you think of Miss de Sor?"

Dear Mr. Mirabel bursts into enthusiasm and makes a charming reply. His large experience of young ladies warns him that they will tell each other what he thinks of them, when they retire for the night; and he is careful on these occasions to say something that will bear repetition.

"I see in Miss de Sor," he declares, "the resolution of a man, tempered by the sweetness of a woman. When that interesting creature marries, her husband will be—shall I use the vulgar word?—henpecked. Dear Miss Plym, he will enjoy it; and he will be quite right too; and, if I am asked to the wedding, I shall say, with heartfelt sincerity, Enviable man!"

In the height of her admiration for Mr. Mirabel's wonderful eye for character, Miss Plym is called away to the piano. Cecilia succeeds to her friend's place—and has her waist taken in charge as a matter of course.

"How do you like Miss Plym?" she asks directly.

Mr. Mirabel smiles, and shows the prettiest little pearly teeth. "I was just thinking of her," he confesses pleasantly; "Miss Plym is so nice and plump, so comforting and domestic—such a perfect clergyman's daughter. You love her, don't you? Is she engaged to be married? In that case—between ourselves, dear Miss Wyvil, a clergyman is obliged to be cautious—I may own that I love her too."

Delicious titillations of flattered self-esteem betray themselves in Cecilia's lovely complexion. She is the chosen confidante of this irresistible man; and she would like to express her sense of obligation. But Mr. Mirabel is a master in the art of putting the right words in the right places; and simple Cecilia distrusts herself and her grammar.

At that moment of embarrassment, a friend leaves the dance, and helps Cecilia out of the difficulty.

Emily approaches the sofa-throne, breathless—followed by her partner, entreating her to give him "one turn more." She is not to be tempted; she means to rest. Cecilia sees an act of mercy, suggested by the presence of the disengaged young man. She seizes his arm, and hurries him off to poor Miss Darnaway; sitting forlorn in a corner, and thinking of the nursery at home. In the meanwhile a circumstance occurs. Mr. Mirabel's all-embracing arm shows itself in a new character, when Emily sits by his side.

It becomes, for the first time, an irresolute arm. It advances a little—and hesitates. Emily at once administers an unexpected check; she insists on preserving a free waist, in her own outspoken language. "No, Mr. Mirabel, keep that for the others. You can't imagine how ridiculous you and the young ladies look, and how absurdly unaware of it you all seem to be." For the first time in his life, the reverend and ready-witted man of the world is at a loss for an answer. Why?

For this simple reason. He too has felt the magnetic attraction of the irresistible little creature whom every one likes. Miss Jethro has been doubly defeated. She has failed to keep them apart; and her unexplained misgivings have not been justified by events: Emily and Mr. Mirabel are good friends already. The brilliant clergyman is poor; his interests in life point to a marriage for money; he has fascinated the heiresses of two rich fathers, Mr. Tyvil and Mr. de Sor—and yet he is conscious of an influence (an alien influence, without a balance at its bankers), which has, in some mysterious way, got between him and his interests.

On Emily's side, the attraction felt is of another nature altogether. Among the merry young people at Monksmoor she is her old happy self again; and she finds in Mr. Mirabel the most agreeable and amusing man whom she has ever met. After those dismal night watches by the bed of her dying aunt, and the dreary weeks of solitude that followed, to live in this new world of luxury and gayety is like escaping from the darkness of night, and basking in the fall brightness of day. Cecilia declares that she looks, once more, like the joyous queen of the bedroom, in the bygone time at school; and Francine (profaning Shakespeare without knowing it), says, "Emily is herself again!"

"Now that your arm is in its right place, reverend sir," she gayly resumes,

"I may admit that there are exceptions to all rules. My waist is at your disposal, in a case of necessity—that is to say, in a case of waltzing."

"The one case of all others," Mirabel answers, with the engaging frankness that has won him so many friends, "which can never happen in my unhappy experience. Waltzing, I blush to own it, means picking me up off the floor, and putting smelling salts to my nostrils. In other words, dear Miss Emily, it is the room that waltzes—not I. I can't look at those whirling couples there, with a steady head. Even the exquisite figure of our young hostess, when it describes flying circles, turns me giddy."

Hearing this allusion to Cecilia, Emily drops to the level of the other girls. She too pays her homage to the Pope of private life. "You promised me your unbiased opinion of Cecilia," she reminds him; "and you haven't given it yet."

The ladies' friend gently remonstrates. "Miss Wyvil's beauty dazzles me. How can I give an unbiased opinion? Besides, I am not thinking of her; I can only think of you."

Emily lifts her eyes, half merrily, half tenderly, and looks at him over the top of her fan. It is her first effort at flirtation. She is tempted to engage in the most interesting of all games to a girl—the game which plays at making love. What has Cecilia told her, in those bedroom gossipings, dear to the hearts of the two friends? Cecilia has whispered, "Mr. Mirabel admires your figure; he calls you 'the Venus of Milo, in a state of perfect abridgment.'" Where is the daughter of Eve, who would not have been flattered by that pretty compliment—who would not have talked soft nonsense in return? "You can only think of Me," Emily repeats coquettishly. "Have you said that to the last young lady who occupied my place, and will you say it again to the next who follows me?"

"Not to one of them! Mere compliments are for the others—not for you."

"What is for me, Mr. Mirabel?"

"What I have just offered you—a confession of the truth."

Emily is startled by the tone in which he replies. He seems to be in earnest; not a vestige is left of the easy gayety of his manner. His face shows an expression of anxiety which she has never seen in it yet. "Do you believe me?" he asks in a whisper.

She tries to change the subject.

"When am I to hear you preach, Mr. Mirabel?"

He persists. "When you believe me," he says.

His eyes add an emphasis to that reply which is not to be mistaken. Emily turns away from him, and notices Francine. She has left the dance, and is looking with marked attention at Emily and Mirabel. "I want to speak to you," she says, and beckons impatiently to Emily.

Mirabel whispers, "Don't go!"

Emily rises nevertheless—ready to avail herself of the first excuse for leaving him. Francine meets her half way, and takes her roughly by the arm.

"What is it?" Emily asks.

"Suppose you leave off flirting with Mr. Mirabel, and make yourself of some use."

"In what way?"

"Use your ears—and look at that girl."

She points disdainfully to innocent Miss Plym. The rector's daughter possesses all the virtues, with one exception—the virtue of having an ear for music. When she sings, she is out of tune; and, when she plays, she murders time.

"Who can dance to such music as that?" says Francine. "Finish the waltz for her."

Emily naturally hesitates. "How can I take her place, unless she asks me?"

Francine laughs scornfully. "Say at once, you want to go back to Mr.

Mirabel."

"Do you think I should have got up, when you beckoned to me," Emily rejoins, "if I had not wanted to get away from Mr. Mirabel?"

Instead of resenting this sharp retort, Francine suddenly breaks into good humor. "Come along, you little spit-fire; I'll manage it for you."

She leads Emily to the piano, and stops Miss Plym without a word of apology: "It's your turn to dance now. Here's Miss Brown waiting to relieve you."

Cecilia has not been unobservant, in her own quiet way, of what has been going on. Waiting until Francine and Miss Plym are out of hearing, she bends over Emily, and says, "My dear, I really do think Francine is in love with Mr. Mirabel."

"After having only been a week in the same house with him!" Emily exclaims.

"At any rate," said Cecilia, more smartly than usual, "she is jealous of you."

CHAPTER XXXIX. FEIGNING.

The next morning, Mr. Mirabel took two members of the circle at Monksmoor by surprise. One of them was Emily; and one of them was the master of the house.

Seeing Emily alone in the garden before breakfast, he left his room and joined her. "Let me say one word," he pleaded, "before we go to breakfast. I am grieved to think that I was so unfortunate as to offend you, last night."

Emily's look of astonishment answered for her before she could speak. "What can I have said or done," she asked, "to make you think that?"

"Now I breathe again!" he cried, with the boyish gayety of manner which was one of the secrets of his popularity among women. "I really feared that I had spoken thoughtlessly. It is a terrible confession for a clergyman to make—but it is not the less true that I am one of the most indiscreet men living. It is my rock ahead in life that I say the first thing which comes uppermost, without stopping to think. Being well aware of my own defects, I naturally distrust myself."

"Even in the pulpit?" Emily inquired.

He laughed with the readiest appreciation of the satire—although it was directed against himself.

"I like that question," he said; "it tells me we are as good friends again as ever. The fact is, the sight of the congregation, when I get into the pulpit, has the same effect upon me that the sight of the footlights has on an actor. All oratory (though my clerical brethren are shy of confessing it) is acting— without the scenery and the costumes. Did you really mean it, last night, when you said you would like to hear me preach?"

"Indeed, I did."

"How very kind of you. I don't think myself the sermon is worth the sacrifice. (There is another specimen of my indiscreet way of talking!) What I mean is, that you will have to get up early on Sunday morning, and drive twelve miles to the damp and dismal little village, in which I officiate for a man with a rich wife who likes the climate of Italy. My congregation works in the fields all the week, and naturally enough goes to sleep in church on Sunday. I have had to counteract that. Not by preaching! I wouldn't puzzle the poor people with my eloquence for the world. No, no: I tell them little stories out of the Bible—in a nice easy gossiping way. A quarter of an hour is my limit of time; and, I am proud to say, some of them (mostly the women) do to a certain extent keep awake. If you and the other ladies decide to honor me, it is needless to say you shall have one of my grand efforts. What will be the effect on my unfortunate flock remains to be seen. I will have the church brushed up, and luncheon of course at the parsonage. Beans, bacon, and beer—I haven't got anything else in the house. Are you rich? I hope not!"

"I suspect I am quite as poor as you are, Mr. Mirabel."

"I am delighted to hear it. (More of my indiscretion!) Our poverty is another bond between us."

Before he could enlarge on this text, the breakfast bell rang.

He gave Emily his arm, quite satisfied with the result of the morning's talk. In speaking seriously to her on the previous night, he had committed the mistake of speaking too soon. To amend this false step, and to recover his position in Emily's estimation, had been his object in view—and it had been successfully accomplished. At the breakfast-table that morning, the companionable clergyman was more amusing than ever.

The meal being over, the company dispersed as usual—with the one exception of Mirabel. Without any apparent reason, he kept his place at the table. Mr. Wyvil, the most courteous and considerate of men, felt it an attention due to his guest not to leave the room first. All that he could venture to do was to give a little hint. "Have you any plans for the morning?" he asked.

"I have a plan that depends entirely on yourself," Mirabel answered; "and I am afraid of being as indiscreet as usual, if I mention it. Your charming daughter tells me you play on the violin."

Modest Mr. Wyvil looked confused. "I hope you have not been annoyed," he said; "I practice in a distant room so that nobody may hear me."

"My dear sir, I am eager to hear you! Music is my passion; and the violin is my favorite instrument."

Mr. Wyvil led the way to his room, positively blushing with pleasure. Since the death of his wife he had been sadly in want of a little encouragement. His daughters and his friends were careful—over-careful, as he thought—of intruding on him in his hours of practice. And, sad to say, his daughters and his friends were, from a musical point of view, perfectly right.

Literature has hardly paid sufficient attention to a social phenomenon of a singularly perplexing kind. We hear enough, and more than enough, of persons who successfully cultivate the Arts—of the remarkable manner in which fitness for their vocation shows itself in early life, of the obstacles which family prejudice places in their way, and of the unremitting devotion which has led to the achievement of glorious results.

But how many writers have noticed those other incomprehensible persons, members of families innocent for generations past of practicing Art or caring for Art, who have notwithstanding displayed from their earliest years the irresistible desire to cultivate poetry, painting, or music; who have surmounted obstacles, and endured disappointments, in the single-hearted resolution to devote their lives to an intellectual pursuit—being absolutely without the capacity which proves the vocation, and justifies the sacrifice. Here is Nature, "unerring Nature," presented in flat contradiction with herself. Here are men bent on performing feats of running, without having legs; and women, hopelessly barren, living in constant expectation of large families to the end of their days. The musician is not to be found more completely deprived than Mr. Wyvil of natural capacity for playing on an instrument—and, for twenty years past, it had been the pride and delight of his heart to let no day of his life go by without practicing on the violin.

"I am sure I must be tiring you," he said politely—after having played without mercy for an hour and more.

No: the insatiable amateur had his own purpose to gain, and was not exhausted yet. Mr. Wyvil got up to look for some more music. In that interval desultory conversation naturally took place. Mirabel contrived to give it the necessary direction—the direction of Emily.

"The most delightful girl I have met with for many a long year past!" Mr. Wyvil declared warmly. "I don't wonder at my daughter being so fond of her. She leads a solitary life at home, poor thing; and I am honestly glad to see her spirits reviving in my house."

"An only child?" Mirabel asked.

In the necessary explanation that followed, Emily's isolated position in the world was revealed in few words. But one more discovery—the most important of all—remained to be made. Had she used a figure of speech in saying that she was as poor as Mirabel himself? or had she told him the shocking truth? He put the question with perfect delicacy—but with unerring directness as well.

Mr. Wyvil, quoting his daughter's authority, described Emily's income as falling short even of two hundred a year. Having made that disheartening reply, he opened another music book. "You know this sonata, of course?" he said. The next moment, the violin was under his chin and the performance began.

While Mirabel was, to all appearance, listening with the utmost attention, he was actually endeavoring to reconcile himself to a serious sacrifice of his own inclinations. If he remained much longer in the same house with Emily, the impression that she had produced on him would be certainly strengthened—and he would be guilty of the folly of making an offer of marriage to a woman who was as poor as himself. The one remedy that could be trusted to preserve him from such infatuation as this, was absence. At the end of the week, he had arranged to return to Vale Regis for his Sunday duty; engaging to join his friends again at Monksmoor on the Monday following. That rash promise, there could be no further doubt about it, must not be fulfilled.

He had arrived at this resolution, when the terrible activity of Mr. Wyvil's bow was suspended by the appearance of a third person in the room.

Cecilia's maid was charged with a neat little three-cornered note from her young lady, to be presented to her master. Wondering why his daughter should write to him, Mr. Wyvil opened the note, and was informed of Cecilia's motive in these words:

"DEAREST PAPA—I hear Mr. Mirabel is with you, and as this is a secret, I must write. Emily has received a very strange letter this morning, which puzzles her and alarms me. When you are quite at liberty, we shall be so much obliged if you will tell us how Emily ought to answer it."

Mr. Wyvil stopped Mirabel, on the point of trying to escape from the music. "A little domestic matter to attend to," he said. "But we will finish the sonata first."

CHAPTER XL. CONSULTING.

Out of the music room, and away from his violin, the sound side of Mr. Wyvil's character was free to assert itself. In his public and in his private capacity, he was an eminently sensible man.

As a member of parliament, he set an example which might have been followed with advantage by many of his colleagues. In the first place he abstained from hastening the downfall of representative institutions by asking questions and making speeches. In the second place, he was able to distinguish between the duty that he owed to his party, and the duty that he owed to his country. When the Legislature acted politically—that is to say, when it dealt with foreign complications, or electoral reforms—he followed his leader. When the Legislature acted socially—that is to say, for the good of the people—he followed his conscience. On the last occasion when the great Russian bugbear provoked a division, he voted submissively with his Conservative allies. But, when the question of opening museums and picture galleries on Sundays arrayed the two parties in hostile camps, he broke into open mutiny, and went over to the Liberals. He consented to help in preventing an extension of the franchise; but he refused to be concerned in obstructing the repeal of taxes on knowledge. "I am doubtful in the first case," he said, "but I am sure in the second." He was asked for an explanation: "Doubtful of what? and sure of what?" To the astonishment of his leader, he answered: "The benefit to the people." The same sound sense appeared in the transactions of his private life. Lazy and dishonest servants found that the gentlest of masters had a side to his character which took them by surprise. And, on certain occasions in the experience of Cecilia and her sister, the most indulgent of fathers proved to be as capable of saying No, as the sternest tyrant who ever ruled a fireside.

Called into council by his daughter and his guest, Mr. Wyvil assisted them by advice which was equally wise and kind—but which afterward proved, under the perverse influence of circumstances, to be advice that he had better not have given.

The letter to Emily which Cecilia had recommended to her father's consideration, had come from Netherwoods, and had been written by Alban Morris.

He assured Emily that he had only decided on writing to her, after some hesitation, in the hope of serving interests which he did not himself understand, but which might prove to be interests worthy of consideration, nevertheless. Having stated his motive in these terms, he proceeded to relate what had passed between Miss Jethro and himself. On the subject of Francine, Alban only ventured to add that she had not produced a favorable impression on him, and that he could not think her likely, on further experience, to prove a desirable friend.

On the last leaf were added some lines, which Emily was at no loss how to answer. She had folded back the page, so that no eyes but her own should see how the poor drawing-master finished his letter: "I wish you all possible happiness, my dear, among your new friends; but don't forget the old friend who thinks of you, and dreams of you, and longs to see you again. The little world I live in is a dreary world, Emily, in your absence. Will you write to me now and then, and encourage me to hope?"

Mr. Wyvil smiled, as he looked at the folded page, which hid the signature.

"I suppose I may take it for granted," he said slyly, "that this gentleman really has your interests at heart? May I know who he is?"

Emily answered the last question readily enough. Mr. Wyvil went on with his inquiries. "About the mysterious lady, with the strange name," he proceeded—"do you know anything of her?"

Emily related what she knew; without revealing the true reason for Miss Jethro's departure from Netherwoods. In after years, it was one of her most treasured remembrances, that she had kept secret the melancholy confession which had startled her, on the last night of her life at school.

Mr. Wyvil looked at Alban's letter again. "Do you know how Miss Jethro became acquainted with Mr. Mirabel?" he asked.

"I didn't even know that they were acquainted."

"Do you think it likely—if Mr. Morris had been talking to you instead of writing to you—that he might have said more than he has said in his letter?"

Cecilia had hitherto remained a model of discretion. Seeing Emily hesitate, temptation overcame her. "Not a doubt of it, papa!" she declared confidently.

"Is Cecilia right?" Mr. Wyvil inquired.

Reminded in this way of her influence over Alban, Emily could only make one honest reply. She admitted that Cecilia was right.

Mr. Wyvil thereupon advised her not to express any opinion, until she was in a better position to judge for herself. "When you write to Mr. Morris," he continued, "say that you will wait to tell him what you think of Miss Jethro, until you see him again."

"I have no prospect at present of seeing him again," Emily said.

"You can see Mr. Morris whenever it suits him to come here," Mr. Wyvil replied. "I will write and ask him to visit us, and you can inclose the invitation in your letter."

"Oh, Mr. Wyvil, how good of you!"

"Oh, papa, the very thing I was going to ask you to do!"

The excellent master of Monksmoor looked unaffectedly surprised. "What are you two young ladies making a fuss about?" he said. "Mr. Morris is a gentleman by profession; and—may I venture to say it, Miss Emily?—a valued friend of yours as well. Who has a better claim to be one of my guests?"

Cecilia stopped her father as he was about to leave the room. "I suppose we mustn't ask Mr. Mirabel what he knows of Miss Jethro?" she said.

"My dear, what can you be thinking of? What right have we to question Mr. Mirabel about Miss Jethro?"

"It's so very unsatisfactory, papa. There must be some reason why Emily and Mr. Mirabel ought not to meet—or why should Miss Jethro have been so very earnest about it?"

"Miss Jethro doesn't intend us to know why, Cecilia. It will perhaps come out in time. Wait for time."

Left together, the girls discussed the course which Alban would probably take, on receiving Mr. Wyvil's invitation.

"He will only be too glad," Cecilia asserted, "to have the opportunity of seeing you again."

"I doubt whether he will care about seeing me again, among strangers," Emily replied. "And you forget that there are obstacles in his way. How is he to leave his class?"

"Quite easily! His class doesn't meet on the Saturday half-holiday. He can be here, if he starts early, in time for luncheon; and he can stay till Monday or Tuesday."

"Who is to take his place at the school?"

"Miss Ladd, to be sure—if you make a point of it. Write to her, as well as to Mr. Morris."

The letters being written—and the order having been given to prepare a room for the expected guest—Emily and Cecilia returned to the drawing-room. They found the elders of the party variously engaged—the men with newspapers, and the ladies with work. Entering the conservatory next, they discovered Cecilia's sister languishing among the flowers in an easy chair. Constitutional laziness, in some young ladies, assumes an invalid character, and presents the interesting spectacle of perpetual convalescence. The doctor declared that the baths at St. Moritz had cured Miss Julia. Miss Julia declined to agree with the doctor.

"Come into the garden with Emily and me," Cecilia said.

"Emily and you don't know what it is to be ill," Julia answered.

The two girls left her, and joined the young people who were amusing themselves in the garden. Francine had taken possession of Mirabel, and had condemned him to hard labor in swinging her. He made an attempt to get away when Emily and Cecilia approached, and was peremptorily recalled to his duty. "Higher!" cried Miss de Sor, in her hardest tones of authority. "I want to swing higher than anybody else!" Mirabel submitted with gentleman-like resignation, and was rewarded by tender encouragement expressed in a look.

"Do you see that?" Cecilia whispered. "He knows how rich she is—I wonder whether he will marry her."

Emily smiled. "I doubt it, while he is in this house," she said. "You are as rich as Francine—and don't forget that you have other attractions as well."

Cecilia shook her head. "Mr. Mirabel is very nice," she admitted; "but I wouldn't marry him. Would you?"

Emily secretly compared Alban with Mirabel. "Not for the world!" she answered.

The next day was the day of Mirabel's departure. His admirers among the ladies followed him out to the door, at which Mr. Wyvil's carriage was waiting. Francine threw a nosegay after the departing guest as he got in. "Mind you come back to us on Monday!" she said. Mirabel bowed and thanked her; but his last look was for Emily, standing apart from the others at the top of the steps. Francine said nothing; her lips closed convulsively—she turned suddenly pale.

CHAPTER XLI. SPEECHIFYING.

On the Monday, a plowboy from Vale Regis arrived at Monksmoor.

In respect of himself, he was a person beneath notice. In respect of his errand, he was sufficiently important to cast a gloom over the household. The faithless Mirabel had broken his engagement, and the plowboy was the herald of misfortune who brought his apology. To his great disappointment (he wrote) he was detained by the affairs of his parish. He could only trust to Mr. Wyvil's indulgence to excuse him, and to communicate his sincere sense of regret (on scented note paper) to the ladies.

Everybody believed in the affairs of the parish—with the exception of Francine. "Mr. Mirabel has made the best excuse he could think of for shortening his visit; and I don't wonder at it," she said, looking significantly at Emily.

Emily was playing with one of the dogs; exercising him in the tricks which he had learned. She balanced a morsel of sugar on his nose—and had no attention to spare for Francine.

Cecilia, as the mistress of the house, felt it her duty to interfere. "That is a strange remark to make," she answered. "Do you mean to say that we have driven Mr. Mirabel away from us?"

"I accuse nobody," Francine began with spiteful candor.

"Now she's going to accuse everybody!" Emily interposed, addressing herself facetiously to the dog.

"But when girls are bent on fascinating men, whether they like it or not," Francine proceeded, "men have only one alternative—they must keep out of the way." She looked again at Emily, more pointedly than ever.

Even gentle Cecilia resented this. "Whom do you refer to?" she said sharply.

"My dear!" Emily remonstrated, "need you ask?" She glanced at Francine as she spoke, and then gave the dog his signal. He tossed up the sugar, and caught it in his mouth. His audience applauded him—and so, for that time, the skirmish ended.

Among the letters of the next morning's delivery, arrived Alban's reply. Emily's anticipations proved to be correct. The drawing-master's du ties would not permit him to leave Netherwoods; and he, like Mirabel, sent his apologies. His short letter to Emily contained no further allusion to Miss Jethro; it began and ended on the first page.

Had he been disappointed by the tone of reserve in which Emily had written to him, under Mr. Wyvil's advice? Or (as Cecilia suggested) had his detention at the school so bitterly disappointed him that he was too disheartened to write at any length? Emily made no attempt to arrive at a conclusion, either one way or the other. She seemed to be in depressed spirits; and she spoke superstitiously, for the first time in Cecilia's experience of her.

"I don't like this reappearance of Miss Jethro," she said. "If the mystery about that woman is ever cleared up, it will bring trouble and sorrow to me—and I believe, in his own secret heart, Alban Morris thinks so too."

"Write, and ask him," Cecilia suggested.

"He is so kind and so unwilling to distress me," Emily answered, "that he wouldn't acknowledge it, even if I am right."

In the middle of the week, the course of private life at Monksmoor suffered an interruption—due to the parliamentary position of the master of the house.

The insatiable appetite for making and hearing speeches, which represents one of the marked peculiarities of the English race (including their cousins in the United States), had seized on Mr. Wyvil's constituents. There was to be a political meeting at the market hall, in the neighboring town; and the member was expected to make an oration, passing in review contemporary events at home and abroad. "Pray don't think of accompanying me," the good man said to his guests. "The hall is badly ventilated, and the speeches, including my own, will not be worth hearing."

This humane warning was ungratefully disregarded. The gentlemen were all interested in "the objects of the meeting"; and the ladies were firm in the resolution not to be left at home by themselves. They dressed with a view to the large assembly of spectators before whom they were about to appear; and they outtalked the men on political subjects, all the way to the town.

The most delightful of surprises was in store for them, when they reached the market hall. Among the crowd of ordinary gentlemen, waiting under the portico until the proceedings began, appeared one person of distinction, whose title was "Reverend," and whose name was Mirabel.

Francine was the first to discover him. She darted up the steps and held out her hand.

396

"This is a pleasure!" she cried. "Have you come here to see—" she was about to say Me, but, observing the strangers round her, altered the word to Us. "Please give me your arm," she whispered, before her young friends had arrived within hearing. "I am so frightened in a crowd!"

She held fast by Mirabel, and kept a jealous watch on him. Was it only her fancy? or did she detect a new charm in his smile when he spoke to Emily?

Before it was possible to decide, the time for the meeting had arrived. Mr. Wyvil's friends were of course accommodated with seats on the platform. Francine, still insisting on her claim to Mirabel's arm, got a chair next to him. As she seated herself, she left him free for a moment. In that moment, the infatuated man took an empty chair on the other side of him, and placed it for Emily. He communicated to that hated rival the information which he ought to have reserved for Francine. "The committee insist," he said, "on my proposing one of the Resolutions. I promise not to bore you; mine shall be the shortest speech delivered at the meeting."

The proceedings began.

Among the earlier speakers not one was inspired by a feeling of mercy for the audience. The chairman reveled in words. The mover and seconder of the first Resolution (not having so much as the ghost of an idea to trouble either of them), poured out language in flowing and overflowing streams, like water from a perpetual spring. The heat exhaled by the crowded audience was already becoming insufferable. Cries of "Sit down!" assailed the orator of the moment. The chairman was obliged to interfere. A man at the back of the hall roared out, "Ventilation!" and broke a window with his stick. He was rewarded with three rounds of cheers; and was ironically invited to mount the platform and take the chair.

Under these embarrassing circumstances, Mirabel rose to speak.

He secured silence, at the outset, by a humorous allusion to the prolix speaker who had preceded him. "Look at the clock, gentlemen," he said; "and limit my speech to an interval of ten minutes." The applause which followed was heard, through the broken window, in the street. The boys among the mob outside intercepted the flow of air by climbing on each other's shoulders and looking in at the meeting, through the gaps left by the shattered glass. Having proposed his Resolution with discreet brevity of speech, Mirabel courted popularity on the plan adopted by the late Lord Palmerston in the House of Commons—he told stories, and made jokes, adapted to the intelligence of the dullest people who were listening to him. The charm of his voice and manner completed his success. Punctually at the tenth minute, he sat down amid cries of "Go on." Francine was the first to take his hand, and to express admiration mutely by pressing it. He returned the pressure—but he looked at the wrong lady—the lady on the other side.

Although she made no complaint, he instantly saw that Emily was overcome by the heat. Her lips were white, and her eyes were closing. "Let me take you out," he said, "or you will faint."

Francine started to her feet to follow them. The lower order of the audience, eager for amusement, put their own humorous construction on the young lady's action. They roared with laughter. "Let the parson and his sweetheart be," they called out; "two's company, miss, and three isn't." Mr. Wyvil interposed his authority and rebuked them. A lady seated behind Francine interfered to good purpose by giving her a chair, which placed her out of sight of the audience. Order was restored—and the proceedings were resumed.

On the conclusion of the meeting, Mirabel and Emily were found waiting for their friends at the door. Mr. Wyvil innocently added fuel to the fire that was burning in Francine. He insisted that Mirabel should return to Monksmoor, and offered him a seat in the carriage at Emily's side.

Later in the evening, when they all met at dinner, there appeared a change in Miss de Sor which surprised everybody but Mirabel. She was gay and good-humored, and especially amiable and attentive to Emily—who sat opposite to her at the table. "What did you and Mr. Mirabel talk about while you were away from us?" she asked innocently. "Politics?"

Emily readily adopted Francine's friendly tone. "Would you have talked politics, in my place?" she asked gayly.

"In your place, I should have had the most delightful of companions," Francine rejoined; "I wish I had been overcome by the heat too!"

Mirabel—attentively observing her—acknowledged the compliment by a bow, and left Emily to continue the conversation. In perfect good faith she owned to having led Mirabel to talk of himself. She had heard from Cecilia that his early life had been devoted to various occupations, and she was interested in knowing how circumstances had led him into devoting himself to the Church. Francine listened with the outward appearance of implicit belief, and with the inward conviction that Emily was deliberately deceiving her. When the little narrative was at an end, she was more agreeable than ever. She admired Emily's dress, and she rivaled Cecilia in enjoyment of the good things on the table; she entertained Mirabel with humorous anecdotes of the priests at St. Domingo, and was so interested in the manufacture of violins, ancient and modern, that Mr. Wyvil promised to show her his famous collection of instruments, after dinner. Her overflowing amiability included even poor Miss Darnaway and the absent brothers and sisters. She heard with flattering sympathy, how they had been ill and had got well again; what amusing tricks they played, what alarming accidents happened to them, and how remarkably clever they were—"including, I do assure you, dear Miss de Sor, the baby only ten months old." When the ladies rose to retire, Francine was, socially speaking, the heroine of the evening.

While the violins were in course of exhibition, Mirabel found an opportunity of speaking to Emily, unobserved.

"Have you said, or done, anything to offend Miss de Sor?" he asked.

"Nothing whatever!" Emily declared, startled by the question. "What makes you think I have offended her?"

"I have been trying to find a reason for the change in her," Mirabel answered—"especially the change toward yourself."

"Well?"

"Well—she means mischief."

"Mischief of what sort?"

"Of a sort which may expose her to discovery—unless she disarms suspicion at the outset. That is (as I believe) exactly what she has been doing this evening. I needn't warn you to be on your guard."

All the next day Emily was on the watch for events—and nothing happened. Not the slightest appearance of jealousy betrayed itself in Francine. She made no attempt to attract to herself the attentions of Mirabel; and she showed no hostility to Emily, either by word, look, or manner.

....

The day after, an event occurred at Netherwoods. Alban Morris received an anonymous letter, addressed to him in these terms:

"A certain young lady, in whom you are supposed to be interested, is forgetting you in your absence. If you are not mean enough to allow yourself to be supplanted by another man, join the party at Monksmoor before it is too late."

CHAPTER XLII. COOKING.

The day after the political meeting was a day of departures, at the pleasant country house.

Miss Darnaway was recalled to the nursery at home. The old squire who did justice to Mr. Wyvil's port-wine went away next, having guests to entertain at his own house. A far more serious loss followed. The three dancing men had engagements which drew them to new spheres of activity in other drawing-rooms. They said, with the same dreary grace of manner, "Very sorry to go"; they drove to the railway, arrayed in the same perfect traveling suits of neutral tint; and they had but one difference of opinion among them—each firmly believed that he was smoking the best cigar to be got in London.

The morning after these departures would have been a dull morning indeed, but for the presence of Mirabel.

When breakfast was over, the invalid Miss Julia established herself on the sofa with a novel. Her father retired to the other end of the house, and profaned the art of music on music's most expressive instrument. Left with

400

Emily, Cecilia, and Francine, Mirabel made one of his happy suggestions. "We are thrown on our own resources," he said. "Let us distinguish ourselves by inventing some entirely new amusement for the day. You young ladies shall sit in council—and I will be secretary." He turned to Cecilia. "The meeting waits to hear the mistress of the house."

Modest Cecilia appealed to her school friends for help; addressing herself in the first instance (by the secretary's advice) to Francine, as the eldest. They all noticed another change in this variable young person. She was silent and subdued; and she said wearily, "I don't care what we do—shall we go out riding?"

The unanswerable objection to riding as a form of amusement, was that it had been more than once tried already. Something clever and surprising was anticipated from Emily when it came to her turn. She, too, disappointed expectation. "Let us sit under the trees," was all that she could suggest, "and ask Mr. Mirabel to tell us a story."

Mirabel laid down his pen and took it on himself to reject this proposal. "Remember," he remonstrated, "that I have an interest in the diversions of the day. You can't expect me to be amused by my own story. I appeal to Miss Wyvil to invent a pleasure which will include the secretary."

Cecilia blushed and looked uneasy. "I think I have got an idea," she announced, after some hesitation. "May I propose that we all go to the keeper's lodge?" There her courage failed her, and she hesitated again.

Mirabel gravely registered the proposal, as far as it went. "What are we to do when we get to the keeper's lodge?" he inquired.

"We are to ask the keeper's wife," Cecilia proceeded, "to lend us her kitchen."

"To lend us her kitchen," Mirabel repeated.

"And what are we to do in the kitchen?"

Cecilia looked down at her pretty hands crossed on her lap, and answered softly, "Cook our own luncheon."

Here was an entirely new amusement, in the most attractive sense of the words! Here was charming Cecilia's interest in the pleasures of the table so happily inspired, that the grateful meeting offered its tribute of applause—even including Francine. The members of the council were young; their daring digestions contemplated without fear the prospect of eating their own amateur cookery. The one question that troubled them now was what they were to cook.

"I can make an omelet," Cecilia ventured to say.

"If there is any cold chicken to be had," Emily added, "I undertake to follow the omelet with a mayonnaise."

"There are clergymen in the Church of England who are even clever enough to fry potatoes," Mirabel announced—"and I am one of them. What shall we have next? A pudding? Miss de Sor, can you make a pudding?"

Francine exhibited another new side to her character—a diffident and humble side. "I am ashamed to say I don't know how to cook anything," she confessed; "you had better leave me out of it."

But Cecilia was now in her element. Her plan of operations was wide enough even to include Francine. "You shall wash the lettuce, my dear, and stone the olives for Emily's mayonnaise. Don't be discouraged! You shall have a companion; we will send to the rectory for Miss Plym—the very person to chop parsley and shallot for my omelet. Oh, Emily, what a morning we are going to have!" Her lovely blue eyes sparkled with joy; she gave Emily a kiss which Mirabel must have been more or less than man not to have coveted. "I declare," cried Cecilia, completely losing her head, "I'm so excited, I don't know what to do with myself!"

Emily's intimate knowledge of her friend applied the right remedy. "You don't know what to do with yourself?" she repeated. "Have you no sense of duty? Give the cook your orders."

Cecilia instantly recovered her presence of mind. She sat down at the writing-table, and made out a list of eatable productions in the animal and vegetable world, in which every other word was underlined two or three times over. Her serious face was a sight to see, when she rang for the cook, and the two held a privy council in a corner.

On the way to the keeper's lodge, the young mistress of the house headed a procession of servants carrying the raw materials. Francine followed, held in custody by Miss Plym—who took her responsibilities seriously, and clamored for instruction in the art of chopping parsley. Mirabel and Emily were together, far behind; they were the only two members of the company whose minds were not occupied in one way or another by the kitchen.

"This child's play of ours doesn't seem to interest you," Mirabel remarked.

"I am thinking," Emily answered, "of what you said to me about Francine."

"I can say something more," he rejoined. "When I noticed the change in her at dinner, I told you she meant mischief. There is another change to-day, which suggests to my mind that the mischief is done."

"And directed against me?" Emily asked.

Mirabel made no direct reply. It was impossible for him to remind her that she had, no matter how innocently, exposed herself to the jealous hatred of Francine. "Time will tell us, what we don't know now," he replied evasively.

"You seem to have faith in time, Mr. Mirabel."

"The greatest faith. Time is the inveterate enemy of deceit. Sooner or later, every hidden thing is a thing doomed to discovery."

"Without exception?"

"Yes," he answered positively, "without exception."

At that moment Francine stopped and looked back at them. Did she think that Emily and Mirabel had been talking together long enough? Miss Plym—with the parsley still on her mind—advanced to consult Emily's experience. The two walked on together, leaving Mirabel to overtake Francine. He saw, in her first look at him, the effort that it cost her to suppress those emotions which the pride of women is most deeply interested in concealing.

Before a word had passed, he regretted that Emily had left them together.

"I wish I had your cheerful disposition," she began, abruptly. "I am out of spirits or out of temper—I don't know which; and I don't know why. Do you ever trouble yourself with thinking of the future?"

"As seldom as possible, Miss de Sor. In such a situation as mine, most people have prospects—I have none."

He spoke gravely, conscious of not feeling at ease on his side. If he had been the most modest man that ever lived, he must have seen in Francine's face that she loved him.

When they had first been presented to each other, she was still under the influence of the meanest instincts in her scheming and selfish nature. She had thought to herself, "With my money to help him, that man's celebrity would do the rest; the best society in England would be glad to receive Mirabel's wife." As the days passed, strong feeling had taken the place of those contemptible aspirations: Mirabel had unconsciously inspired the one passion which was powerful enough to master Francine—sensual passion. Wild hopes rioted in her. Measureless desires which she had never felt before, united themselves with capacities for wickedness, which had been the horrid growth of a few nights—capacities which suggested even viler attempts to rid herself of a supposed rivalry than slandering Emily by means of an anonymous letter. Without waiting for it to be offered, she took Mirabel's arm, and pressed it to her breast as they slowly walked on. The fear of discovery which had troubled her after she had sent her base letter to the post, vanished at that inspiriting moment. She bent her head near enough to him when he spoke to feel his breath on her face.

"There is a strange similarity," she said softly, "between your position and mine. Is there anything cheering in my prospects? I am far away from home—my father and mother wouldn't care if they never saw me again. People talk about my money! What is the use of money to such a lonely wretch as I am? Suppose I write to London, and ask the lawyer if I may give it all away to some deserving person? Why not to you?"

"My dear Miss de Sor—!"

404

"Is there anything wrong, Mr. Mirabel, in wishing that I could make you a prosperous man?"

"You must not even talk of such a thing!"

"How proud you are!" she said submissively.

"Oh, I can't bear to think of you in that miserable village—a position so unworthy of your talents and your claims! And you tell me I must not talk about it. Would you have said that to Emily, if she was as anxious as I am to see you in your right place in the world?"

"I should have answered her exactly as I have answered you."

"She will never embarrass you, Mr. Mirabel, by being as sincere as I am. Emily can keep her own secrets."

"Is she to blame for doing that?"

"It depends on your feeling for her."

"What feeling do you mean?"

"Suppose you heard she was engaged to be married?" Francine suggested.

Mirabel's manner—studiously cold and formal thus far—altered on a sudden. He looked with unconcealed anxiety at Francine. "Do you say that seriously?" he asked.

"I said 'suppose.' I don't exactly know that she is engaged."

"What do you know?"

"Oh, how interested you are in Emily! She is admired by some people. Are you one of them?"

Mirabel's experience of women warned him to try silence as a means of provoking her into speaking plainly. The experiment succeeded: Francine returned to the question that he had put to her, and abruptly answered it.

"You may believe me or not, as you like—I know of a man who is in love with her. He has had his opportunities; and he has made good use of them.

Would you like to know who he is?"

"I should like to know anything which you may wish to tell me." He did his best to make the reply in a tone of commonplace politeness—and he might have succeeded in deceiving a man. The woman's quicker ear told her that he was angry. Francine took the full advantage of that change in her favor.

"I am afraid your good opinion of Emily will be shaken," she quietly resumed, "when I tell you that she has encouraged a man who is only drawing-master at a school. At the same time, a person in her circumstances—I mean she has no money—ought not to be very hard to please. Of course she has never spoken to you of Mr. Alban Morris?"

"Not that I remember."

Only four words—but they satisfied Francine.

The one thing wanting to complete the obstacle which she had now placed in Emily's way, was that Alban Morris should enter on the scene. He might hesitate; but, if he was really fond of Emily, the anonymous letter would sooner or later bring him to Monksmoor. In the meantime, her object was gained. She dropped Mirabel's arm.

"Here is the lodge," she said gayly—"I declare Cecilia has got an apron on already! Come, and cook."

CHAPTER XLIII. SOUNDING.

Mirabel left Francine to enter the lodge by herself. His mind was disturbed: he felt the importance of gaining time for reflection before he and Emily met again.

The keeper's garden was at the back of the lodge. Passing through the wicket-gate, he found a little summer-house at a turn in the path. Nobody was there: he went in and sat down.

At intervals, he had even yet encouraged himself to underrate the true importance of the feeling which Emily had awakened in him. There was an end to all self-deception now. After what Francine had said to him,

406

this shallow and frivolous man no longer resisted the all-absorbing influence of love. He shrank under the one terrible question that forced itself on his mind:—Had that jealous girl spoken the truth?

In what process of investigation could he trust, to set this anxiety at rest? To apply openly to Emily would be to take a liberty, which Emily was the last person in the world to permit. In his recent intercourse with her he had felt more strongly than ever the importance of speaking with reserve. He had been scrupulously careful to take no unfair advantage of his opportunity, when he had removed her from the meeting, and when they had walked together, with hardly a creature to observe them, in the lonely outskirts of the town. Emily's gaiety and good humor had not led him astray: he knew that these were bad signs, viewed in the interests of love. His one hope of touching her deeper sympathies was to wait for the help that might yet come from time and chance. With a bitter sigh, he resigned himself to the necessity of being as agreeable and amusing as ever: it was just possible that he might lure her into alluding to Alban Morris, if he began innocently by making her laugh.

As he rose to return to the lodge, the keeper's little terrier, prowling about the garden, looked into the summer-house. Seeing a stranger, the dog showed his teeth and growled.

Mirabel shrank back against the wall behind him, trembling in every limb. His eyes stared in terror as the dog came nearer: barking in high triumph over the discovery of a frightened man whom he could bully. Mirabel called out for help. A laborer at work in the garden ran to the place—and stopped with a broad grin of amusement at seeing a grown man terrified by a barking dog. "Well," he said to himself, after Mirabel had passed out under protection, "there goes a coward if ever there was one yet!"

Mirabel waited a minute behind the lodge to recover himself. He had been so completely unnerved that his hair was wet with perspiration. While he used his handkerchief, he shuddered at other recollections than the recollection of the dog. "After that night at the inn," he thought, "the least thing frightens me!"

He was received by the young ladies with cries of derisive welcome.

"Oh, for shame! for shame! here are the potatoes already cut, and nobody to fry them!"

Mirabel assumed the mask of cheerfulness—with the desperate resolution of an actor, amusing his audience at a time of domestic distress. He astonished the keeper's wife by showing that he really knew how to use her frying-pan. Cecilia's omelet was tough—but the young ladies ate it. Emily's mayonnaise sauce was almost as liquid as water—they swallowed it nevertheless by the help of spoons. The potatoes followed, crisp and dry and delicious—and Mirabel became more popular than ever. "He is the only one of us," Cecilia sadly acknowledged, "who knows how to cook."

When they all left the lodge for a stroll in the park, Francine attached herself to Cecilia and Miss Plym. She resigned Mirabel to Emily—in the happy belief that she had paved the way for a misunderstanding between them.

The merriment at the luncheon table had revived Emily's good spirits. She had a light-hearted remembrance of the failure of her sauce. Mirabel saw her smiling to herself. "May I ask what amuses you?" he said.

"I was thinking of the debt of gratitude that we owe to Mr. Wyvil," she replied. "If he had not persuaded you to return to Monksmoor, we should never have seen the famous Mr. Mirabel with a frying pan in his hand, and never have tasted the only good dish at our luncheon."

Mirabel tried vainly to adopt his companion's easy tone. Now that he was alone with her, the doubts that Francine had aroused shook the prudent resolution at which he had arrived in the garden. He ran the risk, and told Emily plainly why he had returned to Mr. Wyvil's house.

"Although I am sensible of our host's kindness," he answered, "I should have gone back to my parsonage—but for You."

She declined to understand him seriously. "Then the affairs of your parish are neglected—and I am to blame!" she said.

"Am I the first man who has neglected his duties for your sake?" he asked. "I wonder whether the masters at school had the heart to report you when you neglected your lessons?"

She thought of Alban—and betrayed herself by a heightened color. The moment after, she changed the subject. Mirabel could no longer resist the conclusion that Francine had told him the truth.

"When do you leave us," she inquired.

"To-morrow is Saturday—I must go back as usual."

"And how will your deserted parish receive you?"

He made a desperate effort to be as amusing as usual.

"I am sure of preserving my popularity," he said, "while I have a cask in the cellar, and a few spare sixpences in my pocket. The public spirit of my parishioners asks for nothing but money and beer. Before I went to that wearisome meeting, I told my housekeeper that I was going to make a speech about reform. She didn't know what I meant. I explained that reform might increase the number of British citizens who had the right of voting at elections for parliament. She brightened up directly. 'Ah,' she said, 'I've heard my husband talk about elections. The more there are of them (he says) the more money he'll get for his vote. I'm all for reform.' On my way out of the house, I tried the man who works in my garden on the same subject. He didn't look at the matter from the housekeeper's sanguine point of view. 'I don't deny that parliament once gave me a good dinner for nothing at the public-house,' he admitted. 'But that was years ago—and (you'll excuse me, sir) I hear nothing of another dinner to come. It's a matter of opinion, of course. I don't myself believe in reform.' There are specimens of the state of public spirit in our village!" He paused. Emily was listening—but he had not succeeded in choosing a subject that amused her. He tried a topic more nearly connected with his own interests; the topic of the future. "Our good friend has asked me to prolong my visit, after Sunday's duties are over," he said. "I hope I shall find you here, next week?"

"Will the affairs of your parish allow you to come back?" Emily asked mischievously.

"The affairs of my parish—if you force me to confess it—were only an excuse."

"An excuse for what?"

"An excuse for keeping away from Monksmoor—in the interests of my own tranquillity. The experiment has failed. While you are here, I can't keep away."

She still declined to understand him seriously. "Must I tell you in plain words that flattery is thrown away on me?" she said.

"Flattery is not offered to you," he answered gravely. "I beg your pardon for having led to the mistake by talking of myself." Having appealed to her indulgence by that act of submission, he ventured on another distant allusion to the man whom he hated and feared. "Shall I meet any friends of yours," he resumed, "when I return on Monday?"

"What do you mean?"

"I only meant to ask if Mr. Wyvil expects any new guests?"

As he put the question, Cecilia's voice was heard behind them, calling to Emily. They both turned round. Mr. Wyvil had joined his daughter and her two friends. He advanced to meet Emily.

"I have some news for you that you little expect," he said. "A telegram has just arrived from Netherwoods. Mr. Alban Morris has got leave of absence, and is coming here to-morrow."

CHAPTER XLIV. COMPETING.

Time at Monksmoor had advanced to the half hour before dinner, on Saturday evening.

Cecilia and Francine, Mr. Wyvil and Mirabel, were loitering in the conservatory. In the drawing-room, Emily had been considerately left alone with Alban. He had missed the early train from Netherwoods; but he had arrived in time to dress for dinner, and to offer the necessary explanations.

If it had been possible for Alban to allude to the anonymous letter, he

410

might have owned that his first impulse had led him to destroy it, and to assert his confidence in Emily by refusing Mr. Wyvil's invitation. But try as he might to forget them, the base words that he had read remained in his memory. Irritating him at the outset, they had ended in rousing his jealousy. Under that delusive influence, he persuaded himself that he had acted, in the first instance, without due consideration. It was surely his interest—it might even be his duty—to go to Mr. Wyvil's house, and judge for himself. After some last wretched moments of hesitation, he had decided on effecting a compromise with his own better sense, by consulting Miss Ladd. That excellent lady did exactly what he had expected her to do. She made arrangements which granted him leave of absence, from the Saturday to the Tuesday following. The excuse which had served him, in telegraphing to Mr. Wyvil, must now be repeated, in accounting for his unexpected appearance to Emily. "I found a person to take charge of my class," he said; "and I gladly availed myself of the opportunity of seeing you again."

After observing him attentively, while he was speaking to her, Emily owned, with her customary frankness, that she had noticed something in his manner which left her not quite at her ease.

"I wonder," she said, "if there is any foundation for a doubt that has troubled me?" To his unutterable relief, she at once explained what the doubt was. "I am afraid I offended you, in replying to your letter about Miss Jethro."

In this case, Alban could enjoy the luxury of speaking unreservedly. He confessed that Emily's letter had disappointed him.

"I expected you to answer me with less reserve," he replied; "and I began to think I had acted rashly in writing to you at all. When there is a better opportunity, I may have a word to say—" He was apparently interrupted by something that he saw in the conservatory. Looking that way, Emily perceived that Mirabel was the object which had attracted Alban's attention. The vile anonymous letter was in his mind again. Without a preliminary word to prepare Emily, he suddenly changed the subject. "How do you like the clergyman?" he asked.

"Very much indeed," she replied, without the slightest embarrassment.

"Mr. Mirabel is clever and agreeable—and not at all spoiled by his success. I am sure," she said innocently, "you will like him too."

Alban's face answered her unmistakably in the negative sense—but Emily's attention was drawn the other way by Francine. She joined them at the moment, on the lookout for any signs of an encouraging result which her treachery might already have produced. Alban had been inclined to suspect her when he had received the letter. He rose and bowed as she approached. Something—he was unable to realize what it was—told him, in the moment when they looked at each other, that his suspicion had hit the mark.

In the conservatory the ever-amiable Mirabel had left his friends for a while in search of flowers for Cecilia. She turned to her father when they were alone, and asked him which of the gentlemen was to take her in to dinner—Mr. Mirabel or Mr. Morris?

"Mr. Morris, of course," he answered. "He is the new guest—and he turns out to be more than the equal, socially-speaking, of our other friend. When I showed him his room, I asked if he was related to a man who bore the same name—a fellow student of mine, years and years ago, at college. He is my friend's younger son; one of a ruined family—but persons of high distinction in their day."

Mirabel returned with the flowers, just as dinner was announced.

"You are to take Emily to-day," Cecilia said to him, leading the way out of the conservatory. As they entered the drawing-room, Alban was just offering his arm to Emily. "Papa gives you to me, Mr. Morris," Cecilia explained pleasantly. Alban hesitated, apparently not understanding the allusion. Mirabel interfered with his best grace: "Mr. Wyvil offers you the honor of taking his daughter to the dining-room." Alban's face darkened ominously, as the elegant little clergyman gave his arm to Emily, and followed Mr. Wyvil and Francine out of the room. Cecilia looked at her silent and surly companion, and almost envied her lazy sister, dining—under cover of a convenient headache—in her own room.

Having already made up his mind that Alban Morris required careful handling, Mirabel waited a little before he led the conversation as usual. Between the soup and the fish, he made an interesting confession, addressed to Emily in the strictest confidence.

"I have taken a fancy to your friend Mr. Morris," he said. "First impressions, in my case, decide everything; I like people or dislike them on impulse. That man appeals to my sympathies. Is he a good talker?"

"I should say Yes," Emily answered prettily, "if you were not present."

Mirabel was not to be beaten, even by a woman, in the art of paying compliments. He looked admiringly at Alban (sitting opposite to him), and said: "Let us listen."

This flattering suggestion not only pleased Emily—it artfully served Mirabel's purpose. That is to say, it secured him an opportunity for observation of what was going on at the other side of the table.

Alban's instincts as a gentleman had led him to control his irritation and to regret that he had suffered it to appear. Anxious to please, he presented himself at his best. Gentle Cecilia forgave and forgot the angry look which had startled her. Mr. Wyvil was delighted with the son of his old friend. Emily felt secretly proud of the good opinions which her admirer was gathering; and Francine saw with pleasure that he was asserting his claim to Emily's preference, in the way of all others which would be most likely to discourage his rival. These various impressions—produced while Alban's enemy was ominously silent—began to suffer an imperceptible change, from the moment when Mirabel decided that his time had come to take the lead. A remark made by Alban offered him the chance for which he had been on the watch. He agreed with the remark; he enlarged on the remark; he was brilliant and familiar, and instructive and amusing—and still it was all due to the remark. Alban's temper was once more severely tried. Mirabel's mischievous object had not escaped his penetration. He did his best to put obstacles in the adversary's way—and was baffled, time after time, with the readiest ingenuity. If he interrupted—the sweet-tempered clergyman submitted, and went on. If he differed—modest Mr. Mirabel said, in the most amiable manner, "I daresay I am wrong," and handled the topic from his opponent's point of view. Never had such a perfect Christian sat before at Mr. Wyvil's table: not a hard word, not an impatient look, escaped him. The longer Alban resisted, the more surely he lost ground in the general estimation. Cecilia was disappointed; Emily was grieved; Mr. Wyvil's favorable opinion began to waver; Francine was disgusted. When dinner was over, and the carriage was waiting to take the shepherd back to his flock by moonlight, Mirabel's triumph was complete. He had made Alban the innocent means of publicly exhibiting his perfect temper and perfect politeness, under their best and brightest aspect.

So that day ended. Sunday promised to pass quietly, in the absence of Mirabel. The morning came—and it seemed doubtful whether the promise would be fulfilled.

Francine had passed an uneasy night. No such encouraging result as she had anticipated had hitherto followed the appearance of Alban Morris at Monksmoor. He had clumsily allowed Mirabel to improve his position—while he had himself lost ground—in Emily's estimation. If this first disastrous consequence of the meeting between the two men was permitted to repeat itself on future occasions, Emily and Mirabel would be brought more closely together, and Alban himself would be the unhappy cause of it. Francine rose, on the Sunday morning, before the table was laid for breakfast—resolved to try the effect of a timely word of advice.

Her bedroom was situated in the front of the house. The man she was looking for presently passed within her range of view from the window, on his way to take a morning walk in the park. She followed him immediately.

"Good-morning, Mr. Morris."

He raised his hat and bowed—without speaking, and without looking at her.

"We resemble each other in one particular," she proceeded, graciously; "we both like to breathe the fresh air before breakfast."

He said exactly what common politeness obliged him to say, and no more—he said, "Yes."

Some girls might have been discouraged. Francine went on.

"It is no fault of mine, Mr. Morris, that we have not been better friends. For some reason, into which I don't presume to inquire, you seem to distrust me. I really don't know what I have done to deserve it."

"Are you sure of that?" he asked—eying her suddenly and searchingly as he spoke.

Her hard face settled into a rigid look; her eyes met his eyes with a stony defiant stare. Now, for the first time, she knew that he suspected her of having written the anonymous letter. Every evil quality in her nature steadily defied him. A hardened old woman could not have sustained the shock of discovery with a more devilish composure than this girl displayed. "Perhaps you will explain yourself," she said.

"I have explained myself," he answered.

"Then I must be content," she rejoined, "to remain in the dark. I had intended, out of my regard for Emily, to suggest that you might—with advantage to yourself, and to interests that are very dear to you—be more careful in your behavior to Mr. Mirabel. Are you disposed to listen to me?"

"Do you wish me to answer that question plainly, Miss de Sor?"

"I insist on your answering it plainly."

"Then I am not disposed to listen to you."

"May I know why? or am I to be left in the dark again?"

"You are to be left, if you please, to your own ingenuity."

Francine looked at him, with a malignant smile. "One of these days, Mr. Morris—I will deserve your confidence in my ingenuity." She said it, and went back to the house.

This was the only element of disturbance that troubled the perfect tranquillity of the day. What Francine had proposed to do, with the one idea of making Alban serve her purpose, was accomplished a few hours later by Emily's influence for good over the man who loved her.

They passed the afternoon together uninterruptedly in the distant solitudes of the park. In the course of conversation Emily found an opportunity of discreetly alluding to Mirabel. "You mustn't be jealous of our clever little friend," she said; "I like him, and admire him; but—"

"But you don't love him?"

She smiled at the eager way in which Alban put the question.

"There is no fear of that," she answered brightly.

"Not even if you discovered that he loves you?"

"Not even then. Are you content at last? Promise me not to be rude to Mr. Mirabel again."

"For his sake?"

"No—for my sake. I don't like to see you place yourself at a disadvantage toward another man; I don't like you to disappoint me."

The happiness of hearing her say those words transfigured him—the manly beauty of his earlier and happier years seemed to have returned to Alban. He took her hand—he was too agitated to speak.

"You are forgetting Mr. Mirabel," she reminded him gently.

"I will be all that is civil and kind to Mr. Mirabel; I will like him and admire him as you do. Oh, Emily, are you a little, only a very little, fond of me?"

"I don't quite know."

"May I try to find out?"

"How?" she asked.

Her fair cheek was very near to him. The softly-rising color on it said, Answer me here—and he answered.

CHAPTER XLV. MISCHIEF—MAKING.

On Monday, Mirabel made his appearance—and the demon of discord returned with him.

416

Alban had employed the earlier part of the day in making a sketch in the park—intended as a little present for Emily. Presenting himself in the drawing-room, when his work was completed, he found Cecilia and Francine alone. He asked where Emily was.

The question had been addressed to Cecilia. Francine answered it.

"Emily mustn't be disturbed," she said.

"Why not?"

"She is with Mr. Mirabel in the rose garden. I saw them talking together—evidently feeling the deepest interest in what they were saying to each other. Don't interrupt them—you will only be in the way."

Cecilia at once protested against this last assertion. "She is trying to make mischief, Mr. Morris—don't believe her. I am sure they will be glad to see you, if you join them in the garden."

Francine rose, and left the room. She turned, and looked at Alban as she opened the door. "Try it," she said—"and you will find I am right."

"Francine sometimes talks in a very ill-natured way," Cecilia gently remarked. "Do you think she means it, Mr. Morris?'

"I had better not offer an opinion," Alban replied.

"Why?"

"I can't speak impartially; I dislike Miss de Sor."

There was a pause. Alban's sense of self-respect forbade him to try the experiment which Francine had maliciously suggested. His thoughts—less easy to restrain—wandered in the direction of the garden. The attempt to make him jealous had failed; but he was conscious, at the same time, that Emily had disappointed him. After what they had said to each other in the park, she ought to have remembered that women are at the mercy of appearances. If Mirabel had something of importance to say to her, she might have avoided exposing herself to Francine's spiteful misconstruction: it would have been easy to arrange with Cecilia that a third person should be present at the interview.

While he was absorbed in these reflections, Cecilia—embarrassed by the silence—was trying to find a topic of conversation. Alban roughly pushed his sketch-book away from him, on the table. Was he displeased with Emily? The same question had occurred to Cecilia at the time of the correspondence, on the subject of Miss Jethro. To recall those letters led her, by natural sequence, to another effort of memory. She was reminded of the person who had been the cause of the correspondence: her interest was revived in the mystery of Miss Jethro.

"Has Emily told you that I have seen your letter?" she asked.

He roused himself with a start. "I beg your pardon. What letter are you thinking of?"

"I was thinking of the letter which mentions Miss Jethro's strange visit. Emily was so puzzled and so surprised that she showed it to me—and we both consulted my father. Have you spoken to Emily about Miss Jethro?"

"I have tried—but she seemed to be unwilling to pursue the subject."

"Have you made any discoveries since you wrote to Emily?"

"No. The mystery is as impenetrable as ever."

As he replied in those terms, Mirabel entered the conservatory from the garden, evidently on his way to the drawing-room.

To see the man, whose introduction to Emily it had been Miss Jethro's mysterious object to prevent—at the very moment when he had been speaking of Miss Jethro herself—was, not only a temptation of curiosity, but a direct incentive (in Emily's own interests) to make an effort at discovery. Alban pursued the conversation with Cecilia, in a tone which was loud enough to be heard in the conservatory.

"The one chance of getting any information that I can see," he proceeded, "is to speak to Mr. Mirabel."

"I shall be only too glad, if I can be of any service to Miss Wyvil and

Mr. Morris."

With those obliging words, Mirabel made a dramatic entry, and looked at Cecilia with his irresistible smile. Startled by his sudden appearance, she unconsciously assisted Alban's design. Her silence gave him the opportunity of speaking in her place.

"We were talking," he said quietly to Mirabel, "of a lady with whom you are acquainted."

"Indeed! May I ask the lady's name?"

"Miss Jethro."

Mirabel sustained the shock with extraordinary self-possession—so far as any betrayal by sudden movement was concerned. But his color told the truth: it faded to paleness—it revealed, even to Cecilia's eyes, a man overpowered by fright.

Alban offered him a chair. He refused to take it by a gesture. Alban tried an apology next. "I am afraid I have ignorantly revived some painful associations. Pray excuse me."

The apology roused Mirabel: he felt the necessity of offering some explanation. In timid animals, the one defensive capacity which is always ready for action is cunning. Mirabel was too wily to dispute the inference— the inevitable inference—which any one must have drawn, after seeing the effect on him that the name of Miss Jethro had produced. He admitted that "painful associations" had been revived, and deplored the "nervous sensibility" which had permitted it to be seen.

"No blame can possibly attach to you, my dear sir," he continued, in his most amiable manner. "Will it be indiscreet, on my part, if I ask how you first became acquainted with Miss Jethro?"

"I first became acquainted with her at Miss Ladd's school," Alban answered. "She was, for a short time only, one of the teachers; and she left her situation rather suddenly." He paused—but Mirabel made no remark. "After an interval of a few months," he resumed, "I saw Miss Jethro again. She called on me at my lodgings, near Netherwoods."

"Merely to renew your former acquaintance?"

Mirabel made that inquiry with an eager anxiety for the reply which he was quite unable to conceal. Had he any reason to dread what Miss Jethro might have it in her power to say of him to another person? Alban was in no way pledged to secrecy, and he was determined to leave no means untried of throwing light on Miss Jethro's mysterious warning. He repeated the plain narrative of the interview, which he had communicated by letter to Emily. Mirabel listened without making any remark.

"After what I have told you, can you give me no explanation?" Alban asked.

"I am quite unable, Mr. Morris, to help you."

Was he lying? or speaking, the truth? The impression produced on Alban was that he had spoken the truth.

Women are never so ready as men to resign themselves to the disappointment of their hopes. Cecilia, silently listening up to this time, now ventured to speak—animated by her sisterly interest in Emily.

"Can you not tell us," she said to Mirabel, "why Miss Jethro tried to prevent Emily Brown from meeting you here?"

"I know no more of her motive than you do," Mirabel replied.

Alban interposed. "Miss Jethro left me," he said, "with the intention— quite openly expressed—of trying to prevent you from accepting Mr. Wyvil's invitation. Did she make the attempt?"

Mirabel admitted that she had made the attempt. "But," he added, "without mentioning Miss Emily's name. I was asked to postpone my visit, as a favor to herself, because she had her own reasons for wishing it. I had my reasons" (he bowed with gallantry to Cecilia) "for being eager to have the honor of knowing Mr. Wyvil and his daughter; and I refused."

Once more, the doubt arose: was he lying? or speaking the truth? And, once more, Alban could not resist the conclusion that he was speaking the truth.

"There is one thing I should like to know," Mirabel continued, after some hesitation. "Has Miss Emily been informed of this strange affair?"

"Certainly!"

Mirabel seemed to be disposed to continue his inquiries—and suddenly changed his mind. Was he beginning to doubt if Alban had spoken without concealment, in describing Miss Jethro's visit? Was he still afraid of what Miss Jethro might have said of him? In any case, he changed the subject, and made an excuse for leaving the room.

"I am forgetting my errand," he said to Alban. "Miss Emily was anxious to know if you had finished your sketch. I must tell her that you have returned."

He bowed and withdrew.

Alban rose to follow him—and checked himself.

"No," he thought, "I trust Emily!" He sat down again by Cecilia's side.

Mirabel had indeed returned to the rose garden. He found Emily employed as he had left her, in making a crown of roses, to be worn by Cecilia in the evening. But, in one other respect, there was a change. Francine was present.

"Excuse me for sending you on a needless errand," Emily said to Mirabel; "Miss de Sor tells me Mr. Morris has finished his sketch. She left him in the drawing-room—why didn't you bring him here?"

"He was talking with Miss Wyvil."

Mirabel answered absently—with his eyes on Francine. He gave her one of those significant looks, which says to a third person, "Why are you here?" Francine's jealousy declined to understand him. He tried a broader hint, in words.

"Are you going to walk in the garden?" he said.

Francine was impenetrable. "No," she answered, "I am going to stay here with Emily."

Mirabel had no choice but to yield. Imperative anxieties forced him to say, in Francine's presence, what he had hoped to say to Emily privately.

"When I joined Miss Wyvil and Mr. Morris," he began, "what do you think they were doing? They were talking of—Miss Jethro."

Emily dropped the rose-crown on her lap. It was easy to see that she had been disagreeably surprised.

"Mr. Morris has told me the curious story of Miss Jethro's visit," Mirabel continued; "but I am in some doubt whether he has spoken to me without reserve. Perhaps he expressed himself more freely when he spoke to you. Miss Jethro may have said something to him which tended to lower me in your estimation?"

"Certainly not, Mr. Mirabel—so far as I know. If I had heard anything of the kind, I should have thought it my duty to tell you. Will it relieve your anxiety, if I go at once to Mr. Morris, and ask him plainly whether he has concealed anything from you or from me?"

Mirabel gratefully kissed her hand. "Your kindness overpowers me," he said—speaking, for once, with true emotion.

Emily immediately returned to the house. As soon as she was out of sight, Francine approached Mirabel, trembling with suppressed rage.

CHAPTER XLVI. PRETENDING.

Miss de Sor began cautiously with an apology. "Excuse me, Mr. Mirabel, for reminding you of my presence."

Mr. Mirabel made no reply.

"I beg to say," Francine proceeded, "that I didn't intentionally see you kiss Emily's hand."

Mirabel stood, looking at the roses which Emily had left on her chair, as completely absorbed in his own thoughts as if he had been alone in the garden.

"Am I not even worth notice?" Francine asked. "Ah, I know to whom I am indebted for your neglect!" She took him familiarly by the arm, and burst into a harsh laugh. "Tell me now, in confidence—do you think Emily is fond of you?"

The impression left by Emily's kindness was still fresh in Mirabel's memory: he was in no humor to submit to the jealous resentment of a woman whom he regarded with perfect indifference. Through the varnish of politeness which overlaid his manner, there rose to the surface the underlying insolence, hidden, on all ordinary occasions, from all human eyes. He answered Francine—mercilessly answered her—at last.

"It is the dearest hope of my life that she may be fond of me," he said.

Francine dropped his arm "And fortune favors your hopes," she added, with an ironical assumption of interest in Mirabel's prospects. "When Mr. Morris leaves us to-morrow, he removes the only obstacle you have to fear. Am I right?"

"No; you are wrong."

"In what way, if you please?"

"In this way. I don't regard Mr. Morris as an obstacle. Emily is too delicate and too kind to hurt his feelings—she is not in love with him. There is no absorbing interest in her mind to divert her thoughts from me. She is idle and happy; she thoroughly enjoys her visit to this house, and I am associated with her enjoyment. There is my chance—!"

He suddenly stopped. Listening to him thus far, unnaturally calm and cold, Francine now showed that she felt the lash of his contempt. A hideous smile passed slowly over her white face. It threatened the vengeance which knows no fear, no pity, no remorse—the vengeance of a jealous woman. Hysterical anger, furious language, Mirabel was prepared for. The smile frightened him.

"Well?" she said scornfully, "why don't you go on?"

423

A bolder man might still have maintained the audacious position which he had assumed. Mirabel's faint heart shrank from it. He was eager to shelter himself under the first excuse that he could find. His ingenuity, paralyzed by his fears, was unable to invent anything new. He feebly availed himself of the commonplace trick of evasion which he had read of in novels, and seen in action on the stage.

"Is it possible," he asked, with an overacted assumption of surprise, "that you think I am in earnest?"

In the case of any other person, Francine would have instantly seen through that flimsy pretense. But the love which accepts the meanest crumbs of comfort that can be thrown to it—which fawns and grovels and deliberately deceives itself, in its own intensely selfish interests—was the love that burned in Francine's breast. The wretched girl believed Mirabel with such an ecstatic sense of belief that she trembled in every limb, and dropped into the nearest chair.

"I was in earnest," she said faintly. "Didn't you see it?"

He was perfectly shameless; he denied that he had seen it, in the most positive manner. "Upon my honor, I thought you were mystifying me, and I humored the joke."

She sighed, and looking at him with an expression of tender reproach. "I wonder whether I can believe you," she said softly.

"Indeed you may believe me!" he assured her.

She hesitated—for the pleasure of hesitating. "I don't know. Emily is very much admired by some men. Why not by you?"

"For the best of reasons," he answered "She is poor, and I am poor. Those are facts which speak for themselves."

"Yes—but Emily is bent on attracting you. She would marry you to-morrow, if you asked her. Don't attempt to deny it! Besides, you kissed her hand."

"Oh, Miss de Sor!"

424

"Don't call me 'Miss de Sor'! Call me Francine. I want to know why you kissed her hand."

He humored her with inexhaustible servility. "Allow me to kiss your hand, Francine!—and let me explain that kissing a lady's hand is only a form of thanking her for her kindness. You must own that Emily—"

She interrupted him for the third time. "Emily?" she repeated. "Are you as familiar as that already? Does she call you 'Miles,' when you are by yourselves? Is there any effort at fascination which this charming creature has left untried? She told you no doubt what a lonely life she leads in her poor little home?"

Even Mirabel felt that he must not permit this to pass.

"She has said nothing to me about herself," he answered. "What I know of her, I know from Mr. Wyvil."

"Oh, indeed! You asked Mr. Wyvil about her family, of course? What did he say?"

"He said she lost her mother when she was a child—and he told me her father had died suddenly, a few years since, of heart complaint."

"Well, and what else?—Never mind now! Here is somebody coming."

The person was only one of the servants. Mirabel felt grateful to the man for interrupting them. Animated by sentiments of a precisely opposite nature, Francine spoke to him sharply.

"What do you want here?"

"A message, miss."

"From whom?"

"From Miss Brown."

"For me?"

"No, miss." He turned to Mirabel. "Miss Brown wishes to speak to you, sir, if you are not engaged."

Francine controlled herself until the man was out of hearing.

"Upon my word, this is too shameless!" she declared indignantly. "Emily can't leave you with me for five minutes, without wanting to see you again. If you go to her after all that you have said to me," she cried, threatening Mirabel with her outstretched hand, "you are the meanest of men!"

He was the meanest of men—he carried out his cowardly submission to the last extremity.

"Only say what you wish me to do," he replied.

Even Francine expected some little resistance from a creature bearing the outward appearance of a man. "Oh, do you really mean it?" she asked "I want you to disappoint Emily. Will you stay here, and let me make your excuses?"

"I will do anything to please you."

Francine gave him a farewell look. Her admiration made a desperate effort to express itself appropriately in words. "You are not a man," she said, "you are an angel!"

Left by himself, Mirabel sat down to rest. He reviewed his own conduct with perfect complacency. "Not one man in a hundred could have managed that she-devil as I have done," he thought. "How shall I explain matters to Emily?"

Considering this question, he looked by chance at the unfinished crown of roses. "The very thing to help me!" he said—and took out his pocketbook, and wrote these lines on a blank page: "I have had a scene of jealousy with Miss de Sor, which is beyond all description. To spare you a similar infliction, I have done violence to my own feelings. Instead of instantly obeying the message which you have so kindly sent to me, I remain here for a little while—entirely for your sake."

Having torn out the page, and twisted it up among the roses, so that

426

only a corner of the paper appeared in view, Mirabel called to a lad who was at work in the garden, and gave him his directions, accompanied by a shilling. "Take those flowers to the servants' hall, and tell one of the maids to put them in Miss Brown's room. Stop! Which is the way to the fruit garden?"

The lad gave the necessary directions. Mirabel walked away slowly, with his hands in his pockets. His nerves had been shaken; he thought a little fruit might refresh him.

CHAPTER XLVII. DEBATING.

In the meanwhile Emily had been true to her promise to relieve Mirabel's anxieties, on the subject of Miss Jethro. Entering the drawing-room in search of Alban, she found him talking with Cecilia, and heard her own name mentioned as she opened the door.

"Here she is at last!" Cecilia exclaimed. "What in the world has kept you all this time in the rose garden?"

"Has Mr. Mirabel been more interesting than usual?" Alban asked gayly. Whatever sense of annoyance he might have felt in Emily's absence, was forgotten the moment she appeared; all traces of trouble in his face vanished when they looked at each other.

"You shall judge for yourself," Emily replied with a smile. "Mr. Mirabel has been speaking to me of a relative who is very dear to him—his sister."

Cecilia was surprised. "Why has he never spoken to us of his sister?" she asked.

"It's a sad subject to speak of, my dear. His sister lives a life of suffering— she has been for years a prisoner in her room. He writes to her constantly. His letters from Monksmoor have interested her, poor soul. It seems he said something about me—and she has sent a kind message, inviting me to visit her one of these days. Do you understand it now, Cecilia?"

"Of course I do! Tell me—is Mr. Mirabel's sister older or younger than he is?"

"Older."

"Is she married?"

"She is a widow."

"Does she live with her brother?" Alban asked.

"Oh, no! She has her own house—far away in Northumberland."

"Is she near Sir Jervis Redwood?"

"I fancy not. Her house is on the coast."

"Any children?" Cecilia inquired.

"No; she is quite alone. Now, Cecilia, I have told you all I know—and I have something to say to Mr. Morris. No, you needn't leave us; it's a subject in which you are interested. A subject," she repeated, turning to Alban, "which you may have noticed is not very agreeable to me."

"Miss Jethro?" Alban guessed.

"Yes; Miss Jethro."

Cecilia's curiosity instantly asserted itself.

"We have tried to get Mr. Mirabel to enlighten us, and tried in vain," she said. "You are a favorite. Have you succeeded?"

"I have made no attempt to succeed," Emily replied. "My only object is to relieve Mr. Mirabel's anxiety, if I can—with your help, Mr. Morris."

"In what way can I help you?"

"You mustn't be angry."

"Do I look angry?"

"You look serious. It is a very simple thing. Mr. Mirabel is afraid that Miss Jethro may have said something disagreeable about him, which you might hesitate to repeat. Is he making himself uneasy without any reason?"

"Without the slightest reason. I have concealed nothing from Mr. Mirabel."

428

"Thank you for the explanation." She turned to Cecilia. "May I send one of the servants with a message? I may as well put an end to Mr. Mirabel's suspense."

The man was summoned, and was dispatched with the message. Emily would have done well, after this, if she had abstained from speaking further of Miss Jethro. But Mirabel's doubts had, unhappily, inspired a similar feeling of uncertainty in her own mind. She was now disposed to attribute the tone of mystery in Alban's unlucky letter to some possible concealment suggested by regard for herself. "I wonder whether I have any reason to feel uneasy?" she said—half in jest, half in earnest.

"Uneasy about what?" Alban inquired.

"About Miss Jethro, of course! Has she said anything of me which your kindness has concealed?"

Alban seemed to be a little hurt by the doubt which her question implied. "Was that your motive," he asked, "for answering my letter as cautiously as if you had been writing to a stranger?"

"Indeed you are quite wrong!" Emily earnestly assured him. "I was perplexed and startled—and I took Mr. Wyvil's advice, before I wrote to you. Shall we drop the subject?"

Alban would have willingly dropped the subject—but for that unfortunate allusion to Mr. Wyvil. Emily had unconsciously touched him on a sore place. He had already heard from Cecilia of the consultation over his letter, and had disapproved of it. "I think you were wrong to trouble Mr. Wyvil," he said.

The altered tone of his voice suggested to Emily that he would have spoken more severely, if Cecilia had not been in the room. She thought him needlessly ready to complain of a harmless proceeding—and she too returned to the subject, after having proposed to drop it not a minute since!

"You didn't tell me I was to keep your letter a secret," she replied.

Cecilia made matters worse—with the best intentions. "I'm sure, Mr.

Morris, my father was only too glad to give Emily his advice."

Alban remained silent—ungraciously silent as Emily thought, after Mr. Wyvil's kindness to him.

"The thing to regret," she remarked, "is that Mr. Morris allowed Miss Jethro to leave him without explaining herself. In his place, I should have insisted on knowing why she wanted to prevent me from meeting Mr. Mirabel in this house."

Cecilia made another unlucky attempt at judicious interference. This time, she tried a gentle remonstrance.

"Remember, Emily, how Mr. Morris was situated. He could hardly be rude to a lady. And I daresay Miss Jethro had good reasons for not wishing to explain herself."

Francine opened the drawing-room door and heard Cecilia's last words.

"Miss Jethro again!" she exclaimed.

"Where is Mr. Mirabel?" Emily asked. "I sent him a message."

"He regrets to say he is otherwise engaged for the present," Francine replied with spiteful politeness. "Don't let me interrupt the conversation. Who is this Miss Jethro, whose name is on everybody's lips?"

Alban could keep silent no longer. "We have done with the subject," he said sharply.

"Because I am here?"

"Because we have said more than enough about Miss Jethro already."

"Speak for yourself, Mr. Morris," Emily answered, resenting the masterful tone which Alban's interference had assumed. "I have not done with Miss Jethro yet, I can assure you."

"My dear, you don't know where she lives," Cecilia reminded her.

"Leave me to discover it!" Emily answered hotly. "Perhaps Mr. Mirabel knows. I shall ask Mr. Mirabel."

430

"I thought you would find a reason for returning to Mr. Mirabel," Francine remarked.

Before Emily could reply, one of the maids entered the room with a wreath of roses in her hand.

"Mr. Mirabel sends you these flowers, miss," the woman said, addressing Emily. "The boy told me they were to be taken to your room. I thought it was a mistake, and I have brought them to you here."

Francine, who happened to be nearest to the door, took the roses from the girl on pretense of handing them to Emily. Her jealous vigilance detected the one visible morsel of Mirabel's letter, twisted up with the flowers. Had Emily entrapped him into a secret correspondence with her? "A scrap of waste paper among your roses," she said, crumpling it up in her hand as if she meant to throw it away.

But Emily was too quick for her. She caught Francine by the wrist. "Waste paper or not," she said; "it was among my flowers and it belongs to me."

Francine gave up the letter, with a look which might have startled Emily if she had noticed it. She handed the roses to Cecilia. "I was making a wreath for you to wear this evening, my dear—and I left it in the garden. It's not quite finished yet."

Cecilia was delighted. "How lovely it is!" she exclaimed. "And how very kind of you! I'll finish it myself." She turned away to the conservatory.

"I had no idea I was interfering with a letter," said Francine; watching Emily with fiercely-attentive eyes, while she smoothed out the crumpled paper.

Having read what Mirabel had written to her, Emily looked up, and saw that Alban was on the point of following Cecilia into the conservatory. He had noticed something in Francine's face which he was at a loss to understand, but which made her presence in the room absolutely hateful to him. Emily followed and spoke to him.

431

"I am going back to the rose garden," she said.

"For any particular purpose?" Alban inquired

"For a purpose which, I am afraid, you won't approve of. I mean to ask Mr. Mirabel if he knows Miss Jethro's address."

"I hope he is as ignorant of it as I am," Alban answered gravely.

"Are we going to quarrel over Miss Jethro, as we once quarreled over Mrs. Rook?" Emily asked—with the readiest recovery of her good humor. "Come! come! I am sure you are as anxious, in your own private mind, to have this matter cleared up as I am."

"With one difference—that I think of consequences, and you don't." He said it, in his gentlest and kindest manner, and stepped into the conservatory.

"Never mind the consequences," she called after him, "if we can only get at the truth. I hate being deceived!"

"There is no person living who has better reason than you have to say that."

Emily looked round with a start. Alban was out of hearing. It was Francine who had answered her.

"What do you mean?" she said.

Francine hesitated. A ghastly paleness overspread her face.

"Are you ill?" Emily asked.

"No—I am thinking."

After waiting for a moment in silence, Emily moved away toward the door of the drawing-room. Francine suddenly held up her hand.

"Stop!" she cried.

Emily stood still.

"My mind is made up," Francine said.

"Made up—to what?"

"You asked what I meant, just now."

"I did."

"Well, my mind is made up to answer you. Miss Emily Brown, you are leading a sadly frivolous life in this house. I am going to give you something more serious to think about than your flirtation with Mr. Mirabel. Oh, don't be impatient! I am coming to the point. Without knowing it yourself, you have been the victim of deception for years past—cruel deception—wicked deception that puts on the mask of mercy."

"Are you alluding to Miss Jethro?" Emily asked, in astonishment. "I thought you were strangers to each other. Just now, you wanted to know who she was."

"I know nothing about her. I care nothing about her. I am not thinking of Miss Jethro."

"Who are you thinking of?"

"I am thinking," Francine answered, "of your dead father."

CHAPTER XLVIII. INVESTIGATING.

Having revived his sinking energies in the fruit garden, Mirabel seated himself under the shade of a tree, and reflected on the critical position in which he was placed by Francine's jealousy.

If Miss de Sor continued to be Mr. Wyvil's guest, there seemed to be no other choice before Mirabel than to leave Monksmoor—and to trust to a favorable reply to his sister's invitation for the free enjoyment of Emily's society under another roof. Try as he might, he could arrive at no more satisfactory conclusion than this. In his preoccupied state, time passed quickly. Nearly an hour had elapsed before he rose to return to the house.

Entering the hall, he was startled by a cry of terror in a woman's voice, coming from the upper regions. At the same time Mr. Wyvil, passing along the bedroom corridor after leaving the music-room, was confronted by his daughter, hurrying out of Emily's bedchamber in such a state of alarm that she could hardly speak.

"Gone!" she cried, the moment she saw her father.

Mr. Wyvil took her in his arms and tried to compose her. "Who has gone?" he asked.

"Emily! Oh, papa, Emily has left us! She has heard dreadful news—she told me so herself."

"What news? How did she hear it?"

"I don't know how she heard it. I went back to the drawing-room to show her my roses—"

"Was she alone?"

"Yes! She frightened me—she seemed quite wild. She said, 'Let me be by myself; I shall have to go home.' She kissed me—and ran up to her room. Oh, I am such a fool! Anybody else would have taken care not to lose sight of her."

"How long did you leave her by herself?"

"I can't say. I thought I would go and tell you. And then I got anxious about her, and knocked at her door, and looked into the room. Gone! Gone!"

Mr. Wyvil rang the bell and confided Cecilia to the care of her maid. Mirabel had already joined him in the corridor. They went downstairs together and consulted with Alban. He volunteered to make immediate inquiries at the railway station. Mr. Wyvil followed him, as far as the lodge gate which opened on the highroad—while Mirabel went to a second gate, at the opposite extremity of the park.

Mr. Wyvil obtained the first news of Emily. The lodge keeper had seen her pass him, on her way out of the park, in the greatest haste. He had called after her, "Anything wrong, miss?" and had received no reply. Asked what time had elapsed since this had happened, he was too confused to be able to answer with any certainty. He knew that she had taken the road which led to the station—and he knew no more.

Mr. Wyvil and Mirabel met again at the house, and instituted an examination of the servants. No further discoveries were made.

The question which occurred to everybody was suggested by the words which Cecilia had repeated to her father. Emily had said she had "heard dreadful news"—how had that news reached her? The one postal delivery at Monksmoor was in the morning. Had any special messenger arrived, with a letter for Emily? The servants were absolutely certain that no such person had entered the house. The one remaining conclusion suggested that somebody must have communicated the evil tidings by word of mouth. But here again no evidence was to be obtained. No visitor had called during the day, and no new guests had arrived. Investigation was completely baffled.

Alban returned from the railway, with news of the fugitive.

He had reached the station, some time after the departure of the London train. The clerk at the office recognized his description of Emily, and stated that she had taken her ticket for London. The station-master had opened the carriage door for her, and had noticed that the young lady appeared to be very much agitated. This information obtained, Alban had dispatched a telegram to Emily—in Cecilia's name: "Pray send us a few words to relieve our anxiety, and let us know if we can be of any service to you."

This was plainly all that could be done—but Cecilia was not satisfied. If her father had permitted it, she would have followed Emily. Alban comforted her. He apologized to Mr. Wyvil for shortening his visit, and announced his intention of traveling to London by the next train. "We may renew our inquiries to some advantage," he added, after hearing what had happened in his absence, "if we can find out who was the last person who saw her, and spoke to her, before your daughter found her alone in the drawing-room. When I went out of the room, I left her with Miss de Sor."

The maid who waited on Miss de Sor was sent for. Francine had been out, by herself, walking in the park. She was then in her room, changing her dress. On hearing of Emily's sudden departure, she had been (as the maid reported) "much shocked and quite at a loss to understand what it meant."

Joining her friends a few minutes later, Francine presented, so far as personal appearance went, a strong contrast to the pale and anxious faces round her. She looked wonderfully well, after her walk. In other respects, she was in perfect harmony with the prevalent feeling. She expressed herself with the utmost propriety; her sympathy moved poor Cecilia to tears.

"I am sure, Miss de Sor, you will try to help us?" Mr. Wyvil began

"With the greatest pleasure," Francine answered.

"How long were you and Miss Emily Brown together, after Mr. Morris left you?"

"Not more than a quarter of an hour, I should think."

"Did anything remarkable occur in the course of conversation?"

"Nothing whatever."

Alban interfered for the first time. "Did you say anything," he asked, "which agitated or offended Miss Brown?"

"That's rather an extraordinary question," Francine remarked.

"Have you no other answer to give?" Alban inquired.

"I answer—No!" she said, with a sudden outburst of anger.

There, the matter dropped. While she spoke in reply to Mr. Wyvil, Francine had confronted him without embarrassment. When Alban interposed, she never looked at him—except when he provoked her to anger. Did she remember that the man who was questioning her, was also the man who had suspected her of writing the anonymous letter? Alban was on his guard against himself, knowing how he disliked her. But the conviction in his own mind was not to be resisted. In some unimaginable way, Francine was associated with Emily's flight from the house.

The answer to the telegram sent from the railway station had not arrived, when Alban took his departure for London. Cecilia's suspense began to grow unendurable: she looked to Mirabel for comfort, and found none. His office was to console, and his capacity for performing that office was notorious

436

among his admirers; but he failed to present himself to advantage, when Mr. Wyvil's lovely daughter had need of his services. He was, in truth, too sincerely anxious and distressed to be capable of commanding his customary resources of ready-made sentiment and fluently-pious philosophy. Emily's influence had awakened the only earnest and true feeling which had ever ennobled the popular preacher's life.

Toward evening, the long-expected telegram was received at last. What could be said, under the circumstances, it said in these words:

"Safe at home—don't be uneasy about me—will write soon."

With that promise they were, for the time, forced to be content.

BOOK THE FIFTH—THE COTTAGE.

CHAPTER XLIX. EMILY SUFFERS.

Mrs. Ellmother—left in charge of Emily's place of abode, and feeling sensible of her lonely position from time to time—had just thought of trying the cheering influence of a cup of tea, when she heard a cab draw up at the cottage gate. A violent ring at the bell followed. She opened the door—and found Emily on the steps. One look at that dear and familiar face was enough for the old servant.

"God help us," she cried, "what's wrong now?"

Without a word of reply, Emily led the way into the bedchamber which had been the scene of Miss Letitia's death. Mrs. Ellmother hesitated on the threshold.

"Why do you bring me in here?" she asked.

"Why did you try to keep me out?" Emily answered.

"When did I try to keep you out, miss?"

"When I came home from school, to nurse my aunt. Ah, you remember now! Is it true—I ask you here, where your old mistress died—is it true that my aunt deceived me about my father's death? And that you knew it?"

There was dead silence. Mrs. Ellmother trembled horribly—her lips dropped apart—her eyes wandered round the room with a stare of idiotic terror. "Is it her ghost tells you that?" she whispered. "Where is her ghost? The room whirls round and round, miss—and the air sings in my ears."

Emily sprang forward to support her. She staggered to a chair, and lifted her great bony hands in wild entreaty. "Don't frighten me," she said. "Stand back."

Emily obeyed her. She dashed the cold sweat off her forehead. "You were talking about your father's death just now," she burst out, in desperate defiant tones. "Well! we know it and we are sorry for it—your father died suddenly."

"My father died murdered in the inn at Zeeland! All the long way to London, I have tried to doubt it. Oh, me, I know it now!"

Answering in those words, she looked toward the bed. Harrowing remembrances of her aunt's delirious self-betrayal made the room unendurable to her. She ran out. The parlor door was open. Entering the room, she passed by a portrait of her father, which her aunt had hung on the wall over the fireplace. She threw herself on the sofa and burst into a passionate fit of crying. "Oh, my father—my dear, gentle, loving father; my first, best, truest friend—murdered! murdered! Oh, God, where was your justice, where was your mercy, when he died that dreadful death?"

A hand was laid on her shoulder; a voice said to her, "Hush, my child! God knows best."

Emily looked up, and saw that Mrs. Ellmother had followed her. "You poor old soul," she said, suddenly remembering; "I frightened you in the other room."

"I have got over it, my dear. I am old; and I have lived a hard life. A hard life schools a person. I make no complaints." She stopped, and began to shudder again. "Will you believe me if I tell you something?" she asked. "I warned my self-willed mistress. Standing by your father's coffin, I warned her. Hide the truth as you may (I said), a time will come when our child will know what you are keeping from her now. One or both of us may live to see it. I am the one who has lived; no refuge in the grave for me. I want to hear about it—there's no fear of frightening or hurting me now. I want to hear how you found it out. Was it by accident, my dear? or did a person tell you?"

Emily's mind was far away from Mrs. Ellmother. She rose from the sofa, with her hands held fast over her aching heart.

"The one duty of my life," she said—"I am thinking of the one duty of my life. Look! I am calm now; I am resigned to my hard lot. Never, never again, can the dear memory of my father be what it was! From this time, it is the horrid memory of a crime. The crime has gone unpunished; the man has escaped others. He shall not escape Me." She paused, and looked at Mrs. Ellmother absently. "What did you say just now? You want to hear how I know what I know? Naturally! naturally! Sit down here—sit down, my old friend, on the sofa with me—and take your mind back to Netherwoods. Alban Morris—"

Mrs. Ellmother recoiled from Emily in dismay. "Don't tell me he had anything to do with it! The kindest of men; the best of men!"

"The man of all men living who least deserves your good opinion or mine," Emily answered sternly.

"You!" Mrs. Ellmother exclaimed, "you say that!"

"I say it. He—who won on me to like him—he was in the conspiracy to deceive me; and you know it! He heard me talk of the newspaper story of the murder of my father—I say, he heard me talk of it composedly, talk of it carelessly, in the innocent belief that it was the murder of a stranger—and he never opened his lips to prevent that horrid profanation! He never even said, speak of something else; I won't hear you! No more of him! God forbid I should ever see him again. No! Do what I told you. Carry your mind back to Netherwoods. One night you let Francine de Sor frighten you. You ran away from her into the garden. Keep quiet! At your age, must I set you an example of self-control?

"I want to know, Miss Emily, where Francine de Sor is now?"

"She is at the house in the country, which I have left."

"Where does she go next, if you please? Back to Miss Ladd?"

"I suppose so. What interest have you in knowing where she goes next?"

"I won't interrupt you, miss. It's true that I ran away into the garden. I can guess who followed me. How did she find her way to me and Mr. Morris, in the dark?"

"The smell of tobacco guided her—she knew who smoked—she had seen him talking to you, on that very day—she followed the scent—she heard what you two said to each other—and she has repeated it to me. Oh, my old friend, the malice of a revengeful girl has enlightened me, when you, my nurse—and he, my lover—left me in the dark: it has told me how my father died!"

"That's said bitterly, miss!"

"Is it said truly?"

"No. It isn't said truly of myself. God knows you would never have been kept in the dark, if your aunt had listened to me. I begged and prayed—I went down on my knees to her—I warned her, as I told you just now. Must I tell you what a headstrong woman Miss Letitia was? She insisted. She put the choice before me of leaving her at once and forever—or giving in. I wouldn't have given in to any other creature on the face of this earth. I am obstinate, as you have often told me. Well, your aunt's obstinacy beat mine; I was too fond of her to say No. Besides, if you ask me who was to blame in the first place, I tell you it wasn't your aunt; she was frightened into it."

"Who frightened her?"

"Your godfather—the great London surgeon—he who was visiting in our house at the time."

"Sir Richard?"

"Yes—Sir Richard. He said he wouldn't answer for the consequences, in the delicate state of your health, if we told you the truth. Ah, he had it all his own way after that. He went with Miss Letitia to the inquest; he won over the coroner and the newspaper men to his will; he kept your aunt's name out of the papers; he took charge of the coffin; he hired the undertaker and his men, strangers from London; he wrote the certificate—who but he! Everybody was cap in hand to the famous man!"

"Surely, the servants and the neighbors asked questions?"

"Hundreds of questions! What did that matter to Sir Richard? They were like so many children, in his hands. And, mind you, the luck helped him. To begin with, there was the common name. Who was to pick out your poor father among the thousands of James Browns? Then, again, the house and lands went to the male heir, as they called him—the man your father quarreled with in the bygone time. He brought his own establishment with him. Long before you got back from the friends you were staying with—don't you remember it?—we had cleared out of the house; we were miles and miles away; and the old servants were scattered abroad, finding new situations wherever they could. How could you suspect us? We had nothing to fear in that way; but my conscience pricked me. I made another attempt to prevail on Miss Letitia, when you had recovered your health. I said, 'There's no fear of a relapse now; break it to her gently, but tell her the truth.' No! Your aunt was too fond of you. She daunted me with dreadful fits of crying, when I tried to persuade her. And that wasn't the worst of it. She bade me remember what an excitable man your father was—she reminded me that the misery of your mother's death laid him low with brain fever—she said, 'Emily takes after her father; I have heard you say it yourself; she has his constitution, and his sensitive nerves. Don't you know how she loved him—how she talks of him to this day? Who can tell (if we are not careful) what dreadful mischief we may do?' That was how my mistress worked on me. I got infected with her fears; it was as if I had caught an infection of disease. Oh, my dear, blame me if it must be; but don't forget how I have suffered for it since! I was driven away from my dying mistress, in terror of what she might say, while you were watching at her bedside. I have lived in fear of what you might ask me—and have longed to go back to you—and have not had the courage to do it. Look at me now!"

The poor woman tried to take out her handkerchief; her quivering hand helplessly entangled itself in her dress. "I can't even dry my eyes," she said faintly. "Try to forgive me, miss!"

Emily put her arms round the old nurse's neck. "It is you," she said sadly, "who must forgive me."

For a while they were silent. Through the window that was open to the little garden, came the one sound that could be heard—the gentle trembling of leaves in the evening wind.

The silence was harshly broken by the bell at the cottage door. They both started.

Emily's heart beat fast. "Who can it be?" she said.

Mrs. Ellmother rose. "Shall I say you can't see anybody?" she asked, before leaving the room.

"Yes! yes!"

Emily heard the door opened—heard low voices in the passage. There was a momentary interval. Then, Mrs. Ellmother returned. She said nothing. Emily spoke to her.

"Is it a visitor?"

"Yes."

"Have you said I can't see anybody?"

"I couldn't say it."

"Why not?"

"Don't be hard on him, my dear. It's Mr. Alban Morris."

CHAPTER L. MISS LADD ADVISES.

Mrs. Ellmother sat by the dying embers of the kitchen fire; thinking over the events of the day in perplexity and distress.

She had waited at the cottage door for a friendly word with Alban, after he had left Emily. The stern despair in his face warned her to let him go in silence. She had looked into the parlor next. Pale and cold, Emily lay on the sofa—sunk in helpless depression of body and mind. "Don't speak to me," she whispered; "I am quite worn out." It was but too plain that the view of Alban's conduct which she had already expressed, was the view to which she had adhered at the interview between them. They had parted in grief—-perhaps in anger—perhaps forever. Mrs. Ellmother lifted Emily in compassionate silence, and carried her upstairs, and waited by her until she slept.

In the still hours of the night, the thoughts of the faithful old servant—dwelling for a while on past and present—advanced, by slow degrees, to consideration of the doubtful future. Measuring, to the best of her ability, the responsibility which had fallen on her, she felt that it was more than she could bear, or ought to bear, alone. To whom could she look for help?

The gentlefolks at Monksmoor were strangers to her. Doctor Allday was near at hand—but Emily had said, "Don't send for him; he will torment me with questions—and I want to keep my mind quiet, if I can." But one person was left, to whose ever-ready kindness Mrs. Ellmother could appeal—and that person was Miss Ladd.

It would have been easy to ask the help of the good schoolmistress in comforting and advising the favorite pupil whom she loved. But Mrs. Ellmother had another object in view: she was determined that the cold-blooded cruelty of Emily's treacherous friend should not be allowed to triumph with impunity. If an ignorant old woman could do nothing else, she could tell the plain truth, and could leave Miss Ladd to decide whether such a person as Francine deserved to remain under her care.

To feel justified in taking this step was one thing: to put it all clearly in writing was another. After vainly making the attempt overnight, Mrs. Ellmother tore up her letter, and communicated with Miss Ladd by means of a telegraphic message, in the morning. "Miss Emily is in great distress. I must not leave her. I have something besides to say to you which cannot be put into a letter. Will you please come to us?"

Later in the forenoon, Mrs. Ellmother was called to the door by the arrival of a visitor. The personal appearance of the stranger impressed her favorably. He was a handsome little gentleman; his manners were winning, and his voice was singularly pleasant to hear.

"I have come from Mr. Wyvil's house in the country," he said; "and I bring a letter from his daughter. May I take the opportunity of asking if Miss Emily is well?"

"Far from it, sir, I am sorry to say. She is so poorly that she keeps her bed."

At this reply, the visitor's face revealed such sincere sympathy and regret, that Mrs. Ellmother was interested in him: she added a word more. "My mistress has had a hard trial to bear, sir. I hope there is no bad news for her in the young lady's letter?"

"On the contrary, there is news that she will be glad to hear—Miss Wyvil is coming here this evening. Will you excuse my asking if Miss Emily has had medical advice?"

"She won't hear of seeing the doctor, sir. He's a good friend of hers—and he lives close by. I am unfortunately alone in the house. If I could leave her, I would go at once and ask his advice."

"Let me go!" Mirabel eagerly proposed.

Mrs. Ellmother's face brightened. "That's kindly thought of, sir—if you don't mind the trouble."

"My good lady, nothing is a trouble in your young mistress's service. Give me the doctor's name and address—and tell me what to say to him."

"There's one thing you must be careful of," Mrs. Ellmother answered. "He mustn't come here, as if he had been sent for—she would refuse to see him."

Mirabel understood her. "I will not forget to caution him. Kindly tell Miss Emily I called—my name is Mirabel. I will return to-morrow."

He hastened away on his errand—only to find that he had arrived too late. Doctor Allday had left London; called away to a serious case of illness. He was not expected to get back until late in the afternoon. Mirabel left a message, saying that he would return in the evening.

The next visitor who arrived at the cottage was the trusty friend, in whose generous nature Mrs. Ellmother had wisely placed confidence. Miss Ladd had resolved to answer the telegram in person, the moment she read it.

"If there is bad news," she said, "let me hear it at once. I am not well enough to bear suspense; my busy life at the school is beginning to tell on me."

"There is nothing that need alarm you, ma'am—but there is a great deal to say, before you see Miss Emily. My stupid head turns giddy with thinking of it. I hardly know where to begin."

"Begin with Emily," Miss Ladd suggested.

Mrs. Ellmother took the advice. She described Emily's unexpected arrival on the previous day; and she repeated what had passed between them afterward. Miss Ladd's first impulse, when she had recovered her composure, was to go to Emily without waiting to hear more. Not presuming to stop her, Mrs. Ellmother ventured to put a question "Do you happen to have my telegram about you, ma'am?" Miss Ladd produced it. "Will you please look at the last part of it again?"

Miss Ladd read the words: "I have something besides to say to you which cannot be put into a letter." She at once returned to her chair.

"Does what you have still to tell me refer to any person whom I know?" she said.

"It refers, ma'am, to Miss de Sor. I am afraid I shall distress you."

"What did I say, when I came in?" Miss Ladd asked. "Speak out plainly; and try—it's not easy, I know—but try to begin at the beginning."

Mrs. Ellmother looked back through her memory of past events, and began by alluding to the feeling of curiosity which she had excited in Francine, on the day when Emily had made them known to one another. From this she advanced to the narrative of what had taken place at Netherwoods—to the atrocious attempt to frighten her by means of the image of wax—to the discovery made by Francine in the garden at night—and to the circumstances under which that discovery had been communicated to Emily.

Miss Ladd's face reddened with indignation. "Are you sure of all that you have said?" she asked.

"I am quite sure, ma'am. I hope I have not done wrong," Mrs. Ellmother added simply, "in telling you all this?"

"Wrong?" Miss Ladd repeated warmly. "If that wretched girl has no defense to offer, she is a disgrace to my school—and I owe you a debt of gratitude for showing her to me in her true character. She shall return at once to Netherwoods; and she shall answer me to my entire satisfaction—or leave my house. What cruelty! what duplicity! In all my experience of girls, I have never met with the like of it. Let me go to my dear little Emily—and try to forget what I have heard."

Mrs. Ellmother led the good lady to Emily's room—and, returning to the lower part of the house, went out into the garden. The mental effort that she had made had left its result in an aching head, and in an overpowering sense of depression. "A mouthful of fresh air will revive me," she thought.

The front garden and back garden at the cottage communicated with each other. Walking slowly round and round, Mrs. Ellmother heard footsteps on the road outside, which stopped at the gate. She looked through the grating, and discovered Alban Morris.

"Come in, sir!" she said, rejoiced to see him. He obeyed in silence. The full view of his face shocked Mrs. Ellmother. Never in her experience of the friend who had been so kind to her at Netherwoods, had he looked so old and so haggard as he looked now. "Oh, Mr. Alban, I see how she has distressed you! Don't take her at her word. Keep a good heart, sir—young girls are never long together of the same mind."

Alban gave her his hand. "I mustn't speak about it," he said. "Silence helps me to bear my misfortune as becomes a man. I have had some hard blows in my time: they don't seem to have blunted my sense of feeling as I thought they had. Thank God, she doesn't know how she has made me suffer! I want to ask her pardon for having forgotten myself yesterday. I spoke roughly to her, at one time. No: I won't intrude on her; I have said I am sorry, in writing. Do you mind giving it to her? Good-by—and thank you. I mustn't stay longer; Miss Ladd expects me at Netherwoods."

"Miss Ladd is in the house, sir, at this moment."

"Here, in London!"

"Upstairs, with Miss Emily."

"Upstairs? Is Emily ill?"

"She is getting better, sir. Would you like to see Miss Ladd?"

"I should indeed! I have something to say to her—and time is of importance to me. May I wait in the garden?"

"Why not in the parlor, sir?"

"The parlor reminds me of happier days. In time, I may have courage enough to look at the room again. Not now."

"If she doesn't make it up with that good man," Mrs. Ellmother thought, on her way back to the house, "my nurse-child is what I have never believed her to be yet—she's a fool."

In half an hour more, Miss Ladd joined Alban on the little plot of grass behind the cottage. "I bring Emily's reply to your letter," she said. "Read it, before you speak to me."

Alban read it: "Don't suppose you have offended me—and be assured that I feel gratefully the tone in which your note is written. I try to write forbearingly on my side; I wish I could write acceptably as well. It is not to be done. I am as unable as ever to enter into your motives. You are not my relation; you were under no obligation of secrecy: you heard me speak ignorantly of the murder of my father, as if it had been the murder of a stranger; and yet you kept me—deliberately, cruelly kept me—deceived! The remembrance of it burns me like fire. I cannot—oh, Alban, I cannot restore you to the place in my estimation which you have lost! If you wish to help me to bear my trouble, I entreat you not to write to me again."

Alban offered the letter silently to Miss Ladd. She signed to him to keep it.

"I know what Emily has written," she said; "and I have told her, what I now tell you—she is wrong; in every way, wrong. It is the misfortune of her impetuous nature that she rushes to conclusions—and those conclusions once formed, she holds to them with all the strength of her character. In this matter, she has looked at her side of the question exclusively; she is blind to your side."

"Not willfully!" Alban interposed.

Miss Ladd looked at him with admiration. "You defend Emily?" she said.

"I love her," Alban answered.

Miss Ladd felt for him, as Mrs. Ellmother had felt for him. "Trust to time, Mr. Morris," she resumed. "The danger to be afraid of is—the danger of some headlong action, on her part, in the interval. Who can say what the end may be, if she persists in her present way of thinking? There is something monstrous, in a young girl declaring that it is her duty to pursue a murderer, and to bring him to justice! Don't you see it yourself?"

Alban still defended Emily. "It seems to me to be a natural impulse," he said—"natural, and noble."

"Noble!" Miss Ladd exclaimed.

"Yes—for it grows out of the love which has not died with her father's death."

"Then you encourage her?"

"With my whole heart—if she would give me the opportunity!"

"We won't pursue the subject, Mr. Morris. I am told by Mrs. Ellmother that you have something to say to me. What is it?"

"I have to ask you," Alban replied, "to let me resign my situation at Netherwoods."

Miss Ladd was not only surprised; she was also—a very rare thing with her—inclined to be suspicious. After what he had said to Emily, it occurred to her that Alban might be meditating some desperate project, with the hope of recovering his lost place in her favor.

"Have you heard of some better employment?" she asked.

"I have heard of no employment. My mind is not in a state to give the necessary attention to my pupils."

"Is that your only reason for wishing to leave me?"

"It is one of my reasons."

"The only one which you think it necessary to mention?"

"Yes."

"I shall be sorry to lose you, Mr. Morris."

"Believe me, Miss Ladd, I am not ungrateful for your kindness."

"Will you let me, in all kindness, say something more?" Miss Ladd answered. "I don't intrude on your secrets—I only hope that you have no rash project in view."

"I don't understand you, Miss Ladd."

"Yes, Mr. Morris—you do."

She shook hands with him—and went back to Emily.

CHAPTER LI. THE DOCTOR SEES.

Alban returned to Netherwoods—to continue his services, until another master could be found to take his place.

By a later train Miss Ladd followed him. Emily was too well aware of the importance of the mistress's presence to the well-being of the school, to permit her to remain at the cottage. It was understood that they were to correspond, and that Emily's room was waiting for her at Netherwoods, whenever she felt inclined to occupy it.

Mrs. Ellmother made the tea, that evening, earlier than usual. Being alone again with Emily, it struck her that she might take advantage of her position to say a word in Alban's favor. She had chosen her time unfortunately.

450

The moment she pronounced the name, Emily checked her by a look, and spoke of another person—that person being Miss Jethro.

Mrs. Ellmother at once entered her protest, in her own downright way. "Whatever you do," she said, "don't go back to that! What does Miss Jethro matter to you?"

"I am more interested in her than you suppose—I happen to know why she left the school."

"Begging your pardon, miss, that's quite impossible!"

"She left the school," Emily persisted, "for a serious reason. Miss Ladd discovered that she had used false references."

"Good Lord! who told you that?"

"You see I know it. I asked Miss Ladd how she got her information. She was bound by a promise never to mention the person's name. I didn't say it to her—but I may say it to you. I am afraid I have an idea of who the person was."

"No," Mrs. Ellmother obstinately asserted, "you can't possibly know who it was! How should you know?"

"Do you wish me to repeat what I heard in that room opposite, when my aunt was dying?"

"Drop it, Miss Emily! For God's sake, drop it!"

"I can't drop it. It's dreadful to me to have suspicions of my aunt—and no better reason for them than what she said in a state of delirium. Tell me, if you love me, was it her wandering fancy? or was it the truth?"

"As I hope to be saved, Miss Emily, I can only guess as you do—I don't rightly know. My mistress trusted me half way, as it were. I'm afraid I have a rough tongue of my own sometimes. I offended her—and from that time she kept her own counsel. What she did, she did in the dark, so far as I was concerned."

"How did you offend her?"

451

"I shall be obliged to speak of your father if I tell you how?"

"Speak of him."

"He was not to blame—mind that!" Mrs. Ellmother said earnestly. "If I wasn't certain of what I say now you wouldn't get a word out of me. Good harmless man—there's no denying it—he was in love with Miss Jethro! What's the matter?"

Emily was thinking of her memorable conversation with the disgraced teacher on her last night at school. "Nothing" she answered. "Go on."

"If he had not tried to keep it secret from us," Mrs. Ellmother resumed, "your aunt might never have taken it into her head that he was entangled in a love affair of the shameful sort. I don't deny that I helped her in her inquiries; but it was only because I felt sure from the first that the more she discovered the more certainly my master's innocence would show itself. He used to go away and visit Miss Jethro privately. In the time when your aunt trusted me, we never could find out where. She made that discovery afterward for herself (I can't tell you how long afterward); and she spent money in employing mean wretches to pry into Miss Jethro's past life. She had (if you will excuse me for saying it) an old maid's hatred of the handsome young woman, who lured your father away from home, and set up a secret (in a manner of speaking) between her brother and herself. I won't tell you how we looked at letters and other things which he forgot to leave under lock and key. I will only say there was one bit, in a journal he kept, which made me ashamed of myself. I read it out to Miss Letitia; and I told her in so many words, not to count any more on me. No; I haven't got a copy of the words—I can remember them without a copy. 'Even if my religion did not forbid me to peril my soul by leading a life of sin with this woman whom I love'—that was how it began—'the thought of my daughter would keep me pure. No conduct of mine shall ever make me unworthy of my child's affection and respect.' There! I'm making you cry; I won't stay here any longer. All that I had to say has been said. Nobody but Miss Ladd knows for certain whether your aunt was innocent or guilty in the matter of Miss Jethro's disgrace. Please to excuse me; my work's waiting downstairs."

From time to time, as she pursued her domestic labors, Mrs. Ellmother thought of Mirabel. Hours on hours had passed—and the doctor had not appeared. Was he too busy to spare even a few minutes of his time? Or had the handsome little gentleman, after promising so fairly, failed to perform his errand? This last doubt wronged Mirabel. He had engaged to return to the doctor's house; and he kept his word.

Doctor Allday was at home again, and was seeing patients. Introduced in his turn, Mirabel had no reason to complain of his reception. At the same time, after he had stated the object of his visit, something odd began to show itself in the doctor's manner.

He looked at Mirabel with an appearance of uneasy curiosity; and he contrived an excuse for altering the visitor's position in the room, so that the light fell full on Mirabel's face.

"I fancy I must have seen you," the doctor said, "at some former time."

"I am ashamed to say I don't remember it," Mirabel answered.

"Ah, very likely I'm wrong! I'll call on Miss Emily, sir, you may depend on it."

Left in his consulting-room, Doctor Allday failed to ring the bell which summoned the next patient who was waiting for him. He took his diary from the table drawer, and turned to the daily entries for the past month of July.

Arriving at the fifteenth day of the month, he glanced at the first lines of writing: "A visit from a mysterious lady, calling herself Miss Jethro. Our conference led to some very unexpected results."

No: that was not what he was in search of. He looked a little lower down: and read on regularly, from that point, as follows:

"Called on Miss Emily, in great anxiety about the discoveries which she might make among her aunt's papers. Papers all destroyed, thank God—except the Handbill, offering a reward for discovery of the murderer, which she found in the scrap-book. Gave her back the Handbill. Emily much surprised that the wretch should have escaped, with such a careful description of him circulated everywhere. She read the description aloud to me, in her nice clear voice: 'Supposed age between twenty-five and thirty years. A well-made man of small stature. Fair complexion, delicate features, clear blue eyes. Hair light, and cut rather short. Clean shaven, with the exception of narrow half-whiskers'—and so on. Emily at a loss to understand how the fugitive could disguise himself. Reminded her that he could effectually disguise his head and face (with time to help him) by letting his hair grow long, and cultivating his beard. Emily not convinced, even by this self-evident view of the case. Changed the subject."

The doctor put away his diary, and rang the bell.

"Curious," he thought. "That dandified little clergyman has certainly reminded me of my discussion with Emily, more than two months since. Was it his flowing hair, I wonder? or his splendid beard? Good God! suppose it should turn out—?"

He was interrupted by the appearance of his patient. Other ailing people followed. Doctor Allday's mind was professionally occupied for the rest of the evening.

CHAPTER LII. "IF I COULD FIND A FRIEND!"

Shortly after Miss Ladd had taken her departure, a parcel arrived for Emily, bearing the name of a bookseller printed on the label. It was large, and it was heavy. "Reading enough, I should think, to last for a lifetime," Mrs. Ellmother remarked, after carrying the parcel upstairs.

Emily called her back as she was leaving the room. "I want to caution you," she said, "before Miss Wyvil comes. Don't tell her—don't tell anybody—how my father met his death. If other persons are taken into our confidence, they will talk of it. We don't know how near to us the murderer may be. The slightest hint may put him on his guard."

"Oh, miss, are you still thinking of that!"

"I think of nothing else."

"Bad for your mind, Miss Emily—and bad for your body, as your looks show. I wish you would take counsel with some discreet person, before you move in this matter by yourself."

Emily sighed wearily. "In my situation, where is the person whom I can trust?"

"You can trust the good doctor."

"Can I? Perhaps I was wrong when I told you I wouldn't see him. He might be of some use to me."

Mrs. Ellmother made the most of this concession, in the fear that Emily might change her mind. "Doctor Allday may call on you tomorrow," she said.

"Do you mean that you have sent for him?"

"Don't be angry! I did it for the best—and Mr. Mirabel agreed with me."

"Mr. Mirabel! What have you told Mr. Mirabel?"

"Nothing, except that you are ill. When he heard that, he proposed to go for the doctor. He will be here again to-morrow, to ask for news of your health. Will you see him?"

"I don't know yet—I have other things to think of. Bring Miss Wyvil up here when she comes."

"Am I to get the spare room ready for her?"

"No. She is staying with her father at the London house."

Emily made that reply almost with an air of relief. When Cecilia arrived, it was only by an effort that she could show grateful appreciation of the sympathy of her dearest friend. When the visit came to an end, she felt an ungrateful sense of freedom: the restraint was off her mind; she could think again of the one terrible subject that had any interest for her now. Over love, over friendship, over the natural enjoyment of her young life, predominated the blighting resolution which bound her to avenge her father's death. Her dearest remembrances of him—tender remembrances once—now burned in her (to use her own words) like fire. It was no ordinary love that had bound parent and child together in the bygone time. Emily had grown from infancy to girlhood, owing all the brightness of her life—a life without a mother, without brothers, without sisters—to her father alone. To submit to lose this beloved, this only companion, by the cruel stroke of disease was of all trials of resignation the hardest to bear. But to be severed from him by the murderous hand of a man, was more than Emily's fervent nature could passively endure. Before the garden gate had closed on her friend she had returned to her one thought, she was breathing again her one aspiration. The books that she had ordered, with her own purpose in view—books that might supply her want of experience, and might reveal the perils which beset the course that lay before her—were unpacked and spread out on the table. Hour after hour, when the old servant believed that her mistress was in bed, she was absorbed over biographies in English and French, which related the stratagems by means of which famous policemen had captured the worst criminals of their time. From these, she turned to works of fiction, which found their chief topic of interest in dwelling on the discovery of hidden crime. The night passed, and dawn glimmered through the window—and still she opened book after book with sinking courage—and still she gained nothing but the disheartening conviction of her inability to carry out her own plans. Almost every page that she turned over revealed the immovable obstacles set in her way by her sex and her age. Could she mix with the people, or visit the scenes, familiar to the experience of men (in fact and in fiction), who had traced the homicide to his hiding-place, and had marked him among his harmless fellow-creatures with the brand of Cain? No! A young girl following, or attempting to follow, that career, must reckon with insult and outrage—paying their abominable tribute to her youth and her beauty, at every turn. What proportion would the men who might respect her bear to the men who might make her the object of advances, which it was hardly possible to imagine without shuddering. She crept exhausted to her bed, the most helpless, hopeless creature on the wide surface of the earth—a girl self-devoted to the task of a man.

Careful to perform his promise to Mirabel, without delay, the doctor called on Emily early in the morning—before the hour at which he usually entered his consulting-room.

"Well? What's the matter with the pretty young mistress?" he asked, in his most abrupt manner, when Mrs. Ellmother opened the door. "Is it love? or jealousy? or a new dress with a wrinkle in it?"

"You will hear about it, sir, from Miss Emily herself. I am forbidden to say anything."

"But you mean to say something—for all that?"

"Don't joke, Doctor Allday! The state of things here is a great deal too serious for joking. Make up your mind to be surprised—I say no more."

Before the doctor could ask what this meant, Emily opened the parlor door. "Come in!" she said, impatiently.

Doctor Allday's first greeting was strictly professional. "My dear child, I never expected this," he began. "You are looking wretchedly ill." He attempted to feel her pulse. She drew her hand away from him.

"It's my mind that's ill," she answered. "Feeling my pulse won't cure me of anxiety and distress. I want advice; I want help. Dear old doctor, you have always been a good friend to me—be a better friend than ever now."

"What can I do?"

"Promise you will keep secret what I am going to say to you—and listen, pray listen patiently, till I have done."

Doctor Allday promised, and listened. He had been, in some degree at least, prepared for a surprise—but the disclosure which now burst on him was more than his equanimity could sustain. He looked at Emily in silent dismay. She had surprised and shocked him, not only by what she said, but by what she unconsciously suggested. Was it possible that Mirabel's personal appearance had produced on her the same impression which was present in his own mind? His first impulse, when he was composed enough to speak, urged him to put the question cautiously.

"If you happened to meet with the suspected man," he said, "have you any means of identifying him?"

"None whatever, doctor. If you would only think it over—"

He stopped her there; convinced of the danger of encouraging her, and resolved to act on his conviction.

"I have enough to occupy me in my profession," he said. "Ask your other friend to think it over."

"What other friend?"

"Mr. Alban Morris."

The moment he pronounced the name, he saw that he had touched on some painful association. "Has Mr. Morris refused to help you?" he inquired.

"I have not asked him to help me."

"Why?"

There was no choice (with such a man as Doctor Allday) between offending him or answering him. Emily adopted the last alternative. On this occasion she had no reason to complain of his silence.

"Your view of Mr. Morris's conduct surprises me," he replied—"surprises me more than I can say," he added; remembering that he too was guilty of having kept her in ignorance of the truth, out of regard—mistaken regard, as it now seemed to be—for her peace of mind.

"Be good to me, and pass it over if I am wrong," Emily said: "I can't dispute with you; I can only tell you what I feel. You have always been so kind to me—may I count on your kindness still?"

Doctor Allday relapsed into silence.

"May I at least ask," she went on, "if you know anything of persons—" She paused, discouraged by the cold expression of inquiry in the old man's eyes as he looked at her.

"What persons?" he said.

"Persons whom I suspect."

"Name them."

458

Emily named the landlady of the inn at Zeeland: she could now place the right interpretation on Mrs. Rook's conduct, when the locket had been put into her hand at Netherwoods. Doctor Allday answered shortly and stiffly: he had never even seen Mrs. Rook. Emily mentioned Miss Jethro next—and saw at once that she had interested him.

"What do you suspect Miss Jethro of doing?" he asked.

"I suspect her of knowing more of my father's death than she is willing to acknowledge," Emily replied.

The doctor's manner altered for the better. "I agree with you," he said frankly. "But I have some knowledge of that lady. I warn you not to waste time and trouble in trying to discover the weak side of Miss Jethro."

"That was not my experience of her at school," Emily rejoined. "At the same time I don't know what may have happened since those days. I may perhaps have lost the place I once held in her regard."

"How?"

"Through my aunt."

"Through your aunt?"

"I hope and trust I am wrong," Emily continued; "but I fear my aunt had something to do with Miss Jethro's dismissal from the school—and in that case Miss Jethro may have found it out." Her eyes, resting on the doctor, suddenly brightened. "You know something about it!" she exclaimed.

He considered a little—whether he should or should not tell her of the letter addressed by Miss Ladd to Miss Letitia, which he had found at the cottage.

"If I could satisfy you that your fears are well founded," he asked, "would the discovery keep you away from Miss Jethro?"

"I should be ashamed to speak to her—even if we met."

"Very well. I can tell you positively, that your aunt was the person who

459

turned Miss Jethro out of the school. When I get home, I will send you a letter that proves it."

Emily's head sank on her breast. "Why do I only hear of this now?" she said.

"Because I had no reason for letting you know of it, before to-day. If I have done nothing else, I have at least succeeded in keeping you and Miss Jethro apart."

Emily looked at him in alarm. He went on without appearing to notice that he had startled her. "I wish to God I could as easily put a stop to the mad project which you are contemplating."

"The mad project?" Emily repeated. "Oh, Doctor Allday. Do you cruelly leave me to myself, at the time of all others, when I am most in need of your sympathy?"

That appeal moved him. He spoke more gently; he pitied, while he condemned her.

"My poor dear child, I should be cruel indeed, if I encouraged you. You are giving yourself up to an enterprise, so shockingly unsuited to a young girl like you, that I declare I contemplate it with horror. Think, I entreat you, think; and let me hear that you have yielded—not to my poor entreaties— but to your own better sense!" His voice faltered; his eyes moistened. "I shall make a fool of myself," he burst out furiously, "if I stay here any longer. Good-by."

He left her.

She walked to the window, and looked out at the fair morning. No one to feel for her—no one to understand her—nothing nearer that could speak to poor mortality of hope and encouragement than the bright heaven, so far away! She turned from the window. "The sun shines on the murderer," she thought, "as it shines on me."

She sat down at the table, and tried to quiet her mind; to think steadily to some good purpose. Of the few friends that she possessed, every one had declared that she was in the wrong. Had they lost the one loved being of all beings on earth, and lost him by the hand of a homicide—and that homicide free? All that was faithful, all that was devoted in the girl's nature, held her to her desperate resolution as with a hand of iron. If she shrank at that miserable moment, it was not from her design—it was from the sense of her own helplessness. "Oh, if I had been a man!" she said to herself. "Oh, if I could find a friend!"

CHAPTER LIII. THE FRIEND IS FOUND.

Mrs. Ellmother looked into the parlor. "I told you Mr. Mirabel would call again," she announced. "Here he is."

"Has he asked to see me?"

"He leaves it entirely to you."

For a moment, and a moment only, Emily was undecided. "Show him in," she said.

Mirabel's embarrassment was visible the moment he entered the room. For the first time in his life—in the presence of a woman—the popular preacher was shy. He who had taken hundreds of fair hands with sympathetic pressure—he who had offered fluent consolation, abroad and at home, to beauty in distress—was conscious of a rising color, and was absolutely at a loss for words when Emily received him. And yet, though he appeared at disadvantage—and, worse still, though he was aware of it himself—there was nothing contemptible in his look and manner. His silence and confusion revealed a change in him which inspired respect. Love had developed this spoiled darling of foolish congregations, this effeminate pet of drawing-rooms and boudoirs, into the likeness of a Man—and no woman, in Emily's position, could have failed to see that it was love which she herself had inspired.

Equally ill at ease, they both took refuge in the commonplace phrases suggested by the occasion. These exhausted there was a pause. Mirabel alluded to Cecilia, as a means of continuing the conversation.

"Have you seen Miss Wyvil?" he inquired.

"She was here last night; and I expect to see her again to-day before she returns to Monksmoor with her father. Do you go back with them?"

"Yes—if you do."

"I remain in London."

"Then I remain in London, too."

The strong feeling that was in him had forced its way to expression at last. In happier days—when she had persistently refused to let him speak to her seriously—she would have been ready with a light-hearted reply. She was silent now. Mirabel pleaded with her not to misunderstand him, by an honest confession of his motives which presented him under a new aspect. The easy plausible man, who had hardly ever seemed to be in earnest before—meant, seriously meant, what he said now.

"May I try to explain myself?" he asked.

"Certainly, if you wish it."

"Pray, don't suppose me capable," Mirabel said earnestly, "of presuming to pay you an idle compliment. I cannot think of you, alone and in trouble, without feeling anxiety which can only be relieved in one way—I must be near enough to hear of you, day by day. Not by repeating this visit! Unless you wish it, I will not again cross the threshold of your door. Mrs. Ellmother will tell me if your mind is more at ease; Mrs. Ellmother will tell me if there is any new trial of your fortitude. She needn't even mention that I have been speaking to her at the door; and she may be sure, and you may be sure, that I shall ask no inquisitive questions. I can feel for you in your misfortune, without wishing to know what that misfortune is. If I can ever be of the smallest use, think of me as your other servant. Say to Mrs. Ellmother, 'I want him'—and say no more."

Where is the woman who could have resisted such devotion as this—inspired, truly inspired, by herself? Emily's eyes softened as she answered him.

"You little know how your kindness touches me," she said.

"Don't speak of my kindness until you have put me to the proof," he interposed. "Can a friend (such a friend as I am, I mean) be of any use?"

"Of the greatest use if I could feel justified in trying you."

"I entreat you to try me!"

"But, Mr. Mirabel, you don't know what I am thinking of."

"I don't want to know."

"I may be wrong. My friends all say I am wrong."

"I don't care what your friends say; I don't care about any earthly thing but your tranquillity. Does your dog ask whether you are right or wrong? I am your dog. I think of You, and I think of nothing else."

She looked back through the experience of the last few days. Miss Ladd—Mrs. Ellmother—Doctor Allday: not one of them had felt for her, not one of them had spoken to her, as this man had felt and had spoken. She remembered the dreadful sense of solitude and helplessness which had wrung her heart, in the interval before Mirabel came in. Her father himself could hardly have been kinder to her than this friend of a few weeks only. She looked at him through her tears; she could say nothing that was eloquent, nothing even that was adequate. "You are very good to me," was her only acknowledgment of all that he had offered. How poor it seemed to be! and yet how much it meant!

He rose—saying considerately that he would leave her to recover herself, and would wait to hear if he was wanted.

"No," she said; "I must not let you go. In common gratitude I ought to decide before you leave me, and I do decide to take you into my confidence." She hesitated; her color rose a little. "I know how unselfishly you offer me your help," she resumed; "I know you speak to me as a brother might speak to a sister—"

He gently interrupted her. "No," he said; "I can't honestly claim to do that. And—may I venture to remind you?—you know why."

She started. Her eyes rested on him with a momentary expression of reproach.

"Is it quite fair," she asked, "in my situation, to say that?"

"Would it have been quite fair," he rejoined, "to allow you to deceive yourself? Should I deserve to be taken into your confidence, if I encouraged you to trust me, under false pretenses? Not a word more of those hopes on which the happiness of my life depends shall pass my lips, unless you permit it. In my devotion to your interests, I promise to forget myself. My motives may be misinterpreted; my position may be misunderstood. Ignorant people may take me for that other happier man, who is an object of interest to you—"

"Stop, Mr. Mirabel! The person to whom you refer has no such claim on me as you suppose."

"Dare I say how happy I am to hear it? Will you forgive me?"

"I will forgive you if you say no more."

Their eyes met. Completely overcome by the new hope that she had inspired, Mirabel was unable to answer her. His sensitive nerves trembled under emotion, like the nerves of a woman; his delicate complexion faded away slowly into whiteness. Emily was alarmed—he seemed to be on the point of fainting. She ran to the window to open it more widely.

"Pray don't trouble yourself," he said, "I am easily agitated by any sudden sensation—and I am a little overcome at this moment by my own happiness."

"Let me give you a glass of wine."

"Thank you—I don't need it indeed."

"You really feel better?"

"I feel quite well again—and eager to hear how I can serve you."

"It's a long story, Mr. Mirabel—and a dreadful story."

"Dreadful?"

"Yes! Let me tell you first how you can serve me. I am in search of a man who has done me the cruelest wrong that one human creature can inflict on another. But the chances are all against me—I am only a woman; and I don't know how to take even the first step toward discovery."

"You will know, when I guide you."

He reminded her tenderly of what she might expect from him, and was rewarded by a grateful look. Seeing nothing, suspecting nothing, they advanced together nearer and nearer to the end.

"Once or twice," Emily continued, "I spoke to you of my poor father, when we were at Monksmoor—and I must speak of him again. You could have no interest in inquiring about a stranger—and you cannot have heard how he died."

"Pardon me, I heard from Mr. Wyvil how he died."

"You heard what I had told Mr. Wyvil," Emily said: "I was wrong."

"Wrong!" Mirabel exclaimed, in a tone of courteous surprise. "Was it not a sudden death?"

"It was a sudden death."

"Caused by disease of the heart?"

"Caused by no disease. I have been deceived about my father's death—and I have only discovered it a few days since."

At the impending moment of the frightful shock which she was innocently about to inflict on him, she stopped—doubtful whether it would be best to relate how the discovery had been made, or to pass at once to the result. Mirabel supposed that she had paused to control her agitation. He was so immeasurably far away from the faintest suspicion of what was coming that he exerted his ingenuity, in the hope of sparing her.

"I can anticipate the rest," he said. "Your sad loss has been caused by some fatal accident. Let us change the subject; tell me more of that man whom I must help you to find. It will only distress you to dwell on your father's death."

"Distress me?" she repeated. "His death maddens me!"

"Oh, don't say that!"

"Hear me! hear me! My father died murdered, at Zeeland—and the man you must help me to find is the wretch who killed him."

She started to her feet with a cry of terror. Mirabel dropped from his chair senseless to the floor.

CHAPTER LIV. THE END OF THE FAINTING FIT.

Emily recovered her presence of mind. She opened the door, so as to make a draught of air in the room, and called for water. Returning to Mirabel, she loosened his cravat. Mrs. Ellmother came in, just in time to prevent her from committing a common error in the treatment of fainting persons, by raising Mirabel's head. The current of air, and the sprinkling of water over his face, soon produced their customary effect. "He'll come round, directly," Mrs. Ellmother remarked. "Your aunt was sometimes taken with these swoons, miss; and I know something about them. He looks a poor weak creature, in spite of his big beard. Has anything frightened him?"

Emily little knew how correctly that chance guess had hit on the truth!

"Nothing can possibly have frightened him," she replied; "I am afraid he is in bad health. He turned suddenly pale while we were talking; and I thought he was going to be taken ill; he made light of it, and seemed to recover. Unfortunately, I was right; it was the threatening of a fainting fit—he dropped on the floor a minute afterward."

A sigh fluttered over Mirabel's lips. His eyes opened, looked at Mrs. Ellmother in vacant terror, and closed again. Emily whispered to her to leave the room. The old woman smiled satirically as she opened the door—then looked back, with a sudden change of humor. To see the kind young mistress bending over the feeble little clergyman set her—by some strange association of ideas—thinking of Alban Morris. "Ah," she muttered to herself, on her way out, "I call him a Man!"

There was wine in the sideboard—the wine which Emily had once already offered in vain. Mirabel drank it eagerly, this time. He looked round the room, as if he wished to be sure that they were alone. "Have I fallen to a low place in your estimation?" he asked, smiling faintly. "I am afraid you will think poorly enough of your new ally, after this?"

"I only think you should take more care of your health," Emily replied, with sincere interest in his recovery. "Let me leave you to rest on the sofa."

He refused to remain at the cottage—he asked, with a sudden change to fretfulness, if she would let her servant get him a cab. She ventured to doubt whether he was quite strong enough yet to go away by himself. He reiterated, piteously reiterated, his request. A passing cab was stopped directly. Emily accompanied him to the gate. "I know what to do," he said, in a hurried absent way. "Rest and a little tonic medicine will soon set me right." The clammy coldness of his skin made Emily shudder, as they shook hands. "You won't think the worse of me for this?" he asked.

"How can you imagine such a thing!" she answered warmly.

"Will you see me, if I come to-morrow?"

"I shall be anxious to see you."

So they parted. Emily returned to the house, pitying him with all her heart.

BOOK THE SIXTH—HERE AND THERE.

CHAPTER LV. MIRABEL SEES HIS WAY.

Reaching the hotel at which he was accustomed to stay when he was in London, Mirabel locked the door of his room. He looked at the houses on the opposite side of the street. His mind was in such a state of morbid distrust that he lowered the blind over the window. In solitude and obscurity, the miserable wretch sat down in a corner, and covered his face with his hands, and tried to realize what had happened to him.

Nothing had been said at the fatal interview with Emily, which could have given him the slightest warning of what was to come. Her father's name—absolutely unknown to him when he fled from the inn—had only been communicated to the public by the newspaper reports of the adjourned inquest. At the time when those reports appeared, he was in hiding, under circumstances which prevented him from seeing a newspaper. While the murder was still a subject of conversation, he was in France—far out of the track of English travelers—and he remained on the continent until the summer of eighteen hundred and eighty-one. No exercise of discretion, on his part, could have extricated him from the terrible position in which he was now placed. He stood pledged to Emily to discover the man suspected of the murder of her father; and that man was—himself!

What refuge was left open to him?

If he took to flight, his sudden disappearance would be a suspicious circumstance in itself, and would therefore provoke inquiries which might lead to serious results. Supposing that he overlooked the risk thus presented, would he be capable of enduring a separation from Emily, which might be a separation for life? Even in the first horror of discovering his situation, her influence remained unshaken—the animating spirit of the one manly capacity for resistance which raised him above the reach of his own fears. The only prospect before him which he felt himself to be incapable of contemplating, was the prospect of leaving Emily.

Having arrived at this conclusion, his fears urged him to think of providing for his own safety.

The first precaution to adopt was to separate Emily from friends whose advice might be hostile to his interests—perhaps even subversive of his security. To effect this design, he had need of an ally whom he could trust. That ally was at his disposal, far away in the north.

At the time when Francine's jealousy began to interfere with all freedom of intercourse between Emily and himself at Monksmoor, he had contemplated making arrangements which might enable them to meet at the house of his invalid sister, Mrs. Delvin. He had spoken of her, and of the bodily affliction which confined her to her room, in terms which had already interested Emily. In the present emergency, he decided on returning to the subject, and on hastening the meeting between the two women which he had first suggested at Mr. Wyvil's country seat.

No time was to be lost in carrying out this intention. He wrote to Mrs. Delvin by that day's post; confiding to her, in the first place, the critical position in which he now found himself. This done, he proceeded as follows:

"To your sound judgment, dearest Agatha, it may appear that I am making myself needlessly uneasy about the future. Two persons only know that I am the man who escaped from the inn at Zeeland. You are one of them, and Miss Jethro is the other. On you I can absolutely rely; and, after my experience of her, I ought to feel sure of Miss Jethro. I admit this; but I cannot get over my distrust of Emily's friends. I fear the cunning old doctor; I doubt Mr. Wyvil; I hate Alban Morris.

"Do me a favor, my dear. Invite Emily to be your guest, and so separate her from these friends. The old servant who attends on her will be included in the invitation, of course. Mrs. Ellmother is, as I believe, devoted to the interests of Mr. Alban Morris: she will be well out of the way of doing mischief, while we have her safe in your northern solitude.

"There is no fear that Emily will refuse your invitation.

"In the first place, she is already interested in you. In the second place, I shall consider the small proprieties of social life; and, instead of traveling with her to your house, I shall follow by a later train. In the third place, I am now the chosen adviser in whom she trusts; and what I tell her to do, she will do. It pains me, really and truly pains me, to be compelled to deceive her—but the other alternative is to reveal myself as the wretch of whom she is in search. Was there ever such a situation? And, oh, Agatha, I am so fond of her! If I fail to persuade her to be my wife, I don't care what becomes of me. I used to think disgrace, and death on the scaffold, the most frightful prospect that a man can contemplate. In my present frame of mind, a life without Emily may just as well end in that way as in any other. When we are together in your old sea-beaten tower, do your best, my dear, to incline the heart of this sweet girl toward me. If she remains in London, how do I know that Mr. Morris may not recover the place he has lost in her good opinion? The bare idea of it turns me cold.

"There is one more point on which I must touch, before I can finish my letter.

"When you last wrote, you told me that Sir Jervis Redwood was not expected to live much longer, and that the establishment would be broken up after his death. Can you find out for me what will become, under the circumstances, of Mr. and Mrs. Rook? So far as I am concerned, I don't doubt that the alteration in my personal appearance, which has protected me for years past, may be trusted to preserve me from recognition by these two people. But it is of the utmost importance, remembering the project to which Emily has devoted herself, that she should not meet with Mrs. Rook. They have been already in correspondence; and Mrs. Rook has expressed an intention (if the opportunity offers itself) of calling at the cottage. Another reason, and a pressing reason, for removing Emily from London! We can easily keep the Rooks out of your house; but I own I should feel more at my ease, if I heard that they had left Northumberland."

With that confession, Mrs. Delvin's brother closed his letter.

CHAPTER LVI. ALBAN SEES HIS WAY.

During the first days of Mirabel's sojourn at his hotel in London, events were in progress at Netherwoods, affecting the interests of the man who was the especial object of his distrust. Not long after Miss Ladd had returned to her school, she heard of an artist who was capable of filling the place to be vacated by Alban Morris. It was then the twenty-third of the month. In four days more the new master would be ready to enter on his duties; and Alban would be at liberty.

On the twenty-fourth, Alban received a telegram which startled him. The person sending the message was Mrs. Ellmother; and the words were: "Meet me at your railway station to-day, at two o'clock."

He found the old woman in the waiting-room; and he met with a rough reception.

"Minutes are precious, Mr. Morris," she said; "you are two minutes late. The next train to London stops here in half an hour—and I must go back by it."

"Good heavens, what brings you here? Is Emily—?"

"Emily is well enough in health—if that's what you mean? As to why I come here, the reason is that it's a deal easier for me (worse luck!) to take this journey than to write a letter. One good turn deserves another. I don't forget how kind you were to me, away there at the school—and I can't, and won't, see what's going on at the cottage, behind your back, without letting you know of it. Oh, you needn't be alarmed about her! I've made an excuse to get away for a few hours—but I haven't left her by herself. Miss Wyvil has come to London again; and Mr. Mirabel spends the best part of his time with her. Excuse me for a moment, will you? I'm so thirsty after the journey, I can hardly speak."

She presented herself at the counter in the waiting-room. "I'll trouble you, young woman, for a glass of ale." She returned to Alban in a better humor. "It's not bad stuff, that! When I have said my say, I'll have a drop more—just to wash the taste of Mr. Mirabel out of my mouth. Wait a bit; I

471

have something to ask you. How much longer are you obliged to stop here, teaching the girls to draw?"

"I leave Netherwoods in three days more," Alban replied.

"That's all right! You may be in time to bring Miss Emily to her senses, yet."

"What do you mean?"

"I mean—if you don't stop it—she will marry the parson."

"I can't believe it, Mrs. Ellmother! I won't believe it!"

"Ah, it's a comfort to him, poor fellow, to say that! Look here, Mr. Morris; this is how it stands. You're in disgrace with Miss Emily—and he profits by it. I was fool enough to take a liking to Mr. Mirabel when I first opened the door to him; I know better now. He got on the blind side of me; and now he has got on the blind side of her. Shall I tell you how? By doing what you would have done if you had had the chance. He's helping her—or pretending to help her, I don't know which—to find the man who murdered poor Mr. Brown. After four years! And when all the police in England (with a reward to encourage them) did their best, and it came to nothing!"

"Never mind that!" Alban said impatiently. "I want to know how Mr. Mirabel is helping her?"

"That's more than I can tell you. You don't suppose they take me into their confidence? All I can do is to pick up a word, here and there, when fine weather tempts them out into the garden. She tells him to suspect Mrs. Rook, and to make inquiries after Miss Jethro. And he has his plans; and he writes them down, which is dead against his doing anything useful, in my opinion. I don't hold with your scribblers. At the same time I wouldn't count too positively, in your place, on his being likely to fail. That little Mirabel—if it wasn't for his beard, I should believe he was a woman, and a sickly woman too; he fainted in our house the other day—that little Mirabel is in earnest. Rather than leave Miss Emily from Saturday to Monday, he has got a parson out of employment to do his Sunday work for him. And, what's more, he has persuaded her (for some reasons of his own) to leave London next week."

"Is she going back to Monksmoor?"

"Not she! Mr. Mirabel has got a sister, a widow lady; she's a cripple, or something of the sort. Her name is Mrs. Delvin. She lives far away in the north country, by the sea; and Miss Emily is going to stay with her."

"Are you sure of that?"

"Sure? I've seen the letter."

"Do you mean the letter of invitation?"

"Yes—I do. Miss Emily herself showed it to me. I'm to go with her— 'in attendance on my mistress,' as the lady puts it. This I will say for Mrs. Delvin: her handwriting is a credit to the school that taught her; and the poor bedridden creature words her invitation so nicely, that I myself couldn't have resisted it—and I'm a hard one, as you know. You don't seem to heed me, Mr. Morris."

"I beg your pardon, I was thinking."

"Thinking of what—if I may make so bold?"

"Of going back to London with you, instead of waiting till the new master comes to take my place."

"Don't do that, sir! You would do harm instead of good, if you showed yourself at the cottage now. Besides, it would not be fair to Miss Ladd, to leave her before the other man takes your girls off your hands. Trust me to look after your interests; and don't go near Miss Emily—don't even write to her—unless you have got something to say about the murder, which she will be eager to hear. Make some discovery in that direction, Mr. Morris, while the parson is only trying to do it or pretending to do it—and I'll answer for the result. Look at the clock! In ten minutes more the train will be here. My memory isn't as good as it was; but I do think I have told you all I had to tell."

"You are the best of good friends!" Alban said warmly.

"Never mind about that, sir. If you want to do a friendly thing in return, tell me if you know what has become of Miss de Sor."

"She has returned to Netherwoods."

"Aha! Miss Ladd is as good as her word. Would you mind writing to tell me of it, if Miss de Sor leaves the school again? Good Lord! there she is on the platform with bag and baggage. Don't let her see me, Mr. Morris! If she comes in here, I shall set the marks of my ten finger-nails on that false face of hers, as sure as I am a Christian woman."

Alban placed himself at the door, so as to hide Mrs. Ellmother. There indeed was Francine, accompanied by one of the teachers at the school. She took a seat on the bench outside the booking-office, in a state of sullen indifference—absorbed in herself—noticing nothing. Urged by ungovernable curiosity, Mrs. Ellmother stole on tiptoe to Alban's side to look at her. To a person acquainted with the circumstances there could be no possible doubt of what had happened. Francine had failed to excuse herself, and had been dismissed from Miss Ladd's house.

"I would have traveled to the world's end," Mrs. Ellmother said, "to see that!"

She returned to her place in the waiting-room, perfectly satisfied.

The teacher noticed Alban, on leaving the booking-office after taking the tickets. "I shall be glad," she said, looking toward Francine, "when I have resigned the charge of that young lady to the person who is to receive her in London."

"Is she to be sent back to her parents?" Alban asked.

"We don't know yet. Miss Ladd will write to St. Domingo by the next mail. In the meantime, her father's agent in London—the same person who pays her allowance—takes care of her until he hears from the West Indies."

"Does she consent to this?"

"She doesn't seem to care what becomes of her. Miss Ladd has given her every opportunity of explaining and excusing herself, and has produced no impression. You can see the state she is in. Our good mistress—always hopeful even in the worst cases, as you know—thinks she is feeling ashamed of herself, and is too proud and self-willed to own it. My own idea is, that some secret disappointment is weighing on her mind. Perhaps I am wrong."

No. Miss Ladd was wrong; and the teacher was right.

The passion of revenge, being essentially selfish in its nature, is of all passions the narrowest in its range of view. In gratifying her jealous hatred of Emily, Francine had correctly foreseen consequences, as they might affect the other object of her enmity—Alban Morris. But she had failed to perceive the imminent danger of another result, which in a calmer frame of mind might not have escaped discovery. In triumphing over Emily and Alban, she had been the indirect means of inflicting on herself the bitterest of all disappointments—she had brought Emily and Mirabel together. The first forewarning of this catastrophe had reached her, on hearing that Mirabel would not return to Monksmoor. Her worst fears had been thereafter confirmed by a letter from Cecilia, which had followed her to Netherwoods. From that moment, she, who had made others wretched, paid the penalty in suffering as keen as any that she had inflicted. Completely prostrated; powerless, through ignorance of his address in London, to make a last appeal to Mirabel; she was literally, as had just been said, careless what became of her. When the train approached, she sprang to her feet—advanced to the edge of the platform—and suddenly drew back, shuddering. The teacher looked in terror at Alban. Had the desperate girl meditated throwing herself under the wheels of the engine? The thought had been in both their minds; but neither of them acknowledged it. Francine stepped quietly into the carriage, when the train drew up, and laid her head back in a corner, and closed her eyes. Mrs. Ellmother took her place in another compartment, and beckoned to Alban to speak to her at the window.

"Where can I see you, when you go to London?" she asked.

"At Doctor Allday's house."

"On what day?"

"On Tuesday next."

CHAPTER LVII. APPROACHING THE END.

Alban reached London early enough in the afternoon to find the doctor at his luncheon. "Too late to see Mrs. Ellmother," he announced. "Sit down and have something to eat."

"Has she left any message for me?"

"A message, my good friend, that you won't like to hear. She is off with her mistress, this morning, on a visit to Mr. Mirabel's sister."

"Does he go with them?"

"No; he follows by a later train."

"Has Mrs. Ellmother mentioned the address?"

"There it is, in her own handwriting."

Alban read the address:—"Mrs. Delvin, The Clink, Belford, Northumberland."

"Turn to the back of that bit of paper," the doctor said. "Mrs. Ellmother has written something on it."

She had written these words: "No discoveries made by Mr. Mirabel, up to this time. Sir Jervis Redwood is dead. The Rooks are believed to be in Scotland; and Miss Emily, if need be, is to help the parson to find them. No news of Miss Jethro."

"Now you have got your information," Doctor Allday resumed, "let me have a look at you. You're not in a rage: that's a good sign to begin with."

"I am not the less determined," Alban answered.

"To bring Emily to her senses?" the doctor asked.

"To do what Mirabel has not done—and then to let her choose between us."

"Ay? ay? Your good opinion of her hasn't altered, though she has treated you so badly?"

"My good opinion makes allowance for the state of my poor darling's mind, after the shock that has fallen on her," Alban answered quietly. "She is not my Emily now. She will be my Emily yet. I told her I was convinced of it, in the old days at school—and my conviction is as strong as ever. Have you seen her, since I have been away at Netherwoods?"

"Yes; and she is as angry with me as she is with you."

"For the same reason?"

"No, no. I heard enough to warn me to hold my tongue. I refused to help her—that's all. You are a man, and you may run risks which no young girl ought to encounter. Do you remember when I asked you to drop all further inquiries into the murder, for Emily's sake? The circumstances have altered since that time. Can I be of any use?"

"Of the greatest use, if you can give me Miss Jethro's address."

"Oh! You mean to begin in that way, do you?"

"Yes. You know that Miss Jethro visited me at Netherwoods?"

"Go on."

"She showed me your answer to a letter which she had written to you. Have you got that letter?"

Doctor Allday produced it. The address was at a post-office, in a town on the south coast. Looking up when he had copied it, Alban saw the doctor's eyes fixed on him with an oddly-mingled expression: partly of sympathy, partly of hesitation.

"Have you anything to suggest?" he asked.

"You will get nothing out of Miss Jethro," the doctor answered, "unless—" there he stopped.

"Unless, what?"

"Unless you can frighten her."

"How am I to do that?"

After a little reflection, Doctor Allday returned, without any apparent reason, to the subject of his last visit to Emily.

"There was one thing she said, in the course of our talk," he continued, "which struck me as being sensible: possibly (for we are all more or less conceited), because I agreed with her myself. She suspects Miss Jethro of knowing more about that damnable murder than Miss Jethro is willing to acknowledge. If you want to produce the right effect on her—" he looked hard at Alban and checked himself once more.

"Well? what am I to do?"

"Tell her you have an idea of who the murderer is."

"But I have no idea."

"But I have."

"Good God! what do you mean?"

"Don't mistake me! An impression has been produced on my mind— that's all. Call it a freak or fancy; worth trying perhaps as a bold experiment, and worth nothing more. Come a little nearer. My housekeeper is an excellent woman, but I have once or twice caught her rather too near to that door. I think I'll whisper it."

He did whisper it. In breathless wonder, Alban heard of the doubt which had crossed Doctor Allday's mind, on the evening when Mirabel had called at his house.

"You look as if you didn't believe it," the doctor remarked.

"I'm thinking of Emily. For her sake I hope and trust you are wrong. Ought I to go to her at once? I don't know what to do!"

"Find out first, my good fellow, whether I am right or wrong. You can do it, if you will run the risk with Miss Jethro."

Alban recovered himself. His old friend's advice was clearly the right advice to follow. He examined his railway guide, and then looked at his watch.

"If I can find Miss Jethro," he answered, "I'll risk it before the day is out."

The doctor accompanied him to the door. "You will write to me, won't you?"

"Without fail. Thank you—and good-by."

BOOK THE SEVENTH—THE CLINK.

CHAPTER LVIII. A COUNCIL OF TWO.

Early in the last century one of the picturesque race of robbers and murderers, practicing the vices of humanity on the borderlands watered by the river Tweed, built a tower of stone on the coast of Northumberland. He lived joyously in the perpetration of atrocities; and he died penitent, under the direction of his priest. Since that event, he has figured in poems and pictures; and has been greatly admired by modern ladies and gentlemen, whom he would have outraged and robbed if he had been lucky enough to meet with them in the good old times.

His son succeeded him, and failed to profit by the paternal example: that is to say, he made the fatal mistake of fighting for other people instead of fighting for himself.

In the rebellion of Forty-Five, this northern squire sided to serious purpose with Prince Charles and the Highlanders. He lost his head; and his children lost their inheritance. In the lapse of years, the confiscated property fell into the hands of strangers; the last of whom (having a taste for the turf) discovered, in course of time, that he was in want of money. A retired merchant, named Delvin (originally of French extraction), took a liking to the wild situation, and purchased the tower. His wife—already in failing health—had been ordered by the doctors to live a quiet life by the sea. Her husband's death left her a rich and lonely widow; by day and night alike, a prisoner in her room; wasted by disease, and having but two interests which reconciled her to life—writing poetry in the intervals of pain, and paying the debts of a reverend brother who succeeded in the pulpit, and prospered nowhere else.

In the later days of its life, the tower had been greatly improved as a place of residence. The contrast was remarkable between the dreary gray outer walls, and the luxuriously furnished rooms inside, rising by two at a time to the lofty eighth story of the building. Among the scattered populace of the country round, the tower was still known by the odd name given to it in the bygone time—"The Clink." It had been so called (as was supposed) in allusion to the noise made by loose stones, washed backward and forward at certain times of the tide, in hollows of the rock on which the building stood.

On the evening of her arrival at Mrs. Delvin's retreat, Emily retired at an early hour, fatigued by her long journey. Mirabel had an opportunity of speaking with his sister privately in her own room.

"Send me away, Agatha, if I disturb you," he said, "and let me know when I can see you in the morning."

"My dear Miles, have you forgotten that I am never able to sleep in calm weather? My lullaby, for years past, has been the moaning of the great North Sea, under my window. Listen! There is not a sound outside on this peaceful night. It is the right time of the tide, just now—and yet, 'the clink' is not to be heard. Is the moon up?"

Mirabel opened the curtains. "The whole sky is one great abyss of black," he answered. "If I was superstitious, I should think that horrid darkness a bad omen for the future. Are you suffering, Agatha?"

"Not just now. I suppose I look sadly changed for the worse since you saw me last?"

But for the feverish brightness of her eyes, she would have looked like a corpse. Her wrinkled forehead, her hollow cheeks, her white lips told their terrible tale of the suffering of years. The ghastly appearance of her face was heightened by the furnishing of the room. This doomed woman, dying slowly day by day, delighted in bright colors and sumptuous materials. The paper on the walls, the curtains, the carpet presented the hues of the rainbow. She lay on a couch covered with purple silk, under draperies of green velvet to keep her warm. Rich lace hid her scanty hair, turning prematurely gray; brilliant rings glittered on her bony fingers. The room was in a blaze of light from lamps and candles. Even the wine at her side that kept her alive had been decanted into a bottle of lustrous Venetian glass. "My grave is open," she used to say; "and I want all these beautiful things to keep me from looking at it. I should die at once, if I was left in the dark."

Her brother sat by the couch, thinking "Shall I tell you what is in your mind?" she asked.

Mirabel humored the caprice of the moment. "Tell me!" he said.

"You want to know what I think of Emily," she answered. "Your letter told me you were in love; but I didn't believe your letter. I have always doubted whether you were capable of feeling true love—until I saw Emily. The moment she entered the room, I knew that I had never properly appreciated my brother. You are in love with her, Miles; and you are a better man than I thought you. Does that express my opinion?"

Mirabel took her wasted hand, and kissed it gratefully.

"What a position I am in!" he said. "To love her as I love her; and, if she knew the truth, to be the object of her horror—to be the man whom she would hunt to the scaffold, as an act of duty to the memory of her father!"

"You have left out the worst part of it," Mrs. Delvin reminded him. "You have bound yourself to help her to find the man. Your one hope of persuading her to become your wife rests on your success in finding him. And you are the man. There is your situation! You can't submit to it. How can you escape from it?"

"You are trying to frighten me, Agatha."

"I am trying to encourage you to face your position boldly."

"I am doing my best," Mirabel said, with sullen resignation. "Fortune has favored me so far. I have, really and truly, been unable to satisfy Emily by discovering Miss Jethro. She has left the place at which I saw her last—there is no trace to be found of her—and Emily knows it."

"Don't forget," Mrs. Delvin replied, "that there is a trace to be found of

Mrs. Rook, and that Emily expects you to follow it."

Mirabel shuddered. "I am surrounded by dangers, whichever way I look," he said. "Do what I may, it turns out to be wrong. I was wrong, perhaps, when I brought Emily here."

"No!"

"I could easily make an excuse," Mirabel persisted "and take her back to London."

"And for all you know to the contrary," his wiser sister replied, "Mrs. Rook may go to London; and you may take Emily back in time to receive her at the cottage. In every way you are safer in my old tower. And—don't forget—you have got my money to help you, if you want it. In my belief, Miles, you will want it."

"You are the dearest and best of sisters! What do you recommend me to do?"

"What you would have been obliged to do," Mrs. Delvin answered, "if you had remained in London. You must go to Redwood Hall tomorrow, as Emily has arranged it. If Mrs. Rook is not there, you must ask for her address in Scotland. If nobody knows the address, you must still bestir yourself in trying to find it. And, when you do fall in with Mrs. Rook—"

"Well?"

"Take care, wherever it may be, that you see her privately."

Mirabel was alarmed. "Don't keep me in suspense," he burst out. "Tell me what you propose."

"Never mind what I propose, to-night. Before I can tell you what I have in my mind, I must know whether Mrs. Rook is in England or Scotland. Bring me that information to-morrow, and I shall have something to say to you. Hark! The wind is rising, the rain is falling. There is a chance of sleep for me—I shall soon hear the sea. Good-night."

"Good-night, dearest—and thank you again, and again!"

CHAPTER LIX. THE ACCIDENT AT BELFORD.

Early in the morning Mirabel set forth for Redwood Hall, in one of the vehicles which Mrs. Delvin still kept at "The Clink" for the convenience of visitors. He returned soon after noon; having obtained information of the whereabout of Mrs. Rook and her husband. When they had last been heard of, they were at Lasswade, near Edinburgh. Whether they had, or had not, obtained the situation of which they were in search, neither Miss Redwood nor any one else at the Hall could tell.

In half an hour more, another horse was harnessed, and Mirabel was on his way to the railway station at Belford, to follow Mrs. Rook at Emily's urgent request. Before his departure, he had an interview with his sister.

Mrs. Delvin was rich enough to believe implicitly in the power of money. Her method of extricating her brother from the serious difficulties that beset him, was to make it worth the while of Mr. and Mrs. Rook to leave England. Their passage to America would be secretly paid; and they would take with them a letter of credit addressed to a banker in New York. If Mirabel failed to discover them, after they had sailed, Emily could not blame his want of devotion to her interests. He understood this; but he remained desponding and irresolute, even with the money in his hands. The one person who could rouse his courage and animate his hope, was also the one person who must know nothing of what had passed between his sister and himself. He had no choice but to leave Emily, without being cheered by her bright looks, invigorated by her inspiriting words. Mirabel went away on his doubtful errand with a heavy heart.

"The Clink" was so far from the nearest post town, that the few letters, usually addressed to the tower, were delivered by private arrangement with a messenger. The man's punctuality depended on the convenience of his superiors employed at the office. Sometimes he arrived early, and sometimes he arrived late. On this particular morning he presented himself, at half past one o'clock, with a letter for Emily; and when Mrs. Ellmother smartly reproved him for the delay, he coolly attributed it to the hospitality of friends whom he had met on the road.

The letter, directed to Emily at the cottage, had been forwarded from London by the person left in charge. It addressed her as "Honored Miss." She turned at once to the end—and discovered the signature of Mrs. Rook!

"And Mr. Mirabel has gone," Emily exclaimed, "just when his presence is of the greatest importance to us!"

Shrewd Mrs. Ellmother suggested that it might be as well to read the letter first—and then to form an opinion.

Emily read it.

"Lasswade, near Edinburgh, Sept. 26th.

"HONORED MISS—I take up my pen to bespeak your kind sympathy for my husband and myself; two old people thrown on the world again by the death of our excellent master. We are under a month's notice to leave Redwood Hall.

"Hearing of a situation at this place (also that our expenses would be paid if we applied personally), we got leave of absence, and made our application. The lady and her son are either the stingiest people that ever lived—or they have taken a dislike to me and my husband, and they make money a means of getting rid of us easily. Suffice it to say that we have refused to accept starvation wages, and that we are still out of place. It is just possible that you may have heard of something to suit us. So I write at once, knowing that good chances are often lost through needless delay.

"We stop at Belford on our way back, to see some friends of my husband, and we hope to get to Redwood Hall in good time on the 28th. Would you please address me to care of Miss Redwood, in case you know of any good situation for which we could apply. Perhaps we may be driven to try our luck in London. In this case, will you permit me to have the honor of presenting my respects, as I ventured to propose when I wrote to you a little time since.

"I beg to remain, Honored Miss,

"Your humble servant,

"R. ROOK."

Emily handed the letter to Mrs. Ellmother. "Read it," she said, "and tell me what you think."

"I think you had better be careful."

"Careful of Mrs. Rook?"

"Yes—and careful of Mrs. Delvin too."

Emily was astonished. "Are you really speaking seriously?" she said. "Mrs. Delvin is a most interesting person; so patient under her sufferings; so kind, so clever; so interested in all that interests me. I shall take the letter to her at once, and ask her advice."

"Have your own way, miss. I can't tell you why—but I don't like her!"

Mrs. Delvin's devotion to the interests of her guest took even Emily by surprise. After reading Mrs. Rook's letter, she rang the bell on her table in a frenzy of impatience. "My brother must be instantly recalled," she said. "Telegraph to him in your own name, telling him what has happened. He will find the message waiting for him, at the end of his journey."

The groom, summoned by the bell, was ordered to saddle the third and last horse left in the stables; to take the telegram to Belford, and to wait there until the answer arrived.

"How far is it to Redwood Hall?" Emily asked, when the man had received his orders.

"Ten miles," Mrs. Delvin answered.

"How can I get there to-day?"

"My dear, you can't get there."

"Pardon me, Mrs. Delvin, I must get there."

"Pardon me. My brother represents you in this matter. Leave it to my brother."

The tone taken by Mirabel's sister was positive, to say the least of it.

Emily thought of what her faithful old servant had said, and began to doubt her own discretion in so readily showing the letter. The mistake—if a mistake it was—had however been committed; and, wrong or right, she was not disposed to occupy the subordinate position which Mrs. Delvin had assigned to her.

"If you will look at Mrs. Rook's letter again," Emily replied, "you will see that I ought to answer it. She supposes I am in London."

"Do you propose to tell Mrs. Rook that you are in this house?" Mrs. Delvin asked.

"Certainly."

"You had better consult my brother, before you take any responsibility on yourself."

Emily kept her temper. "Allow me to remind you," she said, "that Mr. Mirabel is not acquainted with Mrs. Rook—and that I am. If I speak to her personally, I can do much to assist the object of our inquiries, before he returns. She is not an easy woman to deal with—"

"And therefore," Mrs. Delvin interposed, "the sort of person who requires careful handling by a man like my brother—a man of the world."

"The sort of person, as I venture to think," Emily persisted, "whom I ought to see with as little loss of time as possible."

Mrs. Delvin waited a while before she replied. In her condition of health, anxiety was not easy to bear. Mrs. Rook's letter and Emily's obstinacy had seriously irritated her. But, like all persons of ability, she was capable, when there was serious occasion for it, of exerting self-control. She really liked and admired Emily; and, as the elder woman and the hostess, she set an example of forbearance and good humor.

"It is out of my power to send you to Redwood Hall at once," she resumed. "The only one of my three horses now at your disposal is the horse which took my brother to the Hall this morning. A distance, there and back, of twenty miles. You are not in too great a hurry, I am sure, to allow the horse time to rest?"

Emily made her excuses with perfect grace and sincerity. "I had no idea the distance was so great," she confessed. "I will wait, dear Mrs. Delvin, as long as you like."

They parted as good friends as ever—with a certain reserve, nevertheless, on either side. Emily's eager nature was depressed and irritated by the prospect of delay. Mrs. Delvin, on the other hand (devoted to her brother's interests), thought hopefully of obstacles which might present themselves with the lapse of time. The horse might prove to be incapable of further exertion for that day. Or the threatening aspect of the weather might end in a storm.

But the hours passed—and the sky cleared—and the horse was reported to be fit for work again. Fortune was against the lady of the tower; she had no choice but to submit.

Mrs. Delvin had just sent word to Emily that the carriage would be ready for her in ten minutes, when the coachman who had driven Mirabel to Belford returned. He brought news which agreeably surprised both the ladies. Mirabel had reached the station five minutes too late; the coachman had left him waiting the arrival of the next train to the North. He would now receive the telegraphic message at Belford, and might return immediately by taking the groom's horse. Mrs. Delvin left it to Emily to decide whether she would proceed by herself to Redwood Hall, or wait for Mirabel's return.

Under the changed circumstances, Emily would have acted ungraciously if she had persisted in holding to her first intention. She consented to wait.

The sea still remained calm. In the stillness of the moorland solitude on the western side of "The Clink," the rapid steps of a horse were heard at some little distance on the highroad.

Emily ran out, followed by careful Mrs. Ellmother, expecting to meet Mirabel.

She was disappointed: it was the groom who had returned. As he pulled up at the house, and dismounted, Emily noticed that the man looked excited.

488

"Is there anything wrong?" she asked.

"There has been an accident, miss."

"Not to Mr. Mirabel!"

"No, no, miss. An accident to a poor foolish woman, traveling from Lasswade."

Emily looked at Mrs. Ellmother. "It can't be Mrs. Rook!" she said.

"That's the name, miss! She got out before the train had quite stopped, and fell on the platform."

"Was she hurt?"

"Seriously hurt, as I heard. They carried her into a house hard by—and sent for the doctor."

"Was Mr. Mirabel one of the people who helped her?"

"He was on the other side of the platform, miss; waiting for the train from London. I got to the station and gave him the telegram, just as the accident took place. We crossed over to hear more about it. Mr. Mirabel was telling me that he would return to 'The Clink' on my horse—when he heard the woman's name mentioned. Upon that, he changed his mind and went to the house."

"Was he let in?"

"The doctor wouldn't hear of it. He was making his examination; and he said nobody was to be in the room but her husband and the woman of the house."

"Is Mr. Mirabel waiting to see her?"

"Yes, miss. He said he would wait all day, if necessary; and he gave me this bit of a note to take to the mistress."

Emily turned to Mrs. Ellmother. "It's impossible to stay here, not knowing whether Mrs. Rook is going to live or die," she said. "I shall go to

Belford—and you will go with me."

The groom interfered. "I beg your pardon, miss. It was Mr. Mirabel's most particular wish that you were not, on any account, to go to Belford."

"Why not?"

"He didn't say."

Emily eyed the note in the man's hand with well-grounded distrust. In all probability, Mirabel's object in writing was to instruct his sister to prevent her guest from going to Belford. The carriage was waiting at the door. With her usual promptness of resolution, Emily decided on taking it for granted that she was free to use as she pleased a carriage which had been already placed at her disposal.

"Tell your mistress," she said to the groom, "that I am going to Belford instead of to Redwood Hall."

In a minute more, she and Mrs. Ellmother were on their way to join Mirabel at the station.

CHAPTER LX. OUTSIDE THE ROOM.

Emily found Mirabel in the waiting room at Belford. Her sudden appearance might well have amazed him; but his face expressed a more serious emotion than surprise—he looked at her as if she had alarmed him.

"Didn't you get my message?" he asked. "I told the groom I wished you to wait for my return. I sent a note to my sister, in case he made any mistake."

"The man made no mistake," Emily answered. "I was in too great a hurry to be able to speak with Mrs. Delvin. Did you really suppose I could endure the suspense of waiting till you came back? Do you think I can be of no use—I who know Mrs. Rook?"

"They won't let you see her."

"Why not? You seem to be waiting to see her."

"I am waiting for the return of the rector of Belford. He is at Berwick;

and he has been sent for at Mrs. Rook's urgent request."

"Is she dying?"

"She is in fear of death—whether rightly or wrongly, I don't know. There is some internal injury from the fall. I hope to see her when the rector returns. As a brother clergyman, I may with perfect propriety ask him to use his influence in my favor."

"I am glad to find you so eager about it."

"I am always eager in your interests."

"Don't think me ungrateful," Emily replied gently. "I am no stranger to Mrs. Rook; and, if I send in my name, I may be able to see her before the clergyman returns."

She stopped. Mirabel suddenly moved so as to place himself between her and the door. "I must really beg of you to give up that idea," he said; "you don't know what horrid sight you may see—what dreadful agonies of pain this unhappy woman may be suffering."

His manner suggested to Emily that he might be acting under some motive which he was unwilling to acknowledge. "If you have a reason for wishing that I should keep away from Mrs. Rook," she said, "let me hear what it is. Surely we trust each other? I have done my best to set the example, at any rate."

Mirabel seemed to be at a loss for a reply.

While he was hesitating, the station-master passed the door. Emily asked him to direct her to the house in which Mrs. Rook had been received. He led the way to the end of the platform, and pointed to the house. Emily and Mrs. Ellmother immediately left the station. Mirabel accompanied them, still remonstrating, still raising obstacles.

The house door was opened by an old man. He looked reproachfully at Mirabel. "You have been told already," he said, "that no strangers are to see my wife?"

Encouraged by discovering that the man was Mr. Rook, Emily mentioned her name. "Perhaps you may have heard Mrs. Rook speak of me," she added.

"I've heard her speak of you oftentimes."

"What does the doctor say?"

"He thinks she may get over it. She doesn't believe him."

"Will you say that I am anxious to see her, if she feels well enough to receive me?"

Mr. Rook looked at Mrs. Ellmother. "Are there two of you wanting to go upstairs?" he inquired.

"This is my old friend and servant," Emily answered. "She will wait for me down here."

"She can wait in the parlor; the good people of this house are well known to me." He pointed to the parlor door—and then led the way to the first floor. Emily followed him. Mirabel, as obstinate as ever, followed Emily.

Mr. Rook opened a door at the end of the landing; and, turning round to speak to Emily, noticed Mirabel standing behind her. Without making any remarks, the old man pointed significantly down the stairs. His resolution was evidently immovable. Mirabel appealed to Emily to help him.

"She will see me, if you ask her," he said, "Let me wait here?"

The sound of his voice was instantly followed by a cry from the bed-chamber—a cry of terror.

Mr. Rook hurried into the room, and closed the door. In less than a minute, he opened it again, with doubt and horror plainly visible in his face. He stepped up to Mirabel—eyed him with the closest scrutiny—and drew back again with a look of relief.

"She's wrong," he said; "you are not the man."

This strange proceeding startled Emily.

"What man do you mean?" she asked.

492

Mr. Rook took no notice of the question. Still looking at Mirabel, he pointed down the stairs once more. With vacant eyes—moving mechanically, like a sleep-walker in his dream—Mirabel silently obeyed. Mr. Rook turned to Emily.

"Are you easily frightened?" he said

"I don't understand you," Emily replied. "Who is going to frighten me? Why did you speak to Mr. Mirabel in that strange way?"

Mr. Rook looked toward the bedroom door. "Maybe you'll hear why, inside there. If I could have my way, you shouldn't see her—but she's not to be reasoned with. A caution, miss. Don't be too ready to believe what my wife may say to you. She's had a fright." He opened the door. "In my belief," he whispered, "she's off her head."

Emily crossed the threshold. Mr. Rook softly closed the door behind her.

CHAPTER LXI. INSIDE THE ROOM.

A decent elderly woman was seated at the bedside. She rose, and spoke to Emily with a mingling of sorrow and confusion strikingly expressed on her face. "It isn't my fault," she said, "that Mrs. Rook receives you in this manner; I am obliged to humor her."

She drew aside, and showed Mrs. Rook with her head supported by many pillows, and her face strangely hidden from view under a veil. Emily started back in horror. "Is her face injured?" she asked.

Mrs. Rook answered the question herself. Her voice was low and weak; but she still spoke with the same nervous hurry of articulation which had been remarked by Alban Morris, on the day when she asked him to direct her to Netherwoods.

"Not exactly injured," she explained; "but one's appearance is a matter of some anxiety even on one's death-bed. I am disfigured by a thoughtless use of water, to bring me to when I had my fall—and I can't get at my toilet-things to put myself right again. I don't wish to shock you. Please excuse the veil."

Emily remembered the rouge on her cheeks, and the dye on her hair, when they had first seen each other at the school. Vanity—of all human frailties the longest-lived—still held its firmly-rooted place in this woman's nature; superior to torment of conscience, unassailable by terror of death!

The good woman of the house waited a moment before she left the room. "What shall I say," she asked, "if the clergyman comes?"

Mrs. Rook lifted her hand solemnly "Say," she answered, "that a dying sinner is making atonement for sin. Say this young lady is present, by the decree of an all-wise Providence. No mortal creature must disturb us." Her hand dropped back heavily on the bed. "Are we alone?" she asked.

"We are alone," Emily answered. "What made you scream just before I came in?"

"No! I can't allow you to remind me of that," Mrs. Rook protested. "I must compose myself. Be quiet. Let me think."

Recovering her composure, she also recovered that sense of enjoyment in talking of herself, which was one of the marked peculiarities in her character.

"You will excuse me if I exhibit religion," she resumed. "My dear parents were exemplary people; I was most carefully brought up. Are you pious? Let us hope so."

Emily was once more reminded of the past.

The bygone time returned to her memory—the time when she had accepted Sir Jervis Redwood's offer of employment, and when Mrs. Rook had arrived at the school to be her traveling companion to the North. The wretched creature had entirely forgotten her own loose talk, after she had drunk Miss Ladd's good wine to the last drop in the bottle. As she was boasting now of her piety, so she had boasted then of her lost faith and hope, and had mockingly declared her free-thinking opinions to be the result of her ill-assorted marriage. Forgotten—all forgotten, in this later time of pain and fear. Prostrate under the dread of death, her innermost nature—stripped of the concealments of her later life—was revealed to view. The early religious training, at which she had scoffed in the insolence of health and strength, revealed its latent influence—intermitted, but a living influence always from first to last. Mrs. Rook was tenderly mindful of her exemplary parents, and proud of exhibiting religion, on the bed from which she was never to rise again.

"Did I tell you that I am a miserable sinner?" she asked, after an interval of silence.

Emily could endure it no longer. "Say that to the clergyman," she answered—"not to me."

"Oh, but I must say it," Mrs. Rook insisted. "I am a miserable sinner. Let me give you an instance of it," she continued, with a shameless relish of the memory of her own frailties. "I have been a drinker, in my time. Anything was welcome, when the fit was on me, as long as it got into my head. Like other persons in liquor, I sometimes talked of things that had better have been kept secret. We bore that in mind—my old man and I—-when we were engaged by Sir Jervis. Miss Redwood wanted to put us in the next bedroom to hers—a risk not to be run. I might have talked of the murder at the inn; and she might have heard me. Please to remark a curious thing. Whatever else I might let out, when I was in my cups, not a word about the pocketbook ever dropped from me. You will ask how I know it. My dear, I should have heard of it from my husband, if I had let that out—and he is as much in the dark as you are. Wonderful are the workings of the human mind, as the poet says; and drink drowns care, as the proverb says. But can drink deliver a person from fear by day, and fear by night? I believe, if I had dropped a word about the pocketbook, it would have sobered me in an instant. Have you any remark to make on this curious circumstance?"

Thus far, Emily had allowed the woman to ramble on, in the hope of getting information which direct inquiry might fail to produce. It was impossible, however, to pass over the allusion to the pocketbook. After giving her time to recover from the exhaustion which her heavy breathing sufficiently revealed, Emily put the question:

"Who did the pocketbook belong to?"

"Wait a little," said Mrs. Rook. "Everything in its right place, is my motto. I mustn't begin with the pocketbook. Why did I begin with it? Do you think this veil on my face confuses me? Suppose I take it off. But you must promise first—solemnly promise you won't look at my face. How can I tell you about the murder (the murder is part of my confession, you know), with this lace tickling my skin? Go away—and stand there with your back to me. Thank you. Now I'll take it off. Ha! the air feels refreshing; I know what I am about. Good heavens, I have forgotten something! I have forgotten him. And after such a fright as he gave me! Did you see him on the landing?"

"Who are you talking of?" Emily asked.

Mrs. Rook's failing voice sank lower still.

"Come closer," she said, "this must be whispered. Who am I talking of?" she repeated. "I am talking of the man who slept in the other bed at the inn; the man who did the deed with his own razor. He was gone when I looked into the outhouse in the gray of the morning. Oh, I have done my duty! I have told Mr. Rook to keep an eye on him downstairs. You haven't an idea how obstinate and stupid my husband is. He says I couldn't know the man, because I didn't see him. Ha! there's such a thing as hearing, when you don't see. I heard—and I knew it again."

Emily turned cold from head to foot.

"What did you know again?" she said.

"His voice," Mrs. Rook answered. "I'll swear to his voice before all the judges in England."

Emily rushed to the bed. She looked at the woman who had said those dreadful words, speechless with horror.

"You're breaking your promise!" cried Mrs. Rook. "You false girl, you're breaking your promise!"

She snatched at the veil, and put it on again. The sight of her face, momentary as it had been, reassured Emily. Her wild eyes, made wilder still by the blurred stains of rouge below them, half washed away—her disheveled hair, with streaks of gray showing through the dye—presented a spectacle which would have been grotesque under other circumstances, but which now reminded Emily of Mr. Rook's last words; warning her not to believe what his wife said, and even declaring his conviction that her intellect was deranged. Emily drew back from the bed, conscious of an overpowering sense of self-reproach. Although it was only for a moment, she had allowed her faith in Mirabel to be shaken by a woman who was out of her mind.

"Try to forgive me," she said. "I didn't willfully break my promise; you frightened me."

Mrs. Rook began to cry. "I was a handsome woman in my time," she murmured. "You would say I was handsome still, if the clumsy fools about me had not spoiled my appearance. Oh, I do feel so weak! Where's my medicine?"

The bottle was on the table. Emily gave her the prescribed dose, and revived her failing strength.

"I am an extraordinary person," she resumed. "My resolution has always been the admiration of every one who knew me. But my mind feels—how shall I express it?—a little vacant. Have mercy on my poor wicked soul! Help me."

"How can I help you?"

"I want to recollect. Something happened in the summer time, when we were talking at Netherwoods. I mean when that impudent master at the school showed his suspicions of me. (Lord! how he frightened me, when he turned up afterward at Sir Jervis's house.) You must have seen yourself he suspected me. How did he show it?"

"He showed you my locket," Emily answered.

"Oh, the horrid reminder of the murder!" Mrs. Rook exclaimed. "I didn't mention it: don't blame Me. You poor innocent, I have something dreadful to tell you."

Emily's horror of the woman forced her to speak. "Don't tell me!" she cried. "I know more than you suppose; I know what I was ignorant of when you saw the locket."

Mrs. Rook took offense at the interruption.

"Clever as you are, there's one thing you don't know," she said. "You asked me, just now, who the pocketbook belonged to. It belonged to your father. What's the matter? Are you crying?"

Emily was thinking of her father. The pocketbook was the last present she had given to him—a present on his birthday. "Is it lost?" she asked sadly.

"No; it's not lost. You will hear more of it directly. Dry your eyes, and expect something interesting—I'm going to talk about love. Love, my dear, means myself. Why shouldn't it? I'm not the only nice-looking woman, married to an old man, who has had a lover."

"Wretch! what has that got to do with it?"

"Everything, you rude girl! My lover was like the rest of them; he would bet on race-horses, and he lost. He owned it to me, on the day when your father came to our inn. He said, 'I must find the money—or be off to America, and say good-by forever.' I was fool enough to be fond of him. It broke my heart to hear him talk in that way. I said, 'If I find the money, and more than the money, will you take me with you wherever you go?' Of course, he said Yes. I suppose you have heard of the inquest held at our old place by the coroner and jury? Oh, what idiots! They believed I was asleep on the night of the murder. I never closed my eyes—I was so miserable, I was so tempted."

"Tempted? What tempted you?"

"Do you think I had any money to spare? Your father's pocketbook tempted me. I had seen him open it, to pay his bill over-night. It was full of bank-notes. Oh, what an overpowering thing love is! Perhaps you have known it yourself."

Emily's indignation once more got the better of her prudence. "Have you no feeling of decency on your death-bed!" she said.

Mrs. Rook forgot her piety; she was ready with an impudent rejoinder. "You hot-headed little woman, your time will come," she answered. "But you're right—I am wandering from the point; I am not sufficiently sensible of this solemn occasion. By-the-by, do you notice my language? I inherit correct English from my mother—a cultivated person, who married beneath her. My paternal grandfather was a gentleman. Did I tell you that there came a time, on that dreadful night, when I could stay in bed no longer? The pocketbook—I did nothing but think of that devilish pocketbook, full of bank-notes. My husband was fast asleep all the time. I got a chair and stood on it. I looked into the place where the two men were sleeping, through the glass in the top of the door. Your father was awake; he was walking up and down the room. What do you say? Was he agitated? I didn't notice. I don't know whether the other man was asleep or awake. I saw nothing but the pocketbook stuck under the pillow, half in and half out. Your father kept on walking up and down. I thought to myself, 'I'll wait till he gets tired, and then I'll have another look at the pocketbook.' Where's the wine? The doctor said I might have a glass of wine when I wanted it."

Emily found the wine and gave it to her. She shuddered as she accidentally touched Mrs. Rook's hand.

The wine helped the sinking woman.

"I must have got up more than once," she resumed. "And more than once my heart must have failed me. I don't clearly remember what I did, till the gray of the morning came. I think that must have been the last time I looked through the glass in the door."

She began to tremble. She tore the veil off her face. She cried out piteously, "Lord, be merciful to me a sinner! Come here," she said to Emily. "Where are you? No! I daren't tell you what I saw; I daren't tell you what I did. When you're possessed by the devil, there's nothing, nothing, nothing you can't do! Where did I find the courage to unlock the door? Where did I find the courage to go in? Any other woman would have lost her senses, when she found blood on her fingers after taking the pocketbook—"

Emily's head swam; her heart beat furiously—she staggered to the door, and opened it to escape from the room.

"I'm guilty of robbing him; but I'm innocent of his blood!" Mrs. Rook called after her wildly. "The deed was done—the yard door was wide open, and the man was gone—when I looked in for the last time. Come back, come back!"

Emily looked round.

"I can't go near you," she said, faintly.

"Come near enough to see this."

She opened her bed-gown at the throat, and drew up a loop of ribbon over her head. The pocketbook was attached to the ribbon. She held it out.

"Your father's book," she said. "Won't you take your father's book?"

For a moment, and only for a moment, Emily was repelled by the profanation associated with her birthday gift. Then, the loving remembrance of the dear hands that had so often touched that relic, drew the faithful daughter back to the woman whom she abhorred. Her eyes rested tenderly on the book. Before it had lain in that guilty bosom, it had been his book. The beloved memory was all that was left to her now; the beloved memory consecrated it to her hand. She took the book.

"Open it," said Mrs. Rook.

There were two five-pound bank-notes in it.

"His?" Emily asked.

"No; mine—the little I have been able to save toward restoring what I stole."

"Oh!" Emily cried, "is there some good in this woman, after all?"

"There's no good in the woman!" Mrs. Rook answered desperately. "There's nothing but fear—fear of hell now; fear of the pocketbook in the past time. Twice I tried to destroy it—and twice it came back, to remind me of the duty that I owed to my miserable soul. I tried to throw it into the fire. It struck

500

the bar, and fell back into the fender at my feet. I went out, and cast it into the well. It came back again in the first bucket of water that was drawn up. From that moment, I began to save what I could. Restitution! Atonement! I tell you the book found a tongue—and those were the grand words it dinned in my ears, morning and night." She stooped to fetch her breath—stopped, and struck her bosom. "I hid it here, so that no person should see it, and no person take it from me. Superstition? Oh, yes, superstition! Shall tell you something? You may find yourself superstitious, if you are ever cut to the heart as I was. He left me! The man I had disgraced myself for, deserted me on the day when I gave him the stolen money. He suspected it was stolen; he took care of his own cowardly self—and left me to the hard mercy of the law, if the theft was found out. What do you call that, in the way of punishment? Haven't I suffered? Haven't I made atonement? Be a Christian—say you forgive me."

"I do forgive you."

"Say you will pray for me."

"I will."

"Ah! that comforts me! Now you can go."

Emily looked at her imploringly. "Don't send me away, knowing no more of the murder than I knew when I came here! Is there nothing, really nothing, you can tell me?"

Mrs. Rook pointed to the door.

"Haven't I told you already? Go downstairs, and see the wretch who escaped in the dawn of the morning!"

"Gently, ma'am, gently! You're talking too loud," cried a mocking voice from outside.

"It's only the doctor," said Mrs. Rook. She crossed her hands over her bosom with a deep-drawn sigh. "I want no doctor, now. My peace is made with my Maker. I'm ready for death; I'm fit for Heaven. Go away! go away!"

501

CHAPTER LXII. DOWNSTAIRS.

In a moment more, the doctor came in—a brisk, smiling, self-sufficient man—smartly dressed, with a flower in his button-hole. A stifling odor of musk filled the room, as he drew out his handkerchief with a flourish, and wiped his forehead.

"Plenty of hard work in my line, just now," he said. "Hullo, Mrs. Rook! somebody has been allowing you to excite yourself. I heard you, before I opened the door. Have you been encouraging her to talk?" he asked, turning to Emily, and shaking his finger at her with an air of facetious remonstrance.

Incapable of answering him; forgetful of the ordinary restraints of social intercourse—with the one doubt that preserved her belief in Mirabel, eager for confirmation—Emily signed to this stranger to follow her into a corner of the room, out of hearing. She made no excuses: she took no notice of his look of surprise. One hope was all she could feel, one word was all she could say, after that second assertion of Mirabel's guilt. Indicating Mrs. Rook by a glance at the bed, she whispered the word:

"Mad?"

Flippant and familiar, the doctor imitated her; he too looked at the bed.

"No more mad than you are, miss. As I said just now, my patient has been exciting herself; I daresay she has talked a little wildly in consequence. Hers isn't a brain to give way, I can tell you. But there's somebody else—"

Emily had fled from the room. He had destroyed her last fragment of belief in Mirabel's innocence. She was on the landing trying to console herself, when the doctor joined her.

"Are you acquainted with the gentleman downstairs?" he asked.

"What gentleman?"

"I haven't heard his name; he looks like a clergyman. If you know him—"

"I do know him. I can't answer questions! My mind—"

"Steady your mind, miss! and take your friend home as soon as you can. He hasn't got Mrs. Rook's hard brain; he's in a state of nervous prostration, which may end badly. Do you know where he lives?"

"He is staying with his sister—Mrs. Delvin."

"Mrs. Delvin! she's a friend and patient of mine. Say I'll look in to-morrow morning, and see what I can do for her brother. In the meantime, get him to bed, and to rest; and don't be afraid of giving him brandy."

The doctor returned to the bedroom. Emily heard Mrs. Ellmother's voice below.

"Are you up there, miss?"

"Yes."

Mrs. Ellmother ascended the stairs. "It was an evil hour," she said, "that you insisted on going to this place. Mr. Mirabel—" The sight of Emily's face suspended the next words on her lips. She took the poor young mistress in her motherly arms. "Oh, my child! what has happened to you?"

"Don't ask me now. Give me your arm—let us go downstairs."

"You won't be startled when you see Mr. Mirabel—will you, my dear? I wouldn't let them disturb you; I said nobody should speak to you but myself. The truth is, Mr. Mirabel has had a dreadful fright. What are you looking for?"

"Is there a garden here? Any place where we can breathe the fresh air?"

There was a courtyard at the back of the house. They found their way to it. A bench was placed against one of the walls. They sat down.

"Shall I wait till you're better before I say any more?" Mrs. Ellmother asked. "No? You want to hear about Mr. Mirabel? My dear, he came into the parlor where I was; and Mr. Rook came in too——and waited, looking at him. Mr. Mirabel sat down in a corner, in a dazed state as I thought. It wasn't for long. He jumped up, and clapped his hand on his heart as if his heart hurt him. 'I must and will know what's going on upstairs,' he says. Mr.

Rook pulled him back, and told him to wait till the young lady came down. Mr. Mirabel wouldn't hear of it. 'Your wife's frightening her,' he says; 'your wife's telling her horrible things about me.' He was taken on a sudden with a shivering fit; his eyes rolled, and his teeth chattered. Mr. Rook made matters worse; he lost his temper. 'I'm damned,' he says, 'if I don't begin to think you are the man, after all; I've half a mind to send for the police.' Mr. Mirabel dropped into his chair. His eyes stared, his mouth fell open. I took hold of his hand. Cold—cold as ice. What it all meant I can't say. Oh, miss, you know! Let me tell you the rest of it some other time."

Emily insisted on hearing more. "The end!" she cried. "How did it end?"

"I don't know how it might have ended, if the doctor hadn't come in—to pay his visit, you know, upstairs. He said some learned words. When he came to plain English, he asked if anybody had frightened the gentleman. I said Mr. Rook had frightened him. The doctor says to Mr. Rook, 'Mind what you are about. If you frighten him again, you may have his death to answer for.' That cowed Mr. Rook. He asked what he had better do. 'Give me some brandy for him first,' says the doctor; 'and then get him home at once.' I found the brandy, and went away to the inn to order the carriage. Your ears are quicker than mine, miss—do I hear it now?"

They rose, and went to the house door. The carriage was there.

Still cowed by what the doctor had said, Mr. Rook appeared, carefully leading Mirabel out. He had revived under the action of the stimulant. Passing Emily he raised his eyes to her—trembled—and looked down again. When Mr. Rook opened the door of the carriage he paused, with one of his feet on the step. A momentary impulse inspired him with a false courage, and brought a flush into his ghastly face. He turned to Emily.

"May I speak to you?" he asked.

She started back from him. He looked at Mrs. Ellmother. "Tell her I am innocent," he said. The trembling seized on him again. Mr. Rook was obliged to lift him into the carriage.

Emily caught at Mrs. Ellmother's arm. "You go with him," she said. "I can't."

"How are you to get back, miss?"

She turned away and spoke to the coachman. "I am not very well. I want the fresh air—I'll sit by you."

Mrs. Ellmother remonstrated and protested, in vain. As Emily had determined it should be, so it was.

"Has he said anything?" she asked, when they had arrived at their journey's end.

"He has been like a man frozen up; he hasn't said a word; he hasn't even moved."

"Take him to his sister; and tell her all that you know. Be careful to repeat what the doctor said. I can't face Mrs. Delvin. Be patient, my good old friend; I have no secrets from you. Only wait till to-morrow; and leave me by myself to-night."

Alone in her room, Emily opened her writing-case. Searching among the letters in it, she drew out a printed paper. It was the Handbill describing the man who had escaped from the inn, and offering a reward for the discovery of him.

At the first line of the personal description of the fugitive, the paper dropped from her hand. Burning tears forced their way into her eyes. Feeling for her handkerchief, she touched the pocketbook which she had received from Mrs. Rook. After a little hesitation she took it out. She looked at it. She opened it.

The sight of the bank-notes repelled her; she hid them in one of the pockets of the book. There was a second pocket which she had not yet examined. She pat her hand into it, and, touching something, drew out a letter.

The envelope (already open) was addressed to "James Brown, Esq., Post Office, Zeeland." Would it be inconsistent with her respect for her father's memory to examine the letter? No; a glance would decide whether she ought to read it or not.

It was without date or address; a startling letter to look at—for it only contained three words:

"I say No."

The words were signed in initials:

"S. J."

In the instant when she read the initials, the name occurred to her.

Sara Jethro.

CHAPTER LXIII. THE DEFENSE OF MIRABEL.

The discovery of the letter gave a new direction to Emily's thoughts—and so, for the time at least, relieved her mind from the burden that weighed on it. To what question, on her father's part, had "I say No" been Miss Jethro's brief and stern reply? Neither letter nor envelope offered the slightest hint that might assist inquiry; even the postmark had been so carelessly impressed that it was illegible.

Emily was still pondering over the three mysterious words, when she was interrupted by Mrs. Ellmother's voice at the door.

"I must ask you to let me come in, miss; though I know you wished to be left by yourself till to-morrow. Mrs. Delvin says she must positively see you to-night. It's my belief that she will send for the servants, and have herself carried in here, if you refuse to do what she asks. You needn't be afraid of seeing Mr. Mirabel."

"Where is he?"

"His sister has given up her bedroom to him," Mrs. Ellmother answered. "She thought of your feelings before she sent me here—and had the curtains closed between the sitting-room and the bedroom. I suspect my nasty temper misled me, when I took a dislike to Mrs. Delvin. She's a good creature; I'm sorry you didn't go to her as soon as we got back."

506

"Did she seem to be angry, when she sent you here?"

"Angry! She was crying when I left her."

Emily hesitated no longer.

She noticed a remarkable change in the invalid's sitting-room—so brilliantly lighted on other occasions—the moment she entered it. The lamps were shaded, and the candles were all extinguished. "My eyes don't bear the light so well as usual," Mrs. Delvin said. "Come and sit near me, Emily; I hope to quiet your mind. I should be grieved if you left my house with a wrong impression of me."

Knowing what she knew, suffering as she must have suffered, the quiet kindness of her tone implied an exercise of self-restraint which appealed irresistibly to Emily's sympathies. "Forgive me," she said, "for having done you an injustice. I am ashamed to think that I shrank from seeing you when I returned from Belford."

"I will endeavor to be worthy of your better opinion of me," Mrs. Delvin replied. "In one respect at least, I may claim to have had your best interests at heart—while we were still personally strangers. I tried to prevail on my poor brother to own the truth, when he discovered the terrible position in which he was placed toward you. He was too conscious of the absence of any proof which might induce you to believe him, if he attempted to defend himself—in one word, he was too timid—to take my advice. He has paid the penalty, and I have paid the penalty, of deceiving you."

Emily started. "In what way have you deceived me?" she asked.

"In the way that was forced on us by our own conduct," Mrs. Delvin said. "We have appeared to help you, without really doing so; we calculated on inducing you to marry my brother, and then (when he could speak with the authority of a husband) on prevailing on you to give up all further inquiries. When you insisted on seeing Mrs. Rook, Miles had the money in his hand to bribe her and her husband to leave England."

"Oh, Mrs. Delvin!"

"I don't attempt to excuse myself. I don't expect you to consider how sorely I was tempted to secure the happiness of my brother's life, by marriage with such a woman as yourself. I don't remind you that I knew—when I put obstacles in your way—that you were blindly devoting yourself to the discovery of an innocent man."

Emily heard her with angry surprise. "Innocent?" she repeated. "Mrs. Rook recognized his voice the instant she heard him speak."

Impenetrable to interruption, Mrs. Delvin went on. "But what I do ask," she persisted, "even after our short acquaintance, is this. Do you suspect me of deliberately scheming to make you the wife of a murderer?"

Emily had never viewed the serious question between them in this light. Warmly, generously, she answered the appeal that had been made to her. "Oh, don't think that of me! I know I spoke thoughtlessly and cruelly to you, just now—"

"You spoke impulsively," Mrs. Delvin interposed; "that was all. My one desire before we part—how can I expect you to remain here, after what has happened?—is to tell you the truth. I have no interested object in view; for all hope of your marriage with my brother is now at an end. May I ask if you have heard that he and your father were strangers, when they met at the inn?"

"Yes; I know that."

"If there had been any conversation between them, when they retired to rest, they might have mentioned their names. But your father was preoccupied; and my brother, after a long day's walk, was so tired that he fell asleep as soon as his head was on the pillow. He only woke when the morning dawned. What he saw when he looked toward the opposite bed might have struck with terror the boldest man that ever lived. His first impulse was naturally to alarm the house. When he got on his feet, he saw his own razor—a blood-stained razor on the bed by the side of the corpse. At that discovery, he lost all control over himself. In a panic of terror, he snatched up his knapsack, unfastened the yard door, and fled from the house. Knowing him, as you and I know him, can we wonder at it? Many a man has been hanged for murder, on circumstantial evidence less direct than the evidence against poor Miles. His horror of his own recollections was so overpowering that he forbade me even to mention the inn at Zeeland in my letters, while he was abroad. 'Never tell me (he wrote) who that wretched murdered stranger was, if I only heard of his name, I believe it would haunt me to my dying day. I ought not to trouble you with these details—and yet, I am surely not without excuse. In the absence of any proof, I cannot expect you to believe as I do in my brother's innocence. But I may at least hope to show you that there is some reason for doubt. Will you give him the benefit of that doubt?"

"Willingly!" Emily replied. "Am I right in supposing that you don't despair of proving his innocence, even yet'?"

"I don't quite despair. But my hopes have grown fainter and fainter, as the years have gone on. There is a person associated with his escape from Zeeland; a person named Jethro—"

"You mean Miss Jethro!"

"Yes. Do you know her?"

"I know her—and my father knew her. I have found a letter, addressed to him, which I have no doubt was written by Miss Jethro. It is barely possible that you may understand what it means. Pray look at it."

"I am quite unable to help you," Mrs. Delvin answered, after reading the letter. "All I know of Miss Jethro is that, but for her interposition, my brother might have fallen into the hands of the police. She saved him."

"Knowing him, of course?"

"That is the remarkable part of it: they were perfect strangers to each other."

"But she must have had some motive."

"There is the foundation of my hope for Miles. Miss Jethro declared, when I wrote and put the question to her, that the one motive by which she was actuated was the motive of mercy. I don't believe her. To my mind, it is

509

in the last degree improbable that she would consent to protect a stranger from discovery, who owned to her (as my brother did) that he was a fugitive suspected of murder. She knows something, I am firmly convinced, of that dreadful event at Zeeland—and she has some reason for keeping it secret. Have you any influence over her?"

"Tell me where I can find her."

"I can't tell you. She has removed from the address at which my brother saw her last. He has made every possible inquiry—without result."

As she replied in those discouraging terms, the curtains which divided Mrs. Delvin's bedroom from her sitting-room were drawn aside. An elderly woman-servant approached her mistress's couch.

"Mr. Mirabel is awake, ma'am. He is very low; I can hardly feel his pulse. Shall I give him some more brandy?"

Mrs. Delvin held out her hand to Emily. "Come to me to-morrow morning," she said—and signed to the servant to wheel her couch into the next room. As the curtain closed over them, Emily heard Mirabel's voice. "Where am I?" he said faintly. "Is it all a dream?"

The prospect of his recovery the next morning was gloomy indeed. He had sunk into a state of deplorable weakness, in mind as well as in body. The little memory of events that he still preserved was regarded by him as the memory of a dream. He alluded to Emily, and to his meeting with her unexpectedly. But from that point his recollection failed him. They had talked of something interesting, he said—but he was unable to remember what it was. And they had waited together at a railway station—but for what purpose he could not tell. He sighed and wondered when Emily would marry him—and so fell asleep again, weaker than ever.

Not having any confidence in the doctor at Belford, Mrs. Delvin had sent an urgent message to a physician at Edinburgh, famous for his skill in treating diseases of the nervous system. "I cannot expect him to reach this remote place, without some delay," she said; "I must bear my suspense as well as I can."

510

"You shall not bear it alone," Emily answered. "I will wait with you till the doctor comes."

Mrs. Delvin lifted her frail wasted hands to Emily's face, drew it a little nearer—and kissed her.

CHAPTER LXIV. ON THE WAY TO LONDON.

The parting words had been spoken. Emily and her companion were on their way to London.

For some little time, they traveled in silence—alone in the railway carriage. After submitting as long as she could to lay an embargo on the use of her tongue, Mrs. Ellmother started the conversation by means of a question: "Do you think Mr. Mirabel will get over it, miss?"

"It's useless to ask me," Emily said. "Even the great man from Edinburgh is not able to decide yet, whether he will recover or not."

"You have taken me into your confidence, Miss Emily, as you promised—and I have got something in my mind in consequence. May I mention it without giving offense?"

"What is it?"

"I wish you had never taken up with Mr. Mirabel."

Emily was silent. Mrs. Ellmother, having a design of her own to accomplish, ventured to speak more plainly. "I often think of Mr. Alban Morris," she proceeded. "I always did like him, and I always shall."

Emily suddenly pulled down her veil. "Don't speak of him!" she said.

"I didn't mean to offend you."

"You don't offend me. You distress me. Oh, how often I have wished—!" She threw herself back in a corner of the carriage and said no more.

Although not remarkable for the possession of delicate tact, Mrs. Ellmother discovered that the best course she could now follow was a course of silence.

Even at the time when she had most implicitly trusted Mirabel, the fear that she might have acted hastily and harshly toward Alban had occasionally troubled Emily's mind. The impression produced by later events had not only intensified this feeling, but had presented the motives of that true friend under an entirely new point of view. If she had been left in ignorance of the manner of her father's death—as Alban had designed to leave her; as she would have been left, but for the treachery of Francine—how happily free she would have been from thoughts which it was now a terror to her to recall. She would have parted from Mirabel, when the visit to the pleasant country house had come to an end, remembering him as an amusing acquaintance and nothing more. He would have been spared, and she would have been spared, the shock that had so cruelly assailed them both. What had she gained by Mrs. Rook's detestable confession? The result had been perpetual disturbance of mind provoked by self-torturing speculations on the subject of the murder. If Mirabel was innocent, who was guilty? The false wife, without pity and without shame—or the brutal husband, who looked capable of any enormity? What was her future to be? How was it all to end? In the despair of that bitter moment—seeing her devoted old servant looking at her with kind compassionate eyes—Emily's troubled spirit sought refuge in impetuous self-betrayal; the very betrayal which she had resolved should not escape her, hardly a minute since!

She bent forward out of her corner, and suddenly drew up her veil. "Do you expect to see Mr. Alban Morris, when we get back?" she asked.

"I should like to see him, miss—if you have no objection."

"Tell him I am ashamed of myself! and say I ask his pardon with all my heart!"

"The Lord be praised!" Mrs. Ellmother burst out—and then, when it was too late, remembered the conventional restraints appropriate to the occasion. "Gracious, what a fool I am!" she said to herself. "Beautiful weather, Miss Emily, isn't it?" she continued, in a desperate hurry to change the subject.

Emily reclined again in her corner of the carriage. She smiled, for the first time since she had become Mrs. Delvin's guest at the tower.

BOOK THE LAST—AT HOME AGAIN.

CHAPTER LXV. CECILIA IN A NEW CHARACTER.

Reaching the cottage at night, Emily found the card of a visitor who had called during the day. It bore the name of "Miss Wyvil," and had a message written on it which strongly excited Emily's curiosity.

"I have seen the telegram which tells your servant that you return to-night. Expect me early to-morrow morning—with news that will deeply interest you."

To what news did Cecilia allude? Emily questioned the woman who had been left in charge of the cottage, and found that she had next to nothing to tell. Miss Wyvil had flushed up, and had looked excited, when she read the telegraphic message—that was all. Emily's impatience was, as usual, not to be concealed. Expert Mrs. Ellmother treated the case in the right way—first with supper, and then with an adjournment to bed. The clock struck twelve, when she put out the young mistress's candle. "Ten hours to pass before Cecilia comes here!" Emily exclaimed. "Not ten minutes," Mrs. Ellmother reminded her, "if you will only go to sleep."

Cecilia arrived before the breakfast-table was cleared; as lovely, as gentle, as affectionate as ever—but looking unusually serious and subdued.

"Out with it at once!" Emily cried. "What have you got to tell me?'

"Perhaps, I had better tell you first," Cecilia said, "that I know what you kept from me when I came here, after you left us at Monksmoor. Don't think, my dear, that I say this by way of complaint. Mr. Alban Morris says you had good reasons for keeping your secret."

"Mr. Alban Morris! Did you get your information from him?"

"Yes. Do I surprise you?"

"More than words can tell!"

"Can you bear another surprise? Mr. Morris has seen Miss Jethro, and has discovered that Mr. Mirabel has been wrongly suspected of a dreadful crime. Our amiable little clergyman is guilty of being a coward—and guilty of nothing else. Are you really quiet enough to read about it?"

She produced some leaves of paper filled with writing. "There," she explained, "is Mr. Morris's own account of all that passed between Miss Jethro and himself."

"But how do you come by it?"

"Mr. Morris gave it to me. He said, 'Show it to Emily as soon as possible; and take care to be with her while she reads it.' There is a reason for this—" Cecilia's voice faltered. On the brink of some explanation, she seemed to recoil from it. "I will tell you by-and-by what the reason is," she said.

Emily looked nervously at the manuscript. "Why doesn't he tell me himself what he has discovered? Is he—" The leaves began to flutter in her trembling fingers—"is he angry with me?"

"Oh, Emily, angry with You! Read what he has written and you shall know why he keeps away."

Emily opened the manuscript.

CHAPTER LXVI. ALBAN'S NARRATIVE.

"The information which I have obtained from Miss Jethro has been communicated to me, on the condition that I shall not disclose the place of her residence. 'Let me pass out of notice (she said) as completely as if I had passed out of life; I wish to be forgotten by some, and to be unknown by others.'" With this one stipulation, she left me free to write the present narrative of what passed at the interview between us. I feel that the discoveries which I have made are too important to the persons interested to be trusted to memory.

1. She Receives Me.

"Finding Miss Jethro's place of abode, with far less difficulty than I had anticipated (thanks to favoring circumstances), I stated plainly the object of my visit. She declined to enter into conversation with me on the subject of the murder at Zeeland.

"I was prepared to meet with this rebuke, and to take the necessary measures for obtaining a more satisfactory reception. 'A person is suspected of having committed the murder,' I said; 'and there is reason to believe that you are in a position to say whether the suspicion is justified or not. Do you refuse to answer me, if I put the question?'

"Miss Jethro asked who the person was.

"I mentioned the name—Mr. Miles Mirabel.

"It is not necessary, and it would certainly be not agreeable to me, to describe the effect which this reply produced on Miss Jethro. After giving her time to compose herself, I entered into certain explanations, in order to convince her at the outset of my good faith. The result justified my anticipations. I was at once admitted to her confidence.

"She said, 'I must not hesitate to do an act of justice to an innocent man. But, in such a serious matter as this, you have a right to judge for yourself whether the person who is now speaking to you is a person whom you can trust. You may believe that I tell the truth about others, if I begin—whatever it may cost me—by telling the truth about myself.'"

2. She Speaks of Herself.

"I shall not attempt to place on record the confession of a most unhappy woman. It was the common story of sin bitterly repented, and of vain effort to recover the lost place in social esteem. Too well known a story, surely, to be told again.

"But I may with perfect propriety repeat what Miss Jethro said to me, in allusion to later events in her life which are connected with my own personal experience. She recalled to my memory a visit which she had paid to me at Netherwoods, and a letter addressed to her by Doctor Allday, which I had read at her express request.

"She said, 'You may remember that the letter contained some severe reflections on my conduct. Among other things, the doctor mentions that he called at the lodging I occupied during my visit to London, and found I had taken to flight: also that he had reason to believe I had entered Miss Ladd's service, under false pretenses.'

"I asked if the doctor had wronged her.

"She answered 'No: in one case, he is ignorant; in the other, he is right. On leaving his house, I found myself followed in the street by the man to whom I owe the shame and misery of my past life. My horror of him is not to be described in words. The one way of escaping was offered by an empty cab that passed me. I reached the railway station safely, and went back to my home in the country. Do you blame me?'

"It was impossible to blame her—and I said so.

"She then confessed the deception which she had practiced on Miss Ladd. 'I have a cousin,' she said, 'who was a Miss Jethro like me. Before her marriage she had been employed as a governess. She pitied me; she sympathized with my longing to recover the character that I had lost. With her permission, I made use of the testimonials which she had earned as a teacher—I was betrayed (to this day I don't know by whom)—and I was dismissed from Netherwoods. Now you know that I deceived Miss Ladd, you may reasonably conclude that I am likely to deceive You.'

"I assured her, with perfect sincerity, that I had drawn no such conclusion. Encouraged by my reply, Miss Jethro proceeded as follows."

3. She Speaks of Mirabel.

"'Four years ago, I was living near Cowes, in the Isle of Wight—in a cottage which had been taken for me by a gentleman who was the owner of a yacht. We had just returned from a short cruise, and the vessel was under orders to sail for Cherbourg with the next tide.

"'While I was walking in my garden, I was startled by the sudden appearance Of a man (evidently a gentleman) who was a perfect stranger to me. He was in a pitiable state of terror, and he implored my protection. In reply to my first inquiries, he mentioned the inn at Zeeland, and the dreadful death of a person unknown to him; whom I recognized (partly by the description given, and partly by comparison of dates) as Mr. James Brown. I shall say nothing of the shock inflicted on me: you don't want to know what I felt. What I did (having literally only a minute left for decision) was to hide the fugitive from discovery, and to exert my influence in his favor with the owner of the yacht. I saw nothing more of him. He was put on board, as soon as the police were out of sight, and was safely landed at Cherbourg.'

"I asked what induced her to run the risk of protecting a stranger, who was under suspicion of having committed a murder.

"She said, 'You shall hear my explanation directly. Let us have done with Mr. Mirabel first. We occasionally corresponded, during the long absence on the continent; never alluding, at his express request, to the horrible event at the inn. His last letter reached me, after he had established himself at Vale Regis. Writing of the society in the neighborhood, he informed me of his introduction to Miss Wyvil, and of the invitation that he had received to meet her friend and schoolfellow at Monksmoor. I knew that Miss Emily possessed a Handbill describing personal peculiarities in Mr. Mirabel, not hidden under the changed appearance of his head and face. If she remembered or happened to refer to that description, while she was living in the same house with him, there was a possibility at least of her suspicion being excited. The fear of this took me to you. It was a morbid fear, and, as events turned out, an unfounded fear: but I was unable to control it. Failing to produce any effect on you, I went to Vale Regis, and tried (vainly again) to induce Mr. Mirabel to send an excuse to Monksmoor. He, like you, wanted to know what my motive was. When I tell you that I acted solely in Miss Emily's interests, and that I knew how she had been deceived about her father's death, need I say why I was afraid to acknowledge my motive?'

"I understood that Miss Jethro might well be afraid of the consequences, if she risked any allusion to Mr. Brown's horrible death, and if it afterward chanced to reach his daughter's ears. But this state of feeling implied an extraordinary interest in the preservation of Emily's peace of mind. I asked

Miss Jethro how that interest had been excited?

"She answered, 'I can only satisfy you in one way. I must speak of her father now.'"

Emily looked up from the manuscript. She felt Cecilia's arm tenderly caressing her. She heard Cecilia say, "My poor dear, there is one last trial of your courage still to come. I am afraid of what you are going to read, when you turn to the next page. And yet—"

"And yet," Emily replied gently, "it must be done. I have learned my hard lesson of endurance, Cecilia, don't be afraid."

Emily turned to the next page.

4. She Speaks of the Dead.

"For the first time, Miss Jethro appeared to be at a loss how to proceed. I could see that she was suffering. She rose, and opening a drawer in her writing table, took a letter from it.

"She said, 'Will you read this? It was written by Miss Emily's father. Perhaps it may say more for me than I can say for myself?'

"I copy the letter. It was thus expressed:

"'You have declared that our farewell to-day is our farewell forever. For the second time, you have refused to be my wife; and you have done this, to use your own words, in mercy to Me.

"'In mercy to Me, I implore you to reconsider your decision.

"'If you condemn me to live without you—I feel it, I know it—you condemn me to despair which I have not fortitude enough to endure. Look at the passages which I have marked for you in the New Testament. Again and again, I say it; your true repentance has made you worthy of the pardon of God. Are you not worthy of the love, admiration, and respect of man? Think! oh, Sara, think of what our lives might be, and let them be united for time and for eternity.

"'I can write no more. A deadly faintness oppresses me. My mind is in a

518

state unknown to me in past years. I am in such confusion that I sometimes think I hate you. And then I recover from my delusion, and know that man never loved woman as I love you.

"'You will have time to write to me by this evening's post. I shall stop at Zeeland to-morrow, on my way back, and ask for a letter at the post office. I forbid explanations and excuses. I forbid heartless allusions to your duty. Let me have an answer which does not keep me for a moment in suspense.

"'For the last time, I ask you: Do you consent to be my wife? Say, Yes—or say, No.'

"I gave her back the letter—with the one comment on it, which the circumstances permitted me to make:

"'You said No?'

"She bent her head in silence.

"I went on—not willingly, for I would have spared her if it had been possible. I said, 'He died, despairing, by his own hand—and you knew it?'

"She looked up. 'No! To say that I knew it is too much. To say that I feared it is the truth.'

"'Did you love him?'

"She eyed me in stern surprise. 'Have I any right to love? Could I disgrace an honorable man by allowing him to marry me? You look as if you held me responsible for his death.'

"'Innocently responsible,' I said.

"She still followed her own train of thought. 'Do you suppose I could for a moment anticipate that he would destroy himself, when I wrote my reply? He was a truly religious man. If he had been in his right mind, he would have shrunk from the idea of suicide as from the idea of a crime.'

"On reflection, I was inclined to agree with her. In his terrible position, it was at least possible that the sight of the razor (placed ready, with the other appliances of the toilet, for his fellow-traveler's use) might have fatally tempted a man whose last hope was crushed, whose mind was tortured by despair. I should have been merciless indeed, if I had held Miss Jethro accountable thus far. But I found it hard to sympathize with the course which she had pursued, in permitting Mr. Brown's death to be attributed to murder without a word of protest. 'Why were you silent?' I said.

"She smiled bitterly.

"'A woman would have known why, without asking,' she replied. 'A woman would have understood that I shrank from a public confession of my shameful past life. A woman would have remembered what reasons I had for pitying the man who loved me, and for accepting any responsibility rather than associate his memory, before the world, with an unworthy passion for a degraded creature, ending in an act of suicide. Even if I had made that cruel sacrifice, would public opinion have believed such a person as I am—against the evidence of a medical man, and the verdict of a jury? No, Mr. Morris! I said nothing, and I was resolved to say nothing, so long as the choice of alternatives was left to me. On the day when Mr. Mirabel implored me to save him, that choice was no longer mine—and you know what I did. And now again when suspicion (after all the long interval that had passed) has followed and found that innocent man, you know what I have done. What more do you ask of me?'

"'Your pardon,' I said, 'for not having understood you—and a last favor. May I repeat what I have heard to the one person of all others who ought to know, and who must know, what you have told me?'

"It was needless to hint more plainly that I was speaking of Emily. Miss Jethro granted my request.

"'It shall be as you please,' she answered. 'Say for me to his daughter, that the grateful remembrance of her is my one refuge from the thoughts that tortured me, when we spoke together on her last night at school. She has made this dead heart of mine feel a reviving breath of life, when I think of her. Never, in our earthly pilgrimage, shall we meet again—I implore her to pity and forget me. Farewell, Mr. Morris; farewell forever.'

"I confess that the tears came into my eyes. When I could see clearly again, I was alone in the room."

CHAPTER LXVII. THE TRUE CONSOLATION.

Emily closed the pages which told her that her father had died by his own hand.

Cecilia still held her tenderly embraced. By slow degrees, her head dropped until it rested on her friend's bosom. Silently she suffered. Silently Cecilia bent forward, and kissed her forehead. The sounds that penetrated to the room were not out of harmony with the time. From a distant house the voices of children were just audible, singing the plaintive melody of a hymn; and, now and then, the breeze blew the first faded leaves of autumn against the window. Neither of the girls knew how long the minutes followed each other uneventfully, before there was a change. Emily raised her head, and looked at Cecilia.

"I have one friend left," she said.

"Not only me, love—oh, I hope not only me!"

"Yes. Only you."

"I want to say something, Emily; but I am afraid of hurting you."

"My dear, do you remember what we once read in a book of history at school? It told of the death of a tortured man, in the old time, who was broken on the wheel. He lived through it long enough to say that the agony, after the first stroke of the club, dulled his capacity for feeling pain when the next blows fell. I fancy pain of the mind must follow the same rule. Nothing you can say will hurt me now."

"I only wanted to ask, Emily, if you were engaged—at one time—to marry Mr. Mirabel. Is it true?"

"False! He pressed me to consent to an engagement—and I said he must not hurry me."

"What made you say that?"

"I thought of Alban Morris."

Vainly Cecilia tried to restrain herself. A cry of joy escaped her.

"Are you glad?" Emily asked. "Why?"

Cecilia made no direct reply. "May I tell you what you wanted to know, a little while since?" she said. "You asked why Mr. Morris left it all to me, instead of speaking to you himself. When I put the same question to him, he told me to read what he had written. 'Not a shadow of suspicion rests on Mr. Mirabel,' he said. 'Emily is free to marry him—and free through Me. Can I tell her that? For her sake, and for mine, it must not be. All that I can do is to leave old remembrances to plead for me. If they fail, I shall know that she will be happier with Mr. Mirabel than with me.' 'And you will submit?' I asked. 'Because I love her,' he answered, 'I must submit.' Oh, how pale you are! Have I distressed you?"

"You have done me good."

"Will you see him?"

Emily pointed to the manuscript. "At such a time as this?" she said.

Cecilia still held to her resolution. "Such a time as this is the right time," she answered. "It is now, when you most want to be comforted, that you ought to see him. Who can quiet your poor aching heart as he can quiet it?" She impulsively snatched at the manuscript and threw it out of sight. "I can't bear to look at it," she said. "Emily! if I have done wrong, will you forgive me? I saw him this morning before I came here. I was afraid of what might happen—I refused to break the dreadful news to you, unless he was somewhere near us. Your good old servant knows where to go. Let me send her—"

Mrs. Ellmother herself opened the door, and stood doubtful on the threshold, hysterically sobbing and laughing at the same time. "I'm everything that's bad!" the good old creature burst out. "I've been listening—I've been lying—I said you wanted him. Turn me out of my situation, if you like. I've got him! Here he is!"

In another moment, Emily was in his arms—and they were alone. On his faithful breast the blessed relief of tears came to her at last: she burst out crying.

"Oh, Alban, can you forgive me?"

He gently raised her head, so that he could see her face.

"My love, let me look at you," he said. "I want to think again of the day when we parted in the garden at school. Do you remember the one conviction that sustained me? I told you, Emily, there was a time of fulfillment to come in our two lives; and I have never wholly lost the dear belief. My own darling, the time has come!"

POSTSCRIPT. GOSSIP IN THE STUDIO.

The winter time had arrived. Alban was clearing his palette, after a hard day's work at the cottage. The servant announced that tea was ready, and that Miss Ladd was waiting to see him in the next room.

Alban ran in, and received the visitor cordially with both hands. "Welcome back to England! I needn't ask if the sea-voyage has done you good. You are looking ten years younger than when you went away."

Miss Ladd smiled. "I shall soon be ten years older again, if I go back to Netherwoods," she replied. "I didn't believe it at the time; but I know better now. Our friend Doctor Allday was right, when he said that my working days were over. I must give up the school to a younger and stronger successor, and make the best I can in retirement of what is left of my life. You and Emily may expect to have me as a near neighbor. Where is Emily?"

"Far away in the North."

"In the North! You don't mean that she has gone back to Mrs. Delvin?"

"She has gone back—with Mrs. Ellmother to take care of her—at my express request. You know what Emily is, when there is an act of mercy to be done. That unhappy man has been sinking (with intervals of partial recovery) for months past. Mrs. Delvin sent word to us that the end was near, and that the one last wish her brother was able to express was the wish to see Emily. He had been for some hours unable to speak when my wife arrived. But he knew her, and smiled faintly. He was just able to lift his hand. She took it, and waited by him, and spoke words of consolation and kindness from time to time. As the night advanced, he sank into sleep, still holding her hand. They only knew that he had passed from sleep to death—passed without a movement or a sigh—when his hand turned cold. Emily remained for a day at the tower to comfort poor Mrs. Delvin—and she comes home, thank God, this evening!"

"I needn't ask if you are happy?" Miss Ladd said.

"Happy? I sing, when I have my bath in the morning. If that isn't happiness (in a man of my age) I don't know what is!"

"And how are you getting on?"

"Famously! I have turned portrait painter, since you were sent away for your health. A portrait of Mr. Wyvil is to decorate the town hall in the place that he represents; and our dear kind-hearted Cecilia has induced a fascinated mayor and corporation to confide the work to my hands."

"Is there no hope yet of that sweet girl being married?" Miss Ladd asked. "We old maids all believe in marriage, Mr. Morris—though some of us don't own it."

"There seems to be a chance," Alban answered. "A young lord has turned up at Monksmoor; a handsome pleasant fellow, and a rising man in politics. He happened to be in the house a few days before Cecilia's birthday; and he asked my advice about the right present to give her. I said, 'Try something new in Tarts.' When he found I was in earnest, what do you think he did? Sent his steam yacht to Rouen for some of the famous pastry! You should have seen Cecilia, when the young lord offered his delicious gift. If I could paint that smile and those eyes, I should be the greatest artist living. I believe she will marry him. Need I say how rich they will be? We shall not envy them—we are rich too. Everything is comparative. The portrait of Mr. Wyvil will put three hundred pounds in my pocket. I have earned a hundred and twenty more by illustrations, since we have been married. And my wife's income (I like to be particular) is only five shillings and tenpence short of two hundred a year. Moral! we are rich as well as happy."

"Without a thought of the future?" Miss Ladd asked slyly.

"Oh, Doctor Allday has taken the future in hand! He revels in the old-fashioned jokes, which used to be addressed to newly-married people, in his time. 'My dear fellow,' he said the other day, 'you may possibly be under a joyful necessity of sending for the doctor, before we are all a year older. In that case, let it be understood that I am Honorary Physician to the family.' The warm-hearted old man talks of getting me another portrait to do. 'The greatest ass in the medical profession (he informed me) has just been made a baronet; and his admiring friends have decided that he is to be painted at full length, with his bandy legs hidden under a gown, and his great globular eyes staring at the spectator—I'll get you the job.' Shall I tell you what he says of Mrs. Rook's recovery?"

Miss Ladd held up her hands in amazement. "Recovery!" she exclaimed.

"And a most remarkable recovery too," Alban informed her. "It is the first case on record of any person getting over such an injury as she has received. Doctor Allday looked grave when he heard of it. 'I begin to believe in the devil,' he said; 'nobody else could have saved Mrs. Rook.' Other people don't take that view. She has been celebrated in all the medical newspapers—and she has been admitted to come excellent almshouse, to live in comfortable idleness to a green old age. The best of it is that she shakes her head, when her wonderful recovery is mentioned. 'It seems such a pity,' she says; 'I was so fit for heaven.' Mr. Rook having got rid of his wife, is in excellent spirits. He is occupied in looking after an imbecile old gentleman; and, when he is asked if he likes the employment, he winks mysteriously and slaps his pocket. Now, Miss Ladd, I think it's my turn to hear some news. What have you got to tell me?"

"I believe I can match your account of Mrs. Rook," Miss Ladd said. "Do you care to hear what has become of Francine?"

Alban, rattling on hitherto in boyish high spirits, suddenly became serious. "I have no doubt Miss de Sor is doing well," he said sternly. "She is too heartless and wicked not to prosper."

"You are getting like your old cynical self again, Mr. Morris—and you are wrong. I called this morning on the agent who had the care of Francine, when I left England. When I mentioned her name, he showed me a telegram, sent to him by her father. 'There's my authority,' he said, 'for letting her leave my house.' The message was short enough to be easily remembered: 'Anything my daughter likes as long as she doesn't come back to us.' In those cruel terms Mr. de Sor wrote of his own child. The agent was just as unfeeling, in his way. He called her the victim of slighted love and clever proselytizing. 'In plain words,' he said, 'the priest of the Catholic chapel close by has converted her; and she is now a novice in a convent of Carmelite nuns in the West of England. Who could have expected it? Who knows how it may end?"

As Miss Ladd spoke, the bell rang at the cottage gate. "Here she is!" Alban cried, leading the way into the hall. "Emily has come home."

LITTLE NOVELS

MRS. ZANT AND THE GHOST.

I.

THE course of this narrative describes the return of a disembodied spirit to earth, and leads the reader on new and strange ground.

Not in the obscurity of midnight, but in the searching light of day, did the supernatural influence assert itself. Neither revealed by a vision, nor announced by a voice, it reached mortal knowledge through the sense which is least easily self-deceived: the sense that feels.

The record of this event will of necessity produce conflicting impressions. It will raise, in some minds, the doubt which reason asserts; it will invigorate, in other minds, the hope which faith justifies; and it will leave the terrible question of the destinies of man, where centuries of vain investigation have left it—in the dark.

Having only undertaken in the present narrative to lead the way along a succession of events, the writer declines to follow modern examples by thrusting himself and his opinions on the public view. He returns to the shadow from which he has emerged, and leaves the opposing forces of incredulity and belief to fight the old battle over again, on the old ground.

II.

THE events happened soon after the first thirty years of the present century had come to an end.

On a fine morning, early in the month of April, a gentleman of middle age (named Rayburn) took his little daughter Lucy out for a walk in the woodland pleasure-ground of Western London, called Kensington Gardens.

The few friends whom he possessed reported of Mr. Rayburn (not unkindly) that he was a reserved and solitary man. He might have been more accurately described as a widower devoted to his only surviving child. Although he was not more than forty years of age, the one pleasure which made life enjoyable to Lucy's father was offered by Lucy herself.

Playing with her ball, the child ran on to the southern limit of the Gardens, at that part of it which still remains nearest to the old Palace of Kensington. Observing close at hand one of those spacious covered seats, called in England "alcoves," Mr. Rayburn was reminded that he had the morning's newspaper in his pocket, and that he might do well to rest and read. At that early hour the place was a solitude.

"Go on playing, my dear," he said; "but take care to keep where I can see you."

Lucy tossed up her ball; and Lucy's father opened his newspaper. He had not been reading for more than ten minutes, when he felt a familiar little hand laid on his knee.

"Tired of playing?" he inquired—with his eyes still on the newspaper.

"I'm frightened, papa."

He looked up directly. The child's pale face startled him. He took her on his knee and kissed her.

"You oughtn't to be frightened, Lucy, when I am with you," he said, gently. "What is it?" He looked out of the alcove as he spoke, and saw a little dog among the trees. "Is it the dog?" he asked.

Lucy answered:

"It's not the dog—it's the lady."

The lady was not visible from the alcove.

"Has she said anything to you?" Mr. Rayburn inquired.

"No."

"What has she done to frighten you?"

530

The child put her arms round her father's neck.

"Whisper, papa," she said; "I'm afraid of her hearing us. I think she's mad."

"Why do you think so, Lucy?"

"She came near to me. I thought she was going to say something. She seemed to be ill."

"Well? And what then?"

"She looked at me."

There, Lucy found herself at a loss how to express what she had to say next—and took refuge in silence.

"Nothing very wonderful, so far," her father suggested.

"Yes, papa—but she didn't seem to see me when she looked."

"Well, and what happened then?"

"The lady was frightened—and that frightened me. I think," the child repeated positively, "she's mad."

It occurred to Mr. Rayburn that the lady might be blind. He rose at once to set the doubt at rest.

"Wait here," he said, "and I'll come back to you."

But Lucy clung to him with both hands; Lucy declared that she was afraid to be by herself. They left the alcove together.

The new point of view at once revealed the stranger, leaning against the trunk of a tree. She was dressed in the deep mourning of a widow. The pallor of her face, the glassy stare in her eyes, more than accounted for the child's terror—it excused the alarming conclusion at which she had arrived.

"Go nearer to her," Lucy whispered.

They advanced a few steps. It was now easy to see that the lady was young, and wasted by illness—but (arriving at a doubtful conclusion perhaps under

531

the present circumstances) apparently possessed of rare personal attractions in happier days. As the father and daughter advanced a little, she discovered them. After some hesitation, she left the tree; approached with an evident intention of speaking; and suddenly paused. A change to astonishment and fear animated her vacant eyes. If it had not been plain before, it was now beyond all doubt that she was not a poor blind creature, deserted and helpless. At the same time, the expression of her face was not easy to understand. She could hardly have looked more amazed and bewildered, if the two strangers who were observing her had suddenly vanished from the place in which they stood.

Mr. Rayburn spoke to her with the utmost kindness of voice and manner.

"I am afraid you are not well," he said. "Is there anything that I can do—"

The next words were suspended on his lips. It was impossible to realize such a state of things; but the strange impression that she had already produced on him was now confirmed. If he could believe his senses, her face did certainly tell him that he was invisible and inaudible to the woman whom he had just addressed! She moved slowly away with a heavy sigh, like a person disappointed and distressed. Following her with his eyes, he saw the dog once more—a little smooth-coated terrier of the ordinary English breed. The dog showed none of the restless activity of his race. With his head down and his tail depressed, he crouched like a creature paralyzed by fear. His mistress roused him by a call. He followed her listlessly as she turned away.

After walking a few paces only, she suddenly stood still.

Mr. Rayburn heard her talking to herself.

"Did I feel it again?" she said, as if perplexed by some doubt that awed or grieved her. After a while her arms rose slowly, and opened with a gentle caressing action—an embrace strangely offered to the empty air! "No," she said to herself, sadly, after waiting a moment. "More perhaps when to-morrow comes—no more to-day." She looked up at the clear blue sky. "The beautiful sunlight! the merciful sunlight!" she murmured. "I should have died if it had happened in the dark."

532

Once more she called to the dog; and once more she walked slowly away.

"Is she going home, papa?' the child asked.

"We will try and find out," the father answered.

He was by this time convinced that the poor creature was in no condition to be permitted to go out without some one to take care of her. From motives of humanity, he was resolved on making the attempt to communicate with her friends.

III.

THE lady left the Gardens by the nearest gate; stopping to lower her veil before she turned into the busy thoroughfare which leads to Kensington. Advancing a little way along the High Street, she entered a house of respectable appearance, with a card in one of the windows which announced that apartments were to let.

Mr. Rayburn waited a minute—then knocked at the door, and asked if he could see the mistress of the house. The servant showed him into a room on the ground floor, neatly but scantily furnished. One little white object varied the grim brown monotony of the empty table. It was a visiting-card.

With a child's unceremonious curiosity Lucy pounced on the card, and spelled the name, letter by letter: "Z, A, N, T," she repeated. "What does that mean?"

Her father looked at the card, as he took it away from her, and put it back on the table. The name was printed, and the address was added in pencil: "Mr. John Zant, Purley's Hotel."

The mistress made her appearance. Mr. Rayburn heartily wished himself out of the house again, the moment he saw her. The ways in which it is possible to cultivate the social virtues are more numerous and more varied than is generally supposed. This lady's way had apparently accustomed her to meet her fellow-creatures on the hard ground of justice without mercy. Something in her eyes, when she looked at Lucy, said: "I wonder whether that child gets punished when she deserves it?"

"Do you wish to see the rooms which I have to let?" she began.

Mr. Rayburn at once stated the object of his visit—as clearly, as civilly, and as concisely as a man could do it. He was conscious (he added) that he had been guilty perhaps of an act of intrusion.

The manner of the mistress of the house showed that she entirely agreed with him. He suggested, however, that his motive might excuse him. The mistress's manner changed, and asserted a difference of opinion.

"I only know the lady whom you mention," she said, "as a person of the highest respectability, in delicate health. She has taken my first-floor apartments, with excellent references; and she gives remarkably little trouble. I have no claim to interfere with her proceedings, and no reason to doubt that she is capable of taking care of herself."

Mr. Rayburn unwisely attempted to say a word in his own defense.

"Allow me to remind you—" he began.

"Of what, sir?"

"Of what I observed, when I happened to see the lady in Kensington Gardens."

"I am not responsible for what you observed in Kensington Gardens. If your time is of any value, pray don't let me detain you."

Dismissed in those terms, Mr. Rayburn took Lucy's hand and withdrew. He had just reached the door, when it was opened from the outer side. The Lady of Kensington Gardens stood before him. In the position which he and his daughter now occupied, their backs were toward the window. Would she remember having seen them for a moment in the Gardens?

"Excuse me for intruding on you," she said to the landlady. "Your servant tells me my brother-in-law called while I was out. He sometimes leaves a message on his card."

She looked for the message, and appeared to be disappointed: there was no writing on the card.

534

Mr. Rayburn lingered a little in the doorway on the chance of hearing something more. The landlady's vigilant eyes discovered him.

"Do you know this gentleman?" she said maliciously to her lodger.

"Not that I remember."

Replying in those words, the lady looked at Mr. Rayburn for the first time; and suddenly drew back from him.

"Yes," she said, correcting herself; "I think we met—"

Her embarrassment overpowered her; she could say no more.

Mr. Rayburn compassionately finished the sentence for her.

"We met accidentally in Kensington Gardens," he said.

She seemed to be incapable of appreciating the kindness of his motive. After hesitating a little she addressed a proposal to him, which seemed to show distrust of the landlady.

"Will you let me speak to you upstairs in my own rooms?" she asked.

Without waiting for a reply, she led the way to the stairs. Mr. Rayburn and Lucy followed. They were just beginning the ascent to the first floor, when the spiteful landlady left the lower room, and called to her lodger over their heads: "Take care what you say to this man, Mrs. Zant! He thinks you're mad."

Mrs. Zant turned round on the landing, and looked at him. Not a word fell from her lips. She suffered, she feared, in silence. Something in the sad submission of her face touched the springs of innocent pity in Lucy's heart. The child burst out crying.

That artless expression of sympathy drew Mrs. Zant down the few stairs which separated her from Lucy.

"May I kiss your dear little girl?" she said to Mr. Rayburn. The landlady, standing on the mat below, expressed her opinion of the value of caresses, as compared with a sounder method of treating young persons in tears: "If that child was mine," she remarked, "I would give her something to cry for."

In the meantime, Mrs. Zant led the way to her rooms.

The first words she spoke showed that the landlady had succeeded but too well in prejudicing her against Mr. Rayburn.

"Will you let me ask your child," she said to him, "why you think me mad?"

He met this strange request with a firm answer.

"You don't know yet what I really do think. Will you give me a minute's attention?"

"No," she said positively. "The child pities me, I want to speak to the child. What did you see me do in the Gardens, my dear, that surprised you?" Lucy turned uneasily to her father; Mrs. Zant persisted. "I first saw you by yourself, and then I saw you with your father," she went on. "When I came nearer to you, did I look very oddly—as if I didn't see you at all?"

Lucy hesitated again; and Mr. Rayburn interfered.

"You are confusing my little girl," he said. "Allow me to answer your questions—or excuse me if I leave you."

There was something in his look, or in his tone, that mastered her. She put her hand to her head.

"I don't think I'm fit for it," she answered vacantly. "My courage has been sorely tried already. If I can get a little rest and sleep, you may find me a different person. I am left a great deal by myself; and I have reasons for trying to compose my mind. Can I see you tomorrow? Or write to you? Where do you live?"

Mr. Rayburn laid his card on the table in silence. She had strongly excited his interest. He honestly desired to be of some service to this forlorn creature—abandoned so cruelly, as it seemed, to her own guidance. But he had no authority to exercise, no sort of claim to direct her actions, even if she consented to accept his advice. As a last resource he ventured on an allusion to the relative of whom she had spoken downstairs.

"When do you expect to see your brother-in-law again?" he said.

"I don't know," she answered. "I should like to see him—he is so kind to me."

She turned aside to take leave of Lucy.

"Good-by, my little friend. If you live to grow up, I hope you will never be such a miserable woman as I am." She suddenly looked round at Mr. Rayburn. "Have you got a wife at home?" she asked.

"My wife is dead."

"And you have a child to comfort you! Please leave me; you harden my heart. Oh, sir, don't you understand? You make me envy you!"

Mr. Rayburn was silent when he and his daughter were out in the street again. Lucy, as became a dutiful child, was silent, too. But there are limits to human endurance—and Lucy's capacity for self-control gave way at last.

"Are you thinking of the lady, papa?" she said.

He only answered by nodding his head. His daughter had interrupted him at that critical moment in a man's reflections, when he is on the point of making up his mind. Before they were at home again Mr. Rayburn had arrived at a decision. Mrs. Zant's brother-in-law was evidently ignorant of any serious necessity for his interference—or he would have made arrangements for immediately repeating his visit. In this state of things, if any evil happened to Mrs. Zant, silence on Mr. Rayburn's part might be indirectly to blame for a serious misfortune. Arriving at that conclusion, he decided upon running the risk of being rudely received, for the second time, by another stranger.

Leaving Lucy under the care of her governess, he went at once to the address that had been written on the visiting-card left at the lodging-house, and sent in his name. A courteous message was returned. Mr. John Zant was at home, and would be happy to see him.

IV.

MR. RAYBURN was shown into one of the private sitting-rooms of the hotel.

He observed that the customary position of the furniture in a room had been, in some respects, altered. An armchair, a side-table, and a footstool had all been removed to one of the windows, and had been placed as close as possible to the light. On the table lay a large open roll of morocco leather, containing rows of elegant little instruments in steel and ivory. Waiting by the table, stood Mr. John Zant. He said "Good-morning" in a bass voice, so profound and so melodious that those two commonplace words assumed a new importance, coming from his lips. His personal appearance was in harmony with his magnificent voice—he was a tall, finely-made man of dark complexion; with big brilliant black eyes, and a noble curling beard, which hid the whole lower part of his face. Having bowed with a happy mingling of dignity and politeness, the conventional side of this gentleman's character suddenly vanished; and a crazy side, to all appearance, took its place. He dropped on his knees in front of the footstool. Had he forgotten to say his prayers that morning, and was he in such a hurry to remedy the fault that he had no time to spare for consulting appearances? The doubt had hardly suggested itself, before it was set at rest in a most unexpected manner. Mr. Zant looked at his visitor with a bland smile, and said:

"Please let me see your feet."

For the moment, Mr. Rayburn lost his presence of mind. He looked at the instruments on the side-table.

"Are you a corn-cutter?" was all he could say.

"Excuse me, sir," returned the polite operator, "the term you use is quite obsolete in our profession." He rose from his knees, and added modestly: "I am a Chiropodist."

"I beg your pardon."

"Don't mention it! You are not, I imagine, in want of my professional services. To what motive may I attribute the honor of your visit?"

By this time Mr. Rayburn had recovered himself.

"I have come here," he answered, "under circumstances which require apology as well as explanation."

Mr. Zant's highly polished manner betrayed signs of alarm; his suspicions pointed to a formidable conclusion—a conclusion that shook him to the innermost recesses of the pocket in which he kept his money.

"The numerous demands on me—" he began.

Mr. Rayburn smiled.

"Make your mind easy," he replied. "I don't want money. My object is to speak with you on the subject of a lady who is a relation of yours."

"My sister-in-law!" Mr. Zant exclaimed. "Pray take a seat."

Doubting if he had chosen a convenient time for his visit, Mr. Rayburn hesitated.

"Am I likely to be in the way of persons who wish to consult you?" he asked.

"Certainly not. My morning hours of attendance on my clients are from eleven to one." The clock on the mantelpiece struck the quarter-past one as he spoke. "I hope you don't bring me bad news?" he said, very earnestly. "When I called on Mrs. Zant this morning, I heard that she had gone out for a walk. Is it indiscreet to ask how you became acquainted with her?"

Mr. Rayburn at once mentioned what he had seen and heard in Kensington Gardens; not forgetting to add a few words, which described his interview afterward with Mrs. Zant.

The lady's brother-in-law listened with an interest and sympathy, which offered the strongest possible contrast to the unprovoked rudeness of the mistress of the lodging-house. He declared that he could only do justice to his sense of obligation by following Mr. Rayburn's example, and expressing himself as frankly as if he had been speaking to an old friend.

"The sad story of my sister-in-law's life," he said, "will, I think, explain certain things which must have naturally perplexed you. My brother was introduced to her at the house of an Australian gentleman, on a visit to England. She was then employed as governess to his daughters. So sincere was the regard felt for her by the family that the parents had, at the entreaty of their children, asked her to accompany them when they returned to the Colony. The governess thankfully accepted the proposal."

"Had she no relations in England?" Mr. Rayburn asked.

"She was literally alone in the world, sir. When I tell you that she had been brought up in the Foundling Hospital, you will understand what I mean. Oh, there is no romance in my sister-in-law's story! She never has known, or will know, who her parents were or why they deserted her. The happiest moment in her life was the moment when she and my brother first met. It was an instance, on both sides, of love at first sight. Though not a rich man, my brother had earned a sufficient income in mercantile pursuits. His character spoke for itself. In a word, he altered all the poor girl's prospects, as we then hoped and believed, for the better. Her employers deferred their return to Australia, so that she might be married from their house. After a happy life of a few weeks only—"

His voice failed him; he paused, and turned his face from the light.

"Pardon me," he said; "I am not able, even yet, to speak composedly of my brother's death. Let me only say that the poor young wife was a widow, before the happy days of the honeymoon were over. That dreadful calamity struck her down. Before my brother had been committed to the grave, her life was in danger from brain-fever."

Those words placed in a new light Mr. Rayburn's first fear that her intellect might be deranged. Looking at him attentively, Mr. Zant seemed to understand what was passing in the mind of his guest.

"No!" he said. "If the opinions of the medical men are to be trusted, the result of the illness is injury to her physical strength—not injury to her mind. I have observed in her, no doubt, a certain waywardness of temper since her illness; but that is a trifle. As an example of what I mean, I may tell you that I invited her, on her recovery, to pay me a visit. My house is not in London—the air doesn't agree with me—my place of residence is at St. Sallins-on-Sea. I am not myself a married man; but my excellent housekeeper would have received Mrs. Zant with the utmost kindness. She was resolved—obstinately resolved, poor thing—to remain in London. It is needless to say that, in her melancholy position, I am attentive to her slightest wishes. I took a lodging for her; and, at her special request, I chose a house which was near Kensington Gardens.

"Is there any association with the Gardens which led Mrs. Zant to make that request?"

"Some association, I believe, with the memory of her husband. By the way, I wish to be sure of finding her at home, when I call to-morrow. Did you say (in the course of your interesting statement) that she intended—as you supposed—to return to Kensington Gardens to-morrow? Or has my memory deceived me?"

"Your memory is perfectly accurate."

"Thank you. I confess I am not only distressed by what you have told me of Mrs. Zant—I am at a loss to know how to act for the best. My only idea, at present, is to try change of air and scene. What do you think yourself?"

"I think you are right."

Mr. Zant still hesitated.

"It would not be easy for me, just now," he said, "to leave my patients and take her abroad."

The obvious reply to this occurred to Mr. Rayburn. A man of larger worldly experience might have felt certain suspicions, and might have remained silent. Mr. Rayburn spoke.

"Why not renew your invitation and take her to your house at the seaside?" he said.

In the perplexed state of Mr. Zant's mind, this plain course of action had apparently failed to present itself. His gloomy face brightened directly.

"The very thing!" he said. "I will certainly take your advice. If the air of St. Sallins does nothing else, it will improve her health and help her to recover her good looks. Did she strike you as having been (in happier days) a pretty woman?"

This was a strangely familiar question to ask—almost an indelicate question, under the circumstances A certain furtive expression in Mr. Zant's fine dark eyes seemed to imply that it had been put with a purpose. Was it possible that he suspected Mr. Rayburn's interest in his sister-in-law to be inspired by any motive which was not perfectly unselfish and perfectly pure? To arrive at such a conclusion as this might be to judge hastily and cruelly of a man who was perhaps only guilty of a want of delicacy of feeling. Mr. Rayburn honestly did his best to assume the charitable point of view. At the same time, it is not to be denied that his words, when he answered, were carefully guarded, and that he rose to take his leave.

Mr. John Zant hospitably protested.

"Why are you in such a hurry? Must you really go? I shall have the honor of returning your visit to-morrow, when I have made arrangements to profit by that excellent suggestion of yours. Good-by. God bless you."

He held out his hand: a hand with a smooth surface and a tawny color, that fervently squeezed the fingers of a departing friend. "Is that man a scoundrel?" was Mr. Rayburn's first thought, after he had left the hotel. His moral sense set all hesitation at rest—and answered: "You're a fool if you doubt it."

V.

DISTURBED by presentiments, Mr. Rayburn returned to his house on foot, by way of trying what exercise would do toward composing his mind.

The experiment failed. He went upstairs and played with Lucy; he drank an extra glass of wine at dinner; he took the child and her governess to a circus in the evening; he ate a little supper, fortified by another glass of wine, before he went to bed—and still those vague forebodings of evil persisted in torturing him. Looking back through his past life, he asked himself if any woman (his late wife of course excepted!) had ever taken the predominant place in his thoughts which Mrs. Zant had assumed—without any discernible reason to account for it? If he had ventured to answer his own question, the reply would have been: Never!

All the next day he waited at home, in expectation of Mr. John Zant's promised visit, and waited in vain.

Toward evening the parlor-maid appeared at the family tea-table, and presented to her master an unusually large envelope sealed with black wax, and addressed in a strange handwriting. The absence of stamp and postmark showed that it had been left at the house by a messenger.

"Who brought this?" Mr. Rayburn asked.

"A lady, sir—in deep mourning."

"Did she leave any message?"

"No, sir."

Having drawn the inevitable conclusion, Mr. Rayburn shut himself up in his library. He was afraid of Lucy's curiosity and Lucy's questions, if he read Mrs. Zant's letter in his daughter's presence.

Looking at the open envelope after he had taken out the leaves of writing which it contained, he noticed these lines traced inside the cover:

"My one excuse for troubling you, when I might have consulted my brother-in-law, will be found in the pages which I inclose. To speak plainly, you have been led to fear that I am not in my right senses. For this very reason, I now appeal to you. Your dreadful doubt of me, sir, is my doubt too. Read what I have written about myself—and then tell me, I entreat you, which I am: A person who has been the object of a supernatural revelation? or an unfortunate creature who is only fit for imprisonment in a mad-house?"

Mr. Rayburn opened the manuscript. With steady attention, which soon quickened to breathless interest, he read what follows:

VI. THE LADY'S MANUSCRIPT.

YESTERDAY morning the sun shone in a clear blue sky—after a succession of cloudy days, counting from the first of the month.

The radiant light had its animating effect on my poor spirits. I had passed the night more peacefully than usual; undisturbed by the dream, so cruelly familiar to me, that my lost husband is still living—the dream from which I always wake in tears. Never, since the dark days of my sorrow, have I been so little troubled by the self-tormenting fancies and fears which beset miserable women, as when I left the house, and turned my steps toward Kensington Gardens—for the first time since my husband's death.

Attended by my only companion, the little dog who had been his favorite as well as mine, I went to the quiet corner of the Gardens which is nearest to Kensington.

On that soft grass, under the shade of those grand trees, we had loitered together in the days of our betrothal. It was his favorite walk; and he had taken me to see it in the early days of our acquaintance. There, he had first asked me to be his wife. There, we had felt the rapture of our first kiss. It was surely natural that I should wish to see once more a place sacred to such memories as these? I am only twenty-three years old; I have no child to comfort me, no companion of my own age, nothing to love but the dumb creature who is so faithfully fond of me.

I went to the tree under which we stood, when my dear one's eyes told his love before he could utter it in words. The sun of that vanished day shone on me again; it was the same noontide hour; the same solitude was around me. I had feared the first effect of the dreadful contrast between past and present. No! I was quiet and resigned. My thoughts, rising higher than earth, dwelt on the better life beyond the grave. Some tears came into my eyes. But I was not unhappy. My memory of all that happened may be trusted, even in trifles which relate only to myself—I was not unhappy.

The first object that I saw, when my eyes were clear again, was the dog. He crouched a few paces away from me, trembling pitiably, but uttering no cry. What had caused the fear that overpowered him?

I was soon to know.

I called to the dog; he remained immovable—conscious of some mysterious coming thing that held him spellbound. I tried to go to the poor creature, and fondle and comfort him.

At the first step forward that I took, something stopped me.

It was not to be seen, and not to be heard. It stopped me.

The still figure of the dog disappeared from my view: the lonely scene round me disappeared—excepting the light from heaven, the tree that sheltered me, and the grass in front of me. A sense of unutterable expectation kept my eyes riveted on the grass. Suddenly, I saw its myriad blades rise erect and shivering. The fear came to me of something passing over them with the invisible swiftness of the wind. The shivering advanced. It was all round me. It crept into the leaves of the tree over my head; they shuddered, without a sound to tell of their agitation; their pleasant natural rustling was struck dumb. The song of the birds had ceased. The cries of the water-fowl on the pond were heard no more. There was a dreadful silence.

But the lovely sunshine poured down on me, as brightly as ever.

In that dazzling light, in that fearful silence, I felt an Invisible Presence near me. It touched me gently.

At the touch, my heart throbbed with an overwhelming joy. Exquisite pleasure thrilled through every nerve in my body. I knew him! From the unseen world—himself unseen—he had returned to me. Oh, I knew him!

And yet, my helpless mortality longed for a sign that might give me assurance of the truth. The yearning in me shaped itself into words. I tried to utter the words. I would have said, if I could have spoken: "Oh, my angel, give me a token that it is You!" But I was like a person struck dumb—I could only think it.

The Invisible Presence read my thought. I felt my lips touched, as my husband's lips used to touch them when he kissed me. And that was my answer. A thought came to me again. I would have said, if I could have spoken: "Are you here to take me to the better world?"

I waited. Nothing that I could feel touched me.

I was conscious of thinking once more. I would have said, if I could have spoken: "Are you here to protect me?"

I felt myself held in a gentle embrace, as my husband's arms used to hold me when he pressed me to his breast. And that was my answer.

The touch that was like the touch of his lips, lingered and was lost; the clasp that was like the clasp of his arms, pressed me and fell away. The garden-scene resumed its natural aspect. I saw a human creature near, a lovely little girl looking at me.

At that moment, when I was my own lonely self again, the sight of the child soothed and attracted me. I advanced, intending to speak to her. To my horror I suddenly ceased to see her. She disappeared as if I had been stricken blind.

And yet I could see the landscape round me; I could see the heaven above me. A time passed—only a few minutes, as I thought—and the child became visible to me again; walking hand-in-hand with her father. I approached them; I was close enough to see that they were looking at me with pity and surprise. My impulse was to ask if they saw anything strange in my face or my manner. Before I could speak, the horrible wonder happened again. They vanished from my view.

Was the Invisible Presence still near? Was it passing between me and my fellow-mortals; forbidding communication, in that place and at that time?

It must have been so. When I turned away in my ignorance, with a heavy heart, the dreadful blankness which had twice shut out from me the beings of my own race, was not between me and my dog. The poor little creature filled me with pity; I called him to me. He moved at the sound of my voice, and followed me languidly; not quite awakened yet from the trance of terror that had possessed him.

Before I had retired by more than a few steps, I thought I was conscious of the Presence again. I held out my longing arms to it. I waited in the hope of a touch to tell me that I might return. Perhaps I was answered by indirect means? I only know that a resolution to return to the same place, at the same hour, came to me, and quieted my mind.

The morning of the next day was dull and cloudy; but the rain held off. I set forth again to the Gardens.

My dog ran on before me into the street—and stopped: waiting to see in which direction I might lead the way. When I turned toward the Gardens, he dropped behind me. In a little while I looked back. He was following me no longer; he stood irresolute. I called to him. He advanced a few steps— hesitated—and ran back to the house.

I went on by myself. Shall I confess my superstition? I thought the dog's desertion of me a bad omen.

Arrived at the tree, I placed myself under it. The minutes followed each other uneventfully. The cloudy sky darkened. The dull surface of the grass showed no shuddering consciousness of an unearthly creature passing over it.

I still waited, with an obstinacy which was fast becoming the obstinacy of despair. How long an interval elapsed, while I kept watch on the ground before me, I am not able to say. I only know that a change came.

Under the dull gray light I saw the grass move—but not as it had moved, on the day before. It shriveled as if a flame had scorched it. No flame appeared. The brown underlying earth showed itself winding onward in a thin strip—which might have been a footpath traced in fire. It frightened me. I longed for the protection of the Invisible Presence. I prayed for a warning of it, if danger was near.

A touch answered me. It was as if a hand unseen had taken my hand— had raised it, little by little—had left it, pointing to the thin brown path that wound toward me under the shriveled blades of grass.

I looked to the far end of the path.

The unseen hand closed on my hand with a warning pressure: the revelation of the coming danger was near me—I waited for it. I saw it.

The figure of a man appeared, advancing toward me along the thin brown path. I looked in his face as he came nearer. It showed me dimly the face of my husband's brother—John Zant.

The consciousness of myself as a living creature left me. I knew nothing; I felt nothing. I was dead.

When the torture of revival made me open my eyes, I found myself on the grass. Gentle hands raised my head, at the moment when I recovered my senses. Who had brought me to life again? Who was taking care of me?

I looked upward, and saw—bending over me—John Zant.

VII.

THERE, the manuscript ended.

Some lines had been added on the last page; but they had been so carefully erased as to be illegible. These words of explanation appeared below the canceled sentences:

"I had begun to write the little that remains to be told, when it struck me that I might, unintentionally, be exercising an unfair influence on your opinion. Let me only remind you that I believe absolutely in the supernatural revelation which I have endeavored to describe. Remember this—and decide for me what I dare not decide for myself."

There was no serious obstacle in the way of compliance with this request.

Judged from the point of view of the materialist, Mrs. Zant might no doubt be the victim of illusions (produced by a diseased state of the nervous system), which have been known to exist—as in the celebrated case of the book-seller, Nicolai, of Berlin—without being accompanied by derangement of the intellectual powers. But Mr. Rayburn was not asked to solve any such intricate problem as this. He had been merely instructed to read the manuscript, and to say what impression it had left on him of the mental condition of the writer; whose doubt of herself had been, in all probability, first suggested by remembrance of the illness from which she had suffered— brain-fever.

Under these circumstances, there could be little difficulty in forming an opinion. The memory which had recalled, and the judgment which had arranged, the succession of events related in the narrative, revealed a mind in full possession of its resources.

Having satisfied himself so far, Mr. Rayburn abstained from considering the more serious question suggested by what he had read.

At any time his habits of life and his ways of thinking would have rendered him unfit to weigh the arguments, which assert or deny supernatural revelation among the creatures of earth. But his mind was now so disturbed by the startling record of experience which he had just read, that he was only conscious of feeling certain impressions—without possessing the capacity to reflect on them. That his anxiety on Mrs. Zant's account had been increased, and that his doubts of Mr. John Zant had been encouraged, were the only practical results of the confidence placed in him of which he was thus far aware. In the ordinary exigencies of life a man of hesitating disposition, his interest in Mrs. Zant's welfare, and his desire to discover what had passed between her brother-in-law and herself, after their meeting in the Gardens, urged him into instant action. In half an hour more, he had arrived at her lodgings. He was at once admitted.

VIII.

MRS. ZANT was alone, in an imperfectly lighted room.

"I hope you will excuse the bad light," she said; "my head has been burning as if the fever had come back again. Oh, don't go away! After what I have suffered, you don't know how dreadful it is to be alone."

The tone of her voice told him that she had been crying. He at once tried the best means of setting the poor lady at ease, by telling her of the conclusion at which he had arrived, after reading her manuscript. The happy result showed itself instantly: her face brightened, her manner changed; she was eager to hear more.

"Have I produced any other impression on you?" she asked.

He understood the allusion. Expressing sincere respect for her own convictions, he told her honestly that he was not prepared to enter on the obscure and terrible question of supernatural interposition. Grateful for the tone in which he had answered her, she wisely and delicately changed the subject.

"I must speak to you of my brother-in-law," she said. "He has told me of your visit; and I am anxious to know what you think of him. Do you like Mr. John Zant?"

Mr. Rayburn hesitated.

The careworn look appeared again in her face. "If you had felt as kindly toward him as he feels toward you," she said, "I might have gone to St. Sallins with a lighter heart."

Mr. Rayburn thought of the supernatural appearances, described at the close of her narrative. "You believe in that terrible warning," he remonstrated; "and yet, you go to your brother-in-law's house!"

"I believe," she answered, "in the spirit of the man who loved me in the days of his earthly bondage. I am under his protection. What have I to do but to cast away my fears, and to wait in faith and hope? It might have helped my resolution if a friend had been near to encourage me." She paused and smiled sadly. "I must remember," she resumed, "that your way of understanding my position is not my way. I ought to have told you that Mr. John Zant feels needless anxiety about my health. He declares that he will not lose sight of me until his mind is at ease. It is useless to attempt to alter his opinion. He says my nerves are shattered—and who that sees me can doubt it? He tells me that my only chance of getting better is to try change of air and perfect repose—how can I contradict him? He reminds me that I have no relation but himself, and no house open to me but his own—and God knows he is right!"

She said those last words in accents of melancholy resignation, which grieved the good man whose one merciful purpose was to serve and console her. He spoke impulsively with the freedom of an old friend,

"I want to know more of you and Mr. John Zant than I know now," he said. "My motive is a better one than mere curiosity. Do you believe that I feel a sincere interest in you?"

"With my whole heart."

That reply encouraged him to proceed with what he had to say. "When you recovered from your fainting-fit," he began, "Mr. John Zant asked questions, of course?"

"He asked what could possibly have happened, in such a quiet place as Kensington Gardens, to make me faint."

"And how did you answer?"

"Answer? I couldn't even look at him!"

"You said nothing?"

"Nothing. I don't know what he thought of me; he might have been surprised, or he might have been offended."

"Is he easily offended?" Mr. Rayburn asked.

"Not in my experience of him."

"Do you mean your experience of him before your illness?"

"Yes. Since my recovery, his engagements with country patients have kept him away from London. I have not seen him since he took these lodgings for me. But he is always considerate. He has written more than once to beg that I will not think him neglectful, and to tell me (what I knew already through my poor husband) that he has no money of his own, and must live by his profession."

"In your husband's lifetime, were the two brothers on good terms?"

"Always. The one complaint I ever heard my husband make of John Zant was that he didn't come to see us often enough, after our marriage. Is there some wickedness in him which we have never suspected? It may be—but how can it be? I have every reason to be grateful to the man against whom I have been supernaturally warned! His conduct to me has been always perfect. I can't tell you what I owe to his influence in quieting my mind, when a dreadful doubt arose about my husband's death."

"Do you mean doubt if he died a natural death?"

"Oh, no! no! He was dying of rapid consumption—but his sudden death took the doctors by surprise. One of them thought that he might have taken an overdose of his sleeping drops, by mistake. The other disputed this conclusion, or there might have been an inquest in the house. Oh, don't speak of it any more! Let us talk of something else. Tell me when I shall see you again."

"I hardly know. When do you and your brother-in-law leave London?"

"To-morrow." She looked at Mr. Rayburn with a piteous entreaty in her eyes; she said, timidly: "Do you ever go to the seaside, and take your dear little girl with you?"

The request, at which she had only dared to hint, touched on the idea which was at that moment in Mr. Rayburn's mind.

Interpreted by his strong prejudice against John Zant, what she had said of her brother-in-law filled him with forebodings of peril to herself; all the more powerful in their influence, for this reason—that he shrank from distinctly realizing them. If another person had been present at the interview, and had said to him afterward: "That man's reluctance to visit his sister-in-law, while her husband was living, is associated with a secret sense of guilt which her innocence cannot even imagine: he, and he alone, knows the cause of her husband's sudden death: his feigned anxiety about her health is adopted as the safest means of enticing her into his house,"—if those formidable conclusions had been urged on Mr. Rayburn, he would have felt it his duty to reject them, as unjustifiable aspersions on an absent man. And yet, when he took leave that evening of Mrs. Zant, he had pledged himself to give Lucy a holiday at the seaside: and he had said, without blushing, that the child really deserved it, as a reward for general good conduct and attention to her lessons!

552

IX.

THREE days later, the father and daughter arrived toward evening at St. Sallins-on-Sea. They found Mrs. Zant at the station.

The poor woman's joy, on seeing them, expressed itself like the joy of a child. "Oh, I am so glad! so glad!" was all she could say when they met. Lucy was half-smothered with kisses, and was made supremely happy by a present of the finest doll she had ever possessed. Mrs. Zant accompanied her friends to the rooms which had been secured at the hotel. She was able to speak confidentially to Mr. Rayburn, while Lucy was in the balcony hugging her doll, and looking at the sea.

The one event that had happened during Mrs. Zant's short residence at St. Sallins was the departure of her brother-in-law that morning, for London. He had been called away to operate on the feet of a wealthy patient who knew the value of his time: his housekeeper expected that he would return to dinner.

As to his conduct toward Mrs. Zant, he was not only as attentive as ever—he was almost oppressively affectionate in his language and manner. There was no service that a man could render which he had not eagerly offered to her. He declared that he already perceived an improvement in her health; he congratulated her on having decided to stay in his house; and (as a proof, perhaps, of his sincerity) he had repeatedly pressed her hand. "Have you any idea what all this means?" she said, simply.

Mr. Rayburn kept his idea to himself. He professed ignorance; and asked next what sort of person the housekeeper was.

Mrs. Zant shook her head ominously.

"Such a strange creature," she said, "and in the habit of taking such liberties that I begin to be afraid she is a little crazy."

"Is she an old woman?"

"No—only middle-aged." This morning, after her master had left the

553

house, she actually asked me what I thought of my brother-in-law! I told her, as coldly as possible, that I thought he was very kind. She was quite insensible to the tone in which I had spoken; she went on from bad to worse. "Do you call him the sort of man who would take the fancy of a young woman?" was her next question. She actually looked at me (I might have been wrong; and I hope I was) as if the "young woman" she had in her mind was myself! I said: "I don't think of such things, and I don't talk about them." Still, she was not in the least discouraged; she made a personal remark next: "Excuse me—but you do look wretchedly pale." I thought she seemed to enjoy the defect in my complexion; I really believe it raised me in her estimation. "We shall get on better in time," she said; "I am beginning to like you." She walked out humming a tune. Don't you agree with me? Don't you think she's crazy?"

"I can hardly give an opinion until I have seen her. Does she look as if she might have been a pretty woman at one time of her life?"

"Not the sort of pretty woman whom I admire!"

Mr. Rayburn smiled. "I was thinking," he resumed, "that this person's odd conduct may perhaps be accounted for. She is probably jealous of any young lady who is invited to her master's house—and (till she noticed your complexion) she began by being jealous of you."

Innocently at a loss to understand how she could become an object of the housekeeper's jealousy, Mrs. Zant looked at Mr. Rayburn in astonishment. Before she could give expression to her feeling of surprise, there was an interruption—a welcome interruption. A waiter entered the room, and announced a visitor; described as "a gentleman."

Mrs. Zant at once rose to retire.

"Who is the gentleman?" Mr. Rayburn asked—detaining Mrs. Zant as he spoke.

A voice which they both recognized answered gayly, from the outer side of the door:

"A friend from London."

X.

"WELCOME to St. Sallins!" cried Mr. John Zant. "I knew that you were expected, my dear sir, and I took my chance at finding you at the hotel." He turned to his sister-in-law, and kissed her hand with an elaborate gallantry worthy of Sir Charles Grandison himself. "When I reached home, my dear, and heard that you had gone out, I guessed that your object was to receive our excellent friend. You have not felt lonely while I have been away? That's right! that's right!" he looked toward the balcony, and discovered Lucy at the open window, staring at the magnificent stranger. "Your little daughter, Mr. Rayburn? Dear child! Come and kiss me."

Lucy answered in one positive word: "No."

Mr. John Zant was not easily discouraged.

"Show me your doll, darling," he said. "Sit on my knee."

Lucy answered in two positive words—"I won't."

Her father approached the window to administer the necessary reproof. Mr. John Zant interfered in the cause of mercy with his best grace. He held up his hands in cordial entreaty. "Dear Mr. Rayburn! The fairies are sometimes shy; and this little fairy doesn't take to strangers at first sight. Dear child! All in good time. And what stay do you make at St. Sallins? May we hope that our poor attractions will tempt you to prolong your visit?"

He put his flattering little question with an ease of manner which was rather too plainly assumed; and he looked at Mr. Rayburn with a watchfulness which appeared to attach undue importance to the reply. When he said: "What stay do you make at St. Sallins?" did he really mean: "How soon do you leave us?" Inclining to adopt this conclusion, Mr. Rayburn answered cautiously that his stay at the seaside would depend on circumstances. Mr. John Zant looked at his sister-in-law, sitting silent in a corner with Lucy on her lap. "Exert your attractions," he said; "make the circumstances agreeable to our good friend. Will you dine with us to-day, my dear sir, and bring your little fairy with you?"

Lucy was far from receiving this complimentary allusion in the spirit in which it had been offered. "I'm not a fairy," she declared. "I'm a child."

"And a naughty child," her father added, with all the severity that he could assume.

"I can't help it, papa; the man with the big beard puts me out."

The man with the big beard was amused—amiably, paternally amused—by Lucy's plain speaking. He repeated his invitation to dinner; and he did his best to look disappointed when Mr. Rayburn made the necessary excuses.

"Another day," he said (without, however, fixing the day). "I think you will find my house comfortable. My housekeeper may perhaps be eccentric—but in all essentials a woman in a thousand. Do you feel the change from London already? Our air at St. Sallins is really worthy of its reputation. Invalids who come here are cured as if by magic. What do you think of Mrs. Zant? How does she look?"

Mr. Rayburn was evidently expected to say that she looked better. He said it. Mr. John Zant seemed to have anticipated a stronger expression of opinion.

"Surprisingly better!" he pronounced. "Infinitely better! We ought both to be grateful. Pray believe that we are grateful."

"If you mean grateful to me," Mr. Rayburn remarked, "I don't quite understand—"

"You don't quite understand? Is it possible that you have forgotten our conversation when I first had the honor of receiving you? Look at Mrs. Zant again."

Mr. Rayburn looked; and Mrs. Zant's brother-in-law explained himself.

"You notice the return of her color, the healthy brightness of her eyes. (No, my dear, I am not paying you idle compliments; I am stating plain facts.) For that happy result, Mr. Rayburn, we are indebted to you."

"Surely not?"

"Surely yes! It was at your valuable suggestion that I thought of inviting my sister-in-law to visit me at St. Sallins. Ah, you remember it now. Forgive me if I look at my watch; the dinner hour is on my mind. Not, as your dear little daughter there seems to think, because I am greedy, but because I am always punctual, in justice to the cook. Shall we see you to-morrow? Call early, and you will find us at home."

He gave Mrs. Zant his arm, and bowed and smiled, and kissed his hand to Lucy, and left the room. Recalling their interview at the hotel in London, Mr. Rayburn now understood John Zant's object (on that occasion) in assuming the character of a helpless man in need of a sensible suggestion. If Mrs. Zant's residence under his roof became associated with evil consequences, he could declare that she would never have entered the house but for Mr. Rayburn's advice.

With the next day came the hateful necessity of returning this man's visit.

Mr. Rayburn was placed between two alternatives. In Mrs. Zant's interests he must remain, no matter at what sacrifice of his own inclinations, on good terms with her brother-in-law—or he must return to London, and leave the poor woman to her fate. His choice, it is needless to say, was never a matter of doubt. He called at the house, and did his innocent best—without in the least deceiving Mr. John Zant—to make himself agreeable during the short duration of his visit. Descending the stairs on his way out, accompanied by Mrs. Zant, he was surprised to see a middle-aged woman in the hall, who looked as if she was waiting there expressly to attract notice.

"The housekeeper," Mrs. Zant whispered. "She is impudent enough to try to make acquaintance with you."

This was exactly what the housekeeper was waiting in the hall to do.

"I hope you like our watering-place, sir," she began. "If I can be of service to you, pray command me. Any friend of this lady's has a claim on me—and you are an old friend, no doubt. I am only the housekeeper; but I presume to take a sincere interest in Mrs. Zant; and I am indeed glad to see you here. We none of us know—do we?—how soon we may want a friend. No offense, I hope? Thank you, sir. Good-morning."

There was nothing in the woman's eyes which indicated an unsettled mind; nothing in the appearance of her lips which suggested habits of intoxication. That her strange outburst of familiarity proceeded from some strong motive seemed to be more than probable. Putting together what Mrs. Zant had already told him, and what he had himself observed, Mr. Rayburn suspected that the motive might be found in the housekeeper's jealousy of her master.

XI.

REFLECTING in the solitude of his own room, Mr. Rayburn felt that the one prudent course to take would be to persuade Mrs. Zant to leave St. Sallins. He tried to prepare her for this strong proceeding, when she came the next day to take Lucy out for a walk.

"If you still regret having forced yourself to accept your brother-in-law's invitation," was all he ventured to say, "don't forget that you are perfect mistress of your own actions. You have only to come to me at the hotel, and I will take you back to London by the next train."

She positively refused to entertain the idea.

"I should be a thankless creature, indeed," she said, "if I accepted your proposal. Do you think I am ungrateful enough to involve you in a personal quarrel with John Zant? No! If I find myself forced to leave the house, I will go away alone."

There was no moving her from this resolution. When she and Lucy had gone out together, Mr. Rayburn remained at the hotel, with a mind ill at ease. A man of readier mental resources might have felt at a loss how to act for the best, in the emergency that now confronted him. While he was still as far as ever from arriving at a decision, some person knocked at the door.

Had Mrs. Zant returned? He looked up as the door was opened, and saw to his astonishment—Mr. John Zant's housekeeper.

"Don't let me alarm you, sir," the woman said. "Mrs. Zant has been taken a little faint, at the door of our house. My master is attending to her."

"Where is the child?" Mr. Rayburn asked.

"I was bringing her back to you, sir, when we met a lady and her little girl at the door of the hotel. They were on their way to the beach—and Miss Lucy begged hard to be allowed to go with them. The lady said the two children were playfellows, and she was sure you would not object."

"The lady is quite right. Mrs. Zant's illness is not serious, I hope?"

"I think not, sir. But I should like to say something in her interests. May I? Thank you." She advanced a step nearer to him, and spoke her next words in a whisper. "Take Mrs. Zant away from this place, and lose no time in doing it."

Mr. Rayburn was on his guard. He merely asked: "Why?"

The housekeeper answered in a curiously indirect manner—partly in jest, as it seemed, and partly in earnest.

"When a man has lost his wife," she said, "there's some difference of opinion in Parliament, as I hear, whether he does right or wrong, if he marries his wife's sister. Wait a bit! I'm coming to the point. My master is one who has a long head on his shoulders; he sees consequences which escape the notice of people like me. In his way of thinking, if one man may marry his wife's sister, and no harm done, where's the objection if another man pays a compliment to the family, and marries his brother's widow? My master, if you please, is that other man. Take the widow away before she marries him."

This was beyond endurance.

"You insult Mrs. Zant," Mr. Rayburn answered, "if you suppose that such a thing is possible!"

"Oh! I insult her, do I? Listen to me. One of three things will happen. She will be entrapped into consenting to it—or frightened into consenting to it—or drugged into consenting to it—"

Mr. Rayburn was too indignant to let her go on.

"You are talking nonsense," he said. "There can be no marriage; the law forbids it."

"Are you one of the people who see no further than their noses?" she asked insolently. "Won't the law take his money? Is he obliged to mention that he is related to her by marriage, when he buys the license?" She paused; her humor changed; she stamped furiously on the floor. The true motive that animated her showed itself in her next words, and warned Mr. Rayburn to grant a more favorable hearing than he had accorded to her yet. "If you won't stop it," she burst out, "I will! If he marries anybody, he is bound to marry ME. Will you take her away? I ask you, for the last time—will you take her away?"

The tone in which she made that final appeal to him had its effect.

"I will go back with you to John Zant's house," he said, "and judge for myself."

She laid her hand on his arm:

"I must go first—or you may not be let in. Follow me in five minutes; and don't knock at the street door."

On the point of leaving him, she abruptly returned.

"We have forgotten something," she said. "Suppose my master refuses to see you. His temper might get the better of him; he might make it so unpleasant for you that you would be obliged to go."

"My temper might get the better of me," Mr. Rayburn replied; "and—if I thought it was in Mrs. Zant's interests—I might refuse to leave the house unless she accompanied me."

"That will never do, sir."

"Why not?"

"Because I should be the person to suffer."

"In what way?"

"In this way. If you picked a quarrel with my master, I should be blamed for it because I showed you upstairs. Besides, think of the lady. You might frighten her out of her senses, if it came to a struggle between you two men."

The language was exaggerated; but there was a force in this last objection which Mr. Rayburn was obliged to acknowledge.

"And, after all," the housekeeper continued, "he has more right over her than you have. He is related to her, and you are only her friend."

Mr. Rayburn declined to let himself be influenced by this consideration, "Mr. John Zant is only related to her by marriage," he said. "If she prefers trusting in me—come what may of it, I will be worthy of her confidence."

The housekeeper shook her head.

"That only means another quarrel," she answered. "The wise way, with a man like my master, is the peaceable way. We must manage to deceive him."

"I don't like deceit."

"In that case, sir, I'll wish you good-by. We will leave Mrs. Zant to do the best she can for herself."

Mr. Rayburn was unreasonable. He positively refused to adopt this alternative.

"Will you hear what I have got to say?" the housekeeper asked.

"There can be no harm in that," he admitted. "Go on."

She took him at his word.

"When you called at our house," she began, "did you notice the doors in the passage, on the first floor? Very well. One of them is the door of the drawing-room, and the other is the door of the library. Do you remember the drawing-room, sir?"

"I thought it a large well-lighted room," Mr. Rayburn answered. "And I noticed a doorway in the wall, with a handsome curtain hanging over it."

"That's enough for our purpose," the housekeeper resumed. "On the

561

other side of the curtain, if you had looked in, you would have found the library. Suppose my master is as polite as usual, and begs to be excused for not receiving you, because it is an inconvenient time. And suppose you are polite on your side and take yourself off by the drawing-room door. You will find me waiting downstairs, on the first landing. Do you see it now?"

"I can't say I do."

"You surprise me, sir. What is to prevent us from getting back softly into the library, by the door in the passage? And why shouldn't we use that second way into the library as a means of discovering what may be going on in the drawing-room? Safe behind the curtain, you will see him if he behaves uncivilly to Mrs. Zant, or you will hear her if she calls for help. In either case, you may be as rough and ready with my master as you find needful; it will be he who has frightened her, and not you. And who can blame the poor housekeeper because Mr. Rayburn did his duty, and protected a helpless woman? There is my plan, sir. Is it worth trying?"

He answered, sharply enough: "I don't like it."

The housekeeper opened the door again, and wished him good-by.

If Mr. Rayburn had felt no more than an ordinary interest in Mrs. Zant, he would have let the woman go. As it was, he stopped her; and, after some further protest (which proved to be useless), he ended in giving way.

"You promise to follow my directions?" she stipulated.

He gave the promise. She smiled, nodded, and left him. True to his instructions, Mr. Rayburn reckoned five minutes by his watch, before he followed her.

XII.

THE housekeeper was waiting for him, with the street-door ajar.

"They are both in the drawing-room," she whispered, leading the way upstairs. "Step softly, and take him by surprise."

A table of oblong shape stood midway between the drawing-room walls.

At the end of it which was nearest to the window, Mrs. Zant was pacing to and fro across the breadth of the room. At the opposite end of the table, John Zant was seated. Taken completely by surprise, he showed himself in his true character. He started to his feet, and protested with an oath against the intrusion which had been committed on him.

Heedless of his action and his language, Mr. Rayburn could look at nothing, could think of nothing, but Mrs. Zant. She was still walking slowly to and fro, unconscious of the words of sympathy which he addressed to her, insensible even as it seemed to the presence of other persons in the room.

John Zant's voice broke the silence. His temper was under control again: he had his reasons for still remaining on friendly terms with Mr. Rayburn.

"I am sorry I forgot myself just now," he said.

Mr. Rayburn's interest was concentrated on Mrs. Zant; he took no notice of the apology.

"When did this happen?" he asked.

"About a quarter of an hour ago. I was fortunately at home. Without speaking to me, without noticing me, she walked upstairs like a person in a dream."

Mr. Rayburn suddenly pointed to Mrs. Zant.

"Look at her!" he said. "There's a change!"

All restlessness in her movements had come to an end. She was standing at the further end of the table, which was nearest to the window, in the full flow of sunlight pouring at that moment over her face. Her eyes looked out straight before her—void of all expression. Her lips were a little parted: her head drooped slightly toward her shoulder, in an attitude which suggested listening for something or waiting for something. In the warm brilliant light, she stood before the two men, a living creature self-isolated in a stillness like the stillness of death.

John Zant was ready with the expression of his opinion.

"A nervous seizure," he said. "Something resembling catalepsy, as you see."

"Have you sent for a doctor?"

"A doctor is not wanted."

"I beg your pardon. It seems to me that medical help is absolutely necessary."

"Be so good as to remember," Mr. John Zant answered, "that the decision rests with me, as the lady's relative. I am sensible of the honor which your visit confers on me. But the time has been unhappily chosen. Forgive me if I suggest that you will do well to retire."

Mr. Rayburn had not forgotten the housekeeper's advice, or the promise which she had exacted from him. But the expression in John Zant's face was a serious trial to his self-control. He hesitated, and looked back at Mrs. Zant.

If he provoked a quarrel by remaining in the room, the one alternative would be the removal of her by force. Fear of the consequences to herself, if she was suddenly and roughly roused from her trance, was the one consideration which reconciled him to submission. He withdrew.

The housekeeper was waiting for him below, on the first landing. When the door of the drawing-room had been closed again, she signed to him to follow her, and returned up the stairs. After another struggle with himself, he obeyed. They entered the library from the corridor—and placed themselves behind the closed curtain which hung over the doorway. It was easy so to arrange the edge of the drapery as to observe, without exciting suspicion, whatever was going on in the next room.

Mrs. Zant's brother-in-law was approaching her at the time when Mr. Rayburn saw him again.

In the instant afterward, she moved—before he had completely passed over the space between them. Her still figure began to tremble. She lifted her drooping head. For a moment there was a shrinking in her—as if she had been touched by something. She seemed to recognize the touch: she was still

564

again.

John Zant watched the change. It suggested to him that she was beginning to recover her senses. He tried the experiment of speaking to her.

"My love, my sweet angel, come to the heart that adores you!"

He advanced again; he passed into the flood of sunlight pouring over her.

"Rouse yourself!" he said.

She still remained in the same position; apparently at his mercy, neither hearing him nor seeing him.

"Rouse yourself!" he repeated. "My darling, come to me!"

At the instant when he attempted to embrace her—at the instant when Mr. Rayburn rushed into the room—John Zant's arms, suddenly turning rigid, remained outstretched. With a shriek of horror, he struggled to draw them back—struggled, in the empty brightness of the sunshine, as if some invisible grip had seized him.

"What has got me?" the wretch screamed. "Who is holding my hands? Oh, the cold of it! the cold of it!"

His features became convulsed; his eyes turned upward until only the white eyeballs were visible. He fell prostrate with a crash that shook the room.

The housekeeper ran in. She knelt by her master's body. With one hand she loosened his cravat. With the other she pointed to the end of the table.

Mrs. Zant still kept her place; but there was another change. Little by little, her eyes recovered their natural living expression—then slowly closed. She tottered backward from the table, and lifted her hands wildly, as if to grasp at something which might support her. Mr. Rayburn hurried to her before she fell—lifted her in his arms—and carried her out of the room.

One of the servants met them in the hall. He sent her for a carriage. In a quarter of an hour more, Mrs. Zant was safe under his care at the hotel.

XIII.

THAT night a note, written by the housekeeper, was delivered to Mrs. Zant.

"The doctors give little hope. The paralytic stroke is spreading upward to his face. If death spares him, he will live a helpless man. I shall take care of him to the last. As for you—forget him."

Mrs. Zant gave the note to Mr. Rayburn.

"Read it, and destroy it," she said. "It is written in ignorance of the terrible truth."

He obeyed—and looked at her in silence, waiting to hear more. She hid her face. The few words she had addressed to him, after a struggle with herself, fell slowly and reluctantly from her lips.

She said: "No mortal hand held the hands of John Zant. The guardian spirit was with me. The promised protection was with me. I know it. I wish to know no more."

Having spoken, she rose to retire. He opened the door for her, seeing that she needed rest in her own room.

Left by himself, he began to consider the prospect that was before him in the future. How was he to regard the woman who had just left him? As a poor creature weakened by disease, the victim of her own nervous delusion? or as the chosen object of a supernatural revelation—unparalleled by any similar revelation that he had heard of, or had found recorded in books? His first discovery of the place that she really held in his estimation dawned on his mind, when he felt himself recoiling from the conclusion which presented her to his pity, and yielding to the nobler conviction which felt with her faith, and raised her to a place apart among other women.

XIV.

THEY left St. Sallins the next day.

Arrived at the end of the journey, Lucy held fast by Mrs. Zant's hand. Tears were rising in the child's eyes.

566

"Are we to bid her good-by?" she said sadly to her father.

He seemed to be unwilling to trust himself to speak; he only said:

"My dear, ask her yourself."

But the result justified him. Lucy was happy again.

MISS MORRIS AND THE STRANGER.

I.

WHEN I first saw him, he was lost in one of the Dead Cities of England—situated on the South Coast, and called Sandwich.

Shall I describe Sandwich? I think not. Let us own the truth; descriptions of places, however nicely they may be written, are always more or less dull. Being a woman, I naturally hate dullness. Perhaps some description of Sandwich may drop out, as it were, from my report of our conversation when we first met as strangers in the street.

He began irritably. "I've lost myself," he said.

"People who don't know the town often do that," I remarked.

He went on: "Which is my way to the Fleur de Lys Inn?"

His way was, in the first place, to retrace his steps. Then to turn to the left. Then to go on until he found two streets meeting. Then to take the street on the right. Then to look out for the second turning on the left. Then to follow the turning until he smelled stables—and there was the inn. I put it in the clearest manner, and never stumbled over a word.

"How the devil am I to remember all that?" he said.

This was rude. We are naturally and properly indignant with any man who is rude to us. But whether we turn our backs on him in contempt, or whether we are merciful and give him a lesson in politeness, depends entirely on the man. He may be a bear, but he may also have his redeeming qualities. This man had redeeming qualities. I cannot positively say that he was either handsome or ugly, young or old, well or ill dressed. But I can speak with certainty to the personal attractions which recommended him to notice. For instance, the tone of his voice was persuasive. (Did you ever read a story, written by one of us, in which we failed to dwell on our hero's voice?) Then, again, his hair was reasonably long. (Are you acquainted with any woman who can endure a man with a cropped head?) Moreover, he was of a good height. (It must be a very tall woman who can feel favorably inclined toward a short man.) Lastly, although his eyes were not more than fairly presentable in form and color, the wretch had in some unaccountable manner become possessed of beautiful eyelashes. They were even better eyelashes than mine. I write quite seriously. There is one woman who is above the common weakness of vanity—and she holds the present pen.

So I gave my lost stranger a lesson in politeness. The lesson took the form of a trap. I asked him if he would like me to show him the way to the inn. He was still annoyed at losing himself. As I had anticipated, he bluntly answered: "Yes."

"When you were a boy, and you wanted something," I said, "did your mother teach you to say 'Please'?"

He positively blushed. "She did," he admitted; "and she taught me to say 'Beg your pardon' when I was rude. I'll say it now: 'Beg your pardon.'"

This curious apology increased my belief in his redeeming qualities. I led the way to the inn. He followed me in silence. No woman who respects herself can endure silence when she is in the company of a man. I made him talk.

"Do you come to us from Ramsgate?" I began. He only nodded his head. "We don't think much of Ramsgate here," I went on. "There is not an old building in the place. And their first Mayor was only elected the other day!"

This point of view seemed to be new to him. He made no attempt to dispute it; he only looked around him, and said: "Sandwich is a melancholy place, miss." He was so rapidly improving in politeness, that I encouraged him by a smile. As a citizen of Sandwich, I may say that we take it as a compliment when we are told that our town is a melancholy place. And why not? Melancholy is connected with dignity. And dignity is associated with age. And we are old. I teach my pupils logic, among other things—there is a specimen. Whatever may be said to the contrary, women can reason. They

569

can also wander; and I must admit that I am wandering. Did I mention, at starting, that I was a governess? If not, that allusion to "pupils" must have come in rather abruptly. Let me make my excuses, and return to my lost stranger.

"Is there any such thing as a straight street in all Sandwich?" he asked.

"Not one straight street in the whole town."

"Any trade, miss?"

"As little as possible—and that is expiring."

"A decayed place, in short?"

"Thoroughly decayed."

My tone seemed to astonish him. "You speak as if you were proud of its being a decayed place," he said.

I quite respected him; this was such an intelligent remark to make. We do enjoy our decay: it is our chief distinction. Progress and prosperity everywhere else; decay and dissolution here. As a necessary consequence, we produce our own impression, and we like to be original. The sea deserted us long ago: it once washed our walls, it is now two miles away from us— we don't regret the sea. We had sometimes ninety-five ships in our harbor, Heaven only knows how many centuries ago; we now have one or two small coasting vessels, half their time aground in a muddy little river—we don't regret our harbor. But one house in the town is daring enough to anticipate the arrival of resident visitors, and announces furnished apartments to let. What a becoming contrast to our modern neighbor, Ramsgate! Our noble market-place exhibits the laws made by the corporation; and every week there are fewer and fewer people to obey the laws. How convenient! Look at our one warehouse by the river side—with the crane generally idle, and the windows mostly boarded up; and perhaps one man at the door, looking out for the job which his better sense tells him cannot possibly come. What a wholesome protest against the devastating hurry and over-work elsewhere, which has shattered the nerves of the nation! "Far from me and from my friends" (to borrow the eloquent language of Doctor Johnson) "be such frigid enthusiasm as shall conduct us indifferent and unmoved" over the bridge by which you enter Sandwich, and pay a toll if you do it in a carriage. "That man is little to be envied (Doctor Johnson again) who can lose himself in our labyrinthine streets, and not feel that he has reached the welcome limits of progress, and found a haven of rest in an age of hurry."

I am wandering again. Bear with the unpremeditated enthusiasm of a citizen who only attained years of discretion at her last birthday. We shall soon have done with Sandwich; we are close to the door of the inn.

"You can't mistake it now, sir," I said. "Good-morning."

He looked down at me from under his beautiful eyelashes (have I mentioned that I am a little woman?), and he asked in his persuasive tones: "Must we say good-by?"

I made him a bow.

"Would you allow me to see you safe home?" he suggested.

Any other man would have offended me. This man blushed like a boy, and looked at the pavement instead of looking at me. By this time I had made up my mind about him. He was not only a gentleman beyond all doubt, but a shy gentleman as well. His bluntness and his odd remarks were, as I thought, partly efforts to disguise his shyness, and partly refuges in which he tried to forget his own sense of it. I answered his audacious proposal amiably and pleasantly. "You would only lose your way again," I said, "and I should have to take you back to the inn for the second time."

Wasted words! My obstinate stranger only made another proposal.

"I have ordered lunch here," he said, "and I am quite alone." He stopped in confusion, and looked as if he rather expected me to box his ears. "I shall be forty next birthday," he went on; "I am old enough to be your father." I all but burst out laughing, and stepped across the street, on my way home. He followed me. "We might invite the landlady to join us," he said, looking the picture of a headlong man, dismayed by the consciousness of his own imprudence. "Couldn't you honor me by lunching with me if we had the landlady?" he asked.

This was a little too much. "Quite out of the question, sir—and you ought to know it," I said with severity. He half put out his hand. "Won't you even shake hands with me?" he inquired piteously. When we have most properly administered a reproof to a man, what is the perversity which makes us weakly pity him the minute afterward? I was fool enough to shake hands with this perfect stranger. And, having done it, I completed the total loss of my dignity by running away. Our dear crooked little streets hid me from him directly.

As I rang at the door-bell of my employer's house, a thought occurred to me which might have been alarming to a better regulated mind than mine.

"Suppose he should come back to Sandwich?"

II.

BEFORE many more days passed I had troubles of my own to contend with, which put the eccentric stranger out of my head for the time.

Unfortunately, my troubles are part of my story; and my early life mixes itself up with them. In consideration of what is to follow, may I say two words relating to the period before I was a governess?

I am the orphan daughter of a shopkeeper of Sandwich. My father died, leaving to his widow and child an honest name and a little income of L80 a year. We kept on the shop—neither gaining nor losing by it. The truth is nobody would buy our poor little business. I was thirteen years old at the time; and I was able to help my mother, whose health was then beginning to fail. Never shall I forget a certain bright summer's day, when I saw a new customer enter our shop. He was an elderly gentleman; and he seemed surprised to find so young a girl as myself in charge of the business, and, what is more, competent to support the charge. I answered his questions in a manner which seemed to please him. He soon discovered that my education (excepting my knowledge of the business) had been sadly neglected; and he inquired if he could see my mother. She was resting on the sofa in the back parlor—and she received him there. When he came out, he patted me on the cheek. "I have taken a fancy to you," he said, "and perhaps I shall come back again." He did come back again. My mother had referred him to the rector for our characters in the town, and he had heard what our clergyman could say for us. Our only relations had emigrated to Australia, and were not doing well there. My mother's death would leave me, so far as relatives were concerned, literally alone in the world. "Give this girl a first-rate education," said our elderly customer, sitting at our tea-table in the back parlor, "and she will do. If you will send her to school, ma'am, I'll pay for her education." My poor mother began to cry at the prospect of parting with me. The old gentleman said: "Think of it," and got up to go. He gave me his card as I opened the shop-door for him. "If you find yourself in trouble," he whispered, so that my mother could not hear him, "be a wise child, and write and tell me of it." I looked at the card. Our kind-hearted customer was no less a person than Sir Gervase Damian, of Garrum Park, Sussex—with landed property in our county as well! He had made himself (through the rector, no doubt) far better acquainted than I was with the true state of my mother's health. In four months from the memorable day when the great man had taken tea with us, my time had come to be alone in the world. I have no courage to dwell on it; my spirits sink, even at this distance of time, when I think of myself in those days. The good rector helped me with his advice—I wrote to Sir Gervase Damian.

A change had come over his life as well as mine in the interval since we had met.

Sir Gervase had married for the second time—and, what was more foolish still, perhaps, at his age, had married a young woman. She was said to be consumptive, and of a jealous temper as well. Her husband's only child by his first wife, a son and heir, was so angry at his father's second marriage that he left the house. The landed property being entailed, Sir Gervase could only express his sense of his son's conduct by making a new will, which left all his property in money to his young wife.

These particulars I gathered from the steward, who was expressly sent to visit me at Sandwich.

"Sir Gervase never makes a promise without keeping it," this gentleman informed me. "I am directed to take you to a first-rate ladies' school in the neighborhood of London, and to make all the necessary arrangements for your remaining there until you are eighteen years of age. Any written communications in the future are to pass, if you please, through the hands of the rector of Sandwich. The delicate health of the new Lady Damian makes it only too likely that the lives of her husband and herself will be passed, for the most part, in a milder climate than the climate of England. I am instructed to say this, and to convey to you Sir Gervase's best wishes."

By the rector's advice, I accepted the position offered to me in this unpleasantly formal manner—concluding (quite correctly, as I afterward discovered) that I was indebted to Lady Damian for the arrangement which personally separated me from my benefactor. Her husband's kindness and my gratitude, meeting on the neutral ground of Garrum Park, were objects of conjugal distrust to this lady. Shocking! shocking! I left a sincerely grateful letter to be forwarded to Sir Gervase; and, escorted by the steward, I went to school—being then just fourteen years old.

I know I am a fool. Never mind. There is some pride in me, though I am only a small shopkeeper's daughter. My new life had its trials—my pride held me up.

For the four years during which I remained at the school, my poor welfare might be a subject of inquiry to the rector, and sometimes even the steward—never to Sir Gervase himself. His winters were no doubt passed abroad; but in the summer time he and Lady Damian were at home again. Not even for a day or two in the holiday time was there pity enough felt for my lonely position to ask me to be the guest of the housekeeper (I expected nothing more) at Garrum Park. But for my pride, I might have felt it bitterly. My pride said to me, "Do justice to yourself." I worked so hard, I behaved so well, that the mistress of the school wrote to Sir Gervase to tell him how thoroughly I had deserved the kindness that he had shown to me. No answer was received. (Oh, Lady Damian!) No change varied the monotony of my life—except when one of my schoolgirl friends sometimes took me home with her for a few days at vacation time. Never mind. My pride held me up.

As the last half-year of my time at school approached, I began to consider the serious question of my future life.

Of course, I could have lived on my eighty pounds a year; but what a lonely, barren existence it promised to be!—unless somebody married me; and where, if you please, was I to find him? My education had thoroughly fitted me to be a governess. Why not try my fortune, and see a little of the world in that way? Even if I fell among ill-conditioned people, I could be independent of them, and retire on my income.

The rector, visiting London, came to see me. He not only approved of my idea—he offered me a means of carrying it out. A worthy family, recently settled at Sandwich, were in want of a governess. The head of the household was partner in a business (the exact nature of which it is needless to mention) having "branches" out of London. He had become superintendent of a new "branch"—tried as a commercial experiment, under special circumstances, at Sandwich. The idea of returning to my native place pleased me—dull as the place was to others. I accepted the situation.

When the steward's usual half-yearly letter arrived soon afterward, inquiring what plans I had formed on leaving school, and what he could do to help them, acting on behalf of Sir Gervase, a delicious tingling filled me from head to foot when I thought of my own independence. It was not ingratitude toward my benefactor; it was only my little private triumph over Lady Damian. Oh, my sisters of the sex, can you not understand and forgive me?

So to Sandwich I returned; and there, for three years, I remained with the kindest people who ever breathed the breath of life. Under their roof I was still living when I met with my lost gentleman in the street.

Ah, me! the end of that quiet, pleasant life was near. When I lightly spoke to the odd stranger of the expiring trade of the town, I never expected that my employer's trade was expiring too. The speculation had turned out to be a losing one; and all his savings had been embarked in it. He could no longer remain at Sandwich, or afford to keep a governess. His wife broke the sad news to me. I was so fond of the children, I proposed to her to give up my salary. Her husband refused even to consider the proposal. It was the old story of poor humanity over again. We cried, we kissed, we parted.

What was I to do next?—Write to Sir Gervase?

I had already written, soon after my return to Sandwich; breaking through the regulations by directly addressing Sir Gervase. I expressed my grateful sense of his generosity to a poor girl who had no family claim on him; and I promised to make the one return in my power by trying to be worthy of the interest he had taken in me. The letter was written without any alloy of mental reserve. My new life as a governess was such a happy one that I had forgotten my paltry bitterness of feeling against Lady Damian.

It was a relief to think of this change for the better, when the secretary at Garrum Park informed me that he had forwarded my letter to Sir Gervase, then at Madeira with his sick wife. She was slowly and steadily wasting away in a decline. Before another year had passed, Sir Gervase was left a widower for the second time, with no child to console him under his loss. No answer came to my grateful letter. I should have been unreasonable indeed if I had expected the bereaved husband to remember me in his grief and loneliness. Could I write to him again, in my own trumpery little interests, under these circumstances? I thought (and still think) that the commonest feeling of delicacy forbade it. The only other alternative was to appeal to the ever-ready friends of the obscure and helpless public. I advertised in the newspapers.

The tone of one of the answers which I received impressed me so favorably, that I forwarded my references. The next post brought my written engagement, and the offer of a salary which doubled my income.

The story of the past is told; and now we may travel on again, with no more stoppages by the way.

III.

THE residence of my present employer was in the north of England. Having to pass through London, I arranged to stay in town for a few days to make some necessary additions to my wardrobe. An old servant of the rector, who kept a lodging-house in the suburbs, received me kindly, and guided my choice in the serious matter of a dressmaker. On the second morning after my arrival an event happened. The post brought me a letter forwarded from the rectory. Imagine my astonishment when my correspondent proved to be Sir Gervase Damian himself!

The letter was dated from his house in London. It briefly invited me to call and see him, for a reason which I should hear from his own lips. He naturally supposed that I was still at Sandwich, and requested me, in a postscript, to consider my journey as made at his expense.

I went to the house the same day. While I was giving my name, a gentleman came out into the hall. He spoke to me without ceremony.

"Sir Gervase," he said, "believes he is going to die. Don't encourage him in that idea. He may live for another year or more, if his friends will only persuade him to be hopeful about himself."

With that, the gentleman left me; the servant said it was the doctor.

The change in my benefactor, since I had seen him last, startled and distressed me. He lay back in a large arm-chair, wearing a grim black dressing-gown, and looking pitiably thin and pinched and worn. I do not think I should have known him again, if we had met by accident. He signed to me to be seated on a little chair by his side.

"I wanted to see you," he said quietly, "before I die. You must have thought me neglectful and unkind, with good reason. My child, you have not been forgotten. If years have passed without a meeting between us, it has not been altogether my fault—"

He stopped. A pained expression passed over his poor worn face; he was evidently thinking of the young wife whom he had lost. I repeated—fervently and sincerely repeated—what I had already said to him in writing. "I owe everything, sir, to your fatherly kindness." Saying this, I ventured a little further. I took his wan white hand, hanging over the arm of the chair, and respectfully put it to my lips.

He gently drew his hand away from me, and sighed as he did it. Perhaps she had sometimes kissed his hand.

"Now tell me about yourself," he said.

I told him of my new situation, and how I had got it. He listened with evident interest.

"I was not self-deceived," he said, "when I first took a fancy to you in the shop. I admire your independent feeling; it's the right kind of courage in a girl like you. But you must let me do something more for you—some little service to remember me by when the end has come. What shall it be?"

"Try to get better, sir; and let me write to you now and then," I answered. "Indeed, indeed, I want nothing more."

"You will accept a little present, at least?" With those words he took from the breast-pocket of his dressing-gown an enameled cross attached to a gold chain. "Think of me sometimes," he said, as he put the chain round my neck. He drew me to him gently, and kissed my forehead. It was too much for me. "Don't cry, my dear," he said; "don't remind me of another sad young face—"

Once more he stopped; once more he was thinking of the lost wife. I pulled down my veil, and ran out of the room.

IV.

THE next day I was on my way to the north. My narrative brightens again—but let us not forget Sir Gervase Damian.

I ask permission to introduce some persons of distinction:—Mrs. Fosdyke, of Carsham Hall, widow of General Fosdyke; also Master Frederick, Miss Ellen, and Miss Eva, the pupils of the new governess; also two ladies and three gentlemen, guests staying in the house.

Discreet and dignified; handsome and well-bred—such was my impression of Mrs. Fosdyke, while she harangued me on the subject of her children, and communicated her views on education. Having heard the views before from others, I assumed a listening position, and privately formed my opinion of the schoolroom. It was large, lofty, perfectly furnished for the purpose; it had a big window and a balcony looking out over the garden terrace and the park beyond—a wonderful schoolroom, in my limited experience. One of the two doors which it possessed was left open, and showed me a sweet little bedroom, with amber draperies and maplewood furniture, devoted to myself. Here were wealth and liberality, in the harmonious combination so seldom discovered by the spectator of small means. I controlled my first feeling of bewilderment just in time to answer Mrs. Fosdyke on the subject of reading and recitation—viewed as minor accomplishments which a good governess might be expected to teach.

"While the organs are young and pliable," the lady remarked, "I regard it as of great importance to practice children in the art of reading aloud, with an agreeable variety of tone and correctness of emphasis. Trained in this way, they will produce a favorable impression on others, even in ordinary conversation, when they grow up. Poetry, committed to memory and recited, is a valuable means toward this end. May I hope that your studies have enabled you to carry out my views?"

Formal enough in language, but courteous and kind in manner. I relieved Mrs. Fosdyke from anxiety by informing her that we had a professor of elocution at school. And then I was left to improve my acquaintance with my three pupils.

They were fairly intelligent children; the boy, as usual, being slower than the girls. I did my best—with many a sad remembrance of the far dearer pupils whom I had left—to make them like me and trust me; and I succeeded in winning their confidence. In a week from the time of my arrival at Carsham Hall, we began to understand each other.

The first day in the week was one of our days for reciting poetry, in obedience to the instructions with which I had been favored by Mrs. Fosdyke. I had done with the girls, and had just opened (perhaps I ought to say profaned) Shakespeare's "Julius Caesar," in the elocutionary interests of Master Freddy. Half of Mark Antony's first glorious speech over Caesar's dead body he had learned by heart; and it was now my duty to teach him, to the best of my small ability, how to speak it. The morning was warm. We had our big window open; the delicious perfume of flowers in the garden beneath filled the room.

I recited the first eight lines, and stopped there feeling that I must not exact too much from the boy at first. "Now, Freddy," I said, "try if you can speak the poetry as I have spoken it."

"Don't do anything of the kind, Freddy," said a voice from the garden; "it's all spoken wrong."

Who was this insolent person? A man unquestionably—and, strange to say, there was something not entirely unfamiliar to me in his voice. The girls began to giggle. Their brother was more explicit. "Oh," says Freddy, "it's only Mr. Sax."

The one becoming course to pursue was to take no notice of the interruption. "Go on," I said. Freddy recited the lines, like a dear good boy, with as near an imitation of my style of elocution as could be expected from him.

"Poor devil!" cried the voice from the garden, insolently pitying my attentive pupil.

I imposed silence on the girls by a look—and then, without stirring from my chair, expressed my sense of the insolence of Mr. Sax in clear and commanding tones. "I shall be obliged to close the window if this is repeated." Having spoken to that effect, I waited in expectation of an apology. Silence was the only apology. It was enough for me that I had produced the right impression. I went on with my recitation.

> *"Here, under leave of Brutus, and the rest*
>
> *(For Brutus is an honorable man;*
>
> *So are they all, all honorable men),*
>
> *Come I to speak in Caesar's funeral.*
>
> *He was my friend, faithful and just to me—"*

"Oh, good heavens, I can't stand that! Why don't you speak the last line properly? Listen to me."

Dignity is a valuable quality, especially in a governess. But there are limits to the most highly trained endurance. I bounced out into the balcony—and there, on the terrace, smoking a cigar, was my lost stranger in the streets of Sandwich!

He recognized me, on his side, the instant I appeared. "Oh, Lord!" he cried in tones of horror, and ran round the corner of the terrace as if my eyes had been mad bulls in close pursuit of him. By this time it is, I fear, useless for me to set myself up as a discreet person in emergencies. Another woman might have controlled herself. I burst into fits of laughter. Freddy and the girls joined me. For the time, it was plainly useless to pursue the business of education. I shut up Shakespeare, and allowed—no, let me tell the truth, encouraged—the children to talk about Mr. Sax.

They only seemed to know what Mr. Sax himself had told them. His father and mother and brothers and sisters had all died in course of time. He was the sixth and last of the children, and he had been christened "Sextus" in consequence, which is Latin (here Freddy interposed) for sixth. Also christened "Cyril" (here the girls recovered the lead) by his mother's request; "Sextus" being such a hideous name. And which of his Christian names does he use? You wouldn't ask if you knew him! "Sextus," of course, because it is the ugliest. Sextus Sax? Not the romantic sort of name that one likes, when one is a woman. But I have no right to be particular. My own name (is it possible that I have not mentioned it in these pages yet?) is only Nancy Morris. Do not despise me—and let us return to Mr. Sax.

Is he married? The eldest girl thought not. She had heard mamma say to a lady, "An old German family, my dear, and, in spite of his oddities, an excellent man; but so poor—barely enough to live on—and blurts out the truth, if people ask his opinion, as if he had twenty thousand a year!" "Your mamma knows him well, of course?" "I should think so, and so do we. He often comes here. They say he's not good company among grown-up people. We think him jolly. He understands dolls, and he's the best back at leap-frog in the whole of England." Thus far we had advanced in the praise of

Sextus Sax, when one of the maids came in with a note for me. She smiled mysteriously, and said, "I'm to wait for an answer, miss."

I opened the note, and read these lines:—

"I am so ashamed of myself, I daren't attempt to make my apologies personally. Will you accept my written excuses? Upon my honor, nobody told me when I got here yesterday that you were in the house. I heard the recitation, and—can you excuse my stupidity?—I thought it was a stage-struck housemaid amusing herself with the children. May I accompany you when you go out with the young ones for your daily walk? One word will do. Yes or no. Penitently yours—S. S."

In my position, there was but one possible answer to this. Governesses must not make appointments with strange gentlemen—even when the children are present in the capacity of witnesses. I said, No. Am I claiming too much for my readiness to forgive injuries, when I add that I should have preferred saying Yes?

We had our early dinner, and then got ready to go out walking as usual. These pages contain a true confession. Let me own that I hoped Mr. Sax would understand my refusal, and ask Mrs. Fosdyke's leave to accompany us. Lingering a little as we went downstairs, I heard him in the hall—actually speaking to Mrs. Fosdyke! What was he saying? That darling boy, Freddy, got into a difficulty with one of his boot-laces exactly at the right moment. I could help him, and listen—and be sadly disappointed by the result. Mr. Sax was offended with me.

"You needn't introduce me to the new governess," I heard him say. "We have met on a former occasion, and I produced a disagreeable impression on her. I beg you will not speak of me to Miss Morris."

Before Mrs. Fosdyke could say a word in reply, Master Freddy changed suddenly from a darling boy to a detestable imp. "I say, Mr. Sax!" he called out, "Miss Morris doesn't mind you a bit—she only laughs at you."

The answer to this was the sudden closing of a door. Mr. Sax had taken refuge from me in one of the ground-floor rooms. I was so mortified, I could almost have cried.

Getting down into the hall, we found Mrs. Fosdyke with her garden hat on, and one of the two ladies who were staying in the house (the unmarried one) whispering to her at the door of the morning-room. The lady—Miss Melbury—looked at me with a certain appearance of curiosity which I was quite at a loss to understand, and suddenly turned away toward the further end of the hall.

"I will walk with you and the children," Mrs. Fosdyke said to me. "Freddy, you can ride your tricycle if you like." She turned to the girls. "My dears, it's cool under the trees. You may take your skipping-ropes."

She had evidently something special to say to me; and she had adopted the necessary measures for keeping the children in front of us, well out of hearing. Freddy led the way on his horse on three wheels; the girls followed, skipping merrily. Mrs. Fosdyke opened the business by the most embarrassing remark that she could possibly have made under the circumstances.

"I find that you are acquainted with Mr. Sax," she began; "and I am surprised to hear that you dislike him."

She smiled pleasantly, as if my supposed dislike of Mr. Sax rather amused her. What "the ruling passion" may be among men, I cannot presume to consider. My own sex, however, I may claim to understand. The ruling passion among women is Conceit. My ridiculous notion of my own consequence was wounded in some way. I assumed a position of the loftiest indifference.

"Really, ma'am," I said, "I can't undertake to answer for any impression that Mr. Sax may have formed. We met by the merest accident. I know nothing about him."

Mrs. Fosdyke eyed me slyly, and appeared to be more amused than ever.

"He is a very odd man," she admitted, "but I can tell you there is a fine nature under that strange surface of his. However," she went on, "I am forgetting that he forbids me to talk about him in your presence. When the opportunity offers, I shall take my own way of teaching you two to understand each other: you will both be grateful to me when I have succeeded. In the meantime, there is a third person who will be sadly disappointed to hear that you know nothing about Mr. Sax."

"May I ask, ma'am, who the person is?"

"Can you keep a secret, Miss Morris? Of course you can! The person is Miss Melbury."

(Miss Melbury was a dark woman. It cannot be because I am a fair woman myself—I hope I am above such narrow prejudices as that—but it is certainly true that I don't admire dark women.)

"She heard Mr. Sax telling me that you particularly disliked him," Mrs. Fosdyke proceeded. "And just as you appeared in the hall, she was asking me to find out what your reason was. My own opinion of Mr. Sax, I ought to tell you, doesn't satisfy her; I am his old friend, and I present him of course from my own favorable point of view. Miss Melbury is anxious to be made acquainted with his faults—and she expected you to be a valuable witness against him."

Thus far we had been walking on. We now stopped, as if by common consent, and looked at one another.

In my previous experience of Mrs. Fosdyke, I had only seen the more constrained and formal side of her character. Without being aware of my own success, I had won the mother's heart in winning the goodwill of her children. Constraint now seized its first opportunity of melting away; the latent sense of humor in the great lady showed itself, while I was inwardly wondering what the nature of Miss Melbury's extraordinary interest in Mr. Sax might be. Easily penetrating my thoughts, she satisfied my curiosity without committing herself to a reply in words. Her large gray eyes sparkled as they rested on my face, and she hummed the tune of the old French song, "C'est l'amour, l'amour, l'amour!" There is no disguising it—something in this disclosure made me excessively angry. Was I angry with Miss Melbury? or with Mr. Sax? or with myself? I think it must have been with myself.

Finding that I had nothing to say on my side, Mrs. Fosdyke looked at her watch, and remembered her domestic duties. To my relief, our interview came to an end.

"I have a dinner-party to-day," she said, "and I have not seen the housekeeper yet. Make yourself beautiful, Miss Morris, and join us in the drawing-room after dinner."

V.

I WORE my best dress; and, in all my life before, I never took such pains with my hair. Nobody will be foolish enough, I hope, to suppose that I did this on Mr. Sax's account. How could I possibly care about a man who was little better than a stranger to me? No! the person I dressed at was Miss Melbury.

She gave me a look, as I modestly placed myself in a corner, which amply rewarded me for the time spent on my toilet. The gentlemen came in. I looked at Mr. Sax (mere curiosity) under shelter of my fan. His appearance was greatly improved by evening dress. He discovered me in my corner, and seemed doubtful whether to approach me or not. I was reminded of our first odd meeting; and I could not help smiling as I called it to mind. Did he presume to think that I was encouraging him? Before I could decide that question, he took the vacant place on the sofa. In any other man—after what had passed in the morning—this would have been an audacious proceeding. He looked so painfully embarrassed, that it became a species of Christian duty to pity him.

"Won't you shake hands?" he said, just as he had said it at Sandwich.

I peeped round the corner of my fan at Miss Melbury. She was looking at us. I shook hands with Mr. Sax.

"What sort of sensation is it," he asked, "when you shake hands with a man whom you hate?"

"I really can't tell you," I answered innocently; "I have never done such a thing."

"You would not lunch with me at Sandwich," he protested; "and, after

585

the humblest apology on my part, you won't forgive me for what I did this morning. Do you expect me to believe that I am not the special object of your antipathy? I wish I had never met with you! At my age, a man gets angry when he is treated cruelly and doesn't deserve it. You don't understand that, I dare say."

"Oh, yes, I do. I heard what you said about me to Mrs. Fosdyke, and I heard you bang the door when you got out of my way."

He received this reply with every appearance of satisfaction. "So you listened, did you? I'm glad to hear that."

"Why?"

"It shows you take some interest in me, after all."

Throughout this frivolous talk (I only venture to report it because it shows that I bore no malice on my side) Miss Melbury was looking at us like the basilisk of the ancients. She owned to being on the wrong side of thirty; and she had a little money—but these were surely no reasons why she should glare at a poor governess. Had some secret understanding of the tender sort been already established between Mr. Sax and herself? She provoked me into trying to find out—especially as the last words he had said offered me the opportunity.

"I can prove that I feel a sincere interest in you," I resumed. "I can resign you to a lady who has a far better claim to your attention than mine. You are neglecting her shamefully."

He stared at me with an appearance of bewilderment, which seemed to imply that the attachment was on the lady's side, so far. It was of course impossible to mention names; I merely turned my eyes in the right direction. He looked where I looked—and his shyness revealed itself, in spite of his resolution to conceal it. His face flushed; he looked mortified and surprised. Miss Melbury could endure it no longer. She rose, took a song from the music-stand, and approached us.

"I am going to sing," she said, handing the music to him. "Please turn over for me, Mr. Sax."

I think he hesitated—but I cannot feel sure that I observed him correctly. It matters little. With or without hesitation, he followed her to the piano.

Miss Melbury sang—with perfect self-possession, and an immense compass of voice. A gentleman near me said she ought to be on the stage. I thought so too. Big as it was, our drawing-room was not large enough for her. The gentleman sang next. No voice at all—but so sweet, such true feeling! I turned over the leaves for him. A dear old lady, sitting near the piano, entered into conversation with me. She spoke of the great singers at the beginning of the present century. Mr. Sax hovered about, with Miss Melbury's eye on him. I was so entranced by the anecdotes of my venerable friend, that I could take no notice of Mr. Sax. Later, when the dinner-party was over, and we were retiring for the night, he still hovered about, and ended in offering me a bedroom candle. I immediately handed it to Miss Melbury. Really a most enjoyable evening!

VI.

THE next morning we were startled by an extraordinary proceeding on the part of one of the guests. Mr. Sax had left Carsham Hall by the first train—nobody knew why.

Nature has laid—so, at least, philosophers say—some heavy burdens upon women. Do those learned persons include in their list the burden of hysterics? If so, I cordially agree with them. It is hardly worth speaking of in my case—a constitutional outbreak in the solitude of my own room, treated with eau-de-cologne and water, and quite forgotten afterward in the absorbing employment of education. My favorite pupil, Freddy, had been up earlier than the rest of us—breathing the morning air in the fruit-garden. He had seen Mr. Sax and had asked him when he was coming back again. And Mr. Sax had said, "I shall be back again next month." (Dear little Freddy!)

In the meanwhile we, in the schoolroom, had the prospect before us of a dull time in an empty house. The remaining guests were to go away at the end of the week, their hostess being engaged to pay a visit to some old friends in Scotland.

During the next three or four days, though I was often alone with Mrs. Fosdyke, she never said one word on the subject of Mr. Sax. Once or twice I caught her looking at me with that unendurably significant smile of hers. Miss Melbury was equally unpleasant in another way. When we accidentally met on the stairs, her black eyes shot at me passing glances of hatred and scorn. Did these two ladies presume to think—?

No; I abstained from completing that inquiry at the time, and I abstain from completing it here.

The end of the week came, and I and the children were left alone at Carsham Hall.

I took advantage of the leisure hours at my disposal to write to Sir Gervase; respectfully inquiring after his health, and informing him that I had been again most fortunate in my engagement as a governess. By return of post an answer arrived. I eagerly opened it. The first lines informed me of Sir Gervase Damian's death.

The letter dropped from my hand. I looked at my little enameled cross. It is not for me to say what I felt. Think of all that I owed to him; and remember how lonely my lot was in the world. I gave the children a holiday; it was only the truth to tell them that I was not well.

How long an interval passed before I could call to mind that I had only read the first lines of the letter, I am not able to say. When I did take it up I was surprised to see that the writing covered two pages. Beginning again where I had left off, my head, in a moment more, began to swim. A horrid fear overpowered me that I might not be in my right mind, after I had read the first three sentences. Here they are, to answer for me that I exaggerate nothing:—

"The will of our deceased client is not yet proved. But, with the sanction of the executors, I inform you confidentially that you are the person chiefly interested in it. Sir Gervase Damian bequeaths to you, absolutely, the whole of his personal property, amounting to the sum of seventy thousand pounds."

If the letter had ended there, I really cannot imagine what extravagances

I might not have committed. But the writer (head partner in the firm of Sir Gervase's lawyers) had something more to say on his own behalf. The manner in which he said it strung up my nerves in an instant. I can not, and will not, copy the words here. It is quite revolting enough to give the substance of them.

The man's object was evidently to let me perceive that he disapproved of the will. So far I do not complain of him—he had, no doubt, good reason for the view he took. But, in expressing his surprise "at this extraordinary proof of the testator's interest in a perfect stranger to the family," he hinted his suspicion of an influence, on my part, exercised over Sir Gervase, so utterly shameful, that I cannot dwell on the subject. The language, I should add, was cunningly guarded. Even I could see that it would bear more than one interpretation, and would thus put me in the wrong if I openly resented it. But the meaning was plain; and part at least of the motive came out in the following sentences:

"The present Sir Gervase, as you are doubtless aware, is not seriously affected by his father's will. He is already more liberally provided for, as heir under the entail to the whole of the landed property. But, to say nothing of old friends who are forgotten, there is a surviving relative of the late Sir Gervase passed over, who is nearly akin to him by blood. In the event of this person disputing the will, you will of course hear from us again, and refer us to your legal adviser."

The letter ended with an apology for delay in writing to me, caused by difficulty in discovering my address.

And what did I do?—Write to the rector, or to Mrs. Fosdyke, for advice? Not I!

At first I was too indignant to be able to think of what I ought to do. Our post-time was late, and my head ached as if it would burst into pieces. I had plenty of leisure to rest and compose myself. When I got cool again, I felt able to take my own part, without asking any one to help me.

Even if I had been treated kindly, I should certainly not have taken the money when there was a relative living with a claim to it. What did I want with a large fortune! To buy a husband with it, perhaps? No, no! from all that I have heard, the great Lord Chancellor was quite right when he said that a woman with money at her own disposal was "either kissed out of it or kicked out of it, six weeks after her marriage." The one difficulty before me was not to give up my legacy, but to express my reply with sufficient severity, and at the same time with due regard to my own self-respect. Here is what I wrote:

"SIR—I will not trouble you by attempting to express my sorrow on hearing of Sir Gervase Damian's death. You would probably form your own opinion on that subject also; and I have no wish to be judged by your unenviable experience of humanity for the second time.

"With regard to the legacy, feeling the sincerest gratitude to my generous benefactor, I nevertheless refuse to receive the money.

"Be pleased to send me the necessary document to sign, for transferring my fortune to that relative of Sir Gervase mentioned in your letter. The one condition on which I insist is, that no expression of thanks shall be addressed to me by the person in whose favor I resign the money. I do not desire (even supposing that justice is done to my motives on this occasion) to be made the object of expressions of gratitude for only doing my duty."

So it ended. I may be wrong, but I call that strong writing.

In due course of post a formal acknowledgment arrived. I was requested to wait for the document until the will had been proved, and was informed that my name should be kept strictly secret in the interval. On this occasion the executors were almost as insolent as the lawyer. They felt it their duty to give me time to reconsider a decision which had been evidently formed on impulse. Ah, how hard men are—at least, some of them! I locked up the acknowledgment in disgust, resolved to think no more of it until the time came for getting rid of my legacy. I kissed poor Sir Gervase's little keepsake. While I was still looking at it, the good children came in, of their own accord, to ask how I was. I was obliged to draw down the blind in my room, or they would have seen the tears in my eyes. For the first time since my mother's death, I felt the heartache. Perhaps the children made me think of the happier time when I was a child myself.

VII.

THE will had been proved, and I was informed that the document was in course of preparation when Mrs. Fosdyke returned from her visit to Scotland.

She thought me looking pale and worn.

"The time seems to me to have come," she said, "when I had better make you and Mr. Sax understand each other. Have you been thinking penitently of your own bad behavior?"

I felt myself blushing. I had been thinking of my conduct to Mr. Sax—and I was heartily ashamed of it, too.

Mrs. Fosdyke went on, half in jest, half in earnest. "Consult your own sense of propriety!" she said. "Was the poor man to blame for not being rude enough to say No, when a lady asked him to turn over her music? Could he help it, if the same lady persisted in flirting with him? He ran away from her the next morning. Did you deserve to be told why he left us? Certainly not—after the vixenish manner in which you handed the bedroom candle to Miss Melbury. You foolish girl! Do you think I couldn't see that you were in love with him? Thank Heaven, he's too poor to marry you, and take you away from my children, for some time to come. There will be a long marriage engagement, even if he is magnanimous enough to forgive you. Shall I ask Miss Melbury to come back with him?"

She took pity on me at last, and sat down to write to Mr. Sax. His reply, dated from a country house some twenty miles distant, announced that he would be at Carsham Hall in three days' time.

On that third day the legal paper that I was to sign arrived by post. It was Sunday morning; I was alone in the schoolroom.

In writing to me, the lawyer had only alluded to "a surviving relative of Sir Gervase, nearly akin to him by blood." The document was more explicit. It described the relative as being a nephew of Sir Gervase, the son of his sister. The name followed.

591

It was Sextus Cyril Sax.

I have tried on three different sheets of paper to describe the effect which this discovery produced on me—and I have torn them up one after another. When I only think of it, my mind seems to fall back into the helpless surprise and confusion of that time. After all that had passed between us—the man himself being then on his way to the house! what would he think of me when he saw my name at the bottom of the document? what, in Heaven's name, was I to do?

How long I sat petrified, with the document on my lap, I never knew. Somebody knocked at the schoolroom door, and looked in and said something, and went out again. Then there was an interval. Then the door was opened again. A hand was laid kindly on my shoulder. I looked up—and there was Mrs. Fosdyke, asking, in the greatest alarm, what was the matter with me.

The tone of her voice roused me into speaking. I could think of nothing but Mr. Sax; I could only say, "Has he come?"

"Yes—and waiting to see you."

Answering in those terms, she glanced at the paper in my lap. In the extremity of my helplessness, I acted like a sensible creature at last. I told Mrs. Fosdyke all that I have told here.

She neither moved nor spoke until I had done. Her first proceeding, after that, was to take me in her arms and give me a kiss. Having so far encouraged me, she next spoke of poor Sir Gervase.

"We all acted like fools," she announced, "in needlessly offending him by protesting against his second marriage. I don't mean you—I mean his son, his nephew, and myself. If his second marriage made him happy, what business had we with the disparity of years between husband and wife? I can tell you this, Sextus was the first of us to regret what he had done. But for his stupid fear of being suspected of an interested motive, Sir Gervase might have known there was that much good in his sister's son."

She snatched up a copy of the will, which I had not even noticed thus far.

"See what the kind old man says of you," she went on, pointing to the words. I could not see them; she was obliged to read them for me. "I leave my money to the one person living who has been more than worthy of the little I have done for her, and whose simple unselfish nature I know that I can trust."

I pressed Mrs. Fosdyke's hand; I was not able to speak. She took up the legal paper next.

"Do justice to yourself, and be above contemptible scruples," she said. "Sextus is fond enough of you to be almost worthy of the sacrifice that you are making. Sign—and I will sign next as the witness."

I hesitated.

"What will he think of me?" I said.

"Sign!" she repeated, "and we will see to that."

I obeyed. She asked for the lawyer's letter. I gave it to her, with the lines which contained the man's vile insinuation folded down, so that only the words above were visible, which proved that I had renounced my legacy, not even knowing whether the person to be benefited was a man or a woman. She took this, with the rough draft of my own letter, and the signed renunciation—and opened the door.

"Pray come back, and tell me about it!" I pleaded.

She smiled, nodded, and went out.

Oh, what a long time passed before I heard the long-expected knock at the door! "Come in," I cried impatiently.

Mrs. Fosdyke had deceived me. Mr. Sax had returned in her place. He closed the door. We two were alone.

He was deadly pale; his eyes, as they rested on me, had a wild startled look. With icy cold fingers he took my hand, and lifted it in silence to his lips. The sight of his agitation encouraged me—I don't to this day know why, unless it appealed in some way to my compassion. I was bold enough to look at him. Still silent, he placed the letters on the table—and then he laid the signed paper beside them. When I saw that, I was bolder still. I spoke first.

"Surely you don't refuse me?" I said.

He answered, "I thank you with my whole heart; I admire you more than words can say. But I can't take it."

"Why not?"

"The fortune is yours," he said gently. "Remember how poor I am, and feel for me if I say no more."

His head sank on his breast. He stretched out one hand, silently imploring me to understand him. I could endure it no longer. I forgot every consideration which a woman, in my position, ought to have remembered. Out came the desperate words, before I could stop them.

"You won't take my gift by itself?" I said.

"No."

"Will you take Me with it?"

That evening, Mrs. Fosdyke indulged her sly sense of humor in a new way. She handed me an almanac.

"After all, my dear," she remarked, "you needn't be ashamed of having spoken first. You have only used the ancient privilege of the sex. This is Leap Year."

MR. COSWAY AND THE LANDLADY.

I.

THE guests would have enjoyed their visit to Sir Peter's country house—but for Mr. Cosway. And to make matters worse, it was not Mr. Cosway but the guests who were to blame. They repeated the old story of Adam and Eve, on a larger scale. The women were the first sinners; and the men were demoralized by the women.

Mr. Cosway's bitterest enemy could not have denied that he was a handsome, well-bred, unassuming man. No mystery of any sort attached to him. He had adopted the Navy as a profession—had grown weary of it after a few years' service—and now lived on the moderate income left to him, after the death of his parents. Out of this unpromising material the lively imaginations of the women built up a romance. The men only noticed that Mr. Cosway was rather silent and thoughtful; that he was not ready with his laugh; and that he had a fancy for taking long walks by himself. Harmless peculiarities, surely? And yet, they excited the curiosity of the women as signs of a mystery in Mr. Cosway's past life, in which some beloved object unknown must have played a chief part.

As a matter of course, the influence of the sex was tried, under every indirect and delicate form of approach, to induce Mr. Cosway to open his heart, and tell the tale of his sorrows. With perfect courtesy, he baffled curiosity, and kept his supposed secret to himself. The most beautiful girl in the house was ready to offer herself and her fortune as consolations, if this impenetrable bachelor would only have taken her into his confidence. He smiled sadly, and changed the subject.

Defeated so far, the women accepted the next alternative.

One of the guests staying in the house was Mr. Cosway's intimate friend—formerly his brother-officer on board ship. This gentleman was now subjected to the delicately directed system of investigation which had failed with his friend. With unruffled composure he referred the ladies, one after another, to Mr. Cosway. His name was Stone. The ladies decided that his nature was worthy of his name.

The last resource left to our fair friends was to rouse the dormant interest of the men, and to trust to the confidential intercourse of the smoking-room for the enlightenment which they had failed to obtain by other means.

In the accomplishment of this purpose, the degree of success which rewarded their efforts was due to a favoring state of affairs in the house. The shooting was not good for much; the billiard-table was under repair; and there were but two really skilled whist-players among the guests. In the atmosphere of dullness thus engendered, the men not only caught the infection of the women's curiosity, but were even ready to listen to the gossip of the servants' hall, repeated to their mistresses by the ladies' maids. The result of such an essentially debased state of feeling as this was not slow in declaring itself. But for a lucky accident, Mr. Cosway would have discovered to what extremities of ill-bred curiosity idleness and folly can lead persons holding the position of ladies and gentlemen, when he joined the company at breakfast on the next morning.

The newspapers came in before the guests had risen from the table. Sir Peter handed one of them to the lady who sat on his right hand.

She first looked, it is needless to say, at the list of births, deaths, and marriages; and then she turned to the general news—the fires, accidents, fashionable departures, and so on. In a few minutes, she indignantly dropped the newspaper in her lap.

"Here is another unfortunate man," she exclaimed, "sacrificed to the stupidity of women! If I had been in his place, I would have used my knowledge of swimming to save myself, and would have left the women to go to the bottom of the river as they deserved!"

"A boat accident, I suppose?" said Sir Peter.

"Oh yes—the old story. A gentleman takes two ladies out in a boat. After a while they get fidgety, and feel an idiotic impulse to change places. The boat upsets as usual; the poor dear man tries to save them—and is drowned along with them for his pains. Shameful! shameful!"

"Are the names mentioned?"

"Yes. They are all strangers to me; I speak on principle." Asserting herself in those words, the indignant lady handed the newspaper to Mr. Cosway, who happened to sit next to her. "When you were in the navy," she continued, "I dare say your life was put in jeopardy by taking women in boats. Read it yourself, and let it be a warning to you for the future."

Mr. Cosway looked at the narrative of the accident—and revealed the romantic mystery of his life by a burst of devout exclamation, expressed in the words:

"Thank God, my wife's drowned!"

II.

To declare that Sir Peter and his guests were all struck speechless, by discovering in this way that Mr. Cosway was a married man, is to say very little. The general impression appeared to be that he was mad. His neighbors at the table all drew back from him, with the one exception of his friend. Mr. Stone looked at the newspaper: pressed Mr. Cosway's hand in silent sympathy—and addressed himself to his host.

"Permit me to make my friend's apologies," he said, "until he is composed enough to act for himself. The circumstances are so extraordinary that I venture to think they excuse him. Will you allow us to speak to you privately?"

Sir Peter, with more apologies addressed to his visitors, opened the door which communicated with his study. Mr. Stone took Mr. Cosway's arm, and led him out of the room. He noticed no one, spoke to no one—he moved mechanically, like a man walking in his sleep.

After an unendurable interval of nearly an hour's duration, Sir Peter returned alone to the breakfast-room. Mr. Cosway and Mr. Stone had already taken their departure for London, with their host's entire approval.

"It is left to my discretion," Sir Peter proceeded, "to repeat to you what I have heard in my study. I will do so, on one condition—that you all consider yourselves bound in honor not to mention the true names and the real places, when you tell the story to others."

Subject to this wise reservation, the narrative is here repeated by one of the company. Considering how he may perform his task to the best advantage, he finds that the events which preceded and followed Mr. Cosway's disastrous marriage resolve themselves into certain well-marked divisions. Adopting this arrangement, he proceeds to relate:

The First Epoch in Mr. Cosway's Life.

The sailing of her Majesty's ship Albicore was deferred by the severe illness of the captain. A gentleman not possessed of political influence might, after the doctor's unpromising report of him, have been superseded by another commanding officer. In the present case, the Lords of the Admiralty showed themselves to be models of patience and sympathy. They kept the vessel in port, waiting the captain's recovery.

Among the unimportant junior officers, not wanted on board under these circumstances, and favored accordingly by obtaining leave to wait for orders on shore, were two young men, aged respectively twenty-two and twenty-three years, and known by the names of Cosway and Stone. The scene which now introduces them opens at a famous seaport on the south coast of England, and discloses the two young gentlemen at dinner in a private room at their inn.

"I think that last bottle of champagne was corked," Cosway remarked. "Let's try another. You're nearest the bell, Stone. Ring."

Stone rang, under protest. He was the elder of the two by a year, and he set an example of discretion.

"I am afraid we are running up a terrible bill," he said. "We have been here more than three weeks—"

"And we have denied ourselves nothing," Cosway added. "We have lived like princes. Another bottle of champagne, waiter. We have our riding-horses, and our carriage, and the best box at the theater, and such cigars as London itself could not produce. I call that making the most of life. Try the new bottle. Glorious drink, isn't it? Why doesn't my father have champagne at the family dinner-table?"

"Is your father a rich man, Cosway?"

"I should say not. He didn't give me anything like the money I expected, when I said good-by—and I rather think he warned me solemnly, at parting, to take the greatest care of it.' There's not a farthing more for you,' he said, 'till your ship returns from her South American station.' Your father is a clergyman, Stone."

"Well, and what of that?"

"And some clergymen are rich."

"My father is not one of them, Cosway."

"Then let us say no more about him. Help yourself, and pass the bottle."

Instead of adopting this suggestion, Stone rose with a very grave face, and once more rang the bell. "Ask the landlady to step up," he said, when the waiter appeared.

"What do you want with the landlady?" Cosway inquired.

"I want the bill."

The landlady—otherwise Mrs. Pounce—entered the room. She was short, and old, and fat, and painted, and a widow. Students of character, as revealed in the face, would have discovered malice and cunning in her bright black eyes, and a bitter vindictive temper in the lines about her thin red lips. Incapable of such subtleties of analysis as these, the two young officers differed widely, nevertheless, in their opinions of Mrs. Pounce. Cosway's reckless sense of humor delighted in pretending to be in love with her. Stone took a dislike to her from the first. When his friend asked for the reason, he made a strangely obscure answer. "Do you remember that morning in the wood when you killed the snake?" he said. "I took a dislike to the snake." Cosway made no further inquiries.

"Well, my young heroes," said Mrs. Pounce (always loud, always cheerful, and always familiar with her guests), "what do you want with me now?"

"Take a glass of champagne, my darling," said Cosway; "and let me try if I can get my arm round your waist. That's all I want with you."

The landlady passed this over without notice. Though she had spoken to both of them, her cunning little eyes rested on Stone from the moment when she appeared in the room. She knew by instinct the man who disliked her—and she waited deliberately for Stone to reply.

"We have been here some time," he said, "and we shall be obliged, ma'am, if you will let us have our bill."

Mrs. Pounce lifted her eyebrows with an expression of innocent surprise.

"Has the captain got well, and must you go on board to-night?" she asked.

"Nothing of the sort!" Cosway interposed. "We have no news of the captain, and we are going to the theater to-night."

"But," persisted Stone, "we want, if you please, to have the bill."

"Certainly, sir," said Mrs. Pounce, with a sudden assumption of respect. "But we are very busy downstairs, and we hope you will not press us for it to-night?"

"Of course not!" cried Cosway.

Mrs. Pounce instantly left the room, without waiting for any further remark from Cosway's friend.

"I wish we had gone to some other house," said Stone. "You mark my words—that woman means to cheat us."

Cosway expressed his dissent from this opinion in the most amiable manner. He filled his friend's glass, and begged him not to say ill-natured things of Mrs. Pounce.

But Stone's usually smooth temper seemed to be ruffled; he insisted on his own view. "She's impudent and inquisitive, if she is not downright dishonest," he said. "What right had she to ask you where we lived when we were at home; and what our Christian names were; and which of us was oldest, you or I? Oh, yes—it's all very well to say she only showed a flattering interest in us! I suppose she showed a flattering interest in my affairs, when I awoke a little earlier than usual, and caught her in my bedroom with my pocketbook in her hand. Do you believe she was going to lock it up for safety's sake? She knows how much money we have got as well as we know it ourselves. Every half-penny we have will be in her pocket tomorrow. And a good thing, too—we shall be obliged to leave the house."

Even this cogent reasoning failed in provoking Cosway to reply. He took Stone's hat, and handed it with the utmost politeness to his foreboding friend. "There's only one remedy for such a state of mind as yours," he said. "Come to the theater."

At ten o'clock the next morning Cosway found himself alone at the breakfast-table. He was informed that Mr. Stone had gone out for a little walk, and would be back directly. Seating himself at the table, he perceived an envelope on his plate, which evidently inclosed the bill. He took up the envelope, considered a little, and put it back again unopened. At the same moment Stone burst into the room in a high state of excitement.

"News that will astonish you!" he cried. "The captain arrived yesterday evening. His doctors say that the sea-voyage will complete his recovery. The ship sails to-day—and we are ordered to report ourselves on board in an hour's time. Where's the bill?"

Cosway pointed to it. Stone took it out of the envelope.

It covered two sides of a prodigiously long sheet of paper. The sum total was brightly decorated with lines in red ink. Stone looked at the total, and passed it in silence to Cosway. For once, even Cosway was prostrated.

In dreadful stillness the two young men produced their pocketbooks; added up their joint stores of money, and compared the result with the bill. Their united resources amounted to a little more than one-third of their debt to the landlady of the inn.

The only alternative that presented itself was to send for Mrs. Pounce; to state the circumstances plainly; and to propose a compromise on the grand commercial basis of credit.

Mrs. Pounce presented herself superbly dressed in walking costume. Was she going out; or had she just returned to the inn? Not a word escaped her; she waited gravely to hear what the gentlemen wanted. Cosway, presuming on his position as favorite, produced the contents of the two pocketbooks and revealed the melancholy truth.

"There is all the money we have," he concluded. "We hope you will not object to receive the balance in a bill at three months."

Mrs. Pounce answered with a stern composure of voice and manner entirely new in the experience of Cosway and Stone.

"I have paid ready money, gentlemen, for the hire of your horses and carriages," she said; "here are the receipts from the livery stables to vouch for me; I never accept bills unless I am quite sure beforehand that they will be honored. I defy you to find an overcharge in the account now rendered; and I expect you to pay it before you leave my house."

Stone looked at his watch.

"In three-quarters of an hour," he said, "we must be on board."

Mrs. Pounce entirely agreed with him. "And if you are not on board," she remarked, "you will be tried by court-martial, and dismissed the service with your characters ruined for life."

"My dear creature, we haven't time to send home, and we know nobody in the town," pleaded Cosway. "For God's sake take our watches and jewelry, and our luggage—and let us go."

"I am not a pawnbroker," said the inflexible lady. "You must either pay your lawful debt to me in honest money, or—"

She paused and looked at Cosway. Her fat face brightened—she smiled graciously for the first time.

Cosway stared at her in unconcealed perplexity. He helplessly repeated her last words. "We must either pay the bill," he said, "or what?"

"Or," answered Mrs. Pounce, "one of you must marry ME."

Was she joking? Was she intoxicated? Was she out of her senses? Neither of the three; she was in perfect possession of herself; her explanation was a model of lucid and convincing arrangement of facts.

"My position here has its drawbacks," she began. "I am a lone widow; I am known to have an excellent business, and to have saved money. The result is that I am pestered to death by a set of needy vagabonds who want to marry me. In this position, I am exposed to slanders and insults. Even if I didn't know that the men were after my money, there is not one of them whom I would venture to marry. He might turn out a tyrant and beat me; or a drunkard, and disgrace me; or a betting man, and ruin me. What I want, you see, for my own peace and protection, is to be able to declare myself married, and to produce the proof in the shape of a certificate. A born gentleman, with a character to lose, and so much younger in years than myself that he wouldn't think of living with me—there is the sort of husband who suits my book! I'm a reasonable woman, gentlemen. I would undertake to part with my husband at the church door—never to attempt to see him or write to him afterward—and only to show my certificate when necessary, without giving any explanations. Your secret would be quite safe in my keeping. I don't care a straw for either of you, so long as you answer my purpose. What do you say to paying my bill (one or the other of you) in this way? I am ready dressed for the altar; and the clergyman has notice at the church. My preference is for Mr. Cosway," proceeded this terrible woman with the cruelest irony, "because he has been so particular in his attentions toward me. The license (which I provided on the chance a fortnight since) is made out in his name. Such is my weakness for Mr. Cosway. But that don't matter if Mr. Stone would like to take his place. He can hail by his friend's name. Oh, yes, he can! I have consulted my lawyer. So long as the bride and bridegroom agree to it, they may be married in any name they like, and it stands good. Look at your watch again, Mr. Stone. The church is in the next street. By my calculation, you have just got five minutes to decide. I'm a punctual woman, my little dears; and I will be back to the moment."

She opened the door, paused, and returned to the room.

"I ought to have mentioned," she resumed, "that I shall make you a present of the bill, receipted, on the conclusion of the ceremony. You will be taken to the ship in my own boat, with all your money in your pockets, and a hamper of good things for the mess. After that I wash my hands of you. You may go to the devil your own way."

With this parting benediction, she left them.

Caught in the landlady's trap, the two victims looked at each other in expressive silence. Without time enough to take legal advice; without friends on shore; without any claim on officers of their own standing in the ship, the prospect before them was literally limited to Marriage or Ruin. Stone made a proposal worthy of a hero.

"One of us must marry her," he said; "I'm ready to toss up for it."

Cosway matched him in generosity. "No," he answered. "It was I who brought you here; and I who led you into these infernal expenses. I ought to pay the penalty—and I will."

Before Stone could remonstrate, the five minutes expired. Punctual Mrs. Pounce appeared again in the doorway.

"Well?" she inquired, "which is it to be—Cosway, or Stone?"

Cosway advanced as reckless as ever, and offered his arm.

"Now then, Fatsides," he said, "come and be married!"

In five-and-twenty minutes more, Mrs. Pounce had become Mrs. Cosway; and the two officers were on their way to the ship.

The Second Epoch in Mr. Cosway's Life.

Four years elapsed before the Albicore returned to the port from which she had sailed.

In that interval, the death of Cosway's parents had taken place. The lawyer who had managed his affairs, during his absence from England, wrote to inform him that his inheritance from his late father's "estate" was eight hundred a year. His mother only possessed a life interest in her fortune; she had left her jewels to her son, and that was all.

Cosway's experience of the life of a naval officer on foreign stations (without political influence to hasten his promotion) had thoroughly disappointed him. He decided on retiring from the service when the ship was "paid off." In the meantime, to the astonishment of his comrades, he seemed to be in no hurry to make use of the leave granted him to go on shore. The faithful Stone was the only man on board who knew that he was afraid of meeting his "wife." This good friend volunteered to go to the inn, and make the necessary investigation with all needful prudence. "Four years is a long time, at her age," he said. "Many things may happen in four years."

An hour later, Stone returned to the ship, and sent a written message on board, addressed to his brother-officer, in these words: "Pack up your things at once, and join me on shore."

"What news?" asked the anxious husband.

Stone looked significantly at the idlers on the landing-place. "Wait," he said, "till we are by ourselves."

"Where are we going?"

"To the railway station."

They got into an empty carriage; and Stone at once relieved his friend of all further suspense.

"Nobody is acquainted with the secret of your marriage, but our two selves," he began quietly. "I don't think, Cosway, you need go into mourning."

"You don't mean to say she's dead!"

"I have seen a letter (written by her own lawyer) which announces her death," Stone replied. "It was so short that I believe I can repeat it word for word: 'Dear Sir—I have received information of the death of my client. Please address your next and last payment, on account of the lease and goodwill of the inn, to the executors of the late Mrs. Cosway.' There, that is the letter. 'Dear Sir' means the present proprietor of the inn. He told me your wife's previous history in two words. After carrying on the business with her customary intelligence for more than three years, her health failed, and she went to London to consult a physician. There she remained under the doctor's care. The next event was the appearance of an agent, instructed to sell the business in consequence of the landlady's declining health. Add the death at a later time—and there is the beginning and the end of the story. Fortune owed you a good turn, Cosway—and Fortune has paid the debt. Accept my best congratulations."

Arrived in London, Stone went on at once to his relations in the North. Cosway proceeded to the office of the family lawyer (Mr. Atherton), who had taken care of his interests in his absence. His father and Mr. Atherton had been schoolfellows and old friends. He was affectionately received, and was invited to pay a visit the next day to the lawyer's villa at Richmond.

"You will be near enough to London to attend to your business at the Admiralty," said Mr. Atherton, "and you will meet a visitor at my house, who is one of the most charming girls in England—the only daughter of the great Mr. Restall. Good heavens! have you never heard of him? My dear sir, he's one of the partners in the famous firm of Benshaw, Restall, and Benshaw."

Cosway was wise enough to accept this last piece of information as quite conclusive. The next day, Mrs. Atherton presented him to the charming Miss Restall; and Mrs. Atherton's young married daughter (who had been his playfellow when they were children) whispered to him, half in jest, half in earnest: "Make the best use of your time; she isn't engaged yet."

Cosway shuddered inwardly at the bare idea of a second marriage. Was Miss Restall the sort of woman to restore his confidence?

She was small and slim and dark—a graceful, well-bred, brightly intelligent person, with a voice exquisitely sweet and winning in tone. Her ears, hands, and feet were objects to worship; and she had an attraction, irresistibly rare among the women of the present time—the attraction of a perfectly natural smile. Before Cosway had been an hour in the house, she discovered that his long term of service on foreign stations had furnished him with subjects of conversation which favorably contrasted with the commonplace gossip addressed to her by other men. Cosway at once became a favorite, as Othello became a favorite in his day.

The ladies of the household all rejoiced in the young officer's success, with the exception of Miss Restall's companion (supposed to hold the place of her lost mother, at a large salary), one Mrs. Margery.

Too cautious to commit herself in words, this lady expressed doubt and disapprobation by her looks. She had white hair, iron-gray eyebrows, and protuberant eyes; her looks were unusually expressive. One evening, she caught poor Mr. Atherton alone, and consulted him confidentially on the subject of Mr. Cosway's income. This was the first warning which opened the eyes of the good lawyer to the nature of the "friendship" already established between his two guests. He knew Miss Restall's illustrious father well, and he feared that it might soon be his disagreeable duty to bring Cosway's visit to an end.

On a certain Saturday afternoon, while Mr. Atherton was still considering how he could most kindly and delicately suggest to Cosway that it was time to say good-by, an empty carriage arrived at the villa. A note from Mr. Restall was delivered to Mrs. Atherton, thanking her with perfect politeness for her kindness to his daughter. "Circumstances," he added, "rendered it necessary that Miss Restall should return home that afternoon."

The "circumstances" were supposed to refer to a garden-party to be given by Mr. Restall in the ensuing week. But why was his daughter wanted at home before the day of the party?

The ladies of the family, still devoted to Cosway's interests, entertained no doubt that Mrs. Margery had privately communicated with Mr. Restall, and that the appearance of the carriage was the natural result. Mrs. Atherton's married daughter did all that could be done: she got rid of Mrs. Margery for one minute, and so arranged it that Cosway and Miss Restall took leave of each other in her own sitting-room.

When the young lady appeared in the hall she had drawn her veil down. Cosway escaped to the road and saw the last of the carriage as it drove away. In a little more than a fortnight his horror of a second marriage had become one of the dead and buried emotions of his nature. He stayed at the villa until Monday morning, as an act of gratitude to his good friends, and then accompanied Mr. Atherton to London. Business at the Admiralty was the excuse. It imposed on nobody. He was evidently on his way to Miss Restall.

"Leave your business in my hands," said the lawyer, on the journey to town, "and go and amuse yourself on the Continent. I can't blame you for falling in love with Miss Restall; I ought to have foreseen the danger, and waited till she had left us before I invited you to my house. But I may at least warn you to carry the matter no further. If you had eight thousand instead of eight hundred a year, Mr. Restall would think it an act of presumption on your part to aspire to his daughter's hand, unless you had a title to throw into the bargain. Look at it in the true light, my dear boy; and one of these days you will thank me for speaking plainly."

Cosway promised to "look at it in the true light."

The result, from his point of view, led him into a change of residence. He left his hotel and took a lodging in the nearest bystreet to Mr. Restall's palace at Kensington.

On the same evening he applied (with the confidence due to a previous arrangement) for a letter at the neighboring post-office, addressed to E. C.—the initials of Edwin Cosway. "Pray be careful," Miss Restall wrote; "I have tried to get you a card for our garden party. But that hateful creature, Margery, has evidently spoken to my father; I am not trusted with any invitation cards. Bear it patiently, dear, as I do, and let me hear if you have succeeded in finding a lodging near us."

Not submitting to this first disappointment very patiently, Cosway sent his reply to the post-office, addressed to A. R.—the initials of Adela Restall. The next day the impatient lover applied for another letter. It was waiting for him, but it was not directed in Adela's handwriting. Had their correspondence been discovered? He opened the letter in the street; and read, with amazement, these lines:

"Dear Mr. Cosway, my heart sympathizes with two faithful lovers, in spite of my age and my duty. I inclose an invitation to the party tomorrow. Pray don't betray me, and don't pay too marked attention to Adela. Discretion is easy. There will be twelve hundred guests. Your friend, in spite of appearances, Louisa Margery."

How infamously they had all misjudged this excellent woman! Cosway went to the party a grateful, as well as a happy man. The first persons known to him, whom he discovered among the crowd of strangers, were the Athertons. They looked, as well they might, astonished to see him. Fidelity to Mrs. Margery forbade him to enter into any explanations. Where was that best and truest friend? With some difficulty he succeeded in finding her. Was there any impropriety in seizing her hand and cordially pressing it? The result of this expression of gratitude was, to say the least of it, perplexing.

Mrs. Margery behaved like the Athertons! She looked astonished to see him and she put precisely the same question: "How did you get here?" Cosway could only conclude that she was joking. "Who should know that, dear lady, better than yourself?" he rejoined. "I don't understand you," Mrs. Margery answered, sharply. After a moment's reflection, Cosway hit on another solution of the mystery. Visitors were near them; and Mrs. Margery had made her own private use of one of Mr. Restall's invitation cards. She might have serious reasons for pushing caution to its last extreme. Cosway looked at her significantly. "The least I can do is not to be indiscreet," he whispered—and left her.

He turned into a side walk; and there he met Adela at last!

It seemed like a fatality. She looked astonished; and she said: "How did you get here?" No intrusive visitors were within hearing, this time. "My dear!" Cosway remonstrated, "Mrs. Margery must have told you, when she sent me my invitation." Adela turned pale. "Mrs. Margery?" she repeated. "Mrs. Margery has said nothing to me; Mrs. Margery detests you. We must have this cleared up. No; not now—I must attend to our guests. Expect a letter; and, for heaven's sake, Edwin, keep out of my father's way. One of our visitors whom he particularly wished to see has sent an excuse—and he is dreadfully angry about it."

She left him before Cosway could explain that he and Mr. Restall had thus far never seen each other.

He wandered away toward the extremity of the grounds, troubled by vague suspicions; hurt at Adela's cold reception of him. Entering a shrubbery, which seemed intended to screen the grounds, at this point, from a lane outside, he suddenly discovered a pretty little summer-house among the trees. A stout gentleman, of mature years, was seated alone in this retreat. He looked up with a frown. Cosway apologized for disturbing him, and entered into conversation as an act of politeness.

"A brilliant assembly to-day, sir."

The stout gentleman replied by an inarticulate sound—something between a grunt and a cough.

"And a splendid house and grounds," Cosway continued.

The stout gentleman repeated the inarticulate sound.

Cosway began to feel amused. Was this curious old man deaf and dumb?

"Excuse my entering into conversation," he persisted. "I feel like a stranger here. There are so many people whom I don't know."

The stout gentleman suddenly burst into speech. Cosway had touched a sympathetic fiber at last.

"There are a good many people here whom I don't know," he said, gruffly. "You are one of them. What's your name?"

"My name is Cosway, sir. What's yours?"

The stout gentleman rose with fury in his looks. He burst out with an oath; and added the in tolerable question, already three times repeated by others: "How did you get here?" The tone was even more offensive than the oath. "Your age protects you, sir," said Cosway, with the loftiest composure. "I'm sorry I gave my name to so rude a person."

"Rude?" shouted the old gentleman. "You want my name in return, I suppose? You young puppy, you shall have it! My name is Restall."

He turned his back and walked off. Cosway took the only course now open to him. He returned to his lodgings.

The next day no letter reached him from Adela. He went to the postoffice. No letter was there. The day wore on to evening—and, with the evening, there appeared a woman who was a stranger to him. She looked like a servant; and she was the bearer of a mysterious message.

"Please be at the garden-door that opens on the lane, at ten o'clock to-morrow morning. Knock three times at the door—and then say 'Adela.' Some one who wishes you well will be alone in the shrubbery, and will let you in. No, sir! I am not to take anything; and I am not to say a word more." She spoke—and vanished.

Cosway was punctual to his appointment. He knocked three times; he pronounced Miss Restall's Christian name. Nothing happened. He waited a while, and tried again. This time Adela's voice answered strangely from the shrubbery in tones of surprise: "Edwin, is it really you?"

"Did you expect any one else?" Cosway asked. "My darling, your message said ten o'clock—and here I am."

The door was suddenly unlocked.

"I sent no message," said Adela, as they confronted each other on the threshold.

In the silence of utter bewilderment they went together into the summer-house. At Adela's request, Cosway repeated the message that he had received, and described the woman who had delivered it. The description applied to no person known to Miss Restall. "Mrs. Margery never sent you the invitation;

and I repeat, I never sent you the message. This meeting has been arranged by some one who knows that I always walk in the shrubbery after breakfast. There is some underhand work going on—"

Still mentally in search of the enemy who had betrayed them, she checked herself, and considered a little. "Is it possible—?" she began, and paused again. Her eyes filled with tears. "My mind is so completely upset," she said, "that I can't think clearly of anything. Oh, Edwin, we have had a happy dream, and it has come to an end. My father knows more than we think for. Some friends of ours are going abroad tomorrow—and I am to go with them. Nothing I can say has the least effect upon my father. He means to part us forever—and this is his cruel way of doing it!"

She put her arm round Cosway's neck and lovingly laid her head on his shoulder. With tenderest kisses they reiterated their vows of eternal fidelity until their voices faltered and failed them. Cosway filled up the pause by the only useful suggestion which it was now in his power to make—he proposed an elopement.

Adela received this bold solution of the difficulty in which they were placed exactly as thousands of other young ladies have received similar proposals before her time, and after.

She first said positively No. Cosway persisted. She began to cry, and asked if he had no respect for her. Cosway declared that his respect was equal to any sacrifice except the sacrifice of parting with her forever. He could, and would, if she preferred it, die for her, but while he was alive he must refuse to give her up. Upon this she shifted her ground. Did he expect her to go away with him alone? Certainly not. Her maid could go with her, or, if her maid was not to be trusted, he would apply to his landlady, and engage "a respectable elderly person" to attend on her until the day of their marriage. Would she have some mercy on him, and just consider it? No: she was afraid to consider it. Did she prefer misery for the rest of her life? Never mind his happiness: it was her happiness only that he had in his mind. Traveling with unsympathetic people; absent from England, no one could say for how long; married, when she did return, to some rich man whom she hated—would she, could she, contemplate that prospect? She contemplated it through tears; she contemplated it to an accompaniment of sighs, kisses, and protestations—she trembled, hesitated, gave way. At an appointed hour of the coming night, when her father would be in the smoking-room, and Mrs. Margery would be in bed, Cosway was to knock at the door in the lane once more; leaving time to make all the necessary arrangements in the interval.

The one pressing necessity, under these circumstances, was to guard against the possibility of betrayal and surprise. Cosway discreetly alluded to the unsolved mysteries of the invitation and the message. "Have you taken anybody into our confidence?" he asked.

Adela answered with some embarrassment. "Only one person," She said—"dear Miss Benshaw."

"Who is Miss Benshaw?"

"Don't you really know, Edwin? She is richer even than papa—she has inherited from her late brother one half-share in the great business in the City. Miss Benshaw is the lady who disappointed papa by not coming to the garden-party. You remember, dear, how happy we were when we were together at Mr. Atherton's? I was very miserable when they took me away. Miss Benshaw happened to call the next day and she noticed it. 'My dear,' she said (Miss Benshaw is quite an elderly lady now), 'I am an old maid, who has missed the happiness of her life, through not having had a friend to guide and advise her when she was young. Are you suffering as I once suffered?' She spoke so nicely—and I was so wretched—that I really couldn't help it. I opened my heart to her."

Cosway looked grave. "Are you sure she is to be trusted?" he asked.

"Perfectly sure."

"Perhaps, my love, she has spoken about us (not meaning any harm) to some friend of hers? Old ladies are so fond of gossip. It's just possible—don't you think so?"

Adela hung her head.

613

"I have thought it just possible myself," she admitted. "There is plenty of time to call on her to-day. I will set our doubts at rest before Miss Benshaw goes out for her afternoon drive."

On that understanding they parted.

Toward evening Cosway's arrangements for the elopement were completed. He was eating his solitary dinner when a note was brought to him. It had been left at the door by a messenger. The man had gone away without waiting for an answer. The note ran thus:

"Miss Benshaw presents her compliments to Mr. Cosway, and will be obliged if he can call on her at nine o'clock this evening, on business which concerns himself."

This invitation was evidently the result of Adela's visit earlier in the day. Cosway presented himself at the house, troubled by natural emotions of anxiety and suspense. His reception was not of a nature to compose him. He was shown into a darkened room. The one lamp on the table was turned down low, and the little light thus given was still further obscured by a shade. The corners of the room were in almost absolute darkness.

A voice out of one of the corners addressed him in a whisper:

"I must beg you to excuse the darkened room. I am suffering from a severe cold. My eyes are inflamed, and my throat is so bad that I can only speak in a whisper. Sit down, sir. I have got news for you."

"Not bad news, I hope, ma'am?" Cosway ventured to inquire.

"The worst possible news," said the whispering voice. "You have an enemy striking at you in the dark."

Cosway asked who it was, and received no answer. He varied the form of inquiry, and asked why the unnamed person struck at him in the dark. The experiment succeeded; he obtained a reply.

"It is reported to me," said Miss Benshaw, "that the person thinks it necessary to give you a lesson, and takes a spiteful pleasure in doing it as mischievously as possible. The person, as I happen to know, sent you your invitation to the party, and made the appointment which took you to the door in the lane. Wait a little, sir; I have not done yet. The person has put it into Mr. Restall's head to send his daughter abroad tomorrow."

Cosway attempted to make her speak more plainly.

"Is this wretch a man or a woman?" he said.

Miss Benshaw proceeded without noticing the interruption.

"You needn't be afraid, Mr. Cosway; Miss Restall will not leave England. Your enemy is all-powerful. Your enemy's object could only be to provoke you into planning an elopement—and, your arrangements once completed, to inform Mr. Restall, and to part you and Miss Adela quite as effectually as if you were at opposite ends of the world. Oh, you will undoubtedly be parted! Spiteful, isn't it? And, what is worse, the mischief is as good as done already."

Cosway rose from his chair.

"Do you wish for any further explanation?" asked Miss Benshaw.

"One thing more," he replied. "Does Adela know of this?"

"No," said Miss Benshaw; "it is left to you to tell her."

There was a moment of silence. Cosway looked at the lamp. Once roused, as usual with men of his character, his temper was not to be trifled with.

"Miss Benshaw," he said, "I dare say you think me a fool; but I can draw my own conclusion, for all that. You are my enemy."

The only reply was a chuckling laugh. All voices can be more or less effectually disguised by a whisper but a laugh carries the revelation of its own identity with it. Cosway suddenly threw off the shade over the lamp and turned up the wick.

The light flooded the room, and showed him—His Wife.

The Third Epoch in Mr. Cosway's Life.

Three days had passed. Cosway sat alone in his lodging—pale and worn: the shadow already of his former self.

He had not seen Adela since the discovery. There was but one way in which he could venture to make the inevitable disclosure—he wrote to her; and Mr. Atherton's daughter took care that the letter should be received. Inquiries made afterward, by help of the same good friend, informed him that Miss Restall was suffering from illness.

The mistress of the house came in.

"Cheer up, sir," said the good woman. "There is better news of Miss Restall to-day."

He raised his head.

"Don't trifle with me!" he answered fretfully; "tell me exactly what the servant said."

The mistress repeated the words. Miss Restall had passed a quieter night, and had been able for a few hours to leave her room. He asked next if any reply to his letter had arrived. No reply had been received.

If Adela definitely abstained from writing to him, the conclusion would be too plain to be mistaken. She had given him up—and who could blame her?

There was a knock at the street-door. The mistress looked out.

"Here's Mr. Stone come back, sir!" she exclaimed joyfully—and hurried away to let him in.

Cosway never looked up when his friend appeared.

"I knew I should succeed," said Stone. "I have seen your wife."

"Don't speak of her," cried Cosway. "I should have murdered her when I saw her face, if I had not instantly left the house. I may be the death of the wretch yet, if you presist in speaking of her!"

Stone put his hand kindly on his friend's shoulder.

"Must I remind you that you owe something to your old comrade?" he asked. "I left my father and mother, the morning I got your letter—and my one thought has been to serve you. Reward me. Be a man, and hear what is your right and duty to know. After that, if you like, we will never refer to the woman again."

Cosway took his hand, in silent acknowledgment that he was right. They sat down together. Stone began.

"She is so entirely shameless," he said, "that I had no difficulty in getting her to speak. And she so cordially hates you that she glories in her own falsehood and treachery."

"Of course, she lies," Cosway said bitterly, "when she calls herself Miss Benshaw?"

"No; she is really the daughter of the man who founded the great house in the City. With every advantage that wealth and position could give her the perverse creature married one of her father's clerks, who had been deservedly dismissed from his situation. From that moment her family discarded her. With the money procured by the sale of her jewels, her husband took the inn which we have such bitter cause to remember—and she managed the house after his death. So much for the past. Carry your mind on now to the time when our ship brought us back to England. At that date, the last surviving member of your wife's family—her elder brother—lay at the point of death. He had taken his father's place in the business, besides inheriting his father's fortune. After a happy married life he was left a widower, without children; and it became necessary that he should alter his will. He deferred performing his duty. It was only at the time of his last illness that he had dictated instructions for a new will, leaving his wealth (excepting certain legacies to old friends) to the hospitals of Great Britain and Ireland. His lawyer lost no time in carrying out the instructions. The new will was ready for signature (the old will having been destroyed by his own hand), when the doctors sent a message to say that their patient was insensible, and might die in that condition."

"Did the doctors prove to be right?"

"Perfectly right. Our wretched landlady, as next of kin, succeeded, not only to the fortune, but (under the deed of partnership) to her late brother's place in the firm: on the one easy condition of resuming the family name. She calls herself "Miss Benshaw." But as a matter of legal necessity she is set down in the deed as "Mrs. Cosway Benshaw." Her partners only now know that her husband is living, and that you are the Cosway whom she privately married. Will you take a little breathing time? or shall I go on, and get done with it?"

Cosway signed to him to go on.

"She doesn't in the least care," Stone proceeded, "for the exposure. 'I am the head partner,' she says 'and the rich one of the firm; they daren't turn their backs on Me.' You remember the information I received—in perfect good faith on his part—from the man who keeps the inn? The visit to the London doctor, and the assertion of failing health, were adopted as the best means of plausibly severing the lady's connection (the great lady now!) with a calling so unworthy of her as the keeping of an inn. Her neighbors at the seaport were all deceived by the stratagem, with two exceptions. They were both men—vagabonds who had pertinaciously tried to delude her into marrying them in the days when she was a widow. They refused to believe in the doctor and the declining health; they had their own suspicion of the motives which had led to the sale of the inn, under very unfavorable circumstances; and they decided on going to London, inspired by the same base hope of making discoveries which might be turned into a means of extorting money."

"She escaped them, of course," said Cosway. "How?"

"By the help of her lawyer, who was not above accepting a handsome private fee. He wrote to the new landlord of the inn, falsely announcing his client's death, in the letter which I repeated to you in the railway carriage on our journey to London. Other precautions were taken to keep up the deception, on which it is needless to dwell. Your natural conclusion that you were free to pay your addresses to Miss Restall, and the poor young lady's innocent confidence in 'Miss Benshaw's' sympathy, gave this unscrupulous woman the means of playing the heartless trick on you which is now exposed. Malice and jealousy—I have it, mind, from herself!—were not her only motives. 'But for that Cosway,' she said (I spare you the epithet which she put before your name), 'with my money and position, I might have married a needy lord, and sunned myself in my old age in the full blaze of the peerage.' Do you understand how she hated you, now? Enough of the subject! The moral of it, my dear Cosway, is to leave this place, and try what change of scene will do for you. I have time to spare; and I will go abroad with you. When shall it be?"

"Let me wait a day or two more," Cosway pleaded.

Stone shook his head. "Still hoping, my poor friend, for a line from Miss Restall? You distress me."

"I am sorry to distress you, Stone. If I can get one pitying word from her, I can submit to the miserable life that lies before me."

"Are you not expecting too much?"

"You wouldn't say so, if you were as fond of her as I am."

They were silent. The evening slowly darkened; and the mistress came in as usual with the candles. She brought with her a letter for Cosway.

He tore it open; read it in an instant; and devoured it with kisses. His highly wrought feelings found their vent in a little allowable exaggeration. "She has saved my life!" he said, as he handed the letter to Stone.

It only contained these lines:

"My love is yours, my promise is yours. Through all trouble, through all profanation, through the hopeless separation that may be before us in this world, I live yours—and die yours. My Edwin, God bless and comfort you."

The Fourth Epoch in Mr. Cosway's Life.

The separation had lasted for nearly two years, when Cosway and Stone paid that visit to the country house which is recorded at the outset of the present narrative. In the interval nothing had been heard of Miss Restall, except through Mr. Atherton. He reported that Adela was leading a very quiet life. The one remarkable event had been an interview between "Miss Benshaw" and herself. No other person had been present; but the little that was reported placed Miss Restall's character above all praise. She had forgiven the woman who had so cruelly injured her!

The two friends, it may be remembered, had traveled to London, immediately after completing the fullest explanation of Cosway's startling behavior at the breakfast-table. Stone was not by nature a sanguine man. "I don't believe in our luck," he said. "Let us be quite sure that we are not the victims of another deception."

The accident had happened on the Thames; and the newspaper narrative proved to be accurate in every respect. Stone personally attended the inquest. From a natural feeling of delicacy toward Adela, Cosway hesitated to write to her on the subject. The ever-helpful Stone wrote in his place.

After some delay, the answer was received. It inclosed a brief statement (communicated officially by legal authority) of the last act of malice on the part of the late head-partner in the house of Benshaw and Company. She had not died intestate, like her brother. The first clause of her will contained the testator's grateful recognition of Adela Restall's Christian act of forgiveness. The second clause (after stating that there were neither relatives nor children to be benefited by the will) left Adela Restall mistress of Mrs. Cosway Benshaw's fortune—on the one merciless condition that she did not marry Edwin Cosway. The third clause—if Adela Restall violated the condition—handed over the whole of the money to the firm in the City, "for the extension of the business, and the benefit of the surviving partners."

Some months later, Adela came of age. To the indignation of Mr. Restall, and the astonishment of the "Company," the money actually went to the firm. The fourth epoch in Mr. Cosway's life witnessed his marriage to a woman who cheerfully paid half a million of money for the happiness of passing her life, on eight hundred a year, with the man whom she loved.

But Cosway felt bound in gratitude to make a rich woman of his wife, if work and resolution could do it. When Stone last heard of him, he was reading for the bar; and Mr. Atherton was ready to give him his first brief.

NOTE.—That "most improbable" part of the present narrative,

which is contained in the division called The First Epoch, is founded on an adventure which actually occurred to no less a person than a cousin of Sir Walter Scott. In Lockhart's delightful "Life," the anecdote will be found as told by Sir Walter to Captain Basil Hall. The remainder of the present story is entirely imaginary. The writer wondered what such a woman as the landlady would do under certain given circumstances, after her marriage to the young midshipman—and here is the result.

MR. MEDHURST AND THE PRINCESS.

I.

THE day before I left London, to occupy the post of second secretary of legation at a small German Court, I took leave of my excellent French singing-master, Monsieur Bonnefoy, and of his young and pretty daughter named Jeanne.

Our farewell interview was saddened by Monsieur Bonnefoy's family anxieties. His elder brother, known in the household as Uncle David, had been secretly summoned to Paris by order of a republican society. Anxious relations in London (whether reasonably or not, I am unable to say) were in some fear of the political consequences that might follow.

At parting, I made Mademoiselle Jeanne a present, in the shape of a plain gold brooch. For some time past, I had taken my lessons at Monsieur Bonnefoy's house; his daughter and I often sang together under his direction. Seeing much of Jeanne, under these circumstances, the little gift that I had offered to her was only the natural expression of a true interest in her welfare. Idle rumor asserted—quite falsely—that I was in love with her. I was sincerely the young lady's friend: no more, no less.

Having alluded to my lessons in singing, it may not be out of place to mention the circumstances under which I became Monsieur Bonnefoy's pupil, and to allude to the change in my life that followed in due course of time.

Our family property—excepting the sum of five thousand pounds left to me by my mother—is landed property strictly entailed. The estates were inherited by my only brother, Lord Medhurst; the kindest, the best, and, I grieve to say it, the unhappiest of men. He lived separated from a bad wife; he had no children to console him; and he only enjoyed at rare intervals the blessing of good health. Having myself nothing to live on but the interest of my mother's little fortune, I had to make my own way in the world. Poor younger sons, not possessed of the commanding ability which achieves distinction, find the roads that lead to prosperity closed to them, with one exception. They can always apply themselves to the social arts which make a man agreeable in society. I had naturally a good voice, and I cultivated it. I was ready to sing, without being subject to the wretched vanity which makes objections and excuses—I pleased the ladies—the ladies spoke favorably of me to their husbands—and some of their husbands were persons of rank and influence. After no very long lapse of time, the result of this combination of circumstances declared itself. Monsieur Bonnefoy's lessons became the indirect means of starting me on a diplomatic career—and the diplomatic career made poor Ernest Medhurst, to his own unutterable astonishment, the hero of a love story!

The story being true, I must beg to be excused, if I abstain from mentioning names, places, and dates, when I enter on German ground. Let it be enough to say that I am writing of a bygone year in the present century, when no such thing as a German Empire existed, and when the revolutionary spirit of France was still an object of well-founded suspicion to tyrants by right divine on the continent of Europe.

II.

ON joining the legation, I was not particularly attracted by my chief, the Minister. His manners were oppressively polite; and his sense of his own importance was not sufficiently influenced by diplomatic reserve. I venture to describe him (mentally speaking) as an empty man, carefully trained to look full on public occasions.

My colleague, the first secretary, was a far more interesting person. Bright, unaffected, and agreeable, he at once interested me when we were introduced to each other. I pay myself a compliment, as I consider, when I add that he became my firm and true friend.

We took a walk together in the palace gardens on the evening of my arrival. Reaching a remote part of the grounds, we were passed by a lean, sallow, sour-looking old man, drawn by a servant in a chair on wheels. My companion stopped, whispered to me, "Here is the Prince," and bowed bareheaded. I followed his example as a matter of course. The Prince feebly returned our salutation. "Is he ill?" I asked, when we had put our hats on again.

"Shakespeare," the secretary replied, "tells us that 'one man in his time plays many parts.' Under what various aspects the Prince's character may have presented itself, in his younger days, I am not able to tell you. Since I have been here, he has played the part of a martyr to illness, misunderstood by his doctors."

"And his daughter, the Princess—what do you say of her?"

"Ah, she is not so easily described! I can only appeal to your memory of other women like her, whom you must often have seen—women who are tall and fair, and fragile and elegant; who have delicate aquiline noses and melting blue eyes—women who have often charmed you by their tender smiles and their supple graces of movement. As for the character of this popular young lady, I must not influence you either way; study it for yourself."

"Without a hint to guide me?"

"With a suggestion," he replied, "which may be worth considering. If you wish to please the Princess, begin by endeavoring to win the good graces of the Baroness."

"Who is the Baroness?"

"One of the ladies in waiting—bosom friend of her Highness, and chosen repository of all her secrets. Personally, not likely to attract you; short and fat, and ill-tempered and ugly. Just at this time, I happen myself to get on with her better than usual. We have discovered that we possess one sympathy in common—we are the only people at Court who don't believe in the Prince's new doctor."

"Is the new doctor a quack?"

The secretary looked round, before he answered, to see that nobody was near us.

"It strikes me," he said, "that the Doctor is a spy. Mind! I have no right to speak of him in that way; it is only my impression—and I ought to add that appearances are all in his favor. He is in the service of our nearest royal neighbor, the Grand Duke; and he has been sent here expressly to relieve the sufferings of the Duke's good friend and brother, our invalid Prince. This is an honorable mission no doubt. And the man himself is handsome, well-bred, and (I don't quite know whether this is an additional recommendation) a countryman of ours. Nevertheless I doubt him, and the Baroness doubts him. You are an independent witness; I shall be anxious to hear if your opinion agrees with ours."

I was presented at Court, toward the end of the week; and, in the course of the next two or three days, I more than once saw the Doctor. The impression that he produced on me surprised my colleague. It was my opinion that he and the Baroness had mistaken the character of a worthy and capable man.

The secretary obstinately adhered to his own view.

"Wait a little," he answered, "and we shall see."

He was quite right. We did see.

III.

BUT the Princess—the gentle, gracious, beautiful Princess—what can I say of her Highness?

I can only say that she enchanted me.

I had been a little discouraged by the reception that I met with from her father. Strictly confining himself within the limits of politeness, he bade me welcome to his Court in the fewest possible words, and then passed me by without further notice. He afterward informed the English Minister that I had been so unfortunate as to try his temper: "Your new secretary irritates me, sir—he is a person in an offensively perfect state of health." The Prince's charming daughter was not of her father's way of thinking; it is impossible to say how graciously, how sweetly I was received. She honored me by speaking to me in my own language, of which she showed herself to be a perfect mistress. I was not only permitted, but encouraged, to talk of my family, and to dwell on my own tastes, amusements, and pursuits. Even when her Highness's attention was claimed by other persons waiting to be presented, I was not forgotten. The Baroness was instructed to invite me for the next evening to the Princess's tea-table; and it was hinted that I should be especially welcome if I brought my music with me, and sang.

My friend the secretary, standing near us at the time, looked at me with a mysterious smile. He had suggested that I should make advances to the Baroness—and here was the Baroness (under royal instructions) making advances to Me!

"We know what that means," he whispered.

In justice to myself, I must declare that I entirely failed to understand him.

On the occasion of my second reception by the Princess, at her little evening party, I detected the Baroness, more than once, in the act of watching her Highness and myself, with an appearance of disapproval in her manner, which puzzled me. When I had taken my leave, she followed me out of the room.

"I have a word of advice to give you," she said. "The best thing you can do, sir, is to make an excuse to your Minister, and go back to England."

I declare again, that I entirely failed to understand the Baroness.

IV.

BEFORE the season came to an end, the Court removed to the Prince's country-seat, in the interests of his Highness's health. Entertainments were given (at the Doctor's suggestion), with a view of raising the patient's depressed spirits. The members of the English legation were among the guests invited. To me it was a delightful visit. I had again every reason to feel gratefully sensible of the Princess's condescending kindness. Meeting the secretary one day in the library, I said that I thought her a perfect creature. Was this an absurd remark to make? I could see nothing absurd in it—and yet my friend burst out laughing.

"My good fellow, nobody is a perfect creature," he said. "The Princess has her faults and failings, like the rest of us."

I denied it positively.

"Use your eyes," he went on; "and you will see, for example, that she is shallow and frivolous. Yesterday was a day of rain. We were all obliged to employ ourselves somehow indoors. Didn't you notice that she had no resources in herself? She can't even read."

"There you are wrong at any rate," I declared. "I saw her reading the newspaper."

"You saw her with the newspaper in her hand. If you had not been deaf and blind to her defects, you would have noticed that she couldn't fix her attention on it. She was always ready to join in the chatter of the ladies about her. When even their stores of gossip were exhausted, she let the newspaper drop on her lap, and sat in vacant idleness smiling at nothing."

I reminded him that she might have met with a dull number of the newspaper. He took no notice of this unanswerable reply.

"You were talking the other day of her warmth of feeling," he proceeded. "She has plenty of sentiment (German sentiment), I grant you, but no true feeling. What happened only this morning, when the Prince was in the breakfast-room, and when the Princess and her ladies were dressed to go out riding? Even she noticed the wretchedly depressed state of her father's spirits. A man of that hypochondriacal temperament suffers acutely, though he may only fancy himself to be ill. The Princess overflowed with sympathy, but she never proposed to stay at home, and try to cheer the old man. Her filial duty was performed to her own entire satisfaction when she had kissed her hand to the Prince. The moment after, she was out of the room—eager to enjoy her ride. We all heard her laughing gayly among the ladies in the hall."

I could have answered this also, if our discussion had not been interrupted at the moment. The Doctor came into the library in search of a book. When he had left us, my colleague's strong prejudice against him instantly declared itself.

"Be on your guard with that man," he said.

"Why?" I asked.

"Haven't you noticed," he replied, "that when the Princess is talking to you, the Doctor always happens to be in that part of the room?"

"What does it matter where the Doctor is?"

My friend looked at me with an oddly mingled expression of doubt and surprise. "Do you really not understand me?" he said.

"I don't indeed."

"My dear Ernest, you are a rare and admirable example to the rest of us—you are a truly modest man."

What did he mean?

V.

EVENTS followed, on the next day, which (as will presently be seen) I have a personal interest in relating.

The Baroness left us suddenly, on leave of absence. The Prince wearied of his residence in the country; and the Court returned to the capital. The charming Princess was reported to be "indisposed," and retired to the seclusion of her own apartments.

A week later, I received a note from the Baroness, marked "private and confidential." It informed me that she had resumed her duties as lady-in-waiting, and that she wished to see me at my earliest convenience. I obeyed at once; and naturally asked if there were better accounts of her Highness's health.

The Baroness's reply a little surprised me. She said, "The Princess is perfectly well."

"Recovered already!" I exclaimed.

"She has never been ill," the Baroness answered. "Her indisposition was a sham; forced on her by me, in her own interests. Her reputation is in peril; and you—you hateful Englishman—are the cause of it."

Not feeling disposed to put up with such language as this, even when it was used by a lady, I requested that she would explain herself. She complied without hesitation. In another minute my eyes were opened to the truth. I knew—no; that is too positive—let me say I had reason to believe that the Princess loved me!

It is simply impossible to convey to the minds of others any idea of the emotions that overwhelmed me at that critical moment of my life. I was in a state of confusion at the time; and, when my memory tries to realize it, I am in a state of confusion now. The one thing I can do is to repeat what the Baroness said to me when I had in some degree recovered my composure.

"I suppose you are aware," she began, "of the disgrace to which the Princess's infatuation exposes her, if it is discovered? On my own responsibility I repeat what I said to you a short time since. Do you refuse to leave this place immediately?"

Does the man live, honored as I was, who would have hesitated to refuse? Find him if you can!

"Very well," she resumed. "As the friend of the Princess, I have no choice now but to take things as they are, and to make the best of them. Let us realize your position to begin with. If you were (like your elder brother) a nobleman possessed of vast estates, my royal mistress might be excused. As it is, whatever you may be in the future, you are nothing now but an obscure young man, without fortune or title. Do you see your duty to the Princess? or must I explain it to you?"

I saw my duty as plainly as she did. "Her Highness's secret is a sacred secret," I said. "I am bound to shrink from no sacrifice which may preserve it."

The Baroness smiled maliciously. "I may have occasion," she answered, "to remind you of what you have just said. In the meanwhile the Princess's secret is in danger of discovery."

"By her father?"

"No. By the Doctor."

At first, I doubted whether she was in jest or in earnest. The next instant, I remembered that the secretary had expressly cautioned me against that man.

"It is evidently one of your virtues," the Baroness proceeded, "to be slow to suspect. Prepare yourself for a disagreeable surprise. The Doctor has been watching the Princess, on every occasion when she speaks to you, with some object of his own in view. During my absence, young sir, I have been engaged in discovering what that object is. My excellent mother lives at the Court of the Grand Duke, and enjoys the confidence of his Ministers. He is still a bachelor; and, in the interests of the succession to the throne, the time has arrived when he must marry. With my mother's assistance, I have found out that the Doctor's medical errand here is a pretense. Influenced by the Princess's beauty the Grand Duke has thought of her first as his future duchess. Whether he has heard slanderous stories, or whether he is only a cautious man, I can't tell you. But this I know: he has instructed his physician—if he had employed a professed diplomatist his motive might have been suspected—to observe her Highness privately, and to communicate the result. The object of the report is to satisfy the Duke that the Princess's reputation is above the reach of scandal; that she is free from entanglements of a certain kind; and that she is in every respect a person to whom he can with propriety offer his hand in marriage. The Doctor, Mr. Ernest, is not disposed to allow you to prevent him from sending in a favorable report. He has drawn his conclusions from the Princess's extraordinary kindness to the second secretary of the English legation; and he is only waiting for a little plainer evidence to communicate his suspicions to the Prince. It rests with you to save the Princess."

"Only tell me how I am to do it!" I said.

"There is but one way of doing it," she answered; "and that way has (comically enough) been suggested to me by the Doctor himself."

Her tone and manner tried my patience.

"Come to the point!" I said.

She seemed to enjoy provoking me.

"No hurry, Mr. Ernest—no hurry! You shall be fully enlightened, if you will only wait a little. The Prince, I must tell you, believes in his daughter's indisposition. When he visited her this morning, he was attended by his medical adviser. I was present at the interview. To do him justice, the Doctor is worthy of the trust reposed in him—he boldly attempted to verify his suspicions of the daughter in the father's presence."

"How?"

"Oh, in the well-known way that has been tried over and over again, under similar circumstances! He merely invented a report that you were engaged in a love-affair with some charming person in the town. Don't be angry; there's no harm done."

"But there is harm done," I insisted. "What must the Princess think of me?"

"Do you suppose she is weak enough to believe the Doctor? Her Highness beat him at his own weapons; not the slightest sign of agitation on her part rewarded his ingenuity. All that you have to do is to help her to mislead this medical spy. It's as easy as lying: and easier. The Doctor's slander declares that you have a love-affair in the town. Take the hint—and astonish the Doctor by proving that he has hit on the truth."

It was a hot day; the Baroness was beginning to get excited. She paused and fanned herself.

"Do I startle you?" she asked.

"You disgust me."

She laughed.

"What a thick-headed man this is!" she said, pleasantly. "Must I put it more plainly still? Engage in what your English prudery calls a 'flirtation,' with some woman here—the lower in degree the better, or the Princess might be jealous—and let the affair be seen and known by everybody about the Court. Sly as he is, the Doctor is not prepared for that! At your age, and with your personal advantages, he will take appearances for granted; he will conclude that he has wronged you, and misinterpreted the motives of the

Princess. The secret of her Highness's weakness will be preserved—thanks to that sacrifice, Mr. Ernest, which you are so willing and so eager to make."

It was useless to remonstrate with such a woman as this. I simply stated my own objection to her artfully devised scheme.

"I don't wish to appear vain," I said; "but the woman to whom I am to pay these attentions may believe that I really admire her—and it is just possible that she may honestly return the feeling which I am only assuming."

"Well—and what then?"

"It's hard on the woman, surely?"

The Baroness was shocked, unaffectedly shocked.

"Good heavens!" she exclaimed, "how can anything that you do for the Princess be hard on a woman of the lower orders? There must be an end of this nonsense, sir! You have heard what I propose, and you know what the circumstances are. My mistress is waiting for your answer. What am I to say?"

"Let me see her Highness, and speak for myself," I said.

"Quite impossible to-day, without running too great a risk. Your reply must be made through me."

There was to be a Court concert at the end of the week. On that occasion I should be able to make my own reply. In the meanwhile I only told the Baroness I wanted time to consider.

"What time?" she asked.

"Until to-morrow. Do you object?"

"On the contrary, I cordially agree. Your base hesitation may lead to results which I have not hitherto dared to anticipate."

"What do you mean?"

"Between this and to-morrow," the horrid woman replied, "the Princess may end in seeing you with my eyes. In that hope I wish you good-morning."

VI.

MY enemies say that I am a weak man, unduly influenced by persons of rank—because of their rank. If this we re true, I should have found little difficulty in consenting to adopt the Baroness's suggestion. As it was, the longer I reflected on the scheme the less I liked it. I tried to think of some alternative that might be acceptably proposed. The time passed, and nothing occurred to me. In this embarrassing position my mind became seriously disturbed; I felt the necessity of obtaining some relief, which might turn my thoughts for a while into a new channel. The secretary called on me, while I was still in doubt what to do. He reminded me that a new prima donna was advertised to appear on that night; and he suggested that we should go to the opera. Feeling as I did at the time, I readily agreed.

We found the theater already filled, before the performance began. Two French gentlemen were seated in the row of stalls behind us. They were talking of the new singer.

"She is advertised as 'Mademoiselle Fontenay,'" one of them said. "That sounds like an assumed name."

"It is an assumed name," the other replied. "She is the daughter of a French singing-master, named Bonnefoy."

To my friend's astonishment I started to my feet, and left him without a word of apology. In another minute I was at the stage-door, and had sent in my card to "Mademoiselle Fontenay." While I was waiting, I had time to think. Was it possible that Jeanne had gone on the stage? Or were there two singing-masters in existence named Bonnefoy? My doubts were soon decided. The French woman-servant whom I remembered when I was Monsieur Bonnefoy's pupil, made her appearance, and conducted me to her young mistress's dressing-room. Dear good Jeanne, how glad she was to see me!

I found her standing before the glass, having just completed her preparations for appearing on the stage. Dressed in her picturesque costume, she was so charming that I expressed my admiration heartily, as became her old friend. "Do you really like me?" she said, with the innocent familiarity which I recollected so well. "See how I look in the glass—that is the great test." It was not easy to apply the test. Instead of looking at her image in the glass, it was far more agreeable to look at herself. We were interrupted—too soon interrupted—by the call-boy. He knocked at the door, and announced that the overture had begun.

"I have a thousand things to ask you," I told her. "What has made this wonderful change in your life? How is it that I don't see your father—"

Her face instantly saddened; her hand trembled as she laid it on my arm to silence me.

"Don't speak of him now," she said, "or you will unnerve me. Come to me to-morrow when the stage will not be waiting; Annette will give you my address." She opened the door to go out, and returned. "Will you think me very unreasonable if I ask you not to make one of my audience to-night? You have reminded me of the dear old days that can never come again. If I feel that I am singing to you—" She left me to understand the rest, and turned away again to the door. As I followed her out, to say good-by, she drew from her bosom the little brooch which had been my parting gift, and held it out to me. "On the stage, or off," she said, "I always wear it. Good-night, Ernest."

I was prepared to hear sad news when we met the next morning.

My good old friend and master had died suddenly. To add to the bitterness of that affliction, he had died in debt to a dear and intimate friend. For his daughter's sake he had endeavored to add to his little savings by speculating with borrowed money on the Stock Exchange. He had failed, and the loan advanced had not been repaid, when a fit of apoplexy struck him down. Offered the opportunity of trying her fortune on the operatic stage, Jeanne made the attempt, and was now nobly employed in earning the money to pay her father's debt.

"It was the only way in which I could do justice to his memory," she said, simply. "I hope you don't object to my going on the stage?"

I took her hand, poor child—and let that simple action answer for me. I was too deeply affected to be able to speak.

"It is not in me to be a great actress," she resumed; "but you know what an admirable musician my father was. He has taught me to sing, so that I can satisfy the critics, as well as please the public. There was what they call a great success last night. It has earned me an engagement for another year to come, and an increase of salary. I have already sent some money to our good old friend at home, and I shall soon send more. It is my one consolation—I feel almost happy again when I am paying my poor father's debt. No more now of my sad story! I want to hear all that you can tell me of yourself." She moved to the window, and looked out. "Oh, the beautiful blue sky! We used sometimes to take a walk, when we were in London, on fine days like this. Is there a park here?"

I took her to the palace gardens, famous for their beauty in that part of Germany.

Arm in arm we loitered along the pleasant walks. The lovely flowers, the bright sun, the fresh fragrant breeze, all helped her to recover her spirits. She began to be like the happy Jeanne of my past experience, as easily pleased as a child. When we sat down to rest, the lap of her dress was full of daisies. "Do you remember," she said, "when you first taught me to make a daisy-chain? Are you too great a man to help me again now?"

We were still engaged with our chain, seated close together, when the smell of tobacco-smoke was wafted to us on the air.

I looked up and saw the Doctor passing us, enjoying his cigar. He bowed; eyed my pretty companion with a malicious smile; and passed on.

"Who is that man?" she asked.

"The Prince's physician," I replied.

"I don't like him," she said; "why did he smile when he looked at me?"

"Perhaps," I suggested, "he thought we were lovers."

She blushed. "Don't let him think that! tell him we are only old friends."

We were not destined to finish our flower chain on that day.

Another person interrupted us, whom I recognized as the elder brother of Monsieur Bonnefoy—already mentioned in these pages, under the name of Uncle David. Having left France for political reasons, the old republican had taken care of his niece after her father's death, and had accepted the position of Jeanne's business manager in her relations with the stage. Uncle David's object, when he joined us in the garden, was to remind her that she was wanted at rehearsal, and must at once return with him to the theater. We parted, having arranged that I was to see the performance on that night.

Later in the day, the Baroness sent for me again.

"Let me apologize for having misunderstood you yesterday," she said: "and let me offer you my best congratulations. You have done wonders already in the way of misleading the Doctor. There is only one objection to that girl at the theater—I hear she is so pretty that she may possibly displease the Princess. In other respects, she is just in the public position which will make your attentions to her look like the beginning of a serious intrigue. Bravo, Mr. Ernest—bravo!"

I was too indignant to place any restraint on the language in which I answered her.

"Understand, if you please," I said, "that I am renewing an old friendship with Mademoiselle Jeanne—begun under the sanction of her father. Respect that young lady, madam, as I respect her."

The detestable Baroness clapped her hands, as if she had been at the theater.

"If you only say that to the Princess," she remarked, "as well as you have said it to me, there will be no danger of arousing her Highness's jealousy. I have a message for you. At the concert, on Saturday, you are to retire to the conservatory, and you may hope for an interview when the singers begin the second part of the programme. Don't let me detain you any longer. Go back to your young lady, Mr. Ernest—pray go back!"

VII.

ON the second night of the opera the applications for places were too numerous to be received. Among the crowded audience, I recognized many of my friends. They persisted in believing an absurd report (first circulated, as I imagine, by the Doctor), which asserted that my interest in the new singer was something more than the interest of an old friend. When I went behind the scenes to congratulate Jeanne on her success, I was annoyed in another way—and by the Doctor again. He followed me to Jeanne's room, to offer his congratulations; and he begged that I would introduce him to the charming prima donna. Having expressed his admiration, he looked at me with his insolently suggestive smile, and said he could not think of prolonging his intrusion. On leaving the room, he noticed Uncle David, waiting as usual to take care of Jeanne on her return from the theater—looked at him attentively—bowed, and went out.

The next morning, I received a note from the Baroness, expressed in these terms:

"More news! My rooms look out on the wing of the palace in which the Doctor is lodged. Half an hour since, I discovered him at his window, giving a letter to a person who is a stranger to me. The man left the palace immediately afterward. My maid followed him, by my directions. Instead of putting the letter in the post, he took a ticket at the railway-station—for what place the servant was unable to discover. Here, you will observe, is a letter important enough to be dispatched by special messenger, and written at a time when we have succeeded in freeing ourselves from the Doctor's suspicions. It is at least possible that he has decided on sending a favorable report of the Princess to the Grand Duke. If this is the case, please consider whether you will not act wisely (in her Highness's interests) by keeping away from the concert."

Viewing this suggestion as another act of impertinence on the part of the Baroness, I persisted in my intention of going to the concert. It was for the Princess to decide what course of conduct I was bound to follow. What did I care for the Doctor's report to the Duke! Shall I own my folly? I do really believe I was jealous of the Duke.

VIII.

ENTERING the Concert Room, I found the Princess alone on the dais, receiving the company. "Nervous prostration" had made it impossible for the

Prince to be present. He was confined to his bed-chamber; and the Doctor was in attendance on him.

I bowed to the Baroness, but she was too seriously offended with me for declining to take her advice to notice my salutation. Passing into the conservatory, it occurred to me that I might be seen, and possibly suspected, in the interval between the first and second parts of the programme, when the music no longer absorbed the attention of the audience. I went on, and waited outside on the steps that led to the garden; keeping the glass door open, so as to hear when the music of the second part of the concert began.

After an interval which seemed to be endless, I saw the Princess approaching me.

She had made the heat in the Concert Room an excuse for retiring for a while; and she had the Baroness in attendance on her to save appearances. Instead of leaving us to ourselves, the malicious creature persisted in paying the most respectful attentions to her mistress. It was impossible to make her understand that she was not wanted any longer until the Princess said sharply, "Go back to the music!" Even then, the detestable woman made a low curtsey, and answered: "I will return, Madam, in five minutes."

I ventured to present myself in the conservatory.

The Princess was dressed with exquisite simplicity, entirely in white. Her only ornaments were white roses in her hair and in her bosom. To say that she looked lovely is to say nothing. She seemed to be the ethereal creature of some higher sphere; too exquisitely delicate and pure to be approached by a mere mortal man like myself. I was awed; I was silent. Her Highness's sweet smile encouraged me to venture a little nearer. She pointed to a footstool which the Baroness had placed for her. "Are you afraid of me, Ernest?" she asked softly.

Her divinely beautiful eyes rested on me with a look of encouragement. I dropped on my knees at her feet. She had asked if I was afraid of her. This, if I may use such an expression, roused my manhood. My own boldness astonished me. I answered: "Madam, I adore you."

She laid her fair hand on my head, and looked at me thoughtfully.

"Forget my rank," she whispered—"have I not set you the example? Suppose that I am nothing but an English Miss. What would you say to Miss?"

"I should say, I love you."

"Say it to Me."

My lips said it on her hand. She bent forward. My heart beats fast at the bare remembrance of it. Oh, heavens, her Highness kissed me!

"There is your reward," she murmured, "for all you have sacrificed for my sake. What an effort it must have been to offer the pretense of love to an obscure stranger! The Baroness tells me this actress—this singer—what is she?—is pretty. Is it true?"

The Baroness was quite mischievous enough to have also mentioned the false impression, prevalent about the Court, that I was in love with Jeanne. I attempted to explain. The gracious Princess refused to hear me.

"Do you think I doubt you?" she said. "Distinguished by me, could you waste a look on a person in that rank of life?" She laughed softly, as if the mere idea of such a thing amused her. It was only for a moment: her thoughts took a new direction—they contemplated the uncertain future. "How is this to end?" she asked. "Dear Ernest, we are not in Paradise; we are in a hard cruel world which insists on distinctions in rank. To what unhappy destiny does the fascination which you exercise over me condemn us both?"

She paused—took one of the white roses out of her bosom—touched it with her lips—and gave it to me.

"I wonder whether you feel the burden of life as I feel it?" she resumed. "It is immaterial to me, whether we are united in this world or in the next. Accept my rose, Ernest, as an assurance that I speak with perfect sincerity. I see but two alternatives before us. One of them (beset with dangers) is elopement. And the other," she added, with truly majestic composure, "is suicide."

Would Englishmen in general have rightly understood such fearless confidence in them as this language implied? I am afraid they might have attributed it to what my friend the secretary called "German sentiment." Perhaps they might even have suspected the Princess of quoting from some old-fashioned German play. Under the irresistible influence of that glorious creature, I contemplated with such equal serenity the perils of elopement and the martyrdom of love, that I was for the moment at a loss how to reply. In that moment, the evil genius of my life appeared in the conservatory. With haste in her steps, with alarm in her face, the Baroness rushed up to her royal mistress, and said, "For God's sake, Madam, come away! The Prince desires to speak with you instantly."

Her Highness rose, calmly superior to the vulgar excitement of her lady in waiting. "Think of it to-night," she said to me, "and let me hear from you to-morrow."

She pressed my hand; she gave me a farewell look. I sank into the chair that she had just left. Did I think of elopement? Did I think of suicide? The elevating influence of the Princess no longer sustained me; my nature became degraded. Horrid doubts rose in my mind. Did her father suspect us?

IX.

NEED I say that I passed a sleepless night?

The morning found me with my pen in my hand, confronting the serious responsibility of writing to the Princess, and not knowing what to say. I had already torn up two letters, when Uncle David presented himself with a message from his niece. Jeanne was in trouble, and wanted to ask my advice.

My state of mind, on hearing this, became simply inexplicable. Here was an interruption which ought to have annoyed me. It did nothing of the kind—it inspired me with a feeling of relief!

I naturally expected that the old Frenchman would return with me to his niece, and tell me what had happened. To my surprise, he begged that I would excuse him, and left me without a word of explanation. I found Jeanne walking up and down her little sitting-room, flushed and angry. Fragments of torn paper and heaps of flowers littered the floor; and three unopen jewel-cases appeared to have been thrown into the empty fireplace. She caught me excitedly by the hand the moment I entered the room.

"You are my true friend," she said; "you were present the other night when I sang. Was there anything in my behavior on the stage which could justify men who call themselves gentlemen in insulting me?"

"My dear, how can you ask the question?"

"I must ask it. Some of them send flowers, and some of them send jewels; and every one of them writes letters—infamous, abominable letters—saying they are in love with me, and asking for appointments as if I was—"

She could say no more. Poor dear Jeanne—her head dropped on my shoulder; she burst out crying. Who could see her so cruelly humiliated—the faithful loving daughter, whose one motive for appearing on the stage had been to preserve her father's good name—and not feel for her as I did? I forgot all considerations of prudence; I thought of nothing but consoling her; I took her in my arms; I dried her tears; I kissed her; I said, "Tell me the name of any one of the wretches who has written to you, and I will make him an example to the rest!" She shook her head, and pointed to the morsels of paper on the floor. "Oh, Ernest, do you think I asked you to come here for any such purpose as that? Those jewels, those hateful jewels, tell me how I can send them back! spare me the sight of them!"

So far it was easy to console her. I sent the jewels at once to the manager of the theater—with a written notice to be posted at the stage door, stating that they were waiting to be returned to the persons who could describe them.

"Try, my dear, to forget what has happened," I said. "Try to find consolation and encouragement in your art."

"I have lost all interest in my success on the stage," she answered, "now I know the penalty I must pay for it. When my father's memory is clear of reproach, I shall leave the theater never to return to it again."

"Take time to consider, Jeanne."

"I will do anything you ask of me."

For a while we were silent. Without any influence to lead to it that

I could trace, I found myself recalling the language that the Princess had used in alluding to Jeanne. When I thought of them now, the words and the tone in which they had been spoken jarred on me. There is surely something mean in an assertion of superiority which depends on nothing better than the accident of birth. I don't know why I took Jeanne's hand; I don't know why I said, "What a good girl you are! how glad I am to have been of some little use to you!" Is my friend the secretary right, when he reproaches me with acting on impulse, like a woman? I don't like to think so; and yet, this I must own— it was well for me that I was obliged to leave her, before I had perhaps said other words which might have been alike unworthy of Jeanne, of the Princess, and of myself. I was called away to speak to my servant. He brought with him the secretary's card, having a line written on it: "I am waiting at your rooms, on business which permits of no delay."

As we shook hands, Jeanne asked me if I knew where her uncle was. I could only tell her that he had left me at my own door. She made no remark; but she seemed to be uneasy on receiving that reply.

X.

WHEN I arrived at my rooms, my colleague hurried to meet me the moment I opened the door.

"I am going to surprise you," he said; "and there is no time to prepare you for it. Our chief, the Minister, has seen the Prince this morning, and has been officially informed of an event of importance in the life of the Princess. She is engaged to be married to the Grand Duke."

Engaged to the Duke—and not a word from her to warn me of it! Engaged—after what she had said to me no longer ago than the past night! Had I been made a plaything to amuse a great lady? Oh, what degradation! I was furious; I snatched up my hat to go to the palace—to force my way to her—to overwhelm her with reproaches. My friend stopped me. He put an official document into my hand.

"There is your leave of absence from the legation," he said; "beginning from to-day. I have informed the Minister, in strict confidence, of the critical position in which you are placed. He agrees with me that the Princess's inexcusable folly is alone to blame. Leave us, Ernest, by the next train. There is some intrigue going on, and I fear you may be involved in it. You know that the rulers of these little German States can exercise despotic authority when they choose?"

"Yes! yes!"

"Whether the Prince has acted of his own free will—or whether he has been influenced by some person about him—I am not able to tell you. He has issued an order to arrest an old Frenchman, known to be a republican, and suspected of associating with one of the secret societies in this part of Germany. The conspirator has taken to flight; having friends, as we suppose, who warned him in time. But this, Ernest, is not the worst of it. That charming singer, that modest, pretty girl—"

"You don't mean Jeanne?"

"I am sorry to say I do. Advantage has been taken of her relationship to the old man, to include that innocent creature in political suspicions which it is simply absurd to suppose that she has deserved. She is ordered to leave the Prince's domains immediately.—Are you going to her?"

"Instantly!" I replied.

Could I feel a moment's hesitation, after the infamous manner in which the Princess had sacrificed me to the Grand Duke? Could I think of the poor girl, friendless, helpless—with nobody near her but a stupid woman-servant, unable to speak the language of the country—and fail to devote myself to the protection of Jeanne? Thank God, I reached her lodgings in time to tell her what had happened, and to take it on myself to receive the police.

XI.

IN three days more, Jeanne was safe in London; having traveled under my escort. I was fortunate enough to find a home for her, in the house of a lady who had been my mother's oldest and dearest friend.

We were separated, a few days afterward, by the distressing news which reached me of the state of my brother's health. I went at once to his house in the country. His medical attendants had lost all hope of saving him: they told me plainly that his release from a life of suffering was near at hand.

While I was still in attendance at his bedside, I heard from the secretary. He inclosed a letter, directed to me in a strange handwriting. I opened the envelope and looked for the signature. My friend had been entrapped into sending me an anonymous letter.

Besides addressing me in French (a language seldom used in my experience at the legation), the writer disguised the identity of the persons mentioned by the use of classical names. In spite of these precautions, I felt no difficulty in arriving at a conclusion. My correspondent's special knowledge of Court secrets, and her malicious way of communicating them, betrayed the Baroness.

I translate the letter; restoring to the persons who figure in it the names under which they are already known. The writer began in these satirically familiar terms:

"When you left the Prince's dominions, my dear sir, you no doubt believed yourself to be a free agent. Quite a mistake! You were a mere puppet; and the strings that moved you were pulled by the Doctor.

"Let me tell you how.

"On a certain night, which you well remember, the Princess was unexpectedly summoned to the presence of her father. His physician's skill had succeeded in relieving the illustrious Prince, prostrate under nervous miseries. He was able to attend to a state affair of importance, revealed to him by the Doctor—who then for the first time acknowledged that he had presented himself at Court in a diplomatic, as well as in a medical capacity.

"This state affair related to a proposal for the hand of the Princess, received from the Grand Duke through the authorized medium of the Doctor. Her Highness, being consulted, refused to consider the proposal. The Prince asked for her reason. She answered: 'I have no wish to be married.' Naturally irritated by such a ridiculous excuse, her father declared positively that the marriage should take place.

644

"The impression produced on the Grand Duke's favorite and emissary was of a different kind.

"Certain suspicions of the Princess and yourself, which you had successfully contrived to dissipate, revived in the Doctor's mind when he heard the lady's reason for refusing to marry his royal master. It was now too late to regret that he had suffered himself to be misled by cleverly managed appearances. He could not recall the favorable report which he had addressed to the Duke—or withdraw the proposal of marriage which he had been commanded to make.

"In this emergency, the one safe course open to him was to get rid of You—and, at the same time, so to handle circumstances as to excite against you the pride and anger of the Princess. In the pursuit of this latter object he was assisted by one of the ladies in waiting, sincerely interested in the welfare of her gracious mistress, and therefore ardently desirous of seeing her Highness married to the Duke.

"A wretched old French conspirator was made the convenient pivot on which the intrigue turned.

"An order for the arrest of this foreign republican having been first obtained, the Prince was prevailed on to extend his distrust of the Frenchman to the Frenchman's niece. You know this already; but you don't know why it was done. Having believed from the first that you were really in love with the young lady, the Doctor reckoned confidently on your devoting yourself to the protection of a friendless girl, cruelly exiled at an hour's notice.

"The one chance against us was that tender considerations, associated with her Highness, might induce you to hesitate. The lady in waiting easily moved this obstacle out of the way. She abstained from delivering a letter addressed to you, intrusted to her by the Princess. When the great lady asked why she had not received your reply, she was informed (quite truly) that you and the charming opera singer had taken your departure together. You may imagine what her Highness thought of you, and said of you, when I mention in conclusion that she consented, the same day, to marry the Duke.

"So, Mr. Ernest, these clever people tricked you into serving their interests, blindfold. In relating how it was done, I hope I may have assisted you in forming a correct estimate of the state of your own intelligence. You have made a serious mistake in adopting your present profession. Give up diplomacy—and get a farmer to employ you in keeping his sheep."

Do I sometimes think regretfully of the Princess?

Permit me to mention a circumstance, and to leave my answer to be inferred. Jeanne is Lady Medhurst.

MR. LISMORE AND THE WIDOW.

I.

LATE in the autumn, not many years since, a public meeting was held at the Mansion House, London, under the direction of the Lord Mayor.

The list of gentlemen invited to address the audience had been chosen with two objects in view. Speakers of celebrity, who would rouse public enthusiasm, were supported by speakers connected with commerce, who would be practically useful in explaining the purpose for which the meeting was convened. Money wisely spent in advertising had produced the customary result—every seat was occupied before the proceedings began.

Among the late arrivals, who had no choice but to stand or to leave the hall, were two ladies. One of them at once decided on leaving the hall. "I shall go back to the carriage," she said, "and wait for you at the door." Her friend answered, "I shan't keep you long. He is advertised to support the second Resolution; I want to see him—and that is all."

An elderly gentleman, seated at the end of a bench, rose and offered his place to the lady who remained. She hesitated to take advantage of his kindness, until he reminded her that he had heard what she said to her friend. Before the third Resolution was proposed, his seat would be at his own disposal again. She thanked him, and without further ceremony took his place He was provided with an opera-glass, which he more than once offered to her, when famous orators appeared on the platform; she made no use of it until a speaker—known in the City as a ship-owner—stepped forward to support the second Resolution.

His name (announced in the advertisements) was Ernest Lismore.

The moment he rose, the lady asked for the opera-glass. She kept it to her eyes for such a length of time, and with such evident interest in Mr. Lismore, that the curiosity of her neighbors was aroused. Had he anything to say in which a lady (evidently a stranger to him) was personally interested? There was nothing in the address that he delivered which appealed to the enthusiasm of women. He was undoubtedly a handsome man, whose appearance proclaimed him to be in the prime of life—midway perhaps between thirty and forty years of age. But why a lady should persist in keeping an opera-glass fixed on him all through his speech, was a question which found the general ingenuity at a loss for a reply.

Having returned the glass with an apology, the lady ventured on putting a question next. "Did it strike you, sir, that Mr. Lismore seemed to be out of spirits?" she asked.

"I can't say it did, ma'am."

"Perhaps you noticed that he left the platform the moment he had done?"

This betrayal of interest in the speaker did not escape the notice of a lady, seated on the bench in front. Before the old gentleman could answer, she volunteered an explanation.

"I am afraid Mr. Lismore is troubled by anxieties connected with his business," she said. "My husband heard it reported in the City yesterday that he was seriously embarrassed by the failure—"

A loud burst of applause made the end of the sentence inaudible. A famous member of Parliament had risen to propose the third Resolution. The polite old man took his seat, and the lady left the hall to join her friend.

"Well, Mrs. Callender, has Mr. Lismore disappointed you?"

"Far from it! But I have heard a report about him which has alarmed me: he is said to be seriously troubled about money matters. How can I find out his address in the City?"

"We can stop at the first stationer's shop we pass, and ask to look at the Directory. Are you going to pay Mr. Lismore a visit?"

"I am going to think about it."

II.

THE next day a clerk entered Mr. Lismore's private room at the office, and presented a visiting-card. Mrs. Callender had reflected, and had arrived at a decision. Underneath her name she had written these explanatory words: "On important business."

"Does she look as if she wanted money?" Mr. Lismore inquired.

"Oh dear, no! She comes in her carriage."

"Is she young or old?"

"Old, sir."

To Mr. Lismore—conscious of the disastrous influence occasionally exercised over busy men by youth and beauty—this was a recommendation in itself. He said: "Show her in."

Observing the lady, as she approached him, with the momentary curiosity of a stranger, he noticed that she still preserved the remains of beauty. She had also escaped the misfortune, common to persons at her time of life, of becoming too fat. Even to a man's eye, her dressmaker appeared to have made the most of that favorable circumstance. Her figure had its defects concealed, and its remaining merits set off to advantage. At the same time she evidently held herself above the common deceptions by which some women seek to conceal their age. She wore her own gray hair; and her complexion bore the test of daylight. On entering the room, she made her apologies with some embarrassment. Being the embarrassment of a stranger (and not of a youthful stranger), it failed to impress Mr. Lismore favorably.

"I am afraid I have chosen an inconvenient time for my visit," she began.

"I am at your service," he answered a little stiffly; "especially if you will be so kind as to mention your business with me in few words."

She was a woman of some spirit, and that reply roused her.

"I will mention it in one word," she said smartly. "My business is—gratitude."

He was completely at a loss to understand what she meant, and he said so plainly. Instead of explaining herself, she put a question.

"Do you remember the night of the eleventh of March, between five and six years since?"

He considered for a moment.

"No," he said, "I don't remember it. Excuse me, Mrs. Callender, I have affairs of my own to attend to which cause me some anxiety—"

"Let me assist your memory, Mr. Lismore; and I will leave you to your affairs. On the date that I have referred to, you were on your way to the railway-station at Bexmore, to catch the night express from the North to London."

As a hint that his time was valuable the ship-owner had hitherto remained standing. He now took his customary seat, and began to listen with some interest. Mrs. Callender had produced her effect on him already.

"It was absolutely necessary," she proceeded, "that you should be on board your ship in the London Docks at nine o'clock the next morning. If you had lost the express, the vessel would have sailed without you."

The expression of his face began to change to surprise. "Who told you that?" he asked.

"You shall hear directly. On your way into the town, your carriage was stopped by an obstruction on the highroad. The people of Bexmore were looking at a house on fire."

He started to his feet.

"Good heavens! are you the lady?"

She held up her hand in satirical protest.

"Gently, sir! You suspected me just now of wasting your valuable time. Don't rashly conclude that I am the lady, until you find that I am acquainted with the circumstances."

"Is there no excuse for my failing to recognize you?" Mr. Lismore asked. "We were on the dark side of the burning house; you were fainting, and I—"

"And you," she interposed, "after saving me at the risk of your own life, turned a deaf ear to my poor husband's entreaties, when he asked you to wait till I had recovered my senses."

"Your poor husband? Surely, Mrs. Callender, he received no serious injury from the fire?"

"The firemen rescued him under circumstances of peril," she answered, "and at his great age he sank under the shock. I have lost the kindest and best of men. Do you remember how you parted from him—burned and bruised in saving me? He liked to talk of it in his last illness. 'At least' (he said to you), 'tell me the name of the man who has preserved my wife from a dreadful death.' You threw your card to him out of the carriage window, and away you went at a gallop to catch your train! In all the years that have passed I have kept that card, and have vainly inquired for my brave sea-captain. Yesterday I saw your name on the list of speakers at the Mansion House. Need I say that I attended the meeting? Need I tell you now why I come here and interrupt you in business hours?"

She held out her hand. Mr. Lismore took it in silence, and pressed it warmly.

"You have not done with me yet," she resumed with a smile. "Do you remember what I said of my errand, when I first came in?"

"You said it was an errand of gratitude."

"Something more than the gratitude which only says 'Thank you,'" she added. "Before I explain myself, however, I want to know what you have been doing, and how it was that my inquiries failed to trace you after that terrible night."

The appearance of depression which Mrs. Callender had noticed at the public meeting showed itself again in Mr. Lismore's face. He sighed as he answered her.

"My story has one merit," he said; "it is soon told. I cannot wonder that you failed to discover me. In the first place, I was not captain of my ship at that time; I was only mate. In the second place, I inherited some money, and ceased to lead a sailor's life, in less than a year from the night of the fire. You will now understand what obstacles were in the way of your tracing me. With my little capital I started successfully in business as a ship-owner. At the time, I naturally congratulated myself on my own good fortune. We little know, Mrs. Callender, what the future has in store for us."

He stopped. His handsome features hardened—as if he was suffering (and concealing) pain. Before it was possible to speak to him, there was a knock at the door. Another visitor, without an appointment, had called; the clerk appeared again, with a card and a message.

"The gentleman begs you will see him, sir. He has something to tell you which is too important to be delayed."

Hearing the message, Mrs. Callender rose immediately.

"It is enough for to-day that we understand each other," she said. "Have you any engagement to-morrow, after the hours of business?"

"None."

She pointed to her card on the writing-table. "Will you come to me to-morrow evening at that address? I am like the gentleman who has just called; I, too, have my reason for wishing to see you."

He gladly accepted the invitation. Mrs. Callender stopped him as he opened the door for her.

"Shall I offend you," she said, "if I ask a strange question before I go? I have a better motive, mind, than mere curiosity. Are you married?"

"No."

"Forgive me again," she resumed. "At my age, you cannot possibly misunderstand me; and yet—"

She hesitated. Mr. Lismore tried to give her confidence. "Pray don't stand on ceremony, Mrs. Callender. Nothing that you can ask me need be prefaced by an apology."

Thus encouraged, she ventured to proceed.

"You may be engaged to be married?" she suggested. "Or you may be in love?"

He found it impossible to conceal his surprise. But he answered without hesitation.

"There is no such bright prospect in my life," he said. "I am not even in love."

She left him with a little sigh. It sounded like a sigh of relief.

Ernest Lismore was thoroughly puzzled. What could be the old lady's object in ascertaining that he was still free from a matrimonial engagement? If the idea had occurred to him in time, he might have alluded to her domestic life, and might have asked if she had children? With a little tact he might have discovered more than this. She had described her feeling toward him as passing the ordinary limits of gratitude; and she was evidently rich enough to be above the imputation of a mercenary motive. Did she propose to brighten those dreary prospects to which he had alluded in speaking of his own life? When he presented himself at her house the next evening, would she introduce him to a charming daughter?

He smiled as the idea occurred to him. "An appropriate time to be thinking of my chances of marriage!" he said to himself. "In another month I may be a ruined man."

III.

THE gentleman who had so urgently requested an interview was a devoted friend—who had obtained a means of helping Ernest at a serious crisis in his affairs.

It had been truly reported that he was in a position of pecuniary embarrassment, owing to the failure of a mercantile house with which he had been intimately connected. Whispers affecting his own solvency had followed on the bankruptcy of the firm. He had already endeavored to obtain advances of money on the usual conditions, and had been met by excuses for delay. His friend had now arrived with a letter of introduction to a capitalist, well known in commercial circles for his daring speculations and for his great wealth.

Looking at the letter, Ernest observed that the envelope was sealed. In spite of that ominous innovation on established usage, in cases of personal introduction, he presented the letter. On this occasion, he was not put off with excuses. The capitalist flatly declined to discount Mr. Lismore's bills, unless they were backed by responsible names.

Ernest made a last effort.

He applied for help to two mercantile men whom he had assisted in their difficulties, and whose names would have satisfied the money-lender. They were most sincerely sorry—but they, too, refused.

The one security that he could offer was open, it must be owned, to serious objections on the score of risk. He wanted an advance of twenty thousand pounds, secured on a homeward-bound ship and cargo. But the vessel was not insured; and, at that stormy season, she was already more than a month overdue. Could grateful colleagues be blamed if they forgot their obligations when they were asked to offer pecuniary help to a merchant in this situation? Ernest returned to his office, without money and without credit.

A man threatened by ruin is in no state of mind to keep an engagement at a lady's tea-table. Ernest sent a letter of apology to Mrs. Callender, alleging extreme pressure of business as the excuse for breaking his engagement.

"Am I to wait for an answer, sir?" the messenger asked.

"No; you are merely to leave the letter."

IV.

IN an hour's time—to Ernest's astonishment—the messenger returned with a reply.

"The lady was just going out, sir, when I rang at the door," he explained, "and she took the letter from me herself. She didn't appear to know your handwriting, and she asked me who I came from. When I mentioned your name, I was ordered to wait."

Ernest opened the letter.

"DEAR MR. LISMORE—One of us must speak out, and your letter of apology forces me to be that one. If you are really so proud and so distrustfull as you seem to be, I shall offend you. If not, I shall prove myself to be your friend.

"Your excuse is 'pressure of business.' The truth (as I have good reason to believe) is 'want of money.' I heard a stranger, at that public meeting, say that you were seriously embarrassed by some failure in the City.

"Let me tell you what my own pecuniary position is in two words. I am the childless widow of a rich man—"

Ernest paused. His anticipated discovery of Mrs. Callender's "charming daughter" was in his mind for the moment. "That little romance must return to the world of dreams," he thought—and went on with the letter.

"After what I owe to you, I don't regard it as repaying an obligation—I consider myself as merely performing a duty when I offer to assist you by a loan of money.

"Wait a little before you throw my letter into the wastepaper basket.

"Circumstances (which it is impossible for me to mention before we meet) put it out of my power to help you—unless I attach to my most sincere offer of service a very unusual and very embarrassing condition. If you are on the brink of ruin, that misfortune will plead my excuse—and your excuse, too, if you accept the loan on my terms. In any case, I rely on the sympathy and forbearance of the man to whom I owe my life.

"After what I have now written, there is only one thing to add. I beg to decline accepting your excuses; and I shall expect to see you tomorrow evening, as we arranged. I am an obstinate old woman—but I am also your faithful friend and servant,

"MARY CALLENDER."

Ernest looked up from the letter. "What can this possibly mean?" he wondered.

But he was too sensible a man to be content with wondering—he decided on keeping his engagement.

V.

WHAT Doctor Johnson called "the insolence of wealth" appears far more frequently in the houses of the rich than in the manners of the rich. The reason is plain enough. Personal ostentation is, in the very nature of it, ridiculous. But the ostentation which exhibits magnificent pictures, priceless china, and splendid furniture, can purchase good taste to guide it, and can assert itself without affording the smallest opening for a word of depreciation, or a look of contempt. If I am worth a million of money, and if I am dying to show it, I don't ask you to look at me—I ask you to look at my house.

Keeping his engagement with Mrs. Callender, Ernest discovered that riches might be lavishly and yet modestly used.

In crossing the hall and ascending the stairs, look where he might, his notice was insensibly won by proofs of the taste which is not to be purchased, and the wealth which uses but never exhibits its purse. Conducted by a man-servant to the landing on the first floor, he found a maid at the door of the boudoir waiting to announce him. Mrs. Callender advanced to welcome her guest, in a simple evening dress perfectly suited to her age. All that had looked worn and faded in her fine face, by daylight, was now softly obscured by shaded lamps. Objects of beauty surrounded her, which glowed with subdued radiance from their background of sober color. The influence of appearances is the strongest of all outward influences, while it lasts. For the moment, the scene produced its impression on Ernest, in spite of the terrible anxieties which consumed him. Mrs. Callender, in his office, was a woman who had stepped out of her appropriate sphere. Mrs. Callender, in her own house, was a woman who had risen to a new place in his estimation.

"I am afraid you don't thank me for forcing you to keep your engagement," she said, with her friendly tones and her pleasant smile.

"Indeed I do thank you," he replied. "Your beautiful house and your gracious welcome have persuaded me into forgetting my troubles—for a while."

The smile passed away from her face. "Then it is true," she said gravely.

"Only too true."

She led him to a seat beside her, and waited to speak again until her maid had brought in the tea.

"Have you read my letter in the same friendly spirit in which I wrote it?" she asked, when they were alone again.

"I have read your letter gratefully, but—"

"But you don't know yet what I have to say. Let us understand each other before we make any objections on either side. Will you tell me what your present position is—at its worst? I can and will speak plainly when my turn comes, if you will honor me with your confidence. Not if it distresses you," she added, observing him attentively.

He was ashamed of his hesitation—and he made amends for it.

"Do you thoroughly understand me?" he asked, when the whole truth had been laid before her without reserve.

She summed up the result in her own words.

"If your overdue ship returns safely, within a month from this time, you can borrow the money you want, without difficulty. If the ship is lost, you have no alternative (when the end of the month comes) but to accept a loan from me or to suspend payment. Is that the hard truth?"

"It is."

"And the sum you require is—twenty thousand pounds?"

"Yes."

"I have twenty times as much money as that, Mr. Lismore, at my sole disposal—on one condition."

"The condition alluded to in your letter?"

"Yes."

"Does the fulfillment of the condition depend in some way on any decision of mine?"

"It depends entirely on you."

That answer closed his lips.

With a composed manner and a steady hand she poured herself out a cup of tea.

"I conceal it from you," she said; "but I want confidence. Here" (she pointed to the cup) "is the friend of women, rich or poor, when they are in trouble. What I have now to say obliges me to speak in praise of myself. I don't like it—let me get it over as soon as I can. My husband was very fond of me: he had the most absolute confidence in my discretion, and in my sense of duty to him and to myself. His last words, before he died, were words that thanked me for making the happiness of his life. As soon as I had in some degree recovered, after the affliction that had fallen on me, his lawyer and executor produced a copy of his will, and said there were two clauses in it which my husband had expressed a wish that I should read. It is needless to say that I obeyed."

She still controlled her agitation—but she was now unable to conceal it. Ernest made an attempt to spare her.

"Am I concerned in this?" he asked.

"Yes. Before I tell you why, I want to know what you would do—in a certain case which I am unwilling even to suppose. I have heard of men, unable to pay the demands made on them, who began business again, and succeeded, and in course of time paid their creditors."

"And you want to know if there is any likelihood of my following their example?" he said. "Have you also heard of men who have made that second effort—who have failed again—and who have doubled the debts they owed to their brethren in business who trusted them? I knew one of those men myself. He committed suicide."

She laid her hand for a moment on his.

"I understand you," she said. "If ruin comes—"

"If ruin comes," he interposed, "a man without money and without credit can make but one last atonement. Don't speak of it now."

She looked at him with horror.

"I didn't mean that!" she said.

"Shall we go back to what you read in the will?" he suggested.

"Yes—if you will give me a minute to compose myself."

VI.

IN less than the minute she had asked for, Mrs. Callender was calm enough to go on.

"I now possess what is called a life-interest in my husband's fortune," she said. "The money is to be divided, at my death, among charitable institutions; excepting a certain event—"

"Which is provided for in the will?" Ernest added, helping her to go on.

"Yes. I am to be absolute mistress of the whole of the four hundred thousand pounds—" her voice dropped, and her eyes looked away from him as she spoke the next words—"on this one condition, that I marry again."

He looked at her in amazement.

"Surely I have mistaken you," he said. "You mean on this one condition, that you do not marry again?"

"No, Mr. Lismore; I mean exactly what I have said. You now know that the recovery of your credit and your peace of mind rests entirely with yourself."

After a moment of reflection he took her hand and raised it respectfully to his lips. "You are a noble woman!" he said.

She made no reply. With drooping head and downcast eyes she waited for his decision. He accepted his responsibility.

"I must not, and dare not, think of the hardship of my own position," he said; "I owe it to you to speak without reference to the future that may be in store for me. No man can be worthy of the sacrifice which your generous forgetfulness of yourself is willing to make. I respect you; I admire you; I thank you with my whole heart. Leave me to my fate, Mrs. Callender—and let me go."

He rose. She stopped him by a gesture.

"A young woman," she answered, "would shrink from saying—what I, as an old woman, mean to say now. I refuse to leave you to your fate. I ask you to prove that you respect me, admire me, and thank me with your whole heart. Take one day to think—and let me hear the result. You promise me this?"

He promised. "Now go," she said.

VII.

NEXT morning Ernest received a letter from Mrs. Callender. She wrote to him as follows:

"There are some considerations which I ought to have mentioned yesterday evening, before you left my house.

"I ought to have reminded you—if you consent to reconsider your decision—that the circumstances do not require you to pledge yourself to me absolutely.

"At my age, I can with perfect propriety assure you that I regard our marriage simply and solely as a formality which we must fulfill, if I am to carry out my intention of standing between you and ruin.

"Therefore—if the missing ship appears in time, the only reason for the marriage is at an end. We shall be as good friends as ever; without the encumbrance of a formal tie to bind us.

"In the other event, I should ask you to submit to certain restrictions which, remembering my position, you will understand and excuse.

"We are to live together, it is unnecessary to say, as mother and son. The marriage ceremony is to be strictly private; and you are so to arrange your affairs that, immediately afterward, we leave England for any foreign place which you prefer. Some of my friends, and (perhaps) some of your friends, will certainly misinterpret our motives—if we stay in our own country—in a manner which would be unendurable to a woman like me.

"As to our future lives, I have the most perfect confidence in you, and I should leave you in the same position of independence which you occupy now. When you wish for my company you will always be welcome. At other times, you are your own master. I live on my side of the house, and you live on yours—and I am to be allowed my hours of solitude every day, in the pursuit of musical occupations, which have been happily associated with all my past life and which I trust confidently to your indulgence.

"A last word, to remind you of what you may be too kind to think of yourself.

"At my age, you cannot, in the course of Nature, be troubled by the society of a grateful old woman for many years. You are young enough to look forward to another marriage, which shall be something more than a mere form. Even if you meet with the happy woman in my lifetime, honestly tell me of it—and I promise to tell her that she has only to wait.

"In the meantime, don't think, because I write composedly, that I write heartlessly. You pleased and interested me, when I first saw you, at the public meeting. I don't think I could have proposed, what you call this sacrifice of myself, to a man who had personally repelled me—though I might have felt my debt of gratitude as sincerely as ever. Whether your ship is saved, or whether your ship is lost, old Mary Callender likes you—and owns it without false shame.

"Let me have your answer this evening, either personally or by letter—whichever you like best."

VIII.

MRS. CALLENDER received a written answer long before the evening. It said much in few words:

"A man impenetrable to kindness might be able to resist your letter. I am not that man. Your great heart has conquered me."

The few formalities which precede marriage by special license were observed by Ernest. While the destiny of their future lives was still in suspense, an unacknowledged feeling of embarrassment, on either side, kept Ernest and Mrs. Callender apart. Every day brought the lady her report of the state of affairs in the City, written always in the same words: "No news of the ship."

IX.

ON the day before the ship-owner's liabilities became due, the terms of the report from the City remained unchanged—and the special license was put to its contemplated use. Mrs. Callender's lawyer and Mrs. Callender's maid were the only persons trusted with the secret. Leaving the chief clerk in charge of the business, with every pecuniary demand on his employer satisfied in full, the strangely married pair quitted England.

They arranged to wait for a few days in Paris, to receive any letters of importance which might have been addressed to Ernest in the interval. On the evening of their arrival, a telegram from London was waiting at their hotel. It announced that the missing ship had passed up Channel—undiscovered in a fog, until she reached the Downs—on the day before Ernest's liabilities fell due.

"Do you regret it?" Mrs. Lismore said to her husband.

"Not for a moment!" he answered.

They decided on pursuing their journey as far as Munich.

Mrs. Lismore's taste for music was matched by Ernest's taste for painting. In his leisure hours he cultivated the art, and delighted in it. The picture-galleries of Munich were almost the only galleries in Europe which he had not seen. True to the engagements to which she had pledged herself, his wife was willing to go wherever it might please him to take her. The one suggestion she made was, that they should hire furnished apartments. If they lived at an hotel, friends of the husband or the wife (visitors like themselves to the famous city) might see their names in the book, or might meet them at the door.

They were soon established in a house large enough to provide them with every accommodation which they required.

Ernest's days were passed in the galleries; Mrs. Lismore remaining at home, devoted to her music, until it was time to go out with her husband for a drive. Living together in perfect amity and concord, they were nevertheless not living happily. Without any visible reason for the change, Mrs. Lismore's spirits were depressed. On the one occasion when Ernest noticed it she made an effort to be cheerful, which it distressed him to see. He allowed her to think that she had relieved him of any further anxiety. Whatever doubts he might feel were doubts delicately concealed from that time forth.

But when two people are living together in a state of artificial tranquillity, it seems to be a law of Nature that the element of disturbance gathers unseen, and that the outburst comes inevitably with the lapse of time.

In ten days from the date of their arrival at Munich, the crisis came. Ernest returned later than usual from the picture-gallery, and—for the first time in his wife's experience—shut himself up in his own room.

He appeared at the dinner-hour with a futile excuse. Mrs. Lismore waited until the servant had withdrawn. "Now, Ernest," she said, "it's time to tell me the truth."

Her manner, when she said those few words, took him by surprise. She was unquestionably confused; and, instead of looking at him, she trifled with the fruit on her plate. Embarrassed on his side, he could only answer:

"I have nothing to tell."

"Were there many visitors at the gallery?" she asked.

"About the same as usual."

"Any that you particularly noticed?" she went on. "I mean, among the ladies."

He laughed uneasily. "You forget how interested I am in the pictures," he said.

There was a pause. She looked up at him—and suddenly looked away again. But he saw it plainly: there were tears in her eyes.

"Do you mind turning down the gas?" she said. "My eyes have been weak all day."

He complied with her request—the more readily, having his own reasons for being glad to escape the glaring scrutiny of the light.

"I think I will rest a little on the sofa," she resumed. In the position which he occupied, his back would have been now turned on her. She stopped him when he tried to move his chair. "I would rather not look at you, Ernest," she said, "when you have lost confidence in me."

Not the words, but the tone, touched all that was generous and noble in his nature. He left his place, and knelt beside her—and opened to her his whole heart.

"Am I not unworthy of you?" he asked, when it was over.

She pressed his hand in silence.

"I should be the most ungrateful wretch living," he said, "if I did not think of you, and you only, now that my confession is made. We will leave Munich to-morrow—and, if resolution can help me, I will only remember the sweetest woman my eyes ever looked on as the creature of a dream."

She hid her face on his breast, and reminded him of that letter of her writing, which had decided the course of their lives.

"When I thought you might meet the happy woman in my life-time, I said to you, 'Tell me of it—and I promise to tell her that she has only to wait.' Time must pass, Ernest, before it can be needful to perform my promise. But you might let me see her. If you find her in the gallery to-morrow, you might bring her here."

Mrs. Lismore's request met with no refusal. Ernest was only at a loss to know how to grant it.

"You tell me she is a copyist of pictures," his wife reminded him. "She will be interested in hearing of the portfolio of drawings by the great French artists which I bought for you in Paris. Ask her to come and see them, and to tell you if she can make some copies. And say, if you like, that I shall be glad to become acquainted with her."

He felt her breath beating fast on his bosom. In the fear that she might lose all control over herself, he tried to relieve her by speaking lightly. "What an invention yours is!" he said. "If my wife ever tries to deceive me, I shall be a mere child in her hands."

She rose abruptly from the sofa—kissed him on the forehead—and said wildly, "I shall be better in bed!" Before he could move or speak, she had left him.

X.

THE next morning he knocked at the door of his wife's room and asked how she had passed the night.

"I have slept badly," she answered, "and I must beg you to excuse my absence at breakfast-time." She called him back as he was about to withdraw. "Remember," she said, "when you return from the gallery to-day, I expect that you will not return alone."

Three hours later he was at home again. The young lady's services as a copyist were at his disposal; she had returned with him to look at the drawings.

The sitting-room was empty when they entered it. He rang for his wife's maid—and was informed that Mrs. Lismore had gone out. Refusing to believe the woman, he went to his wife's apartments. She was not to be found.

When he returned to the sitting-room, the young lady was not unnaturally offended. He could make allowances for her being a little out of temper at the slight that had been put on her; but he was inexpressibly disconcerted by the manner—almost the coarse manner—in which she expressed herself.

"I have been talking to your wife's maid, while you have been away," she said. "I find you have married an old lady for her money. She is jealous of me, of course?"

"Let me beg you to alter your opinion," he answered. "You are wronging my wife; she is incapable of any such feeling as you attribute to her."

The young lady laughed. "At any rate you are a good husband," she said satirically. "Suppose you own the truth? Wouldn't you like her better if she was young and pretty like me?"

He was not merely surprised—he was disgusted. Her beauty had so completely fascinated him, when he first saw her, that the idea of associating any want of refinement and good breeding with such a charming creature never entered his mind. The disenchantment to him was already so complete that he was even disagreeably affected by the tone of her voice: it was almost as repellent to him as the exhibition of unrestrained bad temper which she seemed perfectly careless to conceal.

"I confess you surprise me," he said, coldly.

The reply produced no effect on her. On the contrary, she became more insolent than ever.

"I have a fertile fancy," she went on, "and your absurd way of taking a joke only encourages me! Suppose you could transform this sour old wife of yours, who has insulted me, into the sweetest young creature that ever lived, by only holding up your finger—wouldn't you do it?"

This passed the limits of his endurance. "I have no wish," he said, "to forget the consideration which is due to a woman. You leave me but one

666

alternative." He rose to go out of the room.

She ran to the door as he spoke, and placed herself in the way of his going out.

He signed to her to let him pass.

She suddenly threw her arms round his neck, kissed him passionately, and whispered, with her lips at his ear: "Oh, Ernest, forgive me! Could I have asked you to marry me for my money if I had not taken refuge in a disguise?"

XI.

WHEN he had sufficiently recovered to think, he put her back from him. "Is there an end of the deception now?" he asked, sternly. "Am I to trust you in your new character?"

"You are not to be harder on me than I deserve," she answered, gently. "Did you ever hear of an actress named Miss Max?"

He began to understand her. "Forgive me if I spoke harshly," he said. "You have put me to a severe trial."

She burst into tears. "Love," she murmured, "is my only excuse."

From that moment she had won her pardon. He took her hand, and made her sit by him.

"Yes," he said, "I have heard of Miss Max and of her wonderful powers of personation—and I have always regretted not having seen her while she was on the stage."

"Did you hear anything more of her, Ernest?"

"Yes, I heard that she was a pattern of modesty and good conduct, and that she gave up her profession, at the height of her success, to marry an old man."

"Will you come with me to my room?" she asked. "I have something there which I wish to show you."

It was the copy of her husband's will.

"Read the lines, Ernest, which begin at the top of the page. Let my dead husband speak for me."

The lines ran thus:

"My motive in marrying Miss Max must be stated in this place, in justice to her—and, I will venture to add, in justice to myself. I felt the sincerest sympathy for her position. She was without father, mother, or friends; one of the poor forsaken children, whom the mercy of the Foundling Hospital provides with a home. Her after life on the stage was the life of a virtuous woman: persecuted by profligates; insulted by some of the baser creatures associated with her, to whom she was an object of envy. I offered her a home, and the protection of a father—on the only terms which the world would recognize as worthy of us. My experience of her since our marriage has been the experience of unvarying goodness, sweetness, and sound sense. She has behaved so nobly, in a trying position, that I wish her (even in this life) to have her reward. I entreat her to make a second choice in marriage, which shall not be a mere form. I firmly believe that she will choose well and wisely—that she will make the happiness of a man who is worthy of her—and that, as wife and mother, she will set an example of inestimable value in the social sphere that she occupies. In proof of the heartfelt sincerity with which I pay my tribute to her virtues, I add to this my will the clause that follows."

With the clause that followed, Ernest was already acquainted.

"Will you now believe that I never loved till I saw your face for the first time?" said his wife. "I had no experience to place me on my guard against the fascination—the madness some people might call it—which possesses a woman when all her heart is given to a man. Don't despise me, my dear! Remember that I had to save you from disgrace and ruin. Besides, my old stage remembrances tempted me. I had acted in a play in which the heroine did—what I have done! It didn't end with me, as it did with her in the story. She was represented as rejoicing in the success of her disguise. I have known some miserable hours of doubt and shame since our marriage. When I went to meet you in my own person at the picture-gallery—oh, what relief, what joy I felt, when I saw how you admired me—it was not because I could no longer carry on the disguise. I was able to get hours of rest from the effort; not only at night, but in the daytime, when I was shut up in my retirement in the music-room; and when my maid kept watch against discovery. No, my love! I hurried on the disclosure, because I could no longer endure the hateful triumph of my own deception. Ah, look at that witness against me! I can't bear even to see it!"

She abruptly left him. The drawer that she had opened to take out the copy of the will also contained the false gray hair which she had discarded. It had only that moment attracted her notice. She snatched it up, and turned to the fireplace.

Ernest took it from her, before she could destroy it. "Give it to me," he said.

"Why?"

He drew her gently to his bosom, and answered: "I must not forget my old wife."

MISS JEROMETTE AND THE CLERGYMAN.

I.

MY brother, the clergyman, looked over my shoulder before I was aware of him, and discovered that the volume which completely absorbed my attention was a collection of famous Trials, published in a new edition and in a popular form.

He laid his finger on the Trial which I happened to be reading at the moment. I looked up at him; his face startled me. He had turned pale. His eyes were fixed on the open page of the book with an expression which puzzled and alarmed me.

"My dear fellow," I said, "what in the world is the matter with you?"

He answered in an odd absent manner, still keeping his finger on the open page.

"I had almost forgotten," he said. "And this reminds me."

"Reminds you of what?" I asked. "You don't mean to say you know anything about the Trial?"

"I know this," he said. "The prisoner was guilty."

"Guilty?" I repeated. "Why, the man was acquitted by the jury, with the full approval of the judge! What call you possibly mean?"

"There are circumstances connected with that Trial," my brother answered, "which were never communicated to the judge or the jury—which were never so much as hinted or whispered in court. I know them—of my own knowledge, by my own personal experience. They are very sad, very strange, very terrible. I have mentioned them to no mortal creature. I have done my best to forget them. You—quite innocently—have brought them back to my mind. They oppress, they distress me. I wish I had found you reading any book in your library, except that book!"

My curiosity was now strongly excited. I spoke out plainly.

"Surely," I suggested, "you might tell your brother what you are unwilling to mention to persons less nearly related to you. We have followed different professions, and have lived in different countries, since we were boys at school. But you know you can trust me."

He considered a little with himself.

"Yes," he said. "I know I can trust you." He waited a moment, and then he surprised me by a strange question.

"Do you believe," he asked, "that the spirits of the dead can return to earth, and show themselves to the living?"

I answered cautiously—adopting as my own the words of a great English writer, touching the subject of ghosts.

"You ask me a question," I said, "which, after five thousand years, is yet undecided. On that account alone, it is a question not to be trifled with."

My reply seemed to satisfy him.

"Promise me," he resumed, "that you will keep what I tell you a secret as long as I live. After my death I care little what happens. Let the story of my strange experience be added to the published experience of those other men who have seen what I have seen, and who believe what I believe. The world will not be the worse, and may be the better, for knowing one day what I am now about to trust to your ear alone."

My brother never again alluded to the narrative which he had confided to me, until the later time when I was sitting by his deathbed. He asked if I still remembered the story of Jeromette. "Tell it to others," he said, "as I have told it to you."

I repeat it after his death—as nearly as I can in his own words.

II.

ON a fine summer evening, many years since, I left my chambers in the Temple, to meet a fellow-student, who had proposed to me a night's amusement in the public gardens at Cremorne.

You were then on your way to India; and I had taken my degree at Oxford. I had sadly disappointed my father by choosing the Law as my profession, in preference to the Church. At that time, to own the truth, I had no serious intention of following any special vocation. I simply wanted an excuse for enjoying the pleasures of a London life. The study of the Law supplied me with that excuse. And I chose the Law as my profession accordingly.

On reaching the place at which we had arranged to meet, I found that my friend had not kept his appointment. After waiting vainly for ten minutes, my patience gave way and I went into the Gardens by myself.

I took two or three turns round the platform devoted to the dancers without discovering my fellow-student, and without seeing any other person with whom I happened to be acquainted at that time.

For some reason which I cannot now remember, I was not in my usual good spirits that evening. The noisy music jarred on my nerves, the sight of the gaping crowd round the platform irritated me, the blandishments of the painted ladies of the profession of pleasure saddened and disgusted me. I opened my cigar-case, and turned aside into one of the quiet by-walks of the Gardens.

A man who is habitually careful in choosing his cigar has this advantage over a man who is habitually careless. He can always count on smoking the best cigar in his case, down to the last. I was still absorbed in choosing my cigar, when I heard these words behind me—spoken in a foreign accent and in a woman's voice:

"Leave me directly, sir! I wish to have nothing to say to you."

I turned round and discovered a little lady very simply and tastefully dressed, who looked both angry and alarmed as she rapidly passed me on her way to the more frequented part of the Gardens. A man (evidently the worse for the wine he had drunk in the course of the evening) was following her, and was pressing his tipsy attentions on her with the coarsest insolence of speech and manner. She was young and pretty, and she cast one entreating look at me as she went by, which it was not in manhood—perhaps I ought to say, in young-manhood—to resist.

I instantly stepped forward to protect her, careless whether I involved myself in a discreditable quarrel with a blackguard or not. As a matter of course, the fellow resented my interference, and my temper gave way. Fortunately for me, just as I lifted my hand to knock him down, at policeman appeared who had noticed that he was drunk, and who settled the dispute officially by turning him out of the Gardens.

I led her away from the crowd that had collected. She was evidently frightened—I felt her hand trembling on my arm—but she had one great merit; she made no fuss about it.

"If I can sit down for a few minutes," she said in her pretty foreign accent, "I shall soon be myself again, and I shall not trespass any further on your kindness. I thank you very much, sir, for taking care of me."

We sat down on a bench in a retired par t of the Gardens, near a little fountain. A row of lighted lamps ran round the outer rim of the basin. I could see her plainly.

I have said that she was "a little lady." I could not have described her more correctly in three words.

Her figure was slight and small: she was a well-made miniature of a woman from head to foot. Her hair and her eyes were both dark. The hair curled naturally; the expression of the eyes was quiet, and rather sad; the complexion, as I then saw it, very pale; the little mouth perfectly charming. I was especially attracted, I remembered, by the carriage of her head; it was strikingly graceful and spirited; it distinguished her, little as she was and quiet as she was, among the thousands of other women in the Gardens, as a creature apart. Even the one marked defect in her—a slight "cast" in the left eye—seemed to add, in some strange way, to the quaint attractiveness of her face. I have already spoken of the tasteful simplicity of her dress. I ought now to add that it was not made of any costly material, and that she wore no jewels or ornaments of any sort. My little lady was not rich; even a man's eye could see that.

She was perfectly unembarrassed and unaffected. We fell as easily into talk as if we had been friends instead of strangers.

I asked how it was that she had no companion to take care of her. "You are too young and too pretty," I said in my blunt English way, "to trust yourself alone in such a place as this."

She took no notice of the compliment. She calmly put it away from her as if it had not reached her ears.

"I have no friend to take care of me," she said simply. "I was sad and sorry this evening, all by myself, and I thought I would go to the Gardens and hear the music, just to amuse me. It is not much to pay at the gate; only a shilling."

"No friend to take care of you?" I repeated. "Surely there must be one happy man who might have been here with you to-night?"

"What man do you mean?" she asked.

"The man," I answered thoughtlessly, "whom we call, in England, a Sweetheart."

I would have given worlds to have recalled those foolish words the moment they passed my lips. I felt that I had taken a vulgar liberty with her. Her face saddened; her eyes dropped to the ground. I begged her pardon.

"There is no need to beg my pardon," she said. "If you wish to know, sir—yes, I had once a sweetheart, as you call it in England. He has gone away and left me. No more of him, if you please. I am rested now. I will thank you again, and go home."

She rose to leave me.

I was determined not to part with her in that way. I begged to be allowed to see her safely back to her own door. She hesitated. I took a man's unfair advantage of her, by appealing to her fears. I said, "Suppose the blackguard who annoyed you should be waiting outside the gates?" That decided her.

674

She took my arm. We went away together by the bank of the Thames, in the balmy summer night.

A walk of half an hour brought us to the house in which she lodged—a shabby little house in a by-street, inhabited evidently by very poor people.

She held out her hand at the door, and wished me good-night. I was too much interested in her to consent to leave my little foreign lady without the hope of seeing her again. I asked permission to call on her the next day. We were standing under the light of the street-lamp. She studied my face with a grave and steady attention before she made any reply.

"Yes," she said at last. "I think I do know a gentleman when I see him. You may come, sir, if you please, and call upon me to-morrow."

So we parted. So I entered—doubting nothing, foreboding nothing—on a scene in my life which I now look back on with unfeigned repentance and regret.

III.

I AM speaking at this later time in the position of a clergyman, and in the character of a man of mature age. Remember that; and you will understand why I pass as rapidly as possible over the events of the next year of my life— why I say as little as I can of the errors and the delusions of my youth.

I called on her the next day. I repeated my visits during the days and weeks that followed, until the shabby little house in the by-street had become a second and (I say it with shame and self-reproach) a dearer home to me.

All of herself and her story which she thought fit to confide to me under these circumstances may be repeated to you in few words.

The name by which letters were addressed to her was "Mademoiselle Jeromette." Among the ignorant people of the house and the small tradesmen of the neighborhood—who found her name not easy of pronunciation by the average English tongue—she was known by the friendly nickname of "The French Miss." When I knew her, she was resigned to her lonely life among strangers. Some years had elapsed since she had lost her parents, and had left France. Possessing a small, very small, income of her own, she added to it by coloring miniatures for the photographers. She had relatives still living in France; but she had long since ceased to correspond with them. "Ask me nothing more about my family," she used to say. "I am as good as dead in my own country and among my own people."

This was all—literally all—that she told me of herself. I have never discovered more of her sad story from that day to this.

She never mentioned her family name—never even told me what part of France she came from or how long she had lived in England. That she was by birth and breeding a lady, I could entertain no doubt; her manners, her accomplishments, her ways of thinking and speaking, all proved it. Looking below the surface, her character showed itself in aspects not common among young women in these days. In her quiet way she was an incurable fatalist, and a firm believer in the ghostly reality of apparitions from the dead. Then again in the matter of money, she had strange views of her own. Whenever my purse was in my hand, she held me resolutely at a distance from first to last. She refused to move into better apartments; the shabby little house was clean inside, and the poor people who lived in it were kind to her—and that was enough. The most expensive present that she ever permitted me to offer her was a little enameled ring, the plainest and cheapest thing of the kind in the jeweler's shop. In all relations with me she was sincerity itself. On all occasions, and under all circumstances, she spoke her mind (as the phrase is) with the same uncompromising plainness.

"I like you," she said to me; "I respect you; I shall always be faithful to you while you are faithful to me. But my love has gone from me. There is another man who has taken it away with him, I know not where."

Who was the other man?

She refused to tell me. She kept his rank and his name strict secrets from me. I never discovered how he had met with her, or why he had left her, or whether the guilt was his of making of her an exile from her country and her friends. She despised herself for still loving him; but the passion was too strong for her—she owned it and lamented it with the frankness which was so

676

preeminently a part of her character. More than this, she plainly told me, in the early days of our acquaintance, that she believed he would return to her. It might be to-morrow, or it might be years hence. Even if he failed to repent of his own cruel conduct, the man would still miss her, as something lost out of his life; and, sooner or later, he would come back.

"And will you receive him if he does come back?" I asked.

"I shall receive him," she replied, "against my own better judgment—in spite of my own firm persuasion that the day of his return to me will bring with it the darkest days of my life."

I tried to remonstrate with her.

"You have a will of your own," I said. "Exert it if he attempts to return to you."

"I have no will of my own," she answered quietly, "where he is concerned. It is my misfortune to love him." Her eyes rested for a moment on mine, with the utter self-abandonment of despair. "We have said enough about this," she added abruptly. "Let us say no more."

From that time we never spoke again of the unknown man. During the year that followed our first meeting, she heard nothing of him directly or indirectly. He might be living, or he might be dead. There came no word of him, or from him. I was fond enough of her to be satisfied with this—he never disturbed us.

IV.

THE year passed—and the end came. Not the end as you may have anticipated it, or as I might have foreboded it.

You remember the time when your letters from home informed you of the fatal termination of our mother's illness? It is the time of which I am now speaking. A few hours only before she breathed her last, she called me to her bedside, and desired that we might be left together alone. Reminding me that her death was near, she spoke of my prospects in life; she noticed my want of interest in the studies which were then supposed to be engaging my attention, and she ended by entreating me to reconsider my refusal to enter the Church.

"Your father's heart is set upon it," she said. "Do what I ask of you, my dear, and you will help to comfort him when I am gone."

Her strength failed her: she could say no more. Could I refuse the last request she would ever make to me? I knelt at the bedside, and took her wasted hand in mine, and solemnly promised her the respect which a son owes to his mother's last wishes.

Having bound myself by this sacred engagement, I had no choice but to accept the sacrifice which it imperatively exacted from me. The time had come when I must tear myself free from all unworthy associations. No matter what the effort cost me, I must separate myself at once and forever from the unhappy woman who was not, who never could be, my wife.

At the close of a dull foggy day I set forth with a heavy heart to say the words which were to part us forever.

Her lodging was not far from the banks of the Thames. As I drew near the place the darkness was gathering, and the broad surface of the river was hidden from me in a chill white mist. I stood for a while, with my eyes fixed on the vaporous shroud that brooded over the flowing water—I stood and asked myself in despair the one dreary question: "What am I to say to her?"

The mist chilled me to the bones. I turned from the river-bank, and made my way to her lodgings hard by. "It must be done!" I said to myself, as I took out my key and opened the house door.

She was not at her work, as usual, when I entered her little sitting-room. She was standing by the fire, with her head down and with an open letter in her hand.

The instant she turned to meet me, I saw in her face that something was wrong. Her ordinary manner was the manner of an unusually placid and self-restrained person. Her temperament had little of the liveliness which we associate in England with the French nature. She was not ready with her laugh; and in all my previous experience, I had never yet known her to cry.

Now, for the first time, I saw the quiet face disturbed; I saw tears in the pretty brown eyes. She ran to meet me, and laid her head on my breast, and burst into a passionate fit of weeping that shook her from head to foot.

Could she by any human possibility have heard of the coming change in my life? Was she aware, before I had opened my lips, of the hard necessity which had brought me to the house?

It was simply impossible; the thing could not be.

I waited until her first burst of emotion had worn itself out. Then I asked—with an uneasy conscience, with a sinking heart—what had happened to distress her.

She drew herself away from me, sighing heavily, and gave me the open letter which I had seen in her hand.

"Read that," she said. "And remember I told you what might happen when we first met."

I read the letter.

It was signed in initials only; but the writer plainly revealed himself as the man who had deserted her. He had repented; he had returned to her. In proof of his penitence he was willing to do her the justice which he had hitherto refused—he was willing to marry her, on the condition that she would engage to keep the marriage a secret, so long as his parents lived. Submitting this proposal, he waited to know whether she would consent, on her side, to forgive and forget.

I gave her back the letter in silence. This unknown rival had done me the service of paving the way for our separation. In offering her the atonement of marriage, he had made it, on my part, a matter of duty to her, as well as to myself, to say the parting words. I felt this instantly. And yet, I hated him for helping me.

She took my hand, and led me to the sofa. We sat down, side by side. Her face was composed to a sad tranquillity. She was quiet; she was herself again.

"I have refused to see him," she said, "until I had first spoken to you. You have read his letter. What do you say?"

I could make but one answer. It was my duty to tell her what my own position was in the plainest terms. I did my duty—leaving her free to decide on the future for herself. Those sad words said, it was useless to prolong the wretchedness of our separation. I rose, and took her hand for the last time.

I see her again now, at that final moment, as plainly as if it had happened yesterday. She had been suffering from an affection of the throat; and she had a white silk handkerchief tied loosely round her neck. She wore a simple dress of purple merino, with a black-silk apron over it. Her face was deadly pale; her fingers felt icily cold as they closed round my hand.

"Promise me one thing," I said, "before I go. While I live, I am your friend—if I am nothing more. If you are ever in trouble, promise that you will let me know it."

She started, and drew back from me as if I had struck her with a sudden terror.

"Strange!" she said, speaking to herself. "He feels as I feel. He is afraid of what may happen to me, in my life to come."

I attempted to reassure her. I tried to tell her what was indeed the truth—that I had only been thinking of the ordinary chances and changes of life, when I spoke.

She paid no heed to me; she came back and put her hands on my shoulders and thoughtfully and sadly looked up in my face.

"My mind is not your mind in this matter," she said. "I once owned to you that I had my forebodings, when we first spoke of this man's return. I may tell you now, more than I told you then. I believe I shall die young, and die miserably. If I am right, have you interest enough still left in me to wish to hear of it?"

She paused, shuddering—and added these startling words:

"You shall hear of it."

The tone of steady conviction in which she spoke alarmed and distressed me. My face showed her how deeply and how painfully I was affected.

"There, there!" she said, returning to her natural manner; "don't take what I say too seriously. A poor girl who has led a lonely life like mine thinks strangely and talks strangely—sometimes. Yes; I give you my promise. If I am ever in trouble, I will let you know it. God bless you—you have been very kind to me—good-by!"

A tear dropped on my face as she kissed me. The door closed between us. The dark street received me.

It was raining heavily. I looked up at her window, through the drifting shower. The curtains were parted: she was standing in the gap, dimly lit by the lamp on the table behind her, waiting for our last look at each other. Slowly lifting her hand, she waved her farewell at the window, with the unsought native grace which had charmed me on the night when we first met. The curtain fell again—she disappeared—nothing was before me, nothing was round me, but the darkness and the night.

V.

IN two years from that time, I had redeemed the promise given to my mother on her deathbed. I had entered the Church.

My father's interest made my first step in my new profession an easy one. After serving my preliminary apprenticeship as a curate, I was appointed, before I was thirty years of age, to a living in the West of England.

My new benefice offered me every advantage that I could possibly desire—with the one exception of a sufficient income. Although my wants were few, and although I was still an unmarried man, I found it desirable, on many accounts, to add to my resources. Following the example of other young clergymen in my position, I determined to receive pupils who might stand in need of preparation for a career at the Universities. My relatives exerted themselves; and my good fortune still befriended me. I obtained two pupils to start with. A third would complete the number which I was at present prepared to receive. In course of time, this third pupil made his appearance, under circumstances sufficiently remarkable to merit being mentioned in detail.

It was the summer vacation; and my two pupils had gone home. Thanks to a neighboring clergyman, who kindly undertook to perform my duties for me, I too obtained a fortnight's holiday, which I spent at my father's house in London.

During my sojourn in the metropolis, I was offered an opportunity of preaching in a church, made famous by the eloquence of one of the popular pulpit-orators of our time. In accepting the proposal, I felt naturally anxious to do my best, before the unusually large and unusually intelligent congregation which would be assembled to hear me.

At the period of which I am now speaking, all England had been startled by the discovery of a terrible crime, perpetrated under circumstances of extreme provocation. I chose this crime as the main subject of my sermon. Admitting that the best among us were frail mortal creatures, subject to evil promptings and provocations like the worst among us, my object was to show how a Christian man may find his certain refuge from temptation in the safeguards of his religion. I dwelt minutely on the hardship of the Christian's first struggle to resist the evil influence—on the help which his Christianity inexhaustibly held out to him in the worst relapses of the weaker and viler part of his nature—on the steady and certain gain which was the ultimate reward of his faith and his firmness—and on the blessed sense of peace and happiness which accompanied the final triumph. Preaching to this effect, with the fervent conviction which I really felt, I may say for myself, at least, that I did no discredit to the choice which had placed me in the pulpit. I held the attention of my congregation, from the first word to the last.

While I was resting in the vestry on the conclusion of the service, a note was brought to me written in pencil. A member of my congregation—a gentleman—wished to see me, on a matter of considerable importance to himself. He would call on me at any place, and at any hour, which I might choose to appoint. If I wished to be satisfied of his respectability, he would beg leave to refer me to his father, with whose name I might possibly be acquainted.

The name given in the reference was undoubtedly familiar to me, as the name of a man of some celebrity and influence in the world of London. I sent back my card, appointing an hour for the visit of my correspondent on the afternoon of the next day.

VI.

THE stranger made his appearance punctually. I guessed him to be some two or three years younger than myself. He was undeniably handsome; his manners were the manners of a gentleman—and yet, without knowing why, I felt a strong dislike to him the moment he entered the room.

After the first preliminary words of politeness had been exchanged between us, my visitor informed me as follows of the object which he had in view.

"I believe you live in the country, sir?" he began.

"I live in the West of England," I answered.

"Do you make a long stay in London?"

"No. I go back to my rectory to-morrow."

"May I ask if you take pupils?"

"Yes."

"Have you any vacancy?"

"I have one vacancy."

"Would you object to let me go back with you to-morrow, as your pupil?"

The abruptness of the proposal took me by surprise. I hesitated.

In the first place (as I have already said), I disliked him. In the second place, he was too old to be a fit companion for my other two pupils—both lads in their teens. In the third place, he had asked me to receive him at least three weeks before the vacation came to an end. I had my own pursuits and amusements in prospect during that interval, and saw no reason why I should inconvenience myself by setting them aside.

He noticed my hesitation, and did not conceal from me that I had disappointed him.

"I have it very much at heart," he said, "to repair without delay the time that I have lost. My age is against me, I know. The truth is—I have wasted my opportunities since I left school, and I am anxious, honestly anxious, to mend my ways, before it is too late. I wish to prepare myself for one of the Universities—I wish to show, if I can, that I am not quite unworthy to inherit my father's famous name. You are the man to help me, if I can only persuade you to do it. I was struck by your sermon yesterday; and, if I may venture to make the confession in your presence, I took a strong liking to you. Will you see my father, before you decide to say No? He will be able to explain whatever may seem strange in my present application; and he will be happy to see you this afternoon, if you can spare the time. As to the question of terms, I am quite sure it can be settled to your entire satisfaction."

He was evidently in earnest—gravely, vehemently in earnest. I unwillingly consented to see his father.

Our interview was a long one. All my questions were answered fully and frankly.

The young man had led an idle and desultory life. He was weary of it, and ashamed of it. His disposition was a peculiar one. He stood sorely in need of a guide, a teacher, and a friend, in whom he was disposed to confide. If I disappointed the hopes which he had centered in me, he would be discouraged, and he would relapse into the aimless and indolent existence of which he was now ashamed. Any terms for which I might stipulate were at my disposal if I would consent to receive him, for three months to begin with, on trial.

Still hesitating, I consulted my father and my friends.

They were all of opinion (and justly of opinion so far) that the new connection would be an excellent one for me. They all reproached me for taking a purely capricious dislike to a well-born and well-bred young man, and for permitting it to influence me, at the outset of my career, against my own interests. Pressed by these considerations, I allowed myself to be persuaded to give the new pupil a fair trial. He accompanied me, the next day, on my way back to the rectory.

VII.

LET me be careful to do justice to a man whom I personally disliked. My senior pupil began well: he produced a decidedly favorable impression on the persons attached to my little household.

The women, especially, admired his beautiful light hair, his crisply-curling beard, his delicate complexion, his clear blue eyes, and his finely shaped hands and feet. Even the inveterate reserve in his manner, and the downcast, almost sullen, look which had prejudiced me against him, aroused a common feeling of romantic enthusiasm in my servants' hall. It was decided, on the high authority of the housekeeper herself, that "the new gentleman" was in love—and, more interesting still, that he was the victim of an unhappy attachment which had driven him away from his friends and his home.

For myself, I tried hard, and tried vainly, to get over my first dislike to the senior pupil.

I could find no fault with him. All his habits were quiet and regular; and he devoted himself conscientiously to his reading. But, little by little, I became satisfied that his heart was not in his studies. More than this, I had my reasons for suspecting that he was concealing something from me, and that he felt painfully the reserve on his own part which he could not, or dared not, break through. There were moments when I almost doubted whether he had not chosen my remote country rectory as a safe place of refuge from some person or persons of whom he stood in dread.

For example, his ordinary course of proceeding, in the matter of his correspondence, was, to say the least of it, strange.

He received no letters at my house. They waited for him at the village post office. He invariably called for them himself, and invariably forbore to trust any of my servants with his own letters for the post. Again, when we were out walking together, I more than once caught him looking furtively over his shoulder, as if he suspected some person of following him, for some evil purpose. Being constitutionally a hater of mysteries, I determined, at an early stage of our intercourse, on making an effort to clear matters up. There might be just a chance of my winning the senior pupil's confidence, if I spoke to him while the last days of the summer vacation still left us alone together in the house.

"Excuse me for noticing it," I said to him one morning, while we were engaged over our books—"I cannot help observing that you appear to have some trouble on your mind. Is it indiscreet, on my part, to ask if I can be of any use to you?"

He changed color—looked up at me quickly—looked down again at his book—struggled hard with some secret fear or secret reluctance that was in him—and suddenly burst out with this extraordinary question: "I suppose you were in earnest when you preached that sermon in London?"

"I am astonished that you should doubt it," I replied.

He paused again; struggled with himself again; and startled me by a second outbreak, even stranger than the first.

"I am one of the people you preached at in your sermon," he said. "That's the true reason why I asked you to take me for your pupil. Don't turn me out! When you talked to your congregation of tortured and tempted people, you talked of Me."

I was so astonished by the confession, that I lost my presence of mind. For the moment, I was unable to answer him.

"Don't turn me out!" he repeated. "Help me against myself. I am telling you the truth. As God is my witness, I am telling you the truth!"

"Tell me the whole truth," I said; "and rely on my consoling and helping you—rely on my being your friend."

In the fervor of the moment, I took his hand. It lay cold and still in mine; it mutely warned me that I had a sullen and a secret nature to deal with.

"There must be no concealment between us," I resumed. "You have entered my house, by your own confession, under false pretenses. It is your duty to me, and your duty to yourself, to speak out."

The man's inveterate reserve—cast off for the moment only—renewed its hold on him. He considered, carefully considered, his next words before he permitted them to pass his lips.

"A person is in the way of my prospects in life," he began slowly, with his eyes cast down on his book. "A person provokes me horribly. I feel dreadful temptations (like the man you spoke of in your sermon) when I am in the person's company. Teach me to resist temptation. I am afraid of myself, if I see the person again. You are the only man who can help me. Do it while you can."

He stopped, and passed his handkerchief over his forehead.

"Will that do?" he asked—still with his eyes on his book.

"It will not do," I answered. "You are so far from really opening your heart to me, that you won't even let me know whether it is a man or a woman who stands in the way of your prospects in life. You used the word 'person,' over and over again—rather than say 'he' or 'she' when you speak of the provocation which is trying you. How can I help a man who has so little confidence in me as that?"

My reply evidently found him at the end of his resources. He tried, tried desperately, to say more than he had said yet. No! The words seemed to stick in his throat. Not one of them would pass his lips.

"Give me time," he pleaded piteously. "I can't bring myself to it, all at once. I mean well. Upon my soul, I mean well. But I am slow at this sort of thing. Wait till to-morrow."

To-morrow came—and again he put it off.

"One more day!" he said. "You don't know how hard it is to speak

687

plainly. I am half afraid; I am half ashamed. Give me one more day."

I had hitherto only disliked him. Try as I might (and did) to make merciful allowance for his reserve, I began to despise him now.

VIII.

THE day of the deferred confession came, and brought an event with it, for which both he and I were alike unprepared. Would he really have confided in me but for that event? He must either have done it, or have abandoned the purpose which had led him into my house.

We met as usual at the breakfast-table. My housekeeper brought in my letters of the morning. To my surprise, instead of leaving the room again as usual, she walked round to the other side of the table, and laid a letter before my senior pupil—the first letter, since his residence with me, which had been delivered to him under my roof.

He started, and took up the letter. He looked at the address. A spasm of suppressed fury passed across his face; his breath came quickly; his hand trembled as it held the letter. So far, I said nothing. I waited to see whether he would open the envelope in my presence or not.

He was afraid to open it in my presence. He got on his feet; he said, in tones so low that I could barely hear him: "Please excuse me for a minute"— and left the room.

I waited for half an hour—for a quarter of an hour after that—and then I sent to ask if he had forgotten his breakfast.

In a minute more, I heard his footstep in the hall. He opened the breakfast-room door, and stood on the threshold, with a small traveling-bag in his hand.

"I beg your pardon," he said, still standing at the door. "I must ask for leave of absence for a day or two. Business in London."

"Can I be of any use?" I asked. "I am afraid your letter has brought you bad news?"

"Yes," he said shortly. "Bad news. I have no time for breakfast."

"Wait a few minutes," I urged. "Wait long enough to treat me like your friend—to tell me what your trouble is before you go."

He made no reply. He stepped into the hall and closed the door—then opened it again a little way, without showing himself.

"Business in London," he repeated—as if he thought it highly important to inform me of the nature of his errand. The door closed for the second time. He was gone.

I went into my study, and carefully considered what had happened.

The result of my reflections is easily described. I determined on discontinuing my relations with my senior pupil. In writing to his father (which I did, with all due courtesy and respect, by that day's post), I mentioned as my reason for arriving at this decision:—First, that I had found it impossible to win the confidence of his son. Secondly, that his son had that morning suddenly and mysteriously left my house for London, and that I must decline accepting any further responsibility toward him, as the necessary consequence.

I had put my letter in the post-bag, and was beginning to feel a little easier after having written it, when my housekeeper appeared in the study, with a very grave face, and with something hidden apparently in her closed hand.

"Would you please look, sir, at what we have found in the gentleman's bedroom, since he went away this morning?"

I knew the housekeeper to possess a woman's full share of that amicable weakness of the sex which goes by the name of "Curiosity." I had also, in various indirect ways, become aware that my senior pupil's strange departure had largely increased the disposition among the women of my household to regard him as the victim of an unhappy attachment. The time was ripe, as it seemed to me, for checking any further gossip about him, and any renewed attempts at prying into his affairs in his absence.

"Your only business in my pupil's bedroom," I said to the housekeeper, "is to see that it is kept clean, and that it is properly aired. There must be no interference, if you please, with his letters, or his papers, or with anything else that he has left behind him. Put back directly whatever you may have found in his room."

The housekeeper had her full share of a woman's temper as well as of a woman's curiosity. She listened to me with a rising color, and a just perceptible toss of the head.

"Must I put it back, sir, on the floor, between the bed and the wall?" she inquired, with an ironical assumption of the humblest deference to my wishes. "That's where the girl found it when she was sweeping the room. Anybody can see for themselves," pursued the housekeeper indignantly, "that the poor gentleman has gone away broken-hearted. And there, in my opinion, is the hussy who is the cause of it!"

With those words, she made me a low curtsey, and laid a small photographic portrait on the desk at which I was sitting.

I looked at the photograph.

In an instant, my heart was beating wildly—my head turned giddy— the housekeeper, the furniture, the walls of the room, all swayed and whirled round me.

The portrait that had been found in my senior pupil's bedroom was the portrait of Jeromette!

IX.

I HAD sent the housekeeper out of my study. I was alone, with the photograph of the Frenchwoman on my desk.

There could surely be little doubt about the discovery that had burst upon me. The man who had stolen his way into my house, driven by the terror of a temptation that he dared not reveal, and the man who had been my unknown rival in the by-gone time, were one and the same!

Recovering self-possession enough to realize this plain truth, the inferences that followed forced their way into my mind as a matter of course.

690

The unnamed person who was the obstacle to my pupil's prospects in life, the unnamed person in whose company he was assailed by temptations which made him tremble for himself, stood revealed to me now as being, in all human probability, no other than Jeromette. Had she bound him in the fetters of the marriage which he had himself proposed? Had she discovered his place of refuge in my house? And was the letter that had been delivered to him of her writing? Assuming these questions to be answered in the affirmative, what, in that case, was his "business in London"? I remembered how he had spoken to me of his temptations, I recalled the expression that had crossed his face when he recognized the handwriting on the letter—and the conclusion that followed literally shook me to the soul. Ordering my horse to be saddled, I rode instantly to the railway-station.

The train by which he had traveled to London had reached the terminus nearly an hour since. The one useful course that I could take, by way of quieting the dreadful misgivings crowding one after another on my mind, was to telegraph to Jeromette at the address at which I had last seen her. I sent the subjoined message—prepaying the reply:

"If you are in any trouble, telegraph to me. I will be with you by the first train. Answer, in any case."

There was nothing in the way of the immediate dispatch of my message. And yet the hours passed, and no answer was received. By the advice of the clerk, I sent a second telegram to the London office, requesting an explanation. The reply came back in these terms:

"Improvements in street. Houses pulled down. No trace of person named in telegram."

I mounted my horse, and rode back slowly to the rectory.

"The day of his return to me will bring with it the darkest days of my life.".... "I shall die young, and die miserably. Have you interest enough still left in me to wish to hear of it?" .... "You shall hear of it." Those words were in my memory while I rode home in the cloudless moonlight night. They were so vividly present to me that I could hear again her pretty foreign accent, her quiet clear tones, as she spoke them. For the rest, the emotions of that memorable day had worn me out. The answer from the telegraph office had struck me with a strange and stony despair. My mind was a blank. I had no thoughts. I had no tears.

I was about half-way on my road home, and I had just heard the clock of a village church strike ten, when I became conscious, little by little, of a chilly sensation slowly creeping through and through me to the bones. The warm, balmy air of a summer night was abroad. It was the month of July. In the month of July, was it possible that any living creature (in good health) could feel cold? It was not possible—and yet, the chilly sensation still crept through and through me to the bones.

I looked up. I looked all round me.

My horse was walking along an open highroad. Neither trees nor waters were near me. On either side, the flat fields stretched away bright and broad in the moonlight.

I stopped my horse, and looked round me again.

Yes: I saw it. With my own eyes I saw it. A pillar of white mist—between five and six feet high, as well as I could judge—was moving beside me at the edge of the road, on my left hand. When I stopped, the white mist stopped. When I went on, the white mist went on. I pushed my horse to a trot—the pillar of mist was with me. I urged him to a gallop—the pillar of mist was with me. I stopped him again—the pillar of mist stood still.

The white color of it was the white color of the fog which I had seen over the river—on the night when I had gone to bid her farewell. And the chill which had then crept through me to the bones was the chill that was creeping through me now.

I went on again slowly. The white mist went on again slowly—with the clear bright night all round it.

I was awed rather than frightened. There was one moment, and one only, when the fear came to me that my reason might be shaken. I caught myself

692

keeping time to the slow tramp of the horse's feet with the slow utterances of these words, repeated over and over again: "Jeromette is dead. Jeromette is dead." But my will was still my own: I was able to control myself, to impose silence on my own muttering lips. And I rode on quietly. And the pillar of mist went quietly with me.

My groom was waiting for my return at the rectory gate. I pointed to the mist, passing through the gate with me.

"Do you see anything there?" I said.

The man looked at me in astonishment.

I entered the rectory. The housekeeper met me in the hall. I pointed to the mist, entering with me.

"Do you see anything at my side?" I asked.

The housekeeper looked at me as the groom had looked at me.

"I am afraid you are not well, sir," she said. "Your color is all gone—you are shivering. Let me get you a glass of wine."

I went into my study, on the ground-floor, and took the chair at my desk. The photograph still lay where I had left it. The pillar of mist floated round the table, and stopped opposite to me, behind the photograph.

The housekeeper brought in the wine. I put the glass to my lips, and set it down again. The chill of the mist was in the wine. There was no taste, no reviving spirit in it. The presence of the housekeeper oppressed me. My dog had followed her into the room. The presence of the animal oppressed me. I said to the woman: "Leave me by myself, and take the dog with you."

They went out, and left me alone in the room.

I sat looking at the pillar of mist, hovering opposite to me.

It lengthened slowly, until it reached to the ceiling. As it lengthened, it grew bright and luminous. A time passed, and a shadowy appearance showed itself in the center of the light. Little by little, the shadowy appearance took the outline of a human form. Soft brown eyes, tender and melancholy, looked at me through the unearthly light in the mist. The head and the rest of the face broke next slowly on my view. Then the figure gradually revealed itself, moment by moment, downward and downward to the feet. She stood before me as I had last seen her, in her purple-merino dress, with the black-silk apron, with the white handkerchief tied loosely round her neck. She stood before me, in the gentle beauty that I remembered so well; and looked at me as she had looked when she gave me her last kiss—when her tears had dropped on my cheek.

I fell on my knees at the table. I stretched out my hands to her imploringly. I said: "Speak to me—O, once again speak to me, Jeromette."

Her eyes rested on me with a divine compassion in them. She lifted her hand, and pointed to the photograph on my desk, with a gesture which bade me turn the card. I turned it. The name of the man who had left my house that morning was inscribed on it, in her own handwriting.

I looked up at her again, when I had read it. She lifted her hand once more, and pointed to the handkerchief round her neck. As I looked at it, the fair white silk changed horribly in color—the fair white silk became darkened and drenched in blood.

A moment more—and the vision of her began to grow dim. By slow degrees, the figure, then the face, faded back into the shadowy appearance that I had first seen. The luminous inner light died out in the white mist. The mist itself dropped slowly downward—floated a moment in airy circles on the floor—vanished. Nothing was before me but the familiar wall of the room, and the photograph lying face downward on my desk.

X.

THE next day, the newspapers reported the discovery of a murder in London. A Frenchwoman was the victim. She had been killed by a wound in the throat. The crime had been discovered between ten and eleven o'clock on the previous night.

I leave you to draw your conclusion from what I have related. My own faith in the reality of the apparition is immovable. I say, and believe, that Jeromette kept her word with me. She died young, and died miserably. And I heard of it from herself.

Take up the Trial again, and look at the circumstances that were revealed during the investigation in court. His motive for murdering her is there.

You will see that she did indeed marry him privately; that they lived together contentedly, until the fatal day when she discovered that his fancy had been caught by another woman; that violent quarrels took place between them, from that time to the time when my sermon showed him his own deadly hatred toward her, reflected in the case of another man; that she discovered his place of retreat in my house, and threatened him by letter with the public assertion of her conjugal rights; lastly, that a man, variously described by different witnesses, was seen leaving the door of her lodgings on the night of the murder. The Law—advancing no further than this—may have discovered circumstances of suspicion, but no certainty. The Law, in default of direct evidence to convict the prisoner, may have rightly decided in letting him go free.

But I persisted in believing that the man was guilty. I declare that he, and he alone, was the murderer of Jeromette. And now, you know why.

MISS MINA AND THE GROOM

I.

I HEAR that the "shocking story of my conduct" was widely circulated at the ball, and that public opinion (among the ladies), in every part of the room, declared I had disgraced myself. But there was one dissentient voice in this chorus of general condemnation. You spoke, Madam, with all the authority of your wide celebrity and your high rank. You said: "I am personally a stranger to the young lady who is the subject of remark. If I venture to interfere, it is only to remind you that there are two sides to every question. May I ask if you have waited to pass sentence, until you have heard what the person accused has to say in her own defense?"

These just and generous words produced, if I am correctly informed, a dead silence. Not one of the women who had condemned me had heard me in my own defense. Not one of them ventured to answer you.

How I may stand in the opinions of such persons as these, is a matter of perfect indifference to me. My one anxiety is to show that I am not quite unworthy of your considerate interference in my favor. Will you honor me by reading what I have to say for myself in these pages?

I will pass as rapidly as I can over the subject of my family; and I will abstain (in deference to motives of gratitude and honor) from mentioning surnames in my narrative.

My father was the second son of an English nobleman. A German lady was his first wife, and my mother. Left a widower, he married for the second time; the new wife being of American birth. She took a stepmother's dislike to me—which, in some degree at least, I must own that I deserved.

When the newly married pair went to the United States they left me in England, by my own desire, to live under the protection of my uncle—a General in the army. This good man's marriage had been childless, and his wife (Lady Claudia) was, perhaps on that account, as kindly ready as her husband to receive me in the character of an adopted daughter. I may add here, that I bear my German mother's Christian name, Wilhelmina. All my friends, in the days when I had friends, used to shorten this to Mina. Be my friend so far, and call me Mina, too.

After these few words of introduction, will your patience bear with me, if I try to make you better acquainted with my uncle and aunt, and if I allude to circumstances connected with my new life which had, as I fear, some influence in altering my character for the worse?

II.

WHEN I think of the good General's fatherly kindness to me, I really despair of writing about him in terms that do justice to his nature. To own the truth, the tears get into my eyes, and the lines mingle in such confusion that I cannot read them myself. As for my relations with my aunt, I only tell the truth when I say that she performed her duties toward me without the slightest pretension, and in the most charming manner.

At nearly fifty years old, Lady Claudia was still admired, though she had lost the one attraction which distinguished her before my time—the attraction of a perfectly beautiful figure. With fine hair and expressive eyes, she was otherwise a plain woman. Her unassuming cleverness and her fascinating manners were the qualities no doubt which made her popular everywhere. We never quarreled. Not because I was always amiable, but because my aunt would not allow it. She managed me, as she managed her husband, with perfect tact. With certain occasional checks, she absolutely governed the General. There were eccentricities in his character which made him a man easily ruled by a clever woman. Deferring to his opinion, so far as appearances went, Lady Claudia generally contrived to get her own way in the end. Except when he was at his Club, happy in his gossip, his good dinners, and his whist, my excellent uncle lived under a despotism, in the happy delusion that he was master in his own house.

Prosperous and pleasant as it appeared on the surface, my life had its sad side for a young woman.

In the commonplace routine of our existence, as wealthy people in the upper rank, there was nothing to ripen the growth of any better capacities which may have been in my nature. Heartily as I loved and admired my uncle, he was neither of an age nor of a character to be the chosen depositary of my most secret thoughts, the friend of my inmost heart who could show me how to make the best and the most of my life. With friends and admirers in plenty, I had found no one who could hold this position toward me. In the midst of society I was, unconsciously, a lonely woman.

As I remember them, my hours of happiness were the hours when I took refuge in my music and my books. Out of the house, my one diversion, always welcome and always fresh, was riding. Without, any false modesty, I may mention that I had lovers as well as admirers; but not one of them produced an impression on my heart. In all that related to the tender passion, as it is called, I was an undeveloped being. The influence that men have on women, because they are men, was really and truly a mystery to me. I was ashamed of my own coldness—I tried, honestly tried, to copy other girls; to feel my heart beating in the presence of the one chosen man. It was not to be done. When a man pressed my hand, I felt it in my rings, instead of my heart.

These confessions made, I have done with the past, and may now relate the events which my enemies, among the ladies, have described as presenting a shocking story.

III.

WE were in London for the season. One morning, I went out riding with my uncle, as usual, in Hyde Park.

The General's service in the army had been in a cavalry regiment—service distinguished by merits which justified his rapid rise to the high places in his profession. In the hunting-field, he was noted as one of the most daring and most accomplished riders in our county. He had always delighted in riding young and high-spirited horses; and the habit remained with him after he had quitted the active duties of his profession in later life. From first to last he had met with no accident worth remembering, until the unlucky morning when he went out with me.

His horse, a fiery chestnut, ran away with him, in that part of the Park-ride called Rotten Row. With the purpose of keeping clear of other riders, he spurred his runaway horse at the rail which divides the Row from the grassy inclosure at its side. The terrified animal swerved in taking the leap, and dashed him against a tree. He was dreadfully shaken and injured; but his strong constitution carried him through to recovery—with the serious drawback of an incurable lameness in one leg.

The doctors, on taking leave of their patient, united in warning him (at his age, and bearing in mind his weakened leg) to ride no more restive horses. "A quiet cob, General," they all suggested. My uncle was sorely mortified and offended. "If I am fit for nothing but a quiet cob," he said, bitterly, "I will ride no more." He kept his word. No one ever saw the General on horseback again.

Under these sad circumstances (and my aunt being no horsewoman), I had apparently no other choice than to give up riding also. But my kind-hearted uncle was not the man to let me be sacrificed to his own disappointment. His riding-groom had been one of his soldier-servants in the cavalry regiment—a quaint sour tempered old man, not at all the sort of person to attend on a young lady taking her riding-exercise alone. "We must find a smart fellow who can be trusted," said the General. "I shall inquire at the club."

For a week afterward, a succession of grooms, recommended by friends, applied for the vacant place.

The General found insurmountable objections to all of them. "I'll tell you what I have done," he announced one day, with the air of a man who had hit on a grand discovery; "I have advertised in the papers."

Lady Claudia looked up from her embroidery with the placid smile that was peculiar to her. "I don't quite like advertising for a servant," she said. "You are at the mercy of a stranger; you don't know that you are not engaging a drunkard or a thief."

"Or you may be deceived by a false character," I added on my side. I seldom ventured, at domestic consultations, on giving my opinion unasked—but the new groom represented a subject in which I felt a strong personal interest. In a certain sense, he was to be my groom.

"I'm much obliged to you both for warning me that I am so easy to deceive," the General remarked satirically. "Unfortunately, the mischief is done. Three men have answered my advertisement already. I expect them here tomorrow to be examined for the place."

Lady Claudia looked up from her embroidery again. "Are you going to see them yourself?" she asked softly. "I thought the steward—"

"I have hitherto considered myself a better judge of a groom than my steward," the General interposed. "However, don't be alarmed; I won't act on my own sole responsibility, after the hint you have given me. You and Mina shall lend me your valuable assistance, and discover whether they are thieves, drunkards, and what not, before I feel the smallest suspicion of it, myself."

IV.

WE naturally supposed that the General was joking. No. This was one of those rare occasions on which Lady Claudia's tact—infallible in matters of importance—proved to be at fault in a trifle. My uncle's self-esteem had been touched in a tender place; and he had resolved to make us feel it. The next morning a polite message came, requesting our presence in the library, to see the grooms. My aunt (always ready with her smile, but rarely tempted into laughing outright) did for once laugh heartily. "It is really too ridiculous!" she said. However, she pursued her policy of always yielding, in the first instance. We went together to the library.

The three grooms were received in the order in which they presented themselves for approval. Two of them bore the ineffaceable mark of the public-house so plainly written on their villainous faces, that even I could see it. My uncle ironically asked us to favor him with our opinions. Lady Claudia answered with her sweetest smile: "Pardon me, General—we are here to learn." The words were nothing; but the manner in which they were spoken was perfect. Few men could have resisted that gentle influence—and the General was not one of the few. He stroked his mustache, and returned to his petticoat government. The two grooms were dismissed.

The entry of the third and last man took me completely by surprise.

If the stranger's short coat and light trousers had not proclaimed his vocation in life, I should have taken it for granted that there had been some mistake, and that we were favored with a visit from a gentleman unknown. He was between dark and light in complexion, with frank clear blue eyes; quiet and intelligent, if appearances were to be trusted; easy in his movements; respectful in his manner, but perfectly free from servility. "I say!" the General blurted out, addressing my aunt confidentially, "he looks as if he would do, doesn't he?"

The appearance of the new man seemed to have had the same effect on Lady Claudia which it had produced on me. But she got over her first feeling of surprise sooner than I did. "You know best," she answered, with the air of a woman who declined to trouble herself by giving an opinion.

"Step forward, my man," said the General. The groom advanced from the door, bowed, and stopped at the foot of the table—my uncle sitting at the head, with my aunt and myself on either side of him. The inevitable questions began.

"What is your name?"

"Michael Bloomfield."

"Your age?"

"Twenty-six."

My aunt's want of interest in the proceedings expressed itself by a little weary sigh. She leaned back resignedly in her chair.

The General went on with his questions: "What experience have you had as a groom?"

"I began learning my work, sir, before I was twelve years old."

"Yes! yes! I mean what private families have you served in?"

"Two, sir."

"How long have you been in your two situations?"

"Four years in the first; and three in the second."

The General looked agreeably surprised. "Seven years in only two situations is a good character in itself," he remarked. "Who are your references?"

The groom laid two papers on the table.

"I don't take written references," said the General.

"Be pleased to read my papers, sir," answered the groom.

My uncle looked sharply across the table. The groom sustained the look with respectful but unshaken composure. The General took up the papers, and seemed to be once more favorably impressed as he read them. "Personal references in each case if required in support of strong written recommendations from both his employers," he informed my aunt. "Copy the addresses, Mina. Very satisfactory, I must say. Don't you think so yourself?" he resumed, turning again to my aunt.

Lady Claudia replied by a courteous bend of her head. The General went on with his questions. They related to the management of horses; and they were answered to his complete satisfaction.

"Michael Bloomfield, you know your business," he said, "and you have a good character. Leave your address. When I have consulted your references, you shall hear from me."

The groom took out a blank card, and wrote his name and address on it. I looked over my uncle's shoulder when he received the card. Another surprise! The handwriting was simply irreproachable—the lines running perfectly straight, and every letter completely formed. As this perplexing person made his modest bow, and withdrew, the General, struck by an after-thought, called him back from the door.

"One thing more," said my uncle. "About friends and followers? I consider it my duty to my servants to allow them to see their relations; but I expect them to submit to certain conditions in return—"

"I beg your pardon, sir," the groom interposed. "I shall not give you any trouble on that score. I have no relations."

"No brothers or sisters?" asked the General.

"None, sir."

"Father and mother both dead?"

"I don't know, sir."

"You don't know! What does that mean?"

"I am telling you the plain truth, sir. I never heard who my father and mother were—and I don't expect to hear now."

He said those words with a bitter composure which impressed me painfully. Lady Claudia was far from feeling it as I did. Her languid interest in the engagement of the groom seemed to be completely exhausted—and that was all. She rose, in her easy graceful way, and looked out of the window at the courtyard and fountain, the house-dog in his kennel, and the box of flowers in the coachman's window.

In the meanwhile, the groom remained near the table, respectfully waiting for his dismissal. The General spoke to him sharply, for the first time. I could see that my good uncle had noticed the cruel tone of that passing reference to the parents, and thought of it as I did.

"One word more, before you go," he said. "If I don't find you more mercifully inclined toward my horses than you seem to be toward your father and mother, you won't remain long in my service. You might have told me you had never heard who your parents were, without speaking as if you didn't care to hear."

"May I say a bold word, sir, in my own defense?"

He put the question very quietly, but, at the same time, so firmly that he even surprised my aunt. She looked round from the window—then turned back again, and stretched out her hand toward the curtain, intending, as I supposed, to alter the arrangement of it. The groom went on.

"May I ask, sir, why I should care about a father and mother who deserted me? Mind what you are about, my lady!" he cried—suddenly addressing my aunt. "There's a cat in the folds of that curtain; she might frighten you."

He had barely said the words before the housekeeper's large tabby cat, taking its noonday siesta in the looped-up fold of the curtain, leaped out and made for the door.

Lady Claudia was, naturally enough, a little perplexed by the man's discovery of an animal completely hidden in the curtain. She appeared to think that a person who was only a groom had taken a liberty in presuming to puzzle her. Like her husband, she spoke to Michael sharply.

"Did you see the cat?" she asked.

"No, my lady."

"Then how did you know the creature was in the curtain?"

For the first time since he had entered the room the groom looked a little confused.

"It's a sort of presumption for a man in my position to be subject to a nervous infirmity," he answered. "I am one of those persons (the weakness is not uncommon, as your ladyship is aware) who know by their own unpleasant sensations when a cat is in the room. It goes a little further than that with me. The 'antipathy,' as the gentlefolks call it, tells me in what part of the room the cat is."

My aunt turned to her husband, without attempting to conceal that she took no sort of interest in the groom's antipathies.

"Haven't you done with the man yet?" she asked.

The General gave the groom his dismissal.

"You shall hear from me in three days' time. Good-morning."

Michael Bloomfield seemed to have noticed my aunt's ungracious manner. He looked at her for a moment with steady attention before he left the room.

V.

"You don't mean to engage that man?" said Lady Claudia as the door closed.

"Why not?" asked my uncle.

"I have taken a dislike to him."

This short answer was so entirely out of the character of my aunt that the General took her kindly by the hand, and said:

"I am afraid you are not well."

She irritably withdrew her hand.

"I don't feel well. It doesn't matter."

"It does matter, Claudia. What can I do for you?"

"Write to the man—" She paused and smiled contemptuously. "Imagine a groom with an antipathy to cats!" she said, turning to me. "I don't know what you think, Mina. I have a strong objection, myself, to servants who hold themselves above their position in life. Write," she resumed, addressing her husband, "and tell him to look for another place."

"What objection can I make to him?" the General asked, helplessly.

"Good heavens! can't you make an excuse? Say he is too young."

My uncle looked at me in expressive silence—walked slowly to the writing-table—and glanced at his wife, in the faint hope that she might change her mind. Their eyes met—and she seemed to recover the command of her temper. She put her hand caressingly on the General's shoulder.

"I remember the time," she said, softly, "when any caprice of mine was a command to you. Ah, I was younger then!"

The General's reception of this little advance was thoroughly characteristic

705

of him. He first kissed Lady Claudia's hand, and then he wrote the letter. My aunt rewarded him by a look, and left the library.

"What the deuce is the matter with her?" my uncle said to me when we were alone. "Do you dislike the man, too?"

"Certainly not. As far as I can judge, he appears to be just the sort of person we want."

"And knows thoroughly well how to manage horses, my dear. What can be your aunt's objection to him?"

As the words passed his lips Lady Claudia opened the library door.

"I am so ashamed of myself," she said, sweetly. "At my age, I have been behaving like a spoiled child. How good you are to me, General! Let me try to make amends for my misconduct. Will you permit me?"

She took up the General's letter, without waiting for permission; tore it to pieces, smiling pleasantly all the while; and threw the fragments into the waste-paper basket. "As if you didn't know better than I do!" she said, kissing him on the forehead. "Engage the man by all means."

She left the room for the second time. For the second time my uncle looked at me in blank perplexity—and I looked back at him in the same condition of mind. The sound of the luncheon bell was equally a relief to both of us. Not a word more was spoken on the subject of the new groom. His references were verified; and he entered the General's service in three days' time.

VI.

ALWAYS careful in anything that concerned my welfare, no matter how trifling it might be, my uncle did not trust me alone with the new groom when he first entered our service. Two old friends of the General accompanied me at his special request, and reported the man to be perfectly competent and trustworthy. After that, Michael rode out with me alone; my friends among young ladies seldom caring to accompany me, when I abandoned the park for the quiet country roads on the north and west of London. Was it wrong in me to talk to him on these expeditions? It would surely have been treating a man like a brute never to take the smallest notice of him—especially as his conduct was uniformly respectful toward me. Not once, by word or look, did he presume on the position which my favor permitted him to occupy.

Ought I to blush when I confess (though he was only a groom) that he interested me?

In the first place, there was something romantic in the very blankness of the story of his life.

He had been left, in his infancy, in the stables of a gentleman living in Kent, near the highroad between Gravesend and Rochester. The same day, the stable-boy had met a woman running out of the yard, pursued by the dog. She was a stranger, and was not well-dressed. While the boy was protecting her by chaining the dog to his kennel, she was quick enough to place herself beyond the reach of pursuit.

The infant's clothing proved, on examination, to be of the finest linen. He was warmly wrapped in a beautiful shawl of some foreign manufacture, entirely unknown to all the persons present, including the master and mistress of the house. Among the folds of the shawl there was discovered an open letter, without date, signature, or address, which it was presumed the woman must have forgotten.

Like the shawl, the paper was of foreign manufacture. The handwriting presented a strongly marked character; and the composition plainly revealed the mistakes of a person imperfectly acquainted with the English language. The contents of the letter, after alluding to the means supplied for the support of the child, announced that the writer had committed the folly of inclosing a sum of a hundred pounds in a banknote, "to pay expenses." In a postscript, an appointment was made for a meeting in six months' time, on the eastward side of London Bridge. The stable-boy's description of the woman who had passed him showed that she belonged to the lower class. To such a person a hundred pounds would be a fortune. She had, no doubt, abandoned the child, and made off with the money.

No trace of her was ever discovered. On the day of the appointment the police watched the eastward side of London Bridge without obtaining any result. Through the kindness of the gentleman in whose stable he had been found, the first ten years of the boy's life were passed under the protection of a charitable asylum. They gave him the name of one of the little inmates who had died; and they sent him out to service before he was eleven years old. He was harshly treated and ran away; wandered to some training-stables near Newmarket; attracted the favorable notice of the head-groom, was employed among the other boys, and liked the occupation. Growing up to manhood, he had taken service in private families as a groom. This was the story of twenty-six years of Michael's life.

But there was something in the man himself which attracted attention, and made one think of him in his absence.

I mean by this, that there was a spirit of resistance to his destiny in him, which is very rarely found in serving-men of his order. I remember accompanying the General "on one of his periodical visits of inspection to the stable." He was so well satisfied that he proposed extending his investigations to the groom's own room.

"If you don object, Michael?" he added, with his customary consideration for the self-respect of all persons in his employment. Michael's color rose a little; he looked at me. "I am afraid the young lady will not find my room quite so tidy as it ought to be," he said as he opened the door for us.

The only disorder in the groom's room was produced, to our surprise, by the groom's books and papers.

Cheap editions of the English poets, translations of Latin and Greek classics, handbooks for teaching French and German "without a master," carefully written "exercises" in both languages, manuals of shorthand, with more "exercises" in that art, were scattered over the table, round the central object of a reading-lamp, which spoke plainly of studies by night. "Why, what is all this?" cried the General. "Are you going to leave me, Michael, and set up a school?" Michael answered in sad, submissive tones. "I try to improve myself, sir—though I sometimes lose heart and hope." "Hope of what?" asked my uncle. "Are you not content to be a servant? Must you rise in the world, as the saying is?" The groom shrank a little at that abrupt question. "If I had relations to care for me and help me along the hard ways of life," he said, "I might be satisfied, sir, to remain as I am. As it is, I have no one to think about but myself—and I am foolish enough sometimes to look beyond myself."

So far, I had kept silence; but I could no longer resist giving him a word of encouragement—his confession was so sadly and so patiently made. "You speak too harshly of yourself," I said; "the best and greatest men have begun like you by looking beyond themselves." For a moment our eyes met. I admired the poor lonely fellow trying so modestly and so bravely to teach himself—and I did not care to conceal it. He was the first to look away; some suppressed emotion turned him deadly pale. Was I the cause of it? I felt myself tremble as that bold question came into my mind. The General, with one sharp glance at me, diverted the talk (not very delicately, as I thought) to the misfortune of Michael's birth.

"I have heard of your being deserted in your infancy by some woman unknown," he said. "What has become of the things you were wrapped in, and the letter that was found on you? They might lead to a discovery, one of these days." The groom smiled. "The last master I served thought of it as you do, Sir. He was so good as to write to the gentleman who was first burdened with the care of me—and the things were sent to me in return."

He took up an unlocked leather bag, which opened by touching a brass knob, and showed us the shawl, the linen (sadly faded by time) and the letter. We were puzzled by the shawl. My uncle, who had served in the East, thought it looked like a very rare kind of Persian work. We examined with interest the letter, and the fine linen. When Michael quietly remarked, as we handed them back to him, "They keep the secret, you see," we could only look at each other, and own there was nothing more to be said.

VII.

THAT night, lying awake thinking, I made my first discovery of a great change that had come over me. I felt like a new woman.

Never yet had my life been so enjoyable to me as it was now. I was conscious of a delicious lightness of heart. The simplest things pleased me; I was ready to be kind to everybody, and to admire everything. Even the familiar scenery of my rides in the park developed beauties which I had never noticed before. The enchantments of music affected me to tears. I was absolutely in love with my dogs and my birds—and, as for my maid, I bewildered the girl with presents, and gave her holidays almost before she could ask for them. In a bodily sense, I felt an extraordinary accession of strength and activity. I romped with the dear old General, and actually kissed Lady Claudia, one morning, instead of letting her kiss me as usual. My friends noticed my new outburst of gayety and spirit—and wondered what had produced it. I can honestly say that I wondered too! Only on that wakeful night which followed our visit to Michael's room did I arrive at something like a clear understanding of myself. The next morning completed the process of enlightenment. I went out riding as usual. The instant when Michael put his hand under my foot as I sprang into the saddle, his touch flew all over me like a flame. I knew who had made a new woman of me from that moment.

As to describing the first sense of confusion that overwhelmed me, even if I were a practiced writer I should be incapable of doing it. I pulled down my veil, and rode on in a sort of trance. Fortunately for me, our house looked on the park, and I had only to cross the road. Otherwise I should have met with some accident if I had ridden through the streets. To this day, I don't know where I rode. The horse went his own way quietly—and the groom followed me.

The groom! Is there any human creature so free from the hateful and anti-Christian pride of rank as a woman who loves with all her heart and soul, for the first time in her life? I only tell the truth (in however unfavorable a light it may place me) when I declare that my confusion was entirely due to the discovery that I was in love. I was not ashamed of myself for being in love with the groom. I had given my heart to the man. What did the accident of his position matter? Put money into his pocket and a title before his name—by another accident: in speech, manners, and attainments, he would be a gentleman worthy of his wealth and worthy of his rank.

Even the natural dread of what my relations and friends might say, if they discovered my secret, seemed to be a sensation so unworthy of me and

710

of him, that I looked round, and called to him to speak to me, and asked him questions about himself which kept him riding nearly side by side with me. Ah, how I enjoyed the gentle deference and respect of his manner as he answered me! He was hardly bold enough to raise his eyes to mine, when I looked at him. Absorbed in the Paradise of my own making, I rode on slowly, and was only aware that friends had passed and had recognized me, by seeing him touch his hat. I looked round and discovered the women smiling ironically as they rode by. That one circumstance roused me rudely from my dream. I let Michael fall back again to his proper place, and quickened my horse's pace; angry with myself, angry with the world in general, then suddenly changing, and being fool enough and child enough to feel ready to cry. How long these varying moods lasted, I don't know. On returning, I slipped off my horse without waiting for Michael to help me, and ran into the house without even wishing him "Good-day."

VIII.

AFTER taking off my riding-habit, and cooling my hot face with eau-de-cologne and water, I went down to the room which we called the morning-room. The piano there was my favorite instrument and I had the idea of trying what music would do toward helping me to compose myself.

As I sat down before the piano, I heard the opening of the door of the breakfast-room (separated from me by a curtained archway), and the voice of Lady Claudia asking if Michael had returned to the stable. On the servant's reply in the affirmative, she desired that he might be sent to her immediately.

No doubt, I ought either to have left the morning-room, or to have let my aunt know of my presence there. I did neither the one nor the other. Her first dislike of Michael had, to all appearance, subsided. She had once or twice actually taken opportunities of speaking to him kindly. I believed this was due to the caprice of the moment. The tone of her voice too suggested, on this occasion, that she had some spiteful object in view, in sending for him. I knew it was unworthy of me—and yet, I deliberately waited to hear what passed between them.

Lady Claudia began.

"You were out riding to-day with Miss Mina?"

"Yes, my lady."

"Turn to the light. I wish to see people when I speak to them. You were observed by some friends of mine; your conduct excited remark. Do you know your business as a lady's groom?"

"I have had seven years' experience, my lady."

"Your business is to ride at a certain distance behind your mistress. Has your experience taught you that?"

"Yes, my lady."

"You were not riding behind Miss Mina—your horse was almost side by side with hers. Do you deny it?"

"No, my lady."

"You behaved with the greatest impropriety—you were seen talking to Miss Mina. Do you deny that?"

"No, my lady."

"Leave the room. No! come back. Have you any excuse to make?"

"None, my lady."

"Your insolence is intolerable! I shall speak to the General."

The sound of the closing door followed.

I knew now what the smiles meant on the false faces of those women-friends of mine who had met me in the park. An ordinary man, in Michael's place, would have mentioned my own encouragement of him as a sufficient excuse. He, with the inbred delicacy and reticence of a gentleman, had taken all the blame on himself. Indignant and ashamed, I advanced to the breakfast-room, bent on instantly justifying him. Drawing aside the curtain, I was startled by a sound as of a person sobbing. I cautiously looked in. Lady Claudia was prostrate on the sofa, hiding her face in her hands, in a passion of tears.

I withdrew, completely bewildered. The extraordinary contradictions in my aunt's conduct were not at an end yet. Later in the day, I went to my uncle, resolved to set Michael right in his estimation, and to leave him to speak to Lady Claudia. The General was in the lowest spirits; he shook his head ominously the moment. I mentioned the groom's name. "I dare say the man meant no harm—but the thing has been observed. I can't have you made the subject of scandal, Mina. My wife makes a point of it—Michael must go.

"You don't mean to say that she has insisted on your sending Michael away?"

Before he could answer me, a footman appeared with a message. "My lady wishes to see you, sir."

The General rose directly. My curiosity had got, by this time, beyond all restraint. I was actually indelicate enough to ask if I might go with him! He stared at me, as well he might. I persisted; I said I particularly wished to see Lady Claudia. My uncle's punctilious good breeding still resisted me. "Your aunt may wish to speak to me in private," he said. "Wait a moment, and I will send for you."

I was incapable of waiting: my obstinacy was something superhuman. The bare idea that Michael might lose his place, through my fault, made me desperate, I suppose. "I won't trouble you to send for me," I persisted; "I will go with you at once as far as the door, and wait to hear if I may come in." The footman was still present, holding the door open; the General gave way. I kept so close behind him that my aunt saw me as her husband entered the room. "Come in, Mina," she said, speaking and looking like the charming Lady Claudia of everyday life. Was this the woman whom I had seen crying her heart out on the sofa hardly an hour ago?

"On second thoughts," she continued, turning to the General, "I fear I may have been a little hasty. Pardon me for troubling you about it again—have you spoken to Michael yet? No? Then let us err on the side of kindness; let us look over his misconduct this time."

My uncle was evidently relieved. I seized the opportunity of making my confession, and taking the whole blame on myself. Lady Claudia stopped me with the perfect grace of which she was mistress.

"My good child, don't distress yourself! don't make mountains out of molehills!" She patted me on the cheek with two plump white fingers which felt deadly cold. "I was not always prudent, Mina, when I was your age. Besides, your curiosity is naturally excited about a servant who is—what shall I call him?—a foundling."

She paused and fixed her eyes on me attentively. "What did he tell you?" she asked. "Is it a very romantic story?"

The General began to fidget in his chair. If I had kept my attention on him, I should have seen in his face a warning to me to be silent. But my interest at the moment was absorbed in my aunt. Encouraged by her amiable reception, I was not merely unsuspicious of the trap that she had set for me—I was actually foolish enough to think that I could improve Michael's position in her estimation (remember that I was in love with him!) by telling his story exactly as I have already told it in these pages. I spoke with fervor. Will you believe it?—her humor positively changed again! She flew into a passion with me for the first time in her life.

"Lies!" she cried. "Impudent lies on the face of them—invented to appeal to your interest. How dare you repeat them? General! if Mina had not brought it on herself, this man's audacity would justify you in instantly dismissing him. Don't you agree with me?"

The General's sense of fair play roused him for once into openly opposing his wife.

"You are completely mistaken," he said. "Mina and I have both had the shawl and the letter in our hands—and (what was there besides?)—ah, yes, the very linen the child was wrapped in."

What there was in those words to check Lady Claudia's anger in its full flow I was quite unable to understand. If her husband had put a pistol to her head, he could hardly have silenced her more effectually. She did not appear to be frightened, or ashamed of her outbreak of rage—she sat vacant and speechless, with her eyes on the General and her hands crossed on her lap. After waiting a moment (wondering as I did what it meant) my uncle rose with his customary resignation and left her. I followed him. He was unusually silent and thoughtful; not a word passed between us. I afterward discovered that he was beginning to fear, poor man, that his wife's mind must be affected in some way, and was meditating a consultation with the physician who helped us in cases of need.

As for myself, I was either too stupid or too innocent to feel any positive forewarning of the truth, so far. After luncheon, while I was alone in the conservatory, my maid came to me from Michael, asking if I had any commands for him in the afternoon. I thought this rather odd; but it occurred to me that he might want some hours to himself. I made the inquiry.

To my astonishment, the maid announced that Lady Claudia had employed Michael to go on an errand for her. The nature of the errand was to take a letter to her bookseller, and to bring back the books which she had ordered. With three idle footmen in the house, whose business it was to perform such service as this, why had she taken the groom away from his work? The question obtained such complete possession of my mind that I actually summoned courage enough to go to my aunt. I said I had thought of driving out in my pony-carriage that afternoon, and I asked if she objected to sending one of the three indoor servants for her books in Michael's place.

She received me with a strange hard stare, and answered with obstinate self-possession: "I wish Michael to go!" No explanation followed. With reason or without it, agreeable to me or not agreeable to me, she wished Michael to go.

I begged her pardon for interfering, and replied that I would give up the idea of driving on that day. She made no further remark. I left the room, determining to watch her. There is no defense for my conduct; it was mean and unbecoming, no doubt. I was drawn on, by some force in me which I could not even attempt to resist. Indeed, indeed I am not a mean person by nature!

At first, I thought of speaking to Michael; not with any special motive, but simply because I felt drawn toward him as the guide and helper in whom my heart trusted at this crisis in my life. A little consideration, however, suggested to me that I might be seen speaking to him, and might so do him an injury. While I was still hesitating, the thought came to me that my aunt's motive for sending him to her bookseller might be to get him out of her way.

Out of her way in the house? No: his place was not in the house. Out of her way in the stable? The next instant, the idea flashed across my mind of watching the stable door.

The best bedrooms, my room included, were all in front of the house. I went up to my maid's room, which looked on the courtyard; ready with my excuse, if she happened to be there. She was not there. I placed myself at the window, in full view of the stable opposite.

An interval elapsed—long or short, I cannot say which; I was too much excited to look at my watch. All I know is that I discovered her! She crossed the yard, after waiting to make sure that no one was there to see her; and she entered the stable by the door which led to that part of the building occupied by Michael. This time I looked at my watch.

Forty minutes passed before I saw her again. And then, instead of appearing at the door, she showed herself at the window of Michael's room; throwing it wide open. I concealed myself behind the window curtain, just in time to escape discovery, as she looked up at the house. She next appeared in the yard, hurrying back. I waited a while, trying to compose myself in case I met any one on the stairs. There was little danger of a meeting at that hour. The General was at his club; the servants were at their tea. I reached my own room without being seen by any one, and locked myself in.

What had my aunt been doing for forty minutes in Michael's room? And why had she opened the window?

I spare you my reflections on these perplexing questions. A convenient headache saved me from the ordeal of meeting Lady Claudia at the dinner-table. I passed a restless and miserable night; conscious that I had found my way blindly, as it were, to some terrible secret which might have its influence on my whole future life, and not knowing what to think, or what to do next. Even then, I shrank instinctively from speaking to my uncle. This was not wonderful. But I felt afraid to speak to Michael—and that perplexed and alarmed me. Consideration for Lady Claudia was certainly not the motive that kept me silent, after what I had seen.

The next morning my pale face abundantly justified the assertion that I was still ill.

My aunt, always doing her maternal duty toward me, came herself to inquire after my health before I was out of my room. So certain was she of not having been observed on the previous day—or so prodigious was her power of controlling herself—that she actually advised me to go out riding before lunch, and try what the fresh air and the exercise would do to relieve me! Feeling that I must end in speaking to Michael, it struck me that this would be the one safe way of consulting him in private. I accepted her advice, and had another approving pat on the cheek from her plump white fingers. They no longer struck cold on my skin; the customary vital warmth had returned to them. Her ladyship's mind had recovered its tranquillity.

IX.

I LEFT the house for my morning ride.

Michael was not in his customary spirits. With some difficulty, I induced him to tell me the reason. He had decided on giving notice to leave his situation in the General's employment. As soon as I could command myself, I asked what had happened to justify this incomprehensible proceeding on his part. He silently offered me a letter. It was written by the master whom he had served before he came to us; and it announced that an employment as secretary was offered to him, in the house of a gentleman who was "interested in his creditable efforts to improve his position in the world."

What it cost me to preserve the outward appearance of composure as I handed back the letter, I am ashamed to tell. I spoke to him with some bitterness. "Your wishes are gratified," I said; "I don't wonder that you are eager to leave your place." He reined back his horse and repeated my words.

717

"Eager to leave my place? I am heart-broken at leaving it." I was reckless enough to ask why. His head sank. "I daren't tell you," he said. I went on from one imprudence to another. "What are you afraid of?" I asked. He suddenly looked up at me. His eyes answered: "You."

Is it possible to fathom the folly of a woman in love? Can any sensible person imagine the enormous importance which the veriest trifles assume in her poor little mind? I was perfectly satisfied—even perfectly happy, after that one look. I rode on briskly for a minute or two—then the forgotten scene at the stable recurred to my memory. I resumed a foot-pace and beckoned to him to speak to me.

"Lady Claudia's bookseller lives in the City, doesn't he?" I began.

"Yes, miss."

"Did you walk both ways?"

"Yes."

"You must have felt tired when you got back?"

"I hardly remember what I felt when I got back—I was met by a surprise."

"May I ask what it was?"

"Certainly, miss. Do you remember a black bag of mine?"

"Perfectly."

"When I returned from the City I found the bag open; and the things I kept in it—the shawl, the linen, and the letter—"

"Gone?"

"Gone."

My heart gave one great leap in me, and broke into vehement throbbings, which made it impossible for me to say a word more. I reined up my horse, and fixed my eyes on Michael. He was startled; he asked if I felt faint. I could only sign to him that I was waiting to hear more.

"My own belief," he proceeded, "is that some person burned the things in my absence, and opened the window to prevent any suspicion being excited by the smell. I am certain I shut the window before I left my room. When I closed it on my return, the fresh air had not entirely removed the smell of burning; and, what is more, I found a heap of ashes in the grate. As to the person who has done me this injury, and why it has been done, those are mysteries beyond my fathoming—I beg your pardon, miss—I am sure you are not well. Might I advise you to return to the house?"

I accepted his advice and turned back.

In the tumult of horror and amazement that filled my mind, I could still feel a faint triumph stirring in me through it all, when I saw how alarmed and how anxious he was about me. Nothing more passed between us on the way back. Confronted by the dreadful discovery that I had now made, I was silent and helpless. Of the guilty persons concerned in the concealment of the birth, and in the desertion of the infant, my nobly-born, highly-bred, irreproachable aunt now stood revealed before me as one! An older woman than I might have been hard put to it to preserve her presence of mind, in such a position as mine. Instinct, not reason, served me in my sore need. Instinct, not reason, kept me passively and stupidly silent when I got back to the house. "We will talk about it to-morrow," was all I could say to Michael, when he gently lifted me from my horse.

I excused myself from appearing at the luncheon-table; and I drew down the blinds in my sitting-room, so that my face might not betray me when Lady Claudia's maternal duty brought her upstairs to make inquiries. The same excuse served in both cases—my ride had failed to relieve me of my headache. My aunt's brief visit led to one result which is worth mentioning. The indescribable horror of her that I felt forced the conviction on my mind that we two could live no longer under the same roof. While I was still trying to face this alternative with the needful composure, my uncle presented himself, in some anxiety about my continued illness. I should certainly have burst out crying, when the kind and dear old man condoled with me, if he had not brought news with him which turned back all my thoughts on myself and my aunt. Michael had shown the General his letter and had given notice to leave. Lady Claudia was present at the time. To her husband's amazement, she abruptly interfered with a personal request to Michael to think better of it, and to remain in his place!

"I should not have troubled you, my dear, on this unpleasant subject," said my uncle, "if Michael had not told me that you were aware of the circumstances under which he feels it his duty to leave us. After your aunt's interference (quite incomprehensible to me), the man hardly knows what to do. Being your groom, he begs me to ask if there is any impropriety in his leaving the difficulty to your decision. I tell you of his request, Mina; but I strongly advise you to decline taking any responsibility on yourself."

I answered mechanically, accepting my uncle's suggestion, while my thoughts were wholly absorbed in this last of the many extraordinary proceedings on Lady Claudia's part since Michael had entered the house. There are limits—out of books and plays—to the innocence of a young unmarried woman. After what I had just heard the doubts which had thus far perplexed me were suddenly and completely cleared up. I said to my secret self: "She has some human feeling left. If her son goes away, she knows that they may never meet again!"

From the moment when my mind emerged from the darkness, I recovered the use of such intelligence and courage as I naturally possessed. From this point, you will find that, right or wrong, I saw my way before me, and took it.

To say that I felt for the General with my whole heart, is merely to own that I could be commonly grateful. I sat on his knee, and laid my cheek against his cheek, and thanked him for his long, long years of kindness to me. He stopped me in his simple generous way. "Why, Mina, you talk as if you were going to leave us!" I started up, and went to the window, opening it and complaining of the heat, and so concealing from him that he had unconsciously anticipated the event that was indeed to come. When I returned to my chair, he helped me to recover myself by alluding once more to his wife. He feared that her health was in some way impaired. In the time when they had first met, she was subject to nervous maladies, having their origin in a "calamity" which was never mentioned by either of them in later days. She might possibly be suffering again, from some other form of nervous derangement, and he seriously thought of persuading her to send for medical advice.

Under ordinary circumstances, this vague reference to a "calamity" would not have excited any special interest in me. But my mind was now in a state of morbid suspicion. I had not heard how long my uncle and aunt had been married; but I remembered that Michael had described himself as being twenty-six years old. Bearing these circumstances in mind, it struck me that I might be acting wisely (in Michael's interest) if I persuaded the General to speak further of what had happened, at the time when he met the woman whom an evil destiny had bestowed on him for a wife. Nothing but the consideration of serving the man I loved would have reconciled me to making my own secret use of the recollections which my uncle might innocently confide to me. As it was, I thought the means would, in this case, he for once justified by the end. Before we part, I have little doubt that you will think so too.

I found it an easier task than I had anticipated to turn the talk back again to the days when the General had seen Lady Claudia for the first time. He was proud of the circumstances under which he had won his wife. Ah, how my heart ached for him as I saw his eyes sparkle, and the color mount in his fine rugged face!

This is the substance of what I heard from him. I tell it briefly, because it is still painful to me to tell it at all.

My uncle had met Lady Claudia at her father's country house. She had then reappeared in society, after a period of seclusion, passed partly in England, partly on the Continent. Before the date of her retirement, she had been engaged to marry a French nobleman, equally illustrious by his birth and by his diplomatic services in the East. Within a few weeks of the wedding-day, he was drowned by the wreck of his yacht. This was the calamity to which my uncle had referred.

Lady Claudia's mind was so seriously affected by the dreadful event, that the doctors refused to answer for the consequences, unless she was at once placed in the strictest retirement. Her mother, and a French maid devotedly attached to her, were the only persons whom it was considered safe for the young lady to see, until time and care had in some degree composed her. Her return to her friends and admirers, after the necessary interval of seclusion, was naturally a subject of sincere rejoicing among the guests assembled in her father's house. My uncle's interest in Lady Claudia soon developed into love. They were equals in rank, and well suited to each other in age. The parents raised no obstacles; but they did not conceal from their guest that the disaster which had befallen their daughter was but too likely to disincline her to receive his addresses, or any man's addresses, favorably. To their surprise, they proved to be wrong. The young lady was touched by the simplicity and the delicacy with which her lover urged his suit. She had lived among worldly people. This was a man whose devotion she could believe to be sincere. They were married.

Had no unusual circumstances occurred? Had nothing happened which the General had forgotten? Nothing.

X.

IT is surely needless that I should stop here, to draw the plain inferences from the events just related.

Any person who remembers that the shawl in which the infant was wrapped came from those Eastern regions which were associated with the French nobleman's diplomatic services—also, that the faults of composition in the letter found on the child were exactly the faults likely to have been committed by the French maid—any person who follows these traces can find his way to the truth as I found mine.

Returning for a moment to the hopes which I had formed of being of some service to Michael, I have only to say that they were at once destroyed, when I heard of the death by drowning of the man to whom the evidence pointed as his father. The prospect looked equally barren when I thought of the miserable mother. That she should openly acknowledge her son in her position was perhaps not to be expected of any woman. Had she courage enough, or, in plainer words, heart enough to acknowledge him privately?

I called to mind again some of the apparent caprices and contradictions in Lady Claudia's conduct, on the memorable day when Michael had presented himself to fill the vacant place. Look back with me to the record of what she said and did on that occasion, by the light of your present knowledge, and you will see that his likeness to his father must have struck her when he entered the room, and that his statement of his age must have correctly described the age of her son. Recall the actions that followed, after she had been exhausted by her first successful efforts at self-control—the withdrawal to the window to conceal her face; the clutch at the curtain when she felt herself sinking; the harshness of manner under which she concealed her emotions when she ventured to speak to him; the reiterated inconsistencies and vacillations of conduct that followed, all alike due to the protest of Nature, desperately resisted to the last—and say if I did her injustice when I believed her to be incapable of running the smallest risk of discovery at the prompting of maternal love.

There remained, then, only Michael to think of. I remember how he had spoken of the unknown parents whom he neither expected nor cared to discover. Still, I could not reconcile it to my conscience to accept a chance outbreak of temper as my sufficient justification for keeping him in ignorance of a discovery which so nearly concerned him. It seemed at least to be my duty to make myself acquainted with the true state of his feelings, before I decided to bear the burden of silence with me to my grave.

What I felt it my duty to do in this serious matter, I determined to do at once. Besides, let me honestly own that I felt lonely and desolate, oppressed by the critical situation in which I was placed, and eager for the relief that it would be to me only to hear the sound of Michael's voice. I sent my maid to say that I wished to speak to him immediately. The crisis was already hanging over my head. That one act brought it down.

XI.

He came in, and stood modestly waiting at the door.

After making him take a chair, I began by saying that I had received his message, and that, acting on my uncle's advice, I must abstain from interfering in the question of his leaving, or not leaving, his place. Having in this way established a reason for sending for him, I alluded next to the loss that he had sustained, and asked if he had any prospect of finding out the person who had entered his room in his absence. On his reply in the negative, I spoke of the serious results to him of the act of destruction that had been committed. "Your last chance of discovering your parents," I said, "has been cruelly destroyed."

He smiled sadly. "You know already, miss, that I never expected to discover them."

I ventured a little nearer to the object I had in view.

"Do you never think of your mother?" I asked. "At your age, she might be still living. Can you give up all hope of finding her, without feeling your heart ache?"

"If I have done her wrong, in believing that she deserted me," he answered, "the heart-ache is but a poor way of expressing the remorse that I should feel."

I ventured nearer still.

"Even if you were right," I began—"even it she did desert you—"

He interrupted me sternly. "I would not cross the street to see her," he said. "A woman who deserts her child is a monster. Forgive me for speaking so, miss! When I see good mothers and their children it maddens me when I think of what my childhood was."

Hearing these words, and watching him attentively while he spoke, I could see that my silence would be a mercy, not a crime. I hastened to speak of other things.

724

"If you decide to leave us," I said, "when shall you go?"

His eyes softened instantly. Little by little the color faded out of his face as he answered me.

"The General kindly said, when I spoke of leaving my place—" His voice faltered, and he paused to steady it. "My master," he resumed, "said that I need not keep my new employer waiting by staying for the customary month, provided—provided you were willing to dispense with my services."

So far, I had succeeded in controlling myself. At that reply I felt my resolution failing me. I saw how he suffered; I saw how manfully he struggled to conceal it.

"I am not willing," I said. "I am sorry—very, very sorry to lose you. But I will do anything that is for your good. I can say no more."

He rose suddenly, as if to leave the room; mastered himself; stood for a moment silently looking at me—then looked away again, and said his parting words.

"If I succeed, Miss Mina, in my new employment—if I get on to higher things—is it—is it presuming too much, to ask if I might, some day—perhaps when you are out riding alone—if I might speak to you—only to ask if you are well and happy—"

He could say no more. I saw the tears in his eyes; saw him shaken by the convulsive breathings which break from men in the rare moments when they cry. He forced it back even then. He bowed to me—oh, God, he bowed to me, as if he were only my servant! as if he were too far below me to take my hand, even at that moment! I could have endured anything else; I believe I could still have restrained myself under any other circumstances. It matters little now; my confession must be made, whatever you may think of me. I flew to him like a frenzied creature—I threw my arms round his neck—I said to him, "Oh, Michael, don't you know that I love you?" And then I laid my head on his breast, and held him to me, and said no more.

In that moment of silence, the door of the room was opened. I started, and looked up. Lady Claudia was standing on the threshold.

I saw in her face that she had been listening—she must have followed him when he was on his way to my room. That conviction steadied me. I took his hand in mine, and stood side by side with him, waiting for her to speak first. She looked at Michael, not at me. She advanced a step or two, and addressed him in these words:

"It is just possible that you have some sense of decency left. Leave the room."

That deliberate insult was all that I wanted to make me completely mistress of myself. I told Michael to wait a moment, and opened my writing desk. I wrote on an envelope the address in London of a faithful old servant, who had attended my mother in her last moments. I gave it to Michael. "Call there to-morrow morning," I said. "You will find me waiting for you."

He looked at Lady Claudia, evidently unwilling to leave me alone with her. "Fear nothing," I said; "I am old enough to take care of myself. I have only a word to say to this lady before I leave the house." With that, I took his arm, and walked with him to the door, and said good-by almost as composedly as if we had been husband and wife already.

Lady Claudia's eyes followed me as I shut the door again and crossed the room to a second door which led into my bed-chamber. She suddenly stepped up to me, just as I was entering the room, and laid her hand on my arm.

"What do I see in your face?" she asked as much of herself as of me—with her eyes fixed in keen inquiry on mine.

"You shall know directly," I answered. "Let me get my bonnet and cloak first."

"Do you mean to leave the house?"

"I do."

She rang the bell. I quietly dressed myself, to go out.

The servant answered the bell, as I returned to the sitting-room.

"Tell your master I wish to see him instantly," said Lady Claudia.

"My master has gone out, my lady."

"To his club?"

"I believe so, my lady."

"I will send you with a letter to him. Come back when I ring again." She turned to me as the man withdrew. "Do you refuse to stay here until the General returns?"

"I shall be happy to see the General, if you will inclose my address in your letter to him."

Replying in those terms, I wrote the address for the second time. Lady Claudia knew perfectly well, when I gave it to her, that I was going to a respectable house kept by a woman who had nursed me when I was a child.

"One last question," she said. "Am I to tell the General that it is your intention to marry your groom?"

Her tone stung me into making an answer which I regretted the moment it had passed my lips.

"You can put it more plainly, if you like," I said. "You can tell the General that it is my intention to marry your son."

She was near the door, on the point of leaving me. As I spoke, she turned with a ghastly stare of horror—felt about her with her hands as if she was groping in darkness—and dropped on the floor.

I instantly summoned help. The women-servants carried her to my bed. While they were restoring her to herself, I wrote a few lines telling the miserable woman how I had discovered her secret.

"Your husband's tranquillity," I added, "is as precious to me as my own. As for your son, you know what he thinks of the mother who deserted him. Your secret is safe in my keeping—safe from your husband, safe from your son, to the end of my life."

I sealed up those words, and gave them to her when she had come to herself again. I never heard from her in reply. I have never seen her from that time to this. She knows she can trust me.

And what did my good uncle say, when we next met? I would rather report what he did, when he had got the better of his first feelings of anger and surprise on hearing of my contemplated marriage. He consented to receive us on our wedding-day; and he gave my husband the appointment which places us both in an independent position for life.

But he had his misgivings. He checked me when I tried to thank him.

"Come back in a year's time," he said. "I will wait to be thanked till the experience of your married life tells me that I have deserved it."

The year passed; and the General received the honest expression of my gratitude. He smiled and kissed me; but there was something in his face which suggested that he was not quite satisfied yet.

"Do you believe that I have spoken sincerely?" I asked.

"I firmly believe it," he answered—and there he stopped.

A wiser woman would have taken the hint and dropped the subject. My folly persisted in putting another question:

"Tell me, uncle. Haven't I proved that I was right when I married my groom?"

"No, my dear. You have only proved that you are a lucky woman!"

728

MR. LEPEL AND THE HOUSEKEEPER

FIRST EPOCH.

THE Italians are born actors.

At this conclusion I arrived, sitting in a Roman theater—now many years since. My friend and traveling companion, Rothsay, cordially agreed with me. Experience had given us some claim to form an opinion. We had visited, at that time, nearly every city in Italy. Where-ever a theater was open, we had attended the performances of the companies which travel from place to place; and we had never seen bad acting from first to last. Men and women, whose names are absolutely unknown in England, played (in modern comedy and drama for the most part) with a general level of dramatic ability which I have never seen equaled in the theaters of other nations. Incapable Italian actors there must be, no doubt. For my own part I have only discovered them, by ones and twos, in England; appearing among the persons engaged to support Salvini and Ristori before the audiences of London.

On the occasion of which I am now writing, the night's performances consisted of two plays. An accident, to be presently related, prevented us from seeing more than the introductory part of the second piece. That one act—in respect of the influence which the remembrance of it afterward exercised over Rothsay and myself—claims a place of its own in the opening pages of the present narrative.

The scene of the story was laid in one of the principalities of Italy, in the bygone days of the Carbonaro conspiracies. The chief persons were two young noblemen, friends affectionately attached to each other, and a beautiful girl born in the lower ranks of life.

On the rising of the curtain, the scene before us was the courtyard of a prison. We found the beautiful girl (called Celia as well as I can recollect) in great distress; confiding her sorrows to the jailer's daughter. Her father was pining in the prison, charged with an offense of which he was innocent;

and she herself was suffering the tortures of hopeless love. She was on the point of confiding her secret to her friend, when the appearance of the young nobleman closed her lips. The girls at once withdrew; and the two friends—whom I now only remember as the Marquis and the Count—began the dialogue which prepared us for the story of the play.

The Marquis had been tried for conspiracy against the reigning Prince and his government; had been found guilty, and is condemned to be shot that evening. He accepts his sentence with the resignation of a man who is weary of his life. Young as he is, he has tried the round of pleasures without enjoyment; he has no interests, no aspirations, no hopes; he looks on death as a welcome release. His friend the Count, admitted to a farewell interview, has invented a stratagem by which the prisoner may escape and take to flight. The Marquis expresses a grateful sense of obligation, and prefers being shot. "I don't value my life," he says; "I am not a happy man like you." Upon this the Count mentions circumstances which he has hitherto kept secret. He loves the charming Celia, and loves in vain. Her reputation is unsullied; she possesses every good quality that a man can desire in a wife—but the Count's social position forbids him to marry a woman of low birth. He is heart-broken; and he too finds life without hope a burden that is not to be borne. The Marquis at once sees a way of devoting himself to his friend's interests. He is rich; his money is at his own disposal; he will bequeath a marriage portion to Celia which will make her one of the richest women in Italy. The Count receives this proposal with a sigh. "No money," he says, "will remove the obstacle that still remains. My father's fatal objection to Celia is her rank in life." The Marquis walks apart—considers a little—consults his watch—and returns with a new idea. "I have nearly two hours of life still left," he says. "Send for Celia: she was here just now, and she is probably in her father's cell." The Count is at a loss to understand what this proposal means. The Marquis explains himself. "I ask your permission," he resumes, "to offer marriage to Celia—for your sake. The chaplain of the prison will perform the ceremony. Before dark, the girl you love will be my widow. My widow is a lady of title—a fit wife for the greatest nobleman in the land." The Count protests and refuses in vain. The jailer is sent to find Celia. She appears. Unable to endure the scene, the Count rushes out in horror. The Marquis takes the girl into his confidence, and makes his excuses. If she becomes a

730

widow of rank, she may not only marry the Count, but will be in a position to procure the liberty of the innocent old man, whose strength is failing him under the rigors of imprisonment. Celia hesitates. After a struggle with herself, filial love prevails, and she consents. The jailer announces that the chaplain is waiting; the bride and bridegroom withdraw to the prison chapel. Left on the stage, the jailer hears a distant sound in the city, which he is at a loss to understand. It sinks, increases again, travels nearer to the prison, and now betrays itself as the sound of multitudinous voices in a state of furious uproar. Has the conspiracy broken out again? Yes! The whole population has risen; the soldiers have refused to fire on the people; the terrified Prince has dismissed his ministers, and promises a constitution. The Marquis, returning from the ceremony which has just made Celia his wife, is presented with a free pardon, and with the offer of a high place in the re-formed ministry. A new life is opening before him—and he has innocently ruined his friend's prospects! On this striking situation the drop-curtain falls.

While we were still applauding the first act, Rothsay alarmed me: he dropped from his seat at my side, like a man struck dead. The stifling heat in the theater had proved too much for him. We carried him out at once into the fresh air. When he came to his senses, my friend entreated me to leave him, and see the end of the play. To my mind, he looked as if he might faint again. I insisted on going back with him to our hotel.

On the next day I went to the theater, to ascertain if the play would be repeated. The box-office was closed. The dramatic company had left Rome.

My interest in discovering how the story ended led me next to the booksellers' shops—in the hope of buying the play. Nobody knew anything about it. Nobody could tell me whether it was the original work of an Italian writer, or whether it had been stolen (and probably disfigured) from the French. As a fragment I had seen it. As a fragment it has remained from that time to this.

SECOND EPOCH.

ONE of my objects in writing these lines is to vindicate the character of an innocent woman (formerly in my service as housekeeper) who has been cruelly slandered. Absorbed in the pursuit of my purpose, it has only now occurred to me that strangers may desire to know something more than they know now of myself and my friend. "Give us some idea," they may say, "of what sort of persons you are, if you wish to interest us at the outset of your story."

A most reasonable suggestion, I admit. Unfortunately, I am not the right man to comply with it.

In the first place, I cannot pretend to pronounce judgment on my own character. In the second place, I am incapable of writing impartially of my friend. At the imminent risk of his own life, Rothsay rescued me from a dreadful death by accident, when we were at college together. Who can expect me to speak of his faults? I am not even capable of seeing them.

Under these embarrassing circumstances—and not forgetting, at the same time, that a servant's opinion of his master and his master's friends may generally be trusted not to err on the favorable side—I am tempted to call my valet as a witness to character.

I slept badly on our first night at Rome; and I happened to be awake while the man was talking of us confidentially in the courtyard of the hotel— just under my bedroom window. Here, to the best of my recollection, is a faithful report of what he said to some friend among the servants who understood English:

"My master's well connected, you must know—though he's only plain Mr. Lepel. His uncle's the great lawyer, Lord Lepel; and his late father was a banker. Rich, did you say? I should think he was rich—and be hanged to him! No, not married, and not likely to be. Owns he was forty last birthday; a regular old bachelor. Not a bad sort, taking him altogether. The worst of him is, he is one of the most indiscreet persons I ever met with. Does the queerest things, when the whim takes him, and doesn't care what other people think of it. They say the Lepels have all got a slate loose in the upper story. Oh, no; not a very old family—I mean, nothing compared to the family of his friend, young Rothsay. They count back, as I have heard, to the ancient kings of Scotland. Between ourselves, the ancient kings haven't left the Rothsays much money. They would be glad, I'll be bound, to get my rich master for one of their daughters. Poor as Job, I tell you. This young fellow, traveling with us, has never had a spare five-pound note since he was born. Plenty of brains in his head, I grant you; and a little too apt sometimes to be suspicious of other people. But liberal—oh, give him his due—liberal in a small way. Tips me with a sovereign now and then. I take it—Lord bless you, I take it. What do you say? Has he got any employment? Not he! Dabbles in chemistry (experiments, and that sort of thing) by way of amusing himself; and tells the most infernal lies about it. The other day he showed me a bottle about as big as a thimble, with what looked like water in it, and said it was enough to poison everybody in the hotel. What rot! Isn't that the clock striking again? Near about bedtime, I should say. Wish you good night."

There are our characters—drawn on the principle of justice without mercy, by an impudent rascal who is the best valet in England. Now you know what sort of persons we are; and now we may go on again.

Rothsay and I parted, soon after our night at the theater. He went to Civita Vecchia to join a friend's yacht, waiting for him in the harbor. I turned homeward, traveling at a leisurely rate through the Tyrol and Germany.

After my arrival in England, certain events in my life occurred which did not appear to have any connection at the time. They led, nevertheless, to consequences which seriously altered the relations of happy past years between Rothsay and myself.

The first event took place on my return to my house in London. I found among the letters waiting for me an invitation from Lord Lepel to spend a few weeks with him at his country seat in Sussex.

I had made so many excuses, in past years, when I received invitations from my uncle, that I was really ashamed to plead engagements in London again. There was no unfriendly feeling between us. My only motive for keeping away from him took its rise in dislike of the ordinary modes of life in an English country-house. A man who feels no interest in politics, who cares nothing for field sports, who is impatient of amateur music and incapable of small talk, is a man out of his element in country society. This was my unlucky case. I went to Lord Lepel's house sorely against my will; longing already for the day when it would be time to say good-by.

The routine of my uncle's establishment had remained unaltered since my last experience of it.

I found my lord expressing the same pride in his collection of old masters, and telling the same story of the wonderful escape of his picture-gallery from fire—I renewed my acquaintance with the same members of Parliament among the guests, all on the same side in politics—I joined in the same dreary amusements—I saluted the same resident priest (the Lepels are all born and bred Roman Catholics)—I submitted to the same rigidly early breakfast hour; and inwardly cursed the same peremptory bell, ringing as a means of reminding us of our meals. The one change that presented itself was a change out of the house. Death had removed the lodgekeeper at the park-gate. His widow and daughter (Mrs. Rymer and little Susan) remained in their pretty cottage. They had been allowed by my lord's kindness to take charge of the gate.

Out walking, on the morning after my arrival, I was caught in a shower on my way back to the park, and took shelter in the lodge.

In the bygone days I had respected Mrs. Rymer's husband as a thoroughly worthy man—but Mrs. Rymer herself was no great favorite of mine. She had married beneath her, as the phrase is, and she was a little too conscious of it. A woman with a sharp eye to her own interests; selfishly discontented with her position in life, and not very scrupulous in her choice of means when she had an end in view: that is how I describe Mrs. Rymer. Her daughter, whom I only remembered as a weakly child, astonished me when I saw her again after the interval that had elapsed. The backward flower had bloomed into perfect health. Susan was now a lovely little modest girl of seventeen—with a natural delicacy and refinement of manner, which marked her to my mind as one of Nature's gentlewomen. When I entered the lodge she was writing at a table in a corner, having some books on it, and rose to withdraw. I begged that she would proceed with her employment, and asked if I might know what it was. She answered me with a blush, and a pretty brightening of her clear blue eyes. "I am trying, sir, to teach myself French," she said. The weather showed no signs of improving—I volunteered to help her, and found her such an attentive and intelligent pupil that I looked in at the lodge from time to time afterward, and continued my instructions. The younger men among my uncle's guests set their own stupid construction on my attentions "to the girl at the gate," as they called her—rather too familiarly, according to my notions of propriety. I contrived to remind them that I was old enough to be Susan's father, in a manner which put an end to their jokes; and I was pleased to hear, when I next went to the lodge, that Mrs. Rymer had been wise enough to keep these facetious gentlemen at their proper distance.

The day of my departure arrived. Lord Leper took leave of me kindly, and asked for news of Rothsay. "Let me know when your friend returns," my uncle said; "he belongs to a good old stock. Put me in mind of him when I next invite you to come to my house."

On my way to the train I stopped of course at the lodge to say good-by. Mrs. Rymer came out alone I asked for Susan.

"My daughter is not very well to-day."

"Is she confined to her room?"

"She is in the parlor."

I might have been mistaken, but I thought Mrs. Rymer answered me in no very friendly way. Resolved to judge for myself, I entered the lodge, and found my poor little pupil sitting in a corner, crying. When I asked her what was the matter, the excuse of a "bad headache" was the only reply that I received. The natures of young girls are a hopeless puzzle to me. Susan seemed, for some reason which it was impossible to understand, to be afraid to look at me.

"Have you and your mother been quarreling?" I asked.

"Oh, no!"

She denied it with such evident sincerity that I could not for a moment suspect her of deceiving me. Whatever the cause of her distress might be, it was plain that she had her own reasons for keeping it a secret.

Her French books were on the table. I tried a little allusion to her lessons.

"I hope you will go on regularly with your studies," I said.

"I will do my best, sir—without you to help me."

She said it so sadly that I proposed—purely from the wish to encourage her—a continuation of our lessons through the post.

"Send your exercises to me once a week," I suggested; "and I will return them corrected."

She thanked me in low tones, with a shyness of manner which I had never noticed in her before. I had done my best to cheer her—and I was conscious, as we shook hands at parting, that I had failed. A feeling of disappointment overcomes me when I see young people out of spirits. I was sorry for Susan.

THIRD EPOCH.

ONE of my faults (which has not been included in the list set forth by my valet) is a disinclination to occupy myself with my own domestic affairs. The proceedings of my footman, while I had been away from home, left me no alternative but to dismiss him on my return. With this exertion of authority my interference as chief of the household came to an end. I left it to my excellent housekeeper, Mrs. Mozeen, to find a sober successor to the drunken vagabond who had been sent away. She discovered a respectable young man—tall, plump, and rosy—whose name was Joseph, and whose character was beyond reproach. I have but one excuse for noticing such a trifling event as this. It took its place, at a later period, in the chain which was slowly winding itself round me.

My uncle had asked me to prolong my visit and I should probably have consented, but for anxiety on the subject of a near and dear relative—my sister. Her health had been failing since the death of her husband, to whom she was tenderly attached. I heard news of her while I was in Sussex, which hurried me back to town. In a month more, her death deprived me of my last living relation. She left no children; and my two brothers had both died unmarried while they were still young men.

This affliction placed me in a position of serious embarrassment, in regard to the disposal of my property after my death.

I had hitherto made no will; being well aware that my fortune (which was entirely in money) would go in due course of law to the person of all others who would employ it to the best purpose—that is to say, to my sister as my nearest of kin. As I was now situated, my property would revert to my uncle if I died intestate. He was a richer man than I was. Of his two children, both sons, the eldest would inherit his estates: the youngest had already succeeded to his mother's ample fortune. Having literally no family claims on me, I felt bound to recognize the wider demands of poverty and misfortune, and to devote my superfluous wealth to increasing the revenues of charitable institutions. As to minor legacies, I owed it to my good housekeeper, Mrs. Mozeen, not to forget the faithful services of past years. Need I add—if I had been free to act as I pleased—that I should have gladly made Rothsay the object of a handsome bequest? But this was not to be. My friend was a man morbidly sensitive on the subject of money. In the early days of our intercourse we had been for the first and only time on the verge of a quarrel, when I had asked (as a favor to myself) to be allowed to provide for him in my will.

"It is because I am poor," he explained, "that I refuse to profit by your kindness—though I feel it gratefully."

I failed to understand him—and said so plainly.

"You will understand this," he resumed; "I should never recover my sense of degradation, if a mercenary motive on my side was associated with our friendship. Don't say it's impossible! You know as well as I do that appearances would be against me, in the eyes of the world. Besides, I don't want money; my own small income is enough for me. Make me your executor if you like, and leave me the customary present of five hundred pounds. If you exceed that sum I declare on my word of honor that I will not touch one farthing of it." He took my hand, and pressed it fervently. "Do me a favor," he said. "Never let us speak of this again!"

I understood that I must yield—or lose my friend.

In now making my will, I accordingly appointed Rothsay one of my executors, on the terms that he had prescribed. The minor legacies having been next duly reduced to writing, I left the bulk of my fortune to public charities.

My lawyer laid the fair copy of the will on my table.

"A dreary disposition of property for a man of your age," he said, "I hope to receive a new set of instructions before you are a year older."

"What instructions?" I asked.

"To provide for your wife and children," he answered.

My wife and children! The idea seemed to be so absurd that I burst out laughing. It never occurred to me that there could be any absurdity from my own point of view.

I was sitting alone, after my legal adviser had taken his leave, looking absently at the newly-engrossed will, when I heard a sharp knock at the house-door which I thought I recognized. In another minute Rothsay's bright face enlivened my dull room. He had returned from the Mediterranean that morning.

"Am I interrupting you?" he asked, pointing to the leaves of manuscript before me. "Are you writing a book?"

"I am making my will."

His manner changed; he looked at me seriously.

"Do you remember what I said, when we once talked of your will?" he asked. I set his doubts at rest immediately—but he was not quite satisfied yet. "Can't you put your will away?" he suggested. "I hate the sight of anything that reminds me of death."

"Give me a minute to sign it," I said—and rang to summon the witnesses.

Mrs. Mozeen answered the bell. Rothsay looked at her, as if he wished to have my housekeeper put away as well as my will. From the first moment when he had seen her, he conceived a great dislike to that good creature.

There was nothing, I am sure, personally repellent about her. She was a little slim quiet woman, with a pale complexion and bright brown eyes. Her movements were gentle; her voice was low; her decent gray dress was adapted to her age. Why Rothsay should dislike her was more than he could explain himself. He turned his unreasonable prejudice into a joke—and said he hated a woman who wore slate colored cap-ribbons!

I explained to Mrs. Mozeen that I wanted witnesses to the signature of my will. Naturally enough—being in the room at the time—she asked if she could be one of them.

I was obliged to say No; and not to mortify her, I gave the reason.

"My will recognizes what I owe to your good services," I said. "If you are one of the witnesses, you will lose your legacy. Send up the men-servants."

With her customary tact, Mrs. Mozeen expressed her gratitude silently, by a look—and left the room.

"Why couldn't you tell that woman to send the servants, without mentioning her legacy?" Rothsay asked. "My friend Lepel, you have done a very foolish thing."

"In what way?"

"You have given Mrs. Mozeen an interest in your death."

It was impossible to make a serious reply to this ridiculous exhibition of Rothsay's prejudice against poor Mrs. Mozeen.

"When am I to be murdered?" I asked. "And how is it to be done? Poison?"

"I'm not joking," Rothsay answered. "You are infatuated about your housekeeper. When you spoke of her legacy, did you notice her eyes."

"Yes."

"Did nothing strike you?"

"It struck me that they were unusually well preserved eyes for a woman

739

of her age."

The appearance of the valet and the footman put an end to this idle talk. The will was executed, and locked up. Our conversation turned on Rothsay's travels by sea. The cruise had been in every way successful. The matchless shores of the Mediterranean defied description; the sailing of the famous yacht had proved to be worthy of her reputation; and, to crown all, Rothsay had come back to England, in a fair way, for the first time in his life, of making money.

"I have discovered a treasure," he announced.

"It was a dirty little modern picture, picked up in a by-street at Palermo. It is a Virgin and Child, by Guido."

On further explanation it appeared that the picture exposed for sale was painted on copper. Noticing the contrast between the rare material and the wretchedly bad painting that covered it, Rothsay had called to mind some of the well-known stories of valuable works of art that had been painted over for purposes of disguise. The price asked for the picture amounted to little more than the value of the metal. Rothsay bought it. His knowledge of chemistry enabled him to put his suspicion successfully to the test; and one of the guests on board the yacht—a famous French artist—had declared his conviction that the picture now revealed to view was a genuine work by Guido. Such an opinion as this convinced me that it would be worth while to submit my friend's discovery to the judgment of other experts. Consulted independently, these critics confirmed the view taken by the celebrated personage who had first seen the work. This result having been obtained, Rothsay asked my advice next on the question of selling his picture. I at once thought of my uncle. An undoubted work by Guido would surely be an acquisition to his gallery. I had only (in accordance with his own request) to let him know that my friend had returned to England. We might take the picture with us, when we received our invitation to Lord Lepel's house.

FOURTH EPOCH.

My uncle's answer arrived by return of post. Other engagements obliged him to defer receiving us for a month. At the end of that time, we were

740

cordially invited to visit him, and to stay as long as we liked.

In the interval that now passed, other events occurred—still of the trifling kind.

One afternoon, just as I was thinking of taking my customary ride in the park, the servant appeared charged with a basket of flowers, and with a message from Mrs. Rymer, requesting me to honor her by accepting a little offering from her daughter. Hearing that she was then waiting in the hall, I told the man to show her in. Susan (as I ought to have already mentioned) had sent her exercises to me regularly every week. In returning them corrected, I had once or twice added a word of well-deserved approval. The offering of flowers was evidently intended to express my pupil's grateful sense of the interest taken in her by her teacher.

I had no reason, this time, to suppose that Mrs. Rymer entertained an unfriendly feeling toward me. At the first words of greeting that passed between us I perceived a change in her manner, which ran in the opposite extreme. She overwhelmed me with the most elaborate demonstrations of politeness and respect; dwelling on her gratitude for my kindness in receiving her, and on her pride at seeing her daughter's flowers on my table, until I made a resolute effort to stop her by asking (as if it was actually a matter of importance to me!) whether she was in London on business or on pleasure.

"Oh, on business, sir! My poor husband invested his little savings in bank stock, and I have just been drawing my dividend. I do hope you don't think my girl over-bold in venturing to send you a few flowers. She wouldn't allow me to interfere. I do assure you she would gather and arrange them with her own hands. In themselves I know they are hardly worth accepting; but if you will allow the motive to plead—"

I made another effort to stop Mrs. Rymer; I said her daughter could not have sent me a prettier present.

The inexhaustible woman only went on more fluently than ever.

"She is so grateful, sir, and so proud of your goodness in looking at her exercises. The difficulty of the French language seem as nothing to her,

741

now her motive is to please you. She is so devoted to her studies that I find it difficult to induce her to take the exercise necessary to her health; and, as you may perhaps remember, Susan was always rather weakly as a child. She inherits her father's constitution, Mr. Lepel—not mine."

Here, to my infinite relief, the servant appeared, announcing that my horse was at the door.

Mrs. Rymer opened her mouth. I saw a coming flood of apologies on the point of pouring out—and seized my hat on the spot. I declared I had an appointment; I sent kind remembrances to Susan (pitying her for having such a mother with my whole heart); I said I hoped to return to my uncle's house soon, and to continue the French lessons. The one thing more that I remember was finding myself safe in the saddle, and out of the reach of Mrs. Rymer's tongue.

Reflecting on what had passed, it was plain to me that this woman had some private end in view, and that my abrupt departure had prevented her from finding the way to it. What motive could she possibly have for that obstinate persistence in presenting poor Susan under a favorable aspect, to a man who had already shown that he was honestly interested in her pretty modest daughter? I tried hard to penetrate the mystery—and gave it up in despair.

Three days before the date at which Rothsay and I were to pay our visit to Lord Lepel, I found myself compelled to undergo one of the minor miseries of human life. In other words I became one of the guests at a large dinner-party. It was a rainy day in October. My position at the table placed me between a window that was open and a door that was hardly ever shut. I went to bed shivering; and woke the next morning with a headache and a difficulty in breathing. On consulting the doctor, I found that I was suffering from an attack of bronchitis. There was no reason to be alarmed. If I remained indoors, and submitted to the necessary treatment, I might hope to keep my engagement with my uncle in ten days or a fortnight.

There was no alternative but to submit. I accordingly arranged with Rothsay that he should present himself at Lord Lepel's house (taking the picture with him), on the date appointed for our visit, and that I should follow as soon as I was well enough to travel.

On the day when he was to leave London, my friend kindly came to keep me company for a while. He was followed into my room by Mrs. Mozeen, with a bottle of medicine in her hand. This worthy creature, finding that the doctor's directions occasionally escaped my memory, devoted herself to the duty of administering the remedies at the prescribed intervals of time. When she left the room, having performed her duties as usual, I saw Rothsay's eyes follow her to the door with an expression of sardonic curiosity. He put a strange question to me as soon as we were alone.

"Who engaged that new servant of yours?" he asked. "I mean the fat fellow, with the curly flaxen hair."

"Hiring servants," I replied, "is not much in my way. I left the engagement of the new man to Mrs. Mozeen."

Rothsay walked gravely up to my bedside.

"Lepel," he said, "your respectable housekeeper is in love with the fat young footman."

It is not easy to amuse a man suffering from bronchitis. But this new outbreak of absurdity was more than I could resist, even with a mustard-plaster on my chest.

"I thought I should raise your spirits," Rothsay proceeded. "When I came to your house this morning, the valet opened the door to me. I expressed my surprise at his condescending to take that trouble. He informed me that Joseph was otherwise engaged. 'With anybody in particular?' I asked, humoring the joke. 'Yes, sir, with the housekeeper. She's teaching him how to brush his hair, so as to show off his good looks to the best advantage.' Make up your mind, my friend, to lose Mrs. Mozeen—especially if she happens to have any money."

"Nonsense, Rothsay! The poor woman is old enough to be Joseph's mother."

"My good fellow, that won't make any difference to Joseph. In the days when we were rich enough to keep a man-servant, our footman—as handsome a fellow as ever you saw, and no older than I am—married a witch with a lame leg. When I asked him why he had made such a fool of himself he looked quite indignant, and said: 'Sir! she has got six hundred pounds.' He and the witch keep a public house. What will you bet me that we don't see your housekeeper drawing beer at the bar, and Joseph getting drunk in the parlor, before we are a year older?"

I was not well enough to prolong my enjoyment of Rothsay's boyish humor. Besides, exaggeration to be really amusing must have some relation, no matter how slender it may be, to the truth. My housekeeper belonged to a respectable family, and was essentially a person accustomed to respect herself. Her brother occupied a position of responsibility in the establishment of a firm of chemists whom I had employed for years past. Her late husband had farmed his own land, and had owed his ruin to calamities for which he was in no way responsible. Kind-hearted Mrs. Mozeen was just the woman to take a motherly interest in a well-disposed lad like Joseph; and it was equally characteristic of my valet—especially when Rothsay was thoughtless enough to encourage him—to pervert an innocent action for the sake of indulging in a stupid jest. I took advantage of my privilege as an invalid, and changed the subject.

A week passed. I had expected to hear from Rothsay. To my surprise and disappointment no letter arrived.

Susan was more considerate. She wrote, very modestly and prettily, to say that she and her mother had heard of my illness from Mr. Rothsay, and to express the hope that I should soon be restored to health. A few days later, Mrs. Rymer's politeness carried her to the length of taking the journey to London to make inquiries at my door. I did not see her, of course. She left word that she would have the honor of calling again.

The second week followed. I had by that time perfectly recovered from my attack of bronchitis—and yet I was too ill to leave the house.

The doctor himself seemed to be at a loss to understand the symptoms that now presented themselves. A vile sensation of nausea tried my endurance, and an incomprehensible prostration of strength depressed my spirits. I felt such a strange reluctance to exert myself that I actually left it to Mrs. Mozeen to write to my uncle in my name, and say that I was not yet well enough to visit him. My medical adviser tried various methods of treatment; my housekeeper administered the prescribed medicines with unremitting care; but nothing came of it. A physician of great authority was called into consultation. Being completely puzzled, he retreated to the last refuge of bewildered doctors. I asked him what was the matter with me. And he answered: "Suppressed gout."

FIFTH EPOCH.

MIDWAY in the third week, my uncle wrote to me as follows:

"I have been obliged to request your friend Rothsay to bring his visit to a conclusion. Although he refuses to confess it, I have reason to believe that he has committed the folly of falling seriously in love with the young girl at my lodge gate. I have tried remonstrance in vain; and I write to his father at the same time that I write to you. There is much more that I might say. I reserve it for the time when I hope to have the pleasure of seeing you, restored to health."

Two days after the receipt of this alarming letter Rothsay returned to me.

Ill as I was, I forgot my sufferings the moment I looked at him. Wild and haggard, he stared at me with bloodshot eyes like a man demented.

"Do you think I am mad? I dare say I am. I can't live without her." Those were the first words he said when we shook hands.

But I had more influence over him than any other person; and, weak as I was, I exerted it. Little by little, he became more reasonable; he began to speak like his old self again.

To have expressed any surprise, on my part, at what had happened, would have been not only imprudent, but unworthy of him and of me. My first inquiry was suggested by the fear that he might have been hurried into openly confessing his passion to Susan—although his position forbade him to offer marriage. I had done him an injustice. His honorable nature had shrunk from the cruelty of raising hopes, which, for all he knew to the contrary, might never be realized. At the same time, he had his reasons for believing that he was at least personally acceptable to her.

"She was always glad to see me," said poor Rothsay. "We constantly talked of you. She spoke of your kindness so prettily and so gratefully. Oh, Lepel, it is not her beauty only that has won my heart! Her nature is the nature of an angel."

His voice failed him. For the first time in my remembrance of our long companionship, he burst into tears.

I was so shocked and distressed that I had the greatest difficulty in preserving my own self-control. In the effort to comfort him, I asked if he had ventured to confide in his father.

"You are the favorite son," I reminded him. "Is there no gleam of hope in the future?"

He had written to his father. In silence he gave me the letter in reply.

It was expressed with a moderation which I had hardly dared to expect. Mr. Rothsay the elder admitted that he had himself married for love, and that his wife's rank in the social scale (although higher than Susan's) had not been equal to his own.

"In such a family as ours," he wrote—perhaps with pardonable pride— "we raise our wives to our own degree. But this young person labors under a double disadvantage. She is obscure, and she is poor. What have you to offer her? Nothing. And what have I to give you? Nothing."

This meant, as I interpreted it, that the main obstacle in the way was Susan's poverty. And I was rich! In the excitement that possessed me, I followed the impulse of the moment headlong, like a child.

"While you were away from me," I said to Rothsay, "did you never once think of your old friend? Must I remind you that I can make Susan your wife with one stroke of my pen?" He looked at me in silent surprise. I took my check-book from the drawer of the table, and placed the inkstand within reach. "Susan's marriage portion," I said, "is a matter of a line of writing, with my name at the end of it."

He burst out with an exclamation that stopped me, just as my pen touched the paper.

"Good heavens!" he cried, "you are thinking of that play we saw at Rome! Are we on the stage? Are you performing the part of the Marquis— and am I the Count?"

I was so startled by this wild allusion to the past—I recognized with such astonishment the reproduction of one of the dramatic situations in the play, at a crisis in his life and mine—that the use of the pen remained suspended in my hand. For the first time in my life I was conscious of a sensation which resembled superstitious dread.

Rothsay recovered himself first. He misinterpreted what was passing in my mind.

"Don't think me ungrateful," he said. "You dear, kind, good fellow, consider for a moment, and you will see that it can't be. What would be said of her and of me, if you made Susan rich with your money, and if I married her? The poor innocent would be called your cast-off mistress. People would say: 'He has behaved liberally to her, and his needy friend has taken advantage of it.'"

The point of view which I had failed to see was put with terrible directness of expression: the conviction that I was wrong was literally forced on me. What reply could I make? Rothsay evidently felt for me.

"You are ill," he said, gently; "let me leave you to rest."

He held out his hand to say good-by. I insisted on his taking up his abode with me, for the present at least. Ordinary persuasion failed to induce him to yield. I put it on selfish grounds next.

"You have noticed that I am ill," I said, "I want you to keep me company."

He gave way directly.

Through the wakeful night, I tried to consider what moral remedies might be within our reach. The one useful conclusion at which I could arrive was to induce Rothsay to try what absence and change might do to compose his mind. To advise him to travel alone was out of the question. I wrote to his one other old friend besides myself—the friend who had taken him on a cruise in the Mediterranean.

The owner of the yacht had that very day given directions to have his vessel laid up for the winter season. He at once countermanded the order by telegraph. "I am an idle man," he said, "and I am as fond of Rothsay as you are. I will take him wherever he likes to go." It was not easy to persuade the object of these kind intentions to profit by them. Nothing that I could say roused him. I spoke to him of his picture. He had left it at my uncle's house, and neither knew nor cared to know whether it had been sold or not. The one consideration which ultimately influenced Rothsay was presented by the doctor; speaking as follows (to quote his own explanation) in the interests of my health:

"I warned your friend," he said, "that his conduct was causing anxiety which you were not strong enough to bear. On hearing this he at once promised to follow the advice which you had given to him, and to join the yacht. As you know, he has kept his word. May I ask if he has ever followed the medical profession?"

Replying in the negative, I begged the doctor to tell me why he had put his question.

He answered, "Mr. Rothsay requested me to tell him all that I knew about your illness. I complied, of course; mentioning that I had lately adopted a new method of treatment, and that I had every reason to feel confident of the results. He was so interested in the symptoms of your illness, and in the remedies being tried, that he took notes in his pocketbook of what I had said. When he paid me that compliment, I thought it possible that I might be speaking to a colleague."

I was pleased to hear of my friend's anxiety for my recovery. If I had been in better health, I might have asked myself what reason he could have had for

748

making those entries in his pocketbook.

Three days later, another proof reached me of Rothsay's anxiety for my welfare.

The owner of the yacht wrote to beg that I would send him a report of my health, addressed to a port on the south coast of England, to which they were then bound. "If we don't hear good news," he added, "I have reason to fear that Rothsay will overthrow our plans for the recovery of his peace of mind by leaving the vessel, and making his own inquiries at your bedside."

With no small difficulty I roused myself sufficiently to write a few words with my own hand. They were words that lied—for my poor friend's sake. In a postscript, I begged my correspondent to let me hear if the effect produced on Rothsay had answered to our hopes and expectations.

SIXTH EPOCH.

THE weary days followed each other—and time failed to justify the doctor's confidence in his new remedies. I grew weaker and weaker.

My uncle came to see me. He was so alarmed that he insisted on a consultation being held with his own physician. Another great authority was called in, at the same time, by the urgent request of my own medical man. These distinguished persons held more than one privy council, before they would consent to give a positive opinion. It was an evasive opinion (encumbered with hard words of Greek and Roman origin) when it was at last pronounced. I waited until they had taken their leave, and then appealed to my own doctor. "What do these men really think?" I asked. "Shall I live, or die?"

The doctor answered for himself as well as for his illustrious colleagues. "We have great faith in the new prescriptions," he said.

I understood what that meant. They were afraid to tell me the truth. I insisted on the truth.

"How long shall I live?" I said. "Till the end of the year?"

The reply followed in one terrible word:

"Perhaps."

It was then the first week in December. I understood that I might reckon—at the utmost—on three weeks of life. What I felt, on arriving at this conclusion, I shall not say. It is the one secret I keep from the readers of these lines.

The next day, Mrs. Rymer called once more to make inquiries. Not satisfied with the servant's report, she entreated that I would consent to see her. My housekeeper, with her customary kindness, undertook to convey the message. If she had been a wicked woman, would she have acted in this way? "Mrs. Rymer seems to be sadly distressed," she pleaded. "As I understand, sir, she is suffering under some domestic anxiety which can only be mentioned to yourself."

Did this anxiety relate to Susan? The bare doubt of it decided me. I consented to see Mrs. Rymer. Feeling it necessary to control her in the use of her tongue, I spoke the moment the door was opened.

"I am suffering from illness; and I must ask you to spare me as much as possible. What do you wish to say to me?"

The tone in which I addressed Mrs. Rymer would have offended a more sensitive woman. The truth is, she had chosen an unfortunate time for her visit. There were fluctuations in the progress of my malady; there were days when I felt better, and days when I felt worse—and this was a bad day. Moreover, my uncle had tried my temper that morning. He had called to see me, on his way to winter in the south of France by his physician's advice; and he recommended a trial of change of air in my case also. His country house (only thirty miles from London) was entirely at my disposal; and the railway supplied beds for invalids. It was useless to answer that I was not equal to the effort. He reminded me that I had exerted myself to leave my bedchamber for my arm-chair in the next room, and that a little additional resolution would enable me to follow his advice. We parted in a state of irritation on either side which, so far as I was concerned, had not subsided yet.

"I wish to speak to you, sir, about my daughter," Mrs. Rymer answered.

The mere allusion to Susan had its composing effect on me. I said kindly that I hoped she was well.

"Well in body," Mrs. Rymer announced. "Far from it, sir, in mind."

Before I could ask what this meant, we were interrupted by the appearance of the servant, bringing the letters which had arrived for me by the afternoon post. I told the man, impatiently, to put them on the table at my side.

"What is distressing Susan?" I inquired, without stopping to look at the letters.

"She is fretting, sir, about your illness. Oh, Mr. Lepel, if you would only try the sweet country air! If you only had my good little Susan to nurse you!"

She, too, taking my uncle's view! And talking of Susan as my nurse!

"What are you thinking of?" I asked her. "A young girl like your daughter nursing Me! You ought to have more regard for Susan's good name!"

"I know what you ought to do!" She made that strange reply with a furtive look at me, half in anger, half in alarm.

"Go on," I said.

"Will you turn me out of your house for my impudence?" she asked.

"I will hear what you have to say to me. What ought I to do?"

"Marry Susan."

I heard the woman plainly—and yet, I declare, I doubted the evidence of my senses.

"She's breaking her heart for you," Mrs. Rymer burst out. "She's been in love with you since you first darkened our doors—and it will end in the neighbors finding it out. I did my duty to her; I tried to stop it; I tried to prevent you from seeing her, when you went away. Too late; the mischief was done. When I see my girl fading day by day—crying about you in secret, talking about you in her dreams—I can't stand it; I must speak out. Oh, yes,

I know how far beneath you she is—the daughter of your uncle's servant. But she's your equal, sir, in the sight of Heaven. My lord's priest converted her only last year—and my Susan is as good a Papist as yourself."

How could I let this go on? I felt that I ought to have stopped it before.

"It's possible," I said, "that you may not be deliberately deceiving me. If you are yourself deceived, I am bound to tell you the truth. Mr. Rothsay loves your daughter, and, what is more, Mr. Rothsay has reason to know that Susan—"

"That Susan loves him?" she interposed, with a mocking laugh. "Oh, Mr. Lepel, is it possible that a clever man like you can't see clearer than that? My girl in love with Mr. Rothsay! She wouldn't have looked at him a second time if he hadn't talked to her about you. When I complained privately to my lord of Mr. Rothsay hanging about the lodge, do you think she turned as pale as ashes, and cried when he passed through the gate, and said good-by?"

She had complained of Rothsay to Lord Lepel—I understood her at last! She knew that my friend and all his family were poor. She had put her own construction on the innocent interest that I had taken in her daughter. Careless of the difference in rank, blind to the malady that was killing me, she was now bent on separating Rothsay and Susan, by throwing the girl into the arms of a rich husband like myself!

"You are wasting your breath," I told her; "I don't believe one word you say to me."

"Believe Susan, then!" cried the reckless woman. "Let me bring her here. If she's too shamefaced to own the truth, look at her—that's all I ask—look at her, and judge for yourself!"

This was intolerable. In justice to Susan, in justice to Rothsay, I insisted on silence. "No more of it!" I said. "Take care how you provoke me. Don't you see that I am ill? don't you see that you are irritating me to no purpose?"

She altered her tone. "I'll wait," she said, quietly, "while you compose yourself."

With those words, she walked to the window, and stood there with her back toward me. Was the wretch taking advantage of my helpless condition? I stretched out my hand to ring the bell, and have her sent away—and hesitated to degrade Susan's mother, for Susan's sake. In my state of prostration, how could I arrive at a decision? My mind was dreadfully disturbed; I felt the imperative necessity of turning my thoughts to some other subject. Looking about me, the letters on the table attracted my attention. Mechanically, I took them up; mechanically I put them down again. Two of them slipped from my trembling fingers; my eyes fell on the uppermost of the two. The address was in the handwriting of the good friend with whom Rothsay was sailing.

Just as I had been speaking of Rothsay, here was the news of him for which I had been waiting.

I opened the letter and read these words:

"There is, I fear, but little hope for our friend—unless this girl on whom he has set his heart can (by some lucky change of circumstances) become his wife. He has tried to master his weakness; but his own infatuation is too much for him. He is really and truly in a state of despair. Two evenings since—to give you a melancholy example of what I mean—I was in my cabin, when I heard the alarm of a man overboard. The man was Rothsay. My sailing-master, seeing that he was unable to swim, jumped into the sea and rescued him, as I got on deck. Rothsay declares it to have been an accident; and everybody believes him but myself. I know the state of his mind. Don't be alarmed; I will have him well looked after; and I won't give him up just yet. We are still bound southward, with a fair wind. If the new scenes which I hope to show him prove to be of no avail, I must reluctantly take him back to England. In that case, which I don't like to contemplate, you may see him again—perhaps in a month's time."

He might return in a month's time—return to hear of the death of the one friend, on whose power and will to help him he might have relied. If I failed to employ in his interests the short interval of life still left to me, could I doubt (after what I had just read) what the end would be? How could I help him? Oh, God! how could I help him?

753

Mrs. Rymer left the window, and returned to the chair which she had occupied when I first received her.

"Are you quieter in your mind now?" she asked.

I neither answered her nor looked at her.

Still determined to reach her end, she tried again to force her unhappy daughter on me. "Will you consent," she persisted, "to see Susan?"

If she had been a little nearer to me, I am afraid I should have struck her. "You wretch!" I said, "do you know that I am a dying man?"

"While there's life there's hope," Mrs. Rymer remarked.

I ought to have controlled myself; but it was not to be done.

"Hope of your daughter being my rich widow?" I asked.

Her bitter answer followed instantly.

"Even then," she said, "Susan wouldn't marry Rothsay."

A lie! If circumstances favored her, I knew, on Rothsay's authority, what Susan would do.

The thought burst on my mind, like light bursting on the eyes of a man restored to sight. If Susan agreed to go through the form of marriage with a dying bridegroom, my rich widow could (and would) become Rothsay's wife. Once more, the remembrance of the play at Rome returned, and set the last embers of resolution, which sickness and suffering had left to me, in a flame. The devoted friend of that imaginary story had counted on death to complete his generous purpose in vain: he had been condemned by the tribunal of man, and had been reprieved. I—in his place, and with his self-sacrifice in my mind—might found a firmer trust in the future; for I had been condemned by the tribunal of God.

Encouraged by my silence, the obstinate woman persisted. "Won't you even send a message to Susan?" she asked.

Rashly, madly, without an instant's hesitation, I answered:

754

"Go back to Susan, and say I leave it to her."

Mrs. Rymer started to her feet. "You leave it to Susan to be your wife, if she likes?"

"I do."

"And if she consents?"

"I consent."

In two weeks and a day from that time, the deed was done. When Rothsay returned to England, he would ask for Susan—and he would find my virgin-widow rich and free.

SEVENTH EPOCH.

WHATEVER may be thought of my conduct, let me say this in justice to myself—I was resolved that Susan should not be deceived.

Half an hour after Mrs. Rymer had left my house, I wrote to her daughter, plainly revealing the motive which led me to offer marriage, solely in the future interest of Rothsay and herself. "If you refuse," I said in conclusion, "you may depend on my understanding you and feeling for you. But, if you consent—then I have a favor to ask Never let us speak to one another of the profanation that we have agreed to commit, for your faithful lover's sake."

I had formed a high opinion of Susan—too high an opinion as it seemed. Her reply surprised and disappointed me. In other words, she gave her consent.

I stipulated that the marriage should be kept strictly secret, for a certain period. In my own mind I decided that the interval should be held to expire, either on the day of my death, or on the day when Rothsay returned.

My next proceeding was to write in confidence to the priest whom I have already mentioned, in an earlier part of these pages. He has reasons of his own for not permitting me to disclose the motive which induced him to celebrate my marriage privately in the chapel at Lord Lepel's house. My uncle's desire that I should try change of air, as offering a last chance of recovery, was known to my medical attendant, and served as a sufficient reason (although he protested against the risk) for my removal to the country. I was carried to the station, and placed on a bed—slung by ropes to the ceiling of a saloon carriage, so as to prevent me from feeling the vibration when the train was in motion. Faithful Mrs. Mozeen entreated to be allowed to accompany me. I was reluctantly compelled to refuse compliance with this request, in justice to the claims of my lord's housekeeper; who had been accustomed to exercise undivided authority in the household, and who had made every preparation for my comfort. With her own hands, Mrs. Mozeen packed everything that I required, including the medicines prescribed for the occasion. She was deeply affected, poor soul, when we parted.

I bore the journey—happily for me, it was a short one—better than had been anticipated. For the first few days that followed, the purer air of the country seemed, in some degree, to revive me. But the deadly sense of weakness, the slow sinking of the vital power in me, returned as the time drew near for the marriage. The ceremony was performed at night. Only Susan and her mother were present. No persons in the house but ourselves had the faintest suspicion of what had happened.

I signed my new will (the priest and Mrs. Rymer being the witnesses) in my bed that night. It left everything that I possessed, excepting a legacy to Mrs. Mozeen, to my wife.

Obliged, it is needless to say, to preserve appearances, Susan remained at the lodge as usual. But it was impossible to resist her entreaty to be allowed to attend on me, for a few hours daily, as assistant to the regular nurse. When she was alone with me, and had no inquisitive eyes to dread, the poor girl showed a depth of feeling, which I was unable to reconcile with the motives that could alone have induced her (as I then supposed) to consent to the mockery of our marriage. On occasions when I was so far able to resist the languor that oppressed me as to observe what was passing at my bedside—I saw Susan look at me as if there were thoughts in her pressing for utterance which she hesitated to express. Once, she herself acknowledged this. "I have so much to say to you," she owned, "when you are stronger and fitter to hear me." At other times, her nerves seemed to be shaken by the spectacle of my sufferings. Her kind hands trembled and made mistakes, when they had any nursing duties to perform near me. The servants, noticing her, used to say, "That pretty girl seems to be the most awkward person in the house." On the day that followed the ceremony in the chapel, this want of self-control brought about an accident which led to serious results.

In removing the small chest which held my medicines from the shelf on which it was placed, Susan let it drop on the floor. The two full bottles still left were so completely shattered that not even a teaspoonful of the contents was saved.

Shocked at what she had done, the poor girl volunteered to go herself to my chemist in London by the first train. I refused to allow it. What did it matter to me now, if my death from exhaustion was hastened by a day or two? Why need my life be prolonged artificially by drugs, when I had nothing left to live for? An excuse for me which would satisfy others was easily found. I said that I had been long weary of physic, and that the accident had decided me on refusing to take more.

That night I did not wake quite so often as usual. When she came to me the next day, Susan noticed that I looked better. The day after, the other nurse made the same observation. At the end of the week, I was able to leave my bed, and sit by the fireside, while Susan read to me. Some mysterious change in my health had completely falsified the prediction of the medical men. I sent to London for my doctor—and told him that the improvement in me had begun on the day when I left off taking his remedies. "Can you explain it?" I asked.

He answered that no such "resurrection from the dead" (as he called it) had ever happened in his long experience. On leaving me, he asked for the latest prescriptions that had been written. I inquired what he was going to do with them. "I mean to go to the chemist," he replied, "and to satisfy myself that your medicines have been properly made up."

I owed it to Mrs. Mozeen's true interest in me to tell her what had happened. The same day I wrote to her. I also mentioned what the doctor had said, and asked her to call on him, and ascertain if the prescriptions had been shown to the chemist, and if any mistake had been made.

A more innocently intended letter than this never was written. And yet there are people who have declared that it was inspired by suspicion of Mrs. Mozeen!

EIGHTH EPOCH.

WHETHER I was so weakened by illness as to be incapable of giving my mind to more than one subject for reflection at a time (that subject being now the extraordinary recovery of my health)—or whether I was preoccupied by the effort, which I was in honor bound to make, to resist the growing attraction to me of Susan's society—I cannot presume to say. This only I know: when the discovery of the terrible position toward Rothsay in which I now stood suddenly overwhelmed me, an interval of some days had passed. I cannot account for it. I can only say—so it was.

Susan was in the room. I was wholly unable to hide from her the sudden change of color which betrayed the horror that had overpowered me. She said, anxiously: "What has frightened you?"

I don't think I heard her. The play was in my memory again—the fatal play, which had wound itself into the texture of Rothsay's life and mine. In vivid remembrance, I saw once more the dramatic situation of the first act, and shrank from the reflection of it in the disaster which had fallen on my friend and myself.

"What has frightened you?" Susan repeated.

I answered in one word—I whispered his name: "Rothsay!"

She looked at me in innocent surprise. "Has he met with some misfortune?" she asked, quietly.

"Misfortune"—did she call it? Had I not said enough to disturb her tranquillity in mentioning Rothsay's name? "I am living!" I said. "Living—and likely to live!"

Her answer expressed fervent gratitude. "Thank God for it!"

I looked at her, astonished as she had been astonished when she looked at me.

"Susan, Susan," I cried—"must I own it? I love you!"

She came nearer to me with timid pleasure in her eyes—with the first faint light of a smile playing round her lips.

"You say it very strangely," she murmured. "Surely, my dear one, you ought to love me? Since the first day when you gave me my French lesson—haven't I loved You?"

"You love me?" I repeated. "Have you read—?" My voice failed me; I could say no more.

She turned pale. "Read what?" she asked.

"My letter."

"What letter?"

"The letter I wrote to you before we were married."

Am I a coward? The bare recollection of what followed that reply makes me tremble. Time has passed. I am a new man now; my health is restored; my happiness is assured: I ought to be able to write on. No: it is not to be done. How can I think coolly? how force myself to record the suffering that I innocently, most innocently, inflicted on the sweetest and truest of women? Nothing saved us from a parting as absolute as the parting that follows death but the confession that had been wrung from me at a time when my motive spoke for itself. The artless avowal of her affection had been justified, had been honored, by the words which laid my heart at her feet when I said "I love you."

She had risen to leave me. In a last look, we had silently resigned ourselves to wait, apart from each other, for the day of reckoning that must follow Rothsay's return, when we heard the sound of carriage-wheels on the drive that led to the house. In a minute more the man himself entered the room.

He looked first at Susan—then at me. In both of us he saw the traces that told of agitation endured, but not yet composed. Worn and weary he waited, hesitating, near the door.

"Am I intruding?" he asked.

"We were thinking of you, and speaking of you," I replied, "just before you came in."

"We?" he repeated, turning toward Susan once more. After a pause, he offered me his hand—and drew it back.

"You don't shake hands with me," he said.

"I am waiting, Rothsay, until I know that we are the same firm friends as ever."

For the third time he looked at Susan.

"Will you shake hands?" he asked.

She gave him her hand cordially. "May I stay here?" she said, addressing herself to me.

In my situation at that moment, I understood the generous purpose that animated her. But she had suffered enough already—I led her gently to the door. "It will be better," I whispered, "if you will wait downstairs in the library." She hesitated. "What will they say in the house?" she objected, thinking of the servants and of the humble position which she was still supposed to occupy. "It matters nothing what they say, now," I told her. She left us.

"There seems to be some private understanding between you," Rothsay said, when we were alone.

"You shall hear what it is," I answered. "But I must beg you to excuse me if I speak first of myself."

"Are you alluding to your health?"

"Yes."

"Quite needless, Lepel. I met your doctor this morning. I know that a council of physicians decided you would die before the year was out."

He paused there.

"And they proved to be wrong," I added.

"They might have proved to be right," Rothsay rejoined, "but for the accident which spilled your medicine and the despair of yourself which decided you on taking no more."

I could hardly believe that I understood him. "Do you assert," I said, "that my medicine would have killed me, if I had taken the rest of it?"

"I have no doubt that it would."

"Will you explain what you mean?"

"Let me have your explanation first. I was not prepared to find Susan in your room. I was surprised to see traces of tears in her face. Something has happened in my absence. Am I concerned in it?"

"You are."

I said it quietly—in full possession of myself. The trial of fortitude through which I had already passed seemed to have blunted my customary sense of feeling. I approached the disclosure which I was now bound to make with steady resolution, resigned to the worst that could happen when the truth was known.

"Do you remember the time," I resumed, "when I was so eager to serve you that I proposed to make Susan your wife by making her rich?"

"Yes."

"Do you remember asking me if I was thinking of the play we saw together at Rome? Is the story as present to your mind now, as it was then?"

"Quite as present."

"You asked if I was performing the part of the Marquis—and if you were the Count. Rothsay! the devotion of that ideal character to his friend has been my devotion; his conviction that his death would justify what he had done for his friend's sake, has been my conviction; and as it ended with him, so it has ended with me—his terrible position is my terrible position toward you, at this moment."

"Are you mad?" Rothsay asked, sternly.

I passed over that first outbreak of his anger in silence.

"Do you mean to tell me you have married Susan?" he went on.

"Bear this in mind," I said. "When I married her, I was doomed to death. Nay, more. In your interests—as God is my witness—I welcomed death."

He stepped up to me, in silence, and raised his hand with a threatening gesture.

That action at once deprived me of my self-possession. I spoke with the ungovernable rashness of a boy.

"Carry out your intention," I said. "Insult me."

His hand dropped.

"Insult me," I repeated; "it is one way out of the unendurable situation in which we are placed. You may trust me to challenge you. Duels are still fought on the Continent; I will follow you abroad; I will choose pistols; I will take care that we fight on the fatal foreign system; and I will purposely miss you. Make her what I intended her to be—my rich widow."

He looked at me attentively.

"Is that your refuge?" he asked, scornfully. "No! I won't help you to commit suicide."

God forgive me! I was possessed by a spirit of reckless despair; I did my best to provoke him.

"Reconsider your decision," I said; "and remember—you tried to commit suicide yourself."

He turned quickly to the door, as if he distrusted his own powers of self-control.

"I wish to speak to Susan," he said, keeping his back turned on me.

"You will find her in the library."

He left me.

I went to the window. I opened it and let the cold wintry air blow over my burning head. I don't know how long I sat at the window. There came a time when I saw Rothsay on the house steps. He walked rapidly toward the park gate. His head was down; he never once looked back at the room in which he had left me.

As he passed out of my sight, I felt a hand laid gently on my shoulder. Susan had returned to me.

"He will not come back," she said. "Try still to remember him as your old friend. He asks you to forgive and forget."

She had made the peace between us. I was deeply touched; my eyes filled with tears as I looked at her. She kissed me on the forehead and went out. I afterward asked what had passed between them when Rothsay spoke with her in the library. She never has told me what they said to each other; and she never will. She is right.

Later in the day I was told that Mrs. Rymer had called, and wished to "pay her respects."

I refused to see her. Whatever claim she might have otherwise had on my consideration had been forfeited by the infamy of her conduct, when she intercepted my letter to Susan. Her sense of injury on receiving my message was expressed in writing, and was sent to me the same evening. The last sentence in her letter was characteristic of the woman.

"However your pride may despise me," she wrote, "I am indebted to you for the rise in life that I have always desired. You may refuse to see me—but you can't prevent my being the mother-in-law of a gentleman."

Soon afterward, I received a visit which I had hardly ventured to expect.

Busy as he was in London, my doctor came to see me. He was not in his usual good spirits.

"I hope you don't bring me any bad news?" I said.

"You shall judge for yourself," he replied. "I come from Mr. Rothsay, to say for him what he is not able to say for himself."

"Where is he?"

"He has left England."

"For any purpose that you know of?"

"Yes. He has sailed to join the expedition of rescue—I ought rather to call it the forlorn hope—which is to search for the lost explorers in Central Australia."

In other words, he had gone to seek death in the fatal footsteps of Burke and Wills. I could not trust myself to speak.

The doctor saw that there was a reason for my silence, and that he would do well not to notice it. He changed the subject.

"May I ask," he said, "if you have heard from the servants left in charge at your house in London?"

"Has anything happened?"

"Something has happened which they are evidently afraid to tell you, knowing the high opinion which you have of Mrs. Mozeen. She has suddenly quitted your service, and has gone, nobody knows where. I have taken charge of a letter which she left for you."

He handed me the letter. As soon as I had recovered myself, I looked at it.

There was this inscription on the address: "For my good master, to wait until he returns home." The few lines in the letter itself ran thus:

"Distressing circumstances oblige me to leave you, sir, and do not permit me to enter into particulars. In asking your pardon, I offer my sincere thanks for your kindness, and my fervent prayers for your welfare."

That was all. The date had a special interest for me. Mrs. Mozeen had written on the day when she must have received my letter—the letter which has already appeared in these pages.

"Is there really nothing known of the poor woman's motives?" I asked.

"There are two explanations suggested," the doctor informed me. "One of them, which is offered by your female servants, seems to me absurd. They declare that Mrs. Mozeen, at her mature age, was in love with the young man who is your footman! It is even asserted that she tried to recommend herself to him, by speaking of the money which she expected to bring to the man who would make her his wife. The footman's reply, informing her that he was already engaged to be married, is alleged to be the cause which has driven her from your house."

I begged that the doctor would not trouble himself to repeat more of what my women servants had said.

"If the other explanation," I added, "is equally unworthy of notice—"

"The other explanation," the doctor interposed, "comes from Mr. Rothsay, and is of a very serious kind."

Rothsay's opinion demanded my respect.

"What view does he take?" I inquired.

"A view that startles me," the doctor said. "You remember my telling you of the interest he took in your symptoms, and in the remedies I had employed? Well! Mr. Rothsay accounts for the incomprehensible recovery of your health by asserting that poison—probably administered in small quantities, and intermitted at intervals in fear of discovery—has been mixed with your medicine; and he asserts that the guilty person is Mrs. Mozeen."

It was impossible that I could openly express the indignation that I felt on hearing this. My position toward Rothsay forced me to restrain myself.

"May I ask," the doctor continued, "if Mrs. Mozeen was aware that she

765

had a legacy to expect at your death?"

"Certainly."

"Has she a brother who is one of the dispensers employed by your chemists?"

"Yes."

"Did she know that I doubted if my prescriptions had been properly prepared, and that I intended to make inquiries?"

"I wrote to her myself on the subject."

"Do you think her brother told her that I was referred to him, when I went to the chemists?"

"I have no means of knowing what her brother did."

"Can you at least tell me when she received your letter?"

"She must have received it on the day when she left my house."

The doctor rose with a grave face.

"These are rather extraordinary coincidences," he remarked.

I merely replied, "Mrs. Mozeen is as incapable of poisoning as I am."

The doctor wished me good-morning.

I repeat here my conviction of my housekeeper's innocence. I protest against the cruelty which accuses her. And, whatever may have been her motive in suddenly leaving my service, I declare that she still possesses my sympathy and esteem, and I invite her to return to me if she ever sees these lines.

I have only to add, by way of postscript, that we have heard of the safe return of the expedition of rescue. Time, as my wife and I both hope, may yet convince Rothsay that he will not be wrong in counting on Susan's love—the love of a sister.

In the meanwhile we possess a memorial of our absent friend. We have bought his picture.

MR. CAPTAIN AND THE NYMPH.

I.

"THE Captain is still in the prime of life," the widow remarked. "He has given up his ship; he possesses a sufficient income, and he has nobody to live with him. I should like to know why he doesn't marry."

"The Captain was excessively rude to Me," the widow's younger sister added, on her side. "When we took leave of him in London, I asked if there was any chance of his joining us at Brighton this season. He turned his back on me as if I had mortally offended him; and he made me this extraordinary answer: 'Miss! I hate the sight of the sea.' The man has been a sailor all his life. What does he mean by saying that he hates the sight of the sea?"

These questions were addressed to a third person present—and the person was a man. He was entirely at the mercy of the widow and the widow's sister. The other ladies of the family—who might have taken him under their protection—had gone to an evening concert. He was known to be the Captain's friend, and to be well acquainted with events in the Captain's life. As it happened, he had reasons for hesitating to revive associations connected with those events. But what polite alternative was left to him? He must either inflict disappointment, and, worse still, aggravate curiosity—or he must resign himself to circumstances, and tell the ladies why the Captain would never marry, and why (sailor as he was) he hated the sight of the sea. They were both young women and handsome women—and the person to whom they had appealed (being a man) followed the example of submission to the sex, first set in the garden of Eden. He enlightened the ladies, in the terms that follow:

THE British merchantman, Fortuna, sailed from the port of Liverpool (at a date which it is not necessary to specify) with the morning tide. She was bound for certain islands in the Pacific Ocean, in search of a cargo of sandal-wood—a commodity which, in those days, found a ready and profitable market in the Chinese Empire.

A large discretion was reposed in the Captain by the owners, who knew him to be not only trustworthy, but a man of rare ability, carefully cultivated during the leisure hours of a seafaring life. Devoted heart and soul to his professional duties, he was a hard reader and an excellent linguist as well. Having had considerable experience among the inhabitants of the Pacific Islands, he had attentively studied their characters, and had mastered their language in more than one of its many dialects. Thanks to the valuable information thus obtained, the Captain was never at a loss to conciliate the islanders. He had more than once succeeded in finding a cargo under circumstances in which other captains had failed.

Possessing these merits, he had also his fair share of human defects. For instance, he was a little too conscious of his own good looks—of his bright chestnut hair and whiskers, of his beautiful blue eyes, of his fair white skin, which many a woman had looked at with the admiration that is akin to envy. His shapely hands were protected by gloves; a broad-brimmed hat sheltered his complexion in fine weather from the sun. He was nice in the choice of his perfumes; he never drank spirits, and the smell of tobacco was abhorrent to him. New men among his officers and his crew, seeing him in his cabin, perfectly dressed, washed, and brushed until he was an object speckless to look upon—a merchant-captain soft of voice, careful in his choice of words, devoted to study in his leisure hours—were apt to conclude that they had trusted themselves at sea under a commander who was an anomalous mixture of a schoolmaster and a dandy. But if the slightest infraction of discipline took place, or if the storm rose and the vessel proved to be in peril, it was soon discovered that the gloved hands held a rod of iron; that the soft voice could make itself heard through wind and sea from one end of the deck to the other; and that it issued orders which the greatest fool on board discovered to be orders that had saved the ship. Throughout his professional life, the general impression that this variously gifted man produced on the little world about him was always the same. Some few liked him; everybody respected him; nobody understood him. The Captain accepted these results. He persisted in reading his books and protecting his complexion, with this result: his owners shook hands with him, and put up with his gloves.

The Fortuna touched at Rio for water, and for supplies of food which might prove useful in case of scurvy. In due time the ship rounded Cape Horn, favored by the finest weather ever known in those latitudes by the oldest hand on board. The mate—one Mr. Duncalf—a boozing, wheezing, self-confident old sea-dog, with a flaming face and a vast vocabulary of oaths, swore that he didn't like it. "The foul weather's coming, my lads," said Mr. Duncalf. "Mark my words, there'll be wind enough to take the curl out of the Captain's whiskers before we are many days older!"

For one uneventful week, the ship cruised in search of the islands to which the owners had directed her. At the end of that time the wind took the predicted liberties with the Captain's whiskers; and Mr. Duncalf stood revealed to an admiring crew in the character of a true prophet.

For three days and three nights the Fortuna ran before the storm, at the mercy of wind and sea. On the fourth morning the gale blew itself out, the sun appeared again toward noon, and the Captain was able to take an observation. The result informed him that he was in a part of the Pacific Ocean with which he was entirely unacquainted. Thereupon, the officers were called to a council in the cabin.

Mr. Duncalf, as became his rank, was consulted first. His opinion possessed the merit of brevity. "My lads, this ship's bewitched. Take my word for it, we shall wish ourselves back in our own latitudes before we are many days older." Which, being interpreted, meant that Mr. Duncalf was lost, like his superior officer, in a part of the ocean of which he knew nothing.

The remaining members of the council having no suggestions to offer, left the Captain to take his own way. He decided (the weather being fine again) to stand on under an easy press of sail for four-and-twenty hours more, and to see if anything came of it.

Soon after nightfall, something did come of it. The lookout forward hailed the quarter-deck with the dread cry, "Breakers ahead!" In less than a minute more, everybody heard the crash of the broken water. The Fortuna was put about, and came round slowly in the light wind. Thanks to the timely alarm and the fine weather, the safety of the vessel was easily provided for. They kept her under a short sail; and they waited for the morning.

The dawn showed them in the distance a glorious green island, not marked in the ship's charts—an island girt about by a coral-reef, and having in its midst a high-peaked mountain which looked, through the telescope, like a mountain of volcanic origin. Mr. Duncalf, taking his morning draught of rum and water, shook his groggy old head and said (and swore): "My lads, I don't like the look of that island." The Captain was of a different opinion. He had one of the ship's boats put into the water; he armed himself and four of his crew who accompanied him; and away he went in the morning sunlight to visit the island.

Skirting round the coral reef, they found a natural breach, which proved to be broad enough and deep enough not only for the passage of the boat, but of the ship herself if needful. Crossing the broad inner belt of smooth water, they approached the golden sands of the island, strew ed with magnificent shells, and crowded by the dusky islanders—men, women, and children, all waiting in breathless astonishment to see the strangers land.

The Captain kept the boat off, and examined the islanders carefully. The innocent, simple people danced, and sang, and ran into the water, imploring their wonderful white visitors by gestures to come on shore. Not a creature among them carried arms of any sort; a hospitable curiosity animated the entire population. The men cried out, in their smooth musical language, "Come and eat!" and the plump black-eyed women, all laughing together, added their own invitation, "Come and be kissed!" Was it in mortals to resist such temptations as these? The Captain led the way on shore, and the women surrounded him in an instant, and screamed for joy at the glorious spectacle of his whiskers, his complexion, and his gloves. So the mariners from the far north were welcomed to the newly-discovered island.

III.

THE morning wore on. Mr. Duncalf, in charge of the ship, cursing the island over his rum and water, as a "beastly green strip of a place, not laid down in any Christian chart," was kept waiting four mortal hours before the Captain returned to his command, and reported himself to his officers as follows:

He had found his knowledge of the Polynesian dialects sufficient to make himself in some degree understood by the natives of the new island. Under the guidance of the chief he had made a first journey of exploration, and had seen for himself that the place was a marvel of natural beauty and fertility. The one barren spot in it was the peak of the volcanic mountain, composed of crumbling rock; originally no doubt lava and ashes, which had cooled and consolidated with the lapse of time. So far as he could see, the crater at the top was now an extinct crater. But, if he had understood rightly, the chief had spoken of earthquakes and eruptions at certain bygone periods, some of which lay within his own earliest recollections of the place.

Adverting next to considerations of practical utility, the Captain announced that he had seen sandal-wood enough on the island to load a dozen ships, and that the natives were willing to part with it for a few toys and trinkets generally distributed among them. To the mate's disgust, the Fortuna was taken inside the reef that day, and was anchored before sunset in a natural harbor. Twelve hours of recreation, beginning with the next morning, were granted to the men, under the wise restrictions in such cases established by the Captain. That interval over, the work of cutting the precious wood and loading the ship was to be unremittingly pursued.

Mr. Duncalf had the first watch after the Fortuna had been made snug. He took the boatswain aside (an ancient sea-dog like himself), and he said in a gruff whisper: "My lad, this here ain't the island laid down in our sailing orders. See if mischief don't come of disobeying orders before we are many days older."

Nothing in the shape of mischief happened that night. But at sunrise the next morning a suspicious circumstance occurred; and Mr. Duncalf whispered to the boatswain: "What did I tell you?" The Captain and the chief of the islanders held a private conference in the cabin, and the Captain, after first forbidding any communication with the shore until his return, suddenly left the ship, alone with the chief, in the chief's own canoe.

What did this strange disappearance mean? The Captain himself, when he took his seat in the canoe, would have been puzzled to answer that

771

question. He asked, in the nearest approach that his knowledge could make to the language used in the island, whether he would be a long time or a short time absent from his ship.

The chief answered mysteriously (as the Captain understood him) in these words: "Long time or short time, your life depends on it, and the lives of your men."

Paddling his light little boat in silence over the smooth water inside the reef, the chief took his visitor ashore at a part of the island which was quite new to the Captain. The two crossed a ravine, and ascended an eminence beyond. There the chief stopped, and silently pointed out to sea.

The Captain looked in the direction indicated to him, and discovered a second and a smaller island, lying away to the southwest. Taking out his telescope from the case by which it was slung at his back, he narrowly examined the place. Two of the native canoes were lying off the shore of the new island; and the men in them appeared to be all kneeling or crouching in curiously chosen attitudes. Shifting the range of his glass, he next beheld a white-robed figure, tall and solitary—the one inhabitant of the island whom he could discover. The man was standing on the highest point of a rocky cape. A fire was burning at his feet. Now he lifted his arms solemnly to the sky; now he dropped some invisible fuel into the fire, which made a blue smoke; and now he cast other invisible objects into the canoes floating beneath him, which the islanders reverently received with bodies that crouched in abject submission. Lowering his telescope, the Captain looked round at the chief for an explanation. The chief gave the explanation readily. His language was interpreted by the English stranger in these terms:

"Wonderful white man! the island you see yonder is a Holy Island. As such it is Taboo—an island sanctified and set apart. The honorable person whom you notice on the rock is an all-powerful favorite of the gods. He is by vocation a Sorcerer, and by rank a Priest. You now see him casting charms and blessings into the canoes of our fishermen, who kneel to him for fine weather and great plenty of fish. If any profane person, native or stranger, presumes to set foot on that island, my otherwise peaceful subjects will (in the performance of a religious duty) put that person to death. Mention this to your men. They will be fed by my male people, and fondled by my female people, so long as they keep clear of the Holy Isle. As they value their lives, let them respect this prohibition. Is it understood between us? Wonderful white man! my canoe is waiting for you. Let us go back."

Understanding enough of the chief's language (illustrated by his gestures) to receive in the right spirit the communication thus addressed to him, the Captain repeated the warning to the ship's company in the plainest possible English. The officers and men then took their holiday on shore, with the exception of Mr. Duncalf, who positively refused to leave the ship. For twelve delightful hours they were fed by the male people, and fondled by the female people, and then they were mercilessly torn from the flesh-pots and the arms of their new friends, and set to work on the sandal-wood in good earnest. Mr. Duncalf superintended the loading, and waited for the mischief that was to come of disobeying the owners' orders with a confidence worthy of a better cause.

IV.

STRANGELY enough, chance once more declared itself in favor of the mate's point of view. The mischief did actually come; and the chosen instrument of it was a handsome young islander, who was one of the sons of the chief.

The Captain had taken a fancy to the sweet-tempered, intelligent lad. Pursuing his studies in the dialect of the island, at leisure hours, he had made the chief's son his tutor, and had instructed the youth in English by way of return. More than a month had passed in this intercourse, and the ship's lading was being rapidly completed—when, in an evil hour, the talk between the two turned on the subject of the Holy Island.

"Does nobody live on the island but the Priest?" the Captain asked.

The chief's son looked round him suspiciously. "Promise me you won't tell anybody!" he began very earnestly.

The Captain gave his promise.

"There is one other person on the island," the lad whispered; "a person to feast your eyes upon, if you could only see her! She is the Priest's daughter. Removed to the island in her infancy, she has never left it since. In that sacred solitude she has only looked on two human beings—her father and her mother. I once saw her from my canoe, taking care not to attract her notice, or to approach too near the holy soil. Oh, so young, dear master, and, oh, so beautiful!" The chief's son completed the description by kissing his own hands as an expression of rapture.

The Captain's fine blue eyes sparkled. He asked no more questions; but, later on that day, he took his telescope with him, and paid a secret visit to the eminence which overlooked the Holy Island. The next day, and the next, he privately returned to the same place. On the fourth day, fatal Destiny favored him. He discovered the nymph of the island.

Standing alone upon the cape on which he had already seen her father, she was feeding some tame birds which looked like turtle-doves. The glass showed the Captain her white robe, fluttering in the sea-breeze; her long black hair falling to her feet; her slim and supple young figure; her simple grace of attitude, as she turned this way and that, attending to the wants of her birds. Before her was the blue ocean; behind her rose the lustrous green of the island forest. He looked and looked until his eyes and arms ached. When she disappeared among the trees, followed by her favorite birds, the Captain shut up his telescope with a sigh, and said to himself: "I have seen an angel!"

From that hour he became an altered man; he was languid, silent, interested in nothing. General opinion, on board his ship, decided that he was going to be taken ill.

A week more elapsed, and the officers and crew began to talk of the voyage to their market in China. The Captain refused to fix a day for sailing. He even took offense at being asked to decide. Instead of sleeping in his cabin, he went ashore for the night.

Not many hours afterward (just before daybreak), Mr. Duncalf, snoring in his cabin on deck, was aroused by a hand laid on his shoulder. The swinging lamp, still alight, showed him the dusky face of the chief's son, convulsed with terror. By wild signs, by disconnected words in the little English which he had learned, the lad tried to make the mate understand him. Dense Mr. Duncalf, understanding nothing, hailed the second officer, on the opposite side of the deck. The second officer was young and intelligent; he rightly interpreted the terrible news that had come to the ship.

The Captain had broken his own rules. Watching his opportunity, under cover of the night, he had taken a canoe, and had secretly crossed the channel to the Holy Island. No one had been near him at the time but the chief's son. The lad had vainly tried to induce him to abandon his desperate enterprise, and had vainly waited on the shore in the hope of hearing the sound of the paddle announcing his return. Beyond all reasonable doubt, the infatuated man had set foot on the shores of the tabooed island.

The one chance for his life was to conceal what he had done, until the ship could be got out of the harbor, and then (if no harm had come to him in the interval) to rescue him after nightfall. It was decided to spread the report that he had really been taken ill, and that he was confined to his cabin. The chief's son, whose heart the Captain's kindness had won, could be trusted to do this, and to keep the secret faithfully for his good friend's sake.

Toward noon, the next day, they attempted to take the ship to sea, and failed for want of wind. Hour by hour, the heat grew more oppressive. As the day declined, there were ominous appearances in the western heaven. The natives, who had given some trouble during the day by their anxiety to see the Captain, and by their curiosity to know the cause of the sudden preparations for the ship's departure, all went ashore together, looking suspiciously at the sky, and reappeared no more. Just at midnight, the ship (still in her snug berth inside the reef) suddenly trembled from her keel to her uppermost masts. Mr. Duncalf, surrounded by the startled crew, shook his knotty fist at the island as if he could see it in the dark. "My lads, what did I tell you? That was a shock of earthquake."

With the morning the threatening aspect of the weather unexpectedly disappeared. A faint hot breeze from the land, just enough to give the ship steerage-way, offered Mr. Duncalf a chance of getting to sea. Slowly the

Fortuna, with the mate himself at the wheel, half sailed, half drifted into the open ocean. At a distance of barely two miles from the island the breeze was felt no more, and the vessel lay becalmed for the rest of the day.

At night the men waited their orders, expecting to be sent after their Captain in one of the boats. The intense darkness, the airless heat, and a second shock of earthquake (faintly felt in the ship at her present distance from the land) warned the mate to be cautious. "I smell mischief in the air," said Mr. Duncalf. "The Captain must wait till I am surer of the weather."

Still no change came with the new day. The dead calm continued, and the airless heat. As the day declined, another ominous appearance became visible. A thin line of smoke was discovered through the telescope, ascending from the topmost peak of the mountain on the main island. Was the volcano threatening an eruption? The mate, for one, entertained no doubt of it. "By the Lord, the place is going to burst up!" said Mr. Duncalf. "Come what may of it, we must find the Captain to-night!"

V.

WHAT was the Captain doing? and what chance had the crew of finding him that night?

He had committed himself to his desperate adventure, without forming any plan for the preservation of his own safety; without giving even a momentary consideration to the consequences which might follow the risk that he had run. The charming figure that he had seen haunted him night and day. The image of the innocent creature, secluded from humanity in her island solitude, was the one image that filled his mind. A man, passing a woman in the street, acts on the impulse to turn and follow her, and in that one thoughtless moment shapes the destiny of his future life. The Captain had acted on a similar impulse, when he took the first canoe he had found on the beach, and shaped his reckless course for the tabooed island.

Reaching the shore while it was still dark, he did one sensible thing—he hid the canoe so that it might not betray him when the daylight came. That done, he waited for the morning on the outskirts of the forest.

The trembling light of dawn revealed the mysterious solitude around him. Following the outer limits of the trees, first in one direction, then in another, and finding no trace of any living creature, he decided on penetrating to the interior of the island. He entered the forest.

An hour of walking brought him to rising ground. Continuing the ascent, he got clear of the trees, and stood on the grassy top of a broad cliff which overlooked the sea. An open hut was on the cliff. He cautiously looked in, and discovered that it was empty. The few household utensils left about, and the simple bed of leaves in a corner, were covered with fine sandy dust. Night-birds flew blundering out of the inner cavities of the roof, and took refuge in the shadows of the forest below. It was plain that the hut had not been inhabited for some time past.

Standing at the open doorway and considering what he should do next, the Captain saw a bird flying toward him out of the forest. It was a turtle-dove, so tame that it fluttered close up to him. At the same moment the sound of sweet laughter became audible among the trees. His heart beat fast; he advanced a few steps and stopped. In a moment more the nymph of the island appeared, in her white robe, ascending the cliff in pursuit of her truant bird. She saw the strange man, and suddenly stood still; struck motionless by the amazing discovery that had burst upon her. The Captain approached, smiling and holding out his hand. She never moved; she stood before him in helpless wonderment—her lovely black eyes fixed spellbound on his face; her dusky bosom palpitating above the fallen folds of her robe; her rich red lips parted in mute astonishment. Feasting his eyes on her beauty in silence, the Captain after a while ventured to speak to her in the language of the main island. The sound of his voice, addressing her in the words that she understood, roused the lovely creature to action. She started, stepped close up to him, and dropped on her knees at his feet.

"My father worships invisible deities," she said, softly. "Are you a visible deity? Has my mother sent you?" She pointed as she spoke to the deserted hut behind them. "You appear," she went on, "in the place where my mother died. Is it for her sake that you show yourself to her child? Beautiful deity, come to the Temple—come to my father!"

The Captain gently raised her from the ground. If her father saw him,

777

he was a doomed man.

Infatuated as he was, he had sense enough left to announce himself plainly in his own character, as a mortal creature arriving from a distant land. The girl instantly drew back from him with a look of terror.

"He is not like my father," she said to herself; "he is not like me. Is he the lying demon of the prophecy? Is he the predestined destroyer of our island?"

The Captain's experience of the sex showed him the only sure way out of the awkward position in which he was now placed. He appealed to his personal appearance.

"Do I look like a demon?" he asked.

Her eyes met his eyes; a faint smile trembled on her lips. He ventured on asking what she meant by the predestined destruction of the island. She held up her hand solemnly, and repeated the prophecy.

The Holy Island was threatened with destruction by an evil being, who would one day appear on its shores. To avert the fatality the place had been sanctified and set apart, under the protection of the gods and their priest. Here was the reason for the taboo, and for the extraordinary rigor with which it was enforced. Listening to her with the deepest interest, the Captain took her hand and pressed it gently.

"Do I feel like a demon?" he whispered.

Her slim brown fingers closed frankly on his hand. "You feel soft and friendly," she said with the fearless candor of a child. "Squeeze me again. I like it!"

The next moment she snatched her hand away from him; the sense of his danger had suddenly forced itself on her mind. "If my father sees you," she said, "he will light the signal fire at the Temple, and the people from the other island will come here and put you to death. Where is your canoe? No! It is daylight. My father may see you on the water." She considered a little, and, approaching him, laid her hands on his shoulders. "Stay here till nightfall," she resumed. "My father never comes this way. The sight of the place where my mother died is horrible to him. You are safe here. Promise to stay where you are till night-time."

The Captain gave his promise.

Freed from anxiety so far, the girl's mobile temperament recovered its native cheerfulness, its sweet gayety and spirit. She admired the beautiful stranger as she might have admired a new bird that had flown to her to be fondled with the rest. She patted his fair white skin, and wished she had a skin like it. She lifted the great glossy folds of her long black hair, and compared it with the Captain's bright curly locks, and longed to change colors with him from the bottom of her heart. His dress was a wonder to her; his watch was a new revelation. She rested her head on his shoulder to listen delightedly to the ticking, as he held the watch to her ear. Her fragrant breath played on his face, her warm, supple figure rested against him softly. The Captain's arm stole round her waist, and the Captain's lips gently touched her cheek. She lifted her head with a look of pleased surprise. "Thank you," said the child of Nature, simply. "Kiss me again; I like it. May I kiss you?" The tame turtle-dove perched on her shoulder as she gave the Captain her first kiss, and diverted her thoughts to the pets that she had left, in pursuit of the truant dove. "Come," she said, "and see my birds. I keep them on this side of the forest. There is no danger, so long as you don't show yourself on the other side. My name is Aimata. Aimata will take care of you. Oh, what a beautiful white neck you have!" She put her arm admiringly round his neck. The Captain's arm held her tenderly to him. Slowly the two descended the cliff, and were lost in the leafy solitudes of the forest. And the tame dove fluttered before them, a winged messenger of love, cooing to his mate.

VI.

THE night had come, and the Captain had not left the island.

Aimata's resolution to send him away in the darkness was a forgotten resolution already. She had let him persuade her that he was in no danger, so long as he remained in the hut on the cliff; and she had promised, at parting, to return to him while the Priest was still sleeping, at the dawn of day.

He was alone in the hut. The thought of the innocent creature whom he loved was sorrowfully as well as tenderly present to his mind. He almost regretted his rash visit to the island. "I will take her with me to England," he said to himself. "What does a sailor care for the opinion of the world? Aimata shall be my wife."

The intense heat oppressed him. He stepped out on the cliff, toward midnight, in search of a breath of air.

At that moment, the first shock of earthquake (felt in the ship while she was inside the reef) shook the ground he stood on. He instantly thought of the volcano on the main island. Had he been mistaken in supposing the crater to be extinct? Was the shock that he had just felt a warning from the volcano, communicated through a submarine connection between the two islands? He waited and watched through the hours of darkness, with a vague sense of apprehension, which was not to be reasoned away. With the first light of daybreak he descended into the forest, and saw the lovely being whose safety was already precious to him as his own, hurrying to meet him through the trees.

She waved her hand distractedly as she approached him. "Go!" she cried; "go away in your canoe before our island is destroyed!"

He did his best to quiet her alarm. Was it the shock of earthquake that had frightened her? No: it was more than the shock of earthquake—it was something terrible which had followed the shock. There was a lake near the Temple, the waters of which were supposed to be heated by subterranean fires. The lake had risen with the earthquake, had bubbled furiously, and had then melted away into the earth and been lost. Her father, viewing the portent with horror, had gone to the cape to watch the volcano on the main island, and to implore by prayers and sacrifices the protection of the gods. Hearing this, the Captain entreated Aimata to let him see the emptied lake, in the absence of the Priest. She hesitated; but his influence was all-powerful. He prevailed on her to turn back with him through the forest.

Reaching the furthest limit of the trees, they came out upon open rocky ground which sloped gently downward toward the center of the island.

Having crossed this space, they arrived at a natural amphitheater of rock. On one side of it the Temple appeared, partly excavated, partly formed by a natural cavern. In one of the lateral branches of the cavern was the dwelling of the Priest and his daughter. The mouth of it looked out on the rocky basin of the lake. Stooping over the edge, the Captain discovered, far down in the empty depths, a light cloud of steam. Not a drop of water was visible, look where he might.

Aimata pointed to the abyss, and hid her face on his bosom. "My father says," she whispered, "that it is your doing."

The Captain started. "Does your father know that I am on the island?"

She looked up at him with a quick glance of reproach. "Do you think I would tell him, and put your life in peril?" she asked. "My father felt the destroyer of the island in the earthquake; my father saw the coming destruction in the disappearance of the lake." Her eyes rested on him with a loving languor. "Are you indeed the demon of the prophecy?" she said, winding his hair round her finger. "I am not afraid of you, if you are. I am a creature bewitched; I love the demon." She kissed him passionately. "I don't care if I die," she whispered between the kisses, "if I only die with you!"

The Captain made no attempt to reason with her. He took the wiser way—he appealed to her feelings.

"You will come and live with me happily in my own country," he said. "My ship is waiting for us. I will take you home with me, and you shall be my wife."

She clapped her hands for joy. Then she thought of her father, and drew back from him in tears.

The Captain understood her. "Let us leave this dreary place," he suggested. "We will talk about it in the cool glades of the forest, where you first said you loved me."

She gave him her hand. "Where I first said I loved you!" she repeated, smiling tenderly as she looked at him. They left the lake together.

VII.

THE darkness had fallen again; and the ship was still becalmed at sea.

Mr. Duncalf came on deck after his supper. The thin line of smoke, seen rising from the peak of the mountain that evening, was now succeeded by ominous flashes of fire from the same quarter, intermittently visible. The faint hot breeze from the land was felt once more. "There's just an air of wind," Mr. Duncalf remarked. "I'll try for the Captain while I have the chance."

One of the boats was lowered into the water—under command of the second mate, who had already taken the bearings of the tabooed island by daylight. Four of the men were to go with him, and they were all to be well armed. Mr. Duncalf addressed his final instructions to the officer in the boat.

"You will keep a lookout, sir, with a lantern in the bows. If the natives annoy you, you know what to do. Always shoot natives. When you get anigh the island, you will fire a gun and sing out for the Captain."

"Quite needless," interposed a voice from the sea. "The Captain is here!"

Without taking the slightest notice of the astonishment that he had caused, the commander of the Fortuna paddled his canoe to the side of the ship. Instead of ascending to the deck, he stepped into the boat, waiting alongside. "Lend me your pistols," he said quietly to the second officer, "and oblige me by taking your men back to their duties on board." He looked up at Mr. Duncalf and gave some further directions. "If there is any change in the weather, keep the ship standing off and on, at a safe distance from the land, and throw up a rocket from time to time to show your position. Expect me on board again by sunrise."

"What!" cried the mate. "Do you mean to say you are going back to the island—in that boat—all by yourself?"

"I am going back to the island," answered the Captain, as quietly as ever; "in this boat—all by myself." He pushed off from the ship, and hoisted the sail as he spoke.

"You're deserting your duty!" the old sea-dog shouted, with one of his loudest oaths.

"Attend to my directions," the Captain shouted back, as he drifted away into the darkness.

Mr. Duncalf—violently agitated for the first time in his life—took leave of his superior officer, with a singular mixture of solemnity and politeness, in these words:

"The Lord have mercy on your soul! I wish you good-evening."

VIII.

ALONE in the boat, the Captain looked with a misgiving mind at the flashing of the volcano on the main island.

If events had favored him, he would have removed Aimata to the shelter of the ship on the day when he saw the emptied basin on the lake. But the smoke of the Priest's sacrifice had been discovered by the chief; and he had dispatched two canoes with instructions to make inquiries. One of the canoes had returned; the other was kept in waiting off the cape, to place a means of communicating with the main island at the disposal of the Priest. The second shock of earthquake had naturally increased the alarm of the chief. He had sent messages to the Priest, entreating him to leave the island, and other messages to Aimata suggesting that she should exert her influence over her father, if he hesitated. The Priest refused to leave the Temple. He trusted in his gods and his sacrifices—he believed they might avert the fatality that threatened his sanctuary.

Yielding to the holy man, the chief sent re-enforcements of canoes to take their turn at keeping watch off the headland. Assisted by torches, the islanders were on the alert (in superstitious terror of the demon of the prophecy) by night as well as by day. The Captain had no alternative but to keep in hiding, and to watch his opportunity of approaching the place in which he had concealed his canoe. It was only after Aimata had left him as usual, to return to her father at the close of evening, that the chances declared themselves in his favor. The fire-flashes from the mountain, visible when the night came, had struck terror into the hearts of the men on the watch. They thought of their wives, their children, and their possessions on the main island, and they one and all deserted their Priest. The Captain seized the opportunity of communicating with the ship, and of exchanging a frail canoe which he was ill able to manage, for a swift-sailing boat capable of keeping the sea in the event of stormy weather.

As he now neared the land, certain small sparks of red, moving on the distant water, informed him that the canoes of the sentinels had been ordered back to their duty.

Carefully avoiding the lights, he reached his own side of the island without accident, and, guided by the boat's lantern, anchored under the cliff. He climbed the rocks, advanced to the door of the hut, and was met, to his delight and astonishment, by Aimata on the threshold.

"I dreamed that some dreadful misfortune had parted us forever," she said; "and I came here to see if my dream was true. You have taught me what it is to be miserable; I never felt my heart ache till I looked into the hut and found that you had gone. Now I have seen you, I am satisfied. No! you must not go back with me. My father may be out looking for me. It is you that are in danger, not I. I know the forest as well by dark as by daylight."

The Captain detained her when she tried to leave him.

"Now you are here," he said, "why should I not place you at once in safety? I have been to the ship; I have brought back one of the boats. The darkness will befriend us—let us embark while we can."

She shrank away as he took her hand. "You forget my father!" she said.

"Your father is in no danger, my love. The canoes are waiting for him at the cape; I saw the lights as I passed."

With that reply he drew her out of the hut and led her toward the sea. Not a breath of the breeze was now to be felt. The dead calm had returned—and the boat was too large to be easily managed by one man alone at the oars.

"The breeze may come again," he said. "Wait here, my angel, for the chance."

784

As he spoke, the deep silence of the forest below them was broken by a sound. A harsh wailing voice was heard, calling:

"Aimata! Aimata!"

"My father!" she whispered; "he has missed me. If he comes here you are lost."

She kissed him with passionate fervor; she held him to her for a moment with all her strength.

"Expect me at daybreak," she said, and disappeared down the landward slope of the cliff.

He listened, anxious for her safety. The voices of the father and daughter just reached him from among the trees. The Priest spoke in no angry tones; she had apparently found an acceptable excuse for her absence. Little by little, the failing sound of their voices told him that they were on their way back together to the Temple. The silence fell again. Not a ripple broke on the beach. Not a leaf rustled in the forest. Nothing moved but the reflected flashes of the volcano on the main island over the black sky. It was an airless and an awful calm.

He went into the hut, and laid down on his bed of leaves—not to sleep, but to rest. All his energies might be required to meet the coming events of the morning. After the voyage to and from the ship, and the long watching that had preceded it, strong as he was he stood in need of repose.

For some little time he kept awake, thinking. Insensibly the oppression of the intense heat, aided in its influence by his own fatigue, treacherously closed his eyes. In spite of himself, the weary man fell into a deep sleep.

He was awakened by a roar like the explosion of a park of artillery. The volcano on the main island had burst into a state of eruption. Smoky flame-light overspread the sky, and flashed through the open doorway of the hut. He sprang from his bed—and found himself up to his knees in water.

Had the sea overflowed the land?

He waded out of the hut, and the water rose to his middle. He looked round him by the lurid light of the eruption. The one visible object within the range of view was the sea, stained by reflections from the blood-red sky, swirling and rippling strangely in the dead calm. In a moment more, he became conscious that the earth on which he stood was sinking under his feet. The water rose to his neck; the last vestige of the roof of the hut disappeared.

He looked round again, and the truth burst on him. The island was sinking—slowly, slowly sinking into volcanic depths, below even the depth of the sea! The highest object was the hut, and that had dropped inch by inch under water before his own eyes. Thrown up to the surface by occult volcanic influences, the island had sunk back, under the same influences, to the obscurity from which it had emerged!

A black shadowy object, turning in a wide circle, came slowly near him as the all-destroying ocean washed its bitter waters into his mouth. The buoyant boat, rising as the sea rose, had dragged its anchor, and was floating round in the vortex made by the slowly sinking island. With a last desperate hope that Aimata might have been saved as he had been saved, he swam to the boat, seized the heavy oars with the strength of a giant, and made for the place (so far as he could guess at it now) where the lake and the Temple had once been.

He looked round and round him; he strained his eyes in the vain attempt to penetrate below the surface of the seething dimpling sea. Had the panic-stricken watchers in the canoes saved themselves, without an effort to preserve the father and daughter? Or had they both been suffocated before they could make an attempt to escape? He called to her in his misery, as if she could hear him out of the fathomless depths: "Aimata! Aimata!" The roar of the distant eruption answered him. The mounting fires lit the solitary sea far and near over the sinking island. The boat turned slowly and more slowly in the lessening vortex. Never again would those gentle eyes look at him with unutterable love! Never again would those fresh lips touch his lips with their fervent kiss! Alone, amid the savage forces of Nature in conflict, the miserable mortal lifted his hands in frantic supplication—and the burning sky glared down on him in its pitiless grandeur, and struck him to his knees in the boat. His reason sank with his sinking limbs. In the merciful frenzy that succeeded the shock, he saw afar off, in her white robe, an angel poised on the waters, beckoning him to follow her to the brighter and the better world. He loosened the sail, he seized the oars; and the faster he pursued it, the faster the mocking vision fled from him over the empty and endless sea.

IX.

THE boat was discovered, on the next morning, from the ship.

All that the devotion of the officers of the Fortuna could do for their unhappy commander was done on the homeward voyage. Restored to his own country, and to skilled medical help, the Captain's mind by slow degrees recovered its balance. He has taken his place in society again—he lives and moves and manages his affairs like the rest of us. But his heart is dead to all new emotions; nothing remains in it but the sacred remembrance of his lost love. He neither courts nor avoids the society of women. Their sympathy finds him grateful, but their attractions seem to be lost on him; they pass from his mind as they pass from his eyes—they stir nothing in him but the memory of Aimata.

"Now you know, ladies, why the Captain will never marry, and why (sailor as he is) he hates the sight of the sea."

MR. MARMADUKE AND THE MINISTER.

I.

September 13th.—Winter seems to be upon us, on the Highland Border, already.

I looked out of window, as the evening closed in, before I barred the shutters and drew the curtains for the night. The clouds hid the hilltops on either side of our valley. Fantastic mists parted and met again on the lower slopes, as the varying breeze blew them. The blackening waters of the lake before our window seemed to anticipate the coming darkness. On the more distant hills the torrents were just visible, in the breaks of the mist, stealing their way over the brown ground like threads of silver. It was a dreary scene. The stillness of all things was only interrupted by the splashing of our little waterfall at the back of the house. I was not sorry to close the shutters, and confine the view to the four walls of our sitting-room.

The day happened to be my birthday. I sat by the peat-fire, waiting for the lamp and the tea-tray, and contemplating my past life from the vantage-ground, so to speak, of my fifty-fifth year.

There was wonderfully little to look back on. Nearly thirty years since, it pleased an all-wise Providence to cast my lot in this remote Scottish hamlet, and to make me Minister of Cauldkirk, on a stipend of seventy-four pounds sterling per annum. I and my surroundings have grown quietly older and older together. I have outlived my wife; I have buried one generation among my parishioners, and married another; I have borne the wear and tear of years better than the kirk in which I minister and the manse (or parsonage-house) in which I live—both sadly out of repair, and both still trusting for the means of reparation to the pious benefactions of people richer than myself. Not that I complain, be it understood, of the humble position which I occupy. I possess many blessings; and I thank the Lord for them. I have my little bit of land and my cow. I have also my good daughter, Felicia; named after her deceased mother, but inheriting her comely looks, it is thought, rather from myself.

Neither let me forget my elder sister, Judith; a friendless single person, sheltered under my roof, whose temperament I could wish somewhat less prone to look at persons and things on the gloomy side, but whose compensating virtues Heaven forbid that I should deny. No; I am grateful for what has been given me (from on high), and resigned to what has been taken away. With what fair prospects did I start in life! Springing from a good old Scottish stock, blessed with every advantage of education that the institutions of Scotland and England in turn could offer; with a career at the Bar and in Parliament before me—and all cast to the winds, as it were, by the measureless prodigality of my unhappy father, God forgive him! I doubt if I had five pounds left in my purse, when the compassion of my relatives on the mother's side opened a refuge to me at Cauldkirk, and hid me from the notice of the world for the rest of my life.

September 14th.—Thus far I had posted up my Diary on the evening of the 13th, when an event occurred so completely unexpected by my household and myself, that the pen, I may say, dropped incontinently from my hand.

It was the time when we had finished our tea, or supper—I hardly know which to call it. In the silence, we could hear the rain pouring against the window, and the wind that had risen with the darkness howling round the house. My sister Judith, taking the gloomy view according to custom— copious draughts of good Bohea and two helpings of such a mutton ham as only Scotland can produce had no effect in raising her spirits—my sister, I say, remarked that there would be ships lost at sea and men drowned this night. My daughter Felicia, the brightest-tempered creature of the female sex that I have ever met with, tried to give a cheerful turn to her aunt's depressing prognostication. "If the ships must be lost," she said, "we may surely hope that the men will be saved." "God willing," I put in—thereby giving to my daughter's humane expression of feeling the fit religious tone that was all it wanted—and then went on with my written record of the events and reflections of the day. No more was said. Felicia took up a book. Judith took up her knitting.

On a sudden, the silence was broken by a blow on the house-door.

My two companions, as is the way of women, set up a scream. I was startled myself, wondering who could be out in the rain and the darkness and striking at the door of the house. A stranger it must be. Light or dark, any person in or near Cauldkirk, wanting admission, would know where to find the bell-handle at the side of the door. I waited a while to hear what might happen next. The stroke was repeated, but more softly. It became me as a man and a minister to set an example. I went out into the passage, and I called through the door, "Who's there?"

A man's voice answered—so faintly that I could barely hear him—"A lost traveler."

Immediately upon this my cheerful sister expressed her view of the matter through the open parlor door. "Brother Noah, it's a robber. Don't let him in!"

What would the Good Samaritan have done in my place? Assuredly he would have run the risk and opened the door. I imitated the Good Samaritan.

A man, dripping wet, with a knapsack on his back and a thick stick in his hand, staggered in, and would, I think, have fallen in the passage if I had not caught him by the arm. Judith peeped out at the parlor door, and said, "He's drunk." Felicia was behind her, holding up a lighted candle, the better to see what was going on. "Look at his face, aunt," says she. "Worn out with fatigue, poor man. Bring him in, father—bring him in."

Good Felicia! I was proud of my girl. "He'll spoil the carpet," says sister Judith. I said, "Silence, for shame!" and brought him in, and dropped him dripping into my own armchair. Would the Good Samaritan have thought of his carpet or his chair? I did think of them, but I overcame it. Ah, we are a decadent generation in these latter days!

"Be quick, father'" says Felicia; "he'll faint if you don't give him something!"

I took out one of our little drinking cups (called among us a "Quaigh"), while Felicia, instructed by me, ran to the kitchen for the cream-jug. Filling the cup with whisky and cream in equal proportions, I offered it to him. He drank it off as if it had been so much water. "Stimulant and nourishment, you'll observe, sir, in equal portions," I remarked to him. "How do you feel now?"

"Ready for another," says he.

Felicia burst out laughing. I gave him another. As I turned to hand it to him, sister Judith came behind me, and snatched away the cream-jug. Never a generous person, sister Judith, at the best of times—more especially in the matter of cream.

He handed me back the empty cup. "I believe, sir, you have saved my life," he said. "Under Providence," I put in—adding, "But I would remark, looking to the state of your clothes, that I have yet another service to offer you, before you tell us how you came into this pitiable state." With that reply, I led him upstairs, and set before him the poor resources of my wardrobe, and left him to do the best he could with them. He was rather a small man, and I am in stature nigh on six feet. When he came down to us in my clothes, we had the merriest evening that I can remember for years past. I thought Felicia would have had a hysteric fit; and even sister Judith laughed—he did look such a comical figure in the minister's garments.

As for the misfortune that had befallen him, it offered one more example of the preternatural rashness of the English traveler in countries unknown to him. He was on a walking tour through Scotland; and he had set forth to go twenty miles a-foot, from a town on one side of the Highland Border, to a town on the other, without a guide. The only wonder is that he found his way to Cauldkirk, instead of perishing of exposure among the lonesome hills.

"Will you offer thanks for your preservation to the Throne of Grace, in your prayers to-night?" I asked him. And he answered, "Indeed I will!"

We have a spare room at the manse; but it had not been inhabited for more than a year past. Therefore we made his bed, for that night, on the sofa in the parlor; and so left him, with the fire on one side of his couch, and the whisky and the mutton ham on the other in case of need. He mentioned his name when we bade him good-night. Marmaduke Falmer of London, son of a minister of the English Church Establishment, now deceased. It was plain, I may add, before he spoke, that we had offered the hospitality of the manse to a man of gentle breeding.

September 15th.—I have to record a singularly pleasant day; due partly to a return of the fine weather, partly to the good social gifts of our guest.

Attired again in his own clothing, he was, albeit wanting in height, a finely proportioned man, with remarkably small hands and feet; having also a bright mobile face, and large dark eyes of an extraordinary diversity of expression. Also, he was of a sweet and cheerful humor; easily pleased with little things, and amiably ready to make his gifts agreeable to all of us. At the same time, a person of my experience and penetration could not fail to perceive that he was most content when in company with Felicia. I have already mentioned my daughter's comely looks and good womanly qualities. It was in the order of nature that a young man (to use his own phrase) getting near to his thirty-first birthday should feel drawn by sympathy toward a well-favored young woman in her four-and-twentieth year. In matters of this sort I have always cultivated a liberal turn of mind, not forgetting my own youth.

As the evening closed in, I was sorry to notice a certain change in our guest for the worse. He showed signs of fatigue—falling asleep at intervals in his chair, and waking up and shivering. The spare room was now well aired, having had a roaring fire in it all day.

I begged him not to stand on ceremony, and to betake himself at once to his bed. Felicia (having learned the accomplishment from her excellent mother) made him a warm sleeping-draught of eggs, sugar, nutmeg, and spirits, delicious alike to the senses of smell and taste. Sister Judith waited until he had closed the door behind him, and then favored me with one of her dismal predictions. "You'll rue the day, brother, when you let him into the house. He is going to fall ill on our hands."

II.

November 28th.—God be praised for all His mercies! This day, our guest, Marmaduke Falmer, joined us downstairs in the sitting-room for the first time since his illness.

He is sadly deteriorated, in a bodily sense, by the wasting rheumatic fever that brought him nigh to death; but he is still young, and the doctor (humanly speaking) has no doubt of his speedy and complete recovery. My sister takes the opposite view. She remarked, in his hearing, that nobody ever thoroughly got over a rheumatic fever. Oh, Judith! Judith! it's well for humanity that you're a single person! If haply, there had been any man desperate enough to tackle such a woman in the bonds of marriage, what a pessimist progeny must have proceeded from you!

Looking back over my Diary for the last two months and more, I see one monotonous record of the poor fellow's sufferings; cheered and varied, I am pleased to add, by the devoted services of my daughter at the sick man's bedside. With some help from her aunt (most readily given when he was nearest to the point of death), and with needful services performed in turn by two of our aged women in Cauldkirk, Felicia could not have nursed him more assiduously if he had been her own brother. Half the credit of bringing him through it belonged (as the doctor himself confessed) to the discreet young nurse, always ready through the worst of the illness, and always cheerful through the long convalescence that followed. I must also record to the credit of Marmaduke that he was indeed duly grateful. When I led him into the parlor, and he saw Felicia waiting by the armchair, smiling and patting the pillows for him, he took her by the hand, and burst out crying. Weakness, in part, no doubt—but sincere gratitude at the bottom of it, I am equally sure.

November 29th.—However, there are limits even to sincere gratitude. Of this truth Mr. Marmaduke seems to be insufficiently aware. Entering the sitting-room soon after noon today, I found our convalescent guest and his nurse alone. His head was resting on her shoulder; his arm was round her waist—and (the truth before everything) Felicia was kissing him.

A man may be of a liberal turn of mind, and may yet consistently object to freedom when it takes the form of unlicensed embracing and kissing; the person being his own daughter, and the place his own house. I signed to my girl to leave us; and I advanced to Mr. Marmaduke, with my opinion of his conduct just rising in words to my lips—when he staggered me with amazement by asking for Felicia's hand in marriage.

"You need feel no doubt of my being able to offer to your daughter a position of comfort and respectability," he said. "I have a settled income of eight hundred pounds a year."

His raptures over Felicia; his protestations that she was the first woman he had ever really loved; his profane declaration that he preferred to die, if I refused to let him be her husband—all these flourishes, as I may call them, passed in at one of my ears and out at the other. But eight hundred pounds sterling per annum, descending as it were in a golden avalanche on the mind of a Scottish minister (accustomed to thirty years' annual contemplation of seventy-four pounds)—eight hundred a year, in one young man's pocket, I say, completely overpowered me. I just managed to answer, "Wait till tomorrow"—and hurried out of doors to recover my self-respect, if the thing was to be anywise done. I took my way through the valley. The sun was shining, for a wonder. When I saw my shadow on the hillside, I saw the Golden Calf as an integral part of me, bearing this inscription in letters of flame—"Here's another of them!"

November 30th.—I have made amends for yesterday's backsliding; I have acted as becomes my parental dignity and my sacred calling.

The temptation to do otherwise, has not been wanting. Here is sister Judith's advice: "Make sure that he has got the money first; and, for Heaven's sake, nail him!" Here is Mr. Marmaduke's proposal: "Make any conditions you please, so long as you give me your daughter." And, lastly, here is Felicia's confession: "Father, my heart is set on him. Oh, don't be unkind to me for the first time in your life!"

But I have stood firm. I have refused to hear any more words on the subject from any one of them, for the next six months to come.

"So serious a venture as the venture of marriage," I said, "is not to be undertaken on impulse. As soon as Mr. Marmaduke can travel, I request him to leave us, and not to return again for six months. If, after that interval, he is still of the same mind, and my daughter is still of the same mind, let him return to Cauldkirk, and (premising that I am in all other respects satisfied) let him ask me for his wife."

There were tears, there were protestations; I remained immovable. A week later, Mr. Marmaduke left us, on his way by easy stages to the south. I am not a hard man. I rewarded the lovers for their obedience by keeping sister Judith out of the way, and letting them say their farewell words (accompaniments included) in private.

III.

May 28th.—A letter from Mr. Marmaduke, informing me that I may expect him at Cauldkirk, exactly at the expiration of the six months' interval—viz., on June the seventh.

Writing to this effect, he added a timely word on the subject of his family. Both his parents were dead; his only brother held a civil appointment in India, the place being named. His uncle (his father's brother) was a merchant resident in London; and to this near relative he referred me, if I wished to make inquiries about him. The names of his bankers, authorized to give me every information in respect to his pecuniary affairs, followed. Nothing could be more plain and straightforward. I wrote to his uncle, and I wrote to his bankers. In both cases the replies were perfectly satisfactory—nothing in the slightest degree doubtful, no prevarications, no mysteries. In a word, Mr. Marmaduke himself was thoroughly well vouched for, and Mr. Marmaduke's income was invested in securities beyond fear and beyond reproach. Even sister Judith, bent on picking a hole in the record somewhere, tried hard, and could make nothing of it.

The last sentence in Mr. Marmaduke's letter was the only part of it which I failed to read with pleasure.

He left it to me to fix the day for the marriage, and he entreated that I would make it as early a day as possible. I had a touch of the heartache when I thought of parting with Felicia, and being left at home with nobody but Judith. However, I got over it for that time, and, after consulting my daughter, we decided on naming a fortnight after Mr. Marmaduke's arrival—that is to say, the twenty-first of June. This gave Felicia time for her preparations, besides offering to me the opportunity of becoming better acquainted with my son-in-law's disposition. The happiest marriage does indubitably make its demands on human forbearance; and I was anxious, among other things, to assure myself of Mr. Marmaduke's good temper.

IV.

June 22d.—The happy change in my daughter's life (let me say nothing of the change in my life) has come: they were married yesterday. The manse is a desert; and sister Judith was never so uncongenial a companion to me as I feel her to be now. Her last words to the married pair, when they drove away, were: "Lord help you both; you have all your troubles before you!"

I had no heart to write yesterday's record, yesterday evening, as usual. The absence of Felicia at the supper-table completely overcame me. I, who have so often comforted others in their afflictions, could find no comfort for myself. Even now that the day has passed, the tears come into my eyes, only with writing about it. Sad, sad weakness! Let me close my Diary, and open the Bible—and be myself again.

June 23d.—More resigned since yesterday; a more becoming and more pious frame of mind—obedient to God's holy will, and content in the belief that my dear daughter's married life will be a happy one.

They have gone abroad for their holiday—to Switzerland, by way of France. I was anything rather than pleased when I heard that my son-in-law proposed to take Felicia to that sink of iniquity, Paris. He knows already what I think of balls and playhouses, and similar devils' diversions, and how I have brought up my daughter to think of them—the subject having occurred in conversation among us more than a week since. That he could meditate taking a child of mine to the headquarters of indecent jiggings and abominable stage-plays, of spouting rogues and painted Jezebels, was indeed a heavy blow.

However, Felicia reconciled me to it in the end. She declared that her only desire in going to Paris was to see the picture-galleries, the public buildings, and the fair outward aspect of the city generally. "Your opinions, father, are my opinions," she said; "and Marmaduke, I am sure, will so shape our arrangements as to prevent our passing a Sabbath in Paris." Marmaduke not only consented to this (with the perfect good temper of which I have observed more than one gratifying example in him), but likewise assured me that, speaking for himself personally, it would be a relief to him when they got to the mountains and the lakes. So that matter was happily settled. Go where they may, God bless and prosper them!

Speaking of relief, I must record that Judith has gone away to Aberdeen on a visit to some friends. "You'll be wretched enough here," she said at parting, "all by yourself." Pure vanity and self-complacence! It may be resignation to her absence, or it may be natural force of mind, I began to be more easy and composed the moment I was alone, and this blessed state of feeling has continued uninterruptedly ever since.

V.

September 5th.—A sudden change in my life, which it absolutely startles me to record. I am going to London!

My purpose in taking this most serious step is of a twofold nature. I have a greater and a lesser object in view.

The greater object is to see my daughter, and to judge for myself whether certain doubts on the vital question of her happiness, which now torment me night and day, are unhappily founded on truth. She and her husband returned in August from their wedding-tour, and took up their abode in Marmaduke's new residence in London. Up to this time, Felicia's letters to me were, in very truth, the delight of my life—she was so entirely happy, so amazed and delighted with all the wonderful things she saw, so full of love and admiration for the best husband that ever lived. Since her return to London, I perceive a complete change.

She makes no positive complaint, but she writes in a tone of weariness and discontent; she says next to nothing of Marmaduke, and she dwells perpetually on the one idea of my going to London to see her. I hope with my whole heart that I am wrong; but the rare allusions to her husband, and the constantly repeated desire to see her father (while she has not been yet three months married), seem to me to be bad signs. In brief, my anxiety is too great to be endured. I have so arranged matters with one of my brethren as to be free to travel to London cheaply by steamer; and I begin the journey tomorrow.

My lesser object may be dismissed in two words. Having already decided on going to London, I propose to call on the wealthy nobleman who owns all the land hereabouts, and represent to him the discreditable, and indeed dangerous, condition of the parish kirk for want of means to institute the necessary repairs. If I find myself well received, I shall put in a word for the manse, which is almost in as deplorable a condition as the church. My lord is a wealthy man—may his heart and his purse be opened unto me!

Sister Judith is packing my portmanteau. According to custom, she forbodes the worst. "Never forget," she says, "that I warned you against Marmaduke, on the first night when he entered the house."

VI.

September 10th.—After more delays than one, on land and sea, I was at last set ashore near the Tower, on the afternoon of yesterday. God help us, my worst anticipations have been realized! My beloved Felicia has urgent and serious need of me.

It is not to be denied that I made my entry into my son-in-law's house in a disturbed and irritated frame of mind. First, my temper was tried by the almost interminable journey, in the noisy and comfortless vehicle which they call a cab, from the river-wharf to the west-end of London, where Marmaduke lives. In the second place, I was scandalized and alarmed by an incident which took place—still on the endless journey from east to west—in a street hard by the market of Covent Garden.

We had just approached a large building, most profusely illuminated with gas, and exhibiting prodigious colored placards having inscribed on them nothing but the name of Barrymore. The cab came suddenly to a standstill; and looking out to see what the obstacle might be, I discovered a huge concourse of men and women, drawn across the pavement and road alike, so that it seemed impossible to pass by them. I inquired of my driver what this assembling of the people meant. "Oh," says he, "Barrymore has made another hit." This answer being perfectly unintelligible to me, I requested some further explanation, and discovered that "Barrymore" was the name of a stage-player favored by the populace; that the building was a theater, and that all these creatures with immortal souls were waiting, before the doors opened, to get places at the show!

The emotions of sorrow and indignation caused by this discovery so absorbed me that I failed to notice an attempt the driver made to pass through, where the crowd seemed to be thinner, until the offended people resented the proceeding. Some of them seized the horse's head; others were on the point of pulling the driver off his box, when providentially the police interfered. Under their protection, we drew back, and reached our destination in safety, by another way. I record this otherwise unimportant affair, because it grieved and revolted me (when I thought of the people's souls), and so indisposed my mind to take cheerful views of anything. Under these circumstances, I would fain hope that I have exaggerated the true state of the case, in respect to my daughter's married life.

My good girl almost smothered me with kisses. When I at last got a fair opportunity of observing her, I thought her looking pale and worn and anxious. Query: Should I have arrived at this conclusion if I had met with no example of the wicked dissipations of London, and if I had ridden at my ease in a comfortable vehicle?

They had a succulent meal ready for me, and, what I call, fair enough whisky out of Scotland. Here again I remarked that Felicia ate very little, and Marmaduke nothing at all. He drank wine, too—and, good heavens, champagne wine!—a needless waste of money surely when there was whisky on the table. My appetite being satisfied, my son-in-law went out of the room, and returned with his hat in his hand. "You and Felicia have many things to talk about on your first evening together. I'll leave you for a while—I shall only be in the way." So he spoke. It was in vain that his wife and I assured him he was not in the way at all. He kissed his hand, and smiled pleasantly, and left us.

"There, father!" says Felicia. "For the last ten days he has gone out like that, and left me alone for the whole evening. When we first returned from Switzerland, he left me in the same mysterious way, only it was after breakfast then. Now he stays at home in the daytime, and goes out at night."

I inquired if she had not summoned him to give her some explanation.

"I don't know what to make of his explanation," says Felicia. "When he went away in the daytime, he told me he had business in the City. Since he took to going out at night, he says he goes to his club."

"Have you asked where his club is, my dear?"

"He says it's in Pall Mall. There are dozens of clubs in that street—and he has never told me the name of his club. I am completely shut out of his confidence. Would you believe it, father? he has not introduced one of his friends to me since we came home. I doubt if they know where he lives, since he took this house."

What could I say?

I said nothing, and looked round the room. It was fitted up with perfectly palatial magnificence. I am an ignorant man in matters of this sort, and partly to satisfy my curiosity, partly to change the subject, I asked to see the house. Mercy preserve us, the same grandeur everywhere! I wondered if even such an income as eight hundred a year could suffice for it all. In a moment when I was considering this, a truly frightful suspicion crossed my mind. Did these mysterious absences, taken in connection with the unbridled luxury that surrounded us, mean that my son-in-law was a gamester? a shameless shuffler of cards, or a debauched bettor on horses? While I was still completely overcome by my own previsions of evil, my daughter put her arm in mine to take me to the top of the house.

For the first time I observed a bracelet of dazzling gems on her wrist. "Not diamonds?" I said. She answered, with as much composure as if she had been the wife of a nobleman, "Yes, diamonds—a present from Marmaduke." This was too much for me; my previsions, so to speak, forced their way into words. "Oh, my poor child!" I burst out, "I'm in mortal fear that your husband's a gamester!"

She showed none of the horror I had anticipated; she only shook her head and began to cry.

"Worse than that, I'm afraid," she said.

I was petrified; my tongue refused its office, when I would fain have asked her what she meant. Her besetting sin, poor soul, is a proud spirit. She dried her eyes on a sudden, and spoke out freely, in these words: "I am not going to cry about it. The other day, father, we were out walking in the park. A horrid, bold, yellow-haired woman passed us in an open carriage. She kissed her hand to Marmaduke, and called out to him, 'How are you, Marmy?' I was so indignant that I pushed him away from me, and told him to go and take a drive with his lady. He burst out laughing. 'Nonsense!' he said; 'she has known me for years—you don't understand our easy London manners.' We have made it up since then; but I have my own opinion of the creature in the open carriage."

Morally speaking, this was worse than all. But, logically viewed, it completely failed as a means of accounting for the diamond bracelet and the splendor of the furniture.

We went on to the uppermost story. It was cut off from the rest of the house by a stout partition of wood, and a door covered with green baize.

When I tried the door it was locked. "Ha!" says Felicia, "I wanted you to see it for yourself!" More suspicious proceedings on the part of my son-in-law! He kept the door constantly locked, and the key in his pocket. When his wife asked him what it meant, he answered: "My study is up there—and I like to keep it entirely to myself." After such a reply as that, the preservation of my daughter's dignity permitted but one answer: "Oh, keep it to yourself, by all means!"

My previsions, upon this, assumed another form.

I now asked myself—still in connection with my son-in-law's extravagant expenditure—whether the clew to the mystery might not haply be the forging of bank-notes on the other side of the baize door. My mind was prepared for anything by this time. We descended again into the dining-room. Felicia saw how my spirits were dashed, and came and perched upon my knee. "Enough of my troubles for to-night, father," she said. "I am going to be your little girl again, and we will talk of nothing but Cauldkirk, until Marmaduke comes back." I am one of the firmest men living, but I could not keep the hot tears out of my eyes when she put her arm round my neck and said those words. By good fortune I was sitting with my back to the lamp; she didn't notice me.

A little after eleven o'clock Marmaduke returned. He looked pale and weary. But more champagne, and this time something to eat with it, seemed to set him to rights again—no doubt by relieving him from the reproaches of a guilty conscience.

I had been warned by Felicia to keep what had passed between us a secret from her husband for the present; so we had (superficially speaking) a merry end to the evening. My son-in-law was nearly as good company as ever, and wonderfully fertile in suggestions and expedients when he saw they were wanted. Hearing from his wife, to whom I had mentioned it, that I purposed representing the decayed condition of the kirk and manse to the owner of Cauldkirk and the country round about, he strongly urged me to draw up a list of repairs that were most needful, before I waited on my lord. This advice, vicious and degraded as the man who offered it may be, is sound advice nevertheless. I shall assuredly take it.

So far I had written in my Diary, in the forenoon. Returning to my daily record, after a lapse of some hours, I have a new mystery of iniquity to chronicle. My abominable son-in-law now appears (I blush to write it) to be nothing less than an associate of thieves!

After the meal they call luncheon, I thought it well before recreating myself with the sights of London, to attend first to the crying necessities of the kirk and the manse. Furnished with my written list, I presented myself at his lordship's residence. I was immediately informed that he was otherwise engaged, and could not possibly receive me. If I wished to see my lord's secretary, Mr. Helmsley, I could do so. Consenting to this, rather than fail entirely in my errand, I was shown into the secretary's room.

Mr. Helmsley heard what I had to say civilly enough; expressing, however, grave doubts whether his lordship would do anything for me, the demands on his purse being insupportably numerous already. However, he undertook to place my list before his employer, and to let me know the result. "Where are you staying in London?" he asked. I answered: "With my son-in-law, Mr. Marmaduke Falmer." Before I could add the address, the secretary started to his feet and tossed my list back to me across the table in the most uncivil manner.

"Upon my word," says he, "your assurance exceeds anything I ever heard of. Your son-in-law is concerned in the robbery of her ladyship's diamond bracelet—the discovery was made not an hour ago. Leave the house, sir, and consider yourself lucky that I have no instructions to give you in charge to the police." I protested against this unprovoked outrage, with a violence of language which I would rather not recall. As a minister, I ought, under every provocation, to have preserved my self-control.

The one thing to do next was to drive back to my unhappy daughter.

Her guilty husband was with her. I was too angry to wait for a fit opportunity of speaking. The Christian humility which I have all my life cultivated as the first of virtues sank, as it were, from under me. In terms of burning indignation I told them what had happened. The result was too distressing to be described. It ended in Felicia giving her husband back the bracelet. The hardened reprobate laughed at us. "Wait till I have seen his lordship and Mr. Helmsley," he said, and left the house.

Does he mean to escape to foreign parts? Felicia, womanlike, believes in him still; she is quite convinced that there must be some mistake. I am myself in hourly expectation of the arrival of the police.

With gratitude to Providence, I note before going to bed the harmless termination of the affair of the bracelet—so far as Marmaduke is concerned. The agent who sold him the jewel has been forced to come forward and state the truth. His lordship's wife is the guilty person; the bracelet was hers—a present from her husband. Harassed by debts that she dare not acknowledge, she sold it; my lord discovered that it was gone; and in terror of his anger the wretched woman took refuge in a lie.

She declared that the bracelet had been stolen from her. Asked for the name of the thief, the reckless woman (having no other name in her mind at the moment) mentioned the man who had innocently bought the jewel of her agent, otherwise my unfortunate son-in-law. Oh, the profligacy of the modern Babylon! It was well I went to the secretary when I did or we should really have had the police in the house. Marmaduke found them in consultation over the supposed robbery, asking for his address. There was a dreadful exhibition of violence and recrimination at his lordship's residence: in the end he re-purchased the bracelet. My son-in-law's money has been returned to him; and Mr. Helmsley has sent me a written apology.

In a worldly sense, this would, I suppose, be called a satisfactory ending.

It is not so to my mind. I freely admit that I too hastily distrusted Marmaduke; but am I, on that account, to give him back immediately the place which he once occupied in my esteem? Again this evening he mysteriously quitted the house, leaving me alone with Felicia, and giving no better excuse for his conduct than that he had an engagement. And this when I have a double claim on his consideration, as his father-in-law and his guest.

September 11th.—The day began well enough. At breakfast, Marmaduke spoke feelingly of the unhappy result of my visit to his lordship, and asked me to let him look at the list of repairs. "It is just useless to expect anything from my lord, after what has happened," I said. "Besides, Mr. Helmsley gave me no hope when I stated my case to him." Marmaduke still held out his hand for the list. "Let me try if I can get some subscribers," he replied. This was kindly meant, at any rate. I gave him the list; and I began to recover some of my old friendly feeling for him. Alas! the little gleam of tranquillity proved to be of short duration.

We made out our plans for the day pleasantly enough. The check came when Felicia spoke next of our plans for the evening. "My father has only four days more to pass with us," she said to her husband. "Surely you won't go out again to-night, and leave him?" Marmaduke's face clouded over directly; he looked embarrassed and annoyed. I sat perfectly silent, leaving them to settle it by themselves.

"You will stay with us this evening, won't you?" says Felicia. No: he was not free for the evening. "What! another engagement? Surely you can put it off?" No; impossible to put it off. "Is it a ball, or a party of some kind?" No answer; he changed the subject—he offered Felicia the money repaid to him for the bracelet. "Buy one for yourself, my dear, this time." Felicia handed him back the money, rather too haughtily, perhaps. "I don't want a bracelet," she said; "I want your company in the evening."

He jumped up, good-tempered as he was, in something very like a rage—then looked at me, and checked himself on the point (as I believe) of using profane language. "This is downright persecution!" he burst out, with an angry turn of his head toward his wife. Felicia got up, in her turn. "Your language is an insult to my father and to me!" He looked thoroughly staggered at this: it was evidently their first serious quarrel.

Felicia took no notice of him. "I will get ready directly, father; and we will go out together." He stopped her as she was leaving the room—recovering his good temper with a readiness which it pleased me to see. "Come, come, Felicia! We have not quarreled yet, and we won't quarrel now. Let me off this one time more, and I will devote the next three evenings of your father's visit to him and to you. Give me a kiss, and make it up." My daughter doesn't do things by halves. She gave him a dozen kisses, I should think—and there was a happy end of it.

"But what shall we do to-morrow evening?" says Marmaduke, sitting down by his wife, and patting her hand as it lay in his.

"Take us somewhere," says she. Marmaduke laughed. "Your father objects to public amusements. Where does he want to go to?" Felicia took up the newspaper. "There is an oratorio at Exeter Hall," she said; "my father likes music." He turned to me. "You don't object to oratorios, sir?" "I don't object to music," I answered, "so long as I am not required to enter a theater." Felicia handed the newspaper to me. "Speaking of theaters, father, have you read what they say about the new play? What a pity it can't be given out of a theater!" I looked at her in speechless amazement. She tried to explain herself. "The paper says that the new play is a service rendered to the cause of virtue; and that the great actor, Barrymore, has set an example in producing it which deserves the encouragement of all truly religious people. Do read it, father!" I held up my hands in dismay. My own daughter perverted! pinning her faith on a newspaper! speaking, with a perverse expression of interest, of a stage-play and an actor! Even Marmaduke witnessed this lamentable exhibition of backsliding with some appearance of alarm. "It's not her fault, sir," he said, interceding with me. "It's the fault of the newspaper. Don't blame her!" I held my peace; determining inwardly to pray for her. Shortly afterward my daughter and I went out. Marmaduke accompanied us part of the way, and left us at a telegraph office. "Who are you going to telegraph to?" Felicia asked. Another mystery! He answered, "Business of my own, my dear"—and went into the office.

September 12th.—Is my miserable son-in-law's house under a curse? The yellow-haired woman in the open carriage drove up to the door at half-past ten this morning, in a state of distraction. Felicia and I saw her from the drawing-room balcony—a tall woman in gorgeous garments. She knocked with her own hand at the door—she cried out distractedly, "Where is he? I must see him!" At the sound of her voice, Marmaduke (playing with his little dog in the drawing-room) rushed downstairs and out into the street. "Hold your tongue!" we heard him say to her. "What are you here for?"

What she answered we failed to hear; she was certainly crying. Marmaduke stamped on the pavement like a man beside himself—took her roughly by the arm, and led her into the house.

Before I could utter a word, Felicia left me and flew headlong down the stairs.

She was in time to hear the dining-room locked. Following her, I prevented the poor jealous creature from making a disturbance at the door. God forgive me—not knowing how else to quiet her—I degraded myself by advising her to listen to what they said. She instantly opened the door of the back dining-room, and beckoned to me to follow. I naturally hesitated. "I shall go mad," she whispered, "if you leave me by myself!" What could I do? I degraded myself the second time. For my own child—in pity for my own child!

We heard them, through the flimsy modern folding-doors, at those times when he was most angry, and she most distracted. That is to say, we heard them when they spoke in their loudest tones.

"How did you find out where I live?" says he. "Oh, you're ashamed of me?" says she. "Mr. Helmsley was with us yesterday evening. That's how I found out!" "What do you mean?" "I mean that Mr. Helmsley had your card and address in his pocket. Ah, you were obliged to give your address when you had to clear up that matter of the bracelet! You cruel, cruel man, what have I done to deserve such a note as you sent me this morning?" "Do what the note tells you!" "Do what the note tells me? Did anybody ever hear a man talk so, out of a lunatic asylum? Why, you haven't even the grace to carry out your own wicked deception—you haven't even gone to bed!" There the voices grew less angry, and we missed what followed. Soon the lady burst out again, piteously entreating him this time. "Oh, Marmy, don't ruin me! Has anybody offended you? Is there anything you wish to have altered? Do you want more money? It is too cruel to treat me in this way—it is indeed!" He made some answer, which we were not able to hear; we could only suppose that he had upset her temper again. She went on louder than ever "I've begged and prayed of you—and you're as hard as iron. I've told you about the Prince—and that has had no effect on you. I have done now. We'll see what the doctor says." He got angry, in his turn; we heard him again. "I won't see the doctor!" "Oh, you refuse to see the doctor?—I shall make your refusal known—and if there's law in England, you shall feel it!" Their voices dropped again; some new turn seemed to be taken by the conversation. We heard the lady once more, shrill and joyful this time. "There's a dear! You see it, don't you, in the right light? And you haven't forgotten the old times, have you? You're the same dear, honorable, kind-hearted fellow that you always were!"

I caught hold of Felicia, and put my hand over her mouth.

There was a sound in the next room which might have been—I cannot be certain—the sound of a kiss. The next moment, we heard the door of the room unlocked. Then the door of the house was opened, and the noise of retreating carriage-wheels followed. We met him in the hall, as he entered the house again.

My daughter walked up to him, pale and determined.

"I insist on knowing who that woman is, and what she wants here." Those were her first words. He looked at her like a man in utter confusion. "Wait till this evening; I am in no state to speak to you now!" With that, he snatched his hat off the hall table and rushed out of the house.

It is little more than three weeks since they returned to London from their happy wedding-tour—and it has come to this!

The clock has just struck seven; a letter has been left by a messenger, addressed to my daughter. I had persuaded her, poor soul, to lie down in her own room. God grant that the letter may bring her some tidings of her husband! I please myself in the hope of hearing good news.

My mind has not been kept long in suspense. Felicia's waiting-woman has brought me a morsel of writing paper, with these lines penciled on it in my daughter's handwriting: "Dearest father, make your mind easy. Everything is explained. I cannot trust myself to speak to you about it to-night—and he doesn't wish me to do so. Only wait till tomorrow, and you shall know all. He will be back about eleven o'clock. Please don't wait up for him—he will come straight to me."

September 13th.—The scales have fallen from my eyes; the light is let in on me at last. My bewilderment is not to be uttered in words—I am like a man in a dream.

Before I was out of my room in the morning, my mind was upset by the arrival of a telegram addressed to myself. It was the first thing of the kind I ever received; I trembled under the prevision of some new misfortune as I opened the envelope.

Of all the people in the world, the person sending the telegram was sister Judith! Never before did this distracting relative confound me as she confounded me now. Here is her message: "You can't come back. An architect from Edinburgh asserts his resolution to repair the kirk and the manse. The man only waits for his lawful authority to begin. The money is ready—but who has found it? Mr. Architect is forbidden to tell. We live in awful times. How is Felicia?"

Naturally concluding that Judith's mind must be deranged, I went downstairs to meet my son-in-law (for the first time since the events of yesterday) at the late breakfast which is customary in this house. He was waiting for me—but Felicia was not present. "She breakfasts in her room this morning," says Marmaduke; "and I am to give you the explanation which has already satisfied your daughter. Will you take it at great length, sir? or will you have it in one word?" There was something in his manner that I did not at all like—he seemed to be setting me at defiance. I said, stiffly, "Brevity is best; I will have it in one word."

"Here it is then," he answered. "I am Barrymore."

POSTSCRIPT ADDED BY FELICIA.

If the last line extracted from my dear father's Diary does not contain explanation enough in itself, I add some sentences from Marmaduke's letter to me, sent from the theater last night. (N. B.—I leave out the expressions of endearment: they are my own private property.)

... "Just remember how your father talked about theaters and actors, when I was at Cauldkirk, and how you listened in dutiful agreement with him. Would he have consented to your marriage if he had known that I was one of the 'spouting rogues,' associated with the 'painted Jezebels' of the playhouse? He would never have consented—and you yourself, my darling, would have trembled at the bare idea of marrying an actor.

"Have I been guilty of any serious deception? and have my friends been guilty in helping to keep my secret? My birth, my name, my surviving relatives, my fortune inherited from my father—all these important particulars have been truly stated. The name of Barrymore is nothing but the name that I assumed when I went on the stage.

"As to what has happened, since our return from Switzerland, I own that I ought to have made my confession to you. Forgive me if I weakly hesitated. I was so fond of you; and I so distrusted the Puritanical convictions which your education had rooted in your mind, that I put it off from day to day. Oh, my angel....!

"Yes, I kept the address of my new house a secret from all my friends, knowing they would betray me if they paid us visits. As for my mysteriously-closed study, it was the place in which I privately rehearsed my new part. When I left you in the mornings, it was to go to the theater rehearsals. My evening absences began of course with the first performance.

"Your father's arrival seriously embarrassed me. When you (most properly) insisted on my giving up some of my evenings to him, you necessarily made it impossible for me to appear on the stage. The one excuse I could make to the theater was, that I was too ill to act. It did certainly occur to me to cut the Gordian knot by owning the truth. But your father's horror, when you spoke of the newspaper review of the play, and the shame and fear you showed at your own boldness, daunted me once more.

"The arrival at the theater of my written excuse brought the manageress down upon me, in a state of distraction. Nobody could supply my place; all the seats were taken; and the Prince was expected. There was what we call a scene between the poor lady and myself. I felt I was in the wrong; I saw that the position in which I had impulsively placed myself was unworthy of me— and it ended in my doing my duty to the theater and the public. But for the affair of the bracelet, which obliged me as an honorable man to give my name and address, the manageress would not have discovered me. She, like every one else, only knew of my address at my bachelor chambers. How could you be jealous of the old theatrical comrade of my first days on the stage? Don't you know yet that you are the one woman in the world....?

"A last word relating to your father, and I have done.

"Do you remember my leaving you at the telegraph office? It was to send a message to a friend of mine, an architect in Edinburgh, instructing him to go immediately to Cauldkirk, and provide for the repairs at my expense. The theater, my dear, more than trebles my paternal income, and I can well afford it. Will your father refuse to accept a tribute of respect to a Scottish minister, because it is paid out of an actor's pocket? You shall ask him the question.

"And, I say, Felicia—will you come and see me act? I don't expect your father to enter a theater; but, by way of further reconciling him to his son-in-law, suppose you ask him to hear me read the play?"

MR. PERCY AND THE PROPHET.

PART 1.—THE PREDICTION.

CHAPTER I. THE QUACK.

THE disasters that follow the hateful offense against Christianity, which men call war, were severely felt in England during the peace that ensued on the overthrow of Napoleon at Waterloo. With rare exceptions, distress prevailed among all classes of the community. The starving nation was ripe and ready for a revolutionary rising against its rulers, who had shed the people's blood and wasted the people's substance in a war which had yielded to the popular interests absolutely nothing in return.

Among the unfortunate persons who were driven, during the disastrous early years of this century, to strange shifts and devices to obtain the means of living, was a certain obscure medical man, of French extraction, named Lagarde. The Doctor (duly qualified to bear the title) was an inhabitant of London; living in one of the narrow streets which connect the great thoroughfare of the Strand with the bank of the Thames.

The method of obtaining employment chosen by poor Lagarde, as the one alternative left in the face of starvation, was, and is still considered by the medical profession to be, the method of a quack. He advertised in the public journals.

Addressing himself especially to two classes of the community, the Doctor proceeded in these words:

"I have the honor of inviting to my house, in the first place: Persons afflicted with maladies which ordinary medical practice has failed to cure—

and, in the second place: Persons interested in investigations, the object of which is to penetrate the secrets of the future. Of the means by which I endeavor to alleviate suffering and to enlighten doubt, it is impossible to speak intelligibly within the limits of an advertisement. I can only offer to submit my system to public inquiry, without exacting any preliminary fee from ladies and gentlemen who may honor me with a visit. Those who see sufficient reason to trust me, after personal experience, will find a money-box fixed on the waiting-room table, into which they can drop their offerings according to their means. Those whom I am not fortunate enough to satisfy will be pleased to accept the expression of my regret, and will not be expected to give anything. I shall be found at home every evening between the hours of six and ten."

Toward the close of the year 1816 this strange advertisement became a general topic of conversation among educated people in London. For some weeks the Doctor's invitations were generally accepted—and, all things considered, were not badly remunerated. A faithful few believed in him, and told wonderful stories of what he had pronounced and prophesied in the sanctuary of his consulting-room. The majority of his visitors simply viewed him in the light of a public amusement, and wondered why such a gentlemanlike man should have chosen to gain his living by exhibiting himself as a quack.

CHAPTER II. THE NUMBERS.

ON a raw and snowy evening toward the latter part of January, 1817, a gentleman, walking along the Strand, turned into the street in which Doctor Lagarde lived, and knocked at the physician's door.

He was admitted by an elderly male servant to a waiting-room on the first floor. The light of one little lamp, placed on a bracket fixed to the wall, was so obscured by a dark green shade as to make it difficult, if not impossible, for visitors meeting by accident to recognize each other. The metal money-box fixed to the table was just visible. In the flickering light of a small fire, the stranger perceived the figures of three men seated, apart and silent, who were the only occupants of the room beside himself.

So far as objects were to be seen, there was nothing to attract attention in the waiting-room. The furniture was plain and neat, and nothing more. The elderly servant handed a card, with a number inscribed on it, to the new visitor, said in a whisper, "Your number will be called, sir, in your turn," and disappeared. For some minutes nothing disturbed the deep silence but the faint ticking of a clock. After a while a bell rang from an inner room, a door opened, and a gentleman appeared, whose interview with Doctor Lagarde had terminated. His opinion of the sitting was openly expressed in one emphatic word—"Humbug!" No contribution dropped from his hand as he passed the money-box on his way out.

The next number (being Number Fifteen) was called by the elderly servant, and the first incident occurred in the strange series of events destined to happen in the Doctor's house that night.

One after another the three men who had been waiting rose, examined their cards under the light of the lamp, and sat down again surprised and disappointed.

The servant advanced to investigate the matter. The numbers possessed by the three visitors, instead of being Fifteen, Sixteen and Seventeen, proved to be Sixteen, Seventeen and Eighteen. Turning to the stranger who had arrived the last, the servant said:

"Have I made a mistake, sir? Have I given you Number Fifteen instead of Number Eighteen?"

The gentleman produced his numbered card.

A mistake had certainly been made, but not the mistake that the servant supposed. The card held by the latest visitor turned out to be the card previously held by the dissatisfied stranger who had just left the room— Number Fourteen! As to the card numbered Fifteen, it was only discovered the next morning lying in a corner, dropped on the floor!

Acting on his first impulse, the servant hurried out, calling to the original holder of Fourteen to come back and bear his testimony to that fact. The street-door had been opened for him by the landlady of the house. She was a pretty woman—and the gentleman had fortunately lingered to talk to her.

He was induced, at the intercession of the landlady, to ascend the stairs again.

On returning to the waiting-room, he addressed a characteristic question to the assembled visitors. "More humbug?" asked the gentleman who liked to talk to a pretty woman.

The servant—completely puzzled by his own stupidity—attempted to make his apologies.

"Pray forgive me, gentlemen," he said. "I am afraid I have confused the cards I distribute with the cards returned to me. I think I had better consult my master."

Left by themselves, the visitors began to speak jestingly of the strange situation in which they were placed. The original holder of Number Fourteen described his experience of the Doctor in his own pithy way. "I applied to the fellow to tell my fortune. He first went to sleep over it, and then he said he could tell me nothing. I asked why. 'I don't know,' says he. ' I do,' says I—'humbug!' I'll bet you the long odds, gentlemen, that you find it humbug, too."

Before the wager could be accepted or declined, the door of the inner room was opened again. The tall, spare, black figure of a new personage appeared on the threshold, relieved darkly against the light in the room behind him. He addressed the visitors in these words:

"Gentlemen, I must beg your indulgence. The accident—as we now suppose it to be—which has given to the last comer the number already held by a gentleman who has unsuccessfully consulted me, may have a meaning which we can none of us at present see. If the three visitors who have been so good as to wait will allow the present holder of Number Fourteen to consult me out of his turn—and if the earlier visitor who left me dissatisfied with his consultation will consent to stay here a little longer—something may happen which will justify a trifling sacrifice of your own convenience. Is ten minutes' patience too much to ask of you?"

The three visitors who had waited longest consulted among themselves, and (having nothing better to do with their time) decided on accepting the

Doctor's proposal. The visitor who believed it all to be "humbug" coolly took a gold coin out of his pocket, tossed it into the air, caught it in his closed hand, and walked up to the shaded lamp on the bracket.

"Heads, stay," he said, "Tails, go." He opened his hand, and looked at the coin. "Heads! Very good. Go on with your hocus-pocus, Doctor—I'll wait."

"You believe in chance," said the Doctor, quietly observing him. "That is not my experience of life."

He paused to let the stranger who now held Number Fourteen pass him into the inner room—then followed, closing the door behind him.

CHAPTER III. THE CONSULTATION.

THE consulting-room was better lighted than the waiting-room, and that was the only difference between the two. In the one, as in the other, no attempt was made to impress the imagination. Everywhere, the commonplace furniture of a London lodging-house was left without the slightest effort to alter or improve it by changes of any kind.

Seen under the clearer light, Doctor Lagarde appeared to be the last person living who would consent to degrade himself by an attempt at imposture of any kind. His eyes were the dreamy eyes of a visionary; his look was the prematurely-aged look of a student, accustomed to give the hours to his book which ought to have been given to his bed. To state it briefly, he was a man who might easily be deceived by others, but who was incapable of consciously practicing deception himself.

Signing to his visitor to be seated, he took a chair on the opposite side of the small table that stood between them—waited a moment with his face hidden in his hands, as if to collect himself—and then spoke.

"Do you come to consult me on a case of illness?" he inquired, "or do you ask me to look to the darkness which hides your future life?"

The answer to these questions was frankly and briefly expressed. "I have no need to consult you about my health. I come to hear what you can tell me of my future life."

"I can try," pursued the Doctor; "but I cannot promise to succeed."

"I accept your conditions," the stranger rejoined. "I never believe nor disbelieve. If you will excuse my speaking frankly, I mean to observe you closely, and to decide for myself."

Doctor Lagarde smiled sadly.

"You have heard of me as a charlatan who contrives to amuse a few idle people," he said. "I don't complain of that; my present position leads necessarily to misinterpretation of myself and my motives. Still, I may at least say that I am the victim of a sincere avowal of my belief in a great science. Yes! I repeat it, a great science! New, I dare say, to the generation we live in, though it was known and practiced in the days when pyramids were built. The age is advancing; and the truths which it is my misfortune to advocate, before the time is ripe for them, are steadily forcing their way to recognition. I am resigned to wait. My sincerity in this matter has cost me the income that I derived from my medical practice. Patients distrust me; doctors refuse to consult with me. I could starve if I had no one to think of but myself. But I have another person to consider, who is very dear to me; and I am driven, literally driven, either to turn beggar in the streets, or do what I am doing now."

He paused, and looked round toward the corner of the room behind him. "Mother," he said gently, "are you ready?"

An elderly lady, dressed in deep mourning, rose from her seat in the corner. She had been, thus far, hidden from notice by the high back of the easy-chair in which her son sat. Excepting some folds of fine black lace, laid over her white hair so as to form a head-dress at once simple and picturesque, there was nothing remarkable in her attire. The visitor rose and bowed. She gravely returned his salute, and moved so as to place herself opposite to her son.

"May I ask what this lady is going to do?" said the stranger.

"To be of any use to you," answered Doctor Lagarde, "I must be thrown into the magnetic trance. The person who has the strongest influence over me is the person who will do it to-night."

He turned to his mother. "When you like," he said.

Bending over him, she took both the Doctor's hands, and looked steadily into his eyes. No words passed between them; nothing more took place. In a minute or two, his head was resting against the back of the chair, and his eyelids had closed.

"Are you sleeping?" asked Madame Lagarde.

"I am sleeping," he answered.

She laid his hands gently on the arms of the chair, and turned to address the visitor.

"Let the sleep gain on him for a minute or two more," she said. "Then take one of his hands, and put to him what questions you please."

"Does he hear us now, madam?"

"You might fire off a pistol, sir, close to his ear, and he would not hear it. The vibration might disturb him; that is all. Until you or I touch him, and so establish the nervous sympathy, he is as lost to all sense of our presence here, as if he were dead."

"Are you speaking of the thing called Animal Magnetism, madam?"

"Yes, sir."

"And you believe in it, of course?"

"My son's belief, sir, is my belief in this thing as in other things. I have heard what he has been saying to you. It is for me that he sacrifices himself by holding these exhibitions; it is in my poor interests that his hardly-earned money is made. I am in infirm health; and, remonstrate as I may, my son persists in providing for me, not the bare comforts only, but even the luxuries of life. Whatever I may suffer, I have my compensation; I can still thank God for giving me the greatest happiness that a woman can enjoy, the possession of a good son."

She smiled fondly as she looked at the sleeping man. "Draw your chair nearer to him," she resumed, "and take his hand. You may speak freely in making your inquiries. Nothing that happens in this room goes out of it."

With those words she returned to her place, in the corner behind her son's chair.

The visitor took Doctor Lagarde's hand. As they touched each other, he was conscious of a faintly-titillating sensation in his own hand—a sensation which oddly reminded him of bygone experiments with an electrical machine, in the days when he was a boy at school!

"I wish to question you about my future life," he began. "How ought I to begin?"

The Doctor spoke his first words in the monotonous tones of a man talking in his sleep.

"Own your true motive before you begin," he said. "Your interest in your future life is centered in a woman. You wish to know if her heart will be yours in the time that is to come—and there your interest in your future life ends."

This startling proof of the sleeper's capacity to look, by sympathy, into his mind, and to see there his most secret thoughts, instead of convincing the stranger, excited his suspicions. "You have means of getting information," he said, "that I don't understand."

The Doctor smiled, as if the idea amused him.

Madame Lagarde rose from her seat and interposed.

"Hundreds of strangers come here to consult my son," she said quietly. "If you believe that we know who those strangers are, and that we have the means of inquiring into their private lives before they enter this room, you believe in something much more incredible than the magnetic sleep!"

This was too manifestly true to be disputed. The visitor made his apologies.

"I should like to have some explanation," he added. "The thing is so very extraordinary. How can I prevail upon Doctor Lagarde to enlighten me?"

"He can only tell you what he sees," Madame Lagarde answered; "ask him that, and you will get a direct reply. Say to him: 'Do you see the lady?'"

The stranger repeated the question. The reply followed at once, in these words:

"I see two figures standing side by side. One of them is your figure. The other is the figure of a lady. She only appears dimly. I can discover nothing but that she is taller than women generally are, and that she is dressed in pale blue."

The man to whom he was speaking started at those last words. "Her favorite color!" he thought to himself—forgetting that, while he held the Doctor's hand, the Doctor could think with his mind.

"Yes," added the sleeper quietly, "her favorite color, as you know. She fades and fades as I look at her," he went on. "She is gone. I only see you, under a new aspect. You have a pistol in your hand. Opposite to you, there stands the figure of another man. He, too, has a pistol in his hand. Are you enemies? Are you meeting to fight a duel? Is the lady the cause? I try, but I fail to see her."

"Can you describe the man?"

"Not yet. So far, he is only a shadow in the form of a man."

There was another interval. An appearance of disturbance showed itself on the sleeper's face. Suddenly, he waved his free hand in the direction of the waiting-room.

"Send for the visitors who are there," he said. "They are all to come in. Each one of them is to take one of my hands in turn—while you remain where you are, holding the other hand. Don't let go of me, even for a moment. My mother will ring."

Madame Lagarde touched a bell on the table. The servant received his orders from her and retired. After a short absence, he appeared again in the consulting-room, with one visitor only waiting on the threshold behind him.

CHAPTER IV. THE MAN.

"The other three gentlemen have gone away, madam," the servant explained, addressing Madame Lagarde. "They were tired of waiting. I found this gentleman fast asleep; and I am afraid he is angry with me for taking the liberty of waking him."

"Sleep of the common sort is evidently not allowed in this house." With that remark the gentleman entered the room, and stood revealed as the original owner of the card numbered Fourteen.

Viewed by the clear lamplight, he was a tall, finely-made man, in the prime of life, with a florid complexion, golden-brown hair, and sparkling blue eyes. Noticing Madame Lagarde, he instantly checked the flow of his satire, with the instinctive good-breeding of a gentleman. "I beg your pardon," he said; "I have a great many faults, and a habit of making bad jokes is one of them. Is the servant right, madam, in telling me that I have the honor of presenting myself here at your request?"

Madame Lagarde briefly explained what had passed.

The florid gentleman (still privately believing it to be all "humbug") was delighted to make himself of any use. "I congratulate you, sir," he said, with his easy humor, as he passed the visitor who had become possessed of his card. "Number Fourteen seems to be a luckier number in your keeping than it was in mine."

As he spoke, he took Doctor Lagarde's disengaged hand. The instant they touched each other the sleeper started. His voice rose; his face flushed. "You are the man!" he exclaimed. "I see you plainly now!"

"What am I doing?"

"You are standing opposite to the gentleman here who is holding my other hand; and (as I have said already) you have met to fight a duel."

The unbeliever cast a shrewd look at his companion in the consultation.

"Considering that you and I are total strangers, sir," he said, "don't you think the Doctor had better introduce us, before he goes any further? We have got to fighting a duel already, and we may as well know who we are, before the pistols go off." He turned to Doctor Lagarde. "Dramatic situations don't amuse me out of the theater," he resumed. "Let me put you to a very commonplace test. I want to be introduced to this gentleman. Has he told you his name?"

"No."

"Of course, you know it, without being told?"

"Certainly. I have only to look into your own knowledge of yourselves, while I am in this trance, and while you have got my hands, to know both your names as well as you do."

"Introduce us, then!" retorted the jesting gentleman. "And take my name first."

"Mr. Percy Linwood," replied the Doctor; "I have the honor of presenting you to Captain Bervie, of the Artillery."

With one accord, the gentlemen both dropped Doctor Lagarde's hands, and looked at each other in blank amazement.

"Of course he has discovered our names somehow!" said Mr. Percy Linwood, explaining the mystery to his own perfect satisfaction in that way.

Captain Bervie had not forgotten what Madame Lagarde had said to him, when he too had suspected a trick. He now repeated it (quite ineffectually) for Mr. Linwood's benefit. "If you don't feel the force of that argument as I feel it," he added, "perhaps, as a favor to me, sir, you will not object to our each taking the Doctor's hand again, and hearing what more he can tell us while he remains in the state of trance?"

"With the greatest pleasure!" answered good-humored Mr. Linwood. "Our friend is beginning to amuse me; I am as anxious as you are to know what he is going to see next."

Captain Bervie put the next question.

"You have seen us ready to fight a duel—can you tell us the result?"

"I can tell you nothing more than I have told you already. The figures of the duelists have faded away, like the other figures I saw before them. What I see now looks like the winding gravel-path of a garden. A man and a woman are walking toward me. The man stops, and places a ring on the woman's finger, and kisses her."

Captain Bervie opened his lips to continue his inquiries—turned pale—and checked himself. Mr. Linwood put the next question.

"Who is the happy man?" he asked.

"You are the happy man," was the instantaneous reply.

"Who is the woman?" cried Captain Bervie, before Mr. Linwood could speak again.

"The same woman whom I saw before; dressed in the same color, in pale blue."

Captain Bervie positively insisted on receiving clearer information than this. "Surely you can see something of her personal appearance?" he said.

"I can see that she has long dark-brown hair, falling below her waist. I can see that she has lovely dark-brown eyes. She has the look of a sensitive nervous person. She is quite young. I can see no more."

"Look again at the man who is putting the ring on her finger," said the Captain. "Are you sure that the face you see is the face of Mr. Percy Linwood?"

"I am absolutely sure."

Captain Bervie rose from his chair.

"Thank you, madam," he said to the Doctor's mother. "I have heard enough."

822

He walked to the door. Mr. Percy Linwood dropped Doctor Lagarde's hand, and appealed to the retiring Captain with a broad stare of astonishment.

"You don't really believe this?" he said.

"I only say I have heard enough," Captain Bervie answered.

Mr. Linwood could hardly fail to see that any further attempt to treat the matter lightly might lead to undesirable results.

"It is difficult to speak seriously of this kind of exhibition," he resumed quietly. "But I suppose I may mention a mere matter of fact, without meaning or giving offense. The description of the lady, I can positively declare, does not apply in any single particular to any one whom I know."

Captain Bervie turned round at the door. His patience was in some danger of failing him. Mr. Linwood's unruffled composure, assisted in its influence by the presence of Madame Lagarde, reminded him of the claims of politeness. He restrained the rash words as they rose to his lips. "You may make new acquaintances, sir," was all that he said. "You have the future before you."

Upon that, he went out. Percy Linwood waited a little, reflecting on the Captain's conduct.

Had Doctor Lagarde's description of the lady accidentally answered the description of a living lady whom Captain Bervie knew? Was he by any chance in love with her? and had the Doctor innocently reminded him that his love was not returned? Assuming this to be likely, was it really possible that he believed in prophetic revelations offered to him under the fantastic influence of a trance? Could any man in the possession of his senses go to those lengths? The Captain's conduct was simply incomprehensible.

Pondering these questions, Percy decided on returning to his place by the Doctor's chair. "Of one thing I am certain, at any rate," he thought to himself. "I'll see the whole imposture out before I leave the house!"

He took Doctor Lagarde's hand. "Now, then! what is the next discovery?" he asked.

The sleeper seemed to find some difficulty in answering the question.

"I indistinctly see the man and the woman again," he said.

"Am I the man still?" Percy inquired.

"No. The man, this time, is the Captain. The woman is agitated by something that he is saying to her. He seems to be trying to persuade her to go away with him. She hesitates. He whispers something in her ear. She yields. He leads her away. The darkness gathers behind them. I look and look, and I can see no more."

"Shall we wait awhile?" Percy suggested, "and then try again?"

Doctor Lagarde sighed, and reclined in his chair. "My head is heavy," he said; "my spirits are dull. The darkness baffles me. I have toiled long enough for you. Drop my hand and leave me to rest."

Hearing those words, Madame Lagarde approached her son's chair.

"It will be useless, sir, to ask him any more questions to-night," she said. "He has been weak and nervous all day, and he is worn out by the effort he has made. Pardon me, if I ask you to step aside for a moment, while I give him the repose that he needs."

She laid her right hand gently on the Doctor's head, and kept it there for a minute or so. "Are you at rest now?" she asked.

"I am at rest," he answered, in faint, drowsy tones.

Madame Lagarde returned to Percy. "If you are not yet satisfied," she said, "my son will be at your service to-morrow evening, sir."

"Thank you, madam, I have only one more question to ask, and you can no doubt answer it. When your son wakes, will he remember what he has said to Captain Bervie and to myself?"

"My son will be as absolutely ignorant of everything that he has seen, and of everything that he has said in the trance, as if he had been at the other end of the world."

Percy Linwood swallowed this last outrageous assertion with an effort which he was quite unable to conceal. "Many thanks, madam," he said; "I wish you good-night."

Returning to the waiting-room, he noticed the money-box fixed to the table. "These people look poor," he thought to himself, "and I feel really indebted to them for an amusing evening. Besides, I can afford to be liberal, for I shall certainly never go back." He dropped a five-pound note into the money-box, and left the house.

Walking toward his club, Percy's natural serenity of mind was a little troubled by the remembrance of Captain Bervie's language and conduct. The Captain had interested the young man in spite of himself. His first idea was to write to Bervie, and mention what had happened at the renewed consultation with Doctor Lagarde. On second thoughts, he saw reason to doubt how the Captain might receive such an advance as this, on the part of a stranger. "After all," Percy decided, "the whole thing is too absurd to be worth thinking about seriously. Neither he nor I are likely to meet again, or to see the Doctor again—and there's an end of it."

He never was more mistaken in his life. The end of it was not to come for many a long day yet.

PART II.—THE FULFILLMENT.

CHAPTER V. THE BALLROOM.

WHILE the consultation at Doctor Lagarde's was still fresh in the memory of the persons present at it, Chance or Destiny, occupied in sowing the seeds for the harvest of the future, discovered as one of its fit instruments a retired military officer named Major Mulvany.

The Major was a smart little man, who persisted in setting up the appearance of youth as a means of hiding the reality of fifty. Being still a bachelor, and being always ready to make himself agreeable, he was generally popular in the society of women. In the ballroom he was a really welcome addition to the company. The German waltz had then been imported into England little more than three years since. The outcry raised against the dance, by persons skilled in the discovery of latent impropriety, had not yet lost its influence in certain quarters. Men who could waltz were scarce. The Major had successfully grappled with the difficulties of learning the dance in mature life; and the young ladies rewarded him nobly for the effort. That is to say, they took the assumption of youth for granted in the palpable presence of fifty.

Knowing everybody and being welcome everywhere, playing a good hand at whist, and having an inexhaustible fancy in the invention of a dinner, Major Mulvany naturally belonged to all the best clubs of his time. Percy Linwood and he constantly met in the billiard-room or at the dinner-table. The Major approved of the easy, handsome, pleasant-tempered young man. "I have lost the first freshness of youth," he used to say, with pathetic resignation, "and I see myself revived, as it were, in Percy. Naturally I like Percy."

About three weeks after the memorable evening at Doctor Lagarde's, the two friends encountered each other on the steps of a club.

"Have you got anything to do to-night?" asked the Major.

"Nothing that I know of," said Percy, "unless I go to the theater."

"Let the theater wait, my boy. My old regiment gives a ball at Woolwich to-night. I have got a ticket to spare; and I know several sweet girls who are going. Some of them waltz, Percy! Gather your rosebuds while you may. Come with me."

The invitation was accepted as readily as it was given. The Major found the carriage, and Percy paid for the post-horses. They entered the ballroom among the earlier guests; and the first person whom they met, waiting near the door, was—Captain Bervie.

Percy bowed a little uneasily. "I feel some doubt," he said, laughing, "whether we have been properly introduced to one another or not."

"Not properly introduced!" cried Major Mulvany. "I'll soon set that right. My dear friend, Percy Linwood; my dear friend, Arthur Bervie—be known to each other! esteem each other!"

Captain Bervie acknowledged the introduction by a cold salute. Percy, yielding to the good-natured impulse of the moment, alluded to what had happened in Doctor Lagarde's consulting-room.

"You missed something worth hearing when you left the Doctor the other night," he said. "We continued the sitting; and you turned up again among the persons of the drama, in a new character—"

"Excuse me for interrupting you," said Captain Bervie. "I am a member of the committee, charged with the arrangements of the ball, and I must really attend to my duties."

He withdrew without waiting for a reply. Percy looked round wonderingly at Major Mulvany. "Strange!" he said, "I feel rather attracted toward Captain Bervie; and he seems to have taken such a dislike to me that he can hardly behave with common civility. What does it mean?"

"I'll tell you," answered the Major, confidentially. "Arthur Bervie is madly in love—madly is really the word—with a Miss Bowmore. And (this is between ourselves) the young lady doesn't feel it quite in the same way. A sweet girl; I've often had her on my knee when she was a child. Her father and mother are old friends of mine. She is coming to the ball to-night. That's the true reason why Arthur left you just now. Look at him—waiting to be the first to speak to her. If he could have his way, he wouldn't let another man come near the poor girl all through the evening; he really persecutes her. I'll introduce you to Miss Bowmore; and you will see how he looks at us for presuming to approach her. It's a great pity; she will never marry him. Arthur Bervie is a man in a thousand; but he's fast becoming a perfect bear under the strain on his temper. What's the matter? You don't seem to be listening to me."

This last remark was perfectly justified. In telling the Captain's love-story, Major Mulvany had revived his young friend's memory of the lady in the blue dress, who had haunted the visions of Doctor Lagarde.

"Tell me," said Percy, "what is Miss Bowmore like? Is there anything remarkable in her personal appearance? I have a reason for asking."

As he spoke, there arose among the guests in the rapidly-filling ballroom a low murmur of surprise and admiration. The Major laid one hand on Percy's shoulder, and, lifting the other, pointed to the door.

"What is Miss Bowmore like?" he repeated. "There she is! Let her answer for herself."

Percy turned toward the lower end of the room.

A young lady was entering, dressed in plain silk, and the color of it was a pale blue! Excepting a white rose at her breast, she wore no ornament of any sort. Doubly distinguished by the perfect simplicity of her apparel, and by her tall, supple, commanding figure, she took rank at once as the most remarkable woman in the room. Moving nearer to her through the crowd, under the guidance of the complaisant Major, young Linwood gained a clearer view of her hair, her complexion, and the color of her eyes. In every one of these particulars she was the living image of the woman described by

Doctor Lagarde!

While Percy was absorbed over this strange discovery, Major Mulvany had got within speaking distance of the young lady and of her mother, as they stood together in conversation with Captain Bervie. "My dear Mrs. Bowmore, how well you are looking! My dear Miss Charlotte, what a sensation you have made already! The glorious simplicity (if I may so express myself) of your dress is—is—what was I going to say?—the ideas come thronging on me; I merely want words."

Miss Bowmore's magnificent brown eyes, wandering from the Major to Percy, rested on the young man with a modest and momentary interest, which Captain Bervie's jealous attention instantly detected.

"They are forming a dance," he said, pressing forward impatiently to claim his partner. "If we don't take our places we shall be too late."

"Stop! stop!" cried the Major. "There is a time for everything, and this is the time for presenting my dear friend here, Mr. Percy Linwood. He is like me, Miss Charlotte—he has been struck by your glorious simplicity, and he wants words." At this part of the presentation, he happened to look toward the irate Captain, and instantly gave him a hint on the subject of his temper. "I say, Arthur Bervie! we are all good-humored people here. What have you got on your eyebrows? It looks like a frown; and it doesn't become you. Send for a skilled waiter, and have it brushed off and taken away directly!"

"May I ask, Miss Bowmore, if you are disengaged for the next dance?" said Percy, the moment the Major gave him an opportunity of speaking.

"Miss Bowmore is engaged to me for the next dance," said the angry Captain, before the young lady could answer.

"The third dance, then?" Percy persisted, with his brightest smile.

"With pleasure, Mr. Linwood," said Miss Bowmore. She would have been no true woman if she had not resented the open exhibition of Arthur's jealousy; it was like asserting a right over her to which he had not the shadow of a claim. She threw a look at Percy as her partner led her away, which was the severest punishment she could inflict on the man who ardently loved her.

The third dance stood in the programme as a waltz.

In jealous distrust of Percy, the Captain took the conductor of the band aside, and used his authority as committeeman to substitute another dance. He had no sooner turned his back on the orchestra than the wife of the Colonel of the regiment, who had heard him, spoke to the conductor in her turn, and insisted on the original programme being retained. "Quote the Colonel's authority," said the lady, "if Captain Bervie ventures to object." In the meantime, the Captain, on his way to rejoin Charlotte, was met by one of his brother officers, who summoned him officially to an impending debate of the committee charged with the administrative arrangements of the supper-table. Bervie had no choice but to follow his brother officer to the committee-room.

Barely a minute later the conductor appeared at his desk, and the first notes of the music rose low and plaintive, introducing the third dance.

"Percy, my boy!" cried the Major, recognizing the melody, "you're in luck's way—it's going to be a waltz!"

Almost as he spoke, the notes of the symphony glided by subtle modulations into the inspiriting air of the waltz. Percy claimed his partner's hand. Miss Charlotte hesitated, and looked at her mother.

"Surely you waltz?" said Percy.

"I have learned to waltz," she answered, modestly; "but this is such a large room, and there are so many people!"

"Once round," Percy pleaded; "only once round!"

Miss Bowmore looked again at her mother. Her foot was keeping time with the music, under her dress; her heart was beating with a delicious excitement; kind-hearted Mrs. Bowmore smiled and said: "Once round, my dear, as Mr. Linwood suggests."

In another moment Percy's arm took possession of her waist, and they were away on the wings of the waltz!

Could words describe, could thought realize, the exquisite enjoyment of the dance? Enjoyment? It was more—it was an epoch in Charlotte's life—it was the first time she had waltzed with a man. What a difference between the fervent clasp of Percy's arm and the cold, formal contact of the mistress who had taught her! How brightly his eyes looked down into hers; admiring her with such a tender restraint, that there could surely be no harm in looking up at him now and then in return. Round and round they glided, absorbed in the music and in themselves. Occasionally her bosom just touched him, at those critical moments when she was most in need of support. At other intervals, she almost let her head sink on his shoulder in trying to hide from him the smile which acknowledged his admiration too boldly. "Once round," Percy had suggested; "once round," her mother had said. They had been ten, twenty, thirty times round; they had never stopped to rest like other dancers; they had centered the eyes of the whole room on them—including the eyes of Captain Bervie—without knowing it; her delicately pale complexion had changed to rosy-red; the neat arrangement of her hair had become disturbed; her bosom was rising and falling faster and faster in the effort to breathe—before fatigue and heat overpowered her at last, and forced her to say to him faintly, "I'm very sorry—I can't dance any more!"

Percy led her into the cooler atmosphere of the refreshment-room, and revived her with a glass of lemonade. Her arm still rested on his—she was just about to thank him for the care he had taken of her—when Captain Bervie entered the room.

"Mrs. Bowmore wishes me to take you back to her," he said to Charlotte. Then, turning to Percy, he added: "Will you kindly wait here while I take Miss Bowmore to the ballroom? I have a word to say to you—I will return directly."

The Captain spoke with perfect politeness—but his face betrayed him. It was pale with the sinister whiteness of suppressed rage.

Percy sat down to cool and rest himself. With his experience of the ways of men, he felt no surprise at the marked contrast between Captain

Bervie's face and Captain Bervie's manner. "He has seen us waltzing, and he is coming back to pick a quarrel with me." Such was the interpretation which Mr. Linwood's knowledge of the world placed on Captain Bervie's politeness. In a minute or two more the Captain returned to the refreshment-room, and satisfied Percy that his anticipations had not deceived him.

CHAPTER VI. LOVE.

FOUR days had passed since the night of the ball.

Although it was no later in the year than the month of February, the sun was shining brightly, and the air was as soft as the air of a day in spring. Percy and Charlotte were walking together in the little garden at the back of Mr. Bowmore's cottage, near the town of Dartford, in Kent.

"Mr. Linwood," said the young lady, "you were to have paid us your first visit the day after the ball. Why have you kept us waiting? Have you been too busy to remember your new friends?"

"I have counted the hours since we parted, Miss Charlotte. If I had not been detained by business—"

"I understand! For three days business has controlled you. On the fourth day, you have controlled business—and here you are? I don't believe one word of it, Mr. Linwood!"

There was no answering such a declaration as this. Guiltily conscious that Charlotte was right in refusing to accept his well-worn excuse, Percy made an awkward attempt to change the topic of conversation.

They happened, at the moment, to be standing near a small conservatory at the end of the garden. The glass door was closed, and the few plants and shrubs inside had a lonely, neglected look. "Does nobody ever visit this secluded place?" Percy asked, jocosely, "or does it hide discoveries in the rearing of plants which are forbidden mysteries to a stranger?"

"Satisfy your curiosity, Mr. Linwood, by all means," Charlotte answered in the same tone. "Open the door, and I will follow you."

Percy obeyed. In passing through the doorway, he encountered the bare hanging branches of some creeping plant, long since dead, and detached from its fastenings on the woodwork of the roof. He pushed aside the branches so that Charlotte could easily follow him in, without being aware that his own forced passage through them had a little deranged the folds of spotless white cambric which a well-dressed gentleman wore round his neck in those days. Charlotte seated herself, and directed Percy's attention to the desolate conservatory with a saucy smile.

"The mystery which your lively imagination has associated with this place," she said, "means, being interpreted, that we are too poor to keep a gardener. Make the best of your disappointment, Mr. Linwood, and sit here by me. We are out of hearing and out of sight of mamma's other visitors. You have no excuse now for not telling me what has really kept you away from us."

She fixed her eyes on him as she said those words. Before Percy could think of another excuse, her quick observation detected the disordered condition of his cravat, and discovered the upper edge of a black plaster attached to one side of his neck.

"You have been hurt in the neck!" she said. "That is why you have kept away from us for the last three days!"

"A mere trifle," he answered, in great confusion; "please don't notice it."

Her eyes, still resting on his face, assumed an expression of suspicious inquiry, which Percy was entirely at a loss to understand. Suddenly, she started to her feet, as if a new idea had occurred to her. "Wait here," she said, flushing with excitement, "till I come back: I insist on it!"

Before Percy could ask for an explanation she had left the conservatory.

In a minute or two, Miss Bowmore returned, with a newspaper in her hand. "Read that," she said, pointing to a paragraph distinguished by a line drawn round it in ink.

The passage that she indicated contained an account of a duel which had recently taken place in the neighborhood of London. The names of the duelists were not mentioned. One was described as an officer, and the other as a civilian. They had quarreled at cards, and had fought with pistols. The civilian had had a narrow escape of his life. His antagonist's bullet had passed near enough to the side of his neck to tear the flesh, and had missed the vital parts, literally, by a hair's-breadth.

Charlotte's eyes, riveted on Percy, detected a sudden change of color in his face the moment he looked at the newspaper. That was enough for her. "You are the man!" she cried. "Oh, for shame, for shame! To risk your life for a paltry dispute about cards!"

"I would risk it again," said Percy, "to hear you speak as if you set some value on it."

She looked away from him without a word of reply. Her mind seemed to be busy again with its own thoughts. Did she meditate returning to the subject of the duel? Was she not satisfied with the discovery which she had just made?

No such doubts as these troubled the mind of Percy Linwood. Intoxicated by the charm of her presence, emboldened by her innocent betrayal of the interest that she felt in him, he opened his whole heart to her as unreservedly as if they had known each other from the days of their childhood. There was but one excuse for him. Charlotte was his first love.

"You don't know how completely you have become a part of my life, since we met at the ball," he went on. "That one delightful dance seemed, by some magic which I can't explain, to draw us together in a few minutes as if we had known each other for years. Oh, dear! I could make such a confession of what I felt—only I am afraid of offending you by speaking too soon. Women are so dreadfully difficult to understand. How is a man to know at what time it is considerate toward them to conceal his true feelings; and at what time it is equally considerate to express his true feelings? One doesn't know whether it is a matter of days or weeks or months—there ought to be a law to settle it. Dear Miss Charlotte, when a poor fellow loves you at first sight, as he has never loved any other woman, and when he is tormented by the fear that some other man may be preferred to him, can't you forgive him if he lets out the truth a little too soon?" He ventured, as he put that very downright question, to take her hand. "It really isn't my fault," he said, simply. "My heart is so full of you I can talk of nothing else."

To Percy's delight, the first experimental pressure of his hand, far from being resented, was softly returned. Charlotte looked at him again, with a new resolution in her face.

"I'll forgive you for talking nonsense, Mr. Linwood," she said; "and I will even permit you to come and see me again, on one condition—that you tell the whole truth about the duel. If you conceal the smallest circumstance, our acquaintance is at an end."

"Haven't I owned everything already?" Percy inquired, in great perplexity. "Did I say No, when you told me I was the man?"

"Could you say No, with that plaster on your neck?" was the ready rejoinder. "I am determined to know more than the newspaper tells me. Will you declare, on your word of honor, that Captain Bervie had nothing to do with the duel? Can you look me in the face, and say that the real cause of the quarrel was a disagreement at cards? When you were talking with me just before I left the ball, how did you answer a gentleman who asked you to make one at the whist-table? You said, 'I don't play at cards.' Ah! You thought I had forgotten that? Don't kiss my hand! Trust me with the whole truth, or say good-by forever."

"Only tell me what you wish to know, Miss Charlotte," said Percy humbly. "If you will put the questions, I will give the answers—as well as I can."

On this understanding, Percy's evidence was extracted from him as follows:

"Was it Captain Bervie who quarreled with you?"

"Yes."

"Was it about me?"

"Yes."

"What did he say?"

"He said I had committed an impropriety in waltzing with you."

"Why?"

"Because your parents disapproved of your waltzing in a public ballroom."

"That's not true! What did he say next?"

"He said I had added tenfold to my offense, by waltzing with you in such a manner as to make you the subject of remark to the whole room."

"Oh! did you let him say that?"

"No; I contradicted him instantly. And I said, besides, 'It's an insult to Miss Bowmore, to suppose that she would permit any impropriety.'"

"Quite right! And what did he say?"

"Well, he lost his temper; I would rather not repeat what he said when he was mad with jealousy. There was nothing to be done with him but to give him his way."

"Give him his way? Does that mean fight a duel with him?"

"Don't be angry—it does."

"And you kept my name out of it, by pretending to quarrel at the card-table?"

"Yes. We managed it when the cardroom was emptying at supper-time, and nobody was present but Major Mulvany and another friend as witnesses."

"And when did you fight the duel?"

"The next morning."

"You never thought of me, I suppose?"

"Indeed, I did; I was very glad that you had no suspicion of what we were at."

"Was that all?"

"No; I had your flower with me, the flower you gave me out of your nosegay, at the ball."

"Well?"

"Oh, never mind, it doesn't matter."

"It does matter. What did you do with my flower?"

"I gave it a sly kiss while they were measuring the ground; and (don't tell anybody!) I put it next to my heart to bring me luck."

"Was that just before he shot at you?"

"Yes."

"How did he shoot?"

"He walked (as the seconds had arranged it) ten paces forward; and then he stopped, and lifted his pistol—"

"Don't tell me any more! Oh, to think of my being the miserable cause of such horrors! I'll never dance again as long as I live. Did you think he had killed you, when the bullet wounded your poor neck?"

"No; I hardly felt it at first."

"Hardly felt it? How he talks! And when the wretch had done his best to kill you, and when it came to your turn, what did you do?"

"Nothing."

"What! You didn't walk your ten paces forward?"

"No."

"And you never shot at him in return?"

"No; I had no quarrel with him, poor fellow; I just stood where I was, and fired in the air—"

Before he could stop her, Charlotte seized his hand, and kissed it with an hysterical fervor of admiration, which completely deprived him of his presence of mind.

"Why shouldn't I kiss the hand of a hero?" she cried, with tears of enthusiasm sparkling in her eyes. "Nobody but a hero would have given that man his life; nobody but a hero would have pardoned him, while the blood was streaming from the wound that he had inflicted. I respect you, I admire you. Oh, don't think me bold! I can't control myself when I hear of anything noble and good. You will understand me better when we get to be old friends—won't you?"

She spoke in low sweet tones of entreaty. Percy's arm stole softly round her.

"Are we never to be nearer and dearer to each other than old friends?" he asked in a whisper. "I am not a hero—your goodness overrates me, dear Miss Charlotte. My one ambition is to be the happy man who is worthy enough to win you. At your own time! I wouldn't distress you, I wouldn't confuse you, I wouldn't for the whole world take advantage of the compliment which your sympathy has paid to me. If it offends you, I won't even ask if I may hope."

She sighed as he said the last words; trembled a little, and silently looked at him.

Percy read his answer in her eyes. Without meaning it on either side their heads drew nearer together; their cheeks, then their lips, touched. She started back from him, and rose to leave the conservatory. At the same moment, the sound of slowly-approaching footsteps became audible on the gravel walk of the garden. Charlotte hurried to the door.

"My father!" she exclaimed, turning to Percy. "Come, and be introduced to him."

Percy followed her into the garden.

CHAPTER VII. POLITICS.

JUDGING by appearances, Mr. Bowmore looked like a man prematurely wasted and worn by the cares of a troubled life. His eyes presented the one feature in which his daughter resembled him. In shape and color they were exactly reproduced in Charlotte; the difference was in the expression. The father's look was habitually restless, eager, and suspicious. Not a trace was to be seen in it of the truthfulness and gentleness which made the charm of the daughter's expression. A man whose bitter experience of the world had soured his temper and shaken his faith in his fellow-creatures—such was Mr. Bowmore as he presented himself on the surface. He received Percy politely—but with a preoccupied air. Every now and then, his restless eyes wandered from the visitor to an open letter in his hand. Charlotte, observing him, pointed to the letter.

"Have you any bad news there, papa?" she asked.

"Dreadful news!" Mr. Bowmore answered. "Dreadful news, my child, to every Englishman who respects the liberties which his ancestors won. My correspondent is a man who is in the confidence of the Ministers," he continued, addressing Percy. "What do you think is the remedy that the Government proposes for the universal distress among the population, caused by an infamous and needless war? Despotism, Mr. Linwood; despotism in this free country is the remedy! In one week more, sir, Ministers will bring in a Bill for suspending the Habeas Corpus Act!"

Before Percy could do justice in words to the impression produced on him, Charlotte innocently asked a question which shocked her father.

"What is the Habeas Corpus Act, papa'"

"Good God!" cried Mr. Bowmore, "is it possible that a child of mine has grown up to womanhood, in ignorance of the palladium of English liberty? Oh, Charlotte! Charlotte!"

"I am very sorry, papa. If you will only tell me, I will never forget it."

Mr. Bowmore reverently uncovered his head, saluting an invisible Habeas Corpus Act. He took his daughter by the hand, with a certain parental sternness: his voice trembled with emotion as he spoke his next words:

"The Habeas Corpus Act, my child, forbids the imprisonment of an English subject, unless that imprisonment can be first justified by law.

839

Not even the will of the reigning monarch can prevent us from appearing before the judges of the land, and summoning them to declare whether our committal to prison is legally just."

He put on his hat again. "Never forget what I have told you, Charlotte!" he said solemnly. "I would not remove my hat, sir," he continuing, turning to Percy, "in the presence of the proudest autocrat that ever sat on a throne. I uncover, in homage to the grand law which asserts the sacredness of human liberty. When Parliament has sanctioned the infamous Bill now before it, English patriots may be imprisoned, may even be hanged, on warrants privately obtained by the paid spies and informers of the men who rule us. Perhaps I weary you, sir. You are a young man; the conduct of the Ministry may not interest you."

"On the contrary," said Percy, "I have the strongest personal interest in the conduct of the Ministry."

"How? in what way?" cried Mr. Bowmore eagerly.

"My late father had a claim on government," Percy answered, "for money expended in foreign service. As his heir, I inherit the claim, which has been formally recognized by the present Ministers. My petition for a settlement will be presented by friends of mine who can advocate my interests in the House of Commons."

Mr. Bowmore took Percy's hand, and shook it warmly.

"In such a matter as this you cannot have too many friends to help you," he said. "I myself have some influence, as representing opinion outside the House; and I am entirely at your service. Come tomorrow, and let us talk over the details of your claim at my humble dinner-table. To-day I must attend a meeting of the Branch-Hampden-Club, of which I am vice-president, and to which I am now about to communicate the alarming news which my letter contains. Excuse me for leaving you—and count on a hearty welcome when we see you to-morrow."

The amiable patriot saluted his daughter with a smile, and disappeared.

"I hope you like my father?" said Charlotte. "All our friends say he ought to be in Parliament. He has tried twice. The expenses were dreadful; and each time the other man defeated him. The agent says he would be certainly elected, if he tried again; but there is no money, and we mustn't think of it."

A man of a suspicious turn of mind might have discovered, in those artless words, the secret of Mr. Bowmore's interest in the success of his young friend's claim on the Government. One British subject, with a sum of ready money at his command, may be an inestimably useful person to another British subject (without ready money) who cannot sit comfortably unless he sits in Parliament. But honest Percy Linwood was not a man of a suspicious turn of mind. He had just opened his lips to echo Charlotte's filial glorification of her father, when a shabbily-dressed man-servant met them with a message, for which they were both alike unprepared:

"Captain Bervie has called, Miss, to say good-by, and my mistress requests your company in the parlor."

CHAPTER VIII. THE WARNING.

HAVING delivered his little formula of words, the shabby servant cast a look of furtive curiosity at Percy and withdrew. Charlotte turned to her lover, with indignation sparkling in her eyes and flushing on her cheeks at the bare idea of seeing Captain Bervie again. "Does he think I will breathe the same air," she exclaimed, "with the man who attempted to take your life!"

Percy gently remonstrated with her.

"You are sadly mistaken," he said. "Captain Bervie stood to receive my fire as fairly as I stood to receive his. When I discharged my pistol in the air, he was the first man who ran up to me, and asked if I was seriously hurt. They told him my wound was a trifle; and he fell on his knees and thanked God for preserving my life from his guilty hand. 'I am no longer the rival who hates you,' he said. 'Give me time to try if change of scene will quiet my mind; and I will be your brother, and her brother.' Whatever his faults may be, Charlotte, Arthur Bervie has a great heart. Go in, I entreat you, and be friends with him as I am."

Charlotte listened with downcast eyes and changing color. "You believe

841

him?" she asked in low and trembling tones.

"I believe him as I believe You," Percy answered.

She secretly resented the comparison, and detested the Captain more heartily than ever. "I will go in and see him, if you wish it," she said. "But not by myself. I want you to come with me."

"Why?" Percy asked.

"I want to see what his face says, when you and he meet."

"Do you still doubt him, Charlotte?"

She made no reply. Percy had done his best to convince her, and had evidently failed.

They went together into the cottage. Fixing her eyes steadily on the Captain's face, Charlotte saw it turn pale when Percy followed her into the parlor. The two men greeted one another cordially. Charlotte sat down by her mother, preserving her composure so far as appearances went. "I hear you have called to bid us good-by," she said to Bervie. "Is it to be a long absence?"

"I have got two months' leave," the Captain answered, without looking at her while he spoke.

"Are you going abroad?"

"Yes. I think so."

She turned away to her mother. Bervie seized the opportunity of speaking to Percy. "I have a word of advice for your private ear." At the same moment, Charlotte whispered to her mother: "Don't encourage him to prolong his visit."

The Captain showed no intention to prolong his visit. To Charlotte's surprise, when he took leave of the ladies, Percy also rose to go. "His carriage," he said, "was waiting at the door; and he had offered to take Captain Bervie back to London."

Charlotte instantly suspected an arrangement between the two men for a confidential interview. Her obstinate distrust of Bervie strengthened tenfold. She reluctantly gave him her hand, as he parted from her at the parlor-door. The effort of concealing her true feeling toward him gave a color and a vivacity to her face which made her irresistibly beautiful. Bervie looked at the woman whom he had lost with an immeasurable sadness in his eyes. "When we meet again," he said, "you will see me in a new character." He hurried out of the gate, as if he feared to trust himself for a moment longer in her presence.

Charlotte followed Percy into the passage. "I shall be here to-morrow, dearest!" he said, and tried to raise her hand to his lips. She abruptly drew it away. "Not that hand!" she answered. "Captain Bervie has just touched it. Kiss the other!"

"Do you still doubt the Captain?" said Percy, amused by her petulance.

She put her arm over his shoulder, and touched the plaster on his neck gently with her finger. "There's one thing I don't doubt," she said: "the Captain did that!"

Percy left her, laughing. At the front gate of the cottage he found Arthur Bervie in conversation with the same shabbily-dressed man-servant who had announced the Captain's visit to Charlotte.

"What has become of the other servant?" Bervie asked. "I mean the old man who has been with Mr. Bowmore for so many years."

"He has left his situation, sir."

"Why?"

"As I understand, sir, he spoke disrespectfully to the master."

"Oh! And how came the master to hear of you?"

"I advertised; and Mr. Bowmore answered my advertisement."

Bervie looked hard at the man for a moment, and then joined Percy at the carriage door. The two gentlemen started for London.

"What do you think of Mr. Bowmore's new servant?" asked the Captain as they drove away from the cottage. "I don't like the look of the fellow."

"I didn't particularly notice him," Percy answered.

There was a pause. When the conversation was resumed, it turned on common-place subjects. The Captain looked uneasily out of the carriage window. Percy looked uneasily at the Captain.

They had left Dartford about two miles behind them, when Percy noticed an old gabled house, sheltered by magnificent trees, and standing on an eminence well removed from the high-road. Carriages and saddle-horses were visible on the drive in front, and a flag was hoisted on a staff placed in the middle of the lawn.

"Something seems to be going on there," Percy remarked. "A fine old house! Who does it belong to?"

Bervie smiled. "It belongs to my father," he said. "He is chairman of the bench of local magistrates, and he receives his brother justices to-day, to celebrate the opening of the sessions."

He stopped and looked at Percy with some embarrassment. "I am afraid I have surprised and disappointed you," he resumed, abruptly changing the subject. "I told you when we met just now at Mr. Bowmore's cottage that I had something to say to you; and I have not yet said it. The truth is, I don't feel sure whether I have been long enough your friend to take the liberty of advising you."

"Whatever your advice is," Percy answered, "trust me to take it kindly on my side."

Thus encouraged, the Captain spoke out.

"You will probably pass much of your time at the cottage," he began, "and you will be thrown a great deal into Mr. Bowmore's society. I have known him for many years. Speaking from that knowledge, I most seriously warn you against him as a thoroughly unprincipled and thoroughly dangerous man."

This was strong language—and, naturally enough, Percy said so. The

Captain justified his language.

"Without alluding to Mr. Bowmore's politics," he went on, "I can tell you that the motive of everything he says and does is vanity. To the gratification of that one passion he would sacrifice you or me, his wife or his daughter, without hesitation and without remorse. His one desire is to get into Parliament. You are wealthy, and you can help him. He will leave no effort untried to reach that end; and, if he gets you into political difficulties, he will desert you without scruple."

Percy made a last effort to take Mr. Bowmore's part—for the one irresistible reason that he was Charlotte's father.

"Pray don't think I am unworthy of your kind interest in my welfare," he pleaded. "Can you tell me of any facts which justify what you have just said?"

"I can tell you of three facts," Bervie said. "Mr. Bowmore belongs to one of the most revolutionary clubs in England; he has spoken in the ranks of sedition at public meetings; and his name is already in the black book at the Home Office. So much for the past. As to the future, if the rumor be true that Ministers mean to stop the insurrectionary risings among the population by suspending the Habeas Corpus Act, Mr. Bowmore will certainly be in danger; and it may be my father's duty to grant the warrant that apprehends him. Write to my father to verify what I have said, and I will forward your letter by way of satisfying him that he can trust you. In the meantime, refuse to accept Mr. Bowmore's assistance in the matter of your claim on Parliament; and, above all things, stop him at the outset, when he tries to steal his way into your intimacy. I need not caution you to say nothing against him to his wife and daughter. His wily tongue has long since deluded them. Don't let him delude you! Have you thought any more of our evening at Doctor Lagarde's?" he asked, abruptly changing the subject.

"I hardly know," said Percy, still under the impression of the formidable warning which he had just received.

"Let me jog your memory," the other continued. "You went on with the consultation by yourself, after I had left the Doctor's house. It will be really doing me a favor if you can call to mind what Lagarde saw in the trance—in my absence?"

Thus entreated Percy roused himself. His memory of events were still fresh enough to answer the call that his friend had made on it. In describing what had happened, he accurately repeated all that the Doctor had said.

Bervie dwelt on the words with alarm in his face as well as surprise.

"A man like me, trying to persuade a woman like—" he checked himself, as if he was afraid to let Charlotte's name pass his lips. "Trying to induce a woman to go away with me," he resumed, "and persuading her at last? Pray, go on! What did the Doctor see next?"

"He was too much exhausted, he said, to see any more."

"Surely you returned to consult him again?"

"No; I had had enough of it."

"When we get to London," said the Captain, "we shall pass along the Strand, on the way to your chambers. Will you kindly drop me at the turning that leads to the Doctor's lodgings?"

Percy looked at him in amazement. "You still take it seriously?" he said.

"Is it not serious?" Bervie asked. "Have you and I, so far, not done exactly what this man saw us doing? Did we not meet, in the days when we were rivals (as he saw us meet), with the pistols in our hands? Did you not recognize his description of the lady when you met her at the ball, as I recognized it before you?"

"Mere coincidences!" Percy answered, quoting Charlotte's opinion when they had spoken together of Doctor Lagarde, but taking care not to cite his authority. "How many thousand men have been crossed in love? How many thousand men have fought duels for love? How many thousand women choose blue for their favorite color, and answer to the vague description of the lady whom the Doctor pretended to see?"

"Say that it is so," Bervie rejoined. "The thing is remarkable, even from your point of view. And if more coincidences follow, the result will be more remarkable still."

Arrived at the Strand, Percy set the Captain down at the turning which led to the Doctor's lodgings. "You will call on me or write me word, if anything remarkable happens?" he said.

"You shall hear from me without fail," Bervie replied.

That night, the Captain's pen performed the Captain's promise, in few and startling words.

"Melancholy news! Madame Lagarde is dead. Nothing is known of her son but that he has left England. I have found out that he is a political exile. If he has ventured back to France, it is barely possible that I may hear something of him. I have friends at the English embassy in Paris who will help me to make inquiries; and I start for the Continent in a day or two. Write to me while I am away, to the care of my father, at 'The Manor House, near Dartford.' He will always know my address abroad, and will forward your letters. For your own sake, remember the warning I gave you this afternoon! Your faithful friend, A. B."

CHAPTER IX. OFFICIAL SECRETS

THERE WAS a more serious reason than Bervie was aware of, at the time, for the warning which he had thought it his duty to address to Percy Linwood. The new footman who had entered Mr. Bowmore's service was a Spy.

Well practiced in the infamous vocation that he followed, the wretch had been chosen by the Department of Secret Service at the Home Office, to watch the proceedings of Mr. Bowmore and his friends, and to report the result to his superiors. It may not be amiss to add that the employment of paid spies and informers, by the English Government of that time, was openly acknowledged in the House of Lords, and was defended as a necessary measure in the speeches of Lord Redesdale and Lord Liverpool.*

The reports furnished by the Home Office Spy, under these circumstances, begin with the month of March, and take the form of a series of notes introduced as follows:

"MR. SECRETARY—Since I entered Mr. Bowmore's service, I have the honor to inform you that my eyes and ears have been kept in a state of active observation; and I can further certify that my means of making myself useful in the future to my honorable employers are in no respect diminished. Not the slightest suspicion of my true character is felt by any person in the house.

FIRST NOTE.

"The young gentleman now on a visit to Mr. Bowmore is, as you have been correctly informed, Mr. Percy Linwood. Although he is engaged to be married to Miss Bowmore, he is not discreet enough to conceal a certain want of friendly feeling, on his part, toward her father. The young lady has noticed this, and has resented it. She accuses her lover of having allowed himself to be prejudiced against Mr. Bowmore by some slanderous person unknown.

"Mr. Percy's clumsy defense of himself led (in my hearing) to a quarrel! Nothing but his prompt submission prevented the marriage engagement from being broken off.

"'If you showed a want of confidence in Me' (I heard Miss Charlotte say), 'I might forgive it. But when you show a want of confidence in a man so noble as my father, I have no mercy on you.' After such an expression of filial sentiment as this, Mr. Percy wisely took the readiest way of appealing to the lady's indulgence. The young man has a demand on Parliament for moneys due to his father's estate; and he pleased and flattered Miss Charlotte by asking Mr. Bowmore to advise him as to the best means of asserting his claim. By way of advancing his political interests, Mr. Bowmore introduced him to the local Hampden Club; and Miss Charlotte rewarded him with a generosity which must not be passed over in silence. Her lover was permitted to put an engagement ring on her finger, and to kiss her afterward to his heart's content."

SECOND NOTE.

"Mr. Percy has paid more visits to the Republican Club; and Justice Bervie (father of the Captain) has heard of it, and has written to his son. The result that might have been expected has followed. Captain Bervie announces his return to England, to exert his influence for political good against the influence of Mr. Bowmore for political evil.

"In the meanwhile, Mr. Percy's claim has been brought before the House of Commons, and has been adjourned for further consideration in six months' time. Both the gentlemen are indignant—especially Mr. Bowmore. He has called a meeting of the Club to consider his young friend's wrongs, and has proposed the election of Mr. Percy as a member of that revolutionary society."

THIRD NOTE.

"Mr. Percy has been elected. Captain Bervie has tried to awaken his mind to a sense of the danger that threatens him, if he persists in associating with his republican friends—and has utterly failed. Mr. Bowmore and Mr. Percy have made speeches at the Club, intended to force the latter gentleman's claim on the immediate attention of Government. Mr. Bowmore's flow of frothy eloquence has its influence (as you know from our shorthand writers' previous reports) on thousands of ignorant people. As it seems to me, the reasons for at once putting this man in prison are beyond dispute. Whether it is desirable to include Mr. Percy in the order of arrest, I must not venture to decide. Let me only hint that his seditious speech rivals the more elaborate efforts of Mr. Bowmore himself.

"So much for the present. I may now respectfully direct your attention to the future.

"On the second of April next the Club assembles a public meeting, 'in aid of British liberty,' in a field near Dartford. Mr. Bowmore is to preside, and is to be escorted afterward to Westminster Hall on his way to plead Mr. Percy's cause, in his own person, before the House of Commons. He is quite serious in declaring that 'the minions of Government dare not touch a hair of his head.' Miss Charlotte agrees with her father And Mr. Percy agrees with Miss Charlotte. Such is the state of affairs at the house in which I am acting the part of domestic servant.

"I inclose shorthand reports of the speeches recently delivered at the

Hampden Club, and have the honor of waiting for further orders."

FOURTH NOTE.

"Your commands have reached me by this morning's post.

"I immediately waited on Justice Bervie (in plain clothes, of course), and gave him your official letter, instructing me to arrest Mr. Bowmore and Mr. Percy Linwood.

"The venerable magistrate hesitated.

"He quite understood the necessity for keeping the arrest a strict secret, in the interests of Government. The only reluctance he felt in granting the warrant related to his son's intimate friend. But for the peremptory tone of your letter, I really believe he would have asked you to give Mr. Percy time for consideration. Not being rash enough to proceed to such an extreme as this, he slyly consulted the young man's interests by declining, on formal grounds, to date the warrant earlier than the second of April. Please note that my visit to him was paid at noon, on the thirty-first of March.

"If the object of this delay (to which I was obliged to submit) is to offer a chance of escape to Mr. Percy, the same chance necessarily includes Mr. Bowmore, whose name is also in the warrant. Trust me to keep a watchful eye on both these gentlemen; especially on Mr. Bowmore. He is the most dangerous man of the two, and the most likely, if he feels any suspicions, to slip through the fingers of the law.

"I have also to report that I discovered three persons in the hall of Justice Bervie's house, as I went out.

"One of them was his son, the Captain; one was his daughter, Miss Bervie; and the third was that smooth-tongued old soldier, Major Mulvany. If the escape of Mr. Bowmore and Mr. Linwood is in contemplation, mark my words: the persons whom I have just mentioned will be concerned in it—and perhaps Miss Charlotte herself as well. At present, she is entirely unsuspicious of any misfortune hanging over her head; her attention being absorbed in the preparation of her bridal finery. As an admirer myself of the fair sex, I must own that it seems hard on the girl to have her lover clapped into prison, before the wedding-day.

"I will bring you word of the arrest myself. There will be plenty of time to catch the afternoon coach to London.

"Here—unless something happens which it is impossible to foresee— my report may come to an end."

* Readers who may desire to test the author's authority for this statement, are referred to "The Annual Register" for 1817, Chapters I. and III.; and, further on, to page 66 in the same volume.

CHAPTER X. THE ELOPEMENT.

ON the evening of the first of April, Mrs. Bowmore was left alone with the servants. Mr. Bowmore and Percy had gone out together to attend a special meeting of the Club. Shortly afterward Miss Charlotte had left the cottage, under very extraordinary circumstances.

A few minutes only after the departure of her father and Percy, she received a letter, which appeared to cause her the most violent agitation. She said to Mrs. Bowmore:

"Mamma, I must see Captain Bervie for a few minutes in private, on a matter of serious importance to all of us. He is waiting at the front gate, and he will come in if I show myself at the hall door."

Upon this, Mrs. Bowmore had asked for an explanation.

"There is no time for explanation," was the only answer she received; "I ask you to leave me for five minutes alone with the Captain."

Mrs. Bowmore still hesitated. Charlotte snatched up her garden hat, and declared, wildly, that she would go out to Captain Bervie, if she was not permitted to receive him at home. In the face of this declaration, Mrs. Bowmore yielded, and left the room.

In a minute more the Captain made his appearance.

Although she had given way, Mrs. Bowmore was not disposed to trust her daughter, without supervision, in the society of a man whom Charlotte herself had reviled as a slanderer and a false friend. She took up her position in the veranda outside the parlor, at a safe distance from one of the two windows of the room which had been left partially open to admit the fresh air. Here she waited and listened.

The conversation was for some time carried on in whispers.

As they became more and more excited, both Charlotte and Bervie ended in unconsciously raising their voices.

"I swear it to you on my faith as a Christian!" Mrs. Bowmore heard the Captain say. "I declare before God who hears me that I am speaking the truth!"

And Charlotte had answered, with a burst of tears:

"I can't believe you! I daren't believe you! Oh, how can you ask me to do such a thing? Let me go! let me go!"

Alarmed at those words, Mrs. Bowmore advanced to the window and looked in.

Bervie had put her daughter's arm on his arm, and was trying to induce her to leave the parlor with him. She resisted, and implored him to release her. He dropped her arm, and whispered in her ear. She looked at him—and instantly made up her mind.

"Let me tell my mother where I am going," she said; "and I will consent."

"Be it so!" he answered. "And remember one thing: every minute is precious; the fewest words are the best."

Mrs. Bowmore re-entered the cottage by the adjoining room, and met them in the passage. In few words, Charlotte spoke.

"I must go at once to Justice Bervie's house. Don't be afraid, mamma! I know what I am about, and I know I am right."

"Going to Justice Bervie's!" cried Mrs. Bowmore, in the utmost extremity of astonishment. "What will your father say, what will Percy think, when they come back from the Club?"

"My sister's carriage is waiting for me close by," Bervie answered. "It is entirely at Miss Bowmore's disposal. She can easily get back, if she wishes to keep her visit a secret, before Mr. Bowmore and Mr. Linwood return."

He led her to the door as he spoke. She ran back and kissed her mother tenderly. Mrs. Bowmore called to them to wait.

"I daren't let you go," she said to her daughter, "without your father's leave!"

Charlotte seemed not to hear, the Captain seemed not to hear. They ran across the front garden, and through the gate—and were out of sight in less than a minute.

More than two hours passed; the sun sank below the horizon, and still there were no signs of Charlotte's return.

Feeling seriously uneasy, Mrs. Bowmore crossed the room to ring the bell, and send the man-servant to Justice Bervie's house to hasten her daughter's return.

As she approached the fireplace, she was startled by a sound of stealthy footsteps in the hall, followed by a loud noise as of some heavy object that had dropped on the floor. She rang the bell violently, and opened the door of the parlor. At the same moment, the spy-footman passed her, running out, apparently in pursuit of somebody, at the top of his speed. She followed him, as rapidly as she could, across the little front garden, to the gate. Arrived in the road, she was in time to see him vault upon the luggage-board at the back of a post-chaise before the cottage, just as the postilion started the horses on their way to London. The spy saw Mrs. Bowmore looking at him, and pointed, with an insolent nod of his head, first to the inside of the vehicle, and then over it to the high-road; signing to her that he designed to accompany the person in the post-chaise to the end of the journey.

Turning to go back, Mrs. Bowmore saw her own bewilderment reflected in the faces of the two female servants, who had followed her out.

"Who can the footman be after, ma'am?" asked the cook. "Do you think it's a thief?"

The housemaid pointed to the post-chaise, barely visible in the distance.

"Simpleton!" she said. "Do thieves travel in that way? I wish my master had come back," she proceeded, speaking to herself: "I'm afraid there's something wrong."

Mrs. Bowmore, returning through the garden-gate, instantly stopped and looked at the woman.

"What makes you mention your master's name, Amelia, when you fear that something is wrong?" she asked.

Amelia changed color, and looked confused.

"I am loth to alarm you, ma'am," she said; "and I can't rightly see what it is my duty to do."

Mrs. Bowmore's heart sank within her under the cruelest of all terrors, the terror of something unknown. "Don't keep me in suspense," she said faintly. "Whatever it is, let me know it."

She led the way back to the parlor. The housemaid followed her. The cook (declining to be left alone) followed the housemaid.

"It was something I heard early this afternoon, ma'am," Amelia began. "Cook happened to be busy—"

The cook interposed: she had not forgiven the housemaid for calling her a simpleton. "No, Amelia, if you must bring me into it—not busy. Uneasy in my mind on the subject of the soup."

"I don't know that your mind makes much difference," Amelia resumed. "What it comes to is this—it was I, and not you, who went into the kitchen-garden for the vegetables."

"Not by my wish, Heaven knows!" persisted the cook.

"Leave the room!" said Mrs. Bowmore. Even her patience had given way at last.

The cook looked as if she declined to believe her own ears. Mrs. Bowmore pointed to the door. The cook said "Oh?"—accenting it as a question. Mrs. Bowmore's finger still pointed. The cook, in solemn silence, yielded to circumstances, and banged the door.

"I was getting the vegetables, ma'am," Amelia proceeded, "when I heard voices on the other side of the paling. The wood is so old that one can see through the cracks easy enough. I saw my master, and Mr. Linwood, and Captain Bervie. The Captain seemed to have stopped the other two on the pathway that leads to the field; he stood, as it might be, between them and the back way to the house—and he spoke severely, that he did!"

"What did Captain Bervie say?"

"He said these words, ma'am: 'For the last time, Mr. Bowmore,' says he, 'will you understand that you are in danger, and that Mr. Linwood is in danger, unless you both leave this neighborhood to-night?' My master made light of it. 'For the last time,' says he, 'will you refer us to a proof of what you say, and allow us to judge for ourselves?' 'I have told you already,' says the Captain, 'I am bound by my duty toward another person to keep what I know a secret.' 'Very well,' says my master, 'I am bound by my duty to my country. And I tell you this,' says he, in his high and mighty way, 'neither Government, nor the spies of Government, dare touch a hair of my head: they know it, sir, for the head of the people's friend!'"

"That's quite true," said Mrs. Bowmore, still believing in her husband as firmly as ever.

Amelia went on:

"Captain Bervie didn't seem to think so," she said. "He lost his temper. 'What stuff!' says he; 'there's a Government spy in your house at this moment, disguised as your footman.' My master looked at Mr. Linwood, and burst out laughing. 'You won't beat that, Captain,' says he, 'if you talk till doomsday.' He turned about without a word more, and went home. The Captain caught Mr. Linwood by the arm, as soon as they were alone. 'For God's sake,' says he, 'don't follow that madman's example!'"

Mrs. Bowmore was shocked. "Did he really call my husband a madman?" she asked.

"He did, indeed, ma'am—and he was in earnest about it, too. 'If you value your liberty,' he says to Mr. Linwood; 'if you hope to become Charlotte's husband, consult your own safety. I can give you a passport. Escape to France and wait till this trouble is over.' Mr. Linwood was not in the best of tempers—Mr. Linwood shook him off. 'Charlotte's father will soon be my father,' says he, 'do you think I will desert him? My friends at the Club have taken up my claim; do you think I will forsake them at the meeting to-morrow? You ask me to be unworthy of Charlotte, and unworthy of my friends—you insult me, if you say more.' He whipped round on his heel, and followed my master."

"And what did the Captain do?"

"Lifted up his hands, ma'am, to the heavens, and looked—I declare it turned my blood to see him. If there's truth in mortal man, it's my firm belief—"

What the housemaid's belief was, remained unexpressed. Before she could get to her next word, a shriek of horror from the hall announced that the cook's powers of interruption were not exhausted yet.

Mistress and servant both hurried out in terror of they knew not what. There stood the cook, alone in the hall, confronting the stand on which the overcoats and hats of the men of the family were placed.

"Where's the master's traveling coat?" cried the cook, staring wildly at an unoccupied peg. "And where's his cap to match! Oh Lord, he's off in the post-chaise! and the footman's after him!"

Simpleton as she was, the woman had blundered on a very serious discovery.

Coat and cap—both made after a foreign pattern, and both strikingly remarkable in form and color to English eyes—had unquestionably disappeared. It was equally certain that they were well known to the foot man, whom the Captain had declared to be a spy, as the coat and cap which his master used in traveling. Had Mr. Bowmore discovered (since the afternoon) that he was really in danger? Had the necessities of instant flight only allowed him time enough to snatch his coat and cap out of the hall? And had the treacherous manservant seen him as he was making his escape to the post-chaise? The cook's conclusions answered all these questions in the affirmative—and, if Captain Bervie's words of warning had been correctly reported, the cook's conclusion for once was not to be despised.

Under this last trial of her fortitude, Mrs. Bowmore's feeble reserves of endurance completely gave way. The poor lady turned faint and giddy. Amelia placed her on a chair in the hall, and told the cook to open the front door, and let in the fresh air.

The cook obeyed; and instantly broke out with a second terrific scream; announcing nothing less, this time, than the appearance of Mr. Bowmore himself, alive and hearty, returning with Percy from the meeting at the Club!

The inevitable inquiries and explanations followed.

Fully assured, as he had declared himself to be, of the sanctity of his person (politically speaking), Mr. Bowmore turned pale, nevertheless, when he looked at the unoccupied peg on his clothes stand. Had some man unknown personated him? And had a post-chaise been hired to lead an impending pursuit of him in the wrong direction? What did it mean? Who was the friend to whose services he was indebted? As for the proceedings of the man-servant, but one interpretation could now be placed on them. They distinctly justified what Captain Bervie had said of him. Mr. Bowmore thought of the Captain's other assertion, relating to the urgent necessity for making his escape; and looked at Percy in silent dismay; and turned paler than ever.

Percy's thoughts, diverted for the moment only from the lady of his love, returned to her with renewed fidelity. "Let us hear what Charlotte thinks of it," he said. "Where is she?"

It was impossible to answer this question plainly and in few words.

Terrified at the effect which her attempt at explanation produced on Percy, helplessly ignorant when she was called upon to account for her daughter's absence, Mrs. Bowmore could only shed tears and express a devout trust in Providence. Her husband looked at the new misfortune from a political point of view. He sat down and slapped his forehead theatrically with the palm of his hand. "Thus far," said the patriot, "my political assailants have only struck at me through the newspapers. Now they strike at me through my child!"

Percy made no speeches. There was a look in his eyes which boded ill for Captain Bervie if the two met. "I am going to fetch her," was all he said, "as fast as a horse can carry me."

He hired his horse at an inn in the town, and set forth for Justice Bervie's house at a gallop.

During Percy's absence, Mr. Bowmore secured the front and back entrances to the cottage with his own hands.

These first precautions taken, he ascended to his room and packed his traveling-bag. "Necessaries for my use in prison," he remarked. "The bloodhounds of Government are after me." "Are they after Percy, too?" his wife ventured to ask. Mr. Bowmore looked up impatiently, and cried "Pooh!"—as if Percy was of no consequence. Mrs. Bowmore thought otherwise: the good woman privately packed a bag for Percy, in the sanctuary of her own room.

For an hour, and more than an hour, no event of any sort occurred.

Mr. Bowmore stalked up and down the parlor, meditating. At intervals, ideas of flight presented themselves attractively to his mind. At intervals, ideas of the speech that he had prepared for the public meeting on the next day took their place. "If I fly to-night," he wisely observed, "what will become of my speech? I will not fly to-night! The people shall hear me."

He sat down and crossed his arms fiercely. As he looked at his wife to see what effect he had produced on her, the sound of heavy carriage-wheels and the trampling of horses penetrated to the parlor from the garden-gate.

Mr. Bowmore started to his feet, with every appearance of having suddenly altered his mind on the question of flight. Just as he reached the hall, Percy's voice was heard at the front door. "Let me in. Instantly! Instantly!"

Mrs. Bowmore drew back the bolts before the servants could help her. "Where is Charlotte?" she cried; seeing Percy alone on the doorstep.

"Gone!" Percy answered furiously. "Eloped to Paris with Captain Bervie! Read her own confession. They were just sending the messenger with it, when I reached the house."

He handed a note to Mrs. Bowmore, and turned aside to speak to her husband while she read it. Charlotte wrote to her mother very briefly; promising to explain everything on her return. In the meantime, she had left home under careful protection—she had a lady for her companion on the journey—and she would write again from Paris. So the letter, evidently written in great haste, began and ended.

Percy took Mr. Bowmore to the window, and pointed to a carriage and four horses waiting at the garden-gate.

"Do you come with me, and back me with your authority as her father?" he asked, sternly. "Or do you leave me to go alone?"

Mr. Bowmore was famous among his admirers for his "happy replies." He made one now.

"I am not Brutus," he said. "I am only Bowmore. My daughter before everything. Fetch my traveling-bag."

While the travelers' bags were being placed in the chaise, Mr. Bowmore was struck by an idea.

He produced from his coat-pocket a roll of many papers thickly covered with writing. On the blank leaf in which they were tied up, he wrote in the largest letters: "Frightful domestic calamity! Vice-President Bowmore obliged to leave England! Welfare of a beloved daughter! His speech will be read at the meeting by Secretary Joskin, of the Club. (Private to Joskin. Have these lines printed and posted everywhere. And, when you read my speech, for God's sake don't drop your voice at the ends of the sentences.)"

He threw down the pen, and embraced Mrs. Bowmore in the most summary manner. The poor woman was ordered to send the roll of paper to the Club, without a word to comfort and sustain her from her husband's lips. Percy spoke to her hopefully and kindly, as he kissed her cheek at parting.

On the next morning, a letter, addressed to Mrs. Bowmore, was delivered at the cottage by private messenger.

Opening the letter, she recognized the handwriting of her husband's old friend, and her old friend—Major Mulvany. In breathless amazement, she read these lines:

"DEAR MRS. BOWMORE—In matters of importance, the golden rule is never to waste words. I have performed one of the great actions of my life—I have saved your husband.

"How I discovered that my friend was in danger, I must not tell you at present. Let it be enough if I say that I have been a guest under Justice Bervie's hospitable roof, and that I know of a Home Office spy who has taken you unawares, under pretense of being your footman. If I had not circumvented him, the scoundrel would have imprisoned your husband, and another dear friend of mine. This is how I did it.

"I must begin by appealing to your memory.

"Do you happen to remember that your husband and I are as near as may be of about the same height? Very good, so far. Did you, in the next place, miss Bowmore's traveling coat and cap from their customary peg? I am the thief, dearest lady; I put them on my own humble self. Did you hear a sudden noise in the hall? Oh, forgive me—I made the noise! And it did just what I wanted of it. It brought the spy up from the kitchen, suspecting that something might be wrong.

"What did the wretch see when he got into the hall? His master, in traveling costume, running out. What did he find when he reached the garden? His master escaping, in a post-chaise, on the road to London. What did he do, the born blackguard that he was? Jumped up behind the chaise to make sure of his prisoner. It was dark when we got to London. In a hop, skip, and jump, I was out of the carriage, and in at my own door, before he could look me in the face.

"The date of the warrant, you must know, obliged him to wait till the morning. All that night, he and the Bow Street runners kept watch They came in with the sunrise—and who did they find? Major Mulvany snug in his bed, and as innocent as the babe unborn. Oh, they did their duty! Searched the place from the kitchen to the garrets—and gave it up. There's but one thing I regret—I let the spy off without a good thrashing. No matter. I'll do it yet, one of these days.

"Let me know the first good news of our darling fugitives, and I shall be more than rewarded for what little I have done.

"Your always devoted,

"TERENCE MULVANY."

CHAPTER XI. PURSUIT AND DISCOVERY.

FEELING himself hurried away on the road to Dover, as fast as four horses could carry him, Mr. Bowmore had leisure to criticise Percy's conduct, from his own purely selfish point of view.

"If you had listened to my advice," he said, "you would have treated that man Bervie like the hypocrite and villain that he is. But no! you trusted to your own crude impressions. Having given him your hand after the duel (I would have given him the contents of my pistol!) you hesitated to withdraw it again, when that slanderer appealed to your friendship not to cast him off. Now you see the consequence!"

"Wait till we get to Paris!" All the ingenuity of Percy's traveling companion failed to extract from him any other answer than that.

Foiled so far, Mr. Bowmore began to start difficulties next. Had they money enough for the journey? Percy touched his pocket, and answered shortly, "Plenty." Had they passports? Percy sullenly showed a letter. "There is the necessary voucher from a magistrate," he said. "The consul at Dover will give us our passports. Mind this!" he added, in warning tones, "I have pledged my word of honor to Justice Bervie that we have no political object in view in traveling to France. Keep your politics to yourself, on the other side of the Channel."

Mr. Bowmore listened in blank amazement. Charlotte's lover was appearing in a new character—the character of a man who had lost his respect for Charlotte's father!

It was useless to talk to him. He deliberately checked any further attempts at conversation by leaning back in the carriage, and closing his eyes. The truth is, Mr. Bowmore's own language and conduct were insensibly producing the salutary impression on Percy's mind which Bervie had vainly tried to convey, under the disadvantage of having Charlotte's influence against him. Throughout the journey, Percy did exactly what Bervie had once entreated him to do—he kept Mr. Bowmore at a distance.

At every stage, they inquired after the fugitives. At every stage, they were answered by a more or less intelligible description of Bervie and Charlotte, and of the lady who accompanied them. No disguise had been attempted; no person had in any case been bribed to conceal the truth.

When the first tumult of his emotions had in some degree subsided, this strange circumstance associated itself in Percy's mind with the equally unaccountable conduct of Justice Bervie, on his arrival at the manor house.

The old gentleman met his visitor in the hall, without expressing, and apparently without feeling, any indignation at his son's conduct. It was even useless to appeal to him for information. He only said, "I am not in Arthur's confidence; he is of age, and my daughter (who has volunteered to accompany him) is of age. I have no claim to control them. I believe they have taken Miss Bowmore to Paris; and that is all I know about it."

He had shown the same dense insensibility in giving his official voucher for the passports. Percy had only to satisfy him on the question of politics; and the document was drawn out as a matter of course. Such had been the father's behavior; and the conduct of the son now exhibited the same shameless composure. To what conclusion did this discovery point? Percy abandoned the attempt to answer that question in despair.

They reached Dover toward two o'clock in the morning.

At the pier-head they found a coast-guardsman on duty, and received more information.

In 1817 the communication with France was still by sailing-vessels. Arriving long after the departure of the regular packet, Bervie had hired a lugger, and had sailed with the two ladies for Calais, having a fresh breeze in his favor. Percy's first angry impulse was to follow him instantly. The next moment he remembered the insurmountable obstacle of the passports. The Consul would certainly not grant those essentially necessary documents at two in the morning!

The only alternative was to wait for the regular packet, which sailed some hours later—between eight and nine o'clock in the forenoon. In this case, they might apply for their passports before the regular office hours, if they explained the circumstances, backed by the authority of the magistrate's letter.

Mr. Bowmore followed Percy to the nearest inn that was open, sublimely indifferent to the delays and difficulties of the journey. He ordered refreshments with the air of a man who was performing a melancholy duty to himself, in the name of humanity.

"When I think of my speech," he said, at supper, "my heart bleeds for the people. In a few hours more, they will assemble in their thousands, eager to hear me. And what will they see? Joskin in my place! Joskin with a manuscript in his hand! Joskin, who drops his voice at the ends of his sentences! I will never forgive Charlotte. Waiter, another glass of brandy and water."

After an unusually quick passage across the Channel, the travelers landed on the French coast, before the defeated spy had returned from London to

Dartford by stage-coach. Continuing their journey by post as far as Amiens, they reached that city in time to take their places by the diligence to Paris.

Arrived in Paris, they encountered another incomprehensible proceeding on the part of Captain Bervie.

Among the persons assembled in the yard to see the arrival of the diligence was a man with a morsel of paper in his hand, evidently on the lookout for some person whom he expected to discover among the travelers. After consulting his bit of paper, he looked with steady attention at Percy and Mr. Bowmore, and suddenly approached them. "If you wish to see the Captain," he said, in broken English, "you will find him at that hotel." He handed a printed card to Percy, and disappeared among the crowd before it was possible to question him.

Even Mr. Bowmore gave way to human weakness, and condescended to feel astonished in the face of such an event as this. "What next?" he exclaimed.

"Wait till we get to the hotel," said Percy.

In half an hour more the landlord had received them, and the waiter had led them to the right door. Percy pushed the man aside, and burst into the room.

Captain Bervie was alone, reading a newspaper. Before the first furious words had escaped Percy's lips, Bervie silenced him by pointing to a closed door on the right of the fireplace.

"She is in that room," he said; "speak quietly, or you may frighten her. I know what you are going to say," he added, as Percy stepped nearer to him. "Will you hear me in my own defense, and then decide whether I am the greatest scoundrel living, or the best friend you ever had?"

He put the question kindly, with something that was at once grave and tender in his look and manner. The extraordinary composure with which he acted and spoke had its tranquilizing influence over Percy. He felt himself surprised into giving Bervie a hearing.

"I will tell you first what I have done," the Captain proceeded, "and next why I did it. I have taken it on myself, Mr. Linwood, to make an alteration in your wedding arrangements. Instead of being married at Dartford church, you will be married (if you see no objection) at the chapel of the embassy in Paris, by my old college friend the chaplain."

This was too much for Percy's self-control. "Your audacity is beyond belief," he broke out.

"And beyond endurance," Mr. Bowmore added. "Understand this, sir! Whatever your defense may be, I object, under any circumstances, to be made the victim of a trick."

"You are the victim of your own obstinate refusal to profit by a plain warning," Bervie rejoined. "At the eleventh hour, I entreated you, and I entreated Mr. Linwood, to provide for your own safety; and I spoke in vain."

Percy's patience gave way once more.

"To use your own language," he said, "I have still to decide whether you have behaved toward me like a scoundrel or a friend. You have said nothing to justify yourself yet."

"Very well put!" Mr. Bowmore chimed in. "Come to the point, sir! My daughter's reputation is in question."

"Miss Bowmore's reputation is not in question for a single instant," Bervie answered. "My sister has been the companion of her journey from first to last."

"Journey?" Mr. Bowmore repeated, indignantly. "I want to know, sir, what the journey means. As an outraged father, I ask one plain question. Why did you run away with my daughter?"

Bervie took a slip of paper from his pocket, and handed it to Percy with a smile.

It was a copy of the warrant which Justice Bervie's duty had compelled him to issue for the "arrest of Orlando Bowmore and Percy Linwood." There was no danger in divulging the secret now. British warrants were waste-paper in France, in those days.

"I ran away with the bride," Bervie said coolly, "in the certain knowledge that you and Mr. Bowmore would run after me. If I had not forced you both to follow me out of England on the first of April, you would have been made State prisoners on the second. What do you say to my conduct now?"

"Wait, Percy, before you answer him," Mr. Bowmore interposed. "He is ready enough at excusing himself. But, observe—he hasn't a word to say in justification of my daughter's readiness to run away with him."

"Have you quite done?" Bervie asked, as quietly as ever.

Mr. Bowmore reserved the right of all others which he most prized, the right of using his tongue. "For the present," he answered in his loftiest manner, "I have done."

Bervie proceeded: "Your daughter consented to run away with me, because I took her to my father's house, and prevailed upon him to trust her with the secret of the coming arrests. She had no choice left but to let her obstinate father and her misguided lover go to prison—or to take her place with my sister and me in the traveling-carriage." He appealed once more to Percy. "My friend, you remember the day when you spared my life. Have I remembered it, too?"

For once, there was an Englishman who was not contented to express the noblest emotions that humanity can feel by the commonplace ceremony of shaking hands. Percy's heart overflowed. In an outburst of unutterable gratitude he threw himself on Bervie's breast. As brothers the two men embraced. As brothers they loved and trusted one another, from that day forth.

The door on the right was softly opened from within. A charming face—the dark eyes bright with happy tears, the rosy lips just opening into a smile—peeped into the room. A low sweet voice, with an under-note of trembling in it, made this modest protest, in the form of an inquiry:

"When you have quite done, Percy, with our good friend, perhaps you will have something to say to ME?"

LAST WORDS.

THE persons immediately interested in the marriage of Percy and Charlotte were the only persons present at the ceremony.

At the little breakfast afterward, in the French hotel, Mr. Bowmore insisted on making a speech to a select audience of six; namely, the bride and bridegroom, the bridesmaid, the Chaplain, the Captain, and Mrs. Bowmore. But what does a small audience matter? The English frenzy for making speeches is not to be cooled by such a trifle as that. At the end of the world, the expiring forces of Nature will hear a dreadful voice—the voice of the last Englishman delivering the last speech.

Percy wisely made his honeymoon a long one; he determined to be quite sure of his superior influence over his wife before he trusted her within reach of her father again.

Mr. and Mrs. Bowmore accompanied Captain Bervie and Miss Bervie on their way back to England, as far as Boulogne. In that pleasant town the banished patriot set up his tent. It was a cheaper place to live in than Paris, and it was conveniently close to England, when he had quite made up his mind whether to be an exile on the Continent, or to go back to his own country and be a martyr in prison. In the end, the course of events settled that question for him. Mr. Bowmore returned to England, with the return of the Habeas Corpus Act.

The years passed. Percy and Charlotte (judged from the romantic point of view) became two uninteresting married people. Bervie (always remaining a bachelor) rose steadily in his profession, through the higher grades of military rank. Mr. Bowmore, wisely overlooked by a new Government, sank back again into the obscurity from which shrewd Ministers would never have assisted him to emerge. The one subject of interest left, among the persons of this little drama, was now represented by Doctor Lagarde. Thus far, not a trace had been discovered of the French physician, who had so strangely associated the visions of his magnetic sleep with the destinies of the two men who had consulted him.

Steadfastly maintaining his own opinion of the prediction and the fulfillment, Bervie persisted in believing that he and Lagarde (or Percy and Lagarde) were yet destined to meet, and resume the unfinished consultation at the point where it had been broken off. Persons, happy in the possession of "sound common sense," who declared the prediction to be skilled guesswork, and the fulfillment manifest coincidence, ridiculed the idea of finding Doctor Lagarde as closely akin to that other celebrated idea of finding the needle in the bottle of hay. But Bervie's obstinacy was proverbial. Nothing shook his confidence in his own convictions.

More than thirteen years had elapsed since the consultation at the Doctor's lodgings, when Bervie went to Paris to spend a summer holiday with his friend, the chaplain at the English embassy. His last words to Percy and Charlotte when he took his leave were: "Suppose I meet with Doctor Lagarde?"

It was then the year 1830. Bervie arrived at his friend's rooms on the 24th of July. On the 27th of the month the famous revolution broke out which dethroned Charles the Tenth in three days.

On the second day, Bervie and his host ventured into the streets, watching the revolution (like other reckless Englishmen) at the risk of their lives. In the confusion around them they were separated. Bervie, searching for his companion, found his progress stopped by a barricade, which had been desperately attacked, and desperately defended. Men in blouses and men in uniform lay dead and dying together: the tricolored flag waved over them, in token of the victory of the people.

Bervie had just revived a poor wretch with a drink from an overthrown bowl of water, which still had a few drops left in it, when he felt a hand laid on his shoulder from behind. He turned and discovered a National Guard, who had been watching his charitable action. "Give a helping hand to that poor fellow," said the citizen-soldier, pointing to a workman standing near, grimed with blood and gunpowder. The tears were rolling down the man's cheeks. "I can't see my way, sir, for crying," he said. "Help me to carry that sad burden into the next street." He pointed to a rude wooden litter, on which lay a dead or wounded man, his face and breast covered with an old cloak. "There is the best friend the people ever had," the workman said. "He cured us, comforted us, respected us, loved us. And there he lies, shot dead while he was binding up the wounds of friends and enemies alike!"

"Whoever he is, he has died nobly," Bervie answered, "May I look at him?"

The workman signed that he might look.

Bervie lifted the cloak—and met with Doctor Lagarde once more.

MISS BERTHA AND THE YANKEE.

[PRELIMINARY STATEMENTS OF WITNESSES FOR THE DEFENSE, COLLECTED AT THE OFFICE OF THE SOLICITOR.]

No. 1.—Miss Bertha Laroche, of Nettlegrove Hall, testifies and says:—

I.

TOWARD the middle of June, in the year 1817, I went to take the waters at Maplesworth, in Derbyshire, accompanied by my nearest relative— my aunt.

I am an only child; and I was twenty-one years old at my last birthday. On coming of age I inherited a house and lands in Derbyshire, together with a fortune in money of one hundred thousand pounds. The only education which I have received has been obtained within the last two or three years of my life; and I have thus far seen nothing of Society, in England or in any other civilized part of the world. I can be a competent witness, it seems, in spite of these disadvantages. Anyhow, I mean to tell the truth.

My father was a French colonist in the island of Saint Domingo. He died while I was very young; leaving to my mother and to me just enough to live on, in the remote part of the island in which our little property was situated. My mother was an Englishwoman. Her delicate health made it necessary for her to leave me, for many hours of the day, under the care of our household slaves. I can never forget their kindness to me; but, unfortunately, their ignorance equaled their kindness. If we had been rich enough to send to France or England for a competent governess we might have done very well. But we were not rich enough. I am ashamed to say that I was nearly thirteen years old before I had learned to read and write correctly.

Four more years passed—and then there came a wonderful event in our lives, which was nothing less than the change from Saint Domingo to England.

My mother was distantly related to an ancient and wealthy English family. She seriously offended those proud people by marrying an obscure foreigner, who had nothing to live on but his morsel of land in the West Indies. Having no expectations from her relatives, my mother preferred happiness with the man she loved to every other consideration; and I, for one, think she was right. From that moment she was cast off by the head of the family. For eighteen years of her life, as wife, mother, and widow, no letters came to her from her English home. We had just celebrated my seventeenth birthday when the first letter came. It informed my mother that no less than three lives, which stood between her and the inheritance of certain portions of the family property, had been swept away by death. The estate and the fortune which I have already mentioned had fallen to her in due course of law, and her surviving relatives were magnanimously ready to forgive her at last!

We wound up our affairs at Saint Domingo, and we went to England to take possession of our new wealth.

At first, the return to her native air seemed to have a beneficial effect on my mother's health. But it was a temporary improvement only. Her constitution had been fatally injured by the West Indian climate, and just as we had engaged a competent person to look after my neglected education, my constant attendance was needed at my mother's bedside. We loved each other dearly, and we wanted no strange nurses to come between us. My aunt (my mother's sister) relieved me of my cares in the intervals when I wanted rest.

For seven sad months our dear sufferer lingered. I have only one remembrance to comfort me; my mother's last kiss was mine—she died peacefully with her head on my bosom.

I was nearly nineteen years old before I had sufficiently rallied my courage to be able to think seriously of myself and my prospects.

At that age one does not willingly submit one's self for the first time to the authority of a governess. Having my aunt for a companion and protectress, I proposed to engage my own masters and to superintend my own education.

My plans failed to meet with the approval of the head of the family. He declared (most unjustly, as the event proved) that my aunt was not a fit person to take care of me. She had passed all the later years of her life in retirement. A good creature, he admitted, in her own way, but she had no knowledge of the world, and no firmness of character. The right person to act as my chaperon, and to superintend my education, was the high-minded and accomplished woman who had taught his own daughters.

I declined, with all needful gratitude and respect, to take his advice. The bare idea of living with a stranger so soon after my mother's death revolted me. Besides, I liked my aunt, and my aunt liked me. Being made acquainted with my decision, the head of the family cast me off, exactly as he had cast off my mother before me.

So I lived in retirement with my good aunt, and studied industriously to improve my mind until my twenty-first birthday came. I was now an heiress, privileged to think and act for myself. My aunt kissed me tenderly. We talked of my poor mother, and we cried in each other's arms on the memorable day that made a wealthy woman of me. In a little time more, other troubles than vain regrets for the dead were to try me, and other tears were to fill my eyes than the tears which I had given to the memory of my mother.

II.

I MAY now return to my visit, in June, 1817, to the healing springs at Maplesworth.

This famous inland watering-place was only between nine and ten miles from my new home called Nettlegrove Hall. I had been feeling weak and out of spirits for some months, and our medical adviser recommended change of scene and a trial of the waters at Maplesworth. My aunt and I established ourselves in comfortable apartments, with a letter of introduction to the chief doctor in the place. This otherwise harmless and worthy man proved, strangely enough, to be the innocent cause of the trials and troubles which beset me at the outset of my new life.

The day after we had presented our letter of introduction, we met the doctor on the public walk. He was accompanied by two strangers, both young men, and both (so far as my ignorant opinion went) persons of some distinction, judging by their dress and manners. The doctor said a few kind words to us, and rejoined his two companions. Both the gentlemen looked at me, and both took off their hats as my aunt and I proceeded on our walk.

I own I thought occasionally of the well-bred strangers during the rest of the day, especially of the shortest of the two, who was also the handsomest of the two to my thinking. If this confession seems rather a bold one, remember, if you please, that I had never been taught to conceal my feelings at Saint Domingo, and that the events which followed our arrival in England had kept me completely secluded from the society of other young ladies of my age.

The next day, while I was drinking my glass of healing water (extremely nasty water, by the way) the doctor joined us.

While he was asking me about my health, the two strangers made their appearance again, and took off their hats again. They both looked expectantly at the doctor, and the doctor (in performance of a promise which he had already made, as I privately suspected) formally introduced them to my aunt and to me. First (I put the handsomest man first) Captain Arthur Stanwick, of the army, home from India on leave, and staying at Maplesworth to take the waters; secondly, Mr. Lionel Varleigh, of Boston, in America, visiting England, after traveling all over Europe, and stopping at Maplesworth to keep company with his friend the Captain.

On their introduction, the two gentlemen, observing, no doubt, that I was a little shy, forbore delicately from pressing their society on us.

Captain Stanwick, with a beautiful smile, and with teeth worthy of the smile, stroked his whiskers, and asked me if I had found any benefit from taking the waters. He afterward spoke in great praise of the charming scenery in the neighborhood of Maplesworth, and then, turning away, addressed his next words to my aunt. Mr. Varleigh took his place. Speaking with perfect gravity, and with no whiskers to stroke, he said:

"I have once tried the waters here out of curiosity. I can sympathize, miss, with the expression which I observed on your face when you emptied your glass just now. Permit me to offer you something nice to take the taste of the waters out of your mouth." He produced from his pocket a beautiful little box filled with sugar-plums. "I bought it in Paris," h e explained. "Having lived a good deal in France, I have got into a habit of making little presents of this sort to ladies and children. I wouldn't let the doctor see it, miss, if I were you. He has the usual medical prejudice against sugar-plums." With that quaint warning, he, too, made his bow and discreetly withdrew.

Thinking it over afterward, I acknowledged to myself that the English Captain—although he was the handsomest man of the two, and possessed the smoothest manners—had failed, nevertheless, to overcome my shyness. The American traveler's unaffected sincerity and good-humor, on the other hand, set me quite at my ease. I could look at him and thank him, and feel amused at his sympathy with the grimace I had made, after swallowing the ill-flavored waters. And yet, while I lay awake at night, wondering whether we should meet our new acquaintances on the next day, it was the English Captain that I most wanted to see again, and not the American traveler! At the time, I set this down to nothing more important than my own perversity. Ah, dear! dear! I know better than that now.

The next morning brought the doctor to our hotel on a special visit to my aunt. He invented a pretext for sending me into the next room, which was so plainly a clumsy excuse that my curiosity was aroused. I gratified my curiosity. Must I make my confession plainer still? Must I acknowledge that I was mean enough to listen on the other side of the door?

I heard my dear innocent old aunt say: "Doctor! I hope you don't see anything alarming in the state of Bertha's health."

The doctor burst out laughing. "My dear madam! there is nothing in the state of the young lady's health which need cause the smallest anxiety to you or to me. The object of my visit is to justify myself for presenting those two gentlemen to you yesterday. They are both greatly struck by Miss Bertha's beauty, and they both urgently entreated me to introduce them. Such introductions, I need hardly say, are marked exceptions to my general rule. In ninety-nine cases out of a hundred I should have said No. In the cases of

Captain Stanwick and Mr. Varleigh, however, I saw no reason to hesitate. Permit me to assure you that I am not intruding on your notice two fortune-hunting adventurers. They are both men of position and men of property. The family of the Stanwicks has been well known to me for years; and Mr. Varleigh brought me a letter from my oldest living friend, answering for him as a gentleman in the highest sense of the word. He is the wealthiest man of the two; and it speaks volumes for him, in my opinion, that he has preserved his simplicity of character after a long residence in such places as Paris and Vienna. Captain Stanwick has more polish and ease of manner, but, looking under the surface, I rather fancy there may be something a little impetuous and domineering in his temper. However, we all have our faults. I can only say, for both these young friends of mine, that you need feel no scruple about admitting them to your intimacy, if they happen to please you—and your niece. Having now, I hope, removed any doubts which may have troubled you, pray recall Miss Bertha. I am afraid I have interrupted you in discussing your plans for the day."

The smoothly eloquent doctor paused for the moment; and I darted away from the door.

Our plans for the day included a drive through the famous scenery near the town. My two admirers met us on horseback. Here, again, the Captain had the advantage over his friend. His seat in the saddle and his riding-dress were both perfect things in their way. The Englishman rode on one side of the carriage and the American on the other. They both talked well, but Mr. Varleigh had seen more of the world in general than Captain Stanwick, and he made himself certainly the more interesting and more amusing companion of the two.

On our way back my admiration was excited by a thick wood, beautifully situated on rising ground at a little distance from the high-road: "Oh, dear," I said, "how I should like to take a walk in that wood!" Idle, thoughtless words; but, oh, what remembrances crowd on me as I think of them now!

Captain Stanwick and Mr. Varleigh at once dismounted and offered themselves as my escort. The coachman warned them to be careful; people had often lost themselves, he said, in that wood. I asked the name of it. The name was Herne Wood. My aunt was not very willing to leave her comfortable seat in the carriage, but it ended in her going with us.

Before we entered the wood, Mr. Varleigh noted the position of the high-road by his pocket-compass. Captain Stanwick laughed at him, and offered me his arm. Ignorant as I was of the ways of the world and the rules of coquetry, my instinct (I suppose) warned me not to distinguish one of the gentlemen too readily at the expense of the other. I took my aunt's arm and settled it in that way.

A winding path led us into the wood.

On a nearer view, the place disappointed me; the further we advanced, the more horribly gloomy it grew. The thickly-growing trees shut out the light; the damp stole over me little by little until I shivered; the undergrowth of bushes and thickets rustled at intervals mysteriously, as some invisible creeping creature passed through it. At a turn in the path we reached a sort of clearing, and saw the sky and the sunshine once more. But, even here, a disagreeable incident occurred. A snake wound his undulating way across the open space, passing close by me, and I was fool enough to scream. The Captain killed the creature with his riding-cane, taking a pleasure in doing it which I did not like to see.

We left the clearing and tried another path, and then another. And still the horrid wood preyed on my spirits. I agreed with my aunt that we should do well to return to the carriage. On our way back we missed the right path, and lost ourselves for the moment. Mr. Varleigh consulted his compass, and pointed in one direction. Captain Stanwick, consulting nothing but his own jealous humor, pointed in the other. We followed Mr. Varleigh's guidance, and got back to the clearing. He turned to the Captain, and said, good-humoredly: "You see the compass was right." Captain Stanwick, answered, sharply: "There are more ways than one out of an English wood; you talk as if we were in one of your American forests."

Mr. Varleigh seemed to be at a loss to understand his rudeness; there was a pause. The two men looked at each other, standing face to face on

876

the brown earth of the clearing—the Englishman's ruddy countenance, light auburn hair and whiskers, and well-opened bold blue eyes, contrasting with the pale complexion, the keenly-observant look, the dark closely-cut hair, and the delicately-lined face of the American. It was only for a moment: I had barely time to feel uneasy before they controlled themselves and led us back to the carriage, talking as pleasantly as if nothing had happened. For days afterward, nevertheless, that scene in the clearing—the faces and figures of the two men, the dark line of trees hemming them in on all sides, the brown circular patch of ground on which they stood—haunted my memory, and got in the way of my brighter and happier thoughts. When my aunt inquired if I had enjoyed the day, I surprised her by saying No. And when she asked why, I could only answer: "It was all spoiled by Herne Wood."

III.

THREE weeks passed.

The terror of those dreadful days creeps over me again when I think of them. I mean to tell the truth without shrinking; but I may at least consult my own feelings by dwelling on certain particulars as briefly as I can. I shall describe my conduct toward the two men who courted me in the plainest terms, if I say that I distinguished neither of them. Innocently and stupidly I encouraged them both.

In books, women are generally represented as knowing their own minds in matters which relate to love and marriage. This is not my experience of myself. Day followed day; and, ridiculous as it may appear, I could not decide which of my two admirers I liked best!

Captain Stanwick was, at first, the man of my choice. While he kept his temper under control, h e charmed me. But when he let it escape him, he sometimes disappointed, sometimes irritated me. In that frame of mind I turned for relief to Lionel Varleigh, feeling that he was the more gentle and the more worthy man of the two, and honestly believing, at such times, that I preferred him to his rival. For the first few days after our visit to Herne Wood I had excellent opportunities of comparing them. They paid their visits to us together, and they divided their attentions carefully between me and my aunt. At the end of the week, however, they began to present themselves separately. If I had possessed any experience of the natures of men, I might have known what this meant, and might have seen the future possibility of some more serious estrangement between the two friends, of which I might be the unfortunate cause. As it was; I never once troubled my head about what might be passing out of my presence. Whether they came together, or whether they came separately, their visits were always agreeable to me. and I thought of nothing and cared for nothing more.

But the time that was to enlighten me was not far off.

One day Captain Stanwick called much earlier than usual. My aunt had not yet returned from her morning walk. The Captain made some excuse for presenting himself under these circumstances which I have now forgotten.

Without actually committing himself to a proposal of marriage he spoke with such tender feeling, he managed his hold on my inexperience so delicately, that he entrapped me into saying some words, on my side, which I remembered with a certain dismay as soon as I was left alone again. In half an hour more, Mr. Lionel Varleigh was announced as my next visitor. I at once noticed a certain disturbance in his look and manner which was quite new in my experience of him. I offered him a chair. To my surprise he declined to take it.

"I must trust to your indulgence to permit me to put an embarrassing question to you," he began. "It rests with you, Miss Laroche, to decide whether I shall remain here, or whether I shall relieve you of my presence by leaving the room."

"What can you possibly mean?" I asked.

"Is it your wish," he went on, "that I should pay you no more visits except in Captain Stanwick's company, or by Captain Stanwick's express permission?"

My astonishment deprived me for the moment of the power of answering him. "Do you really mean that Captain Stanwick has forbidden you to call on me?" I asked as soon as I could speak.

"I have exactly repeated what Captain Stanwick said to me half an hour since," Lionel Varleigh answered.

In my indignation at hearing this, I entirely forgot the rash words of encouragement which the Captain had entrapped me into speaking to him. When I think of it now, I am ashamed to repeat the language in which I resented this man's presumptuous assertion of authority over me. Having committed one act of indiscretion already, my anxiety to assert my freedom of action hurried me into committing another. I bade Mr. Varleigh welcome whenever he chose to visit me, in terms which made his face flush under the emotions of pleasure and surprise which I had aroused in him. My wounded vanity acknowledged no restraints. I signed to him to take a seat on the sofa at my side; I engaged to go to his lodgings the next day, with my aunt, and see the collection of curiosities which he had amassed in the course of his travels. I almost believe, if he had tried to kiss me, that I was angry enough with the Captain to have let him do it!

Remember what my life had been—remember how ignorantly I had passed the precious days of my youth, how insidiously a sudden accession of wealth and importance had encouraged my folly and my pride—and try, like good Christians, to make some allowance for me!

My aunt came in from her walk, before Mr. Varleigh's visit had ended. She received him rather coldly, and he perceived it. After reminding me of our appointment for the next day, he took his leave.

"What appointment does Mr. Varleigh mean?" my aunt asked, as soon as we were alone. "Is it wise, under the circumstances, to make appointments with Mr. Varleigh?" she said, when I had answered her question. I naturally inquired what she meant. My aunt replied, "I have met Captain Stanwick while I was out walking. He has told me something which I am quite at a loss to understand. Is it possible, Bertha, that you have received a proposal of marriage from him favorably, without saying one word about your intentions to me?"

I instantly denied it. However rashly I might have spoken, I had certainly said nothing to justify Captain Stanwick in claiming me as his promised wife. In his mean fear of a fair rivalry with Mr. Varleigh, he had deliberately misinterpreted me. "If I marry either of the two," I said, "it will be Mr. Varleigh!"

My aunt shook her head. "These two gentlemen seem to be both in love with you, Bertha. It is a trying position for you between them, and I am afraid you have acted with some indiscretion. Captain Stanwick tells me that he and his friend have come to a separation already. I fear you are the cause of it. Mr. Varleigh has left the hotel at which he was staying with the Captain, in consequence of a disagreement between them this morning. You were not aware of that when you accepted his invitation. Shall I write an excuse for you? We must, at least, put off the visit, my dear, until you have set yourself right with Captain Stanwick."

I began to feel a little alarmed, but I was too obstinate to yield without a struggle. "Give me time to think over it," I said. "To write an excuse seems like acknowledging the Captain's authority. Let us wait till to-morrow morning."

IV.

THE morning brought with it another visit from Captain Stanwick. This time my aunt was present. He looked at her without speaking, and turned to me, with his fiery temper showing itself already in his eyes.

"I have a word to say to you in private," he began.

"I have no secrets from my aunt," I answered. "Whatever you have to say, Captain Stanwick, may be said here."

He opened his lips to reply, and suddenly checked himself. He was controlling his anger by so violent an effort that it turned his ruddy face pale. For the moment he conquered his temper—he addressed himself to me with the outward appearance of respect at least.

"Has that man Varleigh lied?" he asked; "or have you given him hopes, too—after what you said to me yesterday?"

"I said nothing to you yesterday which gives you any right to put that question to me," I rejoined. "You have entirely misunderstood me, if you think so."

My aunt attempted to say a few temperate words, in the hope of soothing him. He waved his hand, refusing to listen to her, and advanced closer to me.

"You have misunderstood me," he said, "if you think I am a man to be made a plaything of in the hands of a coquette!"

My aunt interposed once more, with a resolution which I had not expected from her.

"Captain Stanwick," she said, "you are forgetting yourself."

He paid no heed to her; he persisted in speaking to me. "It is my misfortune to love you," he burst out. "My whole heart is set on you. I mean to be your husband, and no other man living shall stand in my way. After what you said to me yesterday, I have a right to consider that you have favored my addresses. This is not a mere flirtation. Don't think it! I say it's the passion of a life! Do you hear? It's the passion of a man's whole life! I am not to be trifled with. I have had a night of sleepless misery about you—I have suffered enough for you—and you're not worth it. Don't laugh! This is no laughing matter. Take care, Bertha! Take care!"

My aunt rose from her chair. She astonished me. On all ordinary occasions the most retiring, the most feminine of women, she now walked up to Captain Stanwick and looked him full in the face, without flinching for an instant.

"You appear to have forgotten that you are speaking in the presence of two ladies," she said. "Alter your tone, sir, or I shall be obliged to take my niece out of the room."

Half angry, half frightened, I tried to speak in my turn. My aunt signed to me to be silent. The Captain drew back a step as if he felt her reproof. But his eyes, still fixed on me, were as fiercely bright as ever. There the gentleman's superficial good-breeding failed to hide the natural man beneath.

"I will leave you in undisturbed possession of the room," he said to my aunt with bitter politeness. "Before I go, permit me to give your niece an opportunity of reconsidering her conduct before it is too late." My aunt drew back, leaving him free to speak to me. After considering for a moment, he laid his hand firmly, but not roughly, on my arm. "You have accepted Lionel Varleigh's invitation to visit him," he said, "under pretense of seeing his curiosities. Think again before you decide on keeping that engagement. If you go to Varleigh tomorrow, you will repent it to the last day of your life." Saying those words, in a tone which made me tremble in spite of myself, he walked to the door. As he laid his hand on the lock, he turned toward me for the last time. "I forbid you to go to Varleigh's lodgings," he said, very distinctly and quietly. "Understand what I tell you. I forbid it."

With those words he left us.

My aunt sat down by me and took my hand kindly. "There is only one thing to be done," she said; "we must return at once to Nettlegrove. If Captain Stanwick attempts to annoy you in your own house, we have neighbors who will protect us, and we have Mr. Loring, our rector, to appeal to for advice. As for Mr. Varleigh, I will write our excuses myself before we go away."

She put out her hand to ring the bell and order the carriage. I stopped her. My childish pride urged me to assert myself in some way, after the passive position that I had been forced to occupy during the interview with Captain Stanwick.

"No," I said, "it is not acting fairly toward Mr. Varleigh to break our engagement with him. Let us return to Nettlegrove by all means, but let us first call on Mr. Varleigh and take our leave. Are we to behave rudely to a gentleman who has always treated us with the utmost consideration, because Captain Stanwick has tried to frighten us by cowardly threats? The commonest feeling of self-respect forbids it."

My aunt protested against this outbreak of folly with perfect temper and good sense. But my obstinacy (my firmness as I thought it!) was immovable. I left her to choose between going with me to Mr. Varleigh, or letting me go to him by myself. Finding it useless to resist, she decided, it is needless to say, on going with me.

We found Mr. Varleigh very courteous, but more than usually grave and quiet. Our visit only lasted for a few minutes; my aunt using the influence of her age and her position to shorten it. She mentioned family affairs as the motive which recalled us to Nettlegrove. I took it on myself to invite Mr. Varleigh to visit me at my own house. He bowed and thanked me, without engaging himself to accept the invitation. When I offered him my hand at parting, he raised it to his lips, and kissed it with a fervor that agitated me. His eyes looked into mine with a sorrowful admiration, with a lingering regret, as if they were taking their leave of me for a long while. "Don't forget me!" he whispered, as he stood at the door, while I followed my aunt out. "Come to Nettlegrove," I whispered back. His eyes dropped to the ground; he let me go without a word more.

This, I declare solemnly, was all that passed at our visit. By some unexpressed consent among us, no allusion whatever was made to Captain Stanwick; not even his name was mentioned. I never knew that the two men had met, just before we called on Mr. Varleigh. Nothing was said which could suggest to me the slightest suspicion of any arrangement for another meeting between them later in the day. Beyond the vague threats which had escaped Captain Stanwick's lips—threats which I own I was rash enough to despise—I had no warning whatever of the dreadful events which happened at Maplesworth on the day after our return to Nettlegrove Hall.

I can only add that I am ready to submit to any questions that may be put to me. Pray don't think me a heartless woman. My worst fault was ignorance. In those days, I knew nothing of the false pretenses under which men hide what is selfish and savage in their natures from the women whom it is their interest to deceive.

No. 2.—Julius Bender, fencing-master, testifies and says:—

I am of German nationality; established in England as teacher of the use of the sword and the pistol since the beginning of the present year.

Finding business slack in London, it unfortunately occurred to me to try what I could do in the country. I had heard of Maplesworth as a place largely frequented by visitors on account of the scenery, as well as by invalids in need of taking the waters; and I opened a gallery there at the beginning of the season of 1817, for fencing and pistol practice. About the visitors I had not been deceived; there were plenty of idle young gentlemen among them who might have been expected to patronize my establishment. They showed the most barbarous indifference to the noble art of attack and defense—came by twos and threes, looked at my gallery, and never returned. My small means began to fail me. After paying my expenses, I was really at my wits' end to find a few pounds to go on with, in the hope of better days.

One gentleman, I remember, who came to see me, and who behaved most liberally.

He described himself as an American, and said he had traveled a great deal. As my ill luck would have it, he stood in no need of my instructions. On the two or three occasions when he amused himself with my foils and my pistols, he proved to be one of the most expert swordsmen and one of the finest shots that I ever met with. It was not wonderful: he had by nature cool nerves and a quick eye; and he had been taught by the masters of the art in Vienna and Paris.

Early in July—the 9th or 10th of the month, I think—I was sitting alone in my gallery, looking ruefully enough at the last two sovereigns in my purse, when a gentleman was announced who wanted a lesson. "A private lesson," he said, with emphasis, looking at the man who cleaned and took care of my weapons.

I sent the man out of the room. The stranger (an Englishman, and, as I fancied, judging by outward appearances, a military man as well) took from his pocket-book a fifty-pound banknote, and held it up before me. "I have a heavy wager depending on a fencing match," he said, "and I have no time to improve myself. Teach me a trick which will make me a match for a man skilled in the use of the foil, and keep the secret—and there are fifty pounds for you."

I hesitated. I did indeed hesitate, poor as I was. But this devil of a man held his banknote before me whichever way I looked, and I had only two pounds left in the world!

"Are you going to fight a duel?" I asked.

"I have already told you what I am going to do," he answered.

I waited a little. The infernal bank-note still tempted me. In spite of myself, I tried him again.

"If I teach you the trick," I persisted, "will you undertake to make no bad use of your lesson?"

"Yes," he said, impatiently enough.

I was not quite satisfied yet.

"Will you promise it, on your word of honor?" I asked.

"Of course I will," he answered. "Take the money, and don't keep me waiting any longer."

I took the money, and I taught him the trick—and I regretted it almost as soon as it was done. Not that I knew, mind, of any serious consequences that followed; for I returned to London the next morning. My sentiments were those of a man of honor, who felt that he had degraded his art, and who could not be quite sure that he might not have armed the hand of an assassin as well. I have no more to say.

No. 3.—Thomas Outwater, servant to Captain Stanwick, testifies and says:—

If I did not firmly believe my master to be out of his senses, no punishment that I could receive would prevail upon me to tell of him what I am going to tell now.

But I say he is mad, and therefore not accountable for what he has done—mad for love of a young woman. If I could have my way, I should like to twist her neck, though she is a lady, and a great heiress into the bargain. Before she came between them, my master and Mr. Varleigh were more like brothers than anything else. She set them at variance, and whether she meant to do it or not is all the same to me. I own I took a dislike to her when I first saw her. She was one of the light-haired, blue-eyed sort, with an innocent look and a snaky waist—not at all to be depended on, as I have found them.

I hear I am not expected to give an account of the disagreement between the two gentlemen, of which this lady was the cause. I am to state what I did in Maplesworth, and what I saw afterward in Herne Wood. Poor as I am, I would give a five-pound note to anybody who could do it for me. Unfortunately, I must do it for myself.

On the 10th of July, in the evening, my master went, for the second time that day, to Mr. Varleigh's lodgings.

I am certain of the date, because it was the day of publication of the town newspaper, and there was a law report in it which set everybody talking. There had been a duel with pistols, a day or two before, between a resident in the town and a visitor, caused by some dispute about horses. Nothing very serious came of the meeting. One of the men only was hurt, and the wound proved to be of no great importance. The awkward part of the matter was that the constables appeared on the ground, before the wounded man had been removed. He and his two seconds were caught, and the prisoners were committed for trial. Dueling (the magistrates said) was an inhuman and unchristian practice, and they were determined to put the law in force and stop it. This sentence made a great stir in the town, and fixed the date, as I have just said, in my mind.

Having been accidentally within hearing of some of the disputes concerning Miss Laroche between my master and Mr. Varleigh, I had my misgivings about the Captain's second visit to the friend with whom he had quarreled already. A gentleman called on him, soon after he had gone out, on important business. This gave me an excuse for following him to Mr. Varleigh's rooms with the visitor's card, and I took the opportunity.

I heard them at high words on my way upstairs, and waited a little on the landing. The Captain was in one of his furious rages; Mr. Varleigh was firm and cool as usual. After listening for a minute or so, I heard enough (in my opinion) to justify me in entering the room. I caught my master in the act of lifting his cane—threatening to strike Mr. Varleigh. He instantly dropped his hand, and turned on me in a fury at my intrusion. Taking no notice of this outbreak of temper, I gave him his friend's card, and went out. A talk followed in voices too low for me to hear outside the room, and then the Captain approached the door. I got out of his way, feeling very uneasy about what was to come next. I could not presume to question Mr. Varleigh. The only thing I could think of was to tell the young lady's aunt what I had seen and heard, and to plead with Miss Laroche herself to make peace between them. When I inquired for the ladies at their lodgings, I was told that they had left Maplesworth.

I saw no more of the Captain that night.

The next morning he seemed to be quite himself again. He said to me, "Thomas, I am going sketching in Herne Wood. Take the paint-box and the rest of it, and put this into the carriage."

He handed me a packet as thick as my arm, and about three feet long, done up in many folds of canvas. I made bold to ask what it was. He answered that it was an artist's sketching umbrella, packed for traveling.

In an hour's time, the carriage stopped on the road below Herne Wood. My master said he would carry his sketching things himself, and I was to wait with the carriage. In giving him the so-called umbrella, I took the occasion of his eye being off me for the moment to pass my hand over it carefully; and I felt, through the canvas, the hilt of a sword. As an old soldier, I could not be mistaken—the hilt of a sword.

What I thought, on making this discovery, does not much matter. What I did was to watch the Captain into the wood, and then to follow him.

I tracked him along the path to where there was a clearing in the midst of the trees. There he stopped, and I got behind a tree. He undid the canvas, and produced two swords concealed in the packet. If I had felt any doubts before, I was certain of what was coming now. A duel without seconds or witnesses, by way of keeping the town magistrates in the dark—a duel between my master and Mr. Varleigh! As his name came into my mind, the man himself appeared, making his way into the clearing from the other side of the wood.

What could I do to stop it? No human creature was in sight. The nearest village was a mile away, reckoning from the further side of the wood. The coachman was a stupid old man, quite useless in a difficulty, even if I had had time enough to go back to the road and summon him to help me. While I was thinking about it, the Captain and Mr. Varleigh had stripped to their shirts and trousers. When they crossed their swords, I could stand it no longer—I burst in on them. "For God Almighty's sake, gentlemen," I cried out, "don't fight without seconds!" My master turned on me, like the madman he was, and threatened me with the point of his sword. Mr. Varleigh pulled me back out of harm's way. "Don't be afraid," he whispered, as he led me back to the verge of the clearing; "I have chosen the sword instead of the pistol expressly to spare his life."

Those noble words (spoken by as brave and true a man as ever breathed) quieted me. I knew Mr. Varleigh had earned the repute of being one of the finest swordsmen in Europe.

The duel began. I was placed behind my master, and was consequently opposite to his antagonist. The Captain stood on his defense, waiting for the other to attack. Mr. Varleigh made a pass. I was opposite the point of his sword; I saw it touch the Captain's left shoulder. In the same instant of time my master struck up his opponent's sword with his own weapon, seized Mr. Varleigh's right wrist in his left hand, and passed his sword clean through Mr. Varleigh's breast. He fell, the victim of a murderous trick—fell without a word or a cry.

The Captain turned slowly, and faced me with his bloody sword in his hand. I can't tell you how he looked; I can only say that the sight of him turned me faint with terror. I was at Waterloo—I am no coward. But I tell you the cold sweat poured down my face like water. I should have dropped if I had not held by the branch of a tree.

My master waited until I had in a measure recovered myself. "Feel if his heart beats," he said, pointing to the man on the ground.

I obeyed. He was dead—the heart was still; the beat of the pulse was gone. I said, "You have killed him!"

The Captain made no answer. He packed up the two swords again in the canvas, and put them under his arm. Then he told me to follow him with the sketching materials. I drew back from him without speaking; there was a horrid hollow sound in his voice that I did not like. "Do as I tell you," he said: "you have yourself to thank for it if I refuse to lose sight of you now." I managed to say that he might trust me to say nothing. He refused to trust me; he put out his hand to take hold of me. I could not stand that. "I'll go with you," I said; "don't touch me!" We reached the carriage and returned to Maplesworth. The same day we traveled by post to London.

In London I contrived to give the Captain the slip. By the first coach the next morning I want back to Maplesworth, eager to hear what had happened, and if the body had been found. Not a word of news reached me; nothing seemed to be known of the duel in Herne Wood.

I went to the wood—on foot, fearing that I might be traced if I hired a carriage. The country round was as solitary as usual. Not a creature was near when I entered the wood; not a creature was near when I looked into the clearing.

There was nothing on the ground. The body was gone.

No. 4.—The Reverend Alfred Loring, Rector of Nettlegrove, testifies and says:—

I.

EARLY in the month of October, 1817, I was informed that Miss Bertha Laroche had called at my house, and wished to see me in private.

I had first been presented to Miss Laroche on her arrival, with her aunt, to take possession of her property at Nettlegrove Hall. My opportunities of improving my acquaintance with her had not been so numerous as I could have desired, and I sincerely regretted it. She had produced a very favorable impression on me. Singularly inexperienced and impulsive—with an odd mixture of shyness and vivacity in her manner, and subject now and then to outbursts of vanity and petulance which she was divertingly incapable of concealing—I could detect, nevertheless, under the surface the signs which told of a true and generous nature, of a simple and pure heart. Her personal appearance, I should add, was attractive in a remarkable degree. There was something in it so peculiar, and at the same time so fascinating, that I am conscious it may have prejudiced me in her favor. For fear of this acknowledgment being misunderstood, I think it right to add that I am old enough to be her grandfather, and that I am also a married man.

I told the servant to show Miss Laroche into my study.

The moment she entered the room, her appearance alarmed me: she looked literally panic-stricken. I offered to send for my wife; she refused the proposal. I entreated her to take time at least to compose herself. It was not in her impulsive nature to do this. She said, "Give me your hand to encourage me, and let me speak while I can." I gave her my hand, poor soul. I said, "Speak to me, my dear, as if I were your father."

So far as I could understand the incoherent statement which she addressed to me, she had been the object of admiration (while visiting Maplesworth) of two gentlemen, who both desired to marry her. Hesitating between them and perfectly inexperienced in such matters, she had been the unfortunate cause of enmity between the rivals, and had returned to Nettlegrove, at her aunt's suggestion, as the best means of extricating herself from a very embarrassing position. The removal failing to alleviate her distressing recollections of what had happened, she and her aunt had tried a further change by making a tour of two months on the Continent. She had returned in a more quiet frame of mind. To her great surprise, she had heard nothing of either of her two suitors, from the day when she left Maplesworth to the day when she presented herself at my rectory.

Early that morning she was walking, after breakfast, in the park at Nettlegrove when she heard footsteps behind her. She turned, and found herself face to face with one of her suitors at Maplesworth. I am informed that there is no necessity now for my suppressing the name. The gentleman was Captain Stanwick.

He was so fearfully changed for the worse that she hardly knew him again.

After his first glance at her, he held his hand over his bloodshot eyes as if the sunlight hurt them. Without a word to prepare her for the disclosure, he confessed that he had killed Mr. Varleigh in a duel. His remorse (he declared) had unsettled his reason: only a few days had passed since he had been released from confinement in an asylum.

"You are the cause of it," he said wildly. "It is for love of you. I have but one hope left to live for—my hope in you. If you cast me off, my mind is made up. I will give my life for the life that I have taken; I will die by my own hand. Look at me, and you will see that I am in earnest. My future as a living man depends on your decision. Think of it to-day, and meet me here to-morrow. Not at this time; the horrid daylight feels like fire in my eyes, and goes like fire to my brain. Wait till sunset—you will find me here."

He left her as suddenly as he had appeared. When she had sufficiently recovered herself to be able to think, she decided on saying nothing of what had happened to her aunt. She took her way to the rectory to seek my advice.

It is needless to encumber my narrative by any statement of the questions which I felt it my duty to put to her under these circumstances. My inquiries informed me that Captain Stanwick had in the first instance produced a favorable impression on her. The less showy qualities of Mr. Varleigh had afterward grown on her liking; aided greatly by the repelling effect on her mind of the Captain's violent language and conduct when he had reason to suspect that his rival was being preferred to him. When she knew the horrible news of Mr. Varleigh's death, she "knew her own heart" (to repeat her exact words to me) by the shock that she felt. Toward Captain Stanwick the only feeling of which she was now conscious was, naturally, a feeling of the strongest aversion.

My own course in this difficult and painful matter appeared to me to be clear. "It is your duty as a Christian to see this miserable man again," I said. "And it is my duty as your friend and pastor, to sustain you under the trial. I will go with you to-morrow to the place of meeting."

II.

THE next evening we found Captain Stanwick waiting for us in the park.

He drew back on seeing me. I explained to him, temperately and firmly, what my position was. With sullen looks he resigned himself to endure my presence. By degrees I won his confidence. My first impression of him remains unshaken—the man's reason was unsettled. I suspected that the assertion of his release was a falsehood, and that he had really escaped from the asylum. It was impossible to lure him into telling me where the place was. He was too cunning to do this—too cunning to say anything about his relations, when I tried to turn the talk that way next. On the other hand, he spoke with a revolting readiness of the crime that he had committed, and of his settled resolution to destroy himself if Miss Laroche refused to be his wife. "I have nothing else to live for; I am alone in the world," he said. "Even my servant has deserted me. He knows how I killed Lionel Varleigh." He paused and spoke his next words in a whisper to me. "I killed him by a trick—he was the best swordsman of the two."

This confession was so horrible that I could only attribute it to an insane delusion. On pressing my inquiries, I found that the same idea must have occurred to the poor wretch's relations, and to the doctors who signed the certificates for placing him under medical care. This conclusion (as I afterward heard) was greatly strengthened by the fact that Mr. Varleigh's body had not been found on the reported scene of the duel. As to the servant, he had deserted his master in London, and had never reappeared. So far as my poor judgment went, the question before me was not of delivering a self-accused murderer to justice (with no corpse to testify against him), but of restoring an insane man to the care of the persons who had been appointed to restrain him.

I tried to test the strength of his delusion in an interval when he was not urging his shocking entreaties on Miss Laroche. "How do you know that you killed Mr. Varleigh?" I said.

He looked at me with a wild terror in his eyes. Suddenly he lifted his right hand, and shook it in the air, with a moaning cry, which was unmistakably a cry of pain. "Should I see his ghost," he asked, "if I had not killed him? I know it, by the pain that wrings me in the hand that stabbed him. Always in my right hand! always the same pain at the moment when I see him!" He stopped and ground his teeth in the agony and reality of his delusion. "Look!" he cried. "Look between the two trees behind you. There he is—with his dark hair, and his shaven face, and his steady look! There he is, standing before me as he stood in the wood, with his eyes on my eyes, and his sword feeling mine!" He turned to Miss Laroche. "Do you see him too?" he asked eagerly. "Tell me the truth. My whole life depends on your telling me the truth."

She controlled herself with a wonderful courage. "I don't see him," she answered.

He took out his handkerchief, and passed it over his face with a gasp of relief. "There is my last chance!" he said. "If she will be true to me—if she will be always near me, morning, noon, and night, I shall be released from the sight of him. See! he is fading away already! Gone!" h e cried, with a scream of exultation. He fell on his knees, and looked at Miss Laroche like a savage adoring his idol. "Will you cast me off now?" he asked, humbly. "Lionel was fond of you in his lifetime. His spirit is a merciful spirit. He shrinks from frightening you, he has left me for your sake; he will release me for your sake. Pity me, take me to live with you—and I shall never see him again!"

It was dreadful to hear him. I saw that the poor girl could endure no more. "Leave us," I whispered to her; "I will join you at the house."

He heard me, and instantly placed himself between us. "Let her promise, or she shan't go."

She felt, as I felt, the imperative necessity of saying anything that might soothe him. At a sign from me she gave him her promise to return.

He was satisfied—he insisted on kissing her hand, and then he let her go. I had by this time succeeded in inducing him to trust me. He proposed, of his own accord, that I should accompany him to the inn in the village at which he had been staying. The landlord (naturally enough distrusting his wretched guest) had warned him that morning to find some other place of shelter. I engaged to use my influence with the man to make him change his purpose, and I succeeded in effecting the necessary arrangements for having the poor wretch properly looked after. On my return to my own house, I wrote to a brother magistrate living near me, and to the superintendent of our county asylum, requesting them to consult with me on the best means of lawfully restraining Captain Stanwick until we could communicate with his relations. Could I have done more than this? The event of the next morning answered that question—answered it at once and forever.

III.

PRESENTING myself at Nettlegrove Hall toward sunset, to take charge of Miss Laroche, I was met by an obstacle in the shape of a protest from her aunt.

This good lady had been informed of the appearance of Captain Stanwick in the park, and she strongly disapproved of encouraging any further communication with him on the part of her niece. She also considered that I had failed in my duty in still leaving the Captain at liberty. I told her that I was only waiting to act on the advice of competent persons, who would arrive the next day to consult with me; and I did my best to persuade her of the wisdom of the course that I had taken in the meantime. Miss Laroche, on her side, was resolved to be true to the promise that she had given. Between us, we induced her aunt to yield on certain conditions.

"I know the part of the park in which the meeting is to take place," the old lady said; "it is my niece's favorite walk. If she is not brought back to me in half an hour's time, I shall send the men-servants to protect her."

The twilight was falling when we reached the appointed place. We found Captain Stanwick angry and suspicious; it was not easy to pacify him on the subject of our delay. His insanity seemed to me to be now more marked than ever. He had seen, or dreamed of seeing, the ghost during the past night. For the first time (he said) the apparition of the dead man had spoken to him. In solemn words it had condemned him to expiate his crime by giving his life for the life that he had taken. It had warned him not to insist on marriage with Bertha Laroche: "She shall share your punishment if she shares your life. And you shall know it by this sign—She shall see me as you see me."

I tried to compose him. He shook his head in immovable despair. "No," he answered; "if she sees him when I see him, there ends the one hope of

894

release that holds me to life. It will be good-by between us, and good-by forever!"

We had walked on, while we were speaking, to a part of the park through which there flowed a rivulet of clear water. On the further bank, the open ground led down into a wooded valley. On our side of the stream rose a thick plantation of fir-trees intersected by a winding path. Captain Stanwick stopped as we reached the place. His eyes rested, in the darkening twilight, on the narrow space pierced by the path among the trees. On a sudden he lifted his right hand, with the same cry of pain which we had heard before; with his left hand he took Miss Laroche by the arm. "There!" he said. "Look where I look! Do you see him there?"

As the words passed his lips, a dimly-visible figure appeared, advancing toward us along the path.

Was it the figure of a living man? or was it the creation of my own excited fancy? Before I could ask myself the question, the man advanced a step nearer to us. A last gleam of the dying light fell on his face through an opening in the trees. At the same instant Miss Laroche started back from Captain Stanwick with a scream of terror. She would have fallen if I had not been near enough to support her. The Captain was instantly at her side again. "Speak!" he cried. "Do you see it, too?"

She was just able to say "Yes" before she fainted in my arms.

He stooped over her, and touched her cold cheek with his lips. "Goodby!" he said, in tones suddenly and strangely changed to the most exquisite tenderness. "Good-by, forever!"

He leaped the rivulet; he crossed the open ground; he was lost to sight in the valley beyond.

As he disappeared, the visionary man among the fir-trees advanced; passed in silence; crossed the rivulet at a bound; and vanished as the figure of the Captain had vanished before him.

I was left alone with the swooning woman. Not a sound, far or near, broke the stillness of the coming night.

No 5.—Mr. Frederic Darnel, Member of the College of Surgeons, testifies and says:—

IN the intervals of my professional duty I am accustomed to occupy myself in studying Botany, assisted by a friend and neighbor, whose tastes in this respect resemble my own. When I can spare an hour or two from my patients, we go out together searching for specimens. Our favorite place is Herne Wood. It is rich in material for the botanist, and it is only a mile distant from the village in which I live.

Early in July, my friend and I made a discovery in the wood of a very alarming and unexpected kind. We found a man in the clearing, prostrated by a dangerous wound, and to all appearance dead.

We carried him to the gamekeeper's cottage on the outskirts of the woods, and on the side of it nearest to our village. He and his boy were out, but the light cart in which he makes his rounds, in the remoter part of his master's property, was in the outhouse. While my friend was putting the horse to, I examined the stranger's wound. It had been quite recently inflicted, and I doubted whether it had (as yet, at any rate) really killed him. I did what I could with the linen and cold water which the gamekeeper's wife offered to me, and then my friend and I removed him carefully to my house in the cart. I applied the necessary restoratives, and I had the pleasure of satisfying myself that the vital powers had revived. He was perfectly unconscious, of course, but the action of the heart became distinctly perceptible, and I had hopes.

In a few days more I felt fairly sure of him. Then the usual fever set in. I was obliged, in justice to his friends, to search his clothes in presence of a witness. We found his handkerchief, his purse, and his cigar-case, and nothing more. No letters or visiting cards; nothing marked on his clothes but initials. There was no help for it but to wait to identify him until he could speak.

When that time came, he acknowledged to me that he had divested himself purposely of any clew to his identity, in the fear (if some mischance happened to him) of the news of it reaching his father and mother abruptly, by means of the newspapers. He had sent a letter to his bankers in London, to be forwarded to his parents, if the bankers neither saw him nor heard from him in a month's time. His first act was to withdraw this letter. The other particulars which he communicated to me are, I am told, already known. I need only add that I willingly kept his secret, simply speaking of him in the neighborhood as a traveler from foreign parts who had met with an accident.

His convalescence was a long one. It was the beginning of October before he was completely restored to health. When he left us he went to London. He behaved most liberally to me; and we parted with sincere good wishes on either side.

No. 6.—Mr. Lionel Varleigh, of Boston, U. S. A., testifies and says:—

MY first proceeding, on my recovery, was to go to the relations of Captain Stanwick in London, for the purpose of making inquiries about him.

I do not wish to justify myself at the expense of that miserable man. It is true that I loved Miss Laroche too dearly to yield her to any rival except at her own wish. It is also true that Captain Stanwick more than once insulted me, and that I endured it. He had suffered from sunstroke in India, and in his angry moments he was hardly a responsible being. It was only when he threatened me with personal chastisement that my patience gave way. We met sword in hand. In my mind was the resolution to spare his life. In his mind was the resolution to kill me. I have forgiven him. I will say no more.

His relations informed me of the symptoms of insane delusion which he had shown after the duel; of his escape from the asylum in which he had been confined; and of the failure to find him again.

The moment I heard this news the dread crossed my mind that Stanwick had found his way to Miss Laroche. In an hour more I was traveling to Nettlegrove Hall.

I arrived late in the evening, and found Miss Laroche's aunt in great alarm about her niece's safety. The young lady was at that very moment speaking to Stanwick in the park, with only an old man (the rector) to protect her. I volunteered to go at once, and assist in taking care of her. A servant accompanied me to show me the place of meeting. We heard voices indistinctly, but saw no one. The servant pointed to a path through the fir-trees. I went on quickly by myself, leaving the man within call. In a few minutes I came upon them suddenly, at a little distance from me, on the bank of a stream.

The fear of seriously alarming Miss Laroche, if I showed myself too suddenly, deprived me for a moment of my presence of mind. Pausing to consider what it might be best to do, I was less completely protected from discovery by the trees than I had supposed. She had seen me; I heard her cry of alarm. The instant afterward I saw Stanwick leap over the rivulet and take to flight. That action roused me. Without stopping for a word of explanation, I pursued him.

Unhappily, I missed my footing in the obscure light, and fell on the open ground beyond the stream. When I had gained my feet once more, Stanwick had disappeared among the trees which marked the boundary of the park beyond me. I could see nothing of him, and I could hear nothing of him, when I came out on the high-road. There I met with a laboring man who showed me the way to the village. From the inn I sent a letter to Miss Laroche's aunt, explaining what had happened, and asking leave to call at the Hall on the next day.

Early in the morning the rector came to me at the inn. He brought sad news. Miss Laroche was suffering from a nervous attack, and my visit to the Hall must be deferred. Speaking next of the missing man, I heard all that Mr. Loring could tell me. My intimate knowledge of Stanwick enabled me to draw my own conclusion from the facts. The thought instantly crossed my mind that the poor wretch might have committed his expiatory suicide at the very spot on which he had attempted to kill me. Leaving the rector to institute the necessary inquiries, I took post-horses to Maplesworth on my way to Herne Wood.

Advancing from the high-road to the wood, I saw two persons at a little distance from me—a man in the dress of a gamekeeper, and a lad. I was too much agitated to take any special notice of them; I hurried along the path which led to the clearing. My presentiment had not misled me. There he lay, dead on the scene of the duel, with a blood-stained razor by his side! I fell on my knees by the corpse; I took his cold hand in mine; and I thanked God that I had forgiven him in the first days of my recovery.

I was still kneeling, when I felt myself seized from behind. I struggled to my feet, and confronted the gamekeeper. He had noticed my hurry in entering the wood; his suspicions had been aroused, and he and the lad had followed me. There was blood on my clothes; there was horror in my face. Appearances were plainly against me; I had no choice but to accompany the gamekeeper to the nearest magistrate.

My instructions to my solicitor forbade him to vindicate my innocence by taking any technical legal objections to the action of the magistrate or of the coroner. I insisted on my witnesses being summoned to the lawyer's office, and allowed to state, in their own way, what they could truly declare on my behalf; and I left my defense to be founded upon the materials thus obtained. In the meanwhile I was detained in custody, as a matter of course.

With this event the tragedy of the duel reached its culminating point. I was accused of murdering the man who had attempted to take my life!

This last incident having been related, all that is worth noticing in my contribution to the present narrative comes to an end. I was tried in due course of law. The evidence taken at my solicitor's office was necessarily altered in form, though not in substance, by the examination to which the witnesses were subjected in a court of justice. So thoroughly did our defense satisfy the jury, that they became restless toward the close of the proceedings, and returned their verdict of Not Guilty without quitting the box.

When I was a free man again, it is surely needless to dwell on the first use that I made of my honorable acquittal. Whether I deserved the enviable place that I occupied in Bertha's estimation, it is not for me to say. Let me leave the decision to the lady who has ceased to be Miss Laroche—I mean the lady who has been good enough to become my wife.

MISS DULANE AND MY LORD.

Part I. TWO REMONSTRATIONS.

I.

ONE afternoon old Miss Dulane entered her drawing-room; ready to receive visitors, dressed in splendor, and exhibiting every outward appearance of a defiant frame of mind.

Just as a saucy bronze nymph on the mantelpiece struck the quarter to three on an elegant clock under her arm, a visitor was announced—"Mrs. Newsham."

Miss Dulane wore her own undisguised gray hair, dressed in perfect harmony with her time of life. Without an attempt at concealment, she submitted to be too short and too stout. Her appearance (if it had only been made to speak) would have said, in effect: "I am an old woman, and I scorn to disguise it."

Mrs. Newsham, tall and elegant, painted and dyed, acted on the opposite principle in dressing, which confesses nothing. On exhibition before the world, this lady's disguise asserted that she had reached her thirtieth year on her last birthday. Her husband was discreetly silent, and Father Time was discreetly silent: they both knew that her last birthday had happened thirty years since.

"Shall we talk of the weather and the news, my dear? Or shall we come to the object of your visit at once?" So Miss Dulane opened the interview.

"Your tone and manner, my good friend, are no doubt provoked by the report in the newspaper of this morning. In justice to you, I refuse to believe the report." So Mrs. Newsham adopted her friend's suggestion.

"You kindness is thrown away, Elizabeth. The report is true."

"Matilda, you shock me!"

"Why?"

"At your age!"

"If he doesn't object to my age, what does it matter to you?"

"Don't speak of that man!"

"Why not?"

"He is young enough to be your son; and he is marrying you—impudently, undisguisedly marrying you—for your money!"

"And I am marrying him—impudently, undisguisedly marrying him—for his rank."

"You needn't remind me, Matilda, that you are the daughter of a tailor."

"In a week or two more, Elizabeth, I shall remind you that I am the wife of a nobleman's son."

"A younger son; don't forget that."

"A younger son, as you say. He finds the social position, and I find the money—half a million at my own sole disposal. My future husband is a good fellow in his way, and his future wife is another good fellow in her way. To look at your grim face, one would suppose there were no such things in the world as marriages of convenience."

"Not at your time of life. I tell you plainly, your marriage will be a public scandal."

"That doesn't frighten us," Miss Dulane remarked. "We are resigned to every ill-natured thing that our friends can say of us. In course of time, the next nine days' wonder will claim public attention, and we shall be forgotten. I shall be none the less on that account Lady Howel Beaucourt. And my husband will be happy in the enjoyment of every expensive taste which a poor man call gratify, for the first time in his life. Have you any more objections to make? Don't hesitate to speak plainly."

"I have a question to ask, my dear."

"Charmed, I am sure, to answer it—if I can."

"Am I right in supposing that Lord Howel Beaucourt is about half your age?"

"Yes, dear; my future husband is as nearly as possible half as old as I am."

Mrs. Newsham's uneasy virtue shuddered. "What a profanation of marriage!" she exclaimed.

"Nothing of the sort," her friend pronounced positively. "Marriage, by the law of England (as my lawyer tells me), is nothing but a contract. Who ever heard of profaning a contract?"

"Call it what you please, Matilda. Do you expect to live a happy life, at your age, with a young man for your husband?"

"A happy life," Miss Dulane repeated, "because it will be an innocent life." She laid a certain emphasis on the last word but one.

Mrs. Newsham resented the emphasis, and rose to go. Her last words were the bitterest words that she had spoken yet.

"You have secured such a truly remarkable husband, my dear, that I am emboldened to ask a great favor. Will you give me his lordship's photograph?"

"No," said Miss Dulane, "I won't give you his lordship's photograph."

"What is your objection, Matilda?"

"A very serious objection, Elizabeth. You are not pure enough in mind to be worthy of my husband's photograph."

With that reply the first of the remonstrances assumed hostile proportions, and came to an untimely end.

II.

THE second remonstrance was reserved for a happier fate. It took its rise in a conversation between two men who were old and true friends. In

902

other words, it led to no quarreling.

The elder man was one of those admirable human beings who are cordial, gentle, and good-tempered, without any conscious exercise of their own virtues. He was generally known in the world about him by a fond and familiar use of his Christian name. To call him "Sir Richard" in these pages (except in the character of one of his servants) would be simply ridiculous. When he lent his money, his horses, his house, and (sometimes, after unlucky friends had dropped to the lowest social depths) even his clothes, this general benefactor was known, in the best society and the worst society alike, as "Dick." He filled the hundred mouths of Rumor with his nickname, in the days when there was an opera in London, as the proprietor of the "Beauty-box." The ladies who occupied the box were all invited under the same circumstances. They enjoyed operatic music; but their husbands and fathers were not rich enough to be able to gratify that expensive taste. Dick's carriage called for them, and took them home again; and the beauties all agreed (if he ever married) that Mrs. Dick would be the most enviable woman on the face of the civilized earth. Even the false reports, which declared that he was privately married already, and on bad terms with his wife, slandered him cordially under the popular name. And his intimate companions, when they alluded among each other to a romance in his life which would remain a hidden romance to the end of his days, forgot that the occasion justified a serious and severe use of his surname, and blamed him affectionately as "poor dear Dick."

The hour was midnight; and the friends, whom the most hospitable of men delighted to assemble round his dinner-table, had taken their leave with the exception of one guest specially detained by the host, who led him back to the dining-room.

"You were angry with our friends," Dick began, "when they asked you about that report of your marriage. You won't be angry with Me. Are you really going to be the old maid's husband?"

This plain question received a plain reply: "Yes, I am."

Dick took the young lord's hand. Simply and seriously, he said: "Accept my congratulations."

Howel Beaucourt started as if he had received a blow instead of a compliment.

"There isn't another man or woman in the whole circle of my acquaintance," he declared, "who would have congratulated me on marrying Miss Dulane. I believe you would make allowances for me if I had committed murder."

"I hope I should," Dick answered gravely. "When a man is my friend—murder or marriage—I take it for granted that he has a reason for what he does. Wait a minute. You mustn't give me more credit than I deserve. I don't agree with you. If I were a marrying man myself, I shouldn't pick an old maid—I should prefer a young one. That's a matter of taste. You are not like me. You always have a definite object in view. I may not know what the object is. Never mind! I wish you joy all the same."

Beaucourt was not unworthy of the friendship he had inspired. "I should be ungrateful indeed," he said, "if I didn't tell you what my object is. You know that I am poor?"

"The only poor friend of mine," Dick remarked, "who has never borrowed money of me."

Beaucourt went on without noticing this. "I have three expensive tastes," he said. "I want to get into Parliament; I want to have a yacht; I want to collect pictures. Add, if you like, the selfish luxury of helping poverty and wretchedness, and hearing my conscience tell me what an excellent man I am. I can't do all this on five hundred a year—but I can do it on forty times five hundred a year. Moral: marry Miss Dulane."

Listening attentively until the other had done, Dick showed a sardonic side to his character never yet discovered in Beaucourt's experience of him.

"I suppose you have made the necessary arrangements," he said. "When the old lady releases you, she will leave consolation behind her in her will."

"That's the first ill-natured thing I ever heard you say, Dick. When the old lady dies, my sense of honor takes fright, and turns its back on her will. It's a condition on my side, that every farthing of her money shall be left to her relations."

"Don't you call yourself one of them?"

"What a question! Am I her relation because the laws of society force a mock marriage on us? How can I make use of her money unless I am her husband? and how can she make use of my title unless she is my wife? As long as she lives I stand honestly by my side of the bargain. But when she dies the transaction is at an end, and the surviving partner returns to his five hundred a year."

Dick exhibited another surprising side to his character. The most compliant of men now became as obstinate as the proverbial mule.

"All very well," he said, "but it doesn't explain why—if you must sell yourself—you have sold yourself to an old lady. There are plenty of young ones and pretty ones with fortunes to tempt you. It seems odd that you haven't tried your luck with one of them."

"No, Dick. It would have been odd, and worse than odd, if I had tried my luck with a young woman."

"I don't see that."

"You shall see it directly. If I marry an old woman for her money, I have no occasion to be a hypocrite; we both know that our marriage is a mere matter of form. But if I make a young woman my wife because I want her money, and if that young woman happens to be worth a straw, I must deceive her and disgrace myself by shamming love. That, my boy, you may depend upon it, I will never do."

Dick's face suddenly brightened with a mingled expression of relief and triumph.

"Ha! my mercenary friend," he burst out, "there's something mixed up in this business which is worthier of you than anything I have heard yet. Stop! I'm going to be clever for the first time in my life. A man who talks of love as you do, must have felt love himself. Where is the young one and the pretty one? And what has she done, poor dear, to be deserted for an old woman? Good God! how you look at me! I have hurt your feelings—I have been a greater fool than ever—I am more ashamed of myself than words can say!"

Beaucourt stopped him there, gently and firmly.

"You have made a very natural mistake," he said. "There was a young lady. She has refused me—absolutely refused me. There is no more love in my life. It's a dark life and an empty life for the rest of my days. I must see what money can do for me next. When I have thoroughly hardened my heart I may not feel my misfortune as I feel it now. Pity me or despise me. In either case let us say goodnight."

He went out into the hall and took his hat. Dick went out into the hall and took his hat.

"Have your own way," he answered, "I mean to have mine—I'll go home with you."

The man was simply irresistible. Beaucourt sat down resignedly on the nearest of the hall chairs. Dick asked him to return to the dining-room. "No," he said; "it's not worth while. What I can tell you may be told in two minutes." Dick submitted, and took the next of the hall chairs. In that inappropriate place the young lord's unpremeditated confession was forced out of him, by no more formidable exercise of power than the kindness of his friend.

"When you hear where I met with her," he began, "you will most likely not want to hear any more. I saw her, for the first time, on the stage of a music hall."

He looked at Dick. Perfectly quiet and perfectly impenetrable, Dick only said, "Go on." Beaucourt continued in these words:

"She was singing Arne's delicious setting of Ariel's song in the 'Tempest,' with a taste and feeling completely thrown away on the greater part of the audience. That she was beautiful—in my eyes at least—I needn't say. That she had descended to a sphere unworthy of her and new to her, nobody could doubt. Her modest dress, her refinement of manner, seemed rather to puzzle than to please most of the people present; they applauded her, but not very warmly, when she retired. I obtained an introduction through her music-master, who happened to be acquainted professionally with some relatives of mine. He told me that she was a young widow; and he assured me that the calamity through which her family had lost their place in the world had brought no sort of disgrace on them. If I wanted to know more, he referred me to the lady herself. I found her very reserved. A long time passed before I could win her confidence—and a longer time still before I ventured to confess the feeling with which she had inspired me. You know the rest."

"You mean, of course, that you offered her marriage?"

"Certainly."

"And she refused you on account of your position in life."

"No. I had foreseen that obstacle, and had followed the example of the adventurous nobleman in the old story. Like him, I assumed a name, and presented myself as belonging to her own respectable middle class of life. You are too old a friend to suspect me of vanity if I tell you that she had no objection to me, and no suspicion that I had approached her (personally speaking) under a disguise."

"What motive could she possibly have had for refusing you?" Dick asked.

"A motive associated with her dead husband," Beaucourt answered. "He had married her—mind, innocently married her—while his first wife was living. The woman was an inveterate drunkard; they had been separated for years. Her death had been publicly reported in the newspapers, among the persons killed in a railway accident abroad. When she claimed her unhappy husband he was in delicate health. The shock killed him. His widow—I can't, and won't, speak of her misfortune as if it was her fault—knew of no living friends who were in a position to help her. Not a great artist with a wonderful voice, she could still trust to her musical accomplishments to provide for the necessities of life. Plead as I might with her to forget the past, I always got the same reply: 'If I was base enough to let myself be tempted by the happy future that you offer, I should deserve the unmerited disgrace which has fallen on me. Marry a woman whose reputation will bear inquiry, and forget me.' I was mad enough to press my suit once too often. When I visited her on the next day she was gone. Every effort to trace her has failed. Lost, my friend— irretrievably lost to me!"

He offered his hand and said good-night. Dick held him back on the doorstep.

"Break off your mad engagement to Miss Dulane," he said. "Be a man, Howel; wait and hope! You are throwing away your life when happiness is within your reach, if you will only be patient. That poor young creature is worthy of you. Lost? Nonsense! In this narrow little world people are never hopelessly lost till they are dead and underground. Help me to recognize her by a description, and tell me her name. I'll find her; I'll persuade her to come back to you—and, mark my words, you will live to bless the day when you followed my advice."

This well-meant remonstrance was completely thrown away. Beaucourt's despair was deaf to every entreaty that Dick had addressed to him. "Thank you with all my heart," he said. "You don't know her as I do. She is one of the very few women who mean No when they say No. Useless, Dick—useless!"

Those were the last words he said to his friend in the character of a single man.

Part II. PLATONIC MARRIAGE.

III.

"SEVEN months have passed, my dear Dick, since my 'inhuman obstinacy' (those were the words you used) made you one of the witnesses at my marriage to Miss Dulane, sorely against your will. Do you remember your parting prophecy when you were out of the bride's hearing? 'A miserable life is before that woman's husband—and, by Jupiter, he has deserved it!'

"Never, my dear boy, attempt to forecast the future again. Viewed as a prophet you are a complete failure. I have nothing to complain of in my married life.

"But you must not mistake me. I am far from saying that I am a happy man; I only declare myself to be a contented man. My old wife is a marvel of good temper and good sense. She trusts me implicitly, and I have given her no reason to regret it. We have our time for being together, and our time for keeping apart. Within our inevitable limits we understand each other and respect each other, and have a truer feeling of regard on both sides than many people far better matched than we are in point of age. But you shall judge for yourself. Come and dine with us, when I return on Wednesday next from the trial trip of my new yacht. In the meantime I have a service to ask of you.

"My wife's niece has been her companion for years. She has left us to be married to an officer, who has taken her to India; and we are utterly at a loss how to fill her place. The good old lady doesn't want much. A nice-tempered refined girl, who can sing and play to her with some little taste and feeling, and read to her now and then when her eyes are weary—there is what we require; and there, it seems, is more than we can get, after advertising for a week past. Of all the 'companions' who have presented themselves, not one has turned out to be the sort of person whom Lady Howel wants.

"Can you help us? In any case, my wife sends you her kind remembrances; and (true to the old times) I add my love."

On the day which followed the receipt of this letter, Dick paid a visit to Lady Howel Beaucourt.

"You seem to be excited," she said. "Has anything remarkable happened?"

"Pardon me if I ask a question first," Dick replied. "Do you object to a young widow?"

"That depends on the widow."

"Then I have found the very person you want. And, oddly enough, your husband has had something to do with it."

"Do you mean that my husband has recommended her?"

There was an undertone of jealousy in Lady Howel's voice—jealousy excited not altogether without a motive. She had left it to Beaucourt's sense of honor to own the truth, if there had been any love affair in his past life which ought to make him hesitates before he married. He had justified Miss Dulane's confidence in him; acknowledging an attachment to a young widow, and adding that she had positively refused him. "We have not met since," he said, "and we shall never meet again." Under those circumstances, Miss Dulane had considerately abstained from asking for any further details. She had not thought of the young widow again, until Dick's language had innocently inspired her first doubt. Fortunately for both of them, he was an outspoken man; and he reassured her unreservedly in these words: "Your husband knows nothing about it."

"Now," she said, "you may tell me how you came to hear of the lady."

"Through my uncle's library," Dick replied. "His will has left me his collection of books—in such a wretchedly neglected condition that I asked Beaucourt (not being a reading man myself) if he knew of any competent person who could advise me how to set things right. He introduced me to Farleigh & Halford, the well-known publishers. The second partner is a book collector himself, as well as a bookseller. He kindly looks in now and then, to see how his instructions for mending and binding are being carried out. When he called yesterday I thought of you, and I found he could help us to a young lady employed in his office at correcting proof sheets."

"What is the lady's name?"

"Mrs. Evelin."

"Why does she leave her employment?"

"To save her eyes, poor soul. When the senior partner, Mr. Farleigh, met with her, she was reduced by family misfortunes to earn her own living. The publishers would have been only too glad to keep her in their office, but for the oculist's report. He declared that she would run the risk of blindness, if she fatigued her weak eyes much longer. There is the only objection to this otherwise invaluable person—she will not be able to read to you."

"Can she sing and play?"

"Exquisitely. Mr. Farleigh answers for her music."

"And her character?"

"Mr. Halford answers for her character."

"And her manners?"

"A perfect lady. I have seen her and spoken to her; I answer for her manners, and I guarantee her personal appearance. Charming—charming!"

For a moment Lady Howel hesitated. After a little reflection, she decided that it was her duty to trust her excellent husband. "I will receive the charming widow," she said, "to-morrow at twelve o'clock; and, if she produces the right impression, I promise to overlook the weakness of her eyes."

IV.

BEAUCOURT had prolonged the period appointed for the trial trip of his yacht by a whole week. His apology when he returned delighted the kind-hearted old lady who had made him a present of the vessel.

"There isn't such another yacht in the whole world," he declared. "I really hadn't the heart to leave that beautiful vessel after only three days experience of her." He burst out with a torrent of technical praises of the yacht, to which his wife listened as attentively as if she really understood what he was talking about. When his breath and his eloquence were exhausted alike, she said, "Now, my dear, it's my turn. I can match your perfect vessel with my perfect lady."

"What! you have found a companion?"

"Yes."

"Did Dick find her for you?"

"He did indeed. You shall see for yourself how grateful I ought to be to your friend."

She opened a door which led into the next room. "Mary, my dear, come and be introduced to my husband."

Beaucourt started when he heard the name, and instantly recovered himself. He had forgotten how many Marys there are in the world.

Lady Howel returned, leading her favorite by the hand, and gayly introduced her the moment they entered the room.

"Mrs. Evelin; Lord—"

She looked at her husband. The utterance of his name was instantly suspended on her lips. Mrs. Evelin's hand, turning cold at the same moment in her hand, warned her to look round. The face of the woman more than reflected the inconcealable agitation in the face of the man.

The wife's first words, when she recovered herself, were addressed to them both.

"Which of you can I trust," she asked, "to tell me the truth?"

"You can trust both of us," her husband answered.

The firmness of his tone irritated her. "I will judge of that for myself," she said. "Go back to the next room," she added, turning to Mrs. Evelin; "I will hear you separately."

The companion, whose duty it was to obey—whose modesty and

gentleness had won her mistress's heart—refused to retire.

"No," she said; "I have been deceived too. I have my right to hear what Lord Howel has to say for himself."

Beaucourt attempted to support the claim that she had advanced. His wife sternly signed to him to be silent. "What do you mean?" she said, addressing the question to Mrs. Evelin.

"I mean this. The person whom you speak of as a nobleman was presented to me as 'Mr. Vincent, an artist.' But for that deception I should never have set foot in your ladyship's house."

"Is this true, my lord?" Lady Howel asked, with a contemptuous emphasis on the title of nobility.

"Quite true," her husband answered. "I thought it possible that my rank might prove an obstacle in the way of my hopes. The blame rests on me, and on me alone. I ask Mrs. Evelin to pardon me for an act of deception which I deeply regret."

Lady Howel was a just woman. Under other circumstances she might have shown herself to be a generous woman. That brighter side of her character was incapable of revealing itself in the presence of Mrs. Evelin, young and beautiful, and in possession of her husband's heart. She could say, "I beg your pardon, madam; I have not treated you justly." But no self-control was strong enough to restrain the next bitter words from passing her lips. "At my age," she said, "Lord Howel will soon be free; you will not have long to wait for him."

The young widow looked at her sadly—answered her sadly.

"Oh, my lady, your better nature will surely regret having said that!"

For a moment her eyes rested on Beaucourt, dim with rising tears. She left the room—and left the house.

There was silence between the husband and wife. Beaucourt was the first to speak again.

"After what you have just heard, do you persist in your jealousy of that lady, and your jealousy of me?" he asked.

"I have behaved cruelly to her and to you. I am ashamed of myself," was all she said in reply. That expression of sorrow, so simple and so true, did not appeal in vain to the gentler side of Beaucourt's nature. He kissed his wife's hand; he tried to console her.

"You may forgive me," she answered. "I cannot forgive myself. That poor lady's last words have made my heart ache. What I said to her in anger I ought to have said generously. Why should she not wait for you? After your life with me—a life of kindness, a life of self-sacrifice—you deserve your reward. Promise me that you will marry the woman you love—after my death has released you."

"You distress me, and needlessly distress me," he said. "What you are thinking of, my dear, can never happen; no, not even if—" He left the rest unsaid.

"Not even if you were free?" she asked.

"Not even then."

She looked toward the next room. "Go in, Howel, and bring Mrs. Evelin back; I have something to say to her."

The discovery that she had left the house caused no fear that she had taken to flight with the purpose of concealing herself. There was a prospect before the poor lonely woman which might be trusted to preserve her from despair, to say the least of it.

During her brief residence in Beaucourt's house she had shown to Lady Howel a letter received from a relation, who had emigrated to New Zealand with her husband and her infant children some years since. They had steadily prospered; they were living in comfort, and they wanted for nothing but a trustworthy governess to teach their children. The mother had accordingly written, asking if her relative in England could recommend a competent person, and offering a liberal salary. In showing the letter to Lady Howel,

Mrs. Evelin had said: "If I had not been so happy as to attract your notice, I might have offered to be the governess myself."

Assuming that it had now occurred to her to act on this idea, Lady Howel felt assured that she would apply for advice either to the publishers who had recommended her, or to Lord Howel's old friend.

Beaucourt at once offered to make the inquiries which might satisfy his wife that she had not been mistaken. Readily accepting his proposal, she asked at the same time for a few minutes of delay.

"I want to say to you," she explained, "what I had in my mind to say to Mrs. Evelin. Do you object to tell me why she refused to marry you? I couldn't have done it in her place."

"You would have done it, my dear, as I think, if her misfortune had been your misfortune." With those prefatory words he told the miserable story of Mrs. Evelin's marriage.

Lady Howel's sympathies, strongly excited, appeared to have led her to a conclusion which she was not willing to communicate to her husband. She asked him, rather abruptly, if he would leave it to her to find Mrs. Evelin. "I promise," she added, "to tell you what I am thinking of, when I come back."

In two minutes more she was ready to go out, and had hurriedly left the house.

V.

AFTER a long absence Lady Howel returned, accompanied by Dick. His face and manner betrayed unusual agitation; Beaucourt noticed it.

"I may well be excited," Dick declared, "after what I have heard, and after what we have done. Lady Howel, yours is the brain that thinks to some purpose. Make our report—I wait for you."

But my lady preferred waiting for Dick. He consented to speak first, for the thoroughly characteristic reason that he could "get over it in no time."

"I shall try the old division," he said, "into First, Second, and Third.

Don't be afraid; I am not going to preach—quite the contrary; I am going to be quick about it. First, then, Mrs. Evelin has decided, under sound advice, to go to New Zealand. Second, I have telegraphed to her relations at the other end of the world to tell them that she is coming. Third, and last, Farleigh & Halford have sent to the office, and secured a berth for her in the next ship that sails—date the day after to-morrow. Done in half a minute. Now, Lady Howel!"

"I will begin and end in half a minute too," she said, "if I can. First," she continued, turning to her husband, "I found Mrs. Evelin at your friend's house. She kindly let me say all that I could say for the relief of my poor heart. Secondly—"

She hesitated, smiled uneasily, and came to a full stop.

"I can't do it, Howel," she confessed; "I speak to you as usual, or I can never get on. Saying many things in few words—if the ladies who assert our rights will forgive me for confessing it—is an accomplishment in which we are completely beaten by the men. You must have thought me rude, my dear, for leaving you very abruptly, without a word of explanation. The truth is, I had an idea in my head, and I kept it to myself (old people are proverbially cautious, you know) till I had first found out whether it was worth mentioning. When you were speaking of the wretched creature who had claimed Mrs. Evelin's husband as her own, you said she was an inveterate drunkard. A woman in that state of degradation is capable, as I persist in thinking, of any wickedness. I suppose this put it into my head to doubt her—no; I mean, to wonder whether Mr. Evelin—do you know that she keeps her husband's name by his own entreaty addressed to her on his deathbed?—oh, I am losing myself in a crowd of words of my own collecting! Say the rest of it for me, Sir Richard!"

"No, Lady Howel. Not unless you call me 'Dick.'"

"Then say it for me—Dick."

"No, not yet, on reflection. Dick is too short, say 'Dear Dick.'"

"Dear Dick—there!"

"Thank you, my lady. Now we had better remember that your husband is

916

present." He turned to Beaucourt. "Lady Howel had the idea," he proceeded, "which ought to have presented itself to you and to me. It was a serious misfortune (as she thought) that Mr. Evelin's sufferings in his last illness, and his wife's anxiety while she was nursing him, had left them unfit to act in their own defense. They might otherwise not have submitted to the drunken wretch's claim, without first making sure that she had a right to advance it. Taking her character into due consideration, are we quite certain that she was herself free to marry, when Mr. Evelin unfortunately made her his wife? To that serious question we now mean to find an answer. With Mrs. Evelin's knowledge of the affair to help us, we have discovered the woman's address, to begin with. She keeps a small tobacconist's shop at the town of Grailey in the north of England. The rest is in the hands of my lawyer. If we make the discovery that we all hope for, we have your wife to thank for it." He paused, and looked at his watch. "I've got an appointment at the club. The committee will blackball the best fellow that ever lived if I don't go and stop them. Good-by."

The last day of Mrs. Evelin's sojourn in England was memorable in more ways than one.

On the first occasion in Beaucourt's experience of his married life, his wife wrote to him instead of speaking to him, although they were both in the house at the time. It was a little note only containing these words: "I thought you would like to say good-by to Mrs. Evelin. I have told her to expect you in the library, and I will take care that you are not disturbed."

Waiting at the window of her sitting-room, on the upper floor, Lady Howel perceived that the delicate generosity of her conduct had been gratefully felt. The interview in the library barely lasted for five minutes. She saw Mrs. Evelin leave the house with her veil down. Immediately afterward, Beaucourt ascended to his wife's room to thank her. Carefully as he had endeavored to hide them, the traces of tears in his eyes told her how cruelly the parting scene had tried him. It was a bitter moment for his admirable wife. "Do you wish me dead?" she asked with sad self-possession. "Live," he said, "and live happily, if you wish to make me happy too." He drew her to him and kissed her forehead. Lady Howel had her reward.

917

Part III. NEWS FROM THE COLONY.

VI.

FURNISHED with elaborate instructions to guide him, which included golden materials for bribery, a young Jew holding the place of third clerk in the office of Dick's lawyer was sent to the town of Grailey to make discoveries. In the matter of successfully instituting private inquiries, he was justly considered to be a match for any two Christians who might try to put obstacles in his way. His name was Moses Jackling.

Entering the cigar-shop, the Jew discovered that he had presented himself at a critical moment.

A girl and a man were standing behind the counter. The girl looked like a maid-of-all-work: she was rubbing the tears out of her eyes with a big red fist. The man, smart in manner and shabby in dress, received the stranger with a peremptory eagerness to do business. "Now, then! what for you?" Jackling bought the worst cigar he had ever smoked, in the course of an enormous experience of bad tobacco, and tried a few questions with this result. The girl had lost her place; the man was in "possession"; and the stock and furniture had been seized for debt. Jackling thereupon assumed the character of a creditor, and ask to speak with the mistress.

"She's too ill to see you, sir," the girl said.

"Tell the truth, you fool," cried the man in possession. He led the way to a door with a glass in the upper part of it, which opened into a parlor behind the shop. As soon as his back was turned, Jackling whispered to the maid, "When I go, slip out after me; I've got something for you." The man lifted the curtain over the glass. "Look through," he said, "and see what's the matter with her for yourself."

Jackling discovered the mistress flat on her back on the floor, helplessly drunk. That was enough for the clerk—so far. He took leave of the man in possession, with the one joke which never wears out in the estimation of

Englishmen; the joke that foresees the drinker's headache in the morning. In a minute or two more the girl showed herself, carrying an empty jug. She had been sent for the man's beer, and she was expected back directly. Jackling, having first overwhelmed her by a present of five shillings, proposed another appointment in the evening. The maid promised to be at the place of meeting; and in memory of the five shillings she kept her word.

"What wages do you get?" was the first question that astonished her.

"Three pounds a year, sir," the unfortunate creature replied.

"All paid?"

"Only one pound paid—and I say it's a crying shame."

"Say what you like, my dear, so long as you listen to me. I want to know everything that your mistress says and does—first when she's drunk, and then when she's sober. Wait a bit; I haven't done yet. If you tell me everything you can remember—mind everything—I'll pay the rest of your wages."

Madly excited by this golden prospect, the victim of domestic service answered inarticulately with a scream. Jackling's right hand and left hand entered his pockets, and appeared again holding two sovereigns separately between two fingers and thumbs. From that moment, he was at liberty to empty the maid-of-all-work's memory of every saying and doing that it contained.

The sober moments of the mistress yielded little or nothing to investigation. The report of her drunken moments produced something worth hearing. There were two men whom it was her habit to revile bitterly in her cups. One of them was Mr. Evelin, whom she abused—sometimes for the small allowance that he made to her; sometimes for dying before she could prosecute him for bigamy. Her drunken remembrances of the other man were associated with two names. She called him "Septimus"; she called him "Darts"; and she despised him occasionally for being a "common sailor." It was clearly demonstrated that he was one man, and not two. Whether he was "Septimus," or whether he was "Darts," he had always committed the same atrocities. He had taken her money away from her; he had called her by an atrocious name; and he had knocked her down on more than one occasion. Provided with this information, Jackling rewarded the girl, and paid a visit to her mistress the next day.

The miserable woman was exactly in the state of nervous prostration (after the excess of the previous evening) which offered to the clerk his best chance of gaining his end. He presented himself as the representative of friends, bent on helping her, whose modest benevolence had positively forbidden him to mention their names.

"What sum of money must you pay," he asked, "to get rid of the man in possession?"

Too completely bewildered to speak, her trembling hand offered to him a slip of paper on which the amount of the debt and the expenses was set forth: L51 12s. 10d.

With some difficulty the Jew preserved his gravity. "Very well," he resumed. "I will make it up to sixty pounds (to set you going again) on two conditions."

She suddenly recovered her power of speech. "Give me the money!" she cried, with greedy impatience of delay.

"First condition," he continued, without noticing the interruption: "you are not to suffer, either in purse or person, if you give us the information that we want."

She interrupted him again. "Tell me what it is, and be quick about it."

"Second condition," he went on as impenetrably as ever; "you take me to the place where I can find the certificate of your marriage to Septimus Darts."

Her eyes glared at him like the eyes of a wild animal. Furies, hysterics, faintings, denials, threats—Jackling endured them all by turns. It was enough for him that his desperate guess of the evening before, had hit the mark on the morning after. When she had completely exhausted herself he returned to the experiment which he had already tried with the maid. Well aware of the advantage of exhibiting gold instead of notes, when the object is to tempt poverty, he produced the promised bribe in sovereigns, pouring them playfully backward and forward from one big hand to the other.

The temptation was more than the woman could resist. In another half-hour the two were traveling together to a town in one of the midland counties.

The certificate was found in the church register, and duly copied.

It also appeared that one of the witnesses to the marriage was still living. His name and address were duly noted in the clerk's pocketbook. Subsequent inquiry, at the office of the Customs Comptroller, discovered the name of Septimus Darts on the captain's official list of the crew of an outward bound merchant vessel. With this information, and with a photographic portrait to complete it, the man was discovered, alive and hearty, on the return of the ship to her port.

His wife's explanation of her conduct included the customary excuse that she had every reason to believe her husband to be dead, and was followed by a bold assertion that she had married Mr. Evelin for love. In Moses Jackling's opinion she lied when she said this, and lied again when she threatened to prosecute Mr. Evelin for bigamy. "Take my word for it," said this new representative of the unbelieving Jew, "she would have extorted money from him if he had lived." Delirium tremens left this question unsettled, and closed the cigar shop soon afterward, under the authority of death.

The good news, telegraphed to New Zealand, was followed by a letter containing details.

At a later date, a telegram arrived from Mrs. Evelin. She had reached her destination, and had received the dispatch which told her that she had been lawfully married. A letter to Lady Howel was promised by the next mail.

While the necessary term of delay was still unexpired, the newspapers received the intelligence of a volcanic eruption in the northern island of the New Zealand group. Later particulars, announcing a terrible destruction of life and property, included the homestead in which Mrs. Evelin was living. The farm had been overwhelmed, and every member of the household had perished.

Part IV. THE NIGHT NURSE.

VII.

Indorsed as follows: "Reply from Sir Richard, addressed to Farleigh & Halford."

"Your courteous letter has been forwarded to my house in the country.

"I really regret that you should have thought it necessary to apologize for troubling me. Your past kindness to the unhappy Mrs. Evelin gives you a friendly claim on me which I gladly recognize—as you shall soon see.

"'The extraordinary story,' as you very naturally call it, is nevertheless true. I am the only person now at your disposal who can speak as an eye-witness of the events.

"In the first place I must tell you that the dreadful intelligence, received from New Zealand, had an effect on Lord Howel Beaucourt which shocked his friends and inexpressibly distressed his admirable wife. I can only describe him, at that time, as a man struck down in mind and body alike.

"Lady Howel was unremitting in her efforts to console him. He was thankful and gentle. It was true that no complaint could be made of him. It was equally true that no change for the better rewarded the devotion of his wife.

"The state of feeling which this implied imbittered the disappointment that Lady Howel naturally felt. As some relief to her overburdened mind, she associated herself with the work of mercy, carried on under the superintendence of the rector of the parish. I thought he was wrong in permitting a woman, at her advanced time of life, to run the risk encountered in visiting the sick and suffering poor at their own dwelling-places. Circumstances, however, failed to justify my dread of the perilous influences of infection and foul air. The one untoward event that happened, seemed to be too trifling to afford any cause for anxiety. Lady Howel caught cold.

"Unhappily, she treated that apparently trivial accident with indifference. Her husband tried in vain to persuade her to remain at home. On one of her charitable visits she was overtaken by a heavy fall of rain; and a shivering fit seized her on returning to the house. At her age the results were serious. A bronchial attack followed. In a week more, the dearest and best of women had left us nothing to love but the memory of the dead.

"Her last words were faintly whispered to me in her husband's presence: 'Take care of him,' the dying woman said, 'when I am gone.'

"No effort of mine to be worthy of that sacred trust was left untried. How could I hope to succeed where she had failed? My house in London and my house in the country were both open to Beaucourt; I entreated him to live with me, or (if he preferred it) to be my guest for a short time only, or (if he wished to be alone) to choose the place of abode which he liked best for his solitary retreat. With sincere expressions of gratitude, his inflexible despair refused my proposals.

"In one of the ancient 'Inns,' built centuries since for the legal societies of London, he secluded himself from friends and acquaintances alike. One by one, they were driven from his dreary chambers by a reception which admitted them with patient resignation and held out little encouragement to return. After an interval of no great length, I was the last of his friends who intruded on his solitude.

"Poor Lady Howel's will (excepting some special legacies) had left her fortune to me in trust, on certain conditions with which it is needless to trouble you. Beaucourt's resolution not to touch a farthing of his dead wife's money laid a heavy responsibility on my shoulders; the burden being ere long increased by forebodings which alarmed me on the subject of his health.

"He devoted himself to the reading of old books, treating (as I was told) of that branch of useless knowledge generally described as 'occult science.' These unwholesome studies so absorbed him, that he remained shut up in his badly ventilated chambers for weeks together, without once breathing the outer air even for a few minutes. Such defiance of the ordinary laws of nature as this could end but in one way; his health steadily declined and feverish symptoms showed themselves. The doctor said plainly, 'There is no chance for him if he stays in this place.'

"Once more he refused to be removed to my London house. The development of the fever, he reminded me, might lead to consequences dangerous to me and to my household. He had heard of one of the great London hospitals, which reserved certain rooms for the occupation of persons capable of paying for the medical care bestowed on them. If he were to be removed at all, to that hospital he would go. Many advantages, and no objections of importance, were presented by this course of proceeding. We conveyed him to the hospital without a moment's loss of time.

"When I think of the dreadful illness that followed, and when I recall the days of unrelieved suspense passed at the bedside, I have not courage enough to dwell on this part of my story. Besides, you know already that Beaucourt recovered—or, as I might more correctly describe it, that he was snatched back to life when the grasp of death was on him. Of this happier period of his illness I have something to say which may surprise and interest you.

"On one of the earlier days of his convalescence my visit to him was paid later than usual. A matter of importance, neglected while he was in danger, had obliged me to leave town for a few days, after there was nothing to be feared. Returning, I had missed the train which would have brought me to London in better time.

"My appearance evidently produced in Beaucourt a keen feeling of relief. He requested the day nurse, waiting in the room, to leave us by ourselves.

"'I was afraid you might not have come to me to-day,' he said. 'My last moments would have been imbittered, my friend, by your absence.'

"'Are you anticipating your death,' I asked, 'at the very time when the doctors answer for your life?'

"'The doctors have not seen her,' he said; 'I saw her last night.'

"'Of whom are you speaking?'

"'Of my lost angel, who perished miserably in New Zealand. Twice her spirit has appeared to me. I shall see her for the third time, tonight; I shall follow her to the better world.'

"Had the delirium of the worst time of the fever taken possession of him again? In unutterable dread of a relapse, I took his hand. The skin was cool. I laid my fingers on his pulse. It was beating calmly.

"'You think I am wandering in my mind,' he broke out. 'Stay here tonight—I command you, stay!—and see her as I have seen her.'

"I quieted him by promising to do what he had asked of me. He had still one more condition to insist on.

"'I won't be laughed at,' he said. 'Promise that you will not repeat to any living creature what I have just told you.'

"My promise satisfied him. He wearily closed his eyes. In a few minutes more his poor weak body was in peaceful repose.

"The day-nurse returned, and remained with us later than usual. Twilight melted into darkness. The room was obscurely lit by a shaded lamp, placed behind a screen that kept the sun out of the sick man's eyes in the daytime.

"'Are we alone?' Beaucourt asked.

"'Yes.'

"'Watch the door.'

"'Why?'

"'You will see her on the threshold.'

"As he said those words the door slowly opened. In the dim light I could only discern at first the figure of a woman. She slowly advanced toward me. I saw the familiar face in shadow; the eyes were large and faintly luminous—the eyes of Mrs. Evelin.

"The wild words spoken to me by Beaucourt, the stillness and the obscurity in the room, had their effect, I suppose, on my imagination. You will think me a poor creature when I confess it. For the moment I did assuredly feel a thrill of superstitious terror.

"My delusion was dispelled by a change in her face. Its natural expression of surprise, when she saw me, set my mind free to feel the delight inspired by the discovery that she was a living woman. I should have spoken to her if she had not stopped me by a gesture.

"Beaucourt's voice broke the silence. 'Ministering Spirit!' he said, 'free me from the life of earth. Take me with you to the life eternal.'

"She made no attempt to enlighten him. 'Wait,' she answered calmly, 'wait and rest.'

"Silently obeying her, he turned his head on the pillow; we saw his face no more.

"I have related the circumstances exactly as they happened: the ghost story which report has carried to your ears has no other foundation than this.

"Mrs. Evelin led the way to that further end of the room in which the screen stood. Placing ourselves behind it, we could converse in whispers without being heard. Her first words told me that she had been warned by one of the hospital doctors to respect my friend's delusion for the present. His mind partook in some degree of the weakness of his body, and he was not strong enough yet to bear the shock of discovering the truth.

"She had been saved almost by a miracle.

"Released (in a state of insensibility) from the ruins of the house, she had been laid with her dead relatives awaiting burial. Happily for her, an English traveler visiting the island was among the first men who volunteered to render help. He had been in practice as a medical man, and he saved her from being buried alive. Nearly a month passed before she was strong enough to bear removal to Wellington (the capital city) and to be received into the hospital.

"I asked why she had not telegraphed or written to me.

"'When I was strong enough to write,' she said, 'I was strong enough to bear the sea-voyage to England. The expenses so nearly exhausted my small savings that I had no money to spare for the telegraph.'

"On her arrival in London, only a few days since, she had called on me at the time when I had left home on the business which I have already mentioned. She had not heard of Lady Howel's death, and had written ignorantly to prepare that good friend for seeing her. The messenger sent with the letter had found the house in the occupation of strangers, and had been referred to the agent employed in letting it. She went herself to this person, and so heard that Lord Howel Beaucourt had lost his wife, and was reported to be dying in one of the London hospitals.

"'If he had been in his usual state of health,' she said, 'it would have been indelicate on my part—I mean it would have seemed like taking a selfish advantage of the poor lady's death—to have let him know that my life had been saved, in any other way than by writing to him. But when I heard he was dying, I forgot all customary considerations. His name was so well-known in London that I easily discovered at what hospital he had been received. There I heard that the report was false and that he was out of danger. I ought to have been satisfied with that—but oh, how could I be so near him and not long to see him? The old doctor with whom I had been speaking discovered, I suppose, that I was in trouble about something. He was so kind and fatherly, and he seemed to take such interest in me, that I confessed everything to him. After he had made me promise to be careful, he told the night-nurse to let me take her place for a little while, when the dim light in the room would not permit his patient to see me too plainly. He waited at the door when we tried the experiment. Neither he nor I foresaw that Lord Howel would put such a strange interpretation on my presence. The nurse doesn't approve of my coming back—even for a little while only—and taking her place again to-night. She is right. I have had my little glimpse of happiness, and with that little I must be content.'

"What I said in answer to this, and what I did as time advanced, it is surely needless to tell you. You have read the newspapers which announce their marriage, and their departure for Italy. What else is there left for me to say?

"There is, perhaps, a word more still wanting.

"Obstinate Lord Howel persisted in refusing to take the fortune that was waiting for him. In this difficulty, the conditions under which I was acting permitted me to appeal to the bride. When she too said No, I was not to be trifled with. I showed her poor Lady's Howel's will. After reading the terms in which my dear old friend alluded to her she burst out crying. I interpreted those grateful tears as an expression of repentance for the ill-considered reply which I had just received. As yet, I have not been told that I was wrong."

MR. POLICEMAN AND THE COOK.

A FIRST WORD FOR MYSELF.

BEFORE the doctor left me one evening, I asked him how much longer I was likely to live. He answered: "It's not easy to say; you may die before I can get back to you in the morning, or you may live to the end of the month."

I was alive enough on the next morning to think of the needs of my soul, and (being a member of the Roman Catholic Church) to send for the priest.

The history of my sins, related in confession, included blameworthy neglect of a duty which I owed to the laws of my country. In the priest's opinion—and I agreed with him—I was bound to make public acknowledgment of my fault, as an act of penance becoming to a Catholic Englishman. We concluded, thereupon, to try a division of labor. I related the circumstances, while his reverence took the pen and put the matter into shape.

Here follows what came of it:

I.

WHEN I was a young man of five-and-twenty, I became a member of the London police force. After nearly two years' ordinary experience of the responsible and ill-paid duties of that vocation, I found myself employed on my first serious and terrible case of official inquiry—relating to nothing less than the crime of Murder.

The circumstances were these:

I was then attached to a station in the northern district of London—which I beg permission not to mention more particularly. On a certain Monday in the week, I took my turn of night duty. Up to four in the morning, nothing occurred at the station-house out of the ordinary way. It was then springtime, and, between the gas and the fire, the room became rather hot.

I went to the door to get a breath of fresh air—much to the surprise of our Inspector on duty, who was constitutionally a chilly man. There was a fine rain falling; and a nasty damp in the air sent me back to the fireside. I don't suppose I had sat down for more than a minute when the swinging-door was violently pushed open. A frantic woman ran in with a scream, and said: "Is this the station-house?"

Our Inspector (otherwise an excellent officer) had, by some perversity of nature, a hot temper in his chilly constitution. "Why, bless the woman, can't you see it is?" he says. "What's the matter now?"

"Murder's the matter!" she burst out. "For God's sake, come back with me. It's at Mrs. Crosscapel's lodging-house, number 14 Lehigh Street. A young woman has murdered her husband in the night! With a knife, sir. She says she thinks she did it in her sleep."

I confess I was startled by this; and the third man on duty (a sergeant) seemed to feel it too. She was a nice-looking young woman, even in her terrified condition, just out of bed, with her clothes huddled on anyhow. I was partial in those days to a tall figure—and she was, as they say, my style. I put a chair for her; and the sergeant poked the fire. As for the Inspector, nothing ever upset him. He questioned her as coolly as if it had been a case of petty larceny.

"Have you seen the murdered man?" he asked.

"No, sir."

"Or the wife?"

"No, sir. I didn't dare go into the room; I only heard about it!"

"Oh? And who are You? One of the lodgers?"

"No, sir. I'm the cook."

"Isn't there a master in the house?"

"Yes, sir. He's frightened out of his wits. And the housemaid's gone for the doctor. It all falls on the poor servants, of course. Oh, why did I ever set foot in that horrible house?"

The poor soul burst out crying, and shivered from head to foot. The Inspector made a note of her statement, and then asked her to read it, and sign it with her name. The object of this proceeding was to get her to come near enough to give him the opportunity of smelling her breath. "When people make extraordinary statements," he afterward said to me, "it sometimes saves trouble to satisfy yourself that they are not drunk. I've known them to be mad—but not often. You will generally find that in their eyes."

She roused herself and signed her name—"Priscilla Thurlby." The Inspector's own test proved her to be sober; and her eyes—a nice light blue color, mild and pleasant, no doubt, when they were not staring with fear, and red with crying—satisfied him (as I supposed) that she was not mad. He turned the case over to me, in the first instance. I saw that he didn't believe in it, even yet.

"Go back with her to the house," he says. "This may be a stupid hoax, or a quarrel exaggerated. See to it yourself, and hear what the doctor says. If it is serious, send word back here directly, and let nobody enter the place or leave it till we come. Stop! You know the form if any statement is volunteered?"

"Yes, sir. I am to caution the persons that whatever they say will be taken down, and may be used against them."

"Quite right. You'll be an Inspector yourself one of these days. Now, miss!" With that he dismissed her, under my care.

Lehigh Street was not very far off—about twenty minutes' walk from the station. I confess I thought the Inspector had been rather hard on Priscilla. She was herself naturally angry with him. "What does he mean," she says, "by talking of a hoax? I wish he was as frightened as I am. This is the first time I have been out at service, sir—and I did think I had found a respectable place."

I said very little to her—feeling, if the truth must be told, rather anxious about the duty committed to me. On reaching the house the door was opened from within, before I could knock. A gentleman stepped out, who proved to be the doctor. He stopped the moment he saw me.

"You must be careful, policeman," he says. "I found the man lying on his back, in bed, dead—with the knife that had killed him left sticking in the wound."

Hearing this, I felt the necessity of sending at once to the station. Where could I find a trustworthy messenger? I took the liberty of asking the doctor if he would repeat to the police what he had already said to me. The station was not much out of his way home. He kindly granted my request.

The landlady (Mrs. Crosscapel) joined us while we were talking. She was still a young woman; not easily frightened, as far as I could see, even by a murder in the house. Her husband was in the passage behind her. He looked old enough to be her father; and he so trembled with terror that some people might have taken him for the guilty person. I removed the key from the street door, after locking it; and I said to the landlady: "Nobody must leave the house, or enter the house, till the Inspector comes. I must examine the premises to see if any one has broken in."

"There is the key of the area gate," she said, in answer to me. "It's always kept locked. Come downstairs and see for yourself." Priscilla went with us. Her mistress set her to work to light the kitchen fire. "Some of us," says Mrs. Crosscapel, "may be the better for a cup of tea." I remarked that she took things easy, under the circumstances. She answered that the landlady of a London lodging-house could not afford to lose her wits, no matter what might happen.

I found the gate locked, and the shutters of the kitchen window fastened. The back kitchen and back door were secured in the same way. No person was concealed anywhere. Returning upstairs, I examined the front parlor window. There, again, the barred shutters answered for the security of that room. A cracked voice spoke through the door of the back parlor. "The policeman can come in," it said, "if he will promise not to look at me." I turned to the landlady for information. "It's my parlor lodger, Miss Mybus," she said, "a most respectable lady." Going into the room, I saw something rolled up perpendicularly in the bed curtains. Miss Mybus had made herself modestly invisible in that way. Having now satisfied my mind about the security of the lower part of the house, and having the keys safe in my pocket, I was ready to go upstairs.

On our way to the upper regions I asked if there had been any visitors on the previous day. There had been only two visitors, friends of the lodgers—and Mrs. Crosscapel herself had let them both out. My next inquiry related to the lodgers themselves. On the ground floor there was Miss Mybus. On the first floor (occupying both rooms) Mr. Barfield, an old bachelor, employed in a merchant's office. On the second floor, in the front room, Mr. John Zebedee, the murdered man, and his wife. In the back room, Mr. Deluc; described as a cigar agent, and supposed to be a Creole gentleman from Martinique. In the front garret, Mr. and Mrs. Crosscapel. In the back garret, the cook and the housemaid. These were the inhabitants, regularly accounted for. I asked about the servants. "Both excellent characters," says the landlady, "or they would not be in my service."

We reached the second floor, and found the housemaid on the watch outside the door of the front room. Not as nice a woman, personally, as the cook, and sadly frightened of course. Her mistress had posted her, to give the alarm in the case of an outbreak on the part of Mrs. Zebedee, kept locked up in the room. My arrival relieved the housemaid of further responsibility. She ran downstairs to her fellow-servant in the kitchen.

I asked Mrs. Crosscapel how and when the alarm of the murder had been given.

"Soon after three this morning," says she, "I was woke by the screams of Mrs. Zebedee. I found her out here on the landing, and Mr. Deluc, in great alarm, trying to quiet her. Sleeping in the next room he had only to open his door, when her screams woke him. 'My dear John's murdered! I am the miserable wretch—I did it in my sleep!' She repeated these frantic words over and over again, until she dropped in a swoon. Mr. Deluc and I carried her back into the bedroom. We both thought the poor creature had been driven distracted by some dreadful dream. But when we got to the bedside—don't ask me what we saw; the doctor has told you about it already. I was once a nurse in a hospital, and accustomed, as such, to horrid sights. It turned me

933

cold and giddy, notwithstanding. As for Mr. Deluc, I thought he would have had a fainting fit next."

Hearing this, I inquired if Mrs. Zebedee had said or done any strange things since she had been Mrs. Crosscapel's lodger.

"You think she's mad?" says the landlady. "And anybody would be of your mind, when a woman accuses herself of murdering her husband in her sleep. All I can say is that, up to this morning, a more quiet, sensible, well-behaved little person than Mrs. Zebedee I never met with. Only just married, mind, and as fond of her unfortunate husband as a woman could be. I should have called them a pattern couple, in their own line of life."

There was no more to be said on the landing. We unlocked the door and went into the room.

II.

HE lay in bed on his back as the doctor had described him. On the left side of his nightgown, just over his heart, the blood on the linen told its terrible tale. As well as one could judge, looking unwillingly at a dead face, he must have been a handsome young man in his lifetime. It was a sight to sadden anybody—but I think the most painful sensation was when my eyes fell next on his miserable wife.

She was down on the floor, crouched up in a corner—a dark little woman, smartly dressed in gay colors. Her black hair and her big brown eyes made the horrid paleness of her face look even more deadly white than perhaps it really was. She stared straight at us without appearing to see us. We spoke to her, and she never answered a word. She might have been dead—like her husband—except that she perpetually picked at her fingers, and shuddered every now and then as if she was cold. I went to her and tried to lift her up. She shrank back with a cry that well-nigh frightened me—not because it was loud, but because it was more like the cry of some animal than of a human being. However quietly she might have behaved in the landlady's previous experience of her, she was beside herself now. I might have been moved by a natural pity for her, or I might have been completely upset in my mind—I only know this, I could not persuade myself that she was guilty. I even said to

Mrs. Crosscapel, "I don't believe she did it."

While I spoke there was a knock at the door. I went downstairs at once, and admitted (to my great relief) the Inspector, accompanied by one of our men.

He waited downstairs to hear my report, and he approved of what I had done. "It looks as if the murder had been committed by somebody in the house." Saying this, he left the man below, and went up with me to the second floor.

Before he had been a minute in the room, he discovered an object which had escaped my observation.

It was the knife that had done the deed.

The doctor had found it left in the body—had withdrawn it to probe the wound—and had laid it on the bedside table. It was one of those useful knives which contain a saw, a corkscrew, and other like implements. The big blade fastened back, when open, with a spring. Except where the blood was on it, it was as bright as when it had been purchased. A small metal plate was fastened to the horn handle, containing an inscription, only partly engraved, which ran thus: "To John Zebedee, from—" There it stopped, strangely enough.

Who or what had interrupted the engraver's work? It was impossible even to guess. Nevertheless, the Inspector was encouraged.

"This ought to help us," he said—and then he gave an attentive ear (looking all the while at the poor creature in the corner) to what Mrs. Crosscapel had to tell him.

The landlady having done, he said he must now see the lodger who slept in the next bed-chamber.

Mr. Deluc made his appearance, standing at the door of the room, and turning away his head with horror from the sight inside.

He was wrapped in a splendid blue dressing-gown, with a golden girdle and trimmings. His scanty brownish hair curled (whether artificially or not, I

935

am unable to say) in little ringlets. His complexion was yellow; his greenish-brown eyes were of the sort called "goggle"—they looked as if they might drop out of his face, if you held a spoon under them. His mustache and goat's beard were beautifully oiled; and, to complete his equipment, he had a long black cigar in his mouth.

"It isn't insensibility to this terrible tragedy," he explained. "My nerves have been shattered, Mr. Policeman, and I can only repair the mischief in this way. Be pleased to excuse and feel for me."

The Inspector questioned this witness sharply and closely. He was not a man to be misled by appearances; but I could see that he was far from liking, or even trusting, Mr. Deluc. Nothing came of the examination, except what Mrs. Crosscapel had in substance already mentioned to me. Mr. Deluc returned to his room.

"How long has he been lodging with you?" the Inspector asked, as soon as his back was turned.

"Nearly a year," the landlady answered.

"Did he give you a reference?"

"As good a reference as I could wish for." Thereupon, she mentioned the names of a well-known firm of cigar merchants in the city. The Inspector noted the information in his pocketbook.

I would rather not relate in detail what happened next: it is too distressing to be dwelt on. Let me only say that the poor demented woman was taken away in a cab to the station-house. The Inspector possessed himself of the knife, and of a book found on the floor, called "The World of Sleep." The portmanteau containing the luggage was locked—and then the door of the room was secured, the keys in both cases being left in my charge. My instructions were to remain in the house, and allow nobody to leave it, until I heard again shortly from the Inspector.

III.

THE coroner's inquest was adjourned; and the examination before the magistrate ended in a remand—Mrs. Zebedee being in no condition to understand the proceedings in either case. The surgeon reported her to be completely prostrated by a terrible nervous shock. When he was asked if he considered her to have been a sane woman before the murder took place, he refused to answer positively at that time.

A week passed. The murdered man was buried; his old father attending the funeral. I occasionally saw Mrs. Crosscapel, and the two servants, for the purpose of getting such further information as was thought desirable. Both the cook and the housemaid had given their month's notice to quit; declining, in the interest of their characters, to remain in a house which had been the scene of a murder. Mr. Deluc's nerves led also to his removal; his rest was now disturbed by frightful dreams. He paid the necessary forfeit-money, and left without notice. The first-floor lodger, Mr. Barfield, kept his rooms, but obtained leave of absence from his employers, and took refuge with some friends in the country. Miss Mybus alone remained in the parlors. "When I am comfortable," the old lady said, "nothing moves me, at my age. A murder up two pairs of stairs is nearly the same thing as a murder in the next house. Distance, you see, makes all the difference."

It mattered little to the police what the lodgers did. We had men in plain clothes watching the house night and day. Everybody who went away was privately followed; and the police in the district to which they retired were warned to keep an eye on them, after that. As long as we failed to put Mrs. Zebedee's extraordinary statement to any sort of test—to say nothing of having proved unsuccessful, thus far, in tracing the knife to its purchaser—we were bound to let no person living under Mr. Crosscapel's roof, on the night of the murder, slip through our fingers.

IV.

IN a fortnight more, Mrs. Zebedee had sufficiently recovered to make the necessary statement—after the preliminary caution addressed to persons in such cases. The surgeon had no hesitation, now, in reporting her to be a sane woman.

Her station in life had been domestic service. She had lived for four years in her last place as lady's-maid, with a family residing in Dorsetshire.

The one objection to her had been the occasional infirmity of sleep-walking, which made it necessary that one of the other female servants should sleep in the same room, with the door locked and the key under her pillow. In all other respects the lady's-maid was described by her mistress as "a perfect treasure."

In the last six months of her service, a young man named John Zebedee entered the house (with a written character) as a footman. He soon fell in love with the nice little lady's-maid, and she heartily returned the feeling. They might have waited for years before they were in a pecuniary position to marry, but for the death of Zebedee's uncle, who left him a little fortune of two thousand pounds. They were now, for persons in their station, rich enough to please themselves; and they were married from the house in which they had served together, the little daughters of the family showing their affection for Mrs. Zebedee by acting as her bridesmaids.

The young husband was a careful man. He decided to employ his small capital to the best advantage, by sheep-farming in Australia. His wife made no objection; she was ready to go wherever John went.

Accordingly they spent their short honeymoon in London, so as to see for themselves the vessel in which their passage was to be taken. They went to Mrs. Crosscapel's lodging-house because Zebedee's uncle had always stayed there when in London. Ten days were to pass before the day of embarkation arrived. This gave the young couple a welcome holiday, and a prospect of amusing themselves to their heart's content among the sights and shows of the great city.

On their first evening in London they went to the theater. They were both accustomed to the fresh air of the country, and they felt half stifled by the heat and the gas. However, they were so pleased with an amusement which was new to them that they went to another theater on the next evening. On this second occasion, John Zebedee found the heat unendurable. They left the theater, and got back to their lodgings toward ten o'clock.

Let the rest be told in the words used by Mrs. Zebedee herself. She said:

"We sat talking for a little while in our room, and John's headache got worse and worse. I persuaded him to go to bed, and I put out the candle (the fire giving sufficient light to undress by), so that he might the sooner fall asleep. But he was too restless to sleep. He asked me to read him something. Books always made him drowsy at the best of times.

"I had not myself begun to undress. So I lit the candle again, and I opened the only book I had. John had noticed it at the railway bookstall by the name of 'The World of Sleep.' He used to joke with me about my being a sleepwalker; and he said, 'Here's something that's sure to interest you'—and he made me a present of the book.

"Before I had read to him for more than half an hour he was fast asleep. Not feeling that way inclined, I went on reading to myself.

"The book did indeed interest me. There was one terrible story which took a hold on my mind—the story of a man who stabbed his own wife in a sleep-walking dream. I thought of putting down my book after that, and then changed my mind again and went on. The next chapters were not so interesting; they were full of learned accounts of why we fall asleep, and what our brains do in that state, and such like. It ended in my falling asleep, too, in my armchair by the fireside.

"I don't know what o'clock it was when I went to sleep. I don't know how long I slept, or whether I dreamed or not. The candle and the fire had both burned out, and it was pitch dark when I woke. I can't even say why I woke—unless it was the coldness of the room.

"There was a spare candle on the chimney-piece. I found the matchbox, and got a light. Then for the first time, I turned round toward the bed; and I saw—"

She had seen the dead body of her husband, murdered while she was unconsciously at his side—and she fainted, poor creature, at the bare remembrance of it.

The proceedings were adjourned. She received every possible care and attention; the chaplain looking after her welfare as well as the surgeon.

I have said nothing of the evidence of the landlady and servants. It was

939

taken as a mere formality. What little they knew proved nothing against Mrs. Zebedee. The police made no discoveries that supported her first frantic accusation of herself. Her master and mistress, where she had been last in service, spoke of her in the highest terms. We were at a complete deadlock.

It had been thought best not to surprise Mr. Deluc, as yet, by citing him as a witness. The action of the law was, however, hurried in this case by a private communication received from the chaplain.

After twice seeing, and speaking with, Mrs. Zebedee, the reverend gentleman was persuaded that she had no more to do than himself with the murder of her husband. He did not consider that he was justified in repeating a confidential communication—he would only recommend that Mr. Deluc should be summoned to appear at the next examination. This advice was followed.

The police had no evidence against Mrs. Zebedee when the inquiry was resumed. To assist the ends of justice she was now put into the witness-box. The discovery of her murdered husband, when she woke in the small hours of the morning, was passed over as rapidly as possible. Only three questions of importance were put to her.

First, the knife was produced. Had she ever seen it in her husband's possession? Never. Did she know anything about it? Nothing whatever.

Secondly: Did she, or did her husband, lock the bedroom door when they returned from the theater? No. Did she afterward lock the door herself? No.

Thirdly: Had she any sort of reason to give for supposing that she had murdered her husband in a sleep-walking dream? No reason, except that she was beside herself at the time, and the book put the thought into her head.

After this the other witnesses were sent out of court The motive for the chaplain's communication now appeared. Mrs. Zebedee was asked if anything unpleasant had occurred between Mr. Deluc and herself.

Yes. He had caught her alone on the stairs at the lodging-house; had presumed to make love to her; and had carried the insult still farther by attempting to kiss her. She had slapped his face, and had declared that her husband should know of it, if his misconduct was repeated. He was in a furious rage at having his face slapped; and he said to her: "Madam, you may live to regret this."

After consultation, and at the request of our Inspector, it was decided to keep Mr. Deluc in ignorance of Mrs. Zebedee's statement for the present. When the witnesses were recalled, he gave the same evidence which he had already given to the Inspector—and he was then asked if he knew anything of the knife. He looked at it without any guilty signs in his face, and swore that he had never seen it until that moment. The resumed inquiry ended, and still nothing had been discovered.

But we kept an eye on Mr. Deluc. Our next effort was to try if we could associate him with the purchase of the knife.

Here again (there really did seem to be a sort of fatality in this case) we reached no useful result. It was easy enough to find out the wholesale cutlers, who had manufactured the knife at Sheffield, by the mark on the blade. But they made tens of thousands of such knives, and disposed of them to retail dealers all over Great Britain—to say nothing of foreign parts. As to finding out the person who had engraved the imperfect inscription (without knowing where, or by whom, the knife had been purchased) we might as well have looked for the proverbial needle in the bundle of hay. Our last resource was to have the knife photographed, with the inscribed side uppermost, and to send copies to every police-station in the kingdom.

At the same time we reckoned up Mr. Deluc—I mean that we made investigations into his past life—on the chance that he and the murdered man might have known each other, and might have had a quarrel, or a rivalry about a woman, on some former occasion. No such discovery rewarded us.

We found Deluc to have led a dissipated life, and to have mixed with very bad company. But he had kept out of reach of the law. A man may be a profligate vagabond; may insult a lady; may say threatening things to her, in the first stinging sensation of having his face slapped—but it doesn't follow

941

from these blots on his character that he has murdered her husband in the dead of the night.

Once more, then, when we were called upon to report ourselves, we had no evidence to produce. The photographs failed to discover the owner of the knife, and to explain its interrupted inscription. Poor Mrs. Zebedee was allowed to go back to her friends, on entering into her own recognizance to appear again if called upon. Articles in the newspapers began to inquire how many more murderers would succeed in baffling the police. The authorities at the Treasury offered a reward of a hundred pounds for the necessary information. And the weeks passed and nobody claimed the reward.

Our Inspector was not a man to be easily beaten. More inquiries and examinations followed. It is needless to say anything about them. We were defeated—and there, so far as the police and the public were concerned, was an end of it.

The assassination of the poor young husband soon passed out of notice, like other undiscovered murders. One obscure person only was foolish enough, in his leisure hours, to persist in trying to solve the problem of Who Killed Zebedee? He felt that he might rise to the highest position in the police force if he succeeded where his elders and betters had failed—and he held to his own little ambition, though everybody laughed at him. In plain English, I was the man.

V.

WITHOUT meaning it, I have told my story ungratefully.

There were two persons who saw nothing ridiculous in my resolution to continue the investigation, single-handed. One of them was Miss Mybus; and the other was the cook, Priscilla Thurlby.

Mentioning the lady first, Miss Mybus was indignant at the resigned manner in which the police accepted their defeat. She was a little bright-eyed wiry woman; and she spoke her mind freely.

"This comes home to me," she said. "Just look back for a year or two. I can call to mind two cases of persons found murdered in London—and the assassins have never been traced. I am a person, too; and I ask myself if my turn is not coming next. You're a nice-looking fellow and I like your pluck and perseverance. Come here as often as you think right; and say you are my visitor, if they make any difficulty about letting you in. One thing more! I have nothing particular to do, and I am no fool. Here, in the parlors, I see everybody who comes into the house or goes out of the house. Leave me your address—I may get some information for you yet."

With the best intentions, Miss Mybus found no opportunity of helping me. Of the two, Priscilla Thurlby seemed more likely to be of use.

In the first place, she was sharp and active, and (not having succeeded in getting another situation as yet) was mistress of her own movements.

In the second place, she was a woman I could trust. Before she left home to try domestic service in London, the parson of her native parish gave her a written testimonial, of which I append a copy. Thus it ran:

"I gladly recommend Priscilla Thurlby for any respectable employment which she may be competent to undertake. Her father and mother are infirm old people, who have lately suffered a diminution of their income; and they have a younger daughter to maintain. Rather than be a burden on her parents, Priscilla goes to London to find domestic employment, and to devote her earnings to the assistance of her father and mother. This circumstance speaks for itself. I have known the family many years; and I only regret that I have no vacant place in my own household which I can offer to this good girl,

(Signed) "HENRY DEERINGTON, Rector of Roth."

After reading those words, I could safely ask Priscilla to help me in reopening the mysterious murder case to some good purpose.

My notion was that the proceedings of the persons in Mrs. Crosscapel's house had not been closely enough inquired into yet. By way of continuing the investigation, I asked Priscilla if she could tell me anything which associated the housemaid with Mr. Deluc. She was unwilling to answer. "I may be casting suspicion on an innocent person," she said. "Besides, I was for so short a time the housemaid's fellow servant—"

943

"You slept in the same room with her," I remarked; "and you had opportunities of observing her conduct toward the lodgers. If they had asked you, at the examination, what I now ask, you would have answered as an honest woman."

To this argument she yielded. I heard from her certain particulars, which threw a new light on Mr. Deluc, and on the case generally. On that information I acted. It was slow work, owing to the claims on me of my regular duties; but with Priscilla's help, I steadily advanced toward the end I had in view.

Besides this, I owed another obligation to Mrs. Crosscapel's nice-looking cook. The confession must be made sooner or later—and I may as well make it now. I first knew what love was, thanks to Priscilla. I had delicious kisses, thanks to Priscilla. And, when I asked if she would marry me, she didn't say No. She looked, I must own, a little sadly, and she said: "How can two such poor people as we are ever hope to marry?" To this I answered: "It won't be long before I lay my hand on the clew which my Inspector has failed to find. I shall be in a position to marry you, my dear, when that time comes."

At our next meeting we spoke of her parents. I was now her promised husband. Judging by what I had heard of the proceedings of other people in my position, it seemed to be only right that I should be made known to her father and mother. She entirely agreed with me; and she wrote home that day to tell them to expect us at the end of the week.

I took my turn of night-duty, and so gained my liberty for the greater part of the next day. I dressed myself in plain clothes, and we took our tickets on the railway for Yateland, being the nearest station to the village in which Priscilla's parents lived.

VI.

THE train stopped, as usual, at the big town of Waterbank. Supporting herself by her needle, while she was still unprovided with a situation, Priscilla had been at work late in the night—she was tired and thirsty. I left the carriage to get her some soda-water. The stupid girl in the refreshment room failed to pull the cork out of the bottle, and refused to let me help her. She took a corkscrew, and used it crookedly. I lost all patience, and snatched the bottle out of her hand. Just as I drew the cork, the bell rang on the platform. I only waited to pour the soda-water into a glass—but the train was moving as I left the refreshment room. The porters stopped me when I tried to jump on to the step of the carriage. I was left behind.

As soon as I had recovered my temper, I looked at the time-table. We had reached Waterbank at five minutes past one. By good luck, the next train was due at forty-four minutes past one, and arrived at Yateland (the next station) ten minutes afterward. I could only hope that Priscilla would look at the time-table too, and wait for me. If I had attempted to walk the distance between the two places, I should have lost time instead of saving it. The interval before me was not very long; I occupied it in looking over the town.

Speaking with all due respect to the inhabitants, Waterbank (to other people) is a dull place. I went up one street and down another—and stopped to look at a shop which struck me; not from anything in itself, but because it was the only shop in the street with the shutters closed.

A bill was posted on the shutters, announcing that the place was to let. The outgoing tradesman's name and business, announced in the customary painted letters, ran thus: James Wycomb, Cutler, etc.

For the first time, it occurred to me that we had forgotten an obstacle in our way, when we distributed our photographs of the knife. We had none of us remembered that a certain proportion of cutlers might be placed, by circumstances, out of our reach—either by retiring from business or by becoming bankrupt. I always carried a copy of the photograph about me; and I thought to myself, "Here is the ghost of a chance of tracing the knife to Mr. Deluc!"

The shop door was opened, after I had twice rung the bell, by an old man, very dirty and very deaf. He said, "You had better go upstairs, and speak to Mr. Scorrier—top of the house."

I put my lips to the old fellow's ear-trumpet, and asked who Mr. Scorrier was.

"Brother-in-law to Mr. Wycomb. Mr. Wycomb's dead. If you want to buy the business apply to Mr. Scorrier."

Receiving that reply, I went upstairs, and found Mr. Scorrier engaged in engraving a brass door-plate. He was a middle-aged man, with a cadaverous face and dim eyes After the necessary apologies, I produced my photograph.

"May I ask, sir, if you know anything of the inscription on that knife?" I said.

He took his magnifying glass to look at it.

"This is curious," he remarked quietly. "I remember the queer name—Zebedee. Yes, sir; I did the engraving, as far as it goes. I wonder what prevented me from finishing it?"

The name of Zebedee, and the unfinished inscription on the knife, had appeared in every English newspaper. He took the matter so coolly that I was doubtful how to interpret his answer. Was it possible that he had not seen the account of the murder? Or was he an accomplice with prodigious powers of self-control?

"Excuse me," I said, "do you read the newspapers?"

"Never! My eyesight is failing me. I abstain from reading, in the interests of my occupation."

"Have you not heard the name of Zebedee mentioned—particularly by people who do read the newspapers?"

"Very likely; but I didn't attend to it. When the day's work is done, I take my walk. Then I have my supper, my drop of grog, and my pipe. Then I go to bed. A dull existence you think, I daresay! I had a miserable life, sir, when I was young. A bare subsistence, and a little rest, before the last perfect rest in the grave—that is all I want. The world has gone by me long ago. So much the better."

The poor man spoke honestly. I was ashamed of having doubted him. I returned to the subject of the knife.

"Do you know where it was purchased, and by whom?" I asked.

"My memory is not so good as it was," he said; "but I have got something by me that helps it."

He took from a cupboard a dirty old scrapbook. Strips of paper, with writing on them, were pasted on the pages, as well as I could see. He turned to an index, or table of contents, and opened a page. Something like a flash of life showed itself on his dismal face.

"Ha! now I remember," he said. "The knife was bought of my late brother-in-law, in the shop downstairs. It all comes back to me, sir. A person in a state of frenzy burst into this very room, and snatched the knife away from me, when I was only half way through the inscription!"

I felt that I was now close on discovery. "May I see what it is that has assisted your memory?" I asked.

"Oh yes. You must know, sir, I live by engraving inscriptions and addresses, and I paste in this book the manuscript instructions which I receive, with marks of my own on the margin. For one thing, they serve as a reference to new customers. And for another thing, they do certainly help my memory."

He turned the book toward me, and pointed to a slip of paper which occupied the lower half of a page.

I read the complete inscription, intended for the knife that killed Zebedee, and written as follows:

"To John Zebedee. From Priscilla Thurlby."

VII.

I DECLARE that it is impossible for me to describe what I felt when Priscilla's name confronted me like a written confession of guilt. How long it was before I recovered myself in some degree, I cannot say. The only thing I can clearly call to mind is, that I frightened the poor engraver.

My first desire was to get possession of the manuscript inscription. I told him I was a policeman, and summoned him to assist me in the discovery of a crime. I even offered him money. He drew back from my hand. "You shall have it for nothing," he said, "if you will only go away and never come here again." He tried to cut it out of the page—but his trembling hands were helpless. I cut it out myself, and attempted to thank him. He wouldn't hear me. "Go away!" he said, "I don't like the look of you."

It may be here objected that I ought not to have felt so sure as I did of the woman's guilt, until I had got more evidence against her. The knife might have been stolen from her, supposing she was the person who had snatched it out of the engraver's hands, and might have been afterward used by the thief to commit the murder. All very true. But I never had a moment's doubt in my own mind, from the time when I read the damnable line in the engraver's book.

I went back to the railway without any plan in my head. The train by which I had proposed to follow her had left Waterbank. The next train that arrived was for London. I took my place in it—still without any plan in my head.

At Charing Cross a friend met me. He said, "You're looking miserably ill. Come and have a drink."

I went with him. The liquor was what I really wanted; it strung me up, and cleared my head. He went his way, and I went mine. In a little while more, I determined what I would do.

In the first place, I decided to resign my situation in the police, from a motive which will presently appear. In the second place, I took a bed at a public-house. She would no doubt return to London, and she would go to my lodgings to find out why I had broken my appointment. To bring to justice the one woman whom I had dearly loved was too cruel a duty for a poor creature like me. I preferred leaving the police force. On the other hand, if she and I met before time had helped me to control myself, I had a horrid fear that I might turn murderer next, and kill her then and there. The wretch had not only all but misled me into marrying her, but also into charging the innocent housemaid with being concerned in the murder.

948

The same night I hit on a way of clearing up such doubts as still harassed my mind. I wrote to the rector of Roth, informing him that I was engaged to marry her, and asking if he would tell me (in consideration of my position) what her former relations might have been with the person named John Zebedee.

By return of post I got this reply:

"SIR—Under the circumstances, I think I am bound to tell you confidentially what the friends and well-wishers of Priscilla have kept secret, for her sake.

"Zebedee was in service in this neighborhood. I am sorry to say it, of a man who has come to such a miserable end—but his behavior to Priscilla proves him to have been a vicious and heartless wretch. They were engaged—and, I add with indignation, he tried to seduce her under a promise of marriage. Her virtue resisted him, and he pretended to be ashamed of himself. The banns were published in my church. On the next day Zebedee disappeared, and cruelly deserted her. He was a capable servant; and I believe he got another place. I leave you to imagine what the poor girl suffered under the outrage inflicted on her. Going to London, with my recommendation, she answered the first advertisement that she saw, and was unfortunate enough to begin her career in domestic service in the very lodging-house to which (as I gather from the newspaper report of the murder) the man Zebedee took the person whom he married, after deserting Priscilla. Be assured that you are about to unite yourself to an excellent girl, and accept my best wishes for your happiness."

It was plain from this that neither the rector nor the parents and friends knew anything of the purchase of the knife. The one miserable man who knew the truth was the man who had asked her to be his wife.

I owed it to myself—at least so it seemed to me—not to let it be supposed that I, too, had meanly deserted her. Dreadful as the prospect was, I felt that I must see her once more, and for the last time.

She was at work when I went into her room. As I opened the door she started to her feet. Her cheeks reddened, and her eyes flashed with anger. I stepped forward—and she saw my face. My face silenced her.

I spoke in the fewest words I could find.

"I have been to the cutler's shop at Waterbank," I said. "There is the unfinished inscription on the knife, complete in your handwriting. I could hang you by a word. God forgive me—I can't say the word."

Her bright complexion turned to a dreadful clay-color. Her eyes were fixed and staring, like the eyes of a person in a fit. She stood before me, still and silent. Without saying more, I dropped the inscription into the fire. Without saying more, I left her.

I never saw her again.

VIII.

BUT I heard from her a few days later. The letter has long since been burned. I wish I could have forgotten it as well. It sticks to my memory. If I die with my senses about me, Priscilla's letter will be my last recollection on earth.

In substance it repeated what the rector had already told me. Further, it informed me that she had bought the knife as a keepsake for Zebedee, in place of a similar knife which he had lost. On the Saturday, she made the purchase, and left it to be engraved. On the Sunday, the banns were put up. On the Monday, she was deserted; and she snatched the knife from the table while the engraver was at work.

She only knew that Zebedee had added a new sting to the insult inflicted on her when he arrived at the lodgings with his wife. Her duties as cook kept her in the kitchen—and Zebedee never discovered that she was in the house. I still remember the last lines of her confession:

"The devil entered into me when I tried their door, on my way up to bed, and found it unlocked, and listened a while, and peeped in. I saw them by the dying light of the candle—one asleep on the bed, the other asleep by the fireside. I had the knife in my hand, and the thought came to me to do it, so that they might hang her for the murder. I couldn't take the knife out again, when I had done it. Mind this! I did really like you—I didn't say Yes, because you could hardly hang your own wife, if you found out who killed Zebedee."

Since the past time I have never heard again of Priscilla Thurlby; I don't know whether she is living or dead. Many people may think I deserve to be hanged myself for not having given her up to the gallows. They may, perhaps, be disappointed when they see this confession, and hear that I have died decently in my bed. I don't blame them. I am a penitent sinner. I wish all merciful Christians good-by forever.

About Author

Early life

Collins was born at 11 New Cavendish Street, Marylebone, London, the son of a well-known Royal Academician landscape painter, William Collins and his wife, Harriet Geddes. Named after his father, he swiftly became known by his middle name, which honoured his godfather, David Wilkie. The family moved to Pond Street, Hampstead, in 1826. In 1828 Collins's brother Charles Allston Collins was born. Between 1829 and 1830, the Collins family moved twice, first to Hampstead Square and then to Porchester Terrace, Bayswater. Wilkie and Charles received their early education from their mother at home. The Collins family were deeply religious, and Collins's mother enforced strict church attendance on her sons, which Wilkie disliked.

In 1835, Collins began attending school at the Maida Vale academy. From 1836 to 1838, he lived with his parents in Italy and France, which made a great impression on him. He learned Italian while the family was in Italy and began learning French, in which he would eventually become fluent. From 1838 to 1840, he attended the Reverend Cole's private boarding school in Highbury, where he was bullied by a boy who would force Collins to tell him a story before allowing him to go to sleep. "It was this brute who first awakened in me, his poor little victim, a power of which but for him I might never have been aware.... When I left school I continued story telling for my own pleasure", Collins later said.

In 1840 the family moved to 85 Oxford Terrace, Bayswater. In late 1840, he left school and was apprenticed as a clerk to the firm of tea merchants Antrobus & Co, owned by a friend of Wilkie's father. He disliked his clerical work but remained employed by the company for more than five years. Collins's first story The Last Stage Coachman, was published in the Illuminated Magazine in August 1843. In 1844 he travelled to Paris with Charles Ward. That same year he wrote his first novel, Iolani, or Tahiti as It Was; a Romance, which was submitted to Chapman and Hall but rejected in 1845. The novel remained unpublished during his lifetime. Collins said of it:

"My youthful imagination ran riot among the noble savages, in scenes which caused the respectable British publisher to declare that it was impossible to put his name on the title page of such a novel." It was during the writing of this novel that Collins's father first learned that his assumptions that Wilkie would follow him in becoming a painter were mistaken.

William Collins had intended Wilkie for a clergyman and was disappointed in his son's lack of interest. In 1846 he instead entered Lincoln's Inn to study law, on the initiative of his father, who wanted him to have a steady income. Wilkie showed only a slight interest in law and spent most of his time with friends and on working on a second novel, Antonina, or the Fall of Rome. After his father's death in 1847, Collins produced his first published book, Memoirs of the Life of William Collins, Esq., R. A., published in 1848. The family moved to 38 Blandford Square soon afterwards, where they used their drawing room for amateur theatricals. In 1849, Collins exhibited a painting, "The Smugglers' Retreat", at the Royal Academy summer exhibition. Antonina was published by Richard Bentley in February 1850. Collins went on a walking tour of Cornwall with artist Henry Brandling in July and August 1850. He managed to complete his legal studies and be called to the bar in 1851. Though he never formally practised, he used his legal knowledge in many of his novels.

Early writing career

An instrumental event in his career was an introduction in March 1851 to Charles Dickens by a mutual friend, through the painter Augustus Egg. They became lifelong friends and collaborators. In May of that year, Collins acted with Dickens in Edward Bulwer-Lytton's play Not So Bad As We Seem. Among the audience were Queen Victoria and Prince Albert. Collins's story "A Terribly Strange Bed," his first contribution to Household Words, appeared in April, 1852. In May 1852 he went on tour with Dickens's company of amateur actors, again performing Not So Bad As We Seem, but with a more substantial role. Collins's novel Basil was published by Bentley in November. During the writing of Hide and Seek, in early 1853, Collins suffered what was probably his first attack of gout, which would plague him for the rest of his life. He was ill from April to early July. After that he stayed with Dickens in Boulogne from July to September 1853, then toured Switzerland and Italy with Dickens and Egg from October to December. Collins published Hide and Seek in June 1854.

During this period Collins extended the variety of his writing, publishing articles in George Henry Lewes's paper The Leader, short stories and essays for Bentley's Miscellany, dramatic criticism and the travel book Rambles Beyond Railways. His first play, The Lighthouse, was performed by Dickens's theatrical company at Tavistock House, in 1855. His first collection of short stories, After Dark, was published by Smith, Elder in February 1856. His novel A Rogue's Life was serialised in Household Words in March 1856. Around then, Collins began using laudanum regularly to treat his gout. He became addicted and struggled with that problem later in life.

Collins joined the staff of Household Words in October 1856. In 1856–57 he collaborated closely with Dickens on a play, The Frozen Deep, first performed in Tavistock. Collins's novel The Dead Secret was serialised in Household Words from January to June 1857 and published in volume form by Bradbury and Evans. Collins's play The Lighthouse was performed at the Olympic Theatre in August. The Lazy Tour of Two Idle Apprentices, based on Dickens's and Collins's walking tour in the north of England, was serialised in Household Words in October 1857. In 1858 he collaborated with Dickens and other writers on the story "A House to Let".

1860s

According to biographer Melisa Klimaszewski, "The novels Collins published in the 1860s are the best and most enduring of his career. The Woman in White, No Name, Armadale, and The Moonstone, written in less than a decade, show Collins not just as a master of his craft, but as an innovater and provocateur. These four works, which secured him an international reputation, and sold in large numbers, ensured his financial stability, and allowed him to support many others".

The Woman in White was serialised in All the Year Round from November 1859 to August 1860 and was a great success. The novel was published in book form soon after serial publication ended, and it reached an eighth edition by November 1860. His increased stature as a writer made Collins resign his position with All the Year Round in 1862 to focus on novel writing. During the planning of his next novel, No Name, he continued to suffer from gout, and it now especially affected his eyes. Serial publication of No Name began in early 1862 and finished in 1863. By this time the laudanum he was taking for his continual gout became a serious problem.

At the beginning of 1863, he travelled to German spas and Italy for his health, with Caroline Graves. In 1864, he began work on his novel Armadale, travelling in August to do research for it. It was published serially in The Cornhill Magazine in 1864–66. His play No Thoroughfare, co-written with Dickens, was published as the 1867 Christmas number of All the Year Round and dramatised at the Adelphi Theatre on 26 December. It enjoyed a run of 200 nights before being taken on tour.

Collins's search for background information for Armadale took him to the Norfolk Broads and the small village of Winterton-on-Sea. His novel The Moonstone was serialised in All the Year Round from January to August 1868. His mother, Harriet Collins, died that year.

Later years

In 1870, his novel Man and Wife was published. This year also saw the death of Charles Dickens, which caused him great sadness. He said of their early days together, "We saw each other every day, and were as fond of each other as men could be."

The Woman in White was dramatised and produced at the Olympic Theatre in October 1871.

Collins's novel Poor Miss Finch was serialised in Cassell's Magazine from October to March 1872. His short novel Miss or Mrs? was published in the 1872 Christmas number of the Graphic. His novel The New Magdalen was serialised from October 1872 to July 1873. His younger brother, Charles Allston Collins, died later in 1873. Charles had married Dickens's younger daughter, Kate.

In 1873–74, Collins toured the United States and Canada, giving readings of his work. The American writers he met included Oliver Wendell Holmes, Sr., and Mark Twain, and he began a friendship with the photographer Napoleon Sarony, who took several portraits of him.

His novel The Law and the Lady, serialised in the Graphic from September to March 1875, was followed by a short novel, The Haunted Hotel, which was serialised from June to November 1878. His later novels include Jezebel's Daughter (1880), The Black Robe (1881), Heart and Science (1883) and The Evil Genius (1886). In 1884, Collins was elected Vice-President of the Society of Authors, which had been founded by his friend and fellow novelist Walter Besant.

The inconsistent quality of Collins's dramatic and fictional works in the last decade of his life was accompanied by a general decline in his health, including diminished eyesight. He was often unable to leave home and had difficulty writing. During these last years, he focused on mentoring younger writers, including the novelist Hall Caine, and helped to protect other writers from copyright infringement of their works. His writing became a way for him to fight his illness without allowing it to keep him bedridden. His step-daughter Harriet also served as an amanuensis for several years. His last novel, Blind Love, was finished posthumously by Walter Besant.

Death

Collins died at 82 Wimpole Street, following a paralytic stroke. He is buried in Kensal Green Cemetery, West London. His headstone describes him as the author of The Woman in White. Caroline Graves died in 1895 and was buried with Collins. Martha Rudd died in 1919.

Personal life

In 1858 Collins began living with Caroline Graves and her daughter Harriet. Caroline came from a humble family, having married young, had a child, and been widowed. Collins lived close to the small shop kept by Caroline, and the two may have met in the neighborhood in the mid–1850s. He treated Harriet, whom he called Carrie, as his own daughter, and helped to provide for her education. Excepting one short separation, they lived together for the rest of Collins's life. Collins disliked the institution of marriage, but remained dedicated to Caroline and Harriet, considering them to be his family. Caroline had wanted to marry Collins. She left him while he wrote The Moonstone and was suffering an attack of acute gout. She then married a younger man named Joseph Clow, but returned to Collins after two years.

In 1868, Collins met Martha Rudd in Winterton-on-Sea in Norfolk, and the two began a liaison. She was 19 years old and from a large, poor family. She moved to London to be closer to him a few years later. Their daughter Marian was born in 1869, their second daughter, Harriet Constance, in 1871 and their son, William Charles, in 1874. When he was with Martha he assumed the name William Dawson, and she and their children used the last name of Dawson themselves.

For the last 20 years of his life Collins divided his time between Caroline, who lived with him at his home in Gloucester Place, and Martha who was nearby.

Like his friend Charles Dickens, Collins was a professing Christian.

Works

Collins's works were classified at the time as "sensation novels", a genre seen nowadays as the precursor to detective and suspense fiction. He also wrote penetratingly on the plight of women and on the social and domestic issues of his time. For example, his 1854 Hide and Seek contained one of the first portrayals of a deaf character in English literature. As did many writers of his time, Collins published most of his novels as serials in magazines such as Dickens's All the Year Round and was known as a master of the form, creating just the right degree of suspense to keep his audience reading from week to week. Sales of All The Year Round increased when The Woman in White followed A Tale of Two Cities.

Collins enjoyed ten years of great success following publication of The Woman in White in 1859. His next novel, No Name combined social commentary – the absurdity of the law as it applied to children of unmarried parents (see Illegitimacy in fiction) – with a densely plotted revenge thriller.

Armadale, the first and only of Collins's major novels of the 1860s to be serialised in a magazine other than All the Year Round, provoked strong criticism, generally centred upon its transgressive villainess Lydia Gwilt, and provoked in part by Collins's typically confrontational preface. The novel was simultaneously a financial coup for its author and a comparative commercial failure: the sum paid by Cornhill for the serialisation rights was exceptional, eclipsing by a substantial margin the prices paid for the vast majority of similar novels, yet the novel failed to recoup its publisher's investment. The Moonstone, published in 1868, and the last novel of what is generally regarded as the most successful decade of its author's career, was, despite a somewhat cool reception from both Dickens and the critics, a significant return to form and reestablished the market value of an author whose success on the competitive Victorian literary market had been gradually waning in the wake of his first perceived masterpiece. Viewed by many to represent the advent of the detective story within the tradition of the English novel, The Moonstone remains one of Collins's most critically acclaimed productions, identified by T. S. Eliot as "the first, the longest, and the best of modern English detective novels... in a genre invented by Collins and not by Poe," and Dorothy L. Sayers referred to it as "probably the very finest detective story ever written".

After The Moonstone, Collins's novels contained fewer thriller elements and more social commentary. The subject matter continued to be sensational, but his popularity declined. The poet Algernon Charles Swinburne commented: "What brought good Wilkie's genius nigh perdition? / Some demon whispered—'Wilkie! have a mission.'"

Factors most often cited have been the death of Dickens in 1870, and with it the loss of his literary mentoring, Collins's increased dependence upon laudanum, and his penchant for using his fiction to rail against social injustices. His novels and novellas of the 1870s and 1880s are generally regarded as inferior to his previous productions and receive comparatively little critical attention today[when?].

The Woman in White and The Moonstone share an unusual narrative structure, somewhat resembling an epistolary novel, in which different

959

portions of the book have different narrators, each with a distinct narrative voice. Armadale has this to a lesser extent through the correspondence between some characters. (Source: Wikipedia)

CPSIA information can be obtained
at www.ICGtesting.com
Printed in the USA
LVHW092008060120
642672LV00012B/316/P